AMBER R. DUELL

The Dark Dreamer Trilogy

Omnibus

Dream Keeper
Dark Consort
Night Warden

The Dark Dreamer Trilogy Omnibus

www.amberrduell.com

Dust jacket design by Asterielly

Case design by Saint Jupiter

DREAM KEEPER

The invisible dome that encased the Dream Realm burned blue beneath my gloved hand. My magic ached to be released from its rigid confinement—to return to the spiritual place deep in my chest, where it could fuel dreams once again—but this barrier was the only thing standing between me and the Nightmare Realm. Or, more specifically, from the things lurking there. Grotesque or beautiful, animalistic or humanoid, it didn't matter. Each and every nightmare held their own special brand of terror waiting to ensnare an unsuspecting Dreamer.

From this close to the wall, I could easily see into the Weaver's realm. Rolling hills stretched into the distance, and a small stream snaked through the low plains, which were colored in muted greens and blues. The knee-high grass tinkled an eerie, hushed melody as the breeze rippled across it. Hooked barbs, hard as steel and sharp as razors, grew along each blade, invisible to the naked eye. Beyond the hills lay an endless array of landscapes with their own vicious traps.

None of the Weaver's creatures roamed among the swaying grass tonight—at least none I could see. Still, something felt different. A layer of anxiety prowling beneath the calm.

I ignored it the best I could and continued my nightly security inspection—if not to protect the Dream Keeper, then to protect *her* world. Although, if I were being honest with myself, it was no longer the Day World I was concerned with saving from legions of deadly nightmares.

It was the Dream Keeper herself—Nora.

Nora, who would be hunted for the dream I'd placed inside her five years ago—the exact contents unknown even to me. She held the end of an invisible leash keeping the nightmares in the Night World, and the Weaver wouldn't hesitate to regain control of it. Even if that meant helping the creatures slip their collars entirely.

I rolled my shoulders and turned my attention back to the barrier. The worry I carried was ridiculous, a waste of time better spent elsewhere. Nothing more than paranoia. The shields were secure, the Weaver still bound to his realm, and the key to unraveling it all was safely hidden in Nora's mind.

Even still, my magic knotted inside me. *Wrong, wrong, wrong,* it seemed to whisper, insistently. Tendrils of it slid down my arms, flowing from my fingertips. The glimmering beach vibrated beneath my feet, and thousands of pieces of sand floated into the air. Two feet. Three feet. Four. Until the air was filled with sparkling flecks. With a deep breath, I flung my arms out wide, fingers splayed to propel a fresh layer of my magic into the existing barrier. It shot outward, clinging to the dome, and strengthened it in a flash of blue.

With the beach undoubtedly safe for Nora, I looked inward. The cords connecting me to each Dreamer that knew the legend of the Sandman spanned out like a million silver harp strings. Some connections glowed bright, their owner already asleep. Others idled, dull and dreamless, while the person on the other end remained awake.

I knew exactly where to find the cord that led to Nora. Even if I hadn't found it every night since we met, the dream I gave her was made of my magic, and it begged to return home. I tugged off my gloves and reached out as if to touch her cord—as if it were a tangible thing, instead of something spiritual. The silver and navy flecks covering my pale hands shimmered brilliantly.

Unlike Nora's cord.

"What's taking you so long?" I whispered to myself. She was never awake this late. We met in the same place on the other side of the realm like clockwork.

Suddenly, a shadow raced toward me in a blur of black and yellow fur, and I froze. Baku was my only ally in the Night World, even if it was by default. "Enemy of my enemy" and what not. But he knew the rules. He wasn't supposed to be here when I was expecting Nora to arrive. If she ever discovered there were darker things outside of these walls, it would invite trouble.

The chimera dug his tiger paws into the sand, skidding to a halt before me. Baku snorted through the elephant trunk situated between his ivory tusks. Large ears flapped twice on either side of his brindle face, and his cow-like tail snapped back and forth behind him.

I stopped breathing the moment I met the worried gleam in his eyes.

"Something's going on in the Nightmare Realm."

It wasn't a question. Baku spent most of his time on the other side of the barrier which meant he had a front row seat to whatever had happened and there was no reason to challenge his judgment. "Wh—"

The Weaver's maniacal joy shot through me, snaking around my fear, strangling it, and I staggered back a step. I hadn't been able to feel the Weaver since the binding. His magic was always traceable, but *never* his emotions. Dread pooled in my gut. I tried to shove the other sensation out, to pull instead on his location, but his magic registered in every direction. It was like trying to pinpoint the dream cord of an insomniac.

A streak of gold shot across the sky. It splintered its way through the stars, spreading, thinning, and fading. Magic thrummed through my veins, frantic to escape. To rise and protect. To defend. Baku pranced nervously at my side.

"Sandman." A gentle voice traveled down the cord. "Help me sleep."

"Nora." Her name fell from my lips as a single, strangled breath. I clenched the leather gloves in my hands. She hadn't asked for my help in years. *Years.* I gaped at the barrier in awe, utterly perplexed. Checking on the Weaver was important, but so was aiding Nora. If one was safe, they both were. I swallowed hard and drew a leather pouch from my belt loop.

"Find the Weaver," I told Baku. I tugged my gloves on again and snapped the hood of my tunic up over my brown curls. "I'll be right behind you."

Baku gave a curt nod and rushed back through the barrier without pause. Even if he had his hands—rather, paws—full, trying to devour a thousand nightmares tonight, Baku would help me find answers.

The cord between Nora and I grew taut as I careened along it to her bedside. Despite my best efforts not to, my breath still hitched when I caught sight of her platinum hair against the dark sheets. I reached a gloved hand out to brush a few strands from her temple but curled my fingers at the last moment. *You shouldn't*, I admonished myself. *This is off limits.*

I didn't creep around in bedrooms, and I certainly didn't touch anyone without their knowledge. Not even Nora. *Especially* not Nora—even if my chest did ache for the smallest hint of physical contact. It was my own fault we never touched, never high-fived or hugged or held hands. It was one of my rules, my lies, to keep distance between us. A lot of good they did. My body still jolted every night at the first glimpse of her and the adrenaline coursed through me long after she woke every morning. I'd spent an eternity watching people dream of love, but I never understood the appeal until Nora. None had come before her and I knew with absolute certainty that none would come after.

"I don't know why you needed to call me tonight," I said, keeping my voice low. Though she could neither hear nor see me, I fumbled for the edge of my hood, retreating into its shadow.

"But, my magic will take you to the beach. You'll be safe there." Please *be safe there.* "I'm sorry, Nora. But I'll see you soon." Reaching into the ever-present pouch, I pinched a bit of sand between my fingers. "Remember to keep a true heart and a true mind, and that the power of the dream is yours."

Then, I promptly sprinkled the glimmering flecks over her eyes and whispered, "Sleep."

My throat seized, and I choked back the awful truth of what she was, of what I made her, and what consequences we might be facing for it now. After escorting Nora's consciousness to the beach, and once I'd ensured that she was safely inside the barrier, I slipped through the surrounding shield into the perilous terrain of the Nightmare Realm. I flew through the tall grass toward the center of the Nightmare World amid a chorus of harsh metal clinks. The tiny barbs stabbed through my pant legs and pricked against my leather boots. Each cut into my skin was like a slap with a hot poker, but it was a small price to pay for a chance at reaching the Weaver's Keep in time to stop whatever was happening. The scent of burning wool ravaged my senses. *His* magic. Strong and undeniable. A sure sign that his binding must have worn thin—*too* thin, given how little time had passed.

The Day World was still warded against the Weaver's power and would remain so. That is, as long as he didn't find Nora. However, just because he couldn't open the doors without prying the information from the Dream Keeper's mind, that didn't mean he couldn't knock.

Chapter Two

Nora

Shadows danced in the soft warmth of the white mini-lights strung around my bedroom. I hopped around my bed, fumbling with the buckle on my sandals, and tossed my purse in the corner. Something hard—probably my phone—thwacked against the light blue wall.

"Whoops," I muttered, then growled at the metal hook locking my footwear in place. There were places to go, people to see. Or, rather, *one* person, and it was already hours past our usual meeting time. I jerked at the stiff strap. "Get off."

Finally, it popped, and I kicked it triumphantly into the corner with my bag. The other came off without any trouble, and my stomach fluttered in anticipation. I tugged off my jean shorts and stepped into a pair of plaid pajama bottoms, leaving on the

ribbed tank top I wore out tonight. Who cared that a glob of nacho cheese stained the front? The Sandman certainly wouldn't.

Climbing beneath the cool sheets, I dragged in a long breath and released it slowly. A small grin played on my lips as I stared at the lights hanging overhead. Then I shut my eyes and waited. Waited for sleep to claim me. To deliver me. But my body was too tense, and my mind still flipped through the day's events—as ridiculously boring as they were. When the highlight of your day was painting your nails a new color, what was there to mull over?

After a handful of long minutes, I opened my eyes again and bit my lip. I could ask. It had been… Actually, I couldn't remember the last time I asked him for anything. Even this. But I had to be up early for work tomorrow and we'd already missed out on hours together. A grin crept across my face.

"Sandman," I whispered, and closed my eyes again in preparation. "Help me sleep."

It came swiftly then, sweeping me gently from my world to another as easily as the breeze carries a feather. I curled my toes, feeling the powder-like sand of the Sandman's beach beneath my bare feet, and opened my eyes. The endless blanket of bright stars, the luminescent waves, the Sandman… This place, this dream, was like coming home.

"Sorry I'm late," I called with a smile in my voice. The light aroma of lilacs filled my lungs and I sighed, content. "Natalie and Emery dragged me to a party to celebrate our final first day of summer vacation." By this time next year, we would all be high school graduates and legal adults—neither of which I was ready to think about. I stretched my arms over my head and fought a yawn. "Sandman?" There was no reply. I dropped my arms and

spun, searching for a glimpse of the familiar black-clad figure. This was our spot—the place directly below the brightest star. My brows lowered in confusion. So why wasn't he here? He was *always* here. "Where are you?"

The only sound was the soft hush of waves lapping the shore. I turned again, squinting down the beach, but there was no hooded figure in sight. My heart skipped a beat. The dream seemed to yawn open, the emptiness pressing in on me from all sides. He had to be here somewhere. A pit formed in my stomach, and I staggered back, unsteady. *He had to.*

The beach was an addiction I didn't know how to cure myself of—didn't *want* to cure myself of. For every time I had to pretend this place didn't exist, the Sandman was there to absolve me of the lies. There to make me feel like I was good and sane and normal. It didn't matter that he was *also* the reason I didn't feel any of those things were true when I was awake. The Sandman was my anchor, holding me firm when life tried to wash me out to sea. Without him… I swallowed hard. Without him, I would be a ship without sails.

"Sandman!" I jogged down the water's edge, my pulse drumming in my ears. "I'm here."

But he wasn't.

☾

Three thirty-two.

The clock on my nightstand glowed green, the colon blinking in a slow, torturous rhythm. I tapped my fingers on my stomach. The Sandman had never been a no-show before. And if he

wasn't there, maybe that meant *they* were right, and he wasn't real.

No.

I refused to believe that. My mother meant well, but I couldn't face a lifetime of pill-pushing psychiatrists. One white-haired doctor tossing around words like *personality disorder* and *delusional* was enough. By the time the final doctor deemed the Sandman a simple outlet for me to process my parents' divorce, the damage was done.

Don't worry about it, he said. *It will pass*, he said.

That was five years ago.

The divorce was a distant memory. My father moved across the country and my mother remarried, but the Sandman became a permanent fixture. One I'd learned to never, ever talk about.

What's going on? I pushed the thought toward the Sandman even though I knew he couldn't hear me. There was only one call that reached from this side of the Dream World to his, only one cry capable of bringing him here, but it never stopped me from trying.

I flung the sheets back with a huff and grabbed an oversized Lund Valley Community College sweater from the end of my bed. Natalie hoped we would go there together next year but… I wrinkled my nose and glanced at the dresser drawer where my sketchbook was carefully tucked between scarves. If I went to college at all, it would be for art, but that was a big *if*. No one in my family knew I drew, and if my mother was going to let me major in something "impractical," she would want to at least see my work. Unfortunately, each page featured a majestic beach and a man hidden beneath a hood. Both things I was supposed to have forgotten long ago.

Tugging the sweater over my head, I made my way through the dark hallway toward the stairs. My mother and step-father were both working the night shift at the hospital and my sister could sleep through anything, yet I found myself tip-toeing down the hall.

I paused outside Katie's door and listened to the steady, heavy breathing on the other side. Part of me wanted to wake my sister up to talk about what happened, but the other part of me—the part that remembered the piercing fluorescent lights of a therapist's office—knew better. Katie had teased me about the Sandman when we were younger, but she never treated me differently. However, now we were older. Barging into her room to complain that my *imaginary friend* hadn't shown up that night might alienate the last blood relative I could rely on.

Although Katie annoyed me like no one else, I loved her more than I was irritated with her. I needed my big sister on my side—even if it meant hiding a huge part of my life. So, I stepped away from her door and crept silently downstairs to the kitchen.

Maybe because I was about to steal someone's box of frozen Thin Mints.

Sorry, not sorry.

Mist curled out of the open freezer, and I reached behind the chicken before a shrill, heart-wrenching scream tore through the house, squeezing the air from my lungs. It was made of nails and teeth and death. Of danger and fear. My eardrums rattled. Each nerve stood at attention, electricity buzzing over my body.

"Katie?" I yelled, frantically abandoning my pursuit of the cookies.

Confusion laced the edges of my shaky voice, but I was already racing across the kitchen. Instinct twisted my gut, telling

me to turn and run, to save myself, but I couldn't. Not if my sister was in trouble. Not if someone had broken in when no one was home to help. Not if Katie was hurt and scared. I propelled myself up the stairs to the second floor, my skin itching me to go faster, faster, faster. Katie's door was still shut at the front of the hallway. My breath shuddered, and I reached for the handle, pausing with apprehension. The metal was cold in my palm.

"Katie?" Her name came out as a crackling whisper and I forced myself to inhale. Then exhale. Inhale again. My hand shook as I twisted the knob.

I eased the door inward. Without a barrier between us, the sound cut through me like a knife. I slapped a palm against the wall, hitting the light switch, and flinched at the sudden brightness. At what it might reveal.

Katie lay flat on her back, her eyes shut tight, with the sheets snarled in a ball at the end of the bed. Sweat poured down her face, plastering her pink hair to her skin. The wild scream continued, unrelenting, her jaw stretched wide, her neck muscles protruding. But everything else was in its rightful place. Nothing was broken. The lock on the window hugged its latch.

I stepped into the room and spun, bumping into the dresser. My pulse thrashed; it mimicked Katie's scream in pendulum beats. Loud then muffled then loud again. "Katie?" My voice felt tight. I knelt on the mattress and shook my sister's broad shoulders. "Wake up."

The scream cracked. Katie sucked in air as if she were drowning and began again, just as terrified. I used the back of my wrist to wipe the moisture from my forehead. My nails dug into her shoulders, and I shook her rigid body with every ounce of strength I had. The more I yelled her name, the more desperate, more savage, my voice became. Black spots danced in my vision. Nightmares were one thing, but this was something else. Something beyond that. I shook the dizzying fear away and darted into the bathroom across the hall.

I returned with a Dixie cup of cold water and leapt onto the bed. The water hit Katie's face with a splash. "Come *on*," I shouted to no avail.

I fumbled for Katie's cell phone on the nightstand. If our mother didn't know what to do, she could send someone who did. My thumb hovered over the direct number to my mother's unit when a quick, metallic burst of air whooshed in from the hallway. A shiver ravaged my spine, and Katie's pitch reached new heights. I slipped from the bed, my hip smashing into the floor. The phone fell from my hand, seemingly in slow motion. I lunged for the door, and slammed it shut, leaning my back against the wood.

I couldn't think.

Couldn't... I couldn't...

The walls seemed to shrink, boxing me in. Trapping me.

Above the screech, a deep chuckle rumbled in the hall. My heart rose to my throat, and I dove for the phone where it had landed on the rug. I managed to dial *nine* before Katie's scream cut off. Palpable silence penetrated the room. My rapid breathing mixed with my sister's, and I edged up onto shaking knees. Katie rolled onto her side with a twitch.

"Katie?" My voice came out as a squeak.

She snuggled into the pillow, and her breathing returned to normal. *Okay.* She was okay. I turned my attention to the space at the bottom of the door. There was probably no one out there anyway. My sister's screams threw me off after a confusing night, that's all. I was merely tired and scared and was likely imagining the whole thing.

But before I called anyone, I *had* to be sure.

With the phone clutched in my hand, I crawled across the room to where the bright yellow handle of Katie's tennis racket leaned against the wall. I gripped the hard foam and held it to my shoulder. I didn't want to leave Katie alone but what choice did I have? I couldn't call for help if no one was out there. My mother would have a field day.

Clenching my jaw shut to keep my teeth from chattering, I dialed two *one*'s before opening the door. If anyone was on the other side, it would only take a single touch to call for help.

I eased out, holding the racket in front of me, and flicked on the hallway light. The stillness slammed into me like a brick wall. "Okay, okay, okay," I chanted under my breath. This was stupid. And yet… at five-foot-three and a hundred and ten pounds, an intruder wouldn't necessarily need to be armed to overpower me.

My nerves exploded with a burst of adrenaline, and I leapt from room to room until each light bulb on the second floor glowed. I checked every closet, under every bed. The racket shook in my hand. There was nothing. No one. An irrational spike of anger zipped through me at the possibility of my brain's betrayal.

My body moved on its own accord, taking me downstairs one tentative step at a time. One million potential fates I might encounter, if there was someone lying in wait, coursed through my thoughts. The joints in my fingers locked around the phone with my thumb still over the green call button. My tongue was sandpaper against the roof of my mouth, and I crept through the living room.

The freezer was still open, rattling in an attempt to keep the internal temperature down. I chomped down on my lip and inched my way forward to shut it. The rarely-used alarm system beside the back door taunted me—if only I remembered the code.

It seemed like it took ages to finish searching the house. I looked everywhere from the coat closet to beneath the bathroom sink, but it had only been eleven minutes since I had woken up. No time at all, really. I gripped the back of a dining room chair to stay on my feet.

There was no intruder. Katie had a nightmare, and my mind deceived me.

Again.

Always.

Only this time, it wasn't part of my subconscious. I wasn't asleep. Katie had screamed. There was a blast of air. Someone had laughed.

I swallowed the fear rising in my chest.

No one *believed* they were crazy. I wasn't sure what it meant if I thought I was unhinged but constantly persuaded myself to believe I wasn't. Was I? Wasn't I? Not even the doctors could agree on an answer. My sanity was a double-edged sword, and I was fighting to maintain balance on the tip.

I dashed back to Katie and climbed in bed beside her, nestling close. I tucked the wrinkled sheet around us both and tried to ignore the nausea curdling in my stomach. Katie was older than me, bolder and more confident, but in that moment, she felt as fragile as blown glass. I wrapped an arm around her waist and squeezed my eyes shut. My ears strained to hear the slightest sound that could signal danger, but no one else was in the house.

No one had laughed.

The Sandman wasn't real.

I balled the back of Katie's T-shirt in my fist. He was real enough to me, and I needed him. *Please, Sandman*, I called in a silent plea for the second time tonight—the one only he could hear. *Help me sleep.*

Chapter Three

"Crap," I grumbled, rummaging through the papers littering my desk. "Crap, crap, crap."

If I hadn't hit snooze so many times, waiting for the Sandman to come to the beach, I wouldn't have been running so late.

"The power is mine." Ha!

Over the years, I repeated his mantra a million times. The words became such a part of me that I forgot the knowledge existed; they were as natural to me as breathing. The power of the beach was his, I knew, but my dreams—the dreams he claimed I would have if he weren't there—that was mine. But if it were true that I could control things when the Sandman wasn't there, he would have appeared. I clenched my jaw, shaking out a book. My name tag had to be here somewhere. I slammed the hardcover down and gripped my rolling stomach.

Idiot.

Heat tingled my cheeks. Relying on him, missing him, needing him... It was ridiculous. He was part of me, and anything that he could give me, I could give myself. My lungs burned, reminding me to inhale, and I sucked in a dry breath. I needed to get my act together, to get to work, and to stop being my own worst enemy.

My name tag fell from between two notebooks and clicked against the desk. I scooped it up, pinned it on my white dress shirt, and tucked the hem into my khakis. I was *so* late. I flew out of my bedroom, and straight into Paul.

My step-father still wore baby blue scrubs that smelled of rubbing alcohol and latex, his dark hair sticking up at odd angles. "Hey kiddo, what's the rush?"

"I'm running late for work." I forced a smile—something I would have to do all day if I didn't want endless reminders from my boss that a good attitude was 'an essential part of good customer service.' Besides, my step-father was a good guy. Better than my biological father, actually. Nice. Involved. *There.*

Paul made a low "hmm" in the back of his throat. "You didn't drink and drive last night, did you?"

I threw him a scowl. The fact that my mother practically shoved me out the door to go to the party should've been a good indicator. "Natalie drove, and she drank soda all night."

"Had to ask," he grumbled. "Fatherly duty and what not."

I rolled my eyes, but a genuine smirk quirked my lips. "Yeah, yeah. Mom asleep? Tell her I'll do the garbage when I get home."

"I'll take it out." Paul yawned and stepped around me into the bathroom. "Have a good day."

The bathroom door clicked shut behind him, and I glanced toward Katie's room. There were only ten minutes left before my shift started, but the screams still echoed in my ears. A raw, frightening thing. I bit my lip and inched forward to peek inside. The hinges creaked a baleful tune as I nudged the door open enough to slip inside, making the hair on my arms rise in anticipation.

The sheets were pulled up to her shoulders, her mass of bubble gum hair spread across the pillow, exactly how she was when I left sometime near dawn—after jolting awake for a third time.

"You up?" I whispered, creeping toward the bed. Katie's chest moved up and down in a steady rhythm, but she had to be more than breathing. She needed to be *okay*. I poked her shoulder. "Hey."

She growled without opening her eyes, "The house better be on fire."

"I wanted to check on you before I left."

Katie rolled over to face the wall. "Shoo."

I stuck my tongue out at her. Katie was okay, even if her voice sounded a bit hoarse. She was fine, but I wasn't. Not really. My head felt hollow without the Sandman's support, my body heavy. "I'm going, I'm go—"

On the maroon pillowcase, completely invisible without the line of sun coming through the window, were flecks of glittering sand. My knees wobbled. I leaned closer and ran a finger through it. The dust was soft, almost a powder, and shone as brightly as a diamond. I stared, unblinking, at the tiny sparkles stuck in the grooves of my fingertip.

These particles… They played such a big role in my life the last few years. Every night I walked on it. Sat on it. Drew in it. At thirteen, I spent six hours trying to make sand castles from the loose particles, but they refused to stick to one another. At fifteen, I made dozens of snow angels across its surface and, with a flick of a certain someone's wrist, it morphed into actual snow. Heck, last week, I used it to play a game of tic-tac-toe. I would know it anywhere. This was *his* sand.

What was it doing on Katie's pillow? The Sandman had ignored my call while I lay awake for hours waiting for sleep to take me. Unless he *had* come… But then why wasn't he at the beach?

"*Nora.*" Katie flung the sheet over her head. The movement kicked the remaining granules into the air. "Go. Away."

I clutched my hand to my chest and sprinted to the car.

My fingers still trembled as I parked behind Howell's Furniture and Decor. Twenty-four hours ago, I had everything under control. Dreaming about the Sandman was one thing, but disembodied laughter, sand on Katie's pillow... I drew a deep breath and blew it out slowly through puckered lips.

What looked like sand could have been Katie's makeup. She liked glitz and glam. That was it. Eye shadow. I shoved the car keys into my purse and nodded to myself in the rearview mirror.

Since I was seven minutes late, I didn't need to draw more attention to myself and decided to jog around to the main doors, instead of knocking on the back. I saw my boss through the glass and cringed. She was usually doing paperwork in the office this early.

"Hey, Lisa," I called over the cowbell clanging against the door. "Sorry I'm late. It won't happen again."

"I hadn't realized." Lisa, a tall woman with wisps of grey in her hair, glanced up from where she leaned over the desk. She held the phone up to one ear, covering the bottom half as she spoke. "You look... chipper."

I stifled a groan. If by chipper, she meant like a member of the walking dead, then yes. "Long night." *Strange night. Strange morning.*

"Come meet your new coworker." She sidestepped the desk to reveal a boy no older than myself in a swivel chair. "This is Ben. He'll be working the sales floor with you this summer."

Ben glanced up from the paperwork and smiled so warmly it locked me in place. It was a smile of hopes and dreams. Promises. His violet eyes gleamed with a thousand flecks of starlight, and the fluorescent lights that reflected in his pupils stretched into seemingly endless mirrors. A mop of thick, curly ash-brown hair framed high cheekbones, and a narrow nose stopped above the softest looking lips.

I swore his breath caught at the same moment mine did. Looking at him, I felt like I was missing a place I had never been. The way he watched me sent lava racing through my veins. I knew him. *Somehow*, I knew him. The longing for something I didn't understand quickly bubbled into panic, and one foot slid back toward the doors.

"Hello," he said with the sweetest of smiles.

One word, two syllables, and the air evaporated from my lungs. His voice tugged at a vital memory. I nearly stumbled backward into a coffee table but caught myself on a column. I couldn't place the voice exactly. It wasn't anyone I knew, but the sound ached deep in my marrow. I wrung my purse straps, the stiff leather digging into my palm, and forced myself to walk toward the desk.

"Randy," Lisa snapped into the phone. "This isn't funny. Where are you? Call me back." She slammed the receiver down.

I shifted between my feet. "Everything okay?"

"Randy ran the deposit to the bank over an hour ago. I swear, if he went back home to sleep..." Lisa picked the phone up again and dialed. "I'll watch the floor while you give Ben a tour."

"Tour?" I swallowed hard. Howell's wasn't hiring. Someone called at least once a week to ask, and the answer was always no. Maybe if someone was lucky, they needed help with deliveries, but never the sales floor. The walls around my composed facade trembled, threatening my sanity. "What happened to Josh?" I asked.

"He's moving to afternoons." She rounded the desk and held the phone out in front of her to speak directly into the receiver. "Randy, if I have to leave one more voicemail, I swear to God..." She slammed the phone down again.

Ben slid his stack of papers across the desk. "I'm done filling these out."

"Great. Thanks," Lisa said. She motioned him out of her chair and plopped down in his place. "If you have any questions, Nora can fill you in."

I glanced sideways, my eyes level with Ben's shoulders. A spike of nerves shot down the back of my neck, trailing all the way down my spine, and I arched my back against the tingling discomfort. Hints of toned muscle flexed beneath the rolled sleeves of his dress shirt when he reached out to shake my hand. Tattooed specks of navy blue and silver covered his hands, the granules thinning out as they spread up his forearm and disappeared beneath the fabric. It was hard to believe Lisa hired him looking like he did. Crazy contact lenses *and* tattoos? I wasn't even allowed to put unnatural color in my hair. I scowled at the mix of emotions warring inside my head—intrigue, comfort, fear. He looked down at me, oozing charm and mystery and everything that would've drawn my friends closer. I stepped away.

The familiar sensation prickled again, begging me to move toward him, and I stopped myself mid-wince. Five years spent teaching myself to run as a default setting, to block out the fantasies, and yet ignoring his hand was one of the hardest things I'd done in a long time. I took a deep breath, letting it out through the corner of my mouth while pressing a hand against my diaphragm—a technique one of the doctors said might help if I felt stressed. My mother insisted I try, and usually they were right. Today, however, it did nothing.

"After you," he said and tucked his arms behind his back.

I fought against a barrage of crazy ideas—ideas crazier than the one I had when I saw the sand on Katie's pillow. Were my dreams leaking into reality? *No.* The Sandman wasn't real in this world. He wasn't. The stress was simply getting to me.

Ben smiled again, a shy grin, and my defenses cracked.

Lisa waved a frantic hand toward us while holding the receiver to her ear. I sighed and turned my back on them both. *Deep breaths.* Deep breaths and a shred of sanity would get me through the day, then tonight I could ask the Sandman directly if there was more to what I was seeing.

Of course, that was assuming he showed up.

Squaring my shoulders, I led Ben through a collection of couches and chairs. "This is where the living room sets are. The customers can order anything they see here. Lamps, rugs, tables." I flicked a ring of fabric samples tied to the arm of a recliner. "Color swatches and prices are attached to everything, so you don't need to memorize them."

"Got it."

He was close. Too close. His energy curled toward me, and I sidestepped an end table to put space between us. "The dining room sets are in there." I pointed through a wide doorway to the left. "Most tables come with four chairs unless the ticket says otherwise, but they can order more."

"All right."

I picked up the pace, motioning to another room at the back. "Desks, bookcases, cabinets, entertainment centers. Basically, office furniture and miscellaneous things that don't fit out here."

"Should I be writing this down?" A hint of a smile laced his voice.

"Maybe," I snapped, then cringed. He was probably trying to diffuse the tension sparking between us. One of us had to—my shift didn't end for another eight hours. I stopped at the end of the aisle. "That way," I murmured, jerking my elbow at the staircase.

He started toward the narrow, sloping steps, his tattooed hand gliding over the rail. Unspoken words pressed against me. I frowned and watched him climb higher alone. Something about the way he moved left me immobile. For a split second, I saw a man in loose cotton pants and a hooded tunic. The image was gone faster than it came, but the damage was done. I couldn't un-see it.

When the curly haired boy stopped halfway up, I jumped. My teeth clacked against each other in an attempt not to say anything. Ben wasn't the Sandman. Because the Sandman *did not exist.*

"Is something wrong?" he asked innocently.

I lifted my chin, cleared my throat, and sprinted up the first few steps. *Not crazy, not crazy, not crazy.* "Where are you from, Ben?"

He resumed his ascent. "All over, really."

A small, cynical noise escaped my throat before I could stop it. He hadn't done anything wrong. This was my problem, my instability, not his. I couldn't take it out on him because he happened to remind me of someone else. Maybe his family moved around a lot. Maybe he really was from all over. My fingers tingled at the memory of the sand on Katie's pillowcase, and I crossed my arms, pressing them into my sides.

"Dreamer, Dreamer," whispered a low, rasping voice behind me. I spun around, gripping the railing, but no one was there. A metallic taste coated my tongue. "Not a screamer," said the voice, this time right in my ear. Cold dread oozed down my spine. "Snapped his neck and—"

"These stairs," Ben said too loudly, chasing away the whispers. "Bit of a hazard."

I blinked the shock away. "Yeah, they're not the best." I dragged in a breath and shot the rest of the way to the second floor with terror rippling across my back. "Bedroom sets." I forced lightness into the words, but it rang false, even to me. Ben shifted closer. He smelled of lilacs and crisp morning air. I shut my eyes and held my breath against the memories it stirred, but the aroma lent me a moment of clarity, of comfort, offering stability to my voice. "It saves the customer more if they buy the whole thing, but they can buy individual pieces if they want. There's a chart on the back of the tag for pricing." The scent grew overwhelming, tightening my stomach with something other than fear. My gaze fell on him. He ducked his head and reached up to pinch the air beside his temple in a familiar gesture. For a moment, I imagined him tugging at a hood. "You..." I paused. He what? *Ugh.* I needed to take a mental health day.

"Nora," Lisa shouted.

"Up here," I called back, thankful for the interruption.

She popped up in the archway below. "I'm going to run home and see if Randy is there. Can you watch things for me while I'm gone?"

"I..." *Don't leave me alone with him.* "Okay. No problem."

"I'll be back soon," she said, already disappearing.

Ben stepped up beside me. "She's..."

"Yeah," I agreed. There wasn't really a word to describe Lisa, but she was a good boss when she wasn't trying to micromanage everything. Or everyone. "Anyway." I shrugged, diffusing some of the tension between my shoulders. "That's it for the sales floor. I'll show you the stock room after Lisa comes back so we can watch for customers."

His arm brushed against mine, and I nearly jumped out of my skin. "What do we do now?" he asked.

"We wait." I started back down the stairs, my eyes darting from one side of the stairwell to the other. My ears prickled but the voice was gone, if it had ever been there to begin with. I let out a slow breath. "Come on. I'll show you how to check the system to see if something is in stock."

Ben's eyes burned into my back, and he followed me silently to Lisa's desk. Not in a way that bothered me, but in a way that should have. I rolled my shoulders. I didn't know Ben. There wasn't a voice in the stairwell. Katie had a nightmare. No one laughed.

Didn't, didn't, didn't.

I threw myself into the rolling chair, still warm from when Lisa sat in it and clicked the power button on the computer. "It takes a minute for this to get going."

"Okay." He grabbed a chair from the other side of the table used for customers and swung it around to sit beside me.

My finger rapped on the mouse. Twenty minutes down. Seven hours and forty minutes to go. My stomach grumbled, and I brushed my long bangs down to hide the side of my face.

"Hungry?"

"Not at all," I lied. Even if he did notice the rumbling, he didn't have to comment.

He laughed. "Liar. When did you eat last?"

The screen popped up with a system update. I flung myself back in the chair. *Of course.* "This is going to take all day," I said, ignoring his question. The last thing I ate was a grilled cheese sandwich yesterday afternoon and a handful of chips at the party. If Natalie and Emery hadn't guilt-tripped me into going out, I would've chowed down on leftover beef stew before bed. Then my cookie heist was interrupted, but it was none of his business. "While we wait, I can show you—"

"The vending machines?" His eyes glimmered, and my face warmed. "Excellent idea. I already know where they are."

"That's not—"

But he was already out of his seat, striding toward the break room in the back. I leaned my head against the headrest. It wouldn't hurt to eat, but my appetite had vanished along with my sanity. My mother couldn't find out. For two months before the first psychiatric visit, I rarely ate, only wanting to get back to the Sandman. Now, if I so much as left a few bites on my plate, she hovered near my door at night to make sure I wasn't in bed too early. Falling asleep before nine on one of those nights almost guaranteed her looking up the phone number of a doctor again. I dragged my hands down my face. Three years without mentioning the Sandman, and she still refused to let it go.

"Pick your poison." Ben dumped an armful of snacks on the desk. "Each one equally delicious and peanut free."

My eyes narrowed. "Are you allergic to peanuts?"

"No." He lifted a hand to his temple again, tugging at air, and plunked down beside me. He focused on the bags as he arranged all of them to face up. "Pretzels? They had loops and sticks."

I snagged the closest bag—the sticks—and pried it open without looking away from him. There was no way he could have known I was allergic to peanuts. None. Just like there was no way he was a fictional person that lived in my head. Peanuts are a common allergy; maybe he was used to looking out for someone in his family.

"So how did you talk Lisa into hiring you when there were no openings?" I asked.

He held his hands up to his chin. "My charisma?"

"Ha. Ha." My lips curled against my will.

"What? You don't think I'm fascinating? Perhaps I should try harder." He batted his long eyelashes. "How about now?"

I slapped a hand over my mouth before I could laugh a mouthful of pretzel into his face. "I think you should save it for the customers."

A siren wailed in the distance. Whatever spell he cast, broke. The smile fell from my face, and I surged up from the desk. I needed to put some space between us. It was too easy with him, like I wasn't pretending. No good could come of that; my secrets were too important to risk.

I opened one of the doors, wedging a piece of wood beneath it to let in some fresh air, and the siren grew louder, followed by another. "I wonder what's going on," I said more to myself than anything.

Ben was at my side then, his expression tight. A rock settled in my gut. I didn't know him well enough to know where his thoughts were but seeing him like this unsettled me.

"Let me guess. You have a warrant out for your arrest," I joked.

His smile was taut, his eyes following the flashing lights when they turned the corner and whizzed by the store. "Why? Are you into bad boys?"

I snorted. "In your dreams."

His eyes flashed, the tiniest of true smiles breaking through. "Maybe in yours."

My heart squeezed. I opened my mouth to speak but the blast of sirens stole my ability to think. To breathe. I tore my eyes away from his, from the secrets written there—and they *were* there, ringing through every bone in my body.

A black Toyota flew into Howell's gravel parking lot in a cloud of dust. The driver slammed the vehicle into park before it came to a full stop, jerking the car to a halt. Lisa's father climbed out, his face beet red.

"We're closing up," he said in his usual raspy tone. "Go on home. We'll call you when we're ready to reopen."

"What happened?" I asked, craning my neck to follow the police. Ben stood as still as a statue beside me.

Lisa's father brushed by us without another word and flipped the row of light switches. A large ring of keys swung on his belt with a bright orange tassel. *Lisa's keys.*

"Grab your things," he barked.

Katie's screams rose up in the back of my mind again, a faint, distant ringing, mingled with a deep chuckle. I shook my head. It was fine. Everything was fine.

"Are you okay?" Ben asked.

"Yep." I bolted toward the desk where I set my purse.

If Lisa's father wanted us to leave, that was fine by me. Between Ben and the creepy, nonexistent voice playing mind-games with me, I was more than ready to go home.

Where Katie had screamed. And another nonexistent voice chuckled.

I swallowed my secrets, shoved down my doubts.

Fine.

I'm absolutely fine.

When I swept through the front door, my mother poked her head over the kitchen counter, her brunette ponytail limp. "What are you doing home?"

I shrugged and kicked the door shut with my heel. "I thought you were in bed."

"I forgot to put dinner in the crockpot." She glanced at the television. *Breaking News* scrolled across the bottom of the WNOX 11 station. "Shouldn't you be at work?"

"There was..." I started. The reporter stood outside a small ranch house that was surrounded by yellow tape. Countless police lights flashed in the background and an ambulance was backed into the driveway. Officers lingered near the door, speaking with two men in suits. "Turn it up."

My mother set the cutting board down. "Did something happen at the store?" she asked, ignoring the scene on TV.

The reporter motioned an older woman forward. I strained to hear what he said, focusing on his lips, but only caught a *thank you.* I darted around the recliner and knelt in front of the entertainment center, tapping the volume button. "And you were the one who discovered the body?"

"Yes," the woman answered in a shaking voice. "Some of their mail was delivered to my house. I have a key, so I went in to set it on their table, and he was on the couch." She placed her hands on her chest. "His neck was snapped at the most hor—"

One of the people in suits—a bald man with dark skin and silver glasses—touched her shoulder. "That's enough." The reporter opened his mouth to object, but the detective pointed a finger at him. "This is an open murder investigation. You know better."

Open murder investigation. My heart dropped, and I gripped the edge of the television stand. The detective ushered the woman away. The reporter turned back to the camera, his face grim. He lifted a finger to his ear and nodded.

Behind him, the EMT's wheeled out a stretcher. The camera zoomed in to reveal a woman with an oxygen mask on. I gasped, slamming a hand over my mouth. It couldn't be...

"Is that Lisa?" My mother's voice rose to a near screech.

I nodded, my body numb. She was fine when she left the store. Did she walk in on the murderer? But the other woman found the body, and she appeared fine. So, what happened? The blood drained from my head, and I shuffled back to plop on the couch before I fainted.

His, the woman had said. Randy. Randy was dead. Murdered. His neck... *His neck.* The voice from the store echoed in my ears. *Dreamer, Dreamer, not a screamer. Snapped his neck and—*

It knew. The voice knew.

My mother jammed the power button, but I could still see the image of Lisa on the stretcher. My hands shook. If by some miracle I wasn't losing it, I had somehow gained psychic abilities overnight.

Insane, insane, insane.

"Nora? Are you okay?"

Tiny wrinkles formed at the edges of my mother's eyes, and she chewed on the inside of her cheek. I knew that look. It was the I'm-worried-you're-about-to-snap look. The one she got right before she started suggesting I be reevaluated.

"Howell's is closed until further notice," I said in a flat voice and cleared the lump from my throat. *Act normal.* It didn't matter my boss was just killed or my other boss was on the way to the hospital. Any sign of weakness, of an oncoming emotional break, in front of my mother, spelled disaster. I stood and rubbed at my eyes. "We were out late last night, and I had to wake up early, so I think I'll go back to bed for a little while."

"Oh? Are you sure you don't want to stay up? You can help me chop the carrots." She hovered at my shoulder, and I shook my head. "How was the party anyway? Did you have fun?"

I hid my wince behind a yawn. She didn't need help with the carrots, and she certainly didn't care about the party. She only wanted to make sure the horrible news didn't send me swan-diving off the deep end. More than anything, she feared the resurgence of the Sandman, which, in turn, meant she lived in terror of major change. After all, he was born from the stress of her divorce so, why wouldn't her remarriage, Katie moving away for college in the fall, or my final year before graduation bring him back? *Because he never left.* Her list of possible triggers hadn't included people-I-knew-being-murdered before, but I was willing to bet it now held the number one spot.

I forced a smile, skirting around her. "It was lots of fun, Mom."

"Good, good," she said, relieved. But her eyes followed me all the way up the stairs.

Once inside the safety of my room, I dug my sketchbook from its hiding place and threw myself into the desk chair. My hands shook as I flipped through pages full of blues and purples and silvers. Past dozens of sketches of the Sandman—that brought an image of Ben to the front of my mind. Those vivid violet eyes belonged among the other images. I could already feel my hand gliding over the sheet of paper, making the perfect sweep of his eyelashes. Could visualize the thrill that would spark through me, shading those impossible irises until they reflected the same mysterious glint as the real things.

But, instead, I slid the black pencil from the box. The tip scratched against the page with a sharp rush. My hand moved feverishly, leaving harsh, angry lines in its wake. When I was finished, the colored pencil slipped from my grip and rolled off the edge of the desk, clattering to the floor.

The words *Dreamer, Dreamer* swallowed the page. They stared up at me. Mocked me. I slammed the notebook shut and clasped my hands over my ears as if it would stop the voice from coming back.

Chapter Four

The television blurred as I clicked through the channels. Every time I tried to sleep, Katie's scream haunted me. I refused to ask for the Sandman's help again, though. After two full nights without him, I couldn't stomach it if he ignored my call. False hope only led to disappointment; I wasn't going to risk confirming he had vanished completely.

But my body languished with news I couldn't share with anyone but him. The Sandman didn't yet know that I had watched police cars race past Howell's on their way to a murder scene. Didn't know it was Lisa's house where Randy was found murdered. His neck snapped. Just like the voice whispered in the stairwell. Impossibly. Unbelievably. *Why would I hear that? Of all things, why that?*

I hauled the blanket off the back of the couch and wrapped it around myself. *This was so not healthy*. Anything was better than sitting in my living room, feeling sorry for myself, but I couldn't find the energy to move.

The cushions shifted near my feet. "Hey," Katie said around a spoonful of cereal. "What are you watching?"

"Nothing yet. Here." I tossed my sister the remote.

We hadn't spoken about the other night. I wasn't sure Katie remembered having a nightmare, or if she blamed her hoarse voice the next morning on too much singing in the shower. Really, it could have been either, but it was hard to imagine that she could forget a nightmare that vivid.

"I'm surprised you're up," I glared at her puffy eyes, willing her to give me the smallest opening to ask. "It's before noon."

"Well, someone likes to blast the television at the crack of dawn," she said.

The surround sound wasn't *that* loud. "It's not the crack of dawn; it's almost eleven."

"Precisely." Katie slurped another spoonful of breakfast, and I cringed. "I could've slept until two, and still made my date with Jen by four."

I glared at her. "Don't you want to enjoy summer vacation? You're only here for a couple more months."

"I *am* enjoying it." Katie leaned into the cushions and flipped the channel, "Nothing exciting happens before lunch."

"Whatever."

"Howell's is still closed, right?" Katie asked.

"Yep." My stomach churned at the thought of going back there. Paul found out from a coworker that Lisa was fine—the sight of Randy's body triggered a severe asthma attack—but I imagined it would be a long time before she reopened. It would be impossible to walk past the office without remembering all the mornings I found Randy taking a nap inside. Impossible not to wonder how different things could've been if he came back to the store to sleep instead of going home.

"That's so bizarre. I mean, why would someone kill your boss? I heard nothing was missing from the house, and there were no signs of forced entry. That's super fishy. My money is on the wife. She had the opportunity, and I'm sure they'll dig up a motive."

I bolted up and snatched the remote from Katie's hand. "Her name is Lisa," I snarled, pointing the remote in her face, fighting off a flash of heat. "And she didn't kill anybody."

"Alright, alright." She held her hands up in surrender while balancing her bowl on her lap. "Sorry, it's just the biggest thing to happen in Cedarbrook in a long time. I didn't mean anything by it."

"Yeah?" I snapped and threw myself back into the cushions. "Well, maybe you should think before you open your mouth. What if whoever killed him followed him from the store? He was taking the deposit to the bank before. If I wasn't late, maybe I would've seen something."

"Or been killed too," she said.

"Katie!"

She rolled her eyes. "Sorry. You're right. Shutting up now. How's mom taking it?"

"Like mom," I grumbled. *Staring holes into me.*

Silence stretched between us. Katie always knew exactly which of my buttons to push, and exactly when to back away. Only this was a *big* button; my boss' murder wasn't a joke, and I wasn't ready to talk about it. But I could only turn my phone off for so long before Emery showed up at the house. And Natalie, if I didn't reply to her texts before she got back from her family trip to California. I swallowed a groan.

"Sooo, what are you doing today?" Katie finally asked.

I tucked the blanket under my armpits. "This."

"Oh no. You're not going to sit around the house moping again. Weren't you just lecturing me about enjoying vacation?" She hopped up and tapped my knee. "Get dressed."

I wasn't moping. I was processing. And avoiding. My friends weren't the only reason I turned off my phone. Multiple news outlets called to get inside information on Randy like I would know anything about his personal life, and a Detective Bell wanted to ask me a few questions. My parents took his calls.

"Where are we going?" I asked.

"Shopping," Katie sang to the ceiling.

"For what?"

"I'll have a dorm room to decorate soon. Maybe I'll get some new clothes, too," Katie called over her shoulder on the way to the staircase. "Who cares? Mom told me she left some money in the jar. We'll hang out at the mall, grab some lunch, and then you can drop me off at the theater to meet Jen."

I narrowed my eyes. "What you're really saying is that you want me to chauffeur you around all day."

"Maybe." She winked at me over the railing. "But I've been having these creepy dreams, so I need to get the hell out of this house."

I felt the blood drain from my face. *Dreams?* Plural? And *creepy*? Creepy was the furnace kicking on when you were alone in the cellar. It was a portrait with eyes that followed you around the room. It absolutely was not something that made a person scream, like Katie had screamed. I swung my legs off the edge of the couch and untangled myself from the blanket. My head swam, thoughts clouding. "Wh… What do you mean? Creepy dreams?"

"I call dibs on the shower," she yelled in a high sing-song voice.

The Sandman was gone, Katie was having bad dreams, and that voice in the stairwell… *Dreamer, Dreamer.* I rubbed my forehead against the distant echo of it. All of that couldn't be a coincidence, could it? When I shivered, it had nothing to do with the air conditioning.

The sweet aroma of sesame chicken mixed with burnt cheese from the pizzeria behind us. Half of the people jammed into the food court were our age, but I only recognized a handful of them. A handful too many, that is. I prodded my fries around my tray, dunking the occasional one in catsup before eating it. Three boys from my school, juniors, stared in our direction. I tried to ignore their loud whispers, catching only bits and pieces.

Body.

Murder.

It was no secret I worked at Howell's but there was no reason I should know anything. Except the voice knew. *Didn't exist. Didn't happen.* My foot bounced under the table.

"Where to first?" Katie scooped fallen guacamole off a plastic wrapper and shoved it back into her taco.

"This was your idea." And a horrible one at that.

"Ask her," one of the boys said a bit louder.

"No way. You do it."

Katie slammed her palms down on the table and twisted toward them. "Take one step toward this table and you'll be the ones on the news tonight."

A fry flew to the back of my throat, sending me into a coughing fit. The guys bolted, disappearing into the center of the mall, before I regained my composure. "I can't believe you just did that," I wheezed.

"Why? They deserved it," Katie said around another bite of taco. "Anyway, like I was saying. Should we start on the top floor and work our way down?"

"Let's go see what new—" The words stuck in my throat as I spotted Ben walking straight toward our table, a white bag hanging off his wrist. His curls bobbed around his forehead as he focused on the phone in his hand. "Crap."

"New crap? That's vague," Katie said with a snort.

I slid lower, the wire seat grating against my spine. I bowed my head to hide behind my hair. With hundreds of people in the mall, why did he have to be the one in my current vicinity? The last thing I wanted was to be reminded of Howell's or the Sandman. This trip was supposed to get my mind off those things.

"Who are you hiding from?"

Crap. Crap. Crap. "Ben."

"Ben?" Katie shouted and sat up straighter to scan the crowd over my head.

"Shut up."

Quickly, I glanced in Ben's direction, with the feeble hope he was too engrossed in his phone to notice, but it was too late. His head snapped up and our eyes met. Ben's perfect lips parted in surprise and his hand rose to his temple, grabbing at air again. Recognition rippled from my head to my toes but I willed the sensation away. Why did he have to be so impossibly attractive? Even with the weird contacts and tattoos that made no sense, I couldn't help but be drawn to him. Maybe he merely reminded me of the Sandman because I needed to see him so badly. It certainly wasn't because they looked alike; I had never seen an inch of the Sandman that wasn't hidden beneath black cloth.

"Ben, from work?" Kate asked, practically bouncing in her seat.

I gave a small nod. He was two feet from our table now; I had to say something. Perhaps, that we were just leaving or that I had to pee. Any excuse to avoid a conversation.

"Hey," he said brightly.

I slid up in the chair. "Hi."

"How are you?" His eyes never left mine while he waited for an answer.

"Um," I stammered. "I'm... okay. Good. You?"

The corners of his lips curled sympathetically. "Same."

I dropped my gaze to the tattoos on his hands and arms. Looking closely, his fingertips were solid navy blue. It wasn't until after the first knuckle that any hint of silver played along his skin. The specks were more condensed there, spreading out and swirling together the higher up they climbed on his arm, until the cuff of his T-shirt got in the way.

"New phone?" I blurted, hoping for his quick answer and even swifter exit.

He shrugged and dropped the phone into the bag. "I figured it was time to join the twenty-first century."

"You didn't have a phone before today?" Katie asked, her brows raised. I kicked her under the table. "Ouch. What?"

Ben kept watching me, waiting. For what, I wasn't sure, but it felt like more than a few words of casual conversation. "I should have checked in with you sooner. Lisa mentioned you've worked with them for almost a year, so I figure this must be hard."

"Well, you're here now, right?" Katie asked, offering a wide smile. "We're done eating, and I was just about to drag Nora to the jewelry store. Want to come along?"

I shot daggers at Katie from across the table. *I'm going to throttle you*, I promised with a steady gaze. My pursed lips vowed it would be a long, long process. Either she thought I had a secret crush on Ben, or she was developing one herself—not that I could blame her. No part of me wanted to spend the afternoon with him trailing us from shop to shop, though. The corner of my eye twitched. Well, *almost* no part of me.

Regardless, I was definitely not done eating.

"I'm sure he has better things to do than follow us around the mall," I said with a stiff smile.

"I don't!" Ben cut in fast, his voice overlapping the end of my sentence. A rogue blush colored his cheeks. "I mean, if you don't mind me tagging along."

Katie nudged me with her toe and scowled, "Yeah, it's totally fine with her."

Ben beamed, "Here, let me."

He scooped up our trays and headed toward the garbage cans. I eyed the half-eaten food before whipping around to my sister. "What are you doing?" I whispered through my teeth.

Katie shrugged. "He's hot."

"Hot? Since when do you like guys with tattoos?"

"First of all, I meant for you. When it comes to guys, he's not my type, but a girl *can* appreciate beauty when she sees it." Katie squinted at Ben from across the food court. "Secondly, what tattoos? How much have you seen of him exactly?"

"Katie," I snapped. I was in no mood for her games. Not about this. "Seriously? Are you blind? He's covered in them."

"Is he?" She wagged her eyebrows.

"And who wears colored contacts like that?" I added, my voice struggling to stay level.

"Been staring into his eyes, have you?"

I drew in a breath and clenched my hands under the table. If we weren't in public, there was every possibility that I *would* strangle her. Wasn't there some sort of sister code about this stuff? Her baby pictures were *so* coming out the next time Jen came over for dinner, especially the one where she decided to go streaking down our street when she was two. It was currently stuffed in the back of the hutch where my dearest sister assumed no one would find it. I cocked one eyebrow, a dare for her to try anything else.

"All right, all right. You're going to have to tell me all about the tattoos later, but his eyes are brown. If he's going to go through all the trouble of colored contacts, he could've picked something fun. Like red. Oh, or cat eyes. That would be cool."

"You're not funny."

Ben approached the table again with his hands in his pockets—his eyes unmistakably violet. "Ready?" he asked.

Cards full of cheap earrings and necklaces lined the walls of the jewelry shop. Mirrors hung every few feet, interspersed by spinning racks. I broke away from Katie and slowly scanned all the jewelry that I would never wear. Ben kept a respectable distance between us, but it wasn't enough to keep me from fidgeting. Something inside me rustled, a living thing writhing beneath my skin, determined to undermine my decision to stay away from him. However, practice made perfect, and I had years of experience, pretending to appear calm and collected.

I glanced at the cashier—a brunette in a floral shirt—and stepped up to a clearance rack at the end of the counter. A magazine was open on the glass case. The girl's eyes drifted closed, her chin slipping off her palm, before she caught herself from face-planting on a perfume ad. I knew exactly how she felt. She raised a hand in a small, embarrassed wave. Ben, of course, gave her one back.

My eyes grazed over beaded necklaces without really seeing them, latching on a zebra print sleep mask with *Sweet Dreams* embroidered in purple. Katie asked something on the other side of a podium, but her words were far away, drowned out by the memory of her scream echoing in the recesses of my mind. It grew louder and louder. I couldn't decipher Ben's answer to her over the upbeat music coming from the ceiling speaker. My pulse raced, a loud *whomp, whomp, whomp* against my eardrums, seemingly in time with the bass.

"Nora?" Ben touched my wrist with gentle, warm fingers. The sensation tore through me, pushing at the macabre chorus until it was nothing more than a faint ringing in my ears. "Are you okay?"

"Yeah." I turned back to the rack, unable to stand the weight of his stare. It felt as if his gaze burrowed into me and latched onto something hidden. Secret. An enemy invasion and yet, for some reason, a welcomed homecoming. "Yeah, I'm fine."

"You look tired."

I shrugged.

"Are you worried about what happened with Randy?" he asked in a quiet voice. "Or is something else bothering you?"

"Nora." Katie scooted between us with a wide blue headband. "Does this clash with my hair?"

"It's perfect," I told her, and Katie bounced away. "If you want to look like cotton candy," I added under my breath.

Ben chuckled. The sound snapped me awake, warming me to him just a little.

"Don't you want anything?" he asked, glancing around at the myriad of ornamentation.

"No. I try to go through life unnoticed… and everything in here draws attention." I bit my tongue. Did I really say that out loud? Next thing I knew, I would be telling him my whole life story. *Ugh.*

"I noticed you," he said quietly, tugging on one of his curls.

Heat flooded my cheeks. What was I supposed to say to that? Thank you, but don't? Because I was ten pounds of crazy in a five-pound basket. This was the worst time imaginable for someone to take an interest in me, and an even worse time for me to *maybe* be interested back. He was nice. And hot. But I had to figure myself out first. Once I stopped seeing Ben as the Sandman, there might be a chance. Until then, I couldn't afford more confusion.

"Hello?" Katie asked the cashier. "Hey."

"I was thinking—" Ben froze, his eyes wide. I followed his gaze to where my sister reached over to shake the brunette's arm.

The girl leapt from her stool and stumbled back. "Get them off." Her voice cracked. "Get them off. Get them off!"

I stepped forward cautiously, my hands raised. "Get what off?"

"Get *them* off!" She repeated it a dozen times, her voice rising with each scream. Carefully manicured nails dug into her tanned forearms, the white tips disappearing. She dragged her hand back with a horrendous *rip*. Layers of skin disappeared. Bright red blood streamed toward her elbow, dripping on the tile floor.

My feet were cemented to the ground. Suddenly, Ben leapt over the counter, shaking the cashier's shoulders, and pried her fingers away. "Wake up." It was a command, calm and careful. But her eyes were wide open, fixed on the gashes on her arm. "Come on. Wake up," he urged.

"*Off.*" The cashier shoved Ben away with more strength than a girl her size should possess and snatched a glitter pen from the counter. "*Off, off, off.*"

Ben tripped on the fallen stool, knocking them both into the corner. "There's nothing there," he said through his teeth. "Wake up."

"*Get them off!*" She pierced her left hand with the pen. Blood oozed around the tip.

Katie screamed. The old shriek rose up in my mind to join it until I could hear nothing else. My body shook, and I stretched across the counter to grab the girl's good hand. To stop her. To give Ben an extra second to restrain her. But before I could reach her, the girl yanked the pen out. In one swift movement, she shouldered Ben through the counter's gate and into my side. We knocked over a podium as we fell, landing in a tangled heap.

The cashier stabbed again. And again. And again. One blossoming bead of blood after another, moving up, up, up her arm. "*Off! Get them off!*"

"Stop!" I shoved the fallen podium off my foot, but it used time I didn't have. I saw what was coming. I saw it, and there was nothing I could do. Time slowed. The scream in my head rose up, muffling my shouts. "Katie, stop her. Stop her!"

But my sister was frozen in slack-jawed horror, as the girl plunged the pen into her throat.

The world stopped in a spray of crimson.

Katie bolted from the store into a gathering crowd. Ben wrapped strong arms around my waist and dragged me away. It all happened so fast, so immediately, that we reached the doors before the body toppled with a sickening thud. It was only after Ben took my face in his hands and held my gaze that I realized the scream was no longer an echo. It wasn't Katie's. It was mine—torn from some place deep inside. The crowd surged around us, rushing this way and that, calling for help. It snuffed the air from my lungs, and I swallowed against a raw throat.

"It's okay. You're okay," Ben said. I moved back a fraction of an inch, but he held fast. "Keep looking at me, Nora. Don't look in there. Look at me. You're okay. I'm here."

I was too shocked, too utterly depleted, to do anything but lean on the bit of strength he offered. Something shimmered behind his starlit eyes, an undercurrent of blue. The hint of an inner glow peeked out, before fading into the depths.

"Nothing is okay," I breathed, unsteady.

Nausea took hold, and I broke away, running to the nearest garbage can. I dry heaved over the pile of rotting food. The stench wafting up from inside did nothing to help. Saliva filled my mouth, and I let it drool from my bottom lip.

"Dreamer, Dreamer, couldn't free her." It was the same velvety voice from Howell's. A voice like distant rolls of thunder, warning of an oncoming storm. "Saw a beetle who tried to eat her."

I heaved again. This time it wasn't in vain.

A rendering of worlds.

A distortion of nature.

A binding of power.

The Weaver and I had lived through it all together, until the day I trapped him in his realm, snipping the last strand of friendship. I sat on the beach, head in my hands, immersed in the actions of the sand-made figures in front of me. It was as if they were part of a play—these replicas of the Weaver and me. For hours, I watched as we created our realms, clear in purpose, content with our differences. I was the light, he, the dark. The balance was satisfied, and our world was better for it.

But we weren't the only beings that had to live in it. I forced the sand to skip over the parts featuring creatures more ancient than us, molded from anger and violence. They were dormant now, irrelevant. But they weren't completely unrelated either. One in particular was the catalyst that changed everything.

I waved a hand at the scene of us reaching for a blade in unison, and it scattered. A lump formed in my throat. Binding the Weaver gave me no pleasure when once, a millennium ago, we were friends. I raked my hands down my face as longing spread through me. It had been a mistake to watch the past—to allow myself to remember with this much clarity. No matter how guilty I felt now, it was the right thing to do. The *only* thing to do. Locking the Weaver in the Nightmare Realm saved millions of lives.

And yet…

I pressed my fingers against my eyelids.

And yet…

A sound like nails on a chalkboard wrenched me from my turmoil. Razor sharp talons clawed at the fabric of the barrier before me. The magic glowed blue beneath each tapered point as it held the line, buffering each blow. I kept my eyes on the reptilian nightmare and scooped up handfuls of sand. It fell in showers from between my bare fingers, swirling and twisting into kunai throwing knives. They hovered in the air around me, dozens of gleaming, pointed tips aimed at the beast.

"Come on," I whispered the challenge as I stood.

My muscles twitched, my nerves tingling. Nora could never see this. I felt her on the other side of the beach at the same moment the barrier strained, and this needed to be over before she came looking for me. I spent countless hours reinforcing the protections between the Dream and Nightmare Realms after what happened at the mall. Although they were stronger now, they were not completely unbreachable. No magic was.

The Weaver knew exactly what he was doing. While Katie's nightmare and Randy's death came as a surprise to Nora, she wasn't quite as emotionally vulnerable as he would've liked. The Weaver needed the shock of today, the blood and the carnage. The things that called to nightmares like hopes called to dreams. He was turning Nora into a flame in the middle of the dankest dungeon.

I supposed I should be glad it attracted a mindless nightmare instead of a more sophisticated creation, but I couldn't find it in me to be grateful. Intelligent or not, the scaled creature was perfectly capable of ripping a hole in my barrier. The magic around the Dream Realm was as secure as I could make it, but even the strongest metal bent with enough exposure to heat.

A high-pitched shriek rippled across the starry sky. If I didn't act soon, the commotion would attract others. I filled my lungs and blew a handful of sand at the wall. It opened for me, a mere pinhole in the scheme of things, and a forked tongue slipped through followed by the tip of a green scaled nose. The barrier fogged with the creature's hot breath. A single clawed toe slipped inside, and the barrier creaked under the pressure.

I sent the first wave of knives soaring forward. They whizzed through the air, hitting their mark one after another. The giant lizard reared back, exposing a yellow underbelly. The next set of knives rustled my clothes as they flew past me. They hadn't yet hit when padded steps thundered across the invisible domed ceiling.

Black and yellow fur streaked across the sky, and the lizard squealed the most human of sounds. A breath fell from my mouth. *Thanks, Baku.* I lifted another handful of sand and blew it at the breach. The space glowed with blue light, and I turned before it faded to match the rest of the wall, tugging my hood up. There was little worse than watching Baku devour his meals.

The sound, maybe.

Definitely, the sound.

Besides, I had a promise to make good on. I told Nora I would see her soon, though she never heard me say it, but we hadn't met in days. Day Walking didn't count. Even with Nora's ability to see the marks on my arms, she didn't know me in the Day World. How could she? She had never seen me in the Night World. I needed to be more careful with what I let slip around her. There were things I shouldn't know as Ben but taking form in her world—being near her in a way I never could before—it was too easy to forget. The extreme amount of energy it took to be there didn't help my focus either.

With a sigh, I ripped the gloves from inside my tunic and strode across the beach, leaving the gnashing teeth and tearing flesh behind.

Nora's pink sweatpants stood out against the silver sand, where she sat at the edge of the beach. The thin white fabric of her T-shirt allowed the lines of a black bra to show through, and I forced myself not to look. Her wet hair was twisted into a high bun, beads of water still clinging to the messy ends. A line creased the space between her brows.

I hated that line and the fact that I was partially to blame for it. I hated that I hated it.

Nora was the Dream Keeper. That's all she was ever supposed to be. I didn't dare give voice to anything more because it was undoubtedly impossible. I loved her enough to recognize I couldn't give her more than a few stolen hours every night, and she couldn't give me more than a handful of decades before she passed away. It wasn't fair to either of us, but the heart never cared about *fair.*

It was enough that I was her refuge. That I was the one she turned to every night since that first call, five years ago. It *had* to be enough. But it wasn't…not really. I didn't want to be her dirty little secret. To be the thing she had to keep hidden from everyone she loved because the truth would mean more doctors.

My chest ached. That's what I had to be for her—hidden. I took a silent, deep breath, and approached. "Hello, Nora."

Her voice was distant, cool, when she replied, "Hello."

"I'm sorry I'm late." I swallowed hard and knelt in front of her. My hands balled into fists on my thighs—as much from nerves as they did to make sure I followed the rules. The feel of her skin beneath my hands was ingrained in me now. A taste of a drug I would always crave. "I came as soon as I could."

She said nothing for so long, my pulse echoed in my ears. The barriers had thinned more than I expected, and with the Weaver playing hide-and-seek... Hurting Nora was the last thing I ever wanted to do but losing her trust could be deadly. We were bound together, a team, whether she knew it or not—what one of us did affected the other.

It was quickly becoming obvious my time of sheltering her from the truth was ending, though. How much damage would the Weaver inflict before she remembered our first meeting? It was easy to let her forget that night. Anyone could've called out to me at that moment and become the Dream Keeper. If I hadn't been so desperate, I would never have chosen someone so young, so vulnerable, for the task. But fate intervened.

I had explained things the best I could at the time, saying that a bad man was trying to hurt her world, and I needed a safe place to hide the key to his cell. Nora had glared into the shadows of my hood with wide, curious eyes, and granted me permission when I asked for it. But it was a game to her. An adventure in the storybooks. A *dream*. She didn't know the gravitas of the danger.

She couldn't have because as soon as I removed the information from my mind and placed it into hers, I collapsed—broken in every way from the battle with the Weaver.

The balance was upended when I turned his own magic against him, binding him to the Nightmare Realm. Although our circumstances were vastly different, the results were the same: two weakened sides of the same coin. A fact I was both grateful for and loathed. I betrayed the Weaver the night we met to discuss things, but his excuses for invading the Day World were never going to make a difference. I don't remember how I did it—Nora carried that knowledge now—so the Weaver couldn't use the same methods against me. And, though binding him was a necessary evil, it is only right that I suffer for betraying someone I once called a friend.

"Where were you?" Nora asked in a voice so lifeless I hardly recognized it.

"I..." *Not yet.* I couldn't tell her yet. There was still time for me to fix things first. "You were about to have a nightmare," I said softly. It didn't answer her question, but it wasn't a complete lie, either.

“A nightmare.” She was quiet for a heartbeat, her eyes narrowing. “I can’t remember the last time I had a bad dream.”

“I’ve always kept them away.” Something I would not be able to do much longer. Worse yet, the Weaver knew it. Yesterday. Tonight. Tomorrow. On and on, the attacks would continue until he either got what he wanted, or I found a way to rebind him. This was just the beginning of the nightmare. The prelude. My gloves strained against their stitching. This was a battle I wasn’t prepared to fight a second time.

“My boss was murdered. Someone snapped his neck. You’d know that if you were here, of course.” Nora’s green eyes swept over me, dull and distant. “Then today I watched a girl at the mall stab herself to death with a pen.”

There was nothing I could say, nothing I could do, to make her forget what happened. I knew because I saw it too. The Weaver’s wicked joy slammed into me both times, but never soon enough for me to pinpoint his target. All I could do was make sure I was nearby in case he sent a sleepwalker after Nora. Not to kill her, of course—if she died, the dream died with her—but to persuade her in the only way the Weaver knew how: torture.

“I’m sorry,” I said again, letting my sincerity coat each word.

“You don’t happen to know anything about it, do you?”

I stared out from beneath my hood, my heart racing. “Why do you ask?”

She turned her head away from me. “No reason.”

With a clenched jaw, I shoved the image of the cashier from my mind and grabbed a handful of sand. Nora needed to talk about what happened but doing it here would only draw more attention to herself. Besides, Baku was ravenous, but he could only eat so many nightmares in a single night.

The sand shifted and swirled as it took shape. First a pair of sneakers, followed by legs, a torso, arms. I stared at my own face, and the sand lifted my image's lips into a smile. My stomach dipped. It was stupid to be jealous of myself, but a seed of discomfort planted itself anyway. Ben could be there for her in a way I couldn't. The fact that she would never know that particular truth… was sand in my wounds.

At that thought, I cleared my throat. Now was the wrong time to go looking for hope. Walking in her world may have taken more out of me than I could afford, but not going left her vulnerable. I had to concentrate on protecting her from the Weaver. Nothing else.

"That's Ben," Nora said in a flat, distinctly unhappy voice. "Katie and I ran into him today at the mall."

That wasn't intentional—the being spotted part, anyway. I meant to watch from afar in case the Weaver tried anything. Not that it mattered in the end. I drew a deep breath and pushed aside the growing guilt. "And?"

Nora shrugged one shoulder. "And nothing. He works at Howell's."

"*Nothing* doesn't show up in your dreams." Especially not the first one the sand finds. Those are the most important ones—the ones that give Dreamers the peace they need to truly rest.

She flicked a hand at Ben's abdomen, and the image scattered. "It's not a big deal."

"You must like him." I bit my tongue. Hadn't I just decided not to go seeking hope?

"Are you *jealous*?" She smirked, but it fell as fast as it came.

Of course, not—I'm much cuter, I almost joked, but I didn't want her to ask me to prove it. It was hard enough to resist showing myself. I wasn't sure why I bothered to hide anymore; it was meant as another way to keep a wall between us, but that wall had crumbled to dust. There was nothing *other* about my face besides my eyes. Nothing to scare her.

However, she now knew me as Ben. Would she feel lied to? Betrayed?

"Don't worry," Nora said with a sigh. Her nose wrinkled in the way that never failed to fill me with adoration, and she pinched her own cheeks, trying not to smile. "You're still my favorite, and I'm sure you're just as cute. If I ever saw you, I would probably dream about you too."

She thought I was cute? My hand twitched with the impulse to reveal myself, but before I could move, a familiar throb pulsated through my marrow. The Weaver was close. If Nora didn't stop dwelling on what happened, she would light his path right to our doorstep. I grabbed a second handful of sand and willed it into my own creation. A butterfly glided through the air to land on her knee.

"I truly am sorry, Nora," I said in a strained voice. "There were some things I needed to take care of. I didn't mean to stay away."

She nodded and turned her attention to the fluttering wings. "It's okay. Maybe not the *best* time for you to go M.I.A." Her nose wrinkled again, but this time her eyes lacked the playful glint that always accompanied it. "But you're back. That's what matters."

Nora hadn't looked this lost or confused since before we agreed she should lie to her mother about my existence. I felt just as horrible about it then as I do now, but I saw what those doctors were doing to her. The bright-eyed, care-free girl I knew faded slowly. She withdrew from all but two of her friends, tossed her astrology books in the dumpster behind the school, and quit the swim team in her freshman year. Though Nora still sketched, there was always a tightness around her eyes on the rare occasions she talked about it. Everything that might relate to me or this place put her under a microscope, so she replaced the slide that *was* her life with one that could withstand the scrutiny. But her manufactured existence lacked the fiery spark of her soul.

I released another handful of sand and a dozen smaller butterflies took shape. They landed in her hair, fluttering around her with graceful ease.

She reached out a hand to let one rest in her palm. "Can I ask you something?"

"Of course."

"Do you think you'll—" She squinted around me. "What's that?"

The sea shrunk away from the beach, and a tendril of black fog inched across the receding water. "Wake up." The words flew from my throat in a stunned breath. "Nora, wake up."

The fog snapped forward, crushing the butterflies mid-flight. Nora gasped, and I lurched to my feet. Sand rose with me, snapping together to form a long blade in my hand. The curved metal gleamed in the moonlight.

"Wake up," I shouted.

"What?"

"Wake. Up." A whistle sounded above us, and the retreating water rose into a tidal wave. It rushed toward the shore, eclipsing the sky. "Nora!" I screamed in a rush of terror.

She vanished, and I flung an empty hand at the wave. A break wall shot from the shore and caught the impact before collapsing. The mist writhed against the beach, scraping against the sand trying to find purchase. With Nora gone, taking her piece of my power out of play, the Dream Realm was entirely dependent on me, and I held no fear of the Weaver—only of what would happen if he escaped. Without fear, he had nothing to hold over me. Fear was his power, his strength, his everything.

"Weaver," I called. Binding aside, he was forbidden from this place. There were no living things for him to kill here, but his presence was a poison, infecting the beach, tainting the dreams. He had an entire world to govern—generals and soldiers, enemies and allies. There was no reason he should need mine or Nora's. "Show yourself."

The mist paused, and the Weaver's deep voice drifted from its center. "I'd love to, old friend, but it's a tight squeeze. Open a door so we can face each other."

"I will be dead before you step foot in here," I snarled.

A soft chuckle danced across the beach before the mist retreated beneath the water. I watched the last wisps vanish and exhaled. The sword disintegrated from tip to hilt. The barrier wasn't deep enough to keep him out—nothing I did was enough. It was a miracle I managed to bind the Weaver at all. My shoulders sagged. There was no guarantee I could do it again with the barriers and a Dream Keeper siphoning my power. Not when I had to resort to Day Walking to protect Nora.

The Weaver was still weak but keeping him that way meant weakening myself. It didn't matter who was right or wrong. It didn't matter that the Weaver had tried to unleash his beasts on the Day World. The universe always kept the balance.

For every light there was a shadow, for every dream, a nightmare.

I swept through Howell's, systematically adjusting chairs around tables and fidgeting with the decorative centerpieces. The police left the entire store a mess. I rolled my eyes. As if they would find something hidden beneath a vase... But I was thankful for the busy work. It kept me away from the office and Lisa's elderly father, who hadn't moved from the desk all morning. The music from his portable radio drifted through the store and, try as I might, I wasn't able to block out the cheerful rhythm. It fed my anxiety, making me jerk and jump without reason. They may have had to reopen the store to survive, but I didn't need to come back. I shouldn't have. But then again, sitting home wasn't much better.

I paused near the back room where Ben was busy talking to a young couple about office chairs. He smiled and laughed and joked with them. All things I would probably never do again after what happened at the mall. Detective Bell interviewed Katie and me last night. He was the same dark-skinned man that interrupted the woman's TV interview about Randy. He was nice enough, promising we weren't suspects, ensuring it was important to speak with eyewitnesses, but that didn't stop him from giving me a distinct once over. With two strange deaths in the same short span of time and my connection to both, there had to be suspicions.

"Hey, you," Ben said, bobbing his head slightly.

I jumped, nearly dropping a set of fifty-dollar bookends. A breath shuttered out of me as I hugged them to my chest. Break these and it was goodbye fancy new colored pencil set.

"You break it, you buy it," he said with a grin.

I laughed dryly and set the ceramic pieces down on top of a TV stand. "I break it, *you* buy it for scaring me." I rubbed my hands together to hide my shaking fingers.

His grin widened. "If I wanted to scare you, I would have done something a little more fun than saying *hey you.*"

My cheeks warmed. "Did you need something?"

"The computer says a rolling chair is in stock, but I'm not sure where to look."

We still hadn't finished the tour, and it was impossible to explain all the places in the back where the chair could be squirreled away. I chewed on the inside of my cheek. "I'll show you."

I led the way through the swinging doors to the back room with Ben following closely. The dry air tickled my nose, and I held my breath against the scent of wood and cardboard. We passed the motion sensor and fluorescent lights flickered to life overhead. The ones in the very back remained off. Randy was supposed to order more bulbs at the end of the month—I jerked again at the thought, quickly hiding it by pretending to trip over my own feet.

"Careful," Ben said, laced with concern.

I took a deep breath and slipped between two rows of large boxes. "Which model number do they want?"

He hesitated. "It's the brown leather one with an adjustable headrest. I can go get the number."

"No," I said, and he stuffed his hands into his pocket. "It's fine. I know which one you're talking about."

I steadied myself between the rows, gripping the rough, dusty boxes. Industrial staples poked precariously out of a few, and I squinted at the descriptions written on white stickers over the barcode. Last time I checked, there was one stuffed behind some mattresses, but if I could avoid climbing back there, I would. Besides, the longer I took in the back, the less time I had to spend out *there* talking to people. I was convinced half of the customers today were only here to be nosy.

A hard corner scraped my ankle through my khakis. I kicked at the offending cardboard until the overhang sat neatly on the shelf.

"I can get it," Ben offered.

I glanced up to where he stood at the end of the tight aisle, beneath the flickering bulb. It almost seemed like his tattoos glowed a bit in the split seconds between the light, which, of course, made no sense. It had to be a trick of the mind—or a special ink. Something. "Don't worry. I've done this a million times," I said. The hardest part was wedging a box out from between others, but once it hit the concrete floor, it slid down the row without much effort.

"But—"

"Please." I sighed and went back to reading labels. "It's been a rough couple of days, and I'm not in the mood to fight with you about which one of us should handle the manual labor."

He was quiet for a heartbeat. "I'm not trying to fight."

"I know," I admitted. He was trying to be nice, but with my mother's obnoxious, worried glances over dinner last night, that almost made it worse. I was flesh and bone just like he was, with good days and bad days, but on every single one of them, I was capable of carrying a stupid chair. A square box caught my attention at the end of the row, and I shimmied my way further down.

"If..." He paused. "If you ever need someone to talk to, you know, about what happened..."

The Sandman had annoyed me by not showing up and then asking me to leave, and the last few days *had* certainly left me with a lot to say, but I wasn't going to lean on Ben simply because he was available. The way he reminded me of the Sandman was too unnerving to allow anything more than necessary interactions between us. The mall was a mistake. I needed my sanity now more than ever and each time I looked at his handsome face, I wanted to picture it with a hood. "I already have people to talk to, but thanks."

"Your sister?" he asked.

"No. Katie will never talk about what happened again." Not that I blamed her in this case, but she had a way of pretending problems didn't exist. A family trait, I supposed. I couldn't help but wonder if she saw that spray of blood every time she shut her eyes too. If she heard the thump of the body hitting the floor whenever it was just a little too quiet. I leaned over a box and one corner caught me in the ribs. *Keep it together*, I begged myself. *Don't lose it in here.* I backed up and bounced on the balls of my feet.

"I do have friends, you know," I said, forcing myself back to the present.

"I know."

The way he said it made me believe he did know, and not in the everyone-has-friends way. "I found the chair, so if you want to go cash the customer out, I'll bring it up."

He stood there another moment before stepping back. His footsteps echoed off the high ceiling, and I blew out a breath. The last thing I needed was for someone to make me feel so transparent. I had too many deep, dark secrets for that. I shuffled the box back and forth, waiting to hear the swinging doors open, when warm fingers grazed the back of my neck. I clasped a hand over the touch and spun. Boxes were stacked one on top of the other, leaving no room for someone to reach between.

"Ben?" I whispered, the hair on my arm standing on end.

A low, rumbling chuckle brushed my ear. I flattened myself against the boxes and closed my eyes. *It wasn't real.* This was what suppressing my feelings got me—another person in my head, tormenting me. Maybe my brain was simply wired differently. Maybe... maybe... I had no idea. Stress affected people differently, I was told. Hallucinations must have been my go-to coping mechanism.

Lucky me.

A warm brush of air sent goosebumps rippling over my skin.

"Get away from her," a voice hissed. I gripped the edge of the steel shelf. *Sandman?*

"Did you think you could hide her forever?" asked a rich voice with an undercurrent of fury.

I crept down the aisle, my heart jack-hammering in my chest. My knees shook, and I peeked between boxes. Ben's white shirt stood out in the unlit corner. His tattooed hands were balled in fists while he spoke. "Not forever. That's why I took precautions."

The chuckle rose again. "You're already failing."

"Am I?" Ben whispered with enough venom to make a viper jealous.

I snuck into an empty space between two cellophane-wrapped desks. Who was he talking to? I leaned on one desk for support and squinted. The corner was empty. I froze. Maybe the killer was Ben after all—maybe he followed Randy home before coming in and the girl... I didn't know about the girl. The cashier did it to herself, but if I was crazy for talking to someone in my dreams, then Ben was crazy for talking to shadows. Shadows that I heard as clearly as he seemed to. One thing was certain—he had no idea how far voices carried back here.

"You think you're safe from me because you don't hold it yourself." Something moved in the corner, a flash of gold slicing through the black. I slapped a hand over my mouth to keep from screaming. "You've convinced yourself that you have nothing to be afraid of, but I smell it on you, old friend. You reek of fear. My freedom isn't the only weapon I have against you anymore. It hasn't been for a while now."

Then the corner brightened a fraction, and Ben flexed his fingers. I sprinted down the aisle to the chair and gripped the edges of the box. I couldn't listen to another word. To another delusion. With a jolt, I yanked the box forward. It crashed down on my big toe, and I yelped.

"Are you okay?" Ben darted down the narrow aisle and bent to free my foot.

"Yes." I rubbed a dust-covered wrist over my forehead. He couldn't know I overheard anything—either he was crazier than I was, or I was officially ready for an institute. Choice A might put me in danger. Choice B meant outing myself. Neither option was all that appealing. I needed to get away from him, from everyone, and think before I opened my mouth.

"I need to go home early today," I said in a hushed voice as a frenzy of emotions withered in my gut.

Ben walked backward, guiding the chair from my path. "Okay."

"You've got that?" I said, motioning to the chair. "It's the right one?"

His eyes searched my face. Seeing. Too seeing. "Yes."

I bolted from the back, leaving Ben alone with his invisible foe. Only, he wasn't quite invisible—because I saw him. Sort of. Flashes of black and gold. A silhouette.

No. I saw nothing. *Nothing, nothing, nothing.*

"Nora!" someone called.

A moment later, I was tackled from behind. Black spots danced in my vision before I recognized the voice as Natalie's. My friend squeezed my waist, mumbling something about missing me into my shoulder.

"What are you doing here?" I asked, patting the arms that held me in place. Part of me wanted to let her hold me so I didn't fall over with relief, but touchy-feely wasn't really my thing. "I thought you weren't coming back from vacation until Friday."

"It *is* Friday." Natalie released me from the embrace and spun me around. "Why aren't you taking our calls? We've been trying to get a hold of you for days. Emery went to your house yesterday, but Katie said you weren't feeling well."

"I wasn't." I faked a cough, knowing full well she would see the lie. "See?"

"Oh no, don't you play those games with me, missy." She grabbed my hand and dragged me through the store. "You're avoiding us, so you don't have to talk about what happened."

That was exactly what I was doing. After the mall, the press intensified their efforts to get in touch with me and an unmarked police car sat at each end of the block now. Turning off my ringer, ignoring calls and texts, was the best way to prevent reliving the real-life nightmares. The Sandman had the beach on some sort of lockdown—he wouldn't say more than that. I only knew that much because he slipped up during one of the few brief moments we saw each other, mumbling something about barriers.

"We're not going to ask about anything," Natalie continued, "and I've secured you an early release." Lisa's father smiled and waved to us on our way toward the exit.

My stomach churned. "Where are we going?"

"Wait," Ben called, and I tensed. "You forgot your purse."

I turned slowly enough to register the look of shock and awe plastered over Natalie's face. A bolt of unexplained jealousy pierced my chest. I had no claim on Ben and I didn't want one. Did I? He was just talking to shadows, so, if for no other reason,

I shouldn't let myself be interested. I couldn't risk *his* crazy feeding mine.

Besides, Natalie already had a boyfriend. Who I hadn't seen in ages because he graduated last year. And I was busy studying. Or working. Or, really, just having an overall aversion to the whole large-social-gathering thing. *Did* she still have a boyfriend? Surely, she would've told me if they broke up…

"Thanks." I plucked the straps from his hand. "See you later."

Natalie clutched my arm. "Who's this?"

"Natalie, Ben," I said with reluctance. "Ben, Natalie."

She held out her hand, and they shook. "We're heading to the carnival tonight at six," she told him.

"We're what?" I asked. There would be way too many people there—most with prying eyes and curious minds. I clutched my purse to my chest. If I thought the attention from Randy was bad, how much worse would it be now?

"Want to meet us there?" she said, ignoring me.

Ben quirked a mischievous smile. "You'll be there?" he asked me.

"I don't—"

"She'll be there." Natalie tugged me toward the doors again. "See you later."

We were outside then, peeling toward Natalie's rusted heap of a car. I threw myself inside, still hugging my purse, and slammed the door. "I can't believe you did that."

"Listen." She turned the key once, twice, and the engine turned over. "I've waited our whole lives to double date."

Date. With Ben? "No."

"Fine." She scrunched her curls. "Don't date him, but, just know, he's clearly interested. And besides, I can't uninvite him now."

I glared across the seat at her. First Katie, now Natalie. I almost didn't want to date Ben, based solely on principle. "I hate you."

"You love me." She moved to pinch the apple of my cheek, and I leaned out of reach. "Anyway, you'll never guess what my aunt did this year. Go on, guess."

Curses. Natalie always had the best stories after her family reunions. "Did she spike the punch bowl again?"

"That too." Natalie laughed, spitting out the latest story between gasps for air, until we turned into my driveway. Emery's van was parked on the street while she sat on my lawn, plucking blades of grass. I twisted my purse straps. They were my friends, and Natalie promised they wouldn't ask questions. Maybe Katie was right when she said I needed to stop hiding in my room. My bad luck had to be used up for the next few years…going anywhere should be safe.

As safe as the back room at Howell's.

I forced a wide smile and slid from the passenger seat.

"The lost has been found," Emery called. Her red hair was twisted back into a regal bun, making the worry etched on her face stand out.

"Hello to you too," I answered with as much cheer as I could muster.

"Come on," Natalie prodded. "There are movies, pizza, and a present from California waiting inside."

The present turned out to be a small amethyst charm on a thin chain bracelet. I fiddled with my birthstone through the chick-flicks they rented, forcing my attention to remain solely on the movie. They talked around me—summer jobs, family, gossip—and I tried to listen to that too. I tried to engage. It was harder than usual, though. The echoes of the voice in the shadows overrode them, chafing against my skull, until we finally left for the carnival.

Stalls peppered the park. The sugary smell of cotton candy and caramel corn filled the air, and huge lights buzzed with electricity. A rainbow of colored bulbs flashed on the Ferris wheel. Somewhere, someone squealed with joy, and I dug my nails into my palms.

"Hey there, pretty lady," called a man on a microphone. He stood beneath a striped booth with wooden rings in his hand. "Care to give it a try?"

Emery shrugged and stepped up to the counter. Her little brother loved it when she brought him home something. I leaned against Natalie to watch Emery toss the rings at the pins. "Are you having fun?" I asked.

"Yeah," Natalie said, giving me a playful shove. "Are you?"

"Yes." I ground out the word as a spinning ride started a few feet away and another shout rang through the crowd.

"I forgot to tell you earlier, but my grandma is visiting next month."

"Grandma B?" I brightened at the thought. Her grandmother was like the one I never had, and she knew how to spoil a girl. Nothing beat her chili, either. Or her pie. And that pasta chicken thing she made. I was going to need bigger pants. "How long is she staying?"

"Two weeks, and she wants to take us to Miami again." She wagged her eyebrows. "You know what that means?"

"Road trip," we sang at the same time and laughed.

A soft tap touched my arm and I whirled around, all humor instantly gone. "Hi," Ben said, rubbing the back of his neck.

My heart sputtered. He came. He *actually* came. And he looked down at me as if I had painted the moon in the sky. My cheeks burned at the wonderment written all over his face, and it struck me. Maybe Natalie was right. Maybe… Maybe he was interested. "You're here."

"Did you doubt me?" He nudged me with his elbow and gave me his starlit smile. The fire in my face spread down to the pit of my stomach.

Emery cheered for herself, and the man with the microphone handed over a neon green stuffed frog. Natalie backed away from Ben and me, smiling. "Ferris wheel?" she suggested to Emery.

I felt the weight of Emery's eyes on me, curious and wondering. Unless Natalie filled her in on one of my bathroom breaks, she had no idea who Ben was or what he was doing here. But she nodded. Later on, there would be questions. So many questions.

"Do you want to go on it too?" Ben asked, eyeing the ride with a hopeful expression.

Natalie winked at me, and they moved toward the surprisingly short line. Now that Ben was here, my desire to leave peaked. This place, with the crowds and loud music, was suffocating. As always. More than always. I didn't have the energy to pretend things were okay, but I didn't have the energy to fight against my friends' efforts either. "We don't have to," I said.

He shrugged one shoulder and looked up at the hanging seats. "I don't mind."

I did. We would be stuck in close quarters for several long minutes, and I wasn't sure how I felt about that. Or, at least, I wasn't sure how I was supposed to feel. "I'm sort of afraid of heights so..."

He smirked. "No, you're not." He motioned me forward, and I glared at him, too shocked by his surety to insist we stay on the ground. "I promise, I don't bite." He winked and added, "Hard."

I folded my arms across my chest and crinkled my nose. "Sorry, I've seen too many movies to want to hang out with a vampire."

"Fine, fine. No biting," he said with false disappointment. He took my hand and tugged me gently after my friends.

My feet dragged down the line. It felt as if my sandals were made of iron as I stepped into the swaying bucket. Ben slid in beside me, and the attendant slammed a bar across our laps with a deafening *clack*. We jolted backward and stopped to let people into the seat in front of us.

"Sorry if it's weird Natalie asked you to come today," I blurted. It wasn't safe for any words to leave my mouth with so many feelings happening at once.

His hands hung loosely over the metal bar. "Why would it be weird?"

"Because we barely know each other." Although it felt like we did. Maybe it was only weird for me. "And you just met her today."

The ride moved again, this time keeping a steady pace the entire way around. Natalie and Emery twisted in their bucket to look down at us. "You two behave," Emery shouted.

I blushed. What had Natalie told her in the last two minutes? Gross exaggerations, obviously. Ones she would pay for with copious amounts of cheesecake. "Ignore them."

Ben paused, then winked playfully and looked up at my friends. His arm slipped around my shoulders, warm and solid, and Natalie whooped before turning around. When they weren't looking, his arm slid away slowly. I fought the urge to draw it back. The image of him talking to the voice floated through my mind, and I gripped the bar instead. It wasn't the first strange thing he'd done. There was the knowing look on his face when the police flew past Howell's and his odd reaction to the girl with the pen.

"I've been wondering." I pressed my lips together. It wasn't something I could just say. "When we were shopping and... things happened, why did you tell that girl to wake up?"

The muscles in his jaw flexed. "She was nodding off before that, so I guess I just assumed."

"But to do what she did, she would need to be in REM sleep, and that doesn't happen until you've been asleep about ninety minutes." The cashier nodded off but was awake minutes before. That fact bothered me since. I refused to let the thought form before now because if I thought about it, I would be forced to think that something else was going on. Something strange and unexplainable. But that's exactly what was happening.

He nodded. "I see you're a sleep expert."

"I've done a little research," I said flatly.

He shrugged, sobering. "I don't know why I said that to her."

What about the back room was on the tip of my tongue, but I wasn't brave enough to hear him deny the truth outright. First, I had some questions for the Sandman. Mainly, if there was any validity to my thoughts. Then, *then*, I would corner Ben and ask him what he knew.

"How was the rest of work?" I asked to change the subject.

"Did you know there are twenty-seven shades of blue you can order furniture in?"

I cocked an eyebrow. "That boring, huh?"

"Of course. You weren't there," he bantered, but his expression shuttered. He stared out across the brightly lit area, his gaze hyper-focused as he scanned our surroundings. "How was not working?"

"Oh, you know." My hair floated around my face, pieces drifting into Ben's personal space. I gathered it into one hand and held it to the side, away from him. "Apparently we're having a sleepover at Emery's tonight, so the fun never ends."

He looked at me then. A look that knew everything I didn't say out loud. A look that said it was okay that I didn't mean it when I said it would be fun. One that said it was okay if I needed to break a little bit. And maybe I did, or maybe I had to do the impossible and swallow my pride. If I asked my mother to take me back to a doctor, she would. But for that brief second beside him, it didn't feel like I was cracking around the edges.

It drew me closer, the space between us shrinking. I needed that feeling. I needed it like I needed air in my lungs. The outsides of our thighs pressed together. Ben inhaled through parted lips, his eyes glowing as they watched my lips. Before I could think about what I was doing, I stretched up to kiss him. The world exploded in a shower of stars, the Ferris wheel no longer the only thing making me soar. It was everything. Every promise, every hope, every dream.

Ben's body stiffened, and I froze. What was I doing? It was my first kiss, and it was with someone I barely knew. It didn't matter that he felt familiar. He was little more than a stranger. I eased back, but his fingers grazed my jaw. He leaned into me, caressing my lips with his own. A small, almost pained, groan escaped him, and he broke away.

I gasped at the sudden loss of contact. Something tugged deep in my chest, tightening. My mind scrambled to make sense of what just happened. I kissed him. He kissed me back. It was right and wrong and everything between.

"Sorry," I breathed. "I'm an idiot."

Ben ran his middle finger over his bottom lip. "Don't be sorry," he said, his voice slightly husky.

I rubbed my face and groaned. There couldn't be a worse place than a carnival ride for me to make the first move. How much longer would I be trapped?

"Hey." He reached out and flicked my side-swept bangs back in place. "I mean it."

I scooted as far away from him as the bench allowed. "Sure."

We stayed that way—me squished in the corner and Ben staring down at nothing in particular—until the worker unlocked the bar imprisoning us. I bolted off the platform. My friends gaped, and I shoved my way out the exit. "I'm going to find the bathroom," I shouted, and didn't stop running until they were out of sight.

"Nora," Ben called after me. "Nora, wait! Please."

I ducked behind the game tents and gulped the sweet-scented air. "Stupid, stupid, stupid." I groaned. In all my life, of all the idiotic things I'd done, this was the worst. And Ben... He had no idea what he was getting into with someone like me. Unless he knew *exactly* what he was getting because he saw the same things I did. The Sandman hadn't known him but there was no denying what happened earlier today.

The Sandman. How was I going to tell him about what happened? I couldn't hide anything from him when he read my dreams. A kiss—my first kiss—would *definitely* show up. Especially when it was with someone I was maybe into, and when that someone was as hot as Ben was. The Sandman shouldn't care though. Even if he did, it shouldn't matter, but guilt nibbled at my insides anyway.

"Hello, Dream Keeper."

The voice froze me in place. It was louder than before, more direct and less frenzied. "You're not real," I whispered, swallowing.

"Of course, I am." The shadows shifted. A flash of black. A speck of gold. The same thing I saw in the back room. "Don't play hard to get, my little Sun-Kissed one. Give me what I seek."

"You're. Not. Real," I insisted. *Except Ben heard you too.* My eye twitched.

"There are two people who would beg to differ. Alas, you cannot ask them now, can you?"

I turned my back to the shadow and stepped toward the crowd. I wasn't going to stand there and let a bodiless voice twist the knife in my stomach. The deaths weren't jokes. *Those* were real, tangible things. It wasn't a hazy truth like the Sandman.

Everyone acknowledged them, their loved ones living with the fresh scars of loss. I blinked against an imagined splatter of red.

"Your Sandman knows," the voice continued as if reading my mind. "He knows many things, Dream Keeper. Many things you do not. Dangerous things. Dark things. Things that will make you regret and things that will make you hate. Things you don't want to know but things you should. Things, things. Many things. Things that tie us together, little Keeper."

My head tilted back to watch the shadow from the corner of my eye. My heart threatened to explode from my chest. What did he know? What *didn't* I know? And why was he calling me a Dream Keeper?

"Let's make a deal, shall we?" The shadow pressed forward into the hazy outline of a man. "If you give me the dream, now, tonight, then I promise not to torment anyone else you're fond of."

I didn't know who—what—he was, if he was anything, but the offer made my entire body itch. *Torment.* I cringed. That was exactly what happened in the mall. The terror on the cashier's face was more real than anything. My stomach bottomed out. The shadowy-figure wasn't simply recapping the deaths. He was the reason for them. I shook my head to clear away the ridiculous, impossible thoughts, but they refused to go. My pulse throbbed through my body, and I dove back into the masses to find my friends.

The pewter-grey sky of the Nightmare Realm cast everything in long, twisting shadows. I tried to ignore the ones that moved and focused instead on the miles of blackness that stretched out before me on the other side of the barrier. The wall gave beneath my hand, wobbling across the entrance to the Day World. A thousand flecks of sand sputtered along the glimmering wall before going dull. Thousands more had already lost their magic while others struggled to hold the line. Only a few patches remained solid and titanium strong, mainly where it clung to the fabric of the Nightmare Realm. I would have thought the edges would fail first—especially since I just fixed this portion two nights ago.

I drew in a deep breath and squinted at the barrier. If it was fading this quickly, the Weaver was regaining his strength faster than I realized. I would need to double the thickness. Triple it. And I still had to find him. In all the years I'd known him, the Weaver was never this hard to locate.

Baku paced behind me, his claws clicking on the stony ground. "You know," I said over my shoulder. "If there *are* any nightmares lurking nearby, they're not going to come out if they see you."

Baku twisted his head to stare at me and turned for another trek across the wasteland.

I smirked. "You would probably get a quicker meal if you hid until someone got it in their mind to attack me."

Baku brushed against the back of my legs, knocking me forward a step.

"Fine, fine." I laughed. "It was just a suggestion."

I reached into the leather satchel hanging at my hip and scooped up two handfuls of sand. I blew it out in front of me, and the grains froze in a sheet. Setting my fingertips against it, I pressed it into the existing barrier and smoothed it down with my palms. The magic absorbed it, drinking it in, until the area glowed blue, then faded to nothing but a mere shimmer.

Inch by inch the barrier shone with new power. I worked my way down, silently grateful Nora was sleeping at her friend's house tonight. She would be later than usual, if she came at all. It was already past three in the morning so when she finally closed her eyes, she might be too tired to dream.

Still, my gut twisted at the possibility of not seeing her. She never shut me out on purpose, but what if tonight was different? What if our kiss was too much and she couldn't stand the thought of seeing me? She ran off so fast I wasn't sure what to think.

I paused to rub the back of my hand over my tingling lips. When she kissed me, the cord between us had thrashed greedily. It was impossible she hadn't felt it too. My only hope was that she hadn't understood, or had written it off as nerves. A lump formed in my throat.

Besides, it wasn't *our* kiss.

It was her kiss with Ben. Even if she did sense similarities between Ben and me, she would never believe it. Just like she would never have kissed me as my true self—it was probably my fault. I set up the rules. I lied. I omitted and pretended.

It was *definitely* my fault.

But my world had unfurled on the Ferris wheel. The kiss was everything I never knew I was missing and more. It would be wrong to coax her into talking about it tonight when she thought I was a neutral third party, but *damn it*, I needed to know where her thoughts were.

I would have to tell her the truth soon anyway, especially if I planned to continue Day Walking. Truthfully, the best thing to do was to stop going; I wasn't able to stop the Weaver from killing Randy or the girl in the shop, anyway. He had occupied the shadows at the edge of the carnival, lingering outside the lights too. I wasn't doing anything but complicating my friendship with the girl that held the key to my enemy's cage. That's all she could ever be to me. All that was fair. But it was a crushing reality. A pebble here, a boulder there, building up over the last year, but now it felt like a rock slide, on the brink of an avalanche.

I sighed and scanned my work again. The barrier was as clear as it was around the beach now and just as sturdy. Nothing was slipping out.

"That should hold until I recharge," I said to Baku.

"Should it?" the Weaver drawled.

My heart leapt into my throat, and I spun around. Baku was nowhere to be seen but my counterpart stood before me, larger than I remembered. His black hair was smoothed into a tight bun. A long, refined nose ran between his wide brows and below them, his eyes glowed molten gold. The perfect nightmare. Alluring enough to draw someone in, terrifying enough to turn them inside out. And it all but gutted me.

"You've made improvements since I was here last," he said. "But if you need to recharge after such a menial task..."

I bared my teeth.

"Tsk. So hostile." He scanned the wall behind me. The gold embroidery on his sleeveless black vest shifted on its own. Threads of gold and black ran off his left shoulder, hugging his muscular bicep before snaking down to his wrist, looping into a band. The loose ends strummed above his pulse point as if they shared his heartbeat. "Give me what I want, and I'll never bother you again."

"That's all you *would* do, Weaver," I said, my voice even more weary than I was.

Every time I turned around, he was testing me. Coming to the beach for no purpose other than to taint my sand, experimenting with his nightmares to find one to inhabit my slumber. Letting nightmares into the Day World was the last straw, but his antics stretched back to the very beginning. If only the playful intent behind it all had stayed the same, maybe then we could've avoided this mess.

I reached into my satchel for more sand and called power from my reserves. It would take more than I had to re-bind him, not to mention that I had none of his threads to use against him. The playing field was even. I could hurt him as easily as he could hurt me, and which one of us left in better condition came down to one thing: determination. Unfortunately, the Weaver loved power as much as I loved Nora.

"I have thousands of creatures that do my bidding. I have an *army*. What do you have?" His voice was low, bordering angry, but his muscles were loose, relaxed. "Don't you miss it?"

"Miss what?" I snapped.

The hard edges of him softened. "The way things used to be."

My eyes narrowed to slits. "Whose fault is it that they're different?"

"Ours," he said with a defeated sighed. Then his face hardened. "You alone won't be enough to keep me out after tonight."

After tonight. My lungs constricted. "What did you do?"

He grinned, running his thumb over his nails.

"Tell me," I demanded.

"The Dream Keeper is a pretty little thing," he said carefully. "I'd hate for anything to happen to her because you refused to cooperate."

Liar. I tossed the sand into the air but before it could take shape, he disappeared. I turned my focus inside, reaching for the cord that connected me to Nora. She was fine—alive and already asleep. How had I missed it? My magic was trained to catch her subconscious if I had enough power to spare, but I still *felt* it. Unless I was so drained tonight, I hadn't noticed.

The important thing was that she was safe.

I loosened a breath and fled the Nightmare Realm before the Weaver had a chance to change his mind about fighting. He was right—he had an army. Hundreds of years' worth of power prowled his lands and what did I have? A beach full of sand I was too tapped to properly wield? If I was going to beat him a second time, I had to reclaim my strength.

Nora strolled down the edge of the water. Her arms wrapped around her abdomen, and her lip trembled. She couldn't see me yet—not behind the secondary barrier I placed to divide my realm in two. One side was mine, the other hers. Separation. Distance. Neutrality. Yet another wasted effort.

I slid the strap of my satchel over my head and dropped it to the ground. Nora let her head fall back. Her shoulders rose and fell with a deep breath. I tugged on my gloves, flipped my hood low over my face and stepped forward.

She didn't see me coming until I was nearly beside her. When she did, she froze and looked at me like I was a stranger. Like the last five years never happened.

"I'm sorry," I blurted, my heart seizing. "I didn't think you would come tonight."

"I'm sleeping at Emery's," she said, hollow.

"Are..." I swallowed. "Are you okay?"

She shook her head. "I need to get some help."

"Help with what?" I asked, cautiously.

"I can't function like this. Hearing things, seeing you… I can't focus. It's like I'm floating out to sea without a paddle and no one cares because I've been adrift for years anyway."

My breath stuck in my throat. This was worse than the kiss. She meant help with me—to get rid of me. There was nothing the doctors could do to erase my presence, but it hurt all the same. I clenched my jaw until my teeth ached.

"Of course, people care," I said. "I care."

She choked on a sob. "But you aren't *real*, Sandman."

"I've always been real," I whispered.

But she either ignored the comment or didn't hear it. I was here—*really* here. No matter how hard she tried to block me out, I was as fixed as the sun. But, maybe that would be best. I could still protect her dreams from the other side of the beach, the side she never saw, and there would be no distractions.

"Are there other things like you?" she blurted, running her fingers down her arms.

My back straightened, my hands sweating. "I'm the only Sandman."

"That's not what I meant." She advanced two steps. "Is there anything else out there? Something that hurts people?"

"I'm not sure where this is com—"

"Where this is coming from?" she finished for me, her eyes flashing incredulously. "How about the fog last night for starters? You know more than you're telling me."

I swallowed hard. There were so many things I had to tell her that I didn't know where to start. If now was even the right time for it. "I..."

"What's a Dream Keeper?" she snapped.

My blood ran cold. "Where did you hear that?"

"A little birdie told me," she said carefully from between her teeth.

"The Weaver?" I asked before I could stop myself. Rage splashed against my insides. I knew he was up to something but talking directly to Nora? I expected him to be subtler than that. The stairwell and back room at Howell's... Did she hear him then? I thought he was trying to get to me, not her. Maybe if I hadn't been so busy, if I had taken a few minutes to listen to her that first night the Weaver pushed at the barrier between our worlds, I would have known. "Don't listen to him, Nora. He's dangerous."

Her eyes widened, her mouth dropping, then her face pinched. Suspicion lined her features. A flush of anger and fear colored her cheeks. I'd never seen that shade on her before. "What is a Dream Keeper?" she asked again in a low voice, enunciating each word with a stone-cold edge.

I couldn't lie. Not when she asked so directly. Not when she deserved the truth a long time ago. If she was going to learn it now, it was better that it came from me.

"You are," I whispered, my throat tight, and braced myself for her reaction.

She jerked back, eying me like I had just given her a death sentence. I prayed I hadn't.

"Nora—"

"No." She shook her head violently, her fingers digging into the hair around her ears. "Dream Keeper? As in keeping a dream? But he said if I didn't give it to him... And I... Then that means..." Her face fell, draining of color.

Then she vanished.

I stared at the indents her feet left in the sand and willed my lungs to inhale again. That could have gone better. Tomorrow felt like a lifetime to wait for a chance to explain.

Everything.

Before I lost her forever. I tugged on the cord that connected me to Nora, asking her to come back. Begging. But there was no reply.

Chapter Eight

Nora

Darkness enveloped the living room when I woke, leaving my friends as nothing but hazy outlines in the room. I sat up and took deep, shaky breaths. *Dream Keeper.* The title echoed through me over and over, alternating voices between the Weaver and the Sandman, until I slammed my hands over my ears. How could things have gotten so bad so quickly? Imagining the Sandman was manageable, but now I was twisting real life events to fit with my warped fantasy dream-life. *Sick.* I had to be.

But I could never actually ask my mother for help. No matter how much I needed to.

I climbed quietly to my feet so as not to wake anyone, and crept over throw pillows, then Emery. My foot knocked a plastic cup. "Crap," I muttered. Hopefully that was water—her mom was rather proud of the new beige carpet. My foot squished into the liquid, and I cringed as it oozed between my toes.

A night light glowed at the end of the hall. Emery's little brother had a hard time finding the bathroom without it, and I silently thanked him for that as I tip-toed across the tile. A quick stop at the store in the morning to get my own wasn't the worst idea. Maybe more than one. I should count the number of outlets in my room first. All I needed was to wake up to a stand of burnt out mini-lights. I wrinkled my nose. Or maybe I should just start sleeping with the light on and consider it problem solved.

With a quick flick of the bathroom light switch, I shut myself inside. My fingers curled around the edge of the sink, and I leaned forward to place my forehead on the cool mirror. *I've always been real*, the Sandman had said. *You are*, he had answered when I asked about a Dream Keeper.

The words overlapped, bumping and scraping against each other in a bid to be heard. Keeping a true heart and a true mind in my dreams should've meant the beach was safe. *Should have.* If I had remembered to keep both things, that is. I said I trusted the Sandman, but there was someone more important that I had to have faith in: myself. Self-trust was something I hadn't known in years, if ever, and it was becoming increasingly impossible to uphold.

But if I believed in myself, then I would have to believe what the Weaver said at the carnival—that he would hurt someone. He wanted me to give him a dream, but what did that mean? How would I give something like that away? It isn't a material thing I could hand over. More importantly, *why* did he want it? Maybe he wanted access to the Sandman, so he could hurt him. My heart sunk. How was I supposed to justify choosing someone that lived in my head over real people? *But* if one of them was real, so was the other.

Stop it. I couldn't let my delusions run wild. *None of this is real.* None *of it.*

I stood straight and splashed water on my face. "Okay," I said to my reflection. The soft lighting made me appear haggard; the dark circles beneath my eyes looked black, my cheeks, sunken. I was paler than usual, which until that moment, I hadn't thought was possible.

I couldn't stay at Emery's tonight. I wanted—*needed*—the comfort of my own bed. Using the hand-towel, I dried my face and reached for the light again when a shadow flicked near the toilet. My stomach lurched. I swung the door open and leapt into the hall. The shadow followed. My joints locked and I stood, watching little yellow fish float inside the sea-themed night light, willing the impossible away. The house was quiet. Quiet and still. I held my breath and listened. Silence.

Calm down. I sighed and dropped my head. *Everything is fine.*

At my feet, dark toe-prints lined the hallway floor, rows of dark circles staining the grey slate. Somehow, deep down, I knew. I knew it wasn't juice I stepped in. A collection of snapshots flashed before me. The police cars rushing by Howell's. Lisa on the news. The cashier with the pen in her hand. The spray of crimson as her body fell to the floor.

Blood.

It was blood. I could never mistake the sight of it. My stomach dropped.

"Natalie?" I called, my voice tight. "Emery?"

Let them be annoyed that I woke up them up. *Let them.* I took two halting steps back toward the living room. *Let's make a deal*, the Weaver had said earlier. My breath stuck in my throat. That wasn't real. It couldn't have been. But maybe. I swallowed hard.

"You awake?" I shouted down the hall.

Oh please, oh please, oh please.

The hallway tilted, and I lost my balance. My shoulder collided with the wall. I slid my way back to the living room and fumbled with the knob on the tall floor lamp.

I couldn't look.

I had to look.

"Guys?" I pleaded, tears welling in my eyes. "Someone say something."

The ice machine in the refrigerator grumbled, sending me straight into the air. The back of my hand knocked the lampshade. I steadied the rocking light with my other hand, and found the knob, twisting until the bulb clicked on. Light flooded the room, but my gaze stayed on the pleated white fabric of the shade. I waited. Held my breath. Prayed someone would grumble for me to turn it off. But no one did. Not after five seconds. Not after ten.

"Anyone?" I whispered desperately. The silence pressed against me. Pressed and pressed and pressed until, finally, I lifted my eyes.

My soul left my body.

Everywhere. The blood was everywhere—coating the walls, painting the furniture red, turning the floor into a swamp.

Emery's body was sprawled out in the same place as when I stepped over her. Her dull eyes stared up at the ceiling. Long, jagged cuts carved both forearms deep enough to see muscle and bone.

Natalie faced the hall from the recliner, two empty sockets staring across the room. Gleaming red streams coated her cheeks. Clutched in her hands were both eyes.

The room pulsated with light and dark. I fought against the lightheadedness. This wasn't real. Not real. Not...

Across the room, scrawled in blood on the bay window, was *DREAMER, DREAMER* beside a smiley face. Something clicked, every ounce of denial shattering. The surreal feeling fell away, replaced by a rage so blistering the scars would never fade. The scream that tore from my throat engulfed me, tore me down, down, down until I folded in on myself.

I rubbed my puffy eyes against the memory of red and blue lights flickering through the window. Highlighting the words written there. Reflecting off the pools of blood, too much for the carpet to absorb. Against flashes of ivory bone poking through skin and dull, lifeless eyes. *Eyes.* I choked back the swell of acid that ignited the back of my throat.

This was my fault. The Weaver wanted to make a deal, but I didn't listen. I tried so hard to convince myself that he wasn't real when I knew he was. If I had given him the dream, whatever it was, my friends would still be alive. Who else would he hurt to get to me? Who was next on his list? Knowing what I know now, would I say no if he asked again?

"Miss Gallagher, I need you to focus," Detective Bell said. I pressed my back against the steel chair and brought my feet up to the seat, burying my face in my knees. "If you want us to catch who did this to your friends, we need you to tell us what you know."

"Where's my mom?" I croaked, my throat still raw from screaming. "I want my mother."

"She's... filling out the paperwork. You're a witness, not a suspect so we can go ahead without her." He clicked his pen a few times, looking purposely down at his notebook. "You said you didn't hear anything."

"No." I lifted my head weakly. The past few hours cooled my fury to a simmer, waiting. Waiting for the second my head hit the pillow. For the Sandman to show his face. I wasn't sure what my answer would be if the Weaver asked again, but I had to end this before he got the chance. For that, I needed the Sandman's help. This wasn't about me anymore. It hadn't been since Randy was murdered, but now it was personal. Now I didn't simply want the Weaver to go away. I wanted him to pay. In flesh. In blood. In pain and death. And I wanted to be the one to do it.

I could only hope I had the willpower to not give in first.

I drew in a shallow breath. "No," I said again, louder. "I wasn't feeling well when I woke up, so I went to the bathroom. When I came back, I turned on the light..."

Detective Bell scooted his chair closer to the table. "Emery Williams' arms were sliced to ribbons, and Natalie Flores, the girl you've been friends with since preschool, clawed out her own eyes. They're dead. Gone. Horrifically murdered. They'll never get to see their families again. They won't graduate next year. They won't go to college, get married, have families. They won't grow old. Their lives are over, Nora. So, I say to you again, people aren't killed like they were without there being some noise. Likely *a lot* of it, based on the crimes committed. These were not pain-free deaths. If someone threatened to hurt you, if you give names, we can keep you safe."

I wanted to fall from the chair and melt into the linoleum. There was no noise during the murders. No struggle. No intruder. Emery's father double-checked all the doors and windows before we settled in to watch a movie. They were still secured when the police arrived. The *thing* behind their deaths cared nothing about locks. The note on the window left no room for doubt—not that I harbored any. I hadn't imagined the voice or invented fantastical theories. Everyone else saw the message.

It was real.

All of it was real.

"You must be a sound sleeper," Detective Bell said when I was silent.

"Apparently Emery's entire family is," I countered. How could I explain it was the Weaver without landing myself in a padded cell? Besides, I wasn't sure exactly how he killed them yet. Just that he did.

His scowl deepened. "A lot of people are dying under strange circumstances. Your boss." He ticked off a finger. "The cashier. Now your closest friends while you slept right beside them."

I swallowed against the rawness of my throat. "I haven't done anything wrong."

Detective Bell removed his glasses and pinched the bridge of his nose. "This doesn't look good. You understand that, don't you?"

"No. I don't. If I did anything to my friends, why wasn't I covered in blood? And, like you pointed out, how could I have pulled that off without waking someone up? In case it's missing from your file, Natalie was a super athlete. If I tried to gouge her eyes out, don't you think she would have knocked me into next week?" I took a ragged breath. I didn't know how the Weaver managed to do it so quietly, but I certainly couldn't have. It was impossible.

"Besides, you have the girl at the mall on surveillance. How can you possibly think I had anything to do with that?"

The detective cleared his throat. "Just because you didn't commit the murders tonight, doesn't mean you don't know who did. You could have let someone into Emery's tonight and locked the door behind them on their way out."

"I didn't," I said as hard and sharp as an axe.

He settled his glasses back over his nose. "Do you have a problem with anyone? Is there anyone that would want to hurt you by hurting people around you? An ex-boyfriend, maybe?"

As it turned out, I did have someone out to get me, but I answered, "I don't have any ex-boyfriends."

The door creaked open and a young officer looked in. "Detective?"

"What is it?"

"Her mother is demanding to be let in."

Detective Bell tossed his pen to the table. "We're done here. She'll be out in a second."

The officer nodded and disappeared.

"I really don't know anything," I insisted more gently.

He glowered. "I don't have time for lies when someone is out there terrorizing the town."

"Neither do I." I put my palms on the table to slide the chair away. "If I knew anything, I would tell you."

"There's one more thing before you go," he said, his tone softening.

I froze. What else could there possibly be?

"I apologize for withholding this from you, but it's important we find the person responsible for the murders. I didn't want to sidetrack you." He cleared his throat again and stared at his notepad. "Your sister is missing."

The words hit me like a brick. "What do you mean, *missing*?"

"Katie was in bed around one this morning, according to your mother. When we called to tell her about what happened, she looked in her room again, and your sister was gone. Her phone and purse were still in her room, and the back door was left ajar."

"Katie isn't missing," I half asked, half stated.

"I'm sorry." Detective Bell eased out of his chair, his lips pursed. "We're going to need you to take a drug test on the way out."

I blinked rapidly until I was able to focus on Detective Bell standing across the table. My sister was missing, and he was talking about peeing in a cup. "Are you sure she's missing?" I demanded. "Because Katie likes to sneak out for parties sometimes. Maybe she—"

"We've considered all the evidence," he hedged.

"But..." But *how*? "What evidence?"

"Excuse me." Detective Bell adjusted his tie and walked to the door. "Your mother is waiting, and I have a killer to find."

I splayed my fingers on the cool metal table. "It's probably the same person," I blurted. "Right? It has to be."

"We'll be in touch. Don't leave town," he said calmly, though the vein protruding from his forehead told another story.

Then he was gone, leaving me alone to remember how my legs worked. How anything worked. I couldn't breathe. Couldn't speak. The fire inside me roared again, and I knew. Whatever it cost me, whatever price I had to pay, I was going to kill the Weaver.

"Sandman," I screamed the moment my feet hit the beach.

He climbed from the glowing sea, water dripping freely from his hood. His clothes clung to him, accenting muscles I would never have guessed lay beneath all that fabric. "I'm here," he said, breathing hard and fast.

I paused, glancing behind him at the quiet waves. "What are you doing?"

"Fixing something." He shook out his gloved hands. "What happened?"

"They're—" *Tell him. Say the word out loud: Dead.* But I didn't want to say it. Didn't want to admit it and have it become real. I clutched my stomach. "Oh, God. I'm going to be sick."

The sky darkened, a hundred different shapes rushing in from nowhere, jostling together to blot out the blues and purples. Shadows fell over the Sandman's form. Slices of starlight cut through the dark masses.

My mouth hung open. "What the..."

"Whatever happened, don't think about it now or he'll come," the Sandman said, and dipped his hand into the sand.

I gripped his wrist before he could form a dream. "Don't think about it?" I hissed. "My friends were brutally murdered while I slept right next to them. My sister is *missing,* and I shouldn't *think* about it? I should pretend it's all okay? You think you can show me a pretty picture, and it will all go away? I promise you, Sandman, nothing will erase what I saw tonight. Ever."

"Nora," he croaked. The sand fell, lifeless, from his hand. "I… I'm sorry."

Pieces of individual shapes dipped lower in the sky—a hoof, a wing, a human-like arm—and I squared my shoulders. The Sandman's tendons flexed beneath my hand, and I jerked away.

I touched him, and he didn't disappear.

I glared at the place my hand had just been, unable to find the right question. Even if I could, I wouldn't have been able to process his answer with my mind torn in a million different directions. Did he lie? Was I missing something? What the hell was going on?

"I don't have the ability to protect you if those nightmares break through the barrier tonight." His voice was strained.

Nightmares. I lifted my head and shuddered. "Is that him? The Weaver?"

The sopping wet hood shook around his head. "No, but they belong to him."

"That bastard is going to pay for what he did." I bolted across the beach, charging toward the sea. "Right after he gives Katie back."

The Sandman stumbled after me and yanked me back with an arm around my middle. The touch sent electricity through my chest, shocking my heart. It was warm and relaxing yet somehow exhilarating—everything I ever imagined. But it wasn't the right time to feel calm. I needed to be angry. To cling to the hate.

"It's not him, Nora. They don't have your sister."

"But they're the Weaver's so they'll take me to him, won't they?" I growled. He wanted something from me badly enough to go through all this trouble—it seemed safe to assume he needed me alive. If not, I would've been victim number one. "I'm going to kill him with my bare hands."

"The Weaver can't be killed without disrupting the balance." He held me flush against his chest, and I felt each hammer of his pulse. It spurred my own, lighting a new kind of fire. He lowered his face to my neck and breathed in. "Please," he begged. "Don't antagonize them. We'll get Katie back."

"I don't understand." I stopped fighting against him, instead standing still as stone. "How did he get her?"

"If he has her, she's only here as much as you are. Her body is still in your world while her mind is trapped. If someone is prone to sleepwalking, the Weaver can turn them into a puppet; she could be anywhere."

"You're saying she kidnapped herself?" Katie hadn't sleep-walked in years. Not since the night she roamed the house with a flashlight and tried to suck up the *snake* with the hose of the vacuum. The dog had a bald spot on his tail for months. My body sagged against the Sandman. "I have to find her."

"We will." He backed away from me and reached into his tunic. His hand trembled around the ties of a black leather bag. "Take this."

I reached out slowly. "What is it?"

"Sand." He took my hand and set it in my palm. "Use it on your mother and step-father at night. It will keep them safe from the nightmares."

"But—"

"They only want the dream in your head. If you leave right now, I promise to tell you everything tomorrow." I had never heard his voice so low. "I need to do something to make this place safer for you, and I need to do it now."

"What dream hidden in my head?" My voice rose, wavering.

When he didn't reply, I opened my mouth to demand answers when a crack—half breaking glass, half thunder—rocked the beach. A small white line skated across a clear dome I never knew existed. Thick slime oozed beneath a giant worm slithering overhead. It reared back and slammed a sucker-like mouth against the barrier. Blue light flashed against the impact. Dozens of rows of teeth clacked against the hard surface and a forked tongue lapped in search of a tangible flaw.

"Go," he urged.

I swallowed hard. "I want answers first."

"I'm sorry," he whispered. "There isn't time."

I shook my head, my stomach dipping. "I can't leave without my sister."

He gently clasped my face and turned me to him. Water dripped from his hood, pattering gently on his arms. Arms that looked strangely familiar beneath the clingy fabric. I squinted at the outlines of his muscles, took in his height. A name began to surface, a line connecting two dots, but the Sandman's thumbs grazed my cheekbones.

"Never doubt that I'll do whatever is necessary to make this right. Anything you ask, anything you don't, it's yours. All of me is yours," he promised.

I blinked slowly, a blush heating my cheeks, and eyed the worm again. "Will any of them get in?"

"They're only here for the dream."

I gripped his wrists, my gaze drifting upward. "Will you be here the next time I fall asleep?"

"I'll be here," he swore. "And I'll tell you the rest."

"You'll *show* me the rest," I corrected, grabbing the edge of his hood.

His hand flew up to grip my wrist, making sure I didn't try to remove the fabric. "I'll show you."

"Okay." The worm slammed its head down again, and I flinched. "Tomorrow," I agreed and woke up.

The lights above my bed blurred as I blinked the lingering sleep from my eyes. A quiet clicking filled the room. It took a good thirty seconds to realize it was my teeth. Longer to realize my entire body was shaking. Longer still to remember I needed to breathe. I dragged in a breath, the air burning my dry throat.

What was that thing?

Everything felt like a lie. My whole life. The Sandman was supposed to be my constant, but now…

Tomorrow. Tomorrow I would have answers.

My limbs were heavy and sluggish, but I forced myself to move. To climb out of bed and put one foot in front of the other on the cold floor. The dresser drawer seemed to weigh a thousand pounds. I sifted through my scarves until I found my notebook and clutched it to my chest.

As I reached for the colored pencils, the memory of the nightmarish worm trickled to the front of my mind. I gripped the edge of the drawer to steady myself. *No.* That thing would not grace a single sheet of paper. Instead, I would draw Natalie's mischievous grin and Emery's bright eyes. Katie's liveliness. The people in my life that I took for granted. The ones who saw beyond what my own mother saw and accepted me.

I leapt back onto my bed and flipped to the last page—the one that said *Dreamer, Dreamer*—and wrenched it out. This notebook was my lighthouse and would be filled only with happy things to chase away the dark.

The pencils clacked against each other as I dumped the box out onto the bedspread, the red landing on top. I flinched. *Pencil... Pen.* Bloody *pen.* I snatched it up and hurled it into the small waste basket beside my desk. My heart thumped wildly at the reminder, and I focused on the blank paper. *Good things.* I could do that. With a shaky hand, I lifted the pink pencil and began with Katie's hair.

That night, I sketched until my hand cramped. Until the first glimpse of sunlight broke through the window. Until each new drawing was speckled with fallen tears.

Chapter Nine

The Sandman

Flashes of orange lightning highlighted each curve of the clouds and rumbles of thunder followed closely on its heels. Despite there being no rain, the ground in this part of the Nightmare Realm was thick with mud. It sucked at my boots, squelching with each step through the empty field. Traces of the Weaver's presence lingered, his magic prickling against mine, and the strong metallic scent of it mixed with the lighter scent of burning wool. A new nightmare was born here recently. It was too bad Baku was nowhere to be found—he loved the new ones best.

I rubbed at the soft spot in front of my ears. The low, droning moan of the Blood Army followed me around geysers of boiling water, through a darkness alive with glowing eyes, and past a table set for an elaborate dinner party. Landscape after landscape, it lingered.

Luckily, there was no hint of the red mist that followed the army, nor any sign of their leaders. Rowan and Kail weren't mindless beasts like the ones the Weaver used as cannon fodder. They were carefully crafted with minds of their own—elite nightmares, nearly as terrifying as the Weaver himself.

With their mournful song echoing through my head, I followed the Weaver's trail of magic deeper into the storm. He could sense me as easily as I could sense him, and he was a step ahead. This being his home turf, it made sense, but bouncing around his realm was growing old—fast. If he considered my emotions rather than my mere presence, he might be convinced to stop.

I hoped—against every instinct I had, I hoped—that I could talk some sense into the Weaver. That we could come to terms. *Peacefully*. His word was his bond by choice, and it hadn't faltered once over the millennia. Mine, however, was another story. I had lied to him countless times about things I could no longer remember.

It was true I cut the last ties of friendship to him the night of the binding, but maybe he would believe me tonight. I had something worth bargaining for this time: Nora's safety in exchange for lengthening his leash.

A rustling drew my attention to the right. Another flash of lightning revealed thin strings reaching down from the clouds. I squinted and brushed my hood back. The strings shifted. Another rustle came from behind, and I turned just in time to avoid an oval hand aimed at my head. Raw wood carved into simple shapes formed a life-size marionette. It stumbled forward in a series of jerky movements controlled by seven white cords. A hint of sulfur clung to its body, identifying it as the Weaver's latest creation.

It rushed me, strings swaying, head down, arms pumping. I tossed a handful of sand out between us, and it swirled into a tall horizontal bar. The puppet's strings snagged on the steel, jerking its body backward where it clattered to the ground. The metal disintegrated into a pile of lifeless sand. Cords wrapped around the marionette's limbs, looping through its joints. I rubbed the space between my brows. *New and stupid.* I didn't have time for this.

"I rather liked that one," the Weaver said, on the other side of his nightmare. My muscles tensed, my eyes flying to the black and gold threads running from his vest sleeve to his wrist. "I see he needs improving though. I'll have to study him and make adjustments."

"You killed Nora's friends and took her sister." The words were out before I could swallow them. It wasn't the best start to a negotiation.

The Weaver rolled his eyes and approached his nightmare. He ran long fingers over a string, following it up toward the clouds. "I did."

"Weaver—"

"*Sandman.*" He glared at me, his gold eyes fierce. "You never could take a hint."

My lips parted. "What?"

"This." He motioned between us. "If I wanted to talk to you, I would've stayed home. Surprisingly, I don't feel like listening to your empty threats. Let me guess, you were going to start with *stop or feel my wrath.*"

"I wasn't—"

"I'm a busy man so let me make this easy for you." He leaned in and examined a knot around the marionette's elbow joint. "Fetch the dream, and I won't have to bother the Dream Keeper again."

He might not bother her, but she would never be safe with his creatures running around the Day World. No one would be. "You know I can't do that."

"You mean you won't," he said and tugged a string free from where it caught on the puppet's chin.

I circled him, and the marionette strained to reach me. The Weaver slapped its forearm, stilling the nightmare. "You have an entire world at your fingertips," I started.

"Which is more than you have with miles of empty beach. I know, I know. You're like a dog with a bone, aren't you?" The Weaver plucked another string free from the puppet, and it climbed to one foot, the other still caught at the ankle. "Don't pretend you don't want more than this life. I feel your emotions the same as you feel mine. I know what it is you desire."

My lungs deflated, and my abdomen ached the same as if he sucker-punched me. In a way, he did. But our wishes weren't the same. He wanted to invade and destroy. I only wanted Nora.

"The impossible," I whispered. He had spent his entire existence striving for things outside our limits—pushing boundaries, working himself to the bone for *more, more, more*. More power. More territory. But this was the first time I wanted something I couldn't quite reach, and it shook me to my core. "We want the impossible."

"No!" The Weaver leapt around the limping nightmare, his hands in fists near his chest, imploring me to understand. "It isn't impossible, don't you see? You think only inside your little sandbox… If you released me and my nightmares, you would have the strength to stay with the girl in the Day World until you grew bored of it."

I winced against the earnestness in his voice. It was true, but that didn't make it right. Night beings ruled the realms through dreams and nightmares, influencing the Day World in our own way. We weren't meant to force ourselves on the mortals' conscious, but taboo or not, I would continue Day Walking until this mess was cleaned up.

"Or is that the problem? You're worried about tiring of the girl?" The sharp edge of his gaze softened. "You don't have to be. When you come back, you and I can work together again. It would be like old times."

Old times. A volley of memories pierced my mind like arrows, stretching back long before the Night World was cleaved in two. Before boundaries and bargains came between us. When we were both new to this existence—him, born in the Day World's shadow, the embodiment of mortal fears. And I, the manifestation of their optimism, their wishes and goodness. Different yet unified, we had laughed together, grown together, and combined our power for the common good more than once.

But the day we erected the wall between the Day and Night Worlds, something pivotal shifted between us. We drew a line in permanent ink and there was no washing the stain from our fingers. No matter how much either of us might wish to.

"We have to maintain the balance, and part of that is staying where we belong," I said, my voice hoarse.

He groaned and spun on his heels, working the last snarl in his puppet's string. "The balance always rights itself, Sandman.

You should know that better than anyone. Just look at yourself—keeping me prisoner has turned you into one as well."

I pressed my lips into a straight line. He wasn't wrong. I was a shell of myself, but it was a choice I'd make again. "I came to negotiate."

"*Negotiate?*" His muscles tensed beneath his sleeveless shirt. "You want to negotiate. With me." He rolled his neck to the side and shivered. "You're about five years too late, *old friend*."

"I know you might find it hard to trust me after—"

"Do you?" He wound the snarled string around his hand and balled it into a fist. "Your plea might be more effective if you weren't reaching for your precious sand as you said it."

I froze, unaware my hand had drifted in that direction, then snapped it away. "There was nothing for me to barter with last time. As you said, there's something else I want now."

"*Last time*." He scoffed. "You have no idea what I was prepared to offer then. I didn't have the chance to extend the offer, did I?" The Weaver freed the marionette. It staggered on its feet, and he drew a slow breath. "But maybe I should thank you for that. I realize now how foolish it would've been to search for common ground with you."

"The binding is wearing thin," I pressed. Whatever his offer entailed, it wouldn't have been enough. No nightmares could be allowed out. "If you leave Nora alone, I won't seek to strengthen it. The gates will still be locked to your magic—I can't undo them without the dream Nora has, and I won't take it back—but you'll eventually be able to pass through if you're alone."

The offer felt heavy. I didn't want the Weaver roaming the Day World as he pleased any more than I wanted his creations to, but it might be the only way.

"So, your Dream Keeper will be safe, and I'll *eventually* be able to Day Walk?" He cocked an eyebrow. "It seems to me that you'll be getting everything you want while I only get a fraction. If I continue as I am, I *will* have everything. My freedom, now and forever, and open passage to the Day World. The ability to send whatever I want, to whomever I want, whenever I choose is my cost, but that's what you're denying me. There's no incentive for me to agree."

Sometimes wishes were only that. *Wishes.* And I couldn't let regret cloud my actions. There was no choice five years ago and there was no choice now. I had to rebind the Weaver before he could do more damage. To do that, I had to be close enough to steal a thread from his arm. Then I needed enough time to force my power into the unborn nightmare and tether the Weaver to this place.

That was all.

One tiny, impossible feat after another.

My humorless laugh was lost in another roll of thunder. I felt exposed here with only a satchel of sand to work with. Powerless. Useless. I should have been with Nora, helping her through the loss of her friends. My back arched against the thought of how much pain she was in. But this *was* helping her. This was *saving* her. Saving her from making a choice between her loved ones and the world as she knew it.

"How did you find her anyway?" I asked softly, buying myself more time.

"I followed your magic back from the beach. It wasn't hard." He gave me a bored scowl. "It was easy to keep track of her after that. But that doesn't really matter, does it?"

"No." I swallowed hard, forcing myself not to look at his arm and tip him off. "No, I suppose it doesn't."

When he glanced at his marionette, I took the opening, as small as it was, and lunged for the threads wrapped around his wrist. The Weaver threw an elbow into my nose. Blood trickled down my lips, and I landed in the mud with a grunt. He advanced, his fists tight, with the nightmare hobbling behind him. I climbed onto my knees to lunge again, but he kicked me onto my back before I found purchase. He slammed a boot down on my chest. His smile was cruel. Entitled. All traces of the friend I once knew, gone. He drew a thread from his wrist and dangled it over me.

"Is this what you want?" he asked. "Maybe I should give it shape and let you have it. Or," he shook it slightly, "let *it* have you."

"Do it," I dared him through my teeth. My satchel dug into my lower back, cutting off my access to the sand. I gripped his ankle and waited. "If you think the balance will right itself, then do it."

A flash of uncertainty crossed his face. There was a reason we stopped trying to kill each other eons ago, and it had nothing to do with the destruction of the only weapon capable of it. Hurting, tormenting, binding—those were another matter. But the balance did always right itself. Neither of us were brave enough to find out what would happen if the other ceased to exist.

The Weaver bent at the waist, his metallic breath skating over me. "You'll soon find out there are worse things than death."

My hand shot up toward the band of threads around his wrist. The Weaver straightened, snapping his arm away, and my fingertips grazed their target. The marionette, somehow tangled again, flopped into the mud and army-crawled toward me. I ground my teeth together. When I rebound the Weaver, it would be so tight he would never take a single step outside of his Keep.

"Now." The Weaver exhaled quickly. "Get out of my realm."

The heel of his boot ground into my chest. The world spun, and then I found myself at home. Stars twinkled in the sky, their light mirrored on the beach. I groaned and wiped the blood from my face without getting up. He was right there. The threads were *right there.* I lifted my head and let it thud back to the ground. *Useless.* I should have fought harder but…

Next time. Next time I wouldn't hold back. Wouldn't let our connection, our history, stand in the way. Nora was too important to allow it.

Hopefully, the Weaver didn't kill anyone else in the meantime.

I worked the ties holding my tunic tight against my chest until I had enough room to stretch the neck of my undershirt down to expose the mark on my breastbone—a navy blue crescent moon, nearly a semicircle, concave up. From the dip flowed a stream of silver and blue that broke off below the hollow of my throat, reaching toward each collarbone, and cascaded down my arms before reaching my fingertips. The epicenter of my power prickled. The starlight offered its strength, and, beneath me, the sand began to hum.

Chapter Ten

Nora

A frenzy charged the community as desperation to find the killer took root. Calls flooded the tip line, a curfew was set in town, and search parties combed through every surrounding park and forest. The one I joined spanned twenty-three people wide, inching across an empty field next to a new cul-de-sac. My mother trudged on my left with hollow eyes and Paul on my right, a line of sweat shining on his brow. Dry grass pricked my shins, the underbrush crunching beneath my sneakers, and I scanned the ground.

It felt like most people were hoping against hope to find some material clue instead of another body. I couldn't blame them given what had happened lately, and they weren't wrong thinking the killer had my sister. They were just wrong about what was going to save her.

The sun burned hot at my back, and the string holding the Sandman's bag chaffed against my sweaty neck. The bag itself clung to the skin beneath my shirt. I almost left it home, but the thought of ever taking it off sent my heart racing. It was proof—hard, undeniable proof—that none of this was in my head. Each painful rub of the knot against my skin was a reminder. All the murders they blamed on some mystery psychopath, the *suicide* they were now blaming on drugs—it was all the Weaver.

And he had my sister.

Cold fury swept up my body, starting at my feet, and turned my heart to ice. Images of a blood-soaked living room wavered in my mind. I slammed a lid over those haunted thoughts to focus on the one person I still had a chance of saving. My sister needed me—both here and in the other world. That was all that mattered. So, today I would search for where the Weaver hid her body, and tonight, her mind.

I skipped ahead to regain my place in line, fueled by my newfound resolve. I had to believe Katie was more useful to the Weaver alive than she was dead. She was leverage over me. A bargaining chip to get what he wanted. Only this time I knew what would happen if I denied him. Giving him the dream was the last thing I wanted to do, but I wanted my sister alive more.

I balled my hands into fists and glanced over at my mother's worn face. New lines seemed to appear overnight. Her hair frizzed out of its clip, and she still wore yesterday's clothes. She was so focused, so determined, I wasn't sure how to approach her. I wanted to shout that I would save Katie. That I knew what happened, and it would all be fine. I would make sure it was. But

I couldn't promise any of that. Not really. And if I tried, I would be back in a psychiatrist's office faster than I could say *Sandman.*

But, while she watched me before, waiting for something to trigger another *episode*, she barely looked at me today. I would've been grateful under other circumstances, but something told me it wasn't only because she was worried about Katie's disappearance. It was that she was afraid to look at me and see the impending break. To her, it wasn't *if* I would fall to pieces anymore, it was *when.*

A police radio crackled from the end of the line where a young officer helped with our efforts. The sound fizzled in my ears, warping into a chant of *Dreamer, Dreamer.* I shook my head until the imagined voice disappeared, and I concentrated instead on the highway traffic zooming back and forth behind us. I listened for the different sounds the passing cars made and wiped sweat from my brow. Specks of white and grey siding peeked through a copse of trees. The newly built homes around the cul-de-sac had already been searched by the police.

The line narrowed along with the field until we were almost shoulder to shoulder. We continued into the trees. I shivered when the shade cut off the heat from the sun and again when the prickle of watchful eyes crawled across my shoulders. I glanced back but the field was empty save a row of cars parked just off the street. When I turned back, my mother and Paul had closed the gap between them, leaving me behind.

"Dreamer, Dreamer," whispered a familiar voice. This time there was no mistaking it as the real thing. It was too loud, too focused.

I froze, watching as everyone continued, not noticing I had fallen behind. There hadn't been time to find out from the

Sandman exactly what the Weaver wanted from me or why. Yet, if something was important enough for the Sandman to hide, it was probably better that it stayed put. Especially since the Weaver wanted it badly enough to go on a murder spree. Until I knew, I couldn't say yes.

But I couldn't say no either.

A human silhouette appeared between two oak trees and chuckled. "Come closer, my little Sun-Kissed Keeper."

I looked between him and the safety of my parents and crossed my arms. If I held onto the anger, let it overwhelm the fear, maybe, just maybe, I could walk away from this conversation without agreeing to his demands. The bloody words on Emery's window flashed through my mind, but I forced myself not to react. Anger. Not fear. I had to hold my ground.

"What do you want, Weaver?" I hissed.

He moved forward, and I got my first true look at my nemesis. His sculpted face was shrouded in black gossamer, his bright gold eyes gleaming. Halfway down his wide, muscular body, the gossamer tangled and cut him off mid-thigh as if he were floating.

He smirked. "Ah, he told you about me then."

"Give me back my sister, asshole." I strained to keep my voice low.

He lifted a hand and ran it down the cloth encasing him. Flecks of black and gold thread sparkled around his wrist, stretching up his arm to join his sleeveless shirt. The embroidery there moved among the weave of the fabric. "I'll give you what you want when you give me what I want. Say yes, and I swear no one else will die for this."

"For *this*," I snapped. He seemed to take pride in slaughtering people, and I imagined someone with that kind of insanity wouldn't stop. "But they will die, right?"

The Weaver quirked an eyebrow. "I wonder what assets you're hiding. The Sandman doesn't strike me as someone that would gravitate toward angry little sprites." He leaned toward me but came up short as a beam of sunlight broke through the branches. "Make no mistake. I will get the dream that's locked away in that pretty head of yours, one way or another, and everything will be as it should have been. If you cooperate, I can guarantee your safety."

He shifted to avoid another line of light and a slow, angry smile spread across my lips. He needed the shadows. I stepped into the sun, lifting my chin in what I hoped looked like confidence. "Like I would trust your word? My safety is guaranteed if I keep the dream hidden, not the other way around."

Rage flashed across his handsome features, disappearing as fast as it came. "*Yours,* perhaps."

"If you—"

"I see you need a little more time to mull things over," he said in a flat voice. His hand fell away from the gossamer and when he brought it back up, a clump of Katie's bright pink hair laid across his palm. "Think hard, Dream Keeper, and remember—tick tock."

Then he was gone.

I stared at the empty space, my heart thundering. He wouldn't murder Katie yet, but I hadn't said yes. *I didn't say no either.* It was a small victory. Or, it would have been if there wasn't a sinking feeling in the pit of my stomach. Someone I knew was on the chopping block. A wave of white-hot terror washed over me. Who did I fail this time?

"Mom." I bolted toward her narrow, hunched back. "Mom, I have to leave."

She and Paul stopped, the party continuing forward without them. "What do you mean you have to go? What could possibly be more important than finding your sister?"

"Please, Mom, I can't..." I couldn't watch someone else I loved die. I couldn't search a field I knew would be empty. "I can't deal with this right now."

"Nora—"

"Let her go, Val," Paul said. "She's been through a lot, and she's running on two hours sleep."

She held her breath and stared at my chin, refusing to make eye contact. I forced myself not to twitch under the scrutiny. What Paul said was mostly true. I felt everything my mother did—on top of losing Natalie and Emery—but getting two hours of sleep last night would have been a blessing. Even if I wasn't dealing with my delusions becoming real life, it would be too much for a lot of people. It was too much for *me*, but I wasn't going to allow myself to break down. One day I would, but not yet.

"Okay, you're right. I'm sorry." She pulled me into a careful hug. "Lock all the doors behind you and make sure you turn on the alarm. Do you remember the new code?"

I stepped back and nodded. "Call me if you find anything."

I barreled through the house to the bathroom attached to my parent's room. With frequent shift changes at the hospital, both my mother and Paul occasionally took pills to fall asleep. I couldn't risk being scared into waking up again, even if it was for my own protection. The Sandman was the only one who could give me answers, and I needed them now before anyone else got hurt.

I opened the medicine cabinet with shaking hands to reveal a row of orange prescription bottles. This was wrong. I knew it was, but there was too much on the line to care. I gently twisted each bottle to read the label. Old antibiotics, a few I didn't recognize, and finally, the one I was looking for. I swallowed hard and shook three white oval pills into my palm. One should do the trick, but if I needed to do this again, I would be ready.

I replaced the bottle exactly in its original spot, closed the cabinet, and hurried into my room to stuff the extra two pills in my sock drawer. The third sat on my palm, heavy with promise. It would give me hours, maybe. If I was lucky. But luck didn't have much to do with it. Natalie and Emery weren't lucky. Katie wasn't.

Hot tears splashed against my forearm before I knew I was crying. Time stopped then. I stared at the droplets as if they were something foreign. I supposed, to me, they were. More fell, scalding my skin. Without me, everyone would all still be alive. Still be here. Safe.

An agonizing sob ripped free of my chest, and I collapsed to the floor. I pressed my fists over my breastbone, praying for something, anything, to ease the sorrow as I curled in on myself. It felt as if my heart was made of tissue paper. Every second I wept disintegrated another piece of it until all that was left was a tattered mess. I laid there in a fetal position until I heaved. Until each breath was an absolute struggle.

And then I cried some more.

I cried until there were no tears left.

Until I was a husk.

Then I sat up, wiping my nose on the back of my hand. I blinked my swollen eyes until the room came back into clear focus, and climbed onto shaky legs. *Breathe*, I told myself. This wasn't going to help Katie. When she was home again—when I brought her back—there would be time to grieve. I clutched the pill in my hand tighter, and my stomach lurched.

What if the Weaver showed up again and I was stuck? If I was going to do this, if I was going to put myself at risk, I couldn't rely solely on the Sandman to protect me. I dropped the third pill into the top drawer and sprinted to the kitchen. A butcher knife was my first choice, but it came with the risk of stabbing myself in my sleep. I needed to think about getting a pocket knife or a taser tomorrow, but for now, I needed something else.

I dabbed at the raw corners of my eyes and stared into the utensil drawer. An apple corer. A cheese grater. A meat mallet.

Two hard knocks rattled the front door, and I jumped. Bile immediately filled my throat. I glared at the shape on the other side of the frosted glass, praying it wasn't a reporter, or, even worse, one of Natalie's relatives. Cars filled her driveway next door, spilling out onto the side of the road. I couldn't face any of them yet, especially not her parents. Not when I was the reason she was dead. Not when I was the only one to survive. To look at them after seeing... I tapped the heel of my hand on my head, fighting against the memory of the blood-soaked carpet beneath my feet. Something tugged in my chest. A threat. The sense of being buried alive.

The knocks came again.

I blinked the bleariness from my eyes again. I had to keep it together. "Coming," I called, and glanced at the meat mallet again before sliding the drawer shut.

When I cracked the door, my heart lurched. Ben stood on my stoop in khakis and a white dress shirt as if he just came from work. His curly hair drooped, and his eyes lacked a bit of their usual light.

"Hey," he said, a line forming between his brows. "I was worried when I couldn't get a hold of you. Are you okay?"

I scowled and drew my phone from my back pocket. Ten texts and two missed phone calls, all from him. He must have heard the news. Who hadn't? It was all over the television and social media was exploding with goodbye messages to Natalie and Emery. Right alongside them were a dozen different theories on who did it, and I was suspect number one.

"I'm..." *Far from okay.* But I wasn't going to say that. Admitting the truth out loud gave it purchase. It locked it into place and made it undeniable.

"Can I come in?" he asked, tugging at a curl near his temple.

I hesitated. I was home alone, for one thing, and about to grill the Sandman for information. But he heard the Weaver at Howell's. He *talked* to him in the back room like they knew each other. Whatever he knew, I wanted to know it too.

"I promise to be a perfect gentleman," he added when I stared silently at him.

"Okay." I shrugged and moved aside.

Ben stepped into the living room, and I shut the door behind him carefully. My pulse boomed. How did I bring the subject up? He probably wouldn't admit to anything without proof; maybe not even with actual evidence. I certainly wouldn't if I were in his shoes. I lifted a hand to my chest to feel the bag of sand tucked safely beneath the fabric.

"So," he started, gazing down at his shoes.

"So," I repeated.

"You're okay then?" he asked, looking me over, then amended, "You're not hurt?"

I shook my head. The movement sent a heaviness clanking through my skull. It felt as if I could sleep for a week. Despite that, I knew if I saw the nightmares again, answers or no answers, the pill would be the only thing keeping me there. I was out of time to be afraid.

His shoulders slumped forward, and he stuck his hands in his pockets. "I was hoping we could talk."

My eyes narrowed. I wanted to believe that my friends' deaths finally pushed him to come clean about whatever he knew, but, to anyone else, showing up with some crazy tale when I was grieving would make him look worse than crazy. It would make him look like an inconsiderate jerk. Treading carefully about this seemed to be an unwritten rule.

"If this is about what happened on the Ferris wheel—"

"Not about that," he said quietly, his cheeks turning pink.

"Then about the Weaver?" I asked before I could change my mind. There was more to Ben than met the eye, and not only because of the Weaver. He reminded me of the Sandman for a reason. What that reason was, I didn't know, but there had to be a connection somewhere. "Don't say you don't know what I'm talking about."

His eyes widened, his lips parting. "It's... Yes."

My breath caught. There were so many things I could ask next. How did he know the Weaver? What were they arguing about? Does he know how to contact him? Would he help me? If the Sandman helped me there, and Ben helped me here, maybe I could save Katie before the Weaver decided he was tired of waiting. I stared into his violet eyes, my heart thudding. How did Ben fit into everything?

I jumped at another sharp rap on the door.

"Nora, it's Detective Bell."

I ground my teeth together. "What now?" I told him everything. Twice. More than twice. I glanced at my phone again. My mother hadn't called which meant Katie was still missing. "One second," I called.

"What do you know about him?" I asked Ben in a rush.

"The answer to that is a lot longer than we have time for." Ben motioned to the door. "Should I call your parents?"

"Not yet, but..." I held my phone out to him and eyed Detective Bell's silhouette through the frosted glass on the door. If he dragged me out of here in handcuffs under some ridiculous pretense, I didn't want to wait for them to give me my phone call to let them know where I was. "Their numbers are in here, just in case."

Ben took it and slipped it in his back pocket. "Got it."

"This conversation isn't over," I promised.

He nodded and opened the door. Detective Bell stood on the porch in a mint green shirt with buttons in the wrong holes, his glasses resting on top of his head. An unmarked car idled in the driveway. His bloodshot eyes flicked to Ben. "I see you have company."

The way he said it grated against me. Like I was using the opportunity of an empty house to have my boyfriend sneak over. As if I would do something like that when my sister was in trouble. As if Ben was my boyfriend.

"Ben stopped by to see if we needed anything," I said, feigning complacency overtop my annoyance.

He pursed his lips. "There are search parties going on all over town that could use another pair of eyes."

Ben nodded. "I thought the family might need some groceries or errands done."

Detective Bell sniffed before turning back to me. "I hate to do this now, but we need you to come down to the station and finish your statement."

I glared at him. "Did my mom say it was all right?"

"We stopped by the search location you were supposed to be at. She plans to keep looking for your sister but gave us the go-ahead. Your step-father is waiting for us."

I paused. He wasn't really asking, and if I didn't cooperate, things would look bad. *Worse.* If they asked Paul to be there, it meant I wasn't simply considered a witness anymore. It meant the people online weren't the only ones to think of me as a suspect anymore. "All right."

Chapter Eleven

"I don't know what else you want from me," I said, avoiding my reflection in the two-way mirror behind Detective Bell. "I've told you everything."

My step-father was a steady presence at my side in the frigid interrogation room. The red light of a camera blinked down from a corner of the ceiling and the grey brick walls made the room feel like the dankest part of someone's basement. Paul spent the last forty-five minutes scratching the stubble on his chin, staring blankly at a dent in the metal table, but I knew he was absorbing every word. It was his focused face. The one he got when he didn't like what he was hearing but wasn't ready to make his case yet.

"None of this adds up. I want to be sure I understand everything correctly," Detective Bell said. "One murder is a travesty but when they start piling up, it sends people into a panic. It looks like we're dealing with a serial killer here, and we must figure this out before anyone else gets hurt. Right now, you're the only thing connecting all of the victims. And, of course, you were present for the incident at the mall."

I clenched my teeth. I did understand, and if anyone wanted the killer stopped, it was me. Telling him about the Weaver wouldn't do anyone any good, though. It would land me in a straitjacket, and then I would be a sitting duck. The Weaver could get to me anytime. Torture me. Kill people. I couldn't stop him from a locked ward.

"I can't tell you something I don't know," I said, sighing.

Detective Bell clicked his pen. "Is there a new drug you kids are doing? Something that wouldn't appear on the test but would make you do things you wouldn't normally do? Like stab yourself or hurt the people around you, for instance. I don't work in drug enforcement—you can tell me the truth."

"That's enough. Nora *passed* the drug test," Paul said in a low voice. "She's cooperated with you every step of the way and answered all your questions with more patience than I would have. I'm not going to let you harass her so if you want to talk to her again, you can contact our lawyer."

His eyes swiveled to my step-father. "We have to explore all our options."

"You think a girl that weighs one-ten sopping wet broke a man's neck? Can you honestly tell me that you think she looks capable of doing any of those things?"

"Mr. Thompson. With her history—" Detective Bell snapped his notebook shut and slid it off the table with calm fury. "Could we speak in the hall for a moment?" he asked in a strained voice.

Paul shoved up from his seat and stormed from the room. When the door clicked shut behind them, leaving me alone, I rested my head in my hands.

Deep breaths. In. Out.

My history. By now, they had to know about the psychologists I used to see, though the subject matter was confidential. I never threatened to hurt myself or anyone else, so unless my mother told them all the specifics, they had no reason to believe it was for anything other than my parents' divorce.

I scrubbed at my face. My mother may have been watching me like I would break, but she couldn't think... I slammed the door on the thought. My mother couldn't believe I had anything to do with this. Even if I was crazy, she had to know I wouldn't hurt anyone. Not like that. Not like anything.

"Dreamer, Dreamer," the Weaver whispered. "*Such* a schemer."

I jerked back, my spine perfectly straight. He hovered in the corner beneath the video camera. I couldn't reply without someone seeing me talk to an empty room, and I wasn't going to out myself as mentally unstable. A-plus for his effort though.

"Had a secret..." He inched around the shadowed perimeter of the room with a sly grin. "Couldn't keep it."

My hands balled into fists under the table. I couldn't take the bait. *Couldn't.* Even if I wanted to lunge across the table and strangle him with my bare hands.

"Ah, Sun-Kissed Keeper, does that piece of technology frighten you? Do you think they will lock you away if you're recorded talking to me?" His lips curled. "You do. I see it. Smell it. You fear they will assume you lost your mind and killed your friends during one of your episodes. That's the word your mother uses, yes? Episodes?"

I squinted at him. I didn't *think* they would. I knew they would. Doubt reared in the back of my mind. *Give it to him. Give him the dream, and he'll go away.* My family would be safe, and I could return to some semblance of sanity. But at what cost? The Sandman was going to give me answers tonight so I had to wait until then, at least. Besides, I still wanted justice.

Not justice.

Payback. I wanted payback.

"No? Perhaps I'm projecting. That's what the Sandman used to call my… Well, episodes." The Weaver leered at me over his shoulder, something human flitting across his eyes, gone as quickly as it came. "Before they began playing on an endless loop, that is. Who knew one teensy banishment would—" He cleared his throat. "Never mind."

Endless loop this. I tapped my middle finger on the table as casually as possible.

The Weaver cocked an eyebrow, amused, then rose into the air, a gossamer trail stretching behind him, tethering him to the floor. "Impressive," he said and stared into the camera lens. "Unable to capture my image, of course. The only reason you can see me is because of that tiny piece of my world residing in your brain."

Each taunt was gasoline on the fire, an inferno in place of a beating heart. Once Katie was back, I would unleash the heat building in my veins and burn him to the ground. I took a deep breath. He couldn't get to me when I was awake, or he would've had me strung up and tortured by now. I had to wait until I knew how to get the upper hand.

"You know." He lowered himself and turned to face me again. "If you don't wish to give me the dream, you could ask the Sandman to take it back. He could hide it in some other poor soul. As he's so torn up about putting you in danger, I'm sure he would honor the request."

The Weaver knew nothing of what the Sandman felt. He couldn't; he didn't *have* feelings. Besides, if someone else had the dream, he would do the same thing to them. More people would die. Not *my* people, but people nonetheless. And what if they caved? What if they gave him what he wanted? I couldn't take that risk.

"Ah, little Keeper, you look perturbed." He shifted back into the corner, his gold eyes gleaming, and crossed his arms. "We sense each other, you see. I know what the Sandman is feeling as he knows what I am. For example, I know right now, he is worried sick about what I'm doing. He feels it—the thrill of having you so close. Just as he felt my ecstasy this morning when I murdered your father."

I flew to my feet, the interview room echoing with the scrape of metal chair legs. "Wh—"

The door swung open. Detective Bell and Paul looked in with matching looks of confusion. "Everything okay?" my stepfather asked.

"Cramp," I lied, clutching my calf. The Weaver chuckled.

"Maybe you should sit down," Paul said carefully. When I didn't listen, he rolled his shoulders. "Detective, I think we should wait for her mother before making a decision about this."

"About what?" I stammered and rubbed the imaginary cramp away to hide my shaking hands. The room tilted. My father wasn't dead. The Weaver was lying. He had to be because my dad was over a thousand miles away. How would the Weaver even connect us? It was impossible…

"A polygraph," the detective answered.

I plunked back into the chair. They would ask if I knew who was behind the murders. They would ask, and I would fail. Then what? They wouldn't let me leave until I told them everything. "A lie detector test? Is that really necessary?"

"No, it isn't," my mother snapped from the hallway. Relief washed over me. "I just talked to your partner, Detective, and you won't be speaking to my daughter again. You said there were a few things to clear up with her, not that you wanted to put her through an interrogation."

"Ma'am, as we've stated, your daughter isn't a suspect," Detective Bell said with an exasperated sigh.

"You're doing your damnedest to make sure she becomes one." My mother shouldered her way into the room and grabbed my hand. Her eyes were red and glassy with tears, the purple bruising beneath them stark against her ashen face. "We're going home."

I didn't argue; I wanted nothing to do with their investigation. The only way to solve this was to find Katie myself and stop the Weaver before anyone else could die. With the Sandman's help, I could do it. I had to.

When I murdered your father.

Nausea gripped my stomach. He couldn't be dead. Because he was all the way in New York City, like a mile off the ground in a penthouse or something. Or, if he was on a business trip, maybe he was even halfway around the world.

"Val, I think we should talk about this," Paul whispered on our way through the parking lot. The sun felt blistering after being in the air conditioning for so long. "It could put an end to their focus on Nora and let them concentrate on finding who really did this."

My mother pressed the unlock button and the SUV lights flashed. "This is a witch hunt, Paul. It's obvious Nora had nothing to do with what happened to those girls. Right now, all we have to do is find Katie."

Paul raised his hands in surrender. "All right. I'll call a lawyer first thing in the morning."

The leather seats burned my legs when I climbed into the back of the vehicle. To know who my father was, the Weaver would've needed to root around in my head, right? And have dug pretty deep while he was at it because I rarely thought of him these days.

"The *best* lawyer," my mother clarified in a stern voice.

No matter what else my mother thought of me, at least she believed I wasn't capable of *this*. I wrapped my arms around my waist and tried not to fidget. What would happen if the lawyer said I had to take the lie detector test? I absolutely couldn't do it but refusing would look terrible. I'm sure the court could find a way to force me anyway.

First thing's first, though. I had to dust off my father's telephone number. He was a sorry excuse for a dad, but I didn't want him dead. I needed to hear his voice. To know without a doubt that the Nightmare Lord was only waging mental warfare. That was all. *That's all.*

My mother went straight to the computer to read through Katie's social media for clues again, while Paul pried a boxed pizza from the freezer. I watched them from the living room as if they weren't real. As if this were a reality show, and I was a mere observer. But I wasn't. I did this; I ruined my family. Five years ago, and again now.

I gnawed on the inside of my cheek to stop the tears from forming and reached into my back pocket for my phone. Only it wasn't there. Because I gave it to Ben. I hung my head and groaned. "Have you told Dad about Katie?" I asked, weary.

"I sent him a text this morning," my mother said, exhausted with an edge of annoyance. "He didn't reply."

He was busy. That's why he didn't reply. He was *always* busy. He probably saw my mother's name pop up and ignored the message. "Can..." I wasn't sure how to phrase the next question. For however little I cared about my father, my mother cared less. Or maybe she cared more. She couldn't hate him and not care about him at the same time. "Can I call him?"

My mother paused mid-scroll and spun in the office chair beside the stairs. "Why?"

I looked to Paul for help, but he was studiously reading the pizza box. "He deserves to know about Katie."

"If he wanted to know, he would've gotten back to me." She spun back to the computer. "But you don't need my permission to call your father."

"Can I use your phone?" I asked quietly. "I don't have his number."

Her head bobbed, and I scooped it up off the computer desk before she could change her mind. I dialed, my heart thumping in my ears. The phone rang. Once. Twice. Four times. Then a woman answered with a warbled *hello*.

"Hi." I paused. "Is this Michael Gallagher's phone?"

"Yes." The woman sniffled. "Who's this?"

"Nora. His daughter," I added in case he never mentioned me to this woman. It wouldn't surprise me. There was a long pause. "Hello?"

"I'm here."

I stalked away from my mother. "Can I talk to him?"

"No. He's... Maybe I should speak with your mother. Is she there?"

I closed my eyes. The Weaver wasn't lying; he did something. I clutched the lump beneath my shirt that was the Sandman's bag. "Where is he?"

"Your father had a heart attack last night. He—" *Hiccup*. "He didn't make it."

"Oh." The phone almost slipped from my hand. "Okay."

She sniffled into the receiver again. "The doctors said he went to sleep and didn't wake up so there wasn't any pain."

"I see."

"Are you—all right?" she asked.

I eased onto a stool at the kitchen island. "I'm fine."

"Is there—"

I hung up and slid the phone across the counter. *Dead*. He was dead, and more people would be soon. I could protect my mother and Paul, but my father lived so far away when the

Weaver got him. What could I have done? I tightened my grip on the Sandman's sand. It wasn't possible for me to save everyone, but that didn't stop the guilt from clawing at me with its thorny fingers.

"What's wrong?" Paul asked.

I opened my mouth, unable to find the words. The bag of sand weighed heavily against my breastbone. It should hurt more—losing a parent. But I felt nothing. Almost as if someone had jabbed a needle full of Novocain straight into my brain. As if I was made of stone. Maybe I was now. Maybe I had to be, in order for all the deaths not to utterly destroy me.

A quiet, hesitant knock broke the silence.

"I'll get it," I said, slipping off the stool. I half expected it to be Detective Bell standing on the other side of the front door with a warrant, but Ben stood there instead.

One side of his mouth lifted in a grin, but it didn't extend to the rest of his face. His skin was waxen, his expression pinched. "Hi," he said softly.

"What are you doing here?" My voice was raw.

Ben held out my phone. "You can't call for my expert advice without this."

Expert advice indeed. The screen was warm with his body heat, and I hurried to set it on the end table. There was no one left for me to call anyway.

"And you are?" Paul asked from directly behind me.

Ben looked over my shoulder, his violet eyes dull. "Ben, sir."

Paul glanced between us before stepping back. "Come in."

"I really shouldn't," Ben said, chewing his bottom lip.

His eyes met mine in a silent apology, and my chest ached. The thought of going up to my room, of being alone, crushed me. The weight of millions of lives threatened to snap my bones, the strain of my sister's fate choking me.

"Stay." The word was half statement, half question, and one hundred percent desperate. But I didn't care—I was.

He blinked once, slowly, heavily. "Okay."

"Paul, have you ever heard Katie mention *Zach* before?" my mother called.

"We'll be in my room." I took Ben's hand and lead him toward the stairs before they could object.

He followed silently, his fingers loose around mine. My brain might have felt as if it were in some suspended state, but my body certainly didn't. It was the first time I would have a boy in my room. A boy I kissed, no less. Even though I had no intention of going down that awkward path again, it didn't stop my nerves from remembering. From tingling.

I couldn't think about that now. I needed to not be alone. To be with someone who didn't think I was psychotic. Who wouldn't ask questions. Ben knew the Weaver, so he must have some idea of what I was up against. That's what I needed. *Understanding.* And his answers to a hundred questions, but not now. Not tonight. I waited five years for the Sandman's answers and Ben's only a matter of days.

"Are you okay, Nora?" he asked when I kicked my bedroom door closed.

"No," I admitted through gasps. "No, I'm not."

He wrapped an arm around my shoulders and gathered me close. I tucked my face into his shoulder and, for the first time since the night I sketched my friends, hot tears scalded my cheeks. They came as a flash flood, washing away my entire life. I cursed them, hated them. Hated *myself* for letting them fall. I couldn't give in to the sorrow yet; I had to be the stone. Now wasn't the time to lose myself in a vortex. Now was the time to fill the hole inside with something else: revenge. When that was complete, when the Weaver paid for everything he had done, the hole would be there, waiting, but so would Katie.

I balled my hands into fists against the threat of defeat. If all those years of pretending to be normal taught me anything, it was how to pull myself together when it felt like I would fall apart. I stepped away from Ben and turned my back to him to wipe my face. "My father had a heart attack today."

Ben eased down on the edge of the mattress with a small creak. "I'm sorry."

"At least they can't blame me for that one," I grumbled.

"They shouldn't blame you for any of it," he said. "You didn't do anything."

"You know it as well as I do." I bit the inside of my cheek. *The Sandman first.* I owed him a chance to explain as much as he owed me the explanation. I kicked off my sandals and sat down beside him. "Sorry, it's been a long day."

He patted my pillow. "You look exhausted. Why don't you try to get some sleep?"

It was more than exhaustion. Each cell in my body ached as if they wanted to cry as badly as I did. I sat down beside him, still in jean shorts and a loose T-shirt. I had no plans to change tonight; pajamas weren't my choice attire for greeting any enemies that might show up. I eyed the sandals I took off. They would have been helpful, but I couldn't put them back on now.

"Sleep isn't as relaxing as it used to be," I murmured.

Ben's eyes flashed, and he studied the string circling my neck as if he knew it held the pouch of sand beneath my shirt. His fingers trembled, and he slid the neck of my shirt up over my bare shoulder. A blush colored his pale cheeks. "I know."

I rubbed at the spot his fingers grazed, both savoring the warmth left behind and willing it away. That he could bring such a mix of feelings fluttering to the surface when I knew so little about him, made me want to run the other way. Instead, I inched closer and asked, "Will you stay?"

"The next time you open your eyes, I'll be there," he said with a small smile.

My mind struggled to understand his answer, but my eyelids lost the fight to stay open. I laid down. "We're going to finish our conversation tomorrow." The words were thick and slurred with sleep. "You're not getting out of it."

The mattress shifted against his weight. One of his arms slid beneath my head until my cheek rested on his chest. It felt sturdy. Safe. The quick *thump thump thump* of his heart pulsed against me. I snuggled against his side, letting his warmth lull me into slumber.

"Sleep well, Nora," he whispered, and I faded away.

Chapter Twelve

For the first time, it wasn't the humming along our cord that told me the exact moment Nora fell asleep. I felt it in the weight of her head against my chest and the slight change of her breath. Her hand slid down my side, limp. I slipped my arm out from beneath her and gently set her head on the pillow, brushing the hair from her face.

The next time she laid eyes on me, it would change everything about our relationship. The trust we built up over the last five years would shatter in a single instant. Every word I ever spoke, all the promises I ever made, each laugh, each smile, each kind gesture wouldn't make any difference. She would question it all, and she would be right to.

With a sigh, I closed my eyes and followed her consciousness back to the beach.

Sand shifted beneath my boots, my hood and gloves already in place, shielding me a moment longer than I deserved. Nora's eyes burned into my back. The thought of turning around and seeing the look on her face turned my blood to ice.

Before I found the courage to move, she said, "Off with the hood."

My nerves prickled, and I spun, peering at her from the safety of fabric. She crossed her arms, glaring at me from a few feet away. Her eyes were glassy with unshed tears, or maybe it was fear shining back at me. I couldn't tell. Either way, it was my own doing. My own stupid, stupid fault.

"Nora..."

"Sandman," she countered with raised brows.

I grimaced. But maybe if she understood first... Maybe if she knew... "Let me explain."

"Explain what?" she snapped, her arms dropping to her sides. "You said you would take it off tonight."

"I will... I just..." My voice caught in my throat. *I just what?* "Let me start at the beginning and when I'm finished, I'll remove the hood."

Her nostrils flared, but she gave a terse nod.

I stared at my gloved hands held out before me, curling my fingers before letting them drop to my sides. "I thought it was better if we didn't get attached. If a situation arose with the Weaver, I needed to keep the big picture in mind. I thought that if you didn't see me, or know me, or touch me, that it would be impossible to care about each other. But I was wrong. Very wrong."

Her green eyes narrowed. "I have no idea what you're talking about."

"You're right. That isn't the beginning." My voice was weary. Resigned. The first and possibly biggest lie had to come first. I closed my eyes, and said, "The Weaver is the Lord of Nightmares as I am the Lord of Dreams. Everything created from magic has a counter, and he's mine. But where dreams are holograms crafted from my sand, his creatures are living, breathing things that he inserts into people's minds."

"Five years ago, the Weaver found a way to release his nightmares into your world. They tortured and killed hundreds of people all over the world before I was able to bind him and seal the exits against his magic. It left me weak, and I had just enough power left to secure the knowledge of how I changed the fabric between our worlds. It was too dangerous to keep the information when I couldn't defend it, so the night you called to me, instead of giving you good dreams, I gave you something else."

She shook her head, rubbing the back of her neck. "What *did* you give me?"

Each of my breaths wavered, fighting their way into tight lungs. "A dream containing the secret to releasing the Weaver's nightmares into your world. I…I made you a Dream Keeper to save us all."

She stood straighter and took half a step toward me. "That's what a Dream Keeper is? *That's* what I'm keeping?" Her voice was harsh and constrained. "That's what the Weaver wants so much? To bring a cosmic-ton of monsters to my world and kill *more* people?"

I chomped down on the inside of my cheek and backed into my hood, relishing my last moments in shadow. "Yes." Then, riding a tiny wave of unwarranted defensiveness for my foe, I added, "I'm sure whatever his reasons are, they make sense to him."

Nora paled, the freckles stark against her face. Her fingers trembled, and she touched them to her chest. "You want to talk about reasons? *I'm* the reason everyone is dead right now."

My heart stopped. "No, Nora. *No.* It's my fault. Magic isn't infinite; it wears down and frays like well-worn cloth, but I didn't notice. If I had..." If I had, no one would be dead. But I thought there was more time. I stepped forward to touch her, to let her feel my sincerity, but stopped myself. "I wouldn't have done this to you if it weren't absolutely necessary at the time. You understand that, right?"

"I don't understand anything. Are you crazy? I was *twelve.*" Nora sucked in air and paused. She tilted her head, her brows lowering. When she exhaled, her whole body seemed to deflate. "You asked my permission the night we met, didn't you? You were hurt and said you needed my help with something important. And I agreed."

I nodded. It wasn't a fair question to ask her; she was young and didn't know the risks. How could she when I didn't explain any of the details? But I had no choice. It had only been a few hours since the battle, and it was all I could do to keep from bleeding out in front of her. I assumed she had forgotten that night.

"I've spent every night since making sure you didn't accidentally see it," I said. "I've protected you from the consequences of my mistake for the last five years, but it wasn't enough. *I* wasn't enough to keep him from finding you. If he kills you, the dream will be lost forever. By killing people around you, the Weaver is poisoning your dreams in hopes you'll become more susceptible to nightmares—so he can snatch you out of the Dream Realm."

"And if he does?" She dug her fingers into her hair and scanned the beach. "If he gets me?"

Dread oozed through my veins, thick and cold. If the Weaver ever broke through and managed to get his claws into Nora, that would be the end. Everything would have been for nothing. There were too many nightmares for me to take on alone, and if Nora was in his realm, every single one of them would be there. Safeguarding their master while he tortured his way into her mind. Helping him do it. I shuddered. He wouldn't let her go until he got what he wanted, then the entire world would be in peril.

"He may not be able to kill you until you allow him access to the dream, but he *can* keep you from waking up," I told her carefully.

Her head jerked side to side. "If he did that, and I still refused to give it to him…?"

I stepped forward, but my knees threatened to buckle. "You would," I said quietly. The Weaver had an endless supply of terror devices at his disposal. Things that got pleasure from pain. Things that would be more than happy to rip into her. "Trust me, Nora. You would give him anything he asked for."

She stumbled away from me. "This whole time I thought we were friends."

"We were." I reached for her hand and when she didn't pull away, I laced my fingers through hers. "We *are*."

She stared down at where we were joined and scowled. Her eyes flashed with a dozen emotions before she spoke. "I want to know everything." The words were so soft, I barely heard them. "All of it."

A smile tugged at my mouth. She wasn't running. She didn't hate me—at least not completely. Not yet. She was listening, trying to understand, so maybe there was a chance my identity wouldn't ruin us. *Maybe.*

So, I told her everything. I explained the barriers and what was really on the other side of the one around the beach. The Day World and the Night World. The Dream Realm and the Nightmare Realm. About the importance of maintaining the balance and how the universe would find a way to even things out if something disturbed it. About magic and Day Walking and why I was weaker now than I had ever been because of where I chose to allocate my magic. The Weaver and his threads. The connection I had to him and to her. The cords tying me to all the Dreamers who knew my legend. How I needed to find the Weaver to re-bind him, and how I would do it once I had.

I left nothing out while she stood there absorbing every word. Every detail. She didn't interrupt me once, but when I finished speaking, her eyes traveled up to my hood. I braced myself. There was still one thing we hadn't covered. *Me.*

She took her hand from mine, her face set. My feet were rooted in place while I watched the war wage within her. It went on for so long I nearly fell to my knees and begged for forgiveness. She deserved that much, but I might as well finish digging my grave first.

Finally, she whispered, "No more secrets, Sandman."

"No more secrets," I echoed.

Terror coiled through me, and I gripped the edges of my hood. I wasn't ready. I might never be, but there were so many more important things at stake than our friendship. I didn't come so far safeguarding the Day World only to fail because I was afraid of hurting someone I loved. Losing Nora would be the same as having my beating heart torn from my chest, but she was in this, for better or worse. I would rather she be alive and hate me than distrust me and perish for it.

With a steadying breath, I brushed the hood back, letting it fall between my shoulder blades. I felt naked as I slowly lifted my gaze from my boots. Nora's face was unreadable. Blank. Of all the reactions I was anticipating, *nothing* wasn't one of them.

"I didn't mean to lie," I said in a rush. "Not really. I wanted to tell you who I was, but you didn't believe I existed *here*, so I didn't think you would believe I existed *there*." I held my arms out to the side and shrugged. "But now you know."

She didn't take her gaze off me, her eyes locked on mine. "Now I know," she repeated slowly.

My heart pounded in my chest. I pried off my gloves one finger at a time, showing her the rest of what I kept hidden. The marks she saw in her world shifted around my hands, twisting and swirling with exposure to the sand.

"I knew it. *I knew it.* Your voice, something about the way you moved..." Nora reached out and grazed the back of my fingers. A jolt of energy rushed through my body. The marks fluttered, shifting toward her touch. She watched, transfixed, and her fingertips followed the specks up the back of my hand. "I recognized you."

I flipped my hand over and curled my fingers to hold hers. That she would let me... "You're not mad?"

"Are you kidding? I'm furious." She lunged, wrapping her arms around me, and buried her face in my neck. "But I'm relieved more than I'm angry. You're real. *Really* real. I mean, I believed it after you gave me the sand but... I'm not insane."

Her breath danced over my skin, and I brought my arms up to return the embrace. Having her against me felt surreal as if *I* were the one dreaming. I breathed her in, my body buzzing. I didn't know what it meant for us. If she forgave me. Trusted me. Cared for me. She was relieved, that much I could see without being told. Everything everyone told her was broken about herself was false. I was proof of that. Real, living proof. It didn't mean she loved me. It didn't mean she still wanted me here—outside of getting her sister back and stopping the Weaver. If she rejected me now, it would be so much worse. So much more personal. I swallowed hard. The truth was worth it.

"Oh, God." She leaned away.

I blinked at the sudden loss of contact. "What?"

"What do you mean *what*?" Her cheeks blazed. "I *kissed* you."

"You did." I grinned. I couldn't help it.

"Oh, my God." She gently shoved my chest. "I can't believe you let me do that. Are you crazy?"

I grinned wider.

"Sandman! Wipe that smug look off your face." She covered her face with a groan. "This is so embarrassing."

I cocked my head, the smirk fading. The rejection would be more personal, yes, but I had to know. It was already a secret kept too long, and we just agreed not to have any more. I carefully pried her hands away from her face. "If you knew it was me..." I cleared the lump from my throat. Hope I hadn't dared allow before bubbled to the surface. "Would it be so bad?"

"Would what be bad?" she asked, keeping her gaze down.

"If the person you kissed was me?" Her eyes snapped up to mine, silent and probing, and a flood of emotions broke free of their gate. "I've been in love with you for a year," I blurted before I could stop myself. The blood drained from my face. It was too soon to tell her that, but the words were out and there was no rewind.

"You have?" she asked, breathless and half-believing. Her gaze dropped to my chest.

My muscles burned against the strain of remaining upright. I had no regret about my feelings, only pain-laced terror. Her reaction held more power over me than the Weaver ever could. "Yes."

"Oh." Her fingers rose to her lips, her cheeks glowing red. Then slowly, her hand fell. Her blush faded. She met my gaze again, and my heart skipped a beat. "I think I have too."

I froze, not daring to breathe, while I waited for her to change her mind. To say she was kidding. But when she didn't, I leaned down to press my forehead to hers, our noses brushing. She was still there. In front of me. Close to me. Seeing me. *Me.* Not the hood. And she felt the same way. My vision spun. "I'm yours. I'll always be yours."

Her breath hitched, the same break she had before she kissed me on the Ferris wheel. My lips tingled at the reminder. Would she allow me to kiss her? If I asked her permission, whatever spell this was, might break.

Nora tilted her chin up as if sensing the unspoken question. I shifted closer, and her hands skimmed my shoulders. A tremor rolled through me, but I was too afraid to move. She placed a tender kiss at the corner of my mouth, and my fear shattered.

She wrapped her arms around my neck, and the hem of her shirt lifted. When my hands found her waist, they grazed bare skin. I tightened my grip and urged her closer. Our lips collided. My whole world exploded in that moment.

A soft sound escaped her, and we pressed closer. My hands moved to her back, sliding up until my fingers tangled in her hair. I breathed her in. Memorized the feel of her. The taste of her. How long I had wanted this. Wanted her. *This* with *her*.

But if we kept going, if her hands, now sliding down my chest, went any lower, I wouldn't want to stop. I would if she wanted me to, but if she didn't... I brought my hands to her shoulders. If she wanted to, we would. However, as much as I wanted it, it *definitely* wasn't the right time for that. Not with everything that was happening. When—*if*—it happened, I wanted to know it wasn't because she felt lost or lonely. I wanted it to be because she knew she loved me as much as I knew I loved her.

"Nora," I mumbled against her mouth.

She broke the kiss and rocked back off her toes. She watched me, studied me, with an expression I only dreamed about. "You're real," she said, closing her eyes. Her head pressed against my chest, over the epicenter of my power. "You're real."

I wrapped my arms around her and set my chin on top of her head, trying to calm my erratic pulse. "I'm real," I assured her.

I sat beside Nora, drawing circles over her kneecap with my finger, while she told me about her run-ins with the Weaver, the problems with the police, and her mother's wariness. Her head rested on my shoulder, and we sat on the beach, watching the luminescent waves lap the shore. There hadn't been a single nightmare in the sky. Part of me wanted to believe she was too content for the Weaver to pinpoint us. But, even if she was as happy as I was, fear still lurked beneath the surface. It had to; her life was falling apart.

"Don't you have questions?" I asked, breaking the quiet calm.

Nora sighed. "I wish I could say no, but I do. I have so many, Sandman—wait." She shifted her head to look up at me. "What do I call you?"

I nudged her forehead with my nose. "Whatever you want."

"But is Ben your real name?"

"I don't have a name," I said into her hair.

"Everyone should have a name." She set her head back on my shoulder. "Ralph? Sherwood?"

"*Sherwood?*"

"You don't like it? How about Mortimer?"

I wrinkled my nose. "I take it back. Don't call me whatever you want."

"It's a work in progress." She laughed, and we were both silent for a moment before she said, "Why me?"

"What do you mean?"

"Why did you choose me as Dream Keeper? You probably had a million people to choose from."

I hesitated, wondering if she was asking something more than her words. There was nothing special about Nora in the Dreamer sense—or there wasn't before, at least. Did she want there to be more? Would it hurt her to realize there was no special pull between us before I created one? "You called to me at the exact right time," I said, my voice strained. We promised no more lies. "That's all."

She nodded, accepting the truth as easily as she had everything else. "How old are you?"

"How old is the human race?" I asked with a shrug.

"Wow. You're such an old man," she joked, but her eyes widened in honest surprise. "Were you born or… Do you have parents?"

"No. Before humans, there was magic in your world too." I grinned at the awe on her face. "The Weaver and I were both born from it, in a way. The details are a bit fuzzy now, but I remember feeling the magic dying. I think we were its last effort to adapt and survive."

She made a low, contemplative noise in the back of her throat and something heavier clouded her expression. "If… If I asked you to take the dream back, could you do it?"

My heart plummeted. She couldn't know what that meant, but I wasn't sure knowing would change her mind. Too much was already lost to her because of it. Because of me. If she wanted to be free, I would let her go. It was the right thing to do.

"If that's what you want," I said carefully. "But, we wouldn't be able to see each other again. There wouldn't be time. I'd have to hide it in someone else and protect them as I've protected you."

She leaned into me and drew a deep breath. "I'll have to think about it after Katie is home."

"Of course." My hand stilled against her leg. The uncertainty I felt before Nora knew my feelings resurfaced. She cared for me but that didn't mean it would be enough. That *I* would be enough when the trade-off of our relationship was a lifetime of potential terror. "Are there any new leads?"

"No." Her muscles tensed. "The police want me to take a polygraph, and we both know I'll fail. I'm running out of time to stop the Weaver. I need your help."

Stop him. There was nothing she could do to stop him. We could save her sister, I could bind him again, but there was no *stopping* him. He would never give up. Thousands of years ruling the Nightmare Realm left him bored. He wanted to expand his territory. To feel something new. I felt it in him, but I also recognized the same desire in myself.

"I'm doing everything I can, Nora."

She sat up straight, her eyes heavy. "What can I do? There has to be something."

"Once I find Katie on this side, we can figure out how to wake her up. If we can get to her before her body is found, maybe she'll be able to find her own way home. All you can do is keep looking. The Weaver won't kill her while she's of any use to him."

Nora looked up. The stars, bright and endless, danced across her face. "Will she be okay when she wakes up?"

My stomach clenched. "It's best to concentrate on finding her."

"That means no," she said with a frown.

"I didn't say—"

"Sandman." Her gaze cut to me. "I know what you're saying when you don't say things."

"She might be okay again with time." After days of psychological torture, I wouldn't say it was likely. I dug the heels of my boots into the sand. "My associate is searching for her now."

She stared at me with one raised brow. "You have an associate? Since when?"

"Since always." I smirked. "Baku has a thing for nightmares, so we're sort of allies by default."

Her other eyebrow shot up. "By *thing* you mean...?"

I leaned forward, squinting playfully, and whispered, "He eats them."

She cringed. "That's not terrifying at all."

"Would you like to meet him?" I asked.

"I don't know." She paused and wrinkled her nose. "Do I?"

I chuckled, my lips quirking at her expression. "I'll introduce you next time."

"Okay," she said around a yawn.

"Would you like to rest now?"

Nora drew a slow, steady breath and a smile crept over her face. "Not yet."

"Then what—"

But she already shifted away from me. She hovered over the sand on her hands and knees and licked her lips. "I've wanted to do this since the first day I saw you at Howell's, but then everything happened and…" She shook her head slightly and peered at me over her shoulder with that perfectly wrinkled nose. "It's about time I got the chance to draw you."

I watched in awe as her fingers brushed through the sand in long, smooth strokes. Her back muscles shifted through her shirt with each movement, and she kept pausing to tuck her hair behind her ears. *Stars.* How I loved this talented, beautiful woman. The world began and ended with her. And there she was, delicately sketching my face with a gleam in her eyes that rivaled the one I imagined shone in my own.

"There," she said triumphantly. "What do you think?"

"It's perfect," I said in a hoarse voice.

"You're not just saying that?" She lifted her chin, glaring playfully.

"Never."

"The eyes are wrong." She sat back on her haunches and cocked her head to examine her work. "I guess it's hard to really capture them without my colored pencils."

"It's perfect," I repeated. "You're perfect."

She snorted, and I held my hand out to her, asking her silently to sit beside me again. When she shuffled back, I guided her head to my thigh and ran my fingers through her hair. She sighed, content, and my heart nearly burst.

"Close your eyes. You won't be of any help to your sister if you're exhausted. I'll watch over you while you rest."

She yawned again. "I didn't get to use your sand on my parents tonight."

"I'll take care of it when they're ready," I promised.

She tucked her knees to her chest. "Will you be in my room when I wake up tomorrow?"

"No. I need to save my strength for the battle that's coming."

"Will the Weaver try to kill you?" she asked, brushing bits of sand from my pants.

My fingers slowed. "I'm sure he would like to, but no."

She made a soft, skeptical sound in her throat, and her eyes fluttered shut.

The ache began as soon as Nora woke up for the day. A tight, weightlessness in my chest, as if I were trying to expel a helium balloon instead of magic. I was near empty, but the barrier had to be reinforced and Katie had to be found. I clawed at my chest through the layers of fabric, scratching an impossible itch. It would take too long to absorb power from the beach tonight. Time—I didn't have.

I closed my eyes and turned my attention inward. The cords tying me to my Dreamers stretched out before me. I ran my finger over them, feeling the person on the other end until I found a young Dreamer with a cache of dreams brimming in his queue. Gaining power this way hadn't been necessary since I bound the Weaver, but however much I didn't want it to be, it was again essential. I rubbed the space between my brows with my free hand and slowly exhaled.

Then I gripped the cord. My body hurdled down the unfamiliar path to a room I had never seen before and a boy who had never asked for my help. He slept beneath a set of Spiderman sheets, his dark hair mussed by the pillow. For me to find him, someone must have told him about me, but no one actually believed anymore. That didn't stop the sand full of my power from reaching him night after night. More importantly, it was full of his hopes, his innocence, his happiness—everything necessary to amplify the magic.

I leaned closer, my head hanging. "I'm sorry," I whispered.

With the last few drops of power within me, I held my hand over his head and called my power home. Silver and blue swirled from the boy's head, rising to greet my waiting palm. Glimpses of his dreams danced through the air. The wheel of a bicycle.

The fall of a block tower. An old dog with a white peppered snout. They flashed against my skin and disappeared. The power shot up my arm and slammed into my chest like a bullet. I clutched my shirt and staggered into a wall, slumping against it. My lungs drew a haggard breath despite the rush of new energy.

The boy would sleep dreamlessly tonight, and in the morning, he would wake without realizing anything was stolen. He wouldn't know how much he missed these dreams. These answers to questions he didn't know he had. They gave him something his waking hours couldn't—endless possibilities without rules, a conversation with a deceased loved one… *anything*.

I would make up for it one day.

I would repay each child I visited tonight for the things I stole. But first, I had to save them. First, I had to get the Weaver under control.

☾

When I returned to the beach hours later, I practically glowed with stolen dreams. I trudged toward the barrier to begin my work when the sound of racing steps reached my ears. I turned in time to see Baku skid to a halt behind me.

"You found something?" I dropped to my knees in front of him and scooped up handfuls of sand to read his dreams. "Show me."

Chapter Thirteen

Nora

An army of reporters stood below the podium. Cameras lined the back wall on tripods to record the news conference. For whatever reason, the scent of burnt rubber invaded the meeting room at the hotel, and the dry heat threatened to suffocate my last bit of patience. Or maybe it was the clingy capris and high-necked ruffle blouse with cap sleeves. It was too warm for stiff, restricting fabrics, but my mother insisted. People were watching, the police included, and I needed to project a certain degree of respectability. I tried not to take her words offensively since I didn't disagree with the thought behind them, but I also hoped passing out from heat stroke fell under my mother's opinion of acceptable behavior.

While Detective Bell addressed the news stations, I recounted every moment of last night's dream. Ben was the Sandman. The Sandman was Ben. He loved me. Pieces I hadn't realized were missing from the puzzle fell into place. How long had I loved him too? How long had I kept myself from acknowledging that because I didn't believe in him?

I believed now. The Sandman was in my corner. With his help, Katie would be back home soon. Maybe even today. Maybe before dinner. I clung to the thought and let it steel my nerves. The detective rattled off Katie's height and weight. He told the press about the scar on the back of her knee from a bike accident when she was seven. That she would likely be with someone armed and dangerous but as of yet, they had no suspect. Then he introduced me, my mother, and Paul.

We stepped up to the podium as a unit, hands clasped together. A united front. My mother choked back a sob, and Paul rubbed circles on her back. I wanted nothing more than to ease her fears, but the only way to do that was to find Katie. Surveillance proved she hadn't left town on public transportation which meant she was close. All her shoes were accounted for, so she couldn't have walked far.

"Katie, if you're watching this, we love you, we miss you, and we won't stop looking for you until you are home. If..." My mother paused. "If you have my daughter, please let her go. We..."

I stared at my black flats and tuned out the rest of her plea. I couldn't listen to it when I knew I was the reason the Weaver took Katie. When I was the reason my mother was in so much pain. Even knowing the truth about what the Weaver would do with the dream, a raw, aching part of me wanted to give it to him and be finished with all of this. But we would fix it. The Sandman and I would make things right again.

Paul tapped my shoulder when Detective Bell resumed the podium, and I stepped back. After what felt like forever, the reporters finished asking their questions and packed up their equipment.

When Detective Bell turned to speak with my mother, I nudged Paul. "Can I go hang up the posters I made this morning?"

He hesitated. "I don't know about that, kiddo. With everything going on it might not be good for you to be walking around on your own."

"It's the middle of the day, and I'll stay in town." When he didn't reply, I added, "Please?"

"All right, all right." He cleared his throat. "Be home before dinner or your mother will kill me."

"I will." Although I likely wouldn't eat again tonight. I needed to put on a show for my mother and the police, then fall asleep as soon as possible to see if the Sandman or Baku found any trace of my sister.

I ran to my car a block away and leaned into the back seat for the stack of fliers. The door on the other side clicked open. I jumped, slamming my head on the roof. The Sandman stared across the seat at me, his eyes full of life again, and my heart lurched. He said he was saving his strength...

"Who?" I breathed, squinting my eyes.

A small crease formed between his brows. "What?"

"The Weaver. Who did he kill this time?"

"That isn't why I'm here." He took the fliers and wall stapler from the back seat. "We're being watched so let's hang these while we talk."

I eased out of the car and glanced casually back at the hotel. Two police officers stood outside their vehicle, staring down the street in our direction. The Sandman and I walked around the corner in silence.

Tension crackled between us. It felt as if this were a dream with concrete under my feet instead of sand. A sky decorated with clouds instead of stars. But his presence at my side, that was the same. A smile spread across my lips before falling away. "If you're not here because of the Weaver, why are you here?"

"Baku heard a rumor about your sister when he was in the Nightmare Realm," he said, his face a perfect mask of calm.

My heart jumped. "Where is she?"

"I'm not sure." The Sandman glanced over his shoulder and shifted closer.

He stopped at a telephone pole and handed me the top flier. I held it against the wood while he stapled the corners down. Katie's smiling face stared at me, and I smoothed the paper so that he could attach the bottom edge.

My mother chose two photos—one from Katie's birthday six months ago with the rest of the family cropped out, and the other a candid of her smiling on the couch. Probably at something on one of her favorite reality shows. I trailed my fingers over her familiar cheek, so like my own yet freckle free, and a bit rounder.

"Baku doesn't speak so I have to read his dreams, but it looked like she was sleeping on a table or floor. There wasn't anything else in the room, and there weren't any windows to let light in. Do you know of any place like that?"

"Do I know a place with a table or a floor?" I raised an eyebrow at him, my hope plummeting. "You have to give me something more than *no windows.*"

He motioned for me to keep walking. "A shed, maybe?"

"Also, not helpful." I held up the next poster and struggled to keep the disappointment from swallowing me. There was still hope. It was *one thing* more than we knew this morning, as vague and unhelpful as it was. "But it would have to be close by."

His eyes shifted to the police again. "We'll lose them and then head to your neighborhood to see what we can find."

I led the way through the same field the search party and I combed through. My car was parked in a nearby parking lot to avoid suspicion, but I looked over my shoulder every few steps for flashing lights. What would the cops say if they found me sneaking around here? They already thought I had an accomplice and Sandman looked fit enough to have snapped a neck or killed two teenage girls.

The Sandman nudged me with his elbow. "You okay?"

"The police already looked here," I said. "They would have searched the sheds too."

"What if the Weaver moved her? You said he spoke with you during the search party which means this area would be safe to hide her. It's not far from your house so it's worth looking again."

I chewed on my lip. It was a valid point, but I hated wasting time double checking the same places. When we entered the trees near the new cul-de-sac where I spoke to the Weaver, I reached for the Sandman. He wove his fingers through mine. "None of this feels like real life," I whispered. "Not everyone being dead, not Katie, not the Weaver. Not *you*."

He was quiet for a long moment. "I'm sorry, Nora."

I knew he was; I was sorry too. Sorry to Lisa and that cashier's family. To everyone that loved Natalie and Emery, and to the woman who answered my father's cell phone. I wasn't sure my mother would want to know about his heart attack, so I still hadn't told her. The numbness swept back in, erasing the pain that threatened to cripple me. After Katie came back, I would fill the family in.

We reached the edge of the woods, and I squinted toward the brand-new houses. With only two of them occupied, and only one with a visible shed, we shouldn't have much trouble getting in and out. It was the middle of a weekday so with any luck, no one would be home either.

We rushed up to the nearest building, and I plastered myself against the back porch. The Sandman smirked. "I don't think that's necessary," he said.

I stuck my tongue out at him. "Says you. If we get caught you can *magic* your way out of here." I waved a hand at the shed. "Check, please."

"Sure, let me get my invisibility cloak out first."

"Sandman," I growled.

He laughed. "Hold on, Nancy Drew."

He didn't bother hiding; he simply strode over and cracked the unlocked door of the tool shed. He shook his head.

I sighed and tilted my head toward the sun. The roof shielded me from most of it, but it beat down on me like a drum. Of course, Katie wasn't there. But she was under the same sky as me, breathing the same air, so it was only a matter of time. The Sandman brushed a stray piece of hair from my forehead. My heart lurched at the touch.

"We'll find her," he assured me.

I nodded, and a square vent caught my attention at the peak of the house. I shoved away from the siding, accidentally knocking his shoulder. "Do you see that?"

He followed my gaze. "The attic vents?"

"A vent isn't a window." I launched myself up the back porch and peered through the sliding glass door. "It's empty."

"Watch out." The Sandman removed a small pouch from beneath his T-shirt like the one beneath mine. With a grin, he pinched a bit of sand from inside and blew it at the latch. The sand sparkled in the bright light before disappearing into the creases of the frame. A moment later, he twisted the knob and stepped inside, holding the door for me. "Open Sesame."

"That's handy," I mumbled, hesitating before following him into the kitchen. I couldn't be caught breaking-and-entering right now. Detective Bell wanted nothing more than a pliable reason to lock me up—but I needed to see.

The stillness of the house raised the hair on the back of my neck. Each rustle of our clothes as we moved through the hallways scraped my eardrums. Each footstep, a stomp. When we found the hatch to the attic and the Sandman pulled it down, unfolding the ladder, I cringed against the squeak of hinges.

He stepped back and stared into the darkness above.

"You first," I whispered and followed him up the rungs.

The attic was broiling. It wouldn't be possible to survive up here long without overheating. That was the only consolation for finding the space empty. My shoulders drooped. If Katie wasn't in any of these attics, where else should we look? There were so many possibilities that it made knowing impossible. Baku needed to give us something more concrete.

"Did you hear that?" the Sandman asked.

I froze and strained my ears. "What?"

Then the distinct sound of a door opening drifted through the house. "I really think you'll like this one," a woman said. "It's a new build, of course, with all the upgrades."

"A realtor," I hissed. What were the odds?

The Sandman ushered me up the last rung of the ladder and tugged the folding stairs back in place as quietly as possible. "Squeeze into the back corner."

My eyebrows rose, but I shuffled into the narrow space where the floor met the slanted roof. "How is this going to help exactly?"

"Do you have the sand I gave you?" he asked.

I nodded.

"Good." He squeezed in beside me and removed the sack from around his neck. "I need it."

My fingers dove into the ruffles at the base of my throat, and I unfastened the top three buttons. The Sandman's eyes widened. "Relax," I said, and tugged the bag free from the tank top I wore beneath my blouse.

He opened and closed his mouth, the corners of his lips quirking. "If they come up here, pour it into my hands and be as quiet and still as you can."

"Again, how is this going to help?" I asked in a hushed, panicked voice. "You can't put people to sleep on a ladder. They'll fall and break their necks."

"I won't put them to sleep."

"Then what? And if you joke about an invisibility cloak again, I'll strangle you."

He raised an eyebrow, amused. "I'm going to create the illusion of empty space."

My eyes narrowed at the bag of fine, silvery sand. "Huh."

"One day, after this is all over, I'll show more to you than your own dreams," he said. A blush rose on the back of his neck. "I mean, if you want. If you decide you don't want me to take the dream back."

My heart dropped like ice against the floor, sending tiny chips scattering in every direction. It was selfish to want to keep him to myself when the dream put everyone around me in danger. Keeping the secret kept the entire world safe, but that wasn't why I hesitated. I was sure that I wanted no part of it. I wasn't up to a burden like this but... "I don't want you to take it. I can't lose you too."

The backs of his fingers caressed my cheek, leaving a flush in their wake. I inched closer, the voices continuing below our feet. "I promised I would always be yours," he said, earnest. "I will never break that oath."

His breath skated along my temple, and I shivered despite the overwhelming heat. "Sandman..."

He nudged my ear with his nose. "I swear it, Nora. Even if you change your mind later."

"I know." I clamped down on a moan as his lips danced across the edge of my jaw.

"We spent so long not touching that it seems like I'll never get enough. That I'll never get close enough to you. Not like I want to," he whispered. The next kiss was as light as his breath. "You should stop me."

"What if I don't want to?" I asked, surprising myself. My entire body screamed for more. If it weren't for the realtor downstairs, I might have said as much. *Might.* But I felt bold with him. Strong and safe. Secure.

His lips crashed against mine and his blue fingertips rested against the sides of my neck as if I were made of glass. His breathing quickened at the same moment mine did. He tasted like spring. I wanted more. I didn't want to be careful. Not anymore. I nudged his lips with the tip of my tongue and heard a groan catch in his throat. His hair was silken clouds between my fingers.

A creak broke through the attic followed by a bang. "It's a little warm up here right now, but the electrician should be back tomorrow to finish the central air."

The Sandman leaned away and cupped both hands together. "The sand," he rasped.

My fingers fumbled with the tie, and I poured the contents of both bags into his palms. The silver and blue tattoos on his arms came alive, and he turned and blew the contents into the air in front of us. It rippled in a sheet. He flipped his palms outward and the sand froze in place. It glowed for a moment before becoming a single translucent wall like the one around the beach.

A man crawled up first with a flashlight, followed by a woman's head. My pulse roared in my ears. This was it—we were doomed. The Sandman's jaw clenched, his fingers spread wide before him. I wanted to inch closer to his side but didn't for fear of making a sound.

The woman swung a look around and shrugged. "It's a lot of storage space."

"With such a spacious yard, there are some nice options for outdoor storage as well," the realtor said from below. "Or if you need something bigger, a storage facility is only a few minutes' drive."

"I don't think that's necessary," the man said. "This is plenty."

The beam of light swung back down the ladder. It seemed like forever before the ladder slammed shut, sealing us into darkness again.

"That was amazing," I breathed, my heart still racing. "It's like we weren't here at all."

The sheet of magic exploded into nothingness, and the Sandman sagged against the wall. "I can't stay much longer," he admitted. "It uses a lot of energy to be in your world."

I clenched my hands in fists. He couldn't leave; we hadn't found Katie yet. But I saw the tightness around his eyes and labored rise and fall of his chest. "You should go," I said. "I'll keep looking for a while."

He shifted onto his knees and searched my face. "Are you sure?"

No. I didn't want to do this alone, but if I wanted to find Katie, he needed to recharge. "I'm sure."

"I'll see you tonight then." He leaned over and kissed my forehead.

I gripped his shirt, holding him in place. Panic clawed through me, an irrational fear that if he left, I wouldn't see him again. "Sandman?"

"Yes?" he asked, his mouth hovering above my skin.

"If you're always mine, then I'm always yours," I said. Because that was the truth, no matter what happened.

His arms wrapped around me, pressing me against him. My fear withdrew until only a single tendril of it remained. "This will all be over soon," he whispered.

"I hope so."

"I hate to leave you here like this."

"We got in. How hard could getting out be?" I pulled away and shrugged. I couldn't finish the other empty houses without him, but that didn't mean I couldn't look somewhere else.

He glanced around the attic space. "Be careful in the dark."

"Where were you?" my mother asked the second I walked through the door. "You couldn't have been hanging up fliers this whole time."

I wrapped my arms around my mother's waist and hugged her. She stiffened for a moment, probably unsure if it was a tactic to get out of trouble, before hugging me back. I hated that pause. Hated that she didn't show me the same affection other mothers show their children. That she showed Katie. She was afraid of me; she hadn't stopped being afraid since the day I insisted the Sandman was real. I don't think she ever really believed that I stopped seeing him, but she *wanted* to. Every time I zoned out or chose sleep over an invitation from a friend, it reminded her of that year she spent dragging me to doctor after doctor. She loved me—I knew she did—but she didn't know how to show it anymore.

"I was driving around to see if I could find Katie," I answered. As fruitless as it was. I hadn't really expected to see her waltzing down a back road anyway, but after looking in all windows in the cul-de-sac homes, I didn't know where else to go.

She tapped my shoulders, and I let go. "Natalie's father called today to let us know that the funeral is going to be this Saturday," she said, ushering me into the kitchen.

Funeral. A hollow pit opened in my stomach. "Okay."

"I made spaghetti."

I nodded. I could force a few bites down to appease her, but not much more than that. "I'll go change. Be right back."

I ran to my room and shut the door. For a minute, I simply leaned against it with my eyes closed, forcing back the desperate sorrow clawing its way through me. *Funeral.* Because Natalie was gone. Forever. Just like Emery. A thousand memories stacked on top of each other. Building and building and building. I shoved away from the door, knocking over the tower of images, and peeled off my sweaty clothes. I barely had my running shorts and tank top on when warm air curled around my ankles.

"Sun-Kissed Keeper," crooned the Weaver. "Keep digging deeper."

"You've got to be kidding me," I said through clenched teeth. I didn't turn around to face him—I couldn't.

"Has the Sandman told you that the stronger your mind is, the stronger your nightmare is?" The warm air wrapped its way up my leg. "How strong do you think yours is?"

"Strong enough." I yanked my hair up into a ponytail. When I turned, the Weaver's gold eyes watched me carefully from the open closet. "Get out of my room."

"How strong do you think your sister's mind is?" he asked with a tilt of his head. "Some things a person can't come back from. Do you think you'll find her before my nightmares break her?"

"I think *I'll* break *you*," I growled.

He gave me a mock bow, lifting his upturned palm. "I welcome you to the Nightmare Realm, Dream Keeper. Please, do take me up on the invitation."

Break her. Katie was running out of time. I slammed the closet door in his face and bolted back to the kitchen before I could suggest an exchange.

Spaghetti churning in my stomach, I flopped down on my bed, sleep already dragging me under. I took a deep breath and rolled onto my side. The air conditioning blew directly on my legs. My skin prickled against it, but the idea of moving enough to crawl between the sheets seemed too daunting.

I felt myself slipping. Falling. Drifting. The dream was close, beckoning me forward, but something yanked me back. A sharp, terrifying sensation gripped my core, and my eyes flew open.

My mother stood in the hallway. The wall sconce glowed behind her, casting her face in shadow, but I knew she was looking at me. It wasn't an awestruck look a mother sometimes gives her child while they're asleep, nor was it one of concern. It radiated hate. A scathing anger that made the hair on my arms stand on end.

I hesitated. "Mom?"

She lunged into my room, her hands outstretched, and grabbed the pillow from beneath my head. There wasn't time to get out of the way before she slammed it over my face. I thrashed beneath her, clawing at her arms. I tried to scream but the pillow blocked my breath.

Then, as fast as my mother had flown into the room, she was back in the hall. I gasped for air and scrambled from the bed. My mother grinned. My heart stopped, my palms sweating. She threw the pillow at me and disappeared into her bedroom across the hall, slamming the door behind her.

The Weaver's laugh traveled from somewhere down the hall. I held my breath and charged around my bed to shut the door, blocking out the sound. The lock beside the doorknob clicked beneath my thumb, but I wasn't taking any chances. One bobby pin and it would pop open. So, propping myself between the wall and my dresser, I slid the heavy antique in front of the door.

I flung myself into bed a second time, adrenaline pumping, and watched the knob until I had calmed enough to fall asleep.

Chapter Fourteen

"My mother tried to smother me."

My eyes snapped away from the barrier overhead to find Nora stomping across the beach. "*What*?"

"Technically it was the Weaver," she clarified, her breath uneven. "Don't worry. I barricaded myself in my room."

I ground my teeth together. It was only a matter of time before he sent a sleepwalker after her, but he couldn't kill Nora. He needed her alive. It was a warning and a good one at that. Using her mother too…

"Have you found anything?"

"Not yet." I motioned her forward, not taking my eyes off the sky. A crack scarred the barrier. A mere hairline fracture, no longer than my little finger, smaller still from down here. It hadn't been there when I left to help Nora find her sister. "Do you see it?"

She squinted. "See what?"

"There." I moved behind her and held my arm out so that she could follow where I pointed. "A crack."

"I just see the sky," she said, shrugging.

I stepped around her. Maybe it was too far up, too small, for her to notice, but it wasn't too small for nightmares to sneak in. Some were tiny, slippery things. I did a sweep after I returned but came up empty-handed. With a quick flick of my wrist, I sent sand racing through the air to patch it.

"It isn't safe here tonight," I said.

She jerked, her eyes scanning for the imperfection again. "I thought those things from the other night couldn't get in."

"Those things couldn't. The barrier was solid then." I scooped sand into a pouch and handed it to her to replace what we used in the attic. She tossed the string over her neck.

Her sister disappeared three nights ago. Which meant for three nights and two days, she'd suffered torture at the hands of who knew what. If we didn't find her soon, there might not be anything left to save. My first concern had to be Nora though. If she wasn't safe, no one was. I took her face in my hands, my thumbs skimming the freckles along her cheekbone.

"How cozy," came a familiar voice. I spun, shoving Nora behind me, to find the Weaver walking from the sea. Water rolled off him as if he were made of wax. He glanced up at where the crack had been. "And how... lazy."

"You can't be here," I growled, tightening my grip on Nora.

He clucked his tongue. "It took me so long to find a way in." The Weaver circled us, and his heavy metallic scent turned my stomach. "Besides, let's not forget that you waltzed into my realm uninvited first—the least you could do is ask me to stay for tea."

I held my hands out, palms parallel to the ground, and sand shot up to greet them. "Nora, go."

"No," she hissed. "You can't keep telling me to leave every time he shows up. I have to face him sooner or later."

The Weaver grinned at her words. "She must."

"Shut up." Nora sidestepped me, her face red with fury. "Don't ever touch my mother again, and I want my sister back."

A black blur zoomed out from behind the Weaver. Something small and rodent-like, heading straight for her legs. I slammed my fingers into a fist, and the sand followed my movement. I flung my arm toward the nightmare, fingers splayed. A spray of tiny needles met the creature's side. It fell to the sand, black blood pooling beneath its bristly fur. Sharp tusks stuck straight out from its mouth, ready to impale. Yellow liquid oozed from tiny, bulging venom sacks beneath each one.

"Leave," I said again, both to the Weaver and Nora.

"What *is* that thing?" Nora breathed.

The Weaver frowned. "That *was*—"

"It doesn't matter what it was," I hissed, meeting the Weaver's glare. "Only what it could have done. The same goes for all his nightmares."

He shrugged, nonchalant. "You can't blame me for trying."

More sand rose around me, and the ground shifted beneath my boots. I blamed him, yes. For letting nightmares into the Day World. For forcing me to bind him. But, if he was anything, it was consistent. The Weaver relied too much on his minions and not enough on himself.

"Are you going to oust me? With all that overflowing magic?" He grinned. "Or are you going to sick Baku on me? He's causing quite the stir these days. I fear he will become rather obese after turning my realm into an all you can eat buffet."

"She's not giving you the dream," I said, rage coating each syllable.

"I rather think that's not up to you. A tough pill to swallow, I'm sure, after so many years of prancing around like someone dubbed you the Night Emperor." The Weaver leaned sideways to better peer at Nora. "Say yes, little Sun-Kissed Keeper. Give me access."

"Give me my sister," she countered with such calm fury that I shivered.

"Nora, go," I begged. "Please."

"I won't leave you alone with him, and I won't leave without Katie," she said, standing her ground.

The Weaver extracted a string from the band around his wrist. Gold filaments glinted against the black thread. With a flick, it stiffened. "Last chance, Keeper."

"Don't you dare release another one of your filthy creatures in here," I snarled.

He tossed the rigid thread, and it exploded midair in a cloud of black powder. A deep rumble tore across the beach a moment before a hairless, human-like creature with jagged fingers stood beside the Weaver. Grey skin clung to its ribs. The nightmare stared hungrily at Nora through hollow slits, and brown saliva dripped down its chin from between pointed, yellow teeth.

There wasn't time to think, no time to reason with Nora. I couldn't fight this thing and protect her at the same time. There was a chance I wasn't going to be able to protect myself. Sand whirled around us, and I jerked her close, trapping us in the center. "Don't be angry," I whispered. Then I did something I knew I would always regret; I dismissed her decision to stay, and shoved her, hard, from the dream.

Dagger-like fingers dug into my shoulder the moment she was gone, sending me to my knees. I swiped my free hand across the ground. A spray of sand swooped upward toward the nightmare as a blade. The metal sliced through the air with a piercing shriek and the gleaming edge severed its wrist. The hand fell to the ground with a soft thud. The sand faltered around me as the taint of the nightmare's presence grew. The infection crept deeper, the blood seeping beyond the surface of the beach.

I stood on unsteady feet and stumbled backward, away from the creature. Foam fell from its mouth in globs. The Weaver was no longer behind him—his presence registering far away. Anxious. Annoyed. He had left me alone with this *thing* to do his dirty work.

"What?" I snapped. "Is that all it takes to stop you?"

It roared, and spit rained across my face. My fingers twitched, rushing to turn the sand into something useful. But I wasn't fast enough, or maybe it was *too* fast, because in the next instant, razor sharp pain seared up my torso. Blood spilled from vertical claw marks on my chest. I barely drew breath before it raised its remaining hand for a second strike.

I leaned back to avoid the blow and fell, landing flat on my back. A whiff of decay hit me instead of claws. They passed through empty air and impaled the nightmare's own thigh. Its slit-eyes constricted in shock.

I tossed a handful of sand in its face and scrambled to my feet. My cuts screamed in protest when I raised a fist above my head. A curtain of sand rose up behind the creature. The shadow fell first, a grey blanket coating the beach. When I brought my arm down in one violent jerk, the wounds wailed, and the curtain fell. The sand encased the shrieking nightmare in a cyclone. Pulling it. Crushing it. Tearing it. I hated that move. Hated the screams mixing with cracks and crunches. Hated the soft clink of sand against sand that echoed through the pain.

Footsteps beat in my ears, a strange new note to the wretchedness before me. Baku skidded to a halt on the other side of the smaller dead nightmare. His eyes lifted to mine with a flash of hope, and I nodded once. Let him eat it. Let him eat the second one too, as soon as it was dead. It was one less mess I needed to clean.

My knees buckled, my arms falling limp at my sides. I looked away from the disaster playing out on my beach, blocked out the sounds, and pried the torn fabric from the middle gash. It had almost—*almost*—nicked the edge of the crescent moon there. It was hard to look at the wound and consider myself lucky, but I was. There wasn't time to heal from something like that. Not now. It would take months, at least.

I rolled my sleeves up and started the tedious task of drawing out each grain of contaminated sand. Baku swished his cow tail and made his way to my side. He lifted the severed hand with his trunk on his way by, and I cringed. "I hope you found something," I said.

The cyclone narrowed, and the screams reduced to tortured mewls. Baku flopped down beside me with a disgruntled huff, his side pressing against my leg. Then he unhinged his jaw and stuffed the entire hand into his mouth. I slammed my eyes shut. The sound of crunching bones set my nerves on edge.

"Nothing, then," I said, more to myself than him.

My energy faded, leaving me feeling empty and dull. I cracked my eyes open in time to see the sand fall around a mangled corpse. Baku lunged for it while I dug into my reserves again—so soon after stealing dreams.

Too soon.

Chapter Fifteen

Nora

I wrenched out of bed, gasping for air, and clutched the leather string around my neck. Those things... The nightmares... That was what the Weaver wanted to unleash on the world. That's what I was protecting humankind from. Not just the people I loved—but everyone. The Weaver could rot in his realm—there was no way was I giving him the dream. Not now, not ever. I still felt the creature's dead gaze crawling over my skin and the scent of rotting flesh lingered in my nostrils.

And I left the Sandman there alone. *No.* I didn't leave him. He kicked me out. Ejected me somehow. My blood fizzled in my veins. It was my dream—I held the power. I could have done something. Helped.

Don't be angry.

Well, I was. I crossed the room in two steps and yanked the top dresser drawer open. The white pills glared up at me from the bottom. They promised sleep. Sleep I couldn't wake from until morning, at least. There would be no shoving me out again. The Sandman and I were in this—all of this—together, and I needed to pull my own weight.

"Keeper." The voice came in a rushed hiss, hot against my ear.

I slammed the drawer shut and spun on my heel. "*You.*" I advanced one step for each one the Weaver took backward. He cocked his head and smirked. "I swear, if anything happens to him, I'll—"

"You'll what?" he drawled. "Boil me in oil? Dream Keeper, I turned torture into a fine art long before you were a twinkle in your father's eye."

I grabbed my hairbrush off the displaced dresser and threw it at him. Then a pen. A tube of mascara. A hand-mirror. It all bounced off his semi-solid form; the mirror shattered into a dozen pieces. I froze, panting, waiting to hear my mother's hurried footsteps in the hall, but there was only silence.

"Ouch," the Weaver deadpanned.

"Is he alive?" I growled.

"Naturally."

I balled my hands into fists. "If you're lying..."

"What reason do I have to lie? Do stop wasting my time; it grows irksome."

I narrowed my eyes. "I'm going to kill you."

"Yes, yes. Very scary." He smiled as if he was genuinely amused, and the beauty of it made me sick to my stomach. "At least one of you has the courage to try."

I opened my mouth to defend the Sandman, but the words stuck in my throat. He hadn't tried before? *Never*? Not even when the Weaver was letting nightmares loose? The binding had to be Plan B. Weakening himself to keep the wards up, constantly fearing the day they broke. It had to be a last resort. But he'd only ever mentioned trapping the Weaver again. Not once had he said anything about a more permanent solution. About delivering the punishment the Weaver deserved.

"Even if he wanted to, the Sandman will never kill me," the Weaver said as if he knew where my thoughts had wandered. "Why do you think I'm here now? Do you think it's because he was incapable of bringing about my death five years ago? No. My life was in his hands when he did this to me, but we have a history, he and I." He casually waved a hand through the air as if it didn't matter, but the way his voice pitched betrayed him. "Besides, he believes in balance—a darkness to the light." He leaned closer, the amused glint fading from his features. "But I'm tired of being bound, Dream Keeper. Do you understand? We did something that needs undoing. This isn't how things are supposed to be."

I squared my shoulders. The Sandman said the balance always rights itself so what was stopping him? I shifted under the Weaver's scrutiny. "Sucks to be you."

"Give me the dream," he growled. "Enough games."

I folded my arms across my chest, my heart hammering against them. Yes. Enough games, indeed. "You might as well kill me because you're not getting it."

The Weaver rose to loom over me, blocking the moonlight from the window. His golden eyes glowed in the darkness, but I held my ground. He couldn't scare me anymore. There wasn't enough left in me to be afraid, and what did remain was too busy being pissed off.

"I've come to offer one last deal," he said after a long silence. "Give me what I want or everyone you know, everything you care about, will be swallowed by fear."

"Wow." I rolled my eyes, but a metallic tang coated my mouth. *Blood.* The only thing telling me that I chomped down on the inside of my cheek. "What an offer, Weaver. It's almost as if it isn't an offer at all."

His top lip lifted in disgust.

"I want Katie back, safe and sound," I said.

"I gathered as much."

Goosebumps dotted my arms at his tone, but I wasn't backing down. He had my mother smother me in my own bed, sent a nightmare straight for me on the beach, and created the most vulgar thing I'd ever seen to hurt the Sandman. *No.* I was finished letting people walk all over me. It got me nowhere. It got me *here*. To this place with him.

"I want to see her first," I said.

He narrowed his eyes. "I see trust is not your forte."

"Call me crazy." I glared at him, waiting, too nervous to breathe.

"I'll show you your sister." If trust wasn't my forte, bargaining wasn't his. "Then you'll give me the dream."

"*If* Katie is okay," I answered. She had to be. *She had to.*

"Tomorrow at dusk," he said slowly. "52 Maple Street. I'll know if you go looking before that. If you try anything, if you drive by or I see a single police officer near that address, I'll let my Blood Army devour your sister piece-by-piece."

Blood Army? I forced myself not to shiver. "I believe you."

Not that he should believe me. If there was ever the tiniest chance of me giving up the secret, seeing the threat he carried with my own eyes had crushed it. But I was tired of waiting for someone else to find Katie. Tired of fruitlessly searching. The Sandman didn't want me to help him fight nightmares—fine. He was probably right. That didn't mean I was going to sit around while there were things that needed to be done.

"A temporary truce, then. Do not think to cross me." The Weaver backed away, fading into the shadows.

I scrambled back into bed. Of course, I was going to cross the Weaver. He had to know I was.

☾

The carcass of the nightmare that rushed me was gone from the beach, and blissfully, there was no sign of the other one. But the normally smooth sand was covered in divots. Blood so dark it was almost black filled the small pits, and a trail of it led away from the water, following deep drag marks.

Alive suddenly didn't feel as comforting as it did a moment ago. The Sandman could be unconscious. Bleeding out. Tortured. Alive meant nothing except that I wasn't too late *yet.*

The blood led past a tall hill to a part of the beach I had never seen before—and I had explored every nook and cranny over the years. My face fell, taking the color with it, and I ran. My bare feet dug into packed sand, and I scrambled up a foreign dune.

"Sandman," I whisper-yelled. It was lost in the endless stretch of sand. The ground was nearly untouched, the drag marks the only thing disturbing the smooth, glimmering grains. Drag marks and footprints. My feet slid back the way I came.

Whatever did the dragging was distinctly not human. Four oval toes were spaced above the pad of an animal's foot—a foot nearly as big as my head.

My heart pounded. The open terrain suddenly felt too defenseless, like something would fall from the sky and leave me with nowhere to hide. A soft *thump* froze me in place. My muscles tightened until they ached. A tiny, familiar voice whispered doubts in the back of my mind, telling me I wasn't brave enough. Strong enough. Smart enough. It was probably right. I knew I was about to cross the Nightmare Lord, but I had no idea what exactly I was walking into. My plan sounded good in theory. Katie's life depended on my finding the Sandman though—I couldn't do this without his cooperation.

I jumped when another *thump* echoed off the invisible barrier. A stout creature appeared in the distance. It was too far away to see, but I knew it was watching me as closely as I was watching it. Then it moved. I locked my knees, bracing myself. Each footstep was another *thump*. My hands shook at my sides. I wouldn't run. Wouldn't. My right foot slid back a step. *Traitor.*

As the creature neared, he studied me through beady eyes. I fought against a scream, my breath rapid and shallow. He stopped in front of me and his elephant trunk reached out, sniffing my hair. A musk emanated from the thick, furry hide, not entirely disgusting but not something I wanted in my face. The black and yellow brindle fur at the base of his neck rose. If he was anything like a dog, that was a horrible sign. I stared at his curved tusks, tinged pink with what I only hoped wasn't blood, and my stomach dropped.

"Um." I took an involuntary step back and cringed. "Hey, there. Nice...nightmare."

He dropped his trunk and glared. I glared back, not daring to breathe. I could've sworn it frowned before scooping up a bit of sand and tossing it at my ankles. Then he turned and lumbered away. His skinny cow-like tail swished angrily back-and-forth as he followed the drag trail.

"Wait," I called. "Where is—"

He paused and glanced back at me. It was a look of understanding so deep I thought only humans were capable of. It shook my core, tethering me in place. When he moved again, I hurried after him, stepping carefully over each of his gigantic paw prints.

It could have been a trap, but what choice was there? I needed to make sure the Sandman was in one piece. So, I followed him and followed him. And followed him some more until the water was far behind us, endless glittering sand the only thing in sight. Then, finally, he stopped in front of an open structure. Two walls held a thatched roof over a wooden platform almost completely hidden under an array of pillows. On one wall was a series of built-in drawers, and on the other… I blinked to make sure it wasn't a mirage. But the three drawings I'd gifted him over the last six months didn't disappear. My self-portrait—the only one I'd ever done, per his request—and two landscapes of his world hung, evenly spaced, across the second interior wall. I swallowed hard.

The Sandman hid himself from me for five years; he hid this even longer. My visits were regulated to a one mile stretch of beach when there was so much more. My pulse roared, an angry thing. This... this was a secret. There weren't supposed to be any left. What else didn't I know?

The creature dug at the sand just outside the structure with his tiger paws until a groan came from beneath the ground. I slapped a hand over my mouth.

"Not yet," the Sandman croaked as his face appeared from under the sand. "I need more time."

"Sandman?" I asked, louder than I intended. "What are you doing?"

His eyes flew open. Silver flecks swirled around his violet pupils. "Nora? What are you doing here?"

"Looking for you."

"You shouldn't have." He closed his eyes again and sighed. "Things might not have ended well. It was dangerous for you to come back this soon."

"Apparently things didn't end very well, regardless," I said. "Are you okay?"

The creature huffed. I shot him a deadly look, and he strode away.

"Don't mind him," the Sandman said, and the footsteps thumped away.

I eyed the creature cresting a nearby dune. "What is that thing?"

"Baku."

I gaped. "*That* is your associate?"

He cracked his eyes open to look up at me. "He's going back out right now to look for Katie."

I bit my tongue, instantly sorry I called him a thing. He wasn't just the Sandman's associate anymore—he was mine. *By default*, as the Sandman had said, but helpful nonetheless. I squinted at him, following his movements, and he waltzed straight through the barrier.

My face fell. "The barriers are down?"

"Baku has been here as long as I have, perhaps longer, but he belongs to neither the Nightmare nor the Dream Realm. He goes where he pleases." His voice was low and tired.

I faced him again and repeated, "Are you okay?"

He paused. "I will be."

I kneeled beside him. His face was the only thing visible while the rest of him lay hidden, perfectly camouflaged, in the sand. I tucked my feet beneath me, then untucked them, and tucked them again. "Are you sure? Do you need help getting out of there?"

His lips quirked. "It's healing me."

"What?"

He sat up with a quiet grunt and ran a hand through his hair. His tunic was gone, and three long, jagged rips ran up the abdomen of his second shirt. I ran my eyes over him for other injuries before stopping at the gaping holes dotting his shoulder.

"The sand. It's—"

"Yes, yes." I waved my hand at him. "The sand heals you, but you never mentioned being buried in it." I dropped my gaze to scowl at the ground where his waist disappeared. Even after all the explanations, what did I really know about the Sandman? About his life or his abilities? I knew he could conjure up pretty illusions. I knew he could travel into my world and break into houses, but not the *how*. Maybe magic was one of those things that had no explanation, but for all the time I spent here, it felt like I knew absolutely nothing.

"Hey." The Sandman ran his thumb down my cheek. "It's faster this way. I'll be fine."

Of course, he would. Because the sand was healing him. My nostrils flared. *Later.* Later we would talk about this hidden oasis and everything I still didn't know. But right now, I was working on a deadline. "I need your help figuring out something specific."

The weight of his eyes made me twitch. I refused to look up. He said nothing for what felt like forever, but it couldn't have been more than thirty seconds. "I'm not going to like this, am I?"

I gave him a quick, fake smile. "That's a pretty safe assumption."

He released a breath. "All right, but first, would you mind?"

I looked up to find him gently tugging an arm from his sleeve.

"Direct contact will speed things up, and Baku doesn't exactly have opposable thumbs."

I hesitated. I wanted to help, to do something I knew was undoubtedly useful, but the crate holding all my doubt weighed heavy, dragging me deeper into uncertainty. And not just about my plan with the Weaver. The Sandman was so certain of his feelings for me—he'd had a year to be sure—but it was new to me. I felt the same way but what if it was my relief tricking me? What if I loved him as a friend? What if I did love him more than a friend but I could never trust him like I had before?

I leaned forward anyway, brushing the thoughts away. My feelings could wait in line. Right now, the Sandman needed to get better so that he could help me trick the Weaver and save my sister. My fingers grazed his stomach, and his breath caught. I pinched the hem of his shirt. The stretchy material clung to him, squelching as it separated from his bloodstained skin.

His abs flexed, and he shifted to lift his arms over his head. My eyes caught on the tattoo over his breastbone. Thousands of blue and silver specks blinked in and out, spilling from a thick, navy-blue crescent moon. My fingertips hovered over it, but I was too afraid to make contact. There had always been so many layers between us that touching bare skin still seemed forbidden.

The Sandman's fingers carefully circled my wrist, and he brought my hand forward. My palm almost covered the moon, only the pointed tips peeked out on either side of my knuckles. Electricity zipped through my arm, leaving peace in its wake. I gasped, my eyelids drooping. I hadn't felt this calm in ages.

"My magic lives in you," he said in a hoarse voice. "The dream I gave you fused with your own power, but it remembers where it came from."

"I don't have power for it to fuse with." The pulsating rhythm beneath my hand was like a second heartbeat.

"Of course, you do." He released my wrist and placed his palm over my collarbone. "It lives here. In your heart." He trailed his fingers up the side of my neck and skimmed my temples. A blush burned my cheeks. "And here."

I wanted to tell him he was crazy, that what he said made no sense, but maybe he wasn't. Maybe it did. *Keep a true mind and a true heart.* I blinked slowly, watching the tattoo shimmer.

He sighed, his hand falling away. "I would love for you to stay, but it isn't safe yet."

"It is tonight," I said quietly. "I talked to the Weaver again."

His muscles stiffened beneath my hand. "Nora, no. Whatever you're thinking, the answer is no."

I broke contact, my skin tingling, and forced my eyes up to his. "Hear me out first."

"Do I have a choice?" he grumbled.

"Of course." I shrugged, one corner of my mouth lifting. "But only one of your options is *really* an option."

The Sandman's face grew tighter with every word as I explained my encounter with the Weaver and my intent to cross him, his chest barely moving with each shallow breath. "If I didn't know better, I'd ask if you had a death wish," he said when I finished.

I clenched my jaw. "My sister is wrapped up in this because of us, and we're going to get her out of it."

"Baku is still searching the—"

"There has to be another way." I inched closer. "There has to be a way for me to do something from my side other than search blindly for where he's hidden her."

The muscle in his jaw twitched. "If we could get one of the threads he wears on his arm, I could use it to track down Katie's subconscious in his realm but—"

"Great," I blurted, hope swelling. "How do we do that?"

"Nora." He leveled a serious look at me. "If it were that easy, I would have rebound him and none of this would be happening. He's not stupid. He knows I'll go for them if I'm close by."

"*You*. But not me." My voice wavered. I didn't want to be close enough to the Weaver to touch him, assuming I could when he wasn't completely in my world, but Katie needed me. "Tell me how to get one."

"If I gave you a…" He paused and clamped his mouth shut. "No. I won't let you risk it."

"Then I'll find a way into the Nightmare Realm and look for her myself." My heart raced at the idea, my palms sweating. No part of me wanted to go there. None. I would do it though.

"You really do have a death wish." He closed his eyes and scooped a handful of sand. The granules moved painfully slow across his palm. "You have to do *exactly* what I tell you. Once you get the thread, the Weaver will pull out all the stops. We'll have a little time before he recovers, but not forever."

Chapter Sixteen

Nora

A fog light illuminated the sign for MJ's U-Store It. I paused at the stop sign a hundred feet from the address the Weaver gave me and eyed the rows of grey steel boxes behind a chain-link fence. *A place with no windows.* The last remnants of sunlight glowed pink across the otherwise empty field, creating a dusk too beautiful to be spent double-crossing an evil lord.

I tugged the sleeve of my fleece sweater down over the heel of my hand. Four hair bands circled my left wrist and forearm beneath it, securing the box cutter the Sandman created. The warm metal dug into my skin—a promise of safety, a threat of failure. Really, the plan could go either way. However, as long as I saved Katie, I could deal with the consequences. I took a deep breath and eased the car forward.

The tires crunched against the gravel drive of the twenty-four-hour storage facility. I knew this was the right place thanks to the internet, but there were at least a hundred tan and green units. Katie was so close. *So close.* It took every ounce of willpower not to call the police the second I knew where she was, but for this plan to work, the Weaver couldn't sense my deceit.

My heart flopped, and I tugged at my sleeves again. If I was going to save Katie and move against the Weaver, I had to be braver than I felt. If I couldn't do that, then I had already lost.

I pulled into the center row, halfway down from where another aisle cut horizontally, and put the car in park. Easing out of the driver's seat, I slammed the door and willed away my nerves. The gentle purr of the engine felt reassuring, although the extra few seconds it would give me to escape wouldn't matter against someone like the Weaver. I rapped my fingers against the hood of the car and squinted into the shadows.

"You didn't back out." The Weaver stepped around the corner of the nearest row, the gossamer shroud still tying him down. "I admit to having my doubts."

"What choice did I have?" I snapped, the anger palpable.

He shrugged one shoulder. "There's always a choice."

I wiped sweaty palms on my grey leggings. What if I couldn't do it? What if I missed my mark? But it was too late for doubts. The ride had started and there was no getting off. "Which unit is she in?"

"Follow me," he said. I took one step toward him when he vanished. His voice drifted across the parking lot. "This way, Sun-Kissed Keeper."

I stomped toward the back of the units where his shadow flickered and strained to hear his voice again. "I have a name, you know," I shouted.

The Weaver popped up beside me. I jumped, hitting a unit door with a clang, and he grinned. "I care nothing for your name, *Keeper*. Only what's behind that freckled forehead of yours." He bopped the air in front of my hairline with a finger.

I locked my knees, refusing to step away and show an ounce of the fear storming through me. "Where is she?"

His eyes narrowed, and he clucked his tongue. "Your Dreamer is here." He vanished, reappearing at the last door in the row.

My sneakers ground into the tiny stones beneath my feet, and I flexed my tingling fingers. *Okay*. Go in, make sure there's a clear path to the exit, check Katie's pulse, slide the box cutter out, open the blade, swing, grab the thread, run. *Easy*. Just like I practiced on the Sandman last night. I swallowed hard. I could do this. I had to.

When I stepped up to the Weaver, he grinned before disappearing, popping up a few units in the opposite direction. "Here, here." His voice bounced through my head. "She's so near."

"I'm going to kill you," I said under my breath.

He materialized an inch from me. "Now, now. Don't ruin the fun."

I scowled. "This isn't a game."

"Of course, it is." He stalked around me in a circle. "I let my nightmares out of the Night World. The Sandman bound me and slammed the doors shut. Now I do something to free myself, he comes running after me, etcetera, etcetera. The question is, who wins?"

"You were letting your monsters run loose through the Day World. What did you expect him to do?"

"People need something real to fear. They *crave* it." He tossed a hand at me. "How many horror movies have you seen? How many ghost stories have you enjoyed?"

"People like horror movies because they aren't real, not because they think being murdered is enjoyable." I pressed my arm against my hip, letting the cutter dig through my leggings and into my thigh. He had to believe I was going through with the deal. "Forget it. Do you remember your promise to ensure my safety?"

One of his eyebrows lifted. "If I want to torment the Sandman's favorite toy now and then, it's my prerogative, but yes, I recall what I said."

Comforting. "I want it extended to my family."

"You're hardly in a place to make demands."

I crossed my arms.

"Fine, fine." He dipped his head and flicked his fingers toward me. "Your family too."

"Good." If this were real, I would ask him for clarification, but his vague half-promise was enough. Let him think I was an idiot. It only helped my cause. "Then, Katie. Now."

"You'll take my word on the deal but not on your sister's wellbeing?"

I sneered, my muscles trembling. "If my sister isn't okay, the deal is off. Consider this proof of purchase."

He shrugged and lifted a long finger to point at the unit directly behind me. "The combination is 22-7-10."

I lunged for the silver lock and fumbled with the dial. "How did you even get a lock on this thing?" I grumbled to myself.

"Katie isn't the only sleepwalker in the world. I'd think that was obvious. How *is* your mother, by the way?" He hovered at my shoulder, and I jerked the arrow too far past the second number. "Seven."

"I know," I snapped. I wiped the sweat from my palms and spun the black knob to start over. It was too hot for this sweater. Too stressful. But I had to hide the weapon and the leggings offered the best range of motion. Neither of which would matter if I passed out from nerves.

When the lock popped open, I yanked the overhead door up and rushed inside. Katie was still in her favorite pajamas—skull and crossbones shorts and a faded graphic T-shirt. Her hair was slick with grease, but her chest rose and fell in an even rhythm, her features smooth. No screaming, no tense muscles. Other than the fact that she was in the middle of a storage unit, she appeared to be having a regular nap.

"Don't worry. She received plenty of breaks to keep her heart ticking. I didn't want her to expire before I was ready—like your father did," he said reassuringly.

My heart twisted painfully. *Stay calm. Don't ruin the plan.*

"And now you see the proof," he added, a saccharine smile glittering on his features.

I dropped to my knees, my back to the Weaver, and pressed my fingers to her neck like I was taking her pulse. With my other hand, I slipped my fingers into my sleeve and slid the box cutter free. My fingers fumbled to grip the smooth surface. I sucked in a ragged breath and slid the blade from the tip. "Hang in there," I whispered to Katie. "It will all be over soon."

"Dream Keeper." The Weaver's voice was stern yet thick with anxiety. "It's time for you to keep your end of the bargain."

"How...?" I asked, stalling. I knew how. The Sandman told me I would have to fall asleep and reject the safety of the beach. Then the Weaver would snatch me away to his realm where I would allow him access. Like there was any chance of me letting him drag me off to his home turf. Deal or no deal, I had no doubt he would torture me if he had the chance. Once he had the dream, I was as good as dead.

"It's easy." He knelt on the other side of Katie. I shifted the box cutter so that it pressed between my knee and Katie's upper arm. "You go to sleep. I'll meet you on the other side and then you say yes."

"Will it hurt?" The black and gold band of threads on his wrist gleamed through the gossamer, stretching up his bicep to attach to his ever-moving shirt. I just needed one of them.

He trailed a finger over Katie's cheek without really touching her. "Not so very much."

"I see." I took a deep breath and fussed with my sister's shirt, smoothing the bottom down where the hem had flipped over. The Sandman sounded so sure this would work, and I trusted him with my life, but maybe whatever piece of his magic I carried wasn't enough to breach the barrier between our worlds. Maybe the dream didn't hold enough sway, even with the weapon made of sand to amplify it. *Be quick*, he warned. The binding would close itself almost immediately, and I didn't want to lose a hand when it did. I took a deep breath. "Well, then..."

I moved without thinking. The blade ripped through the fabric, tearing through the top layer of flesh below the Weaver's elbow. The threads floated away from him, squirming in an attempt to return to their master, and the blade slipped from my hand. I gripped the band around his wrist and yanked with every muscle I had. Three broke away, falling with me to the floor.

The gossamer flashed blue, and the Weaver's nails clawed against the resealed binding, his eyes darting wildly across its surface. "You," he bellowed.

"Yes." I scrambled off the floor, tying the three threads into a knot to keep them together. They twitched in my palm. "Me."

He bent, gasping over my sister's sleeping body. "I will personally peel the skin from her body while you watch."

My legs shook beneath me. I knew he would threaten Katie after I did this. I knew it, but I *also* knew it was the only way to save her in time. "Not if I skin you first."

"Foolish Keeper," he rasped. "You are no match for me."

"I appreciate being underestimated. It makes winning that much sweeter." I tucked my prize into the pocket of my fleece and zipped it shut. He would have more soon—apparently, all it took was a trip to his loom to replenish what was lost. Twenty-four hours until he had a full arsenal wrapped around his arm again.

I looped my elbows under Katie's armpits and dragged her toward the waiting car. The Weaver watched every step with fury blazing in his golden irises. Surely, he was imagining each way he would torture me for this betrayal, but I couldn't think about that now. I had to get Katie to the hospital, then find her in the Nightmare Realm before the Weaver paid her a visit.

A nurse in teal scrubs wheeled Katie back into the curtained area of the emergency room, an IV bag swaying from a metal pole. They planned to run every test to discover why she was in a coma, explore every avenue of possibilities, but so far, they'd come up empty-handed. Of course, they had, unless there was some sort of supernatural CT scan. My mother shuffled after them, speaking in a low voice to one of her coworkers from the maternity ward while I stood silently in the hall with Paul.

My eyelids threatened to slam shut where I stood, but I couldn't give in yet. When I finally fell asleep, it had to be somewhere safe. Somewhere no one would be tempted to wake me before the Sandman and I did what had to be done. He was waiting for me now, waiting for the strands of thread in my pocket, so we could follow one of them straight to Katie. Time was ticking. The Weaver wouldn't leave himself vulnerable by attacking her while weak, but there was nothing stopping him from telling his creatures to up their game. Nothing except some sort of sick satisfaction of doing it himself. The Sandman assured me that would be the case.

Katie still appeared calm. The heart monitor beeped in a regular, steady rhythm, and that had to count for something.

"She'll be fine," Paul whispered to me. "You did good."

But not good enough.

I pressed my lips together and nodded. By the way Detective Bell hovered near the nurses' station, casting suspicious looks in my direction, I guessed I was firmly up Shit Creek without a paddle. I could almost hear his questions now. How did I know where to find Katie? How did I know the combination to the lock? Why hadn't I called the police first? Was I hiding something? Did I turn on my hypothetical partner in crime? I couldn't handle it yet.

"It's going to be a long night." Paul fished the keys from his pocket. "Let's head home, huh? We could both use some rest."

I cast a glance at my mother. Her coworker held her up while another nurse went over Katie's chart, line by line. "What about Mom?"

"She won't leave until your sister does."

I knew he was right, but I just found Katie again. I didn't want to leave her, not even to save her, for fear she would disappear again. She was waiting though, stuck in the Night World. I had lost enough people to the Weaver for my sister to be next.

"Okay," I said. Twenty-four hours suddenly felt like minutes on the countdown, and I'd already wasted two of them. "Let's go."

Chapter Seventeen

An identical long-sleeved shirt replaced the Sandman's torn one, his old tunic gone. My pulse thundered in my ears, and I ran, my feet pumping nearly as fast as my heart. The Sandman moved toward me so fast I barely noticed him in front of me before he swept me into a crushing embrace. I closed my eyes, breathed in his light lilac scent. Allowed myself this moment of calm before venturing into the Nightmare Realm.

"I got it," I squeaked.

His breath shuddered against my hair. "Please, never ask me to help you do something that reckless again."

"It worked though," I said with defiant cheer and fisted the fabric of his shirt to hold him close.

"Should that make me feel better?" He stepped back and scanned my face. "We haven't even begun the dangerous part of this plan, and I feel as if I've died a thousand deaths. Are you sure you won't reconsider? Wait here or go be with your sister at the hospital while I wake her up?"

The idea was tempting. I had no idea what we would find in the Nightmare Realm, what we would face. If the things waiting for us were anything like the creatures that the Weaver brought here... I swallowed. "I have to go with you. Katie doesn't know who you are. I can get through to her and convince her to wake up. She might think you're one of them."

His eyes flashed. "I could never be mistaken for a nightmare, Nora."

"I didn't mean it like that."

"I know." He chewed on his bottom lip. "I know. Sorry, I'm a little tense."

I squeezed his forearm with one hand and opened the pocket of my fleece with the other. At least the weather here was always comfortable, so I wasn't dying of heat anymore. I hoped the same could be said about the Nightmare Realm. My stomach churned with a mix of hope and dread. I pinched the threads between my fingers and held them up. They wriggled weakly before falling limp. "Here."

"We just need one." He loosened the knot and plucked a single thread from my grip, wincing. "Put the other two away. It isn't enough to bind the Weaver but keep them safe in case we need to do this again."

"Will we?" I whispered, my brows lowered, watching him work.

"I hope not." A thin, almost invisible line of sand rose up to join the thread, surrounding it, then slowly sank into the fibers. The thread squirmed in the Sandman's palm.

"What are you doing?"

His eyes flicked up to mine, his head cocked. "I'm... giving it a lobotomy, I guess. Taking control of its mind."

"Its' mind?" I squinted at the piece of thread. The other two suddenly weighed down my pocket. "Are you saying they're alive?"

"It's an unborn nightmare." The Sandman picked it up between his index finger and thumb and shook it.

"You had me steal *nightmares*?" My jaw hung open, and I lightly punched his shoulder. "Are you crazy? Why would you let me do that?"

He raised his eyebrows. "I didn't *let you* do anything. As I recall, I explained what we would need, then tried talking you out of it."

"You could have warned me," I half shouted. "I've been carrying those...things...around with me for hours."

"If I warned you, you still would've done it." He gave me a knowing half-smile. "I'm sorry I didn't tell you, okay? I will next time."

"Next time," I grumbled. There had better not be a next time. I was lucky I didn't pee my pants in that storage unit. "Now what?"

The Sandman pinched the thread until it stiffened, as straight as a needle, and took my hand. "Now, we try not to be afraid."

I bit my lip. Even if I didn't want to be afraid, even if I somehow managed to talk myself into feeling safe, there were going to be things I couldn't shake. I remembered the small nightmare that ran at me and the one that followed. How many more were there? How many were worse? I shivered.

"We can find another way," he offered.

"*Is* there another way?" If there were, if it were preferable to this, I imagined we would have done it already. And now the Weaver was pissed. We were out of time and options.

He pressed his lips into a straight line and tightened his grip on my hand, giving me my answer. "I've linked the nightmare to Katie's cord. I'll use that connection to guide us through the Nightmare Realm to where the Weaver is keeping her mind."

Jealousy sparked in my chest at the mention of the other cords. I knew he helped other people in a vague sense, that he had a life outside the hours I spent with him, but I never realized how little I knew about it. He knew everything about me—my friends, my family, school, work. What did I know about him? A laundry list of how his world worked? I knew his morals though. His subtle movements, his habits, his likes and dislikes. That seemed like enough when I didn't believe he was real, but now I wasn't sure. "I'm ready to go."

He turned, looking down at me with an expression that rocked my resolve. It was a look full of knowledge and pity. He knew exactly what we would find outside of his Dream Realm. Not the specific nightmares, perhaps, but the scope of what waited for us. All the things I never faced because he had shielded me, and now he was leading me straight into the heart of their world. To where one wrong move could place me in the Weaver's hands.

"You're sure you won't stay?" he asked again.

"Positive."

He drew in a deep breath and kissed my temple. "Then don't let go."

Darkness swallowed the world, dragging us from beneath the bright starlit sky and into an inky black. It pulsed around us, a thousand times stronger than when I felt it the first time in Katie's room. The familiar tang of metal coated my tongue, throwing me back to the first night I felt the brush of air and found Katie screaming in her bed. I reached my free hand out to grip the Sandman's shirt.

"I can't see anything," I whispered in a shaky voice.

"Wait," came his reply, soft, steady, and close.

Soon, shapes appeared in the lightening landscape. The sky faded to slate blue, the grass balsam. As more colors emerged, each maintaining a grey hue, I realized we were standing at the bottom of a jagged cliff. A smooth, silver lake reflected the peak. Low lying vines with pointed red and yellow thorns surrounded us. They scraped faintly at my ankles without drawing blood.

"Sandman?" I asked, needing to hear his voice again.

"This way." He tip-toed toward the lake. I followed in his exact footsteps. Each one was long and leaping until the thorns gave way to packed dirt. "Stay on this side of me," he said under his breath, moving to stand between me and the water.

I stared at the pond, and something broke the mirror-like surface. Two eyes protruded upward from a thick scaly forehead. The black orbs blinked, matching my stare. "What is that?"

"It would be impossible to know all their names. Don't stare," the Sandman warned. "It might take it as a sign of aggression."

Two more sets of eyes joined the first. I shifted so the Sandman's side blocked them from view. My heart was probably pounding, but I felt nothing. I was too numb, too stunned. I expected to enter a fiery cavern, complete with walls covered in shackles and echoing screams of tortured Dreamers. Not this. The stark setting was almost pretty in a macabre way, but I felt the danger hidden behind it. Lurking. Waiting. The unknown threat scraped against my skin, ached like a sickness in my bones. This was not a place to admire the scenery.

The thread in the Sandman's hand swiveled right, and he altered our course away from the water's edge. I breathed a sigh of relief, though I still felt the dark eyes of the water creatures at my back.

"They know who we are," he said. "They'll report our presence to the Weaver."

I shuffled closer. "Not what you want to tell me if I shouldn't be scared."

But of course, they would. Deep down I'd assumed as much, which was why we had to be quick. How far was the Weaver's Keep from this place? How close was he to finishing his new threads? I shouldn't have stayed at the hospital so long. Two and a half hours passed by the time I made it into my bed. Less than twenty-two left until he was undoubtedly ready to come for us. For me. Unless he decided to attack with his old nightmares.

The Sandman inched closer. "Katie isn't far."

I leaned into him, forcing myself to look straight ahead. "Is she okay? Did they hurt her?"

"I… don't know."

For as well as I knew him, I had no idea what his face revealed. I knew that pause though, so I studied him, concentrating on memorizing what his worried face looked like instead of the distant metal-on-stone scraping I heard to our left. The slight droop of his mouth. The strain around his eyes.

"What I told you before about holding all the power in your dreams?" He turned to follow the thread's direction again. "It doesn't hold true for nightmares. The creatures that live here are their own beings."

I discreetly patted the meat mallet I tucked in my waistband before bed. "I'll do whatever I need to do to save my sister."

"Good," the Sandman said. We slowed and approached the entrance to a cave. "Here's your chance."

The opening in the mountainside seemed to stretch forever into the darkness. A putrid odor wafted from the narrow crevice—rot and decay with an undercurrent of something sweeter. I slapped a hand over my mouth and nose. "What *is* that?" I asked without breathing.

"Your guess is as good as mine."

I gagged. "Katie's in there?"

"It seems so." He turned his head and hid a cough in his shoulder. "Any idea what she's afraid of?"

Nothing scared my sister. She rode every rollercoaster she found, went skydiving for her eighteenth birthday, and was the official killer-of-bugs in our house. She ate weird food. Got a tattoo. Katie faced life with a fearlessness that I had admired my entire life. "She isn't afraid of anything."

He wheezed. "Everyone is afraid of something."

My lungs screamed for air, and I forced myself to inhale. *Kettle corn.* The sweetness in the air was kettle corn. Like the kind Katie accidentally dumped on the woman in front of us at the circus when we were little. Right before she ran, screaming and crying, from the striped tent. "Clowns," I said. "She's afraid of clowns."

The Sandman paled, his jaw set. His hand dipped into the leather satchel at his hip. The sand was swirling together before he had it out of the bag. Once it stopped shifting, he held out a small gleaming knife and gave me the smallest wisp of a grin. "You can never have too many ways to defend yourself."

I tugged the meat mallet out of my waistband, holding a weapon in each hand. "Noticed this, did you?"

His grin widened a fraction. "It isn't exactly subtle."

I blushed. "So, should we...?"

"I can't." He scanned the rocky ledges above the opening. It wasn't until the scraping sound came again that I realized it had stopped. And now it was right on top of us. "It's planning to defend its territory."

"All the more reason to come inside." I followed where he was looking, then glanced at the opening again.

He shook his head. "We can't risk getting boxed in. If I'm wounded too severely by anything, I can't guarantee we'll get out before the Weaver finds us."

"But—"

"Go wake Katie up. I'll kill it and be right behind you." His hand dove into the satchel again. "Go, Nora."

A high-pitched laugh echoed from somewhere above our heads. My heart rammed against my chest, and I threw myself into the dark passage. The walls narrowed the further I went, scraping my arms through my sweater. Then, without warning, it widened again, opening into a vast cavern. The ground squished, sponge-like, beneath my feet, releasing a fresh wave of the pungent odor.

"Oh, my God." I breathed into the crook of my elbow and tightened my grip on the weapons.

I squinted into the darkness, blinking hard until my eyes adjusted enough to see Katie shackled to a hospital bed floating in thick pink goop. My pulse roared. There was no way to reach her, no bridge or rope to swing on. How did the nightmares reach her? Unless they didn't. My chest tightened. It wasn't the time for foolish wishes. Of course, they did, and there was no telling what state she would be in. If I didn't want anything worse to happen, I had to get over there and wake her up.

I nudged the goop with the toe of my sneaker. It wasn't as thick as it looked, and it didn't eat away at my shoe, but that didn't mean it was safe. If it was, there wouldn't be a point to floating Katie in its middle, but there was no other way to get to her.

With a deep, shaking breath, I waded into the reeking liquid. A spotlight on the ceiling flickered to life with the movement. "All right," I said both to myself and Katie. "No big deal, right?

The sharp snap of popping bubbles was the only reply. *Bubbles.* Great. Bubbles meant air. Air below the surface of the pink goop meant... I didn't know what it meant in this place. Nothing good.

"Katie?" I sloshed the last few feet to the bed. "Can you hear me?" Her body remained still, the only sign she was alive was the shallow movement of her chest. I set the knife and mallet down on the mattress and worked the buckle of the brown leather cuff around her wrist. "It's me. Nora. You have to wake up, Katie. We have to go home."

The cuff splashed into the thick pink liquid, and I reached across the bed to free her other wrist.

A series of thuds resonated through the entrance to the cavern followed by a manic laugh. My stomach heaved. How long could the Sandman fight? He said he wasn't strong enough to beat the Weaver again, but he had to be strong enough to beat a nightmare or two otherwise we wouldn't be here.

"Wake up, wake up, wake up," I shouted in Katie's ear.

Katie stirred with a soft moan. I slapped her face so hard my palm stung. "No," she murmured. "No more."

"That's right. No more." I sloshed to the end of the bed to free her ankles. "Wake up so we can go home."

Her eyes fluttered open. "Nora?" Her voice cracked. "Is that you?"

"Yes. It's me." I smiled, laughing despite myself. She was conscious—a step in the right direction. My fingers fumbled with the last buckle. "Come on."

"No." She kicked out at my hands, one foot still tethered. "It's not you."

I hurried to her side and snatched the weapons up before they fell. "Katie—"

"Get away," she shrieked.

"It's me."

Katie shoved me, and I stumbled back, the goop splashing up to my shoulders.

"*Katie.*"

"Go away, go away, go away." She covered her face with both hands. A million angry red pinpricks covered her skin. "Please go away."

A large bubble *bloop*-ed between us. Ripples danced across the surface, and I froze mid-step. Fear swelled in my chest. I scrambled to shove the panic down before whatever lurked nearby noticed. *Clowns and...* I had no idea what else the Weaver would use to torment her. "We have to go," I said slowly. "Right now."

Katie sobbed on the bed, curling around herself.

More manic laughter floated down the tunnel, followed by the Sandman's roar. We didn't have long. I took wide steps toward Katie, twisting my body with each one, and something slithered against my kneecaps. I bolted onto the bed beside my sister and wrapped my arms around her shoulders. "It's me," I whispered. "Nora. Your sister. Your birthday is December Fifteenth. You have a scar on your knee from falling off your bike when you were nine, and I have one on the top of my foot from when you dropped the curling iron the day of mom's wedding. Our dog, Bear, was fourteen when we put him down. You slept with his collar for a month."

The longer I spoke, the less Katie's shoulders shook, but there wasn't time for a complete history of our childhood. A flash of white broke the surface before disappearing into the sludge again. I choked back a scream.

"Do you remember those hideous shoes you begged mom for?" Another flash of white. "The ones for homecoming?"

The head of a snake broke the water, rising up, up, up. Its underbelly was covered in pearly white scales, and the fur lining its back was sticky with the foul-smelling liquid. I met its yellow eyes and words froze in my throat. A thin black tongue sliced the air before its jaw unhinged to reveal several rows of razor-sharp teeth. Its hood flared, black and white speckled feathers spanning the width of the cavern, and a spray of pink splattered the walls. Its hiss filled the cave.

I dug my fingers into Katie's shoulders. "Wake up," I screamed.

The snake lunged.

"Katie!" I stood, straddling her legs, and slashed with the knife. Swung with the mallet. They both met nothing but air. "Open your damn eyes."

I didn't mind happy clowns with big hair and colorful clothes. Those were fine, but these... Clowns in the Nightmare Realm were the reason people had phobias. One glance had the potential to ruin someone for life. I shook out my hands. "Come on," I said under my breath.

There wasn't an infinite amount of sand here, only what I brought with me in my satchel. Each grain had to count. I scooped a healthy amount into my palm and formed a metal handle across my palm, with one end sharpened to a point. From the other, a heavy spiked ball hung at the bottom of a thick chain. I tested the flail, swinging it gently, and turned my attention to the opening Nora disappeared into.

The biggest danger lay outside, but that didn't mean the cave was safe. It was a risk—a horrible, stupid risk, but one we had to take. If too many nightmares found us, if I was too wounded to defend her, this would all have been for nothing. It was best if nothing followed Nora inside. She was strong and independent. There was nothing I could do to stop her from going after her sister. Nothing I was willing to do, anyway, so I had to trust her the same way she trusted me. If there was anything in there with Katie, it would know better than to kill Nora when the Weaver needed her alive. If anything came out of the cave with her, I wouldn't let it take her, but she may have to fight. She would *likely* have to fight. Why hadn't I spent the last five years teaching her combat skills?

A small pebble bounced down the cliff. I squared my feet and scanned the area it fell from. A blur of white and red with a blip of yellow flashed against the dreary rock. I gripped the smooth handle of the flail as two grating honks sounded from behind me. My back prickled, and I knew without turning that the nightmare was there. In one swift motion, I bent, ducking, and spun while throwing the spiked ball at his knees. The clown leapt over it as if he were jumping rope, and his oversized shoes squeaked when he landed. I backed away to give myself more room to maneuver.

The clown watched me silently, and I tried not to shudder. His pasty white skin peeled away from his mouth and eyes, leaving exposed muscle and tendons in place of makeup. The red tip of his bulbous nose oozed pus and tufts of crimson hair dotted his head. The upturn of skin around his mouth made him appear like he was smiling, and in truth, he might have been. A twinkle filled his solid black eyes. On his black and white suit were three enormous mustard-colored pom-poms and a polka-dot bow tie with a black flower at its center.

"Sandman." His voice raked against my eardrums like nails on a chalkboard and his head bobbed erratically. "A pleasure to meet the legend."

I would waste no breath engaging the clown in conversation. We weren't there to chat but to tear each other apart. I smashed the spiked ball into his arm. Ruby blood seeped into the surrounding fabric. He laughed, a high-squeal. I struck again and again, hitting limbs, but the clown stood in place, taking each hit when he should have been writhing on the ground. His head continued to bob, growing faster by the second, until it seemed it would separate from his neck. The laugh rose and fell. I clutched the flail's handle and took a step closer, a bud of unease growing. If I could get close enough, I could stab the pointed end through his heart and end it.

But the clown's laugh grew and grew and grew. A spray of green acid shot from the flower at the base of his throat and hit my chin, searing a trail down my neck. I roared against the pain, and the flail fell to the ground in a rain of sand. I lifted the neck of my tunic and swiped at the liquid, but it only made it worse.

The clown darted into the mouth of the cave. I stumbled after him, gathering more sand into my hands, and let the darkness of the narrow crevice swallow me.

The acoustics carried Nora's voice toward me, and it gave me the incentive I needed to steel myself against the blazing pain of the clown's acid. He tapped my shoulder. I spun, but he was gone. Another tap, again from behind. I drew a shaky breath, the sound echoing in my head, and pretended to turn. Instead, I leapt back outside the cave. When the clown appeared again, his back was to me, facing the spot where I should have been.

I lunged, stretching my sand into a piece of wire between two blocks of wood, and wrapped it around his pale neck. He lurched forward but the wire sliced into his flesh. He gurgled a laugh. A splash of blood flew from his mouth, then his head turned slowly. Bit by bit, crack by crack, his face made the trek around to look me in the eye.

My muscles tensed, and I braced myself against the narrow walls.

With his body still facing away from me, the clown coughed. "Lord of Dreams." He grinned, his teeth red with blood. "Our master is coming for you."

I wrenched both blocks and his head thumped to the floor. *Our*. I dropped the wire and ran deeper into the cave. I knew it was a risk to send Nora in alone, just as my rushing in to help was, but none of that mattered. I had to wake her and her sister up before it was too late.

I sloshed into putrid pink liquid.

"Nor—" I tried, but it came out as a wheeze. I lifted a hand to the widening hole in my neck.

An enormous serpentine nightmare arched from the water. Nora screamed for her sister to wake up, and a hiss pierced the air. The snake lunged. Nora swung. I stepped forward, but it was too late. There wasn't time to reach them.

A flash of silver, another swing of the knife. The snake hissed again and knocked into the bed in the middle of the room. My heart dropped to my stomach. Nora gripped the edge of the mattress before she could fall backward. The knife I gave her was covered in slick, black blood. It ran down her hand, her arm, dripping on her thigh.

The snake flopped into the liquid, one feather of its hood hanging, half severed. Nora gasped. I moved toward her again, conscious of the danger swimming so close. She jerked at the sight of me, her fingers digging into Katie's arm. The meat mallet was gone.

"Go back," she called.

I shook my head.

"Go. Back. It's not safe." She turned to her sister. "Wake up, Katie. I swear if any of us die saving you, I will haunt you for all eternity."

"I can't wake up." Her voice cracked. "I can't."

Nora said something to her sister, but the roaring in my head prevented me from hearing. She was still talking when Katie vanished. Nora fell forward without her sister's body there to lean into. I tried to speak again but my vocal cords were too damaged. I had to get back to the beach and heal. The Weaver wasn't going to take this lying down. We had to be ready.

Nora pushed up onto her elbows and scanned me from head to toe. Her eyes widened at the sight of my neck, then again when they reached my knees. A series of bubbles popped a foot away. "Run!" When I hesitated, she said, "Sandman, go. I'll see you soon."

Then she vanished.

The snake shot out from the pink goop, straight at the empty hospital bed. Its jaws clamped down on the metal frame, and it shrieked in fury. I shifted back toward the crevice, where the decapitated clown lay across the entrance to the cave. The nightmare paused, watching me with a flick of clear eyelids. It inched forward. Once it decided to lunge at me, it would be over. I eased out of the liquid, watching each subtle movement the serpent made, then spun and darted back into the passageway. The snake slammed into the narrow crevice a mere second after I slid safely inside.

I reached deep inside myself, focusing on the beach, and shuffled sideways toward the opening. Darkness faded. My center shifted, then sand was beneath my feet instead of stone. I stumbled backward, hitting the ground. There was barely enough time to register the familiar sky above me before the sand swathed my wounds, burying me, knitting me back together. I closed my eyes and let the hum of it fill me.

We did it. Nora did it.

A faint smile spread across my lips, and I faded into unconsciousness.

Chapter Nineteen

I woke in a pool of sweat. My heart pounded in my ears, and I stared at the ceiling, gasping for air. The scent of rot lingered, but there was no mistaking where I was. Moonlight filtered into my bedroom and Paul's snores traveled through the door over the purr of the air conditioning. *I did it.* I woke up before the snake could strike again, and Katie woke up before me. Safe from the Weaver.

I kicked free of the tangled sheet and grabbed my phone from the dresser. My mom's cell went straight to voicemail. I shoved my dresser away from the door—a permanently necessary precaution—and bolted from the room. "Paul," I shouted, banging on his door. "Paul, we have to go back to the hospital." His snoring stopped, but there was no reply. I pounded on the wood again. "I'm taking the car."

There was a thud inside his room followed by a series of footsteps. When the door swung open, my step-father blinked the sleep from his eyes. "What's going on?"

Every second I stood there was torture. I had to know it worked. I had to be sure that I didn't go through all of that for nothing. That the Sandman and I hadn't risked our lives and failed. The blood drained from my face. *Sandman*. He got out—he had to. But his face. The skin on his chin and neck was gone, leaving a red blistering wound. I gripped the door frame. I had to get back, but first I had to know Katie was safe because the next time I went to the Night World, I wasn't leaving without the Weaver's head on a platter. "Hurry. We have to go back to the hospital."

He stood straighter. "What happened?"

"I don't know." I couldn't tell him I thought my sister might be awake or why. "Probably nothing, but I need to see Katie."

He grabbed a clean shirt off the top of the folded laundry in a basket. "Have you talked to your mother?"

"She's not picking up," I answered, barely keeping the jitters at bay.

He nodded. "Give me a second. I'll drive."

With that, I ran outside to wait in the car, my head pounding.

My muscles strained with the effort to not race to the elevator, but I didn't want to call unwanted attention to myself. I already had enough of that between my mother and Detective Bell.

Finding Katie on my own was going to lead back to an interrogation room. Unless Katie cleared me. Unless she remembered something. I'm not sure which would be worse for her though—remembering or forgetting. *Remembering.*

When the doors pinged open on the third floor, I jumped. Paul scowled at me but thankfully said nothing. He led the way past the officer standing outside Katie's room and into a whirl of activity. Machines beeped steadily while two nurses stood beside the bed, checking tubes and screens. A doctor on the far side of the room was deep in a hushed conversation with my mother but paused in his speech when we entered the room. "Can I help you?" he asked with a thick accent.

My mother started. "What are you two doing here?"

My vision tunneled to the bed. Katie's feet and legs were hidden beneath a white blanket, unmoving. I bulldozed into the room, knocking into the nurse standing at a laptop on a rolling podium. "Katie?"

"Nora?" My sister sat up. Her big, bright, beautiful eyes were wide open. Haunted, but open. "Nora!"

I flung myself at her to a chorus of shocked complaints, but Katie latched onto me, sobbing into my shoulder. Her hands shook against my back, and I tightened my embrace. This was real life, not a dream. She was here. She was safe. The pit in my stomach filled with relief. "Thank God," I breathed.

"Thank you," Katie said. Her voice was dry. Broken. "Thank you, thank you, thank you."

I held so tightly it felt as if her ribs would crack. Hushed voices resumed behind us, rushed and confused. "I'm sorry." I shivered. "This is my fault."

"I had this awful dream," she said quietly so only I heard.

I buried my face in her hair and nodded.

"You were there," she said, half questioning the idea.

"I was there."

She sniffled. "But how?"

A shadow flickered near the closet. Gold eyes blinked in and out, and I tensed. He was less present than before—a flat image against the gossamer screen. I glanced at the clock. We should have another eighteen hours before he was ready, yet he was strong enough to press against the barrier between Day and Night. My elation drained away, dread taking its place. But my sister was back, and she was never going there again.

My mother's hand landed on my shoulder. "We should let the staff finish their tests."

"No. I want to talk to Nora," Katie said. When no one moved, she added, "*Alone*."

I clasped Katie's hands, begging her with a look not to make me discuss everything then and there. Now that I knew she was awake, I had to make sure the Sandman made it out of that cave. The pit in my stomach yawned open. He was hurt when I saw him last—what if it was too much? What if he couldn't escape? That would be my fault too. I pressed a hand over the ache in my chest.

"Now," Katie insisted, her nostrils flared.

The room fell silent, a million unanswered questions pressing down on us. What happened the night she went missing? Who took her? Had she been in the storage unit the whole time? Why was she unconscious? Was anything physically wrong? Emotionally, there was going to be a plethora. I knew it, the doctors knew it, and the Weaver lurking in the corner knew it. The only one that might be in denial was our mother. She already had one crazy daughter, after all. But hopefully talking to professionals would help my sister come to terms with whatever it was she needed. Not that it had for me.

The doctor, an older man, moved first, ushering the nurses from the room. Paul practically dragged our mother out after them, whispering to her. When the door clicked shut, the officer stationed outside shifted in front of the small window.

"Tell me," she demanded.

"There's too much to tell." I glanced at the Weaver who grinned back. My heart slammed against my ribcage. I wouldn't give him the reaction he was looking for. Wouldn't let him see my panic or my fear. "All the deaths... They're because I have something someone wants. He took you to get to me."

"Oh, please," she hissed. "What could you possibly have that someone would want that bad? I mean, what the hell, Nora? It was like I was transported to some sort of alternate reality."

"You wouldn't believe me if I told you." *Breathe.* I had the same questions she did once. She deserved answers, but not with the Weaver listening in. Not before I made sure the Sandman was okay.

"You just waltzed into my head. I didn't imagine you there. It was real."

If anyone understood the feeling that something was real when everyone else thought it was imaginary, I did. There was a difference in someone being part of your dream and someone actually being in your head. I couldn't remember what the former felt like, not really, but I distinctly remembered how the first night with the Sandman jarred me. How different it felt.

"No, you didn't imagine anything," I agreed. The Weaver shifted closer. *Ignore him. Ignore him. Ignore him.* "The Sandman and I came to wake you up before the Weaver could destroy you."

Katie blinked puffy eyes. "*The Sandman*? Are you talking about that freak you used to dream about? God, Nora, seriously?"

"Don't call him a freak," I snapped. "We just risked everything for you. After what you saw over there, you still don't believe me? You just admitted my presence there was real, so why couldn't he be real too?"

"So... You've seen him this whole time?" She narrowed her eyes, head tilted in disbelief. "He never went away?"

"I don't have time to explain." I launched off the bed to pace between my sister and the Nightmare Lord. My hands shook at my sides. *Don't look at him.* "The Weaver is here, and he's pissed."

"Keeper," the Weaver chimed in. "*Pissed* doesn't come close to describing what I am."

Katie didn't react. Surviving the nightmare hadn't given her the ability to see him now that she was awake. I didn't know why I expected it to. Her gaze darted around the room, the machine beeping faster, and climbed to her knees. "The clown? It's here?"

"The clown is dead," the Weaver said.

"Not the clown. The clown is dead," I relayed before I could stop myself.

My sister slumped against the pillows and covered her face. "He was... Nora, he did so many things."

"I know." I turned to glare at the Weaver. "I saw the marks."

"Needles," she said with a shiver.

I glanced over my shoulder at the tattoo on her inner wrist. "Since when are you afraid of needles?"

"Since always." When she saw me staring, she lifted her wrist, exposing her tattoo. "I was trying to face my fears or whatever."

"Do you want to know what else they did in the cave?" the Weaver asked.

I whirred back to the shadowed corner. "Shut up," I snapped, spittle flying.

"Who are you talking to?" Katie asked.

The Weaver shifted, his face straining with the effort to get closer to me. "I must say, I admire you for leaving the Sandman to die alone."

My knees wobbled. "What?"

"*What?*" Katie parroted. "Nora, are you having a meltdown?"

"I'm not talking to you," I said to my sister. Then to the Weaver, "Repeat what you just said."

"Winning is a subjective thing, is it not?" he asked.

My heart dropped. Exploded. Shattered. "You're lying."

"You would know what a liar looked like, wouldn't you? But when have *I* ever lied to *you*, Dream Keeper? Why would I need to when I have so many of your people left to toy with?"

I fell onto the edge of the bed. Katie shook my arm, her voice droning in my ears. "You can't kill each other. He said so."

"Half true." He pressed against the fabric holding him back. "Technically, I suppose." He sighed dramatically. "But I did not lay a hand on your precious Dream Lord. I didn't need to."

"*Liar.*"

"Nora!" Katie yanked my hair. "What are you doing?"

I ripped the bag of sand from around my neck and pressed it into her hand. "Sprinkle this in your eyes if you're going to sleep and you'll be safe. Don't let them see it. Don't go to sleep without it."

"Please," she begged. "Stop. You're scaring me. Tell me what's going on."

I kissed her forehead. "Trust me. I'll fix everything."

She gripped my wrist. "You're always running away from things, but you can't run away from this. I need to know what happened to me."

"I'm not running," I promised. *Not anymore.*

The door swung open and Detective Bell stood in the doorway, the knot of his tie loose, his shirt wrinkled. Energy jolted my body, not because I was worried about another line of questioning but because I needed to get home to sleep. The Sandman wasn't dead. He couldn't be dead. *He couldn't.*

"I'm glad to see you awake," the detective said. He glanced at me, then back to my sister. "Are you feeling up to a few questions?"

"I..."

Our mother bustled into the room. "Is this really necessary right now?" she demanded. "She only woke up an hour ago."

"We need to know what happened," he replied. "It could help us locate the killer."

"Killer?" Katie asked.

I tore my wrist from Katie's grip, unable to listen to them explain what happened the night she disappeared, and ran. I nearly slammed into Paul on my way around the corner. He juggled two cups of coffee, nearly spilling one all over himself. "Where are you headed?" he asked.

"Home." I forced a smile. "Katie asked me to get some of her things from the house. Her phone and toothbrush, stuff like that. Can I have the keys?" He glared at me. I could see the wheels turning in his head. *Maybe her mother is right,* he was thinking. *Maybe she is crazy. Maybe she* did *have something to do with everything.* A whole list of maybes I didn't care to know. He could question my sanity all he wanted if he gave me the keys. "Please? I'll be right back. I swear."

For a moment I thought he would say no, or he would insist on driving me again, but then he handed me his coffee so he could dig through his pocket.

I hurried upstairs to my bedroom with unsteady steps, my breath equally so. Putting nothing past the Weaver, I shoved my dresser in front of the door. I yanked open the top drawer and fished through my socks until I found the three white pills at the bottom. Opening wide, I tossed them to the back of my throat and swallowed. I took a deep, shuddering breath. He wasn't dead. *He was not.* If this was a trick by the Weaver to force me to return, it worked.

I tossed a grey bag from the local WalMart Supercenter on my desk and dumped out the Swiss Army knife I picked up on my way home. I pried the plastic away from the cardboard, my teeth chattering. The meat mallet was gone, lost somewhere in the cave, and I wasn't going back empty-handed. After fiddling with the attachments—five different blades, a corkscrew, and a screwdriver—I stuffed it into the pocket of my fleece and froze.

The Weaver's threads were still there. Still shifting with life. I held them up and glared at them through narrowed eyes. Without the Sandman, they weren't of any use to me; I couldn't control the sand. Besides, the only person I needed to track down after finding the Sandman was the Nightmare Lord, and together we could do that without help.

I didn't relish the idea of carrying nightmares around in my pocket any longer than I had to, so I opened the top drawer of the desk and rifled through crumpled post-its, white-out, and paperclips until I found a narrow tin pencil case. Dumping the pens out into the mess, I set the threads inside and stashed the case at the back of the drawer. My fingers drummed on the desktop. We could destroy them later if we didn't need them. After I found the Sandman. After we stopped the Weaver.

Seventeen hours and counting.

I took a deep breath, letting it out through my mouth, and climbed into bed.

True heart.

True mind.

I closed my eyes.

I'm coming. I pushed the thought toward the Sandman. *Please be okay.*

Chapter Twenty

Nora

I blinked into the darkness. *Darkness.* Not the beach. The Sandman wasn't there to make sure I went straight to a safe place. My chest tightened, fear weighing me down, locking my joints. I couldn't let what the Weaver said get to me; the Sandman was alive. He was hiding maybe or lost. Healing—he definitely needed it. The last time he was hurt, he had healed enough for his magic to catch me but this time…

There could be a million reasons his magic wasn't here to greet me.

For the first time in five years.

After we ventured into the Nightmare Realm, and he fought whatever horrible thing was outside the cave... I winced. This train of thought wasn't helping.

As my eyes adjusted, I found myself amid low swooping vines. Thin, willowy trees dotted the landscape, and my feet sunk into the mossy ground, releasing a whiff of stagnant water with each step. Insects buzzed, and frogs croaked. Dim lights flickered in the distance, floating, swooping. I rubbed the chill from my upper arms.

"Sandman?" I whispered.

Everything fell silent and still the instant the word left my tongue. My pulse revved. This was not the place to invoke his name, to draw unnecessary attention to myself. The Weaver was real here, and if he found me first, it was all over. I would never be able to withstand the torture my sister had. The Sandman had sheltered me from my nightmares, so I didn't know what my subconscious feared, but I knew I feared drowning. Small spaces. The monkeys from the Wizard of Oz. Whatever waited for me here, it would break me. Maybe not right away, but it would.

My feet squished the entire way around the outskirts of the swamp, cool water leaking into my sneakers. Eyes burned down at me from treetops, but I kept mine forward. Looking would make the fear worse. Other things peered from behind fallen logs or boulders, the creatures they belong to mostly hidden. I shivered. How many enemies surrounded me? I hugged myself tighter, my fingers digging into my sweater, and walked faster.

The lights flashed again in hypnotic irregularity, and a drone like a distant jet roared overhead. I bit back a scream and flung my arms over my ears, ducking. The buzzing stayed steady, warring with my booming pulse. Six legs hovered over me. Translucent wings with cobwebbed lines kicked up fragments of God-knows-what. Two long antennae twitched, smelling, tasting, and domed black eyes seemed to look at nothing and everything. Its abdomen flashed. I let out a breath. A lightning bug. I could handle bugs. Not spiders though. Or those things with a million legs. My lips parted, and I watched it hover. My parents used to drive Katie and me miles to find and catch them on early summer nights.

The giant bug surged forward, its light flickering lazily, and the noise exploded around me. Chirps and whistles, growls and snaps. Buzzing. Splashing. I ran. My arms pumped furiously, and I gasped for air. I wasn't afraid exactly, but I didn't want to stick around and find out if there was something nearby that would change that.

The outline of a mountain loomed in the distance. If I made it there, I could get an aerial view. Maybe find that cave again. I shuddered. But the clown was dead, and I didn't have to go back inside the cavern. Those things watching me from the lake... Well, I wouldn't get close enough to find out what they were, but that's where I last saw the Sandman.

The ground shifted beneath me. My shoulder rammed hard into a tree trunk, and I tripped over a log hidden beneath ferns. A pair of milky-white, lifeless eyes popped open on a tree root, staring skyward. A woman's face shifted, emerging slowly, the pattern of lines on her brown skin camouflaging her to blend with the bark. A sliver of skull peeked through a crack in her forehead and, when her jaw stretched open, maggots wriggled in place of a tongue. I scrambled to my feet and swerved right, then left.

Something large crashed through the brush behind me, but I was almost free. The trees thinned. A brighter shade of grey filtered down, showing the end of the swamp. A low, confidant growl rumbled from somewhere nearby. Too near. I propelled myself harder, my lungs sucking in stale air, and emerged on the other side of the tree line.

Only there was nowhere to go because the ground wasn't the ground at all, but the thick, bumpy hide of an alligator. I was twenty feet in the air, trapped. The trees creaked behind me, and I looked. I didn't mean to. I shouldn't have. Birds—what I assumed were birds—with giant wingspans and clawed feet took to the air. Something shifted in the trees. Something large and orange. *Nope.* I wasn't facing whatever that was. I wouldn't win, but more importantly, I couldn't fail, especially not so soon. I turned and barreled along the alligator's neck. One gigantic reptilian eye blinked, and I inched toward its left flank.

I couldn't go back, and I couldn't go forward either. Not without going down. I grabbed onto one of the smaller ridges lining the alligator's back and swung to the outer side, peering down at the hard, rocky ground. "Oh, this is a bad idea," I mumbled.

Heights themselves weren't a problem, but that gut-twisting sensation of falling was. I could climb a mountain or fly on a plane without a second thought, but bungee-jumping was out of the question. And doing this... There was a ninety-percent chance I would fall to my death but under the circumstances, it was my only choice.

I cracked my knuckles and got down on my stomach. The alligator's head swung in my direction. "Don't mind me," I said as if I were talking to an angry dog. Its mouth cracked into a grin like it knew what would happen: I would fall, and my body would be his dinner, which was probably the same thing that would happen if I made it down in one piece.

My dreams are only as strong as I am.

Dreams. Not nightmares.

I blew out a breath and skidded down until the toe of my sneaker found a groove between scales. The alligator kept walking. Kept watching, waiting, while I worked my way down to the next edge. The growl above turned to a low whine. I bit my lip. This had to work. But each lumbering step jarred my hold. The alligator dragged its toes, flinging its foot out. The front and back feet on opposite sides moved together. The back leg slammed down beside me.

One. Two. Three. I took a breath. *Four. Five. Six.*

The front leg moved. I dug my fingers into the crevice and closed my eyes to wait for the impact. *Thud.* I moved as fast as I dared, sliding more than climbing, and counted again. Every time I missed my mark, each time I didn't catch a scale with my hands or feet, my stomach rose to my throat.

I was halfway there.

Halfway.

And the giant animal stopped.

Steam curled off the surface of a pond in front of us. If I didn't get down now, I would be in that water. Dragged to the bottom where I would either drown or be eaten. Or worse. There wasn't a doubt in my mind that other things lived in there. Snakes, fish, leeches, plants to catch my ankles and anchor me in the murky depths. Without thinking, I maneuvered around to the front of the leg. The farther I went, the faster I went, the scales scraping against my palms like razors.

I had to slow down, to stop and start again. My jaw ached from clenching. I curled my fingers to catch a groove, but the friction tore my nails back. I hissed. Then my foot struck something solid and the impact rattled my brain. I pressed myself against the cool leg. It moved again. Another drag, and slam of its front leg.

"Crap," I squeaked.

Five feet from safety. I held my breath and let go, free-falling. Pinpricks covered my body. I forced my eyes open until they burned, but I wouldn't be blindsided. My teeth slammed together when I hit the ground—the sweet, beautiful ground—and I swore a molar cracked. But I was alive.

My body screamed when I launched myself up. Muscles I didn't know existed cried out in protest, but I had to keep moving. Had to. I shook a wave of dizziness from my head. Without giving myself time to object, I bolted, staying beneath the alligator's soft belly where I wouldn't be seen.

I had to figure out where to go next. Nowhere was safe, but I couldn't stay out in the open. There wasn't much time left before I reached the alligator's tail; I would have to run straight for the mountain in the distance.

A splash sounded behind me. The alligator shifted violently and the things living on its back shrieked in unison. The squelching sound popped against my eardrums. I covered my ears and darted out from beneath the gigantic nightmare before it could crush me. Running, I looked back and my blood ran cold. Large maroon tentacles reached from the water, wrapping around the alligator's nose. It attempted to gnash at the bits skimming too close to its teeth. More sticky, rubber-like suction cups crawled over the ground toward the enormous clawed feet. Nightmares leapt from the alligator's back, some making the drop and others hitting with a sickening crunch. The ones that flew blotted out the grey sky.

I pushed myself harder, as hard as my body would allow. Away from the things fleeing whatever occupied that water. Away before they could decide to pursue me, to offer me to their Nightmare Lord.

Yellow fireflies blinked here and there among the black silhouettes. It was as if I were inside an engine with all the hums and clicks. The mountain suddenly seemed even farther away. Too far. I would never make it in time—I needed somewhere else to hide. A flutter of legs grazed my skin. I jerked forward, lowering my head.

Then I was off the ground. Two spindly black legs held me, veering away from the swarm of escaping nightmares, and I choked back a scream before I attracted more attention. I twisted and turned to loosen the bug's grip. Pushed and pulled at the legs. Pounded my fists against them. The bug dipped in response and dropped me in a field of dry, cracked dirt. It landed on a boulder beside me, glaring before taking off.

Thanks a lot, I growled in my head. Although, I was strangely certain it meant to help and positive it did just that. Whatever danger lurked in the swamp was now running loose. It was good I was nowhere near it, but he could have taken me toward my destination instead of away from it. The boulder was the only thing in the surrounding landscape. I was helpless; a rod in a thunderstorm, waiting to be struck.

Sandman? I thought toward him. Nothing. And I didn't dare speak his name out loud again.

I gathered my hair back with a rubber band from my wrist and took a steadying breath. "Okay." *I can do this.* A laugh bubbled from my chest before I could stop it. Who was I kidding? This was the worst idea I'd ever had. A death wish. But if I didn't do something, if I didn't try, these creatures would be in my world. I trudged across the scarred earth and trained my eyes on my target. Walking. Marching. Keeping a straight path to the mountain.

"Nora," something whispered. "Noraaa."

I froze. Not some*thing*. Someone. Natalie. My heart slammed into my chest. I spun, and there she was. Her dark curly hair hung loose down her back, her tan arms relaxed at her side. She wasn't alone—Emery was beside her. My mother. My father. Paul. Katie. They stood in a line, a few feet from each other, each facing the same direction: away from me.

"What..." I licked my lips. "What are you doing here?"

Silence.

"Guys?"

I took one step forward, and they mirrored the movement. Again. Three times.

Goosebumps raised on my arms and my chin quivered slightly. "This isn't funny."

More silence. I breathed into my hands. This wasn't real. It couldn't be real. I ran toward them, and they vanished in a swirl of smoke. The landscape widened. Deepened. For as far as I could see, there was nothing. The mountain was a mere hill in the distance. I spun, my mind racing, and when I faced the mountain again, a familiar hooded figure stood a few yards away. My heart leapt in relief.

"Sandman!"

He was okay. Alive. I took one step forward, and he dashed away, disappearing like the others had. A hollow space cracked inside me. Emptying me. Swallowing me into its depths. I was alone; no one was coming to help me. This was a trick. A nightmare.

"This isn't happening," I said, my voice cracking.

But it was. So, I took a step, my limbs heavy, and lumbered away from the emptiness, toward the only thing that existed. That tiny blip of a mountain on the horizon.

I bent over Nora in her bedroom and placed two fingers against her throat. Her pulse slammed against my fingertips, her eyes moving frantically beneath their lids. I should have known she wasn't going to wait. If things were reversed, I wouldn't have. I wasn't conscious to catch her when she fell asleep. My power was tapped, leaving only enough to heal me, which meant she fell smack dab into enemy territory.

"Nora?" I whispered in her ear. I repeated it again, a little louder.

She wasn't screaming or thrashing about which had to be a good sign. Maybe the Weaver hadn't found her yet. Maybe there was still time to extract her from whatever nightmare she found herself in.

"Wake up, Nora. Please." I needed to shout, but footsteps pounded on the stairs. Nora's step-father called her name. I shook her shoulders. "*Please*."

When she didn't stir, I gripped her headboard until my knuckles turned white. She was in too deep. Something had found her, and they weren't letting her go. My stomach twisted. "Hold on." I placed a soft kiss on each of her temples. "I'm coming."

☾

Thunder rumbled over the beach. This time it wasn't the Weaver coming for me, not when what he really wanted was in his own backyard. The thunder was anger, my determination. I would tear down the walls of the entire Night World if I had to, and I would do it happily. I would run my power dry to save her. Anything. Whatever I had to do.

Baku paced the water's edge, his pupils dilated. I ran to his side and fell to my knees. "Nora is stuck in the Nightmare Realm." I ground my bare knuckles into the sand. If the Weaver touched her… But of course, he would; it's what he promised. I winced. "I don't know where. Will you find her? Bring her here?"

Baku's trunk reached out to rub the soft skin that healed over my acid burns.

I brushed him off. "I'm fine. I need to steal more dreams first, but I'll be right behind you."

He flicked some sand at me. *Don't do anything you'll regret*, he seemed to say.

"Don't worry," I assured him. What I was about to do was reckless, but I would never regret it. "I'm going to raze the ground they walk on."

Baku's wide lips curled ever so slightly before he leapt from the beach.

If I found Nora before the Weaver did, I wouldn't let her out of my sight until this was finished and she was safe. The nightmare she was living would never become part of her reality.

The mountain was a mere pinprick through the tears spilling freely down my face. The longer I walked, the smaller it became. The chasm in my chest deepened with every step. I would never make it. Never survive. Never find the Sandman. Never stop the Weaver.

Never. Never. Never.

I wasn't good enough. Strong enough. Smart enough.

Not enough. Not enough. Not enough.

It was all my fault Katie was hurt. People had died. The world would soon be doomed.

All my fault. All my fault. All my fault.

The guilt gnawed from the inside out until each cell in my body ached. I lacked in every way that mattered. Why had I ever thought this was a good idea? Who was I to save anyone, let alone an immortal, unearthly *magical* being like the Sandman? Who did I think I was that I could stop someone like the Weaver? I was a Dream Keeper. A container. A custodian. Not a warrior. My entire life, I hadn't taken so much as a self-defense class, and it wasn't for lack of trying on my father's part. He was a black belt. A lot of good it did him in the end.

My knees gave out, and I plopped to the parched earth with a sob. "I'm sorry," I said to the emptiness. I wasn't sure what I was sorry for exactly—maybe everything. Maybe nothing. What did my apology mean to the people who lost their loved ones? *Nothing.* Another sob wracked my shoulders. *I* was nothing.

"That's her?" snapped a male's voice. "Look at her. She's pitiful."

I didn't move. My fate had come, and I was ready for this to end. They would take me to their lord and master where he would repay me for my treachery. In pain and blood and death. The exact things I had planned to repay him in. It was everything I deserved.

"Shh," urged a feminine voice.

I sighed and closed my eyes. Cold palms cupped my cheeks, injecting prickling pain down into my marrow. My eyes flew open again, my jaw hanging open in a silent scream. The agony was too much to muster a real one, stealing my breath, solidifying my body.

The woman kneeling before me removed her hands from my skin, taking most of the pain with her, and stood. She wore a red silk ball gown with strings of beads that draped off her shoulders. Large black wings jutted from her back like branches from a winter tree, breaking off in a million jagged directions. Her skin was so pale I could practically see through it, and long, pin-straight black hair fell to her waist with a crown of raven beaks perched on her head. Red flecked eyes roamed my face.

"Hello, child," she said. Her voice was surprisingly soft. "You do not fear touch, so you must not fear me."

The pain her hands caused lingered, but I said nothing about her blatant lie. Instead, I stared at the beautiful woman, feeling as if I were nothing more than a husk, and what did pain matter to an empty thing anyway?

"I am Rowan." She motioned behind her. "Kail."

A man with golden brown skin stepped forward wearing a white half-mask with a long-pointed beak that curled away from his nose. Black hair fell out of place, skimming just above his left eye, and his lips pressed into a straight line. Black lace-like designs ran over the shoulders and waist of a black trench coat. "Leave her, Ro."

"You do not fear the unknown, so you must not fear him," she continued in a light voice.

"Rowan."

She bent and grabbed the back of my sweater, forcing me to my feet. "She will be fine once she leaves this place."

"But *we* won't be," he snarled.

Rowan nudged my back, the pressure of her hands through my sweater a dull warning, until my feet moved of their own accord. I managed to stumble three feet before stopping dead. Two black horses with clawed feet and spiked tails snorted steam. Behind them stretched a mass of people hidden beneath black cloaks. Red mist coiled around their ankles, hissing against the flowing fabric. A collective moan rose to fill the air, and I scanned the line of nightmares.

"You do not fear blood," Rowan said. "So, you must not fear the Blood Army."

Kail lifted me onto the smaller horse and swung himself onto the larger. Being hauled away by a horde of nightmares should've terrified me, but the edges of fear were dull. As we marched away from the parched ground, part of my brain responded, a spark of something igniting deep in my brain. Feeling crept back into my mind and body, bit by bit. It seemed like it took forever but couldn't have been more than five minutes before we reached the foot of the mountain. I blinked back my surprise.

"See?" Rowan walked between the two horses, smug. "She's coming back already."

Kail harrumphed.

"What—" I clamped my mouth shut. The world slowly came back to me, falling in place like pieces of a puzzle. *What happened?* I wanted to ask but ignorance was a weakness I couldn't afford to display. Everything was a weakness here. Everything but me. I wasn't empty. I wasn't nothing. This wasn't my fault, and I *would* find the Sandman. I *would* fix things.

"You fear many things." Rowan smiled kindly. "All humans do. That was one of your plagues."

"The lightning bug," I said before I could stop myself. "He brought me there."

"If you do not fear a thing, it will not see you as other. It likely misread your fear of the Barren as a longing for it when you fled. Not all nightmares are highly intelligent. It thought it was doing you a service, I'm sure."

How long had they been watching me? And the Blood Army… The Weaver mentioned them once. Mentioned letting them devour my sister. I shifted in the saddle made of bone—*bone*—and the horse whipped his head around to nip at my ankle.

"You fear horses." A small smirk curled on Kail's lips. "In case that was unclear."

"Do I?" I sneered. I wanted to point out that this wasn't a horse. Horses had hooves, unlike this beast, but I had bigger problems.

We fell into silence, the only sound, the sizzling of blood droplets hitting the ground and fueling the mist that traveled around the army. *The Barren*, she called it. The place that sucked me dry, made me feel worthless and alone, had a name. If that was only one of the things I feared, I had no interest in meeting the others. I needed to escape sooner rather than later, but I was lucky to have survived as long as I had. These people were going to take me right to the Weaver. Why else wouldn't they hurt me? Another touch from Rowan would be enough to send me tumbling to the ground. I rubbed at my tingling cheeks. There had to be a way out of this.

Kail whispered to Rowan. She replied, but I couldn't hear well enough to understand over the surge of wailing from the Blood Army. I took the reins and gave the horse a small, steady tug. His claws dug into the ground, and he wheeled on me. A single fang shot out from his top gums. He arched his head, aiming for my thigh.

Rowan tsked, and the creature froze. "Do not try to escape, Dream Keeper. This is our realm." She rubbed the horse's velvety nose until the fang disappeared. "Even if Poz cooperated in carrying you away from us, there are eyes and ears everywhere. It would do you no good."

"Does *he* know I'm here?" I spat, sure if the Weaver saw everything, he would come to get me himself. Unless he wanted the will tortured out of me before I was dropped at his feet to save himself the trouble

"The Weaver? He awaits your arrival."

Of course, he does. I leapt from the ivory saddle and landed in the middle of the Blood Army. Their crimson mist instantly boiled me, turning the blood in my veins to a river of fire. A scream ripped from my throat, and I flailed, reaching desperately for the stirrup. The horse sidestepped me.

"Kail," Rowan ordered.

He jumped down beside me and lifted me from the ground. A dusting of the mist clung to my clothes. Itching. Burning. I was going to die. I clung to Kail's neck and gasped for breath. The faint hint of cloves calmed my scream. Called my mind forward. *It isn't real. None of this is real. It's all happening in my head.* But it was real. Terrifyingly real. The truth was like being dunked in an ice bath. I shuddered. I should never have taken those pills. Never.

Kail tossed me into the saddle of his own horse. "Brainless girl." He swung up behind me and gathered the reins. "I bet you won't be trying that again."

"Shut it," I grumbled, my voice scratchy.

"You..." He smiled wryly down at me. His eyes flashed through an array of colors—blue, yellow, red, green, brown—never settling on one for more than a second. "You *are* afraid of me. Just a little."

"Am not," I wheezed.

"Don't lie."

He jabbed his heels into the horse and, with Rowan back on her own steed, we galloped toward a stone tower with flowing blood taking the place of mortar. My breath caught. I would never get out of there. Not with the hundreds of soldiers stoking the mist around the base. I pinched my arm until I broke the skin. The pain was real, as real as it was in the mist, but it did nothing to pull me from sleep.

Kail chuckled. "Nice try."

"No one asked you."

He stared down at me, his eye color changing faster. "Better." He looked over at Rowan. "But not enough."

"It will be," she said, completely confident in her words.

I pretended to fidget and reached for the knife in the pocket of my fleece. "What will be what?" I asked.

"You will be." Rowan slid gracefully from her horse, her skirts puffing around her, and waved the army away. They moved in unison, turning around, seemingly floating along the mist on their way around the tower. "Come. It's safe to talk inside."

I cast another glance at the moving unit of cloaked nightmares. Their moans changed to a dull murmur. "Let me guess." I motioned to where the cloaked figures disappeared. Kail practically tossed me to the ground. I stumbled and scowled back at him, blowing the hair from my face. "Zombies?"

"The Blood Army is the Blood Army." Rowan's eyes narrowed. "Pray you don't run into a zombie."

Kail landed on his feet beside me, too close. He grinned. "After you."

Rowan opened the door and disappeared inside. I planted my feet. No way. I wasn't going in there. Not in a million years. No.

"Problem?" Kail asked.

I jumped sideways away from him, but his hand shot out and gripped my upper arm. I glowered at him, anger replacing the fear, and brought my knee up, hard, between his legs. With my free hand, I flicked opened one of the attachments on the knife. "I don't know, Kail. Is there?"

He groaned, his teeth bared under the hooked nose of his mask and tightened his grip on my arm. I would have a bruise later.

"You…"

My pulse throbbed in my temples, the rest of his sentence lost to the ringing in my ears. Sweat beaded on my upper lip, and I swung my arm up in an arch, driving the corkscrew into his left eye with a pop. There was no blood, but his remaining eye flashed so fast I couldn't catch any single color. The world slowed. I forgot how to breathe. To move.

He released my arm and staggered back, his steps uneven. "I will *gut* you," he howled. There wasn't time to decide if it was a legitimate threat before razor sharp agony blasted through my skull.

I knew nothing then. Only the spinning darkness of the fall.

Fire exploded from the mouth of the cave where Nora's sister was tortured. The heat from my magic curled over my shoulders and blew my hood around my face. Flames snapped and popped, spreading over the thorny brush, drowning out the screech from the serpent inside. I strode through it untouched. One person's dream was another person's nightmare, after all, and I was the sand's master no matter what form it took.

I had hoped Nora would return to the only place that was familiar to look for a way into my realm, but there was no trace of her. Cold dread filled my veins. If I had to draw the attention of every nightmare in this realm to find someone who knew her whereabouts, I would do it. Let the Weaver come for me. I had the power of a thousand dreams while he had broken threads.

Three of the scaled creatures living in the lake broke the surface, watching the blaze with hungry black eyes.

"Where is she?" I roared.

Two dove back into the depths. The third smiled.

Smiled.

Fury rumbled in my chest. The crack in my heart widened, the fissures racing throughout my body. If this creature wouldn't tell me where Nora was, it was of no use to me.

I flung a handful of sand at the water's surface and bubbles emerged from the bottom. Boiling. Scalding. I drew in a steady, satisfied breath. The scent of charred meat from behind me mingled with the wave of rancid seafood in front of me. I held my breath. The bodies of two dozen hidden nightmares bobbed to the surface, rocking between bubbles.

I turned my back on the pond, on the destruction, and walked away, my shoulders squared, with another handful of sand in my fist.

Chapter Twenty-Four

Nora

When I regained consciousness, it was in a bed of heavy silks. Sweeping sheer curtains rustled around the wooden bedposts in a nonexistent breeze. A dozen candles glowed on scrolled stands inside a corner fireplace. Their light flickered across deep red walls—the color of freshly dried blood—and danced across the dark wooden floor. Through the window, the grey skies had turned charcoal.

How long had I been out? More importantly, how long did I have left?

I flung back the warm blankets and pain seared its way through my skull. I pressed the heels of my hands against my temples with a hiss. *Rowan.* I took a steadying breath and pieced together what happened. The Barren already felt like a distant memory, but the blistering misery of the red mist was clear as day. So was what happened just before my head exploded.

I lowered my hands, flexing the one I used to stab Kail in the eye. It was a small consolation considering I was now trapped in enemy territory without a way to defend myself. I shifted to the edge of the mattress and peered over it. Cliché or not, I wasn't willing to bet on there being a literal monster under the bed. I snagged one of the six feather pillows and tossed it on the ground. When nothing lunged out to attack, I eased my feet down to the ground, my sneakers still tied tight, and leapt across the room to the single window.

My heart struck the ground. The Blood Army that followed Rowan and Kail wasn't the entire army; it was a mere fraction. A single drop of water in a deep well. There were thousands of them. Their mist coiled and rose, the steady hiss reaching me three stories up. Luckily their moaning had stopped.

"Crap." My breath fogged the window pane.

I was doomed. There was no way I was sneaking out. Not with so many of those things out there waiting. My blood pulsed in my ears, warning me. Telling me to remember what the mist could do and not to do anything stupid, but I didn't need a reminder. Still... If Rowan and Kail were handing me to the Weaver, I had to be in one piece. They couldn't allow me to boil alive if they heard my escape attempt end in agonizing screams. I swallowed hard. Either way, if I was going down, I would do it fighting. I ripped a sheet from the bed and wrapped it around my shoulders, knotting the fabric. Maybe it would help shield me from the mist once I got outside. The cloaks seemed to work for the nightmares anyway.

There was no door to the room, simply an archway into a hall lit with wall torches that burned green fire. The brown and black wallpaper boasted large medallions and between wide planks of hardwood floor oozed a bit of black sludge. "Crap," I muttered again, and gingerly eased onto my tip-toes.

My fingers skimmed the wall to keep my balance and the wallpaper shifted beneath my touch. I froze, squinting. It moved again. Bile rose to the back of my throat. The medallions weren't a design at all, but black tarantulas with their legs pressed tightly against their bodies. What I thought to be an off-white design at the center turned out to be a single unblinking eye on their abdomen. "*Crap, crap, crap.*"

Something cool licked my ankle. I leapt back, leaving tiny strands of the sludge reaching up from the floor, patting the ground in search of the foot they just touched.

A door swung open behind me and the goo darted back below the floor. Kail stood in the doorway, dangling my knife between his index finger and thumb. "Hello, again."

I ran as fast and hard as I could. My heartbeat drummed against the lingering pain in my temples, nearly blinding me. I swerved right, following the green lights, and thundered down a set of stairs. Three identical doors appeared at the landing where a moment ago there was another hallway. My knife whizzed past my head, pinning a tarantula to the wall with a tiny squeal.

"Perhaps I was wrong about you being completely pathetic," Kail said, sauntering down the last few steps. He smelled of rich spices with an undercurrent of cedar now instead of cloves. He approached slowly, carefully, like a tiger stalking its prey, and my feet slid back. He chuckled. "Perhaps not."

I spun to rip the knife from the wall, but he got there first. The arachnid hit the floor with a tiny *plop*. Another morphed from the wall, and my stomach flopped. "That's mine," I said, determined not to let him see how he affected me.

"Not anymore, Dream Keeper." His eyes were cold behind his mask. The one I stabbed had healed but remained steady on blue while his right eye flashed between colors.

I grabbed the long-pointed beak and tugged. The mask didn't budge. Curiosity prodded against a flash of fear. Was the mask actually part of his face or was it well secured? What did he look like underneath?

He swatted my hands away. "Excuse you."

"Let me out of here," I growled, refusing to acknowledge the blush that swept up the back of my neck.

"Oh, of course," he drawled. "Since you asked so nicely, let me show you the front door. Never mind all the trouble we went through to find you first. Never mind the risk we took bringing you here. That's all irrelevant."

I balled my hands into fists, ready to strike. More than ready.

"Save your strength, human. You'll need it."

He wasn't wrong, but all the strength in my body wouldn't do me any good if I was forever trapped here. So, I swung. My fist met only air, the momentum nearly throwing my body to the ground. I pressed my lips together and straightened myself. He was on guard against me now. My next attack would have to be subtle and well-timed.

"Rowan is waiting." He flicked the knotted sheet at my throat, and his top lip lifted into a sneer. "She has a tonic for your head. If you behave, I won't smash the cup before you have a chance to drink it."

I snorted. "Like I'd drink anything either of you offered me."

His lips turned down into a sarcastic frown. He raised a calloused brown hand up to my ear. And snapped his fingers. The sound crashed through my head. My stomach bottomed out, and every drop of blood drained from my face. I wouldn't give him the satisfaction of collapsing to the floor. *I wouldn't.*

He smirked. "Follow me." He started up the stairs, his black trench coat flaring with each step, but I stayed firmly planted in front of the three doors. "Pick the middle one," he drawled over his shoulder. "The endless free-fall is a particular favorite of mine, although the other two aren't half bad."

I stared at the doors again, weighing his words. It could be a lie. One of them could be the way out, and he was just trying to scare me into walking away, but somehow, I didn't think he would need to trick me. Judging by the size of his arms, he could toss me over his shoulder and carry me to Rowan without breaking a sweat. *He needs me alive.* I didn't doubt there were worse things here than the wall decor so if I wanted to stay in one piece, I had little choice but to go with him. At least for now.

"Asshole."

"Oh stop. You're going to hurt my feelings," he said, raising the pitch of his voice.

"I'll hurt *something*, but it won't be your feelings," I muttered.

He stopped and turned back to glare at me. "Are you coming?"

I slowly placed a foot on the bottom step without looking away from his flashing iris and gave him the finger. He huffed but said nothing.

We didn't speak as we passed through hallway after hallway. Each was identical, but I still got the feeling he was walking me in circles. If he was trying to make me lose my bearings, he succeeded. I wasn't even sure what floor we were on anymore, let alone which passageway. Not that it mattered—the Blood Army was still outside.

Think, Nora. Think.

Kail stopped so fast I rammed into him, his back solid as concrete. I rubbed my nose expecting to find blood, but the back of my hand came away clean.

"Inside." He pressed open a narrow panel in the wall.

I peered around him to find the warm glow of a regular fire lighting a richly decorated den. A brown leather sofa sat across from two matching chairs, a thick red throw rug beneath all three. The mantel above the fire shelved a massive clock. The hands shifted backward and forward, not pointing to numbers but strange symbols. "I'll pass, thanks."

He grunted and gripped my arm, shoving me into the room. Rowan stood in the corner, thumbing through a book. "How are you feeling?" she asked.

"Super."

"Drink that." She motioned to a clay cup with steaming liquid. "I need to speak to you with a clear mind."

I folded my arms. "Trust me, it's clear."

She set the book down and crossed the room with rustling skirts, her strange wings scraping the ceiling. She lifted the cup and held it out. "I don't need to poison you, Dream Keeper. If I wanted you dead, you would be."

I pursed my lips. The pain in my head wasn't *that* bad. It had already receded to a dull, aching pressure—nothing a couple Tylenol couldn't cure. Or maybe something a little stronger than Tylenol. *A lot stronger.*

Still, there was no way I was drinking anything they offered me. Maybe it wasn't poisonous, but that didn't mean it wouldn't have other side effects. Like sprouting gills or stealing my willpower. Plus, it was probably made from the liver of some sort of creepy crawly creature.

"Pass," I insisted in a flat voice.

Her eyes narrowed slightly before she set the cup back down and smoothed her features. "Sit. Please. We mean you no harm."

My eyebrows shot up but before I could contradict her, Kail snapped, "You stabbed me in the eye! You deserved what happened outside. And you leapt into the mist yourself so don't try pinning that on us."

"I thought I didn't need to fear you or the Blood Army," I accused Rowan. "You said I didn't fear being touched or blood, so I didn't need to be afraid."

"Without your fear, we have no desire to harm you, and we certainly get nothing from it, but that doesn't mean we can't." She pointed to the sofa again. "Sit."

I adjusted the sheet around my shoulders. "No."

"We just want to talk."

Kail barked a laugh from the doorway. "We can't trust her, Ro. Forget it."

"*You* can't trust *me*?" I shouted. "Are you joking? Everyone here wants to crack my head open like a walnut to find the dream the Sandman hid there. Then whatever's left of me will be tossed away or fed to something with a lot of pointy teeth."

Rowan hovered beside me, and I held my breath against the scent of black licorice wafting from her body. "We saved you from the Barren and brought you safely here. You tried to run twice now." She glared at the fabric tied at my neck with unspoken accusations of a third attempt. "And you stabbed my friend with your tiny knife. I rather think we're being quite accommodating."

Kail poked the area between my shoulder blades, and I stumbled to the center of the room. *Fine.* I would sit, I would listen to them, but my eyes scanned the room for potential weapons. Anything I could use to free myself before the Weaver arrived. If I was going to escape him, I needed the element of surprise. Given Rowan's ability, the Weaver would probably walk in and expect to see me sitting, resigned to my fate, on their couch. I had to be part of the shadow. To use his world against him.

Rowan perched on the edge of a chair across from me. "We want to work with you."

"What?" Books lined shelves, but nothing sharp. Nothing I could wield in a fight. "Me?"

"The Weaver..." Rowan glanced at Kail. "He forces us to do things."

"To kill people," Kail clarified.

"Most of us don't want to. Killing is unnecessary; it culls our source of energy and serves no purpose other than to be cruel." She ran her hands down the hair that cascaded over her shoulders. "We are not all evil."

I very much doubted that, but Rowan had my attention. "Did you kill my friends? Any of the people I knew?"

They exchanged a glance before shaking their heads.

My eyes narrowed. "But you know who did?"

"The Weaver killed them himself, except your two friends. He was busy with the Sandman at the time, so he delegated."

"I want names." As soon as the Weaver was dealt with, they would be next. It wouldn't be painless either. They would feel each twinge of pain I locked away. Each unshed tear.

"We want to make a deal with you." Rowan shifted, her hands folded neatly in her lap. "We all want the same thing."

"*We* is an overstatement," Kail grumbled.

My nostrils flared. *Focus.* "How would you know what I want?"

"You want the Weaver gone." Kail flung himself in the empty chair and rapped his fingers on the arm. "If he's dead, your friends and family will be safe. Your world. There would be no more waiting around for bindings to wear down and barriers to break. For the rest of your life, you could live free of this place."

I looked between them. Kail with the lower half of his face set, his shoulders squared and tight. Rowan, sitting as if she came straight from a finishing school two hundred years ago, her face blank. Waiting. Patient. What did they want me to say? It wasn't exactly a secret I wanted the Weaver dead or that I would try my hardest to make that happen, but if I was being honest with myself, I knew it was impossible. It was the idea that kept me going. Pushed me forward. Not the hope of it coming true.

"And?" I asked suspiciously.

"And." Rowan paused. "The Weaver would expect an assassination attempt from us. His defenses would be up and when we failed, he would kill us. But you? He wouldn't think twice about turning his back on you."

I blinked. Once. Twice. They were serious. A harsh laugh flew from my throat. "*Me*? You're asking *me* to kill him when you're the ones with the power here? This is a joke, right?"

Silence. Thick, suffocating silence.

Finally, Kail said, "I told you this wouldn't work. Now what? We can't kill her, but if he digs through her head, he'll find out we tried to betray him."

"She hasn't said no." Rowan wiped her hands on her skirt. "If she does this, so many people would be spared. *We* would be."

I gaped at them while they discussed me like I wasn't right in front of them. "Why would I want to spare either of you?"

"Because." Kail stood and strode to the mantle over the fireplace. He pressed a brick. A hole opened in the wall, and he removed a blade. It was no bigger than a hunting knife with glowing red liquid embedded in a long crystal that ran down the center. The metal handle was woven from black and gold, blue and silver, a patchwork of dreams and nightmares. The power sucked the air from the room. "We have this, and you do not. Without it, you may be able to bind him again, but we would be back in this position a few years from now."

Rowan nodded, smiling. "In exchange, we will take care of the nightmares that killed your friends."

I could do it; I could kill the Weaver. Avenge the people that died. Live without fear of more death. I could stop watching the shadows. The Sandman didn't think we should because of the balance, but with this, I could do it alone. But did I trust them? Enough to betray someone I *did* trust? Cold sweat trickled down my spine.

"I can't do anything without the Sandman," I said. *And he might be dead.* I balled my hands into fists.

Rowan quirked an eyebrow. "Then what did you come here for?"

Nerves prickled beneath my skin. She was right. Why did I come if it wasn't to do something about the Weaver? After I found the Sandman, what did I think we would do together? It wasn't enough to find him alive and prove the Weaver a liar. To stop this, I was going to have to help the Sandman put an end to the threat. But what if the Weaver hadn't been lying? I couldn't walk away from this chance.

"She thinks her boyfriend is dead," Kail said with a smirk.

The room spun. "He's not?" My extremities went numb, my vision blurring behind a lens of unshed tears.

"The Sandman is not dead," Rowan said slowly, her head cocked. "He left the cave for the Dream World. I don't know precisely where he is now, but it would be easy enough to track him down."

The lightness in my chest made me feel as if I were floating away, out of this horrible place toward something better. I gripped the couch cushion so hard my knuckles turned white. I wasn't floating anywhere. I was trapped here until they decided to let me go. Or not let me go, depending on how this conversation went.

Kail snorted and flipped my knife into the air, catching it.

I ground my teeth together. If he wanted my help, he had a strange way of showing it. Were the offer not so tempting, I would pry that ridiculous mask off his face and beat him over the head with it. But it *was* tempting. And they could get me back to the Sandman—something I was apparently unable to do for myself.

"What do you want me to do, exactly?" I asked.

Rowan's red-stained lips turned up. "With the Sandman at your side, it won't be impossible for you to reach the Weaver's Keep. Get the Weaver alone—that shouldn't be overly difficult either considering it's exactly what he wants—and use the blade. It contains both Dream and Nightmare magic, so it can kill both lords."

I glared at the blade. It could kill the Sandman, yet they hadn't used it. Why? Surely, they hated him as much as their lord did. Had they tried and failed? If so, I imagine they would be dead, or at the very least the Weaver would have heard of the attempt and confiscated the blade. Or killed them. Maybe both. If he would expect Rowan and Kail to try killing him, he had to know they would use such a weapon against him eventually.

But the answers scared me more than those questions did. This was my chance to take the Weaver down. Probably my only one since the Sandman was so adamant about rebinding him. I needed to believe they never tried using this against the Sandman if I was going to accept their help.

"The Sandman can't know about this plan," Rowan added.

"Why not?" I asked. I knew my own answer but if *they* didn't want the Sandman to know, there was a good chance I shouldn't be doing it. There was so much I didn't know about this place, about the creatures here... I could be walking into something I couldn't walk out of.

"He believes everything needs a counter," Kail explained. "That his mirror image must exist for things to work, but we are capable of ruling ourselves."

So, for the same reason I wouldn't tell him. I rapped my fingers on my thigh. "This plan doesn't seem like much of a plan."

"You'll figure it out if you want your revenge." Kail's voice was cool. Flippant.

I would do anything to spare my remaining loved ones the same fate as the others but lying to the Sandman didn't feel right. I wasn't sure I could lead him into the heart of the Nightmare Realm and go behind his back. He risked everything to help me bring Katie back. He would risk everything again to protect me and the Day World.

But, if the Weaver was gone... Really and truly gone...

"Is there even time for me to get to the Weaver before he's finished weaving?" I asked. All sense of time was lost to me, but it felt like an eternity since I crawled into my bed.

Rowan's wings scraped loudly against the back of the chair. "He's strong enough to fight, but he's still working. If he's going to face the Sandman and win, he'll want an overflow."

I nodded. He was still occupied then. "You'll take me to the Sandman?"

Kail laughed and Rowan leveled a look in his direction. "We cannot be seen helping you, of course. But we'll provide a guide tasked with taking you to the Weaver. He won't know that isn't your true destination. You'll know when it's time to part ways; listen to the Sandman's magic inside you. It will lead you in the right direction, and then an ally will locate you."

Listen to the magic? I didn't even know how to begin to find it. I narrowed my eyes. "That's ridiculously non-informative. How am I supposed to get away from this guide?"

"I'll return your knife before you go," Kail said, tossing a hand in my direction.

I narrowed my eyes at him. "You can't be serious."

"Do I look like I'm kidding?"

"Will you do this?" Rowan asked quickly. "Will you kill him?"

"I..." Would I? I couldn't promise anything, but I could try. I wanted the Weaver dead. Deciding what to tell the Sandman could happen later, after I saw he was okay with my own eyes. I took a deep breath and let it out slowly. "Give me that thing."

Rowan smiled. "Excellent."

Kail turned back to the strange clock and collected a sheath. "Don't take the blade out until it's time to use it, or the Weaver will know you have it."

"You'll need better clothes before you go too," Rowan said.

Kail dropped the light knife on my lap and strode from the room without another word.

"Ignore him," Rowan whispered. "He thinks this is too dangerous."

"He's not the only one," I grumbled. But it didn't matter. Battles weren't won by cowards.

Chapter Twenty-Five

My footsteps echoed through the narrow canyon. Dull yellow stone rose a hundred stories on both sides, the sky nothing more than a shard of grey, yet its light reached all the way to the bits of crumbling boulders littering the path. I surveyed the walls from beneath my hood and ground my teeth. Seventy-one nightmares dead, nearly half my power depleted, and still no sign of Nora.

Rocks tumbled down the canyon walls, kicking up a cloud of dust. My heart lurched, and I fisted sand from my satchel. "I know you're there," I called, and broke into a jog. "Show yourself."

Heavy silence rang while the debris settled. The hair on the back of my neck stood on end, and I screeched to a halt. Cracks rent the air. The ground lurched, nearly knocking me to my feet, and the mountainside trembled. Pebbles rained down, and I flung myself behind a boulder. They pelted me one after another like nails on wood, puncturing and gouging through my clothes. I tugged my hood down to protect my face, dropping the sand. A dust storm devoured me. Blinded me. I held my breath and waited with strained ears.

Forever passed before the canyon finally cleared again. I wiped away the blood beading on my hands and cracked my neck. A grinding swelled in the canyon, plucking at my nerves. The sand I held when I took shelter was now scattered at my feet under a layer of powder. I leaned forward to rest on my knees and grabbed another handful from my sack. Whatever nightmare was on the other side of the boulder had one chance to tell me where Nora was. *One.* Just like the others.

But when I stood, my blood froze. A twenty-foot man made of solid yellow rock glared down at me with molten eyes. He staggered toward me and more gravel flew from his joints. I planted my feet. The sand hummed in my hand, and I squeezed it tight. When I opened my fingers, it spilled to the ground, forming a wooden crate with a black fuse poking through the wooden slats.

"Where is the Dream Keeper?" I bellowed.

He bent, ready to tackle, and took a deep, gasping breath. The crevices in his abdomen glowed, steam leaking out from between his lips. It didn't matter what came next. I wouldn't ask him again.

I flicked a pinch of sand at the crate and snapped my fingers. Sparks flew from the fuse. I planted my feet, locked my knees, and lowered my head. The creature gurgled and took another step forward. *Good.* The closer the better.

The fuse disappeared. Sand burst from my satchel and wrapped itself tightly around my body in protection. A moment of calm vengeance filled my heart.

Then the canyon ignited into fiery chaos.

Seventy-two nightmares dead.

Chapter Twenty-Six

Nora

Rowan led me back through the tarantula lined walls. Now that I met her approval, dressed in a form-fitting black T-shirt with a leather vest, tight cotton pants, and boots that came halfway to my knee, it was time to leave. The blade rested against my spine, the handle an inch from the bottom hem of the vest. When the time came, I would simply need to flick a clasp and unsheathe the weapon.

Already I was questioning my decision to go along with this disaster of a plan. The idea of killing the Weaver was appealing but to risk my life to do it? Hadn't I given enough?

But the entire world was at stake. How could I turn away from that? I was only one person. If I failed, millions upon millions would be affected. Including me, if I managed to get out of here alive. I forced my muscles to relax. This was this right thing to do. So, after I found the Sandman, we would go to the Weaver's Keep with a plan to bind him. A plan I would deviate from. The lies I would need to tell curdled in my stomach like sour milk.

Rowan opened a side door at the back of their bloody tower. An icy wind blasted me in the face, and an explosion rumbled somewhere in the distance. I shivered at the smoke pluming in the distance.

"Follow Elkmar and no other," Rowan said.

Something clicked and clomped toward us. A solid shadow, faded in parts and darker in others, lumbered forward. It had a humanoid body with cow hooves for feet and long, frog-like fingers. The head was that of a gazelle, complete with two ribbed horns and empty eye sockets. With knees that bent backward, it didn't walk so much as creep.

I shook my head. "Tell me that's not Elkmar."

"He won't touch you," she assured me with a casual wave of her hand.

The creature opened its mouth and made a series of clicks. I winced at the stale, musty odor wafting off of him. "Comforting."

"Take the advice—follow no one else." Kail bumped against my back, the point of his mask grazing my shoulder. "There will be others that want to take credit for finding you. Don't listen to them, no matter how friendly they appear on the surface."

I snorted. It was good advice, except I would add them to the list of nightmares that wanted to use me. The others to gain favor with the Weaver, Rowan and Kail to kill him. Although it was completely possible they would betray me. What could they tell him that he didn't already know though? That I wanted him dead? That I planned on trying? He wasn't stupid. The only thing they could tell him was that I had the blade, but I saw no advantage to that.

Unless their plan was to turn the Sandman against me.

Let them try. If he learned I was keeping a secret from him, he would forgive me just as I forgave him. Hopefully. Worst case scenario, he would never forget my betrayal, but even then, he would never actively work against me.

Kail twisted me around and draped the knotted sheet back around my shoulders. "Don't forget your cape."

I flung my fist into his stomach and, when he doubled over, I grinned, tossing the fabric back at him. It wasn't as damaging as I had hoped my next assault to be, but it would do. Rowan ran her red-flecked eyes up and down my body. A cold sweat broke out against her examination. "What?" I snapped.

She shrugged, her skeletal wing shifting. "Nothing."

"I don't trust you," I said slowly, enunciating each syllable, and narrowed my eyes.

Another shrug.

Kail straightened. His blue eye fixed on me, his other flashing so fast the colors blurred together. He grabbed my hand, slammed the Swiss Army knife into my palm, and shoved me out the door. "Prove me wrong. Be braver than I think you are."

Elkmar clicked again, and the Blood Army parted. My muscles burned with tension, and I followed him away from the bleeding tower. Away from Rowan and Kail and their penetrating gazes. I knew then, with their eyes like daggers on my back, that they wanted something other than the Weaver's death, that they were using me to get more than they let on, but as long as the Weaver was dead and the dream inside me was safe, I couldn't care less what hellish plan they wanted to unleash on their brethren. Let this realm implode—I would never be back.

☾

Elkmar walked a single step ahead of me. If I slowed to put space between us, he slowed with me. If I inched to the side, so did he. The proximity filled me with tension. It balled in my center, a twisting, aching thing. Pricks of cold broke through the heat radiating from his body, but at least he didn't have fangs or rotting flesh like the other nightmares I'd seen.

I didn't know how long ago we left the tower. The mist of the Blood Army had long since disappeared from the horizon, and my feet threatened to cramp inside my boots. The scenery hadn't changed. I was positive that was the same rock we passed five times now, but Elkmar continued with purpose. So, I followed. And I waited. Rowan said I would know when to run, but I didn't see how. And if I wasn't to trust anyone, how would I know the ally they mentioned? Maybe if I was a nightmare I could sense it, but I wasn't. I was just a human, a Dreamer, with no special abilities to my name. I crossed my arms, rubbing away a chill.

The blade they had given me wasn't heavy enough to weigh down the back of my vest, but it was sturdy enough to scrape against my spine when I moved the wrong way. I practiced masking my discomfort as we traveled. The leather was stiff yet flexible, hiding the blade in its decoratively sewn lines. The fabric smelled like *them* though. Bitter, and a little bit sweet. Like the bargain I struck. For all the Weaver had done and all he planned to do, I would gladly shove the dagger into his chest. Even if it cost me everything.

But Rowan and Kail were right about something else too. The Sandman wouldn't like it. He explained how he and the Weaver shouldn't kill each other because the universe wouldn't like it or some nonsense, but he never mentioned whether they were vulnerable to others. Maybe it was because he didn't know about the blade or he assumed no one else would be strong enough to get the job done, but I doubted that. On this account, the nightmares were more honest than he was. I dug my fingers into my upper arms. This once, I was going to do something I knew deep down was wrong. Something that was also right.

Elkmar screeched to a halt, and I slammed into him, flying backward. I caught myself on my palms, but the impact still sent pain racing up my tailbone. "What the—"

My voice stuck in my throat, and Elkmar leaned awkwardly over my outstretched legs. Silver flashed overhead, the source hidden behind my guide's form. The air rang with the sound of slicing metal. Glowing orange sparks rained down on us, and I ducked my head.

Elkmar let out a single low click and lowered into a crouch. That's when I saw it. A woman's naked torso connected to two scissor blades at the hip and another at each wrist. She stepped forward, steady on the pointed ends, and Elkmar lunged. I stayed frozen on the ground as they collided. The scissor woman fell sideways, stabbing at my shadow guide, and they rolled with each other.

I scrambled to my feet. Was this it? Should I run? Elkmar was distracted, but I was no closer to finding the Sandman than

I was when I first fell asleep. His magic wasn't calling me in any specific direction. My head was void of everything but the rapid thud of my pulse.

I couldn't chance missing my moment though. With no idea where I was headed, I bolted toward the distant forest. It didn't matter what I was running toward as long as it bought me enough time to gain my bearings and catch my breath.

The sound of scraping metal faded last, but even then, the memory of it grated against my ears like rusted gears trying to turn. I kept going over the rocky landscape until I tripped over my own feet and skidded across the ground into a shallow puddle of oily blue liquid. Gagging on the scent of rotten eggs, I charged to my feet, my body screaming in protest.

A drip fell in front of my face, sending ripples across the surface of the puddle. Then another and another. I knew I shouldn't look up, but my eyes lifted anyway. A thin rope nailed to a tree held a giant, translucent pod aloft. Red veins snaked across the surface. Inside, a school of goldfish swam in circles, their mouths open wide in silent screams. Their scales fell off one at a time and floated to the surface where they bubbled and foamed over the lip.

I winced and backed away, straight into something solid. Elkmar glowered down at me, a puff of smoke flying from his nostrils. "Hey," I said in a light tone. "I... got lost."

The empty eye sockets narrowed, and he flung his head back the way we came. No doubt he expected me to follow when he turned, but I inched toward the blue puddle. Pulling the Swiss Army knife from my pocket, I sawed at the rope holding the pod up. I leaned my weight into the tree, and the coarse rope burned my raw, scraped hands. If the water inside was as slippery as it looked, maybe it would trip up Elkmar long enough for me to hide. I gritted my teeth against the guttural scream building in my chest.

A shadow fell over me from above, and I sawed faster. Hooves clacked against the stone. Elkmar must have noticed I wasn't behind him. I wasn't brave enough to look. Abandoning the rope with a single strand intact, I ran again. There was another set of clicks followed by a squelch which I could only assume was the pod, but still, I didn't glance back.

I ran until my calves cramped and my lungs begged for air. Until the endless rocky scenery gave way to a grassy plain dotted with an array of colorful wildflowers. Insects buzzed harmlessly from one to another. At first glance, they weren't any different than the ones in the Day World, and I wasn't about to get close enough to discover their differences. Every few feet, tall metal posts rose into the air, disappearing into a cover of grey clouds.

I slipped between them and collapsed on a patch of bare dirt. *Think*, I told myself. There was a way out somewhere—I just had to find it. Unless... Dread slithered into my limbs, making a home for itself beside the quivering muscles. Unless the sand was the only way into the Dream Realm, and I gave it all to Katie. Not that I could have wielded it anyway. My eyes closed for the briefest moment, and I grappled with my fate. Why had I taken those pills? *Why*? When would they wear off?

A breeze kicked up around me paired with a soft fluttering. My eyes popped open in time to see a wave of bees flee from the pink and yellow flowers nearby. *Now what*? I was careful not to move in case whatever it was hadn't noticed me yet. Something cooed. A soft, happy sound, and I pressed myself into the ground. A stronger breeze skated over the field, the flowers trembling. Then a hooked beak nuzzled the top of my head. My breath caught. Another coo. Above me, a green parrot the size of an ostrich tilted its head back and forth. Black eyes reflected my disheveled appearance.

Don't eat me, I urged silently, not daring to speak.

Its clawed feet scraped lazily across the ground, tearing up a row of flowers. It seemed to have no interest in me other than curiosity, but that could be part of its charm. A lure. I eased up onto my elbows and looked harder at my surroundings while keeping the bird in my peripheral vision. All around me, more metal posts rose, forming a circle. A shifting in the clouds revealed a swinging perch. *A cage*. I was in its cage.

Something black and yellow galloped around the outer limits of the bars. The parrot squawked. Its wings beat furiously, and it soared into the air, the wind blowing dirt in my eyes. "Wake up, wake up, wake up," I begged myself. I could try again. I could get the Sandman's pouch back from Katie and pray there was enough left for me to get to the beach.

The blur halted on the other side of the cage and stared at me. I blinked. "Baku?" Relief washed over me so quickly I was sure I would faint.

The chimera motioned me toward him with a bob of his head. I struggled to my feet, feeling every tiny scrape and bruise. My legs wobbled with each step toward the Sandman's friend. The bird's eyes burned into my back in what felt like a warning. Perhaps it was—perhaps the bird expected I would be eaten like it would have been.

"Where is he?" I slipped through the cage bars beside him. "Is he okay?"

Baku nodded.

A breath fell from deep in my chest, taking a slice of anxiety with it. "Where is he? How do I get there?"

Baku turned slowly, his trunk reaching over to skim each bar as we passed. The bird flew into a frenzy of beating wings and high-pitched cries. I bit the inside of my cheek. There was no choice but to trust Baku as the Sandman did if I wanted to escape, but I couldn't forget what he was. A predator. I might not have been on the menu but letting myself become too comfortable seemed dangerous.

Chapter Twenty-Seven

The hollowness in my chest ached, a dull, throbbing pain, begging for relief. I sat on the edge of my two-walled pavilion and shrugged out of my tunic. It smelled of iron and death. Remnants from 164 nightmares decorated the fabric, but I was still no closer to finding Nora. My muscles ached, and I kicked off my boots, contorting this way and that to remove the rest of my soiled clothes. I would cleanse the sand later. There wasn't time to waste washing myself, let alone the beach. As soon as I recharged enough to steal more dreams, I had to go back.

I leaned across the pillows and dragged a clean pair of pants from a built-in drawer on the wall. I tugged them on without standing up. The pillows cradled me, and sand crept up to my chest. The magic murmured against my tattoo. My eyes fluttered shut but flew open again when my imagination threw pictures of Nora's face skewed in agony across my lids. If I could, I would take the dream from her now. Turn their attention to someone else, *anyone* else, long enough for me to rescue her. But she would have to give me permission. She had asked if I would be willing to, not if I would, and as small as it was, there was a difference. Besides, she was clear that day in the attic when she said she wanted to keep it. Even if there was the hint of consent before, she recanted it.

"Sandman!"

And now I was hearing Nora's voice. I winced, pressing further into the pillows.

"Sandman?"

I jerked into a sitting position. Nora ran toward me clad completely in black, her blond hair pulled back in a loose braid. It had to be an illusion. A nightmare disguised as my deepest wish. The barriers around the beach must've worn down when I was busy in the Nightmare Realm, but finding Nora was more important. If the barriers to the Day World were in working order, she would be safe when I woke her.

I called the sand up to my hand and closed my fingers around the handle of a whip. The light-weight thong coiled beside me. The nightmare was two feet away when she lunged. I braced myself for the attack. For claws or teeth. But none came. My grip loosened on the handle, and Nora's arms wrapped around me. She buried her face in my neck, her shoulders shaking. She must have been crying because her cheeks were slick against my skin.

It was really her. I dropped the whip and pressed her to me. "Nora?"

"The Weaver said you were dead," she whispered. "I didn't want to believe him but when I fell asleep, you weren't there."

"I was unconscious. Why didn't you wait for me?"

She paused, and her arms tightened around me. "What if you never came?"

"I'll always come. You know that." I leaned back and smoothed the tears from her cheeks with my thumbs. She nodded but doubt still lingered in her eyes. A dull worry. "You're okay? Nothing hurt you?"

"I'm still in one piece." She hesitated, then recounted her journey so fast I had trouble keeping up. "Then Rowan and Kail came with the Blood Army—"

"The Blood Army?" I blurted. I scanned her over for wounds, but her fingers dug into my biceps, drawing my attention back to her face. To the dirt smudged against her freckles and the pieces of hair falling out of place. My heart cracked. "Why didn't you wake up?"

She pressed her lips into a straight line. "I'm fine."

I wanted to demand to know what happened, to know which nightmares I had to kill first for trapping her, but that wasn't us. Nora and I had never forced the other to talk. Pushed maybe, but never demanded, so I bit my tongue. *Later.* After we were finished binding the Weaver. "Where did you get these?" I plucked at the sleeve of her leather vest.

"Rowan."

My eyes narrowed. "Why would she give you clothes?"

"She and Kail helped me escape the Barren." Nora looked behind me, the moonlight reflected in her green eyes. "I wasn't sure I would see this place again."

Neither was I. My hands ran up and down her arms. Feeling her. Memorizing her. Her legs straddled mine, the heat from her hands now warming my neck. *Rowan and Kail helped her escape.* Why? I opened my mouth to find out, but she spoke first.

"Why did you keep this place hidden?"

Because I didn't want to share this place with her or anyone else. At first because I knew I shouldn't get too close to the Dream Keeper but, when I realized I already had, I needed this sanctuary more than ever. I came here every time my chest ached with want of someone I would never have. The one person I shouldn't want. But I couldn't admit that, so instead I shrugged.

"We have to finish this," she said in a flat, quiet voice. "Now. Before it's too late."

"There's time to regroup."

"No." The word was sharp as a nail.

I blinked, my heart squeezing. "Nora, are you sure you're okay? I can bind the Weaver alone. I've done it before."

"Your energy wasn't spread all over the Night World before," she said matter-of-factly.

She wasn't wrong. I was stronger the first time. Without warding every entrance to the Day World and protecting her dreams, I might've been able to rebind the Weaver a long time ago. If I had bothered to check in with him before now, I wouldn't have to. "I'm sorry I brought you into this," I said. "I didn't know things would end like this."

"I'm sorry too." Her forehead *thunk*-ed on my shoulder.

I stroked her hair. "What do you possibly have to be sorry for?"

"Lying by omission?" She tensed against me. "I wasn't trapped here because of a nightmare. I took three of my mother's sleeping pills tonight to make sure I didn't wake up before I had time to find you."

"Nora." My hand stilled, my fingers twined in the base of her braid. "You shouldn't have done that. What if you needed to wake up to survive? What if the pills hurt your body?"

"I know, okay?" She shuddered. "Trust me, I know."

There wasn't a doubt in my mind that she did. Or that she would wake up right then if she could, and maybe never come back. I rested my chin on her head. The bittersweet scent of nightmares clung to her, and I kissed her hair.

"You said Rowan and Kail helped you escape," I said gently, trying not to think of what they could have done to her.

She nodded.

That didn't make any sense. They were the head of the Weaver's largest force. They should have taken the Blood Army and marched her straight to his doorstep. The only person more powerful than Rowan was the Weaver himself—she would never risk her life to betray him.

And Kail.

I never really understood his role in things. Rowan's second, her friend, maybe her lover. They were a team, but when I faced them before binding the Weaver, he seemed almost hesitant to fight me. The unknown was his forte, however. If I spent a hundred years studying him, he would still remain a mystery.

But one thing I knew, whatever happened to Nora in the Nightmare Realm, Rowan and Kail would never risk losing her. Delivering the most wanted person to the Weaver would earn them an express ticket to the Day World once the gates were open or grant them creatures to torture. Whatever struck their fancy. But to let her go? It was impossible.

"When can we go back?" Nora asked, glancing at my tattoo. "Are you ready now or do you need more time to recharge?"

"Slow down." I understood her anxiety but rushing into things would only lead to failure. Her mind would crack wide open for the Weaver if we were caught, but not before he made sure I was far away, unable to help. "I'm not sure if it's a good idea for you to come with me."

She tensed on top of me. "You can't stop me."

"No," I agreed. She was her own person; I wouldn't force her to stay, even if I thought it was for her own good. Even if I wanted to, she would probably find a way to go on her own. It was safer if we stuck together.

"Then what's your plan?"

There was only one plan—the one where I went alone. What could I ask her to do that I wouldn't hate myself for later? How much risk could I expect her to take on? "First we'll have to break into the Weaver's Keep and steal more thread."

"I still have the other two," she said.

I shook my head. "We'll need more—whatever he's woven. Then, once the Weaver's inside his Keep, I'll wrap the thread around the building to trap him inside his own nightmare. It won't take him long to break out of it, but it should buy enough time for me to get close to him and reinforce the binding."

She stilled. "I'll get the thread then. If I'm inside, we know he will be too."

"Absolutely not," I said. Her fingers pressed into the tender muscle at the back of my neck. In a softer tone, I added, "I won't use you as bait."

"Why not? It makes sense."

I shook my head. "I'm not trapping you in the nightmare with him. What do you think the Lord of Nightmares could possibly fear that wouldn't destroy you? Besides, if he gets you, this whole thing will have been for nothing."

"I'll get out. Don't worry."

"Don't worry?" I laughed, mirthless. "You're asking the impossible of me."

Nora lifted her head from my shoulder and looked me in the eyes. A clear, determined expression steeled her face. "Don't think I'm not just as worried about you. The Weaver won't kill you but that doesn't mean he can't do something worse. Besides, what else do you want me to do?"

Stay away. But I knew she wouldn't. She had lost too much and come too far to turn back now. My gaze fell to her mouth. Neither of us spoke, and the air thickened with panic-fueled urgency. This could be our last moment together—the eye of our hurricane. On the other side waited a storm capable of destroying everything and everyone.

Nora shifted, bringing her calves closer to my thighs. Her hands trailed down the edges of my chest. My breath hitched. She lowered her lips to mine, and I leaned in to better meet them, clutching her waist. I drank in the taste of her, the feel of her, savoring each moment. Committing it to memory.

Her fingers blazed a path lower and lower. My grip tightened, and she arched into me. A groan escaped my throat before I could stop myself. She reached the edge of my waistband, and my heart threatened to explode, but it still wasn't the right time. She was nervous and afraid of our return to the Nightmare Realm. If we weren't about to face our enemy, I doubt she would want to move so fast. Not when we hadn't talked about a relationship. I didn't want right now with her—I wanted always. And I wouldn't get that by messing things up right out of the starting gate.

I stilled her hands. "We can't."

Her brows lowered, her breath uneven. "I thought..."

"It's not that I don't want to." *How I wanted to.*

She brushed the hair from my forehead. "If you're worried because I've never been with anyone before, I'm not afraid. And if things don't go well, we might never—"

"Nora." I winced. She wasn't going to make this easy. "It has nothing to do with that. But… we can't. Not yet. Things won't go wrong; we have time."

You terrify me, I wanted to say. *What you could do to me if you woke up a day, a week, a month from now and realized you were confused. That it was all an awful mistake.*

"Besides, you might change your mind about having the dream taken away," I skimmed my knuckles down her cheek. "Even if you decide to keep it, there's a chance you'll never want to see me again. After you've had time to process everything and realize what I did to you by making you a Dream Keeper, you could very well hate me."

She took my hand before I could pull it back, keeping it against her cheek. "You're not the only one with feelings on the line, Sandman. If my only choice was between my sanity and losing you, I would keep this dream until the day I died. It's other people's lives that are in danger because of what I am, but I already told you, I want to keep it. Do you think I don't love you? Do you think I kissed Ben for any reason other than that he reminded me of you? That he *was* you? You may have realized it first but that doesn't make my feelings any less true now. I'll never be able to break your heart without breaking my own. Why do you think I'm going through all of this? To save people, yes, but also to make it safe for us to stay together."

My heart soared, only to slam against an invisible ceiling and crash back down around me. She loved me, but she shouldn't risk herself like this to be with me. My future was a lot longer than hers, and if I regretted any part of tonight, I would never forgive myself.

I leaned forward and nuzzled her neck, placing a soft kiss at the hollow of her throat. "After we take care of the Weaver, I'll do whatever you want. I'll take the dream if you ask me to. I'll disappear or stay. We can go back to the way things were or we can finish this." I laid my forehead on her collarbone. "All I want is for you to be happy and safe again."

Her hands landed gently on my back, tracing lines up and down the sides of my shoulder blades. It warmed me from the inside out, drawing out my worries until I felt boneless. I leaned away from her. She needed an outlet for her anxiety as much as I did, and just because we weren't going to take our relationship to another level, that didn't mean my body couldn't offer her some comfort.

Her eyes widened when I pressed her palm against my tattoo. The bit of my magic within her stirred with recognition and rose to meet mine. She sagged against me, her breath skating over my shoulders and down my back. "Lay down with me," she said in my ear, shifting from my lap.

I eased back into the pillows and did as she asked. We faced each other, and her hand found my chest again. Her head came to rest in the dip near my shoulder, her nose against my neck. I rested a hand carefully on her hip, my other rising to play with her hair. A sneakered foot slipped between my ankles. I sighed silently, my heart both calm and frantic. I would gladly stay cocooned together like this until the sky fell around us, but that wasn't possible.

"Tell me where to find the loom," she said against my skin.

My eyes slid shut. I told her everything I knew about the Weaver's Keep and what we might expect to find when we got there, but even I didn't know the extent of what awaited us. A lot could change in five years.

Chapter Twenty-Eight

Nora

The Sandman asked me to keep my eyes closed for the trip to the Weaver's Keep. The less afraid I was, the less attention we would attract, but each sound that reached my ears sent fear rushing to the surface. Clicks and scrapes, hisses and growls. I was glad I couldn't see what was making them. Gladder still that nothing decided to risk an attack as he led me blindly over the ever-changing terrain. It didn't help that our plan was riddled with holes we couldn't fill without knowing exactly what we would find when we arrived.

There would be sentries, of course. With the Weaver working, he would need extra protection, especially if he sensed the Sandman coming. *When* he sensed him.

Really, our success hinged on how well the Sandman stalled him, so I could get inside through the basement window. There, I would work my way up the hidden staircase to the top of the tower where the loom was. *Do not use the outer stairs*, he warned. The Weaver might notice and go after me instead of him. The same for the patrols. I pressed a hand against my back pocket where I tucked the skeleton key the Sandman made in case of locked doors.

The skin on my back was raw where the knife chaffed through my shirt. It was a good thing the Sandman stopped us from going too far. What had I been thinking? If my clothes started to come off along with his and he saw it, everything would have fallen apart. But I *hadn't* been thinking. My mind completely shut down and the urge to be close to him took over. It still lingered in the pit of my belly. He was right to stop me, and not just because of the knife.

My treachery seemed so much worse beside him. The sensation his touch created, the way my heart flopped, I was risking it all. I hadn't realized I was doing all this, in part, for us until I said it. If nothing else, the panic made my real feelings for him crystal clear. Protection for the Day World mattered, but I would have it whether I went with his plan or stuck with mine. The chances of the Sandman forgiving me for killing the Weaver seemed smaller the longer I spent with him. Smaller and deadlier. After losing so much already, losing him would destroy me.

"We're almost there," he said in a soft, reassuring voice, his breath warm against my temple.

I nodded, sweat beading on my upper lip. *Almost there.* The odds of surviving this wasn't in our favor; these could be my last few moments with the Sandman. I inched closer until my arm pressed against his. "Is that supposed to be comforting?"

"That depends. Was it?"

I laughed dryly. "Not particularly."

"Then I lied. We're so far away that our feet will probably fall off before we make it to the Keep."

I nudged him with my side. "Oh, good. I was worried this would be too easy, but if we're going to fight the Weaver without feet…"

He chuckled. "I'm glad I could clear that up for you."

I smiled, but it didn't last long. I tightened my grip on his arm. "In case this doesn't work, can you promise me something?"

He paused for a moment before asking, "What?"

"Two things, actually." I swallowed. "If the Weaver gets me, take the dream. After seeing Katie and... and learning what's out there… I don't want to be responsible for destroying my world. Take it somewhere safe."

"He's not going to get you," he said in a sure, solid voice. "I won't let him."

I opened my eyes and focused on him, ignoring the dark swirling storm clouds surrounding us. "Promise me anyway."

He pressed his lips into a tight line. "What's the second thing?"

"Take care of my family."

"No." He squeezed my hand so hard that my fingers straightened. "I won't promise you either of those things because it won't come to that. We'll bind him, and you'll wake up safe in your bed."

"Sandman—"

"You will." His voice was hard. Final.

I blew a frustrated breath through flared nostrils. "Wouldn't it be easier to kill him?"

"You know I can't." He looked straight ahead, his eyes glazing over.

"But I can," I said quietly.

His mouth opened, and he paused. A thought flashed through his eyes, harsh and unspoken, before he shook his head. "Don't get any crazy ideas. We're going to bind him. It's safer for everyone that way."

I studied the grim lines on his face. That was as close as I would come to asking permission. I would obviously never get it, but I didn't need his blessing. He said himself the balance would find a way to compensate. Kail was right when he said the nightmares could govern themselves. I was sure someone else could step up as their leader, and on the plus side, there would be no new creatures.

The Sandman stopped at the edge of an empty moat and crouched in the tall grass. I followed suit, batting a cattail from my face. On the other side of the ditch rose a black marble building veined with gold. Half of the rectangular third floor was domed, while the other half was surrounded by glassless arched openings. A simple wooden staircase ran up both ends to allow access to the upper floors from the outside. Going through the basement seemed a waste of time when there was such a direct route. I bit my lip. It was important to stick to the plan. At least this part of it.

"I thought it would be bigger," I whispered.

"It was. A lot of it was destroyed during our last battle." The Sandman's gaze swept over the other side of the ditch. There was no sign of nightmares, large or small. "The loom is in the dome. I'm going to distract them over there." He nodded to the far end. "The basement window is there." He pointed to a small window just big enough for me to fit through at the base of the building. "Hurry inside as soon as you think it's safe. I'll keep them away long enough for you to get in and get the thread, then I'll meet you in the open tower."

Just like we said an hour ago. "But there aren't any nightmares."

"They're here," he promised.

Hiding. Waiting. A chill ran over me. What would I do when the moment came? Kill the Weaver? Help bind him? The chance may not present itself to use the knife Kail and Rowan gave me. Then I wouldn't have to decide. But if it did... I cleared my throat. "How am I supposed to get to the tower from the dome?"

"There's a hatch. You can't miss it once you're inside."

"Okay." I eyed the path to my destination, and ice prickled along my skin.

The Sandman hooked my chin with his finger and turned me toward him. Looking at him hurt. It made me question everything. Doubt it all. Was I a murderer? Could I do this and not lose myself? Lose us?

"Be careful," he said, his voice soft, wistful.

"You too." His eyes traveled over my face, drinking me in like he would never get another chance. The threat of tears burned, but I blinked them away. I would see him again. *I would.* And one way or the other, we would sort things out. "I love you."

He drew a sharp breath before pressing his lips to mine. It was a hard, desperate kiss that was over as quickly as it came. "I love you too."

Then he was gone, running away from me with a satchel of sand at his hip.

I crouched in the grass and held my breath. The moment he disappeared around the corner, the world felt as if it stopped. My ears strained against the silence, the hair on the back of my neck lifting. Nothing. I shifted to the balls of my feet. Was he wrong? Was nothing waiting? Or, more likely, was there an ambush? My lungs ached, and I released the breath I forgot I was holding. We never agreed on a signal and if I waited for one, I might not make it on time. I crept from my hiding spot.

A series of popping clicks raked the air, and a shadow moved in the open tower. Four long finger bones reached up over the sill. The nightmare launched itself over the edge, and I slammed a hand over my mouth before I could scream. Both two-fingered hands were attached to straight ivory bones held together at the elbow with a swiveling joint. The head was distinctly human but four times the size with a mass of flowing brown hair. She slithered down the side of the brick, her body nothing but an exposed spine, proportionate to her skull. It sliced through the air, sliding back and forth like a snake, and hit the ground with a crunch. She shot around the corner of the building where the Sandman disappeared, using her bony, pronged fingers to hurtle forward.

The moment she was out of sight, I raced headlong through the ditch and across the open lawn. My heart hammered, my pulse thundering in my ears. The basement window was two hundred feet away. One hundred. Fifty. A light flashed through the glass. Once. Twice. I dug my heels into the soft dirt, nearly falling forward. The light came again, this time stopping on the other side of the glass. Two bright eyes swayed gently from side to side. Then the bat-like nightmare flew straight at the window, slamming its body against the glass. A shrill cry rattled the frame. Leathery wings slapped against the pane and pointed white teeth snapped together below a wrinkled snout.

That there might be something inside was a given after being in Rowan and Kail's tower, but I didn't expect anything to try attacking me before I was in and able to find a place to hide. There wasn't time to deal with it. Even if I killed it, it was likely already drawing the attention of other things.

The clacking bones of the creature the Sandman fought echoed around me. I looked up at the outer staircase, then back to the trapped creature. A gamble to remain unseen versus a sure thing. I clenched my jaw shut and bolted to the outer stairs.

The railing was rough beneath my palm, splinters impaling my skin. Each step felt heavier than the last, each taking me farther and farther away from where I needed to be, until I barreled through an unlocked door at the top. I kicked it shut behind me and leaned my back against the smooth metal, gasping for air. The overwhelming scent of burned cotton strangled me, but I made it without being seen or followed.

A nervous laugh bubbled from my chest, and I straightened to find a loom taking up nearly the entire space. Black threads passed over the beams, casting the room in an eerie glow. Wood creaked, parts of the loom moving, guiding new threads through from an invisible source. I stepped toward it, and the smile fell from my face. The Weaver had to infuse the thread with his power to make his nightmares which meant...

A bench scraped the floor, clattering as it toppled, and the machine came to an abrupt stop. My heart sputtered. I didn't see the Weaver, didn't hear his footsteps, until he was right in front of me, his hands around my throat. "Hello, Dream Keeper." He beamed.

My mouth dried, my tongue sandpaper in my mouth. His grip was tight enough to keep me from speaking but not hard enough to prevent air from reaching my lungs.

"How brave you are," he continued, unruffled. "How stupid *he* is."

I gripped his arm, the solid muscle flexing beneath my hand. Thin, wispy filaments hung limp at his shoulder where he must have ripped the cut threads from his sleeve. The embroidery on his vest, missing. I drew a shallow breath, refusing to meet his stare. A pile of thread pooled at the corner of the loom, a single piece running into the machine four feet away, gold-filaments twined throughout.

"Don't even think about it," he growled. I forced my eyes up to his, and he dragged me away from the machine until my back slammed into the wall. The knife jammed into my spine, and I cringed. "You were right; I underestimated you. It won't happen again."

Except you already have. I opened my mouth to tell him to go to Hell but only a wheeze came out.

He gave me a crooked grin. "The Sandman is foolish enough to expect me outside right now, isn't he? Why else would he send you in here alone? But I am not so vain as to need to take him down personally. What good is an army if they don't fight for you, hmm?"

My heart leapt to my throat. I dug my nails into his arm, but his grip was steel. He stepped forward, leaving no space between us. His breath tickled my cheek. "I am faster than you, stronger than you. Did you think you could steal my thread again without being caught? That I would let anyone bind me a second time?" He forced my chin up and smoothed the hair from my forehead, staring at the space between my eyes. "Give me the dream."

"No," I squeaked.

The muscles in his jaw jumped. "You don't want to play this game with me, Keeper. You're in my house now."

Of course, I didn't want to. I wasn't giving up yet though. If things went wrong, the Sandman would do as I asked and take the dream, even if he hadn't made the promise.

Be braver than I think you are, Kail had said.

With my body screaming in fear, I didn't feel very brave. The Weaver was in front of me, choking me, promising to torture me, yet I hesitated because the Sandman wouldn't like it. Because the balance was so important to him.

But I knew I couldn't go through this again. Even if the Sandman took the dream from me after rebinding the Weaver, I wouldn't be safe. Not really. The next time he broke free, I would be first on his list. *No*. Not first. He would kill the little family I had left before he got around to me, but he *would* get to me for everything I've done. It wouldn't be a quick death either. My stomach rolled, and I wedged a hand between my back and the wall, gripping the knife. The handle was icy against my palm.

"Listen." The Weaver pushed the hatch open overhead and a dozen different horrifying cries bounced off the domed ceiling. "He can't save you. Give me the dream now, and I'll allow you to return to your regular life. Keep testing me, and you won't be the only one to suffer."

"Why?" I croaked. I was stalling, biding time before I made the switch from prison guard to executioner. His death wasn't necessary. Not for the rest of the world anyway. He could be rebound, live his life here until the next time the magic wore down, but this was personal. And it was time I did something to save myself instead of worrying about everyone else. "Why do you want to let them out?"

His gold eyes glimmered. "This place is suffocating me, Dream Keeper. Can you imagine being trapped in a single room for your entire life? Watching millennium pass by while your four walls stay the same? I want more from life, and so do my nightmares. Things were never supposed to be like this—I told you that." His grip loosened ever so slightly. "The Sandman and I… we did this to ourselves, you know? But this is going to fix everything."

His words were a lightning bolt to my chest. A twist to my gut. Randy was dead. The cashier. Natalie. Emery. My father. All of them murdered on his order, my sister trapped and tortured in a cave, because he had a severe case of cabin fever. Because he thought bloodshed would fix something.

"What are you talking about?" I rasped.

I flicked the snap holding the knife in place. The hurt and anger I'd kept locked away boiled over, the flames licking through my body. Burning my veins. Scarring my heart. I tightened my grip on the handle. The Weaver tipped his head toward the hatch and closed his eyes, inhaling the acrid scent of metal and decay that wafted from the opening.

"Smell that, Keeper?" he asked, ignoring my question. "Death is coming."

The world slowed. My arm moved as if detached. As if I had no control. A brief flicker of recognition lit the Weaver's face as he sensed the knife's magic, but it was too late. I rammed the blade into his chest. It tore through flesh. Ripped past muscle. Scraped against bone. Sunk into his heart. I stood immobile. His gold eye dimmed, his mouth hanging open. It might have been my imagination, but I swore I felt every flutter of his pulse echo through the weapon.

He stumbled away from me then. Air whooshed into my lungs, and I nearly collapsed. The Weaver tumbled into the loom, his boots crushing the pile of thread. It bucked and coiled beneath him until he fell to the ground. Blood oozed from the corner of his mouth, and a cough sent it flying at my knees.

I knelt beside him and gripped the gleaming handle. "You're right." My voice was low and scratchy, and I yanked the blade free. "Death *is* coming."

A bittersweet grin played at his crimson lips. His hand snapped out, gripping my wrist. "You have no idea what you've done to yourself, Dream Keeper."

Stars danced in my vision. I shook my head, blinking hard. "What...?"

"Dreamer, Dreamer. Couldn't redeem her." The Weaver's half-cough, half-laugh splashed hot blood across my cheek. "You stupid, stupid girl. I wish—" Another cough. "I wish I could be here to see the Sandman's face."

A whistle rose up from nowhere, growing louder and louder until I was sure my eardrums would explode. I tried to tug myself free of the Weaver's grip, but he held tight. His lips were moving.

Speaking. Saying something. My body seized. I couldn't breathe. Couldn't think. Feel. See.

Then the Weaver's hand fell away.

My senses returned one by one.

The Weaver's body slumped against the loom. His blood pooled around us on the black and gold marble, soaking through my pants. I took a single shaking breath, and a burst of agonizing pain sent me flying backward. My skull cracked against the wall, my brain rattling. It was as if I were on fire. As if every bone was breaking. Every vein collapsing. The room blinked in and out. I struggled to my hands and knees. I had to get out. To run before any of his creatures found me like this and tried to avenge their leader. I needed the Sandman.

The woven thread snapped up, circling the same wrist the Weaver held moments ago. I gripped the coil, yanking it, but it only tightened. The blood flow ceased, and my fingers tingled. I screamed then. An angry, tormented sound rising from the depths of my soul. Waves of pain rocked my body. My muscles tightened and cramped. I was going to die here. Alone. In a puddle of the Weaver's blood.

I fell to the cool, slick marble. My legs convulsed, splashing blood across the floor. With my last burst of strength, I screamed again. This time a name. The only name I ever loved. The one I had just betrayed.

"Sandman!"

Chapter Twenty-Nine

The Sandman

The field was stained red and black with blood, both mine and the nightmares'. Mostly theirs. It weighed down my sleeves and dripped from my fingers. I stood in the middle of the carnage, panting. Each breath was tight against my broken ribs. Giant cats, humanoid beings, and a prehistoric creature littered the yard. At least fifty different nightmares, some powerful, some not. But Despina was different.

I held little hope of truly defeating her before my power ran out. For a spine with two forked hands and a giant skull, she was clever. There wasn't much to aim at. She had no vital organs, she felt no pain. I wasn't sure who I hated facing more—her or the Weaver. I needed to hurry though. Nora should've made it to the tower by now, and the Weaver was nowhere to be seen.

I stepped around and over lifeless forms, my boots sloshing against the blood-soaked ground. A cut in my leg still oozed, and my jaw throbbed from a punch I took. Despina's clicking bones sounded behind me. I scooped a handful of sand from my satchel and tossed it out in front of me. A giant web sprung between two trees, and I leapt through a rectangular gap. I heard the soft thud of her over-sized head hitting the fine strands, but I was already sprinting. It wouldn't hold her long, but I only needed a head start. Once I reached the stairs, I could better deflect her attacks. She wouldn't want to break what was left of the Weaver's home which meant she would pull her punches. At least until I reached the top where she would have me cornered, but by then I should have the thread I needed.

An explosion of terror shot through me. Not mine, but his. The Weaver's fear, close and undiluted. I spun around, grabbing another handful of sand. Despina was still untangling herself, but there wasn't another living nightmare to be seen. My brows lowered, and I scanned the area. *Where are you, Weaver? And what are you afra—*

Sharp, blinding pain lanced my chest. Stinging. Burning. My heart sputtered, and the ground rose up to meet me.

I lay there, in the blood and dirt, gasping for what were surely my last breaths. I rubbed a shaking hand over the fatal wound, but there was no mark. A cloud descended over me, wrapping around my mind. No matter which way I looked, I understood nothing. Nothing but blazing agony. Nothing but a desire for it to end.

I flipped to my back to find Despina hovering over me. Only her hair moved, her empty eye sockets focused on the fortress. *Nora.* A crackling breath broke free from my throat. Something went wrong. The Weaver never came... I forced myself up onto my elbows and scrambled out from under the skeletal nightmare. Despina didn't so much as glance in my direction, and I willed myself onto unsteady feet.

Ice filled my chest, chasing the magic from my center. Each breath threatened to crumble my lungs, each step, my bones. My jaw trembled. Teeth clacked. I wasn't going to make it. I stumbled over my own feet. The ground warped before me, an upheaval, and I flung my arms out to catch my balance.

A scream blasted across the battlefield, nearly sending me back to my knees. Then another scream. "Sandman!"

"Nora," I tried to call back, but my voice was gone. Lost. I sucked in air. What was he doing to her? What had she done to him? Despina's bones clacked again. Quick. Erratic. I tried to move faster, to run, but my vision blurred. The nightmare zipped past me, the wind she kicked up the only thing to touch me. A blur of ivory bones snaked up the side of the black wall.

The pain gripping my chest faded. This was surely what dying felt like; the bliss before the nothing. But then my vision cleared. The shaking in my legs dulled to a tremor. Heat exploded behind my tattoo, branching out through my arms. The sand at my hip buzzed through the satchel with new vigor. I flexed the numbness from my fingers.

A cry rang down from the distant sky. Something large and angry was coming. I could question everything later, after I found Nora and we were out of danger. My boots pounded across the lawn, the memory of pain slowing my movements, and my ragged breath echoed in my ears.

"Nora?" I propelled myself up the outer stairs. Despina clicked and scraped her way over the domed roof. We reached the door at the same time, and I threw a handful of sand at her. It exploded in a series of tiny white fireworks. She reeled back. I flung myself inside and slammed the door behind me.

"Nora?"

Blood was everywhere. Splattered on the walls. The loom. Pooling beneath the bodies. *Bodies.*

The air left me, wringing my lungs. Suffocating me.

I was wrong. I hadn't been dying before. *This* was dying. This was death.

I slid across the soaked floor on my knees and scooped Nora into my arms. Her skin was like ice, her face white as a sheet. Blood matted her hair and speckled her face like a second layer of freckles. Tears pricked my eyes. "Nora?" I smoothed her hair back, wiped at the blood on her skin. It smeared, the streak reaching all the way down her jaw. "No, no, no. Open your eyes. Please, Nora. Please, wake up."

Another screech joined the first outside. Let them come. Let them see their master dead on the floor. Let them see who did it. Let them rip me apart so that my body matched my heart.

I glared at the knife in Nora's hand with its red, glowing center. Recognition struck, and my stomach churned. I hadn't seen it in a thousand years. The Weaver and I had agreed... My mouth ran dry. It was supposed to be lost. Buried. Burned. At the bottom of an ocean. Destroyed. Somewhere neither the Weaver nor I would ever find it and try to demolish the balance. I hooked my arm under Nora's shoulders and leaned forward, yanking the blade from her grip. No one should have this much power. No one. I leaned away from the Weaver's body, resting on my heels.

"Why?" I choked. "We had a plan."

She answered with a groan.

"Nora!" The knife clattered to the ground, and I lifted her up. "Nora? Can you hear me?"

She winced. "Sandman?"

I crushed her against me. Hot tears spilled down my cheeks. "You're alive."

"Debatable," she mumbled into my chest.

"What happened? You were only supposed to get the thread. Where did you find that knife?" I blurted, the words overlapping.

"I..." She shifted, and I loosened my grip. "Rowan and Kail gave it to me to kill him. I wasn't sure I would be able to do it, but he... I had no choice."

Rowan and Kail. But how did they find it? My fingers dug into Nora's shoulders, and she sat up gingerly. We were supposed to bind the Weaver. That was it. Anything else had the potential to destroy the Night World, and now... My eyes locked onto the Weaver's waxen face, and I stilled. My friend. My enemy. Emotions funneled through me faster than I could register them. My entire life was woven with strands of his existence, and now… Now it felt as if my heart was cleaved in two—his half gone and Nora's hemorrhaging. "You killed him," I rasped.

She nodded, and her hands flew up to press against her temples. Beneath the Weaver's blood, her fingers and hands were black, the mat color reaching up toward her elbow like a glove. Each of her frantic heartbeats sent a visible pulse of gold along the veins beneath. Thread coiled around her wrist like a manacle, the other end still attached to the loom. My blood drained to my feet. *Magic.* The Weaver's magic. The pain I felt outside... That was the Weaver's death, and the release of it was because the balance was restored. My connection to the Weaver wasn't gone—it was transferred.

To her.

My jaw hung open, my voice raw. "No."

"I'm sorry. I know it wasn't the plan, and I should have told you."

I pried her hands away from her head, holding them between us. "Look."

Her eyes flashed. She snatched her arms from my grip and scrubbed frantically at her skin. "What is this?"

Outside, the creatures had arrived, screeching over our heads. Others came too. Bellowing and shouting and roaring. No one had come close to killing one of us before, and with the nightmares, there was no way to know if they were here for revenge or to welcome Nora as their new lord. *Lady.* But whatever their reason, now wasn't the time. We had to get out of here and regroup.

"We have to leave," I said. She didn't move except to continue scratching at her arms. "*Now.*"

I scooped the blade off the floor, tucking it into my belt, and hauled her up by her elbows. A low moan beat against my eardrums. The Blood Army. Rowan and Kail had come to claim their prize—whatever they hoped it would be. I grabbed the thread where it connected to the loom and raked it across a sharp metal edge. It whipped itself free of me and fastened around Nora's arm, melding into the sleeve of her black T-shirt.

"Sandman," she cried.

The terror in her voice cut like glass, gouging my soul. Pain poured from the wound and spread its acidic burn through my body until every beat of my heart made it feel as if I would combust. Nora… My Nora. What had she *done*?

I spared a final glance at the Weaver's corpse and regret pinched my chest. Surely, this wasn't real. He would open his gold eyes and bark out a loud curse any moment now. Much worse had happened to us in the past and he—*we*—survived. Except I'd seen too much death since our creation not to recognize its pallor. My power pulsed at the brutal realization, threatening to knock me off my feet.

The Weaver, my friend, my nemesis… was gone.

But this wasn't the time to mourn. If I should mourn at all. So I steeled myself and gripped Nora's hand. The color on her arms would fade as the magic sunk deeper into her being, but the consequences of her actions—never. "I'm sorry," I whispered and ripped her from the Nightmare Realm.

Her realm.

Chapter Thirty

The pain continued to tremble through my body. A pinch here, a poke there. My muscles cramped, and joints ached, but the worst of it had faded. My vision was clear by the time the Sandman escorted me back to the beach. He released his grip on my elbows, and I fell to my knees into glorious, glorious sand. A sob stuck in my throat.

"No," the Sandman shouted. I snapped my head up to find Baku crouching low, a hungry gleam in his eyes. "No." His voice was softer this time, his hands held out in my defense.

Baku flicked a look between us but didn't straighten from his position.

A cold sweat broke out on my skin. "Sandman?"

"*No*. She's not... She... You can't." His shoulders slumped, and he stepped between us. "Give us a few minutes, Baku."

I didn't see Baku get up or walk away, but I sensed his distance growing on the other side of the Sandman. It was a small weight lifted from inside. A sprinkle of calm amid the chaos. "I'm so sorry," I blurted through building tears. I wanted to reach out to him but found I didn't have the courage to try. "I didn't know. I thought..." *I thought I would fix everything.* I held my arms out in front of me, stained and foreign. They prickled with a power I couldn't explain, the threads holding me in a vice grip. "What's happening to me?"

The Sandman shook his head once. Dirt and debris were caked in his hair. A smudge of something else marked his face. His chest was covered in mud and tacky blood, his legs drenched. The fabric of his pants clung to his thigh where a large gash continued to bleed, but most of it came from somewhere else. I looked past my arms to the blood splattered over my entire body, and my heart shuttered.

My eyes sought his, desperate for answers, but even with all the signs of a vicious fight, they were the worst to look at. Stars danced a duet across the vibrant violet—love and hate, relief and fear.

Despair shook through me like an earthquake. Whatever this was, whatever was happening, it was as bad as it seemed. Worse. "Stop looking at me like that," I said, sounding as broken and desperate as I felt. "Tell me what this is before I find a saw and start—"

"The balance." His eyes fell to my arms, and he reached out to stroke his fingertips over my tense wrists. "I wasn't sure what killing him would do exactly, or I would have warned you." He ran his hands through his hair. "Or, maybe I wouldn't have because I didn't know you were planning this. And the knife? You had it on you when you came back? No." He winced. "Don't answer that. I know you did."

"It wasn't like that." I inched closer, still not daring to reach out. But it *was* like that. It was a conscious decision to lie and betray. "I wanted the Weaver dead, Sandman. I *needed* him dead and for this to be over. I knew you would've stopped me if I told you. I second guessed myself until the end, but he wasn't going to let me go."

"I know he wasn't," he mumbled, his head hanging. "I know, I know. But, Nora... I told you the universe kept the balance. You could've..."

I stared at him. The words were all over his face, his body, aching to be free yet too afraid to surface. "Just say it."

He shook his head, his eyes pressed shut. "It doesn't matter. It's done."

"But what's happening to me?"

"Apparently to kill the Weaver is to become the Weaver," he said, his voice dead. He met my gaze, his pupils wide. "To become the Weaver is to become a target."

I shook my head. He couldn't mean that. This was a trick, a nightmare. This wasn't the beach, but another mind game the Weaver's world was playing on me. I couldn't be the Weaver. The Weaver was the Weaver, dead or alive.

"What are you saying? That I'm a nightmare now?" I sucked in the lilac-scented air and almost gagged. *Sweet. Too sweet.* "Why would I be a target?"

"You're the Lady of Nightmares. Not quite a nightmare, but not quite human either. Someone has to rule over them, keep them in line, create them."

"No. Rowan said they could—"

"Rowan used you. She was no match for the Weaver, but you? If killing the Weaver makes you the next ruler of the Nightmare Realm, you were never meant to last long."

"No..." But it rang true. Once I killed the Weaver, she planned to kill me. I leapt to my feet, scrubbing at the stain on my arms again. "*No.* There has to be something we can do. Can't I just pass the torch or something? If Rowan wants this, she can have it."

The Sandman shook his head. "If there is a way, I know nothing of it."

The beach spun, and I latched onto his arm. My lungs cried for air but no matter how much I drew, no matter how quickly I drew it, there wasn't enough. My pulse hammered through me. *Weaver.* I blinked through wet eyes. "There has to be *something.*"

Thunder boomed overhead. Lightning followed on its heels, outlining a thousand different shapes, all coming straight toward us. A splash of orange, a towering set of horns, a slithering figure in the sky. The low moan of the Blood Army.

The Sandman reached into the satchel still hanging at his hip. "You have to leave."

"You can't face that many alone," I cried. The volume of their march alone was unlike anything I'd ever heard. The ground trembled with it.

The Sandman scooped up enough sand to make a pair of scissors and snipped the thread from my wrist, then again at the sleeve of my shirt. I felt naked, weak, wrong without it. I wanted to snatch the long tangle from his hands. Protect it. Keep it. But the deep need for it scared me more than the Sandman destroying it did. I curled my hands into fists. "If I really am the new Weaver, I'm going to stay and fight."

"You have no idea how to use the magic coursing through your veins," he said, not unkindly. "Besides, they're coming because I kidnapped their new leader. If you're not here, they'll look for you somewhere else."

The black and gold thread writhed in his arms, reaching for me, but I stepped back. "You didn't kidnap me."

"Technically, I did," he said. "And whatever their feelings are about this power shift, they won't stand for it. What they will do after they have you back… is anyone's guess."

"But..." I blinked at the mass of creatures coming toward the Dream Realm and something swelled in my breast. A sickening hope. A brimming hate. I clamped a hand over my mouth to keep from speaking about things I didn't understand.

"I'm going to put the entire Nightmare Realm on lockdown until you've gained enough strength to face them. The nightmares already can't get out, but I'll make it so that no one can get in. Who knows what they'll do to a Dreamer without someone to enforce the rules, as few as they are. If you're here, you'll be bound too. And..." He slammed his mouth shut and swallowed hard. "And, that means you need to wake up."

I tore my eyes away from the darkening sky. "You can do that? Stop everyone from having a nightmare?"

"It will take everything I have, but without the Weaver fighting me, it's possible." He stepped closer and lifted my chin. His lips pressed against mine, hard and unapologetic. "Everything will be fine, okay? I'll see you later. I promise."

Baku appeared at his side again, shifting between his paws, and the hoard slowed. Slowed but didn't stop. Even if I wasn't here, if they believed he had taken me, they would want their pound of flesh. Both their anger and anticipation tingled along my nerves.

"Distract them," he said to Baku.

Baku snorted his agreement, if only out of excitement for having caged prey, and an irrational spike of anger hit me. I focused on the Sandman's hands, and he called sand up to encase the long, thrashing strand of thread. Invading it. Stealing its allegiance. I balled my hands into fists. The nightmares were close enough to the thinning barrier now that flashes of muted color broke through the darkness. A wicked gleam filled the chimera's eyes.

"Wake up, Nora," the Sandman warned.

I crossed my arms, saw the darkness there, and slipped them behind my back instead. "Baku gets a choice."

"Baku knows what he's doing." The Sandman whipped the coil of thread out and it fell to the ground, limp.

I could help him. I could fight or order the nightmares back to where they belonged. They should have to listen to me now. It was worth a shot anyway. The Dream Realm didn't have to be the only safe place for a Dreamer. Not anymore. Together, the Sandman and I could destroy everything on the other side of the beach's barrier. I saw the walls clearly now—a dome of shimmering magic—and felt the strain of its fading power.

"I love you," he said in a final tone.

"Wait—"

Before I could finish my plea, he shoved me awake.

Waking up felt like having my soul ripped away, torn to shreds, and stuffed back into a body that no longer fit. I flew up in bed, crisp white sheets pooling in my lap. A scream lodged in my throat, and I fought to breathe. Monitors beeped furiously all around me. Wires streamed out from the neck of a white and blue hospital gown, and a needle was stuck in my arm, delivering IV fluids. I reached up to tear the wires from my chest and froze. My hands and arms were still as black as night, my veins glowing gold beneath. The place where the thread had circled my wrist was raw and aching.

A nurse in colorful scrubs flew into the room with my mother two steps behind. Katie rushed in beside her dressed in a pair of jeans and a plaid shirt, not the hospital clothes I last saw her in. Her hair was dyed dark brown, her face free of makeup.

My heart dropped. What was I doing here? It couldn't be later than mid-day. The pills I took shouldn't have been enough to warrant a trip to the emergency room. My mother broke down just inside the door, clinging to Katie, whispering *thank you, thank you, thank you.*

"What am I doing here?" I asked in a hoarse voice.

The nurse stuck her head out the door, calling for someone to page the doctor, and rushed over to check the monitors. "How do you feel?"

Like I got hit by a truck. "Someone better tell me what's going on," I said, harsher than intended.

"You've been unconscious for two days." The nurse spoke calmly as she checked the IV bag. "We almost lost you twice."

"Almost lost me?" I looked to my mother with her wrinkled sweats and greasy hair, the old mascara trails running down her cheeks. *When?* My eyes lost focus, my thoughts turning inward. What were the things that almost killed me? Becoming the Weaver, probably, but what else? "I..."

Katie slipped past the nurse and placed her hand in mine. "We thought it might have been a reaction to the pills you took, but they pumped your stomach and everything." Her eyes bored into mine. She knew. "The doctor said your heart gave out a couple times this afternoon but righted itself somehow."

"It's all over now." I squeezed my sister's hand. It was only partially a lie. The Weaver was gone, our torment over, but there was so much more to think about. How long could I stay with my family? The Sandman never lasted long in the Day World, and he was stronger than I was, but I forced a weak smile for their sake. "I'm awake now. Everything can go back to normal."

"Normal?" my mother asked. "We're moving, and you're never leaving the house again. Either of you."

"Mom," Katie groaned.

She glared, her face tight. "You think I'm kidding?"

I blinked, forcing my smile to stay put. Even if it wouldn't be for long, I wanted to stay in our house, surrounded by a lifetime of memories. When I left them for the Nightmare Realm, my mother would be glad for them. I gripped the railing of the bed. Or maybe she was right—maybe moving was better. She deserved a fresh start away from the things that would remind her of her delusional, runaway daughter.

Already I felt the strain of this place. It clawed at me like a drowning man would claw at the surface of a lake. The bright fluorescent lights stung my exposed skin, and my pupils constricted against the faint sunlight filtering through the tinted window.

But no one noticed my arms. They couldn't see the power raging beneath my skin or comprehend my ability to bring a nightmare crashing into their slumber. It was my new secret, the hidden truth that mortals couldn't see, just as no one had noticed the Sandman's tattoos or his starlit eyes. Even then, before I knew the Sandman was real or who Ben really was, I wasn't completely human. I carried a piece of the Sandman inside me.

I still did.

Now I belonged to something darker though. It lurked beneath my skin, grinning as it spread. The idea should have terrified me. By my own hand, I created a different identity for myself. Something new. Something legends never spoke of. A Weaver. *The* Weaver. Ruler of all things that go bump in the night.

Yes, I should have been terrified, and a large part of me was.

But another part of me grinned back, and that terrified me more than anything else.

I flopped back on the flat pillow and slammed my eyes shut, ignoring the sudden rush of medical staff that flooded into the room. While they thought I slept for two days, I was awake.

Running.

Fighting.

Plotting.

Killing.

And I was exhausted.

Please come, I plead silently to the Sandman. *Please help me. I need you.*

Chapter Thirty-One

I ripped myself out of the crazed darkness, back to the Dream Realm. The force of my back hitting the ground knocked my teeth together. The sand reached up to cradle me, a few grains sneaking beneath my clothes. The binding was done. I had no way of knowing how long it would last, but it bought me some time. Enough to recharge and prepare. This wouldn't be like last time. I would check the binding every day and tighten it down.

Baku glared at me, shaking his head. Blood stained the fur around his mouth and paws.

"I know, Baku." I sighed. "I'll train her. She'll learn and take up her rightful place. A year—"

He huffed.

"Six months," I conceded. The nightmares needed someone to lead them before they tore each other apart. "Six months, and she'll be ready."

He gave a laugh-like grumble and walked away, disappearing through the barrier.

Nora wouldn't be ready in six months, nor would she be in a year. Or two, or three. Being trapped would only fuel the nightmares volatile behavior. The mindless ones wouldn't be much of a problem if she proved she wouldn't put up with their behavior, but the others... They would undoubtedly line up for an opportunity to crush her, either for her power or because they were angry she abandoned them. I had the knife now, but they wouldn't need a special weapon to kill the Weaver like everyone else did. They were her and she was them. It would be nothing more than severing a limb to them now that they knew without a doubt what a Weaver's death meant.

I shifted into a sitting position, setting my elbows on my knees, and my chin hit my chest. There was nothing I could do to protect her there. Not anymore. So, I closed my eyes and called on the sand that Nora's presence tainted, working it through my fingers while trying not to crumble.

It took nearly four hours to regain enough strength to Day Walk and another to track down Nora's location. Our cord was severed now, dead and dull, but I was connected to her in another way. As my opposite, I could feel her proximity, her feelings. The fear and confusion laced with a near giddiness, which brought on a stronger wave of fear.

I almost didn't recognize Katie staring at the wall in the waiting room of the hospital. Her hair was dark now, and the brightness gone from her expression. She clasped the leather bag I gave Nora in one hand. The other toyed with the strings, the knotted ends fraying under the constant touch. I tucked my hands in my back pockets. Did she believe now? It would be easier for Nora if she had someone on this side to confide in now that I... Now that she couldn't come to the beach without infecting it.

"Where's Nora?" I asked, cringing at the clear misery in my voice.

Katie looked me up and down slowly, recognition filtering in through her pain. "Ben, right?"

I nodded.

"I'll show you." Katie stood, her movements stiff and slow, and motioned me to follow her down the hall. "She's awake now."

I didn't trust myself to speak so I nodded again.

"Fair warning. She's a little off right now," she added. Her fingers curled around the bag, squeezing. "The doctors keep ordering more tests and someone is constantly in and out to poke at her, so I think she's just tired but..." She shrugged.

"Is she alone now?"

"Our mom and Paul are in the cafeteria, and Nora threw the last nurse out before she got halfway to the bed." She stopped outside of an open door. "This is her."

"Thanks." I gave her a wisp of a smile. "I'll take my chances."

"Good luck."

I waited for her to walk back down the hall and turn into the small seating area before slipping inside. A blue curtain was drawn across the room, but I shut the door anyway. I wiped sweaty hands on my pants and stepped around the cloth. Nora stood in front of a monitor with colored lines, pressing button after button with her charcoal fingers. A thin line of blood ran from the crease of her elbow where she must have ripped a needle out.

"What are you doing?" I asked.

She jumped and slammed a hand to her chest. "Sandman." Her shoulders squared. "I thought you were one of them."

"One of who?"

"The hospital staff. Or maybe Detective Bell. I overheard him talking to my mother in the hall about wanting to personally apologize, but I pretended to be asleep." She bit her lip, turning back to the screen. "Help me shut this thing off so I can sneak out of here."

My mouth ran dry. I moved slowly to her side and guided her hand away from the machine. She jerked against the touch, then squeezed my fingers, clinging to me while she trembled. "The Nightmare Realm is bound," I said. "It should last for a few months, at least, but I'll keep reinforcing it to give you more time."

"More time," she echoed and started jabbing the buttons with her other hand.

I watched her, unsure what to say or do. "You should make the most of it with your family. They need you."

"Well, *I* need *you*," she shouted.

My lips pressed into a frown. She was still Nora, my Nora, but for the first time, I was at a loss of how to react. How was I supposed to make this better for her? "You have me," I promised.

"I called for you." Her fingers stilled on the monitor. "You didn't come."

I closed my eyes and twisted my neck so that she couldn't see my face distort. If I heard her, I would have come the second I was able. But I couldn't. I never could again. "I won't be able to hear you anymore," I said gently.

A small, pained sound escaped her throat. "Now that I'm the Weaver, you mean? Now that we're enemies?" Her voice cracked.

"No." I spun and gripped her face, forcing her to look at me and me at her. My stomach clenched. "I will never be your enemy, Nora. I'll train you so when the time comes you're ready to go back, but you will never be anything but *you*. Forever. You will have me no matter what."

Tears brimmed in her green eyes, and she tugged me closer, burying her face into my shirt. "I'm scared."

My words were trapped beneath a heavy blanket of sorrow. I tried to stomp the feeling down, to move beyond it. There was already enough suffering inside her that she didn't need to confuse mine with her own, but it was a boulder. A mountain. Immovable. She was what everyone feared now—she should fear nothing. She needed to fear nothing if she was going to survive.

"It'll be okay, Nora," I finally managed. My fingers shook, and I ran a hand over her head. "We'll get through this."

Her tears soaked through my shirt, her back shaking with each sob. "I'm going to have to leave everyone, even you, and live in that horrible place for the rest of my miserable life."

I held her so tight she had to feel my heart pounding against her cheek. It was true she would have to leave this world, but she could learn to Day Walk to visit her family. I didn't know what it meant for us yet, but I didn't want to give her up. I wouldn't. No matter what it took, we would find a way for it to work. "You'll never have to leave me. I'm always yours, remember?"

She tilted her head back to study me, her chin trembling. I would have given anything to know what she was thinking in that moment. Disbelief raged across her face, then a softer flash of hope, followed by a tiny crease between her brows. She wanted to believe me, but I understood the hesitation. It seemed impossible to me right now too, but things would settle down. A path might open to us when our minds were clear. It had to. A block of ice formed in my gut, frozen guilt and shame. I drew a shuddering breath.

"And I'm always yours," she finally whispered.

I kissed her, tasting the salt from her tears, and let myself forget everything for that brief moment. Nora would be okay. We would be okay. Eventually. Six months would have to be enough time to become who she needed to be—no longer a mere Dream Keeper but a powerful new entity. A Lady of Nightmares with kindness in her heart and steel in her soul.

DARK CONSORT

Chapter One

Somewhere, a Dreamer screamed.

It was the type of scream that quickened the blood and curdled the stomach. I'd heard the same cry over and over from different mouths since I'd reopened the barrier keeping Dreamers from the Nightmare Realm. Baku was right to scoff at my plan to keep it intact until Nora returned to claim her title as Lady of Nightmares. Five months of pent-up energy had the nightmares tearing themselves apart; if I hadn't let Dreamers trickle back in to appease the ravenous creatures, there might be nothing left to claim.

Not that I would mind a major culling of nightmares, but Nora needed them. Rowan was gathering nightmares to her side from the safety of the Keep in a bid to become the next Weaver.

To do that, she would have to kill Nora. Ideally, Rowan would first have to go through thousands of nightmares pledging loyalty to Nora. Unfortunately, this wasn't a battle I could win on Nora's behalf—not if she wanted to earn the respect of her subjects. So there I was: constantly chasing down Dreamers in the Nightmare Realm before they died both here and in the Day World.

Shame tightened my chest as the scream cut through the air again. Baku and I froze and listened. This landscape was particularly fearsome, composed of roughly fifty acres of steep, sudden valleys and hills, as if an enormous creature had dragged its claws repeatedly across the ground. It threw sound in whatever direction it felt like. The scream came again from just below our current position only to bounce somewhere to the north. *Finally.* The source was close enough to catch the cry before it was carried away.

I threw my hood up, feeling the hum of my sand at my hip. "Ready?"

Baku flicked his elephant ears once in response.

White sound waves spiraled silently up the grassy hill toward us, the rings widening the closer they got. I pulled sand from my satchel to form a barrier against the unseen nightmare's attack, but before I could give it shape, the force of a coil whipped it from my palm. *Not good.* Without sand, there was little I could do to defend myself, let alone the Dreamer. The closest known shelter was nearly four hundred yards away, but we'd never make it to the small, rundown shack in time.

I dug my boots into the dirt and looked straight into the tunnel of sound waves. "This is going to hurt," I said through clenched teeth.

Baku widened his stance, the black and yellow brindle fur on the back of his neck rising in anticipation.

The waves slammed into us, and a high-pitched whine pierced my eardrums. My bones rattled. Baku lowered his head and pressed forward. His ears laid flat against the side of his head, and his tiger paws clawed up patches of grass with each step. The hunger I was so accustomed to seeing in his eyes had faded and was replaced with anger. At me. At the nightmares. He didn't speak, so I had no true way of knowing without reading his dreams, but he was a loyal friend, even after everything. Of course, I often left a trail of dead nightmares in my wake. Hunting them down was a thrill for Baku, but having his meals handed to him didn't hurt either.

The Dreamer bellowed again, his low tones a clear contrast to the nightmare's, and I shuddered. Movement caught my eye ahead. A young man in a white t-shirt and plaid boxers climbed from one of the deep gouges and scrambled toward the shack at the edge of the forest.

"No!" I shouted, but the landscape carried my voice off. We had to get to that shelter before the Dreamer did. There was no telling what sort of nightmare waited inside, but there was undoubtedly *something* there. There always was. I veered toward the man, but moving sideways through the rings was harder than heading straight toward them, and I slipped in my rush. My ribs banged into a rock jutting from the ground. Baku lunged after me, struggling not to be swept away himself.

A puff of black fur, no larger than a hedgehog, rolled up the hill. The nightmare had no visible legs, no eyes or mouth, but the sound waves twisting off its back moved to follow the Dreamer. I braced myself against the shifting noise as it proceeded with clear purpose.

The moment the waves released us, I was on my feet, gripping a handful of sand. I barreled forward while forming the sand into two ski poles. There was only one path that would let me reach the Dreamer in time. Without thinking, I took a deep breath and leapt back into the waves. My eyes instantly watered as the noise filled my head, but I pressed on, the dirt giving way beneath the pointed poles.

The puff of fur froze, and the sound waves slowed. I knew in that moment that it could see, with or without eyes. I felt its invisible gaze pierce me as hard as the rings beat my eardrums, but I kept moving. There was no other choice.

Then the sound cut off.

I blinked, too stunned to take another step, but Baku wasted no time sprinting toward the small creature. Saliva dripped from the base of his tusks. The puff let out a single small chirp, and the ground rumbled. I wasn't about to stay to find out why. I hurried after the Dreamer, catching up to him just before he reached the shelter. "Wake up," I snapped, ripping him back by the neck of his shirt. "You're having a nightmare. Wake up."

My hood had fallen back, and the man met my eyes for the briefest of moments. He relaxed for half a second, and I thought he would take my advice. Instead, he shoved me away with a punch to my chest. "Stay back," he demanded.

I raised my hands between us and tilted my head sideways to check on Baku. He was nearly at the puff now, but the ground trembled so hard the rickety shack behind the Dreamer swayed in time with the earth's movements. "Listen to me," I said slowly. "This isn't real."

He bent and snagged a fist-sized rock from the ground. "*Stay back.*"

I blew out a breath. Whose idea was it to let the Dreamers back in again? *Right.* I scowled. *Mine.* And now I had the privilege of traipsing all over the Nightmare Realm saving them when I should've been training Nora to do it herself—as useless as that had proven so far.

"Just wake up," I grumbled as I tossed a pinch of sand in his face.

The man swung out with the rock, nearly colliding with the side of my head before he vanished. The rock crashed to the ground, then bounced back up as a chorus of chirps raked the air. I winced, knowing without looking that there would be more screeching puffs behind me, and sprinted to Baku's side.

Nothing could've prepared me for what the nightmares were doing. Thousands of them scurried up to the first nightmare, creating a sea of black. Then, one-by-one, their fur fused together. They formed paws as big as Baku, legs wider than I was tall. Their creation grew quickly—too quickly. More puffs raced up the legs to form an elongated body, and my stomach dropped.

"We should go," I suggested.

Baku pranced closer to me but continued to eye the growing nightmare with a predatory gaze.

The body rounded, a tail stretching out behind it, and its head morphed with three rows of pointed teeth. A massive fisher cat stared down at us as the last few puffs rolled into place.

"Now." I stepped back. "We should go *now.*"

Baku shook his head.

There was little I wanted less than to fight this thing. It was mindless, driven by instinct, and would align itself with whomever exerted dominance. It was no threat to Nora if she didn't allow it to be one, and I hated to kill a potential ally. She would need everyone she could get when the time came.

"Baku, we can't—"

He charged the nightmare, mouth curled in a wicked smile.

I hesitated. Maybe the nightmare would run when we proved we weren't an easy target, or maybe Baku would give up when he realized I wasn't helping. Or not. Because Baku could handle himself. I groaned and reluctantly followed him.

When the nightmare saw Baku coming, it lunged toward him. I moved swiftly, throwing sand-made blades through the air. They glinted, their path true, and a single puff of fur fell with each slash. My jaw tightened. *Seriously, Baku*… I didn't have enough sand to take each one out individually.

The nightmare lifted a massive paw, and Baku slid beneath it on his side. Once under the beast, he climbed its hind leg as easily as a cat climbed a tree. His sharp claws shredded through the puffs, and they fell one after another. The fisher cat rose onto its back legs and threw itself over. My breath stuck in my throat. I rushed forward, sand at the ready. The fallen puffs popped like balloons beneath my boots. "Baku!"

The fisher cat lifted itself back onto all fours and swung its head in my direction. A collective hush from the puffs chilled my body. Then each one bellowed, sending countless sound waves in every direction. They knocked me flat on my back, and I struggled to breathe. My sand would only be swept away again if I tried to use it. Where had I put those ski poles?

An orange and black blur shot across the nightmare's snout and dove between its teeth. "Baku, you idiot," I hissed. I was nearly back on my feet when the sound came to a sudden stop. The smaller balls tumbled down on each other in one giant mound with Baku sitting at the top, shoveling them into his mouth with his trunk. The chorus of chirps sounded across the landscape, both far and near, as they began to reform. I took a heaping mound of sand from my satchel and flung it at the base of the pile. Baku leapt out of the way and circled to my side. The fisher cat was forming yet again when I called on the sand's magic to mimic the puffs' own cry. I compressed the sound into one wave that blasted through the entire mass.

Black fur wove gently back and forth in the air around us and settled in the creases of my clothing, my hair, my bag. My head rang. I rubbed the soft spot in front of my raw ears and my fingertips came away sticky with blood. "That was unnecessary." I could barely hear my own voice. My shoulders hunched, and I squeezed my eyes shut for a moment. "They could've proved useful to Nora."

Baku lifted a flattened puff with his trunk and stuck it slowly, defiantly, into his mouth.

"Fine," I said with a sigh. "I'm going home. Are you coming with me?"

He scooped up another trunk-full of dead puffs, slid them into my open satchel, and nodded with an amused glint in his eyes.

"Baku!" I stared at the half-deflated nightmares, my mouth open. "You're finishing these before we get back to the beach."

His only answer was a swish of his cow tail as he walked away.

I chuckled and followed him, ignoring the heat leeching through my satchel. Baku reached in and grabbed one after another as we made our way through the Nightmare Realm, and I tried not to shudder.

The only cries we heard on the way back to the Dream Realm were inhuman. At one point, something resembling a giant cabbage bounced past us, followed by what looked like a radioactive rabbit, but neither entity spared us a glance. Baku watched them, popping another puff as if it was popcorn.

"Please tell me they're almost gone." I peeked inside my bag to find it empty. *Thank the stars.* Baku's ears perked up and the fur rose on the back of his neck. "Relax. I'm sure you'll find something else to—"

My magic snapped against my chest like a rubber band, reaching out for sand I didn't have. Something was wrong. Very wrong. I raced to the barrier of the Dream Realm with Baku at my side. Barbed grass bit at my boots and pants, but Baku didn't seem to notice it beneath his tiger paws. What I saw waiting for me turned me to ice.

A half-emaciated giant stood at the edge of the Dream Realm wearing nothing but black pants with thick chains wrapped around his torso. Pieces of orange flesh had rotted away, leaving putrid wounds and exposed bones. He hoisted a five-foot sledgehammer, nearly half his size, over his bald head and swung.

"No!" I screamed as it sailed toward the barrier.

How did he know it was there? Intelligent nightmares had ways of tracking the Dream Realm even though it reflected the surrounding nightmare landscape, and sure, some of the others stumbled upon it occasionally, but giants were far from smart.

The hammer smashed into the barrier. Blue light burst at the impact and webbed over the dome.

"You will pay," came a tiny voice. Then another and another. Hundreds of them, saying the same thing, their voices overlapping until I could barely make out individual words.

"Leave us be."

Then I saw them. Hundreds of spotted red mushrooms with knobby arms and legs scurried through the tall grass at my feet. The grass parted for them, keeping its razor-sharp barbs from impaling the small nightmares. Beyond them, the giant lifted his hammer again.

Absolutely not.

I would not allow these creatures to destroy my realm. My *home*. What I was doing wasn't an act of war—it was an act of preservation for everyone involved. They needed the Dreamers' fear, but I needed the Dreamers to stay alive. And Nora needed a realm that wasn't imploding. There would be no fight between her nightmares and myself.

But that was the problem—they weren't Nora's yet. Right now, they were Rowan's. And Rowan… She *did* mean war, though this was the first time she took an offensive position against me.

I called on the sand within the barrier. It burst from within, using the place weakened by the giant's attack, and formed a spear the second it was clear. The tip pierced the giant between the eyes, and he fell backward, landing with a resounding boom.

The mushrooms fell silent at the sight of their dead comrade, and I flicked a look at Baku to see if he wanted the kill, but his intense gaze was fixed on the giant. So I let the sand rain down. Tiny squeals mixed with the clink of metallic barbs as the grass sought to protect itself from the acidic raindrops. The attack didn't stop until every blade of grass before me fizzled away.

I walked further down to where the grass was still alive, happy to leave the steaming pile of liquefied nightmares behind. Baku trotted over to the giant's corpse like it was a Thanksgiving feast. I shook my head and crossed back into the Dream Realm. With a flick of my hand, I sent sand in every direction to make sure nothing got inside, then set to work repairing the gaping hole in the ceiling.

The longer I wove my magic, the more my hands shook. It wasn't exhaustion—I had more than enough power now—but fury. And fear. What would Nora be walking into in three weeks? How many more attacks would Rowan send to my doorstep before then? Rowan had used Nora to kill the Weaver; now all she had to do was use her growing number of followers to bring Nora to her doorstep, and the realm would be hers. Rowan had to know the time for Nora's return was close. Things were only going to get worse from here, but I had no idea how to tell Nora that.

Baku waltzed through the barrier with a piece of the giant dangling from his mouth. As he chewed, he dipped his trunk down and wrote in the sand. When he was finished, he shoved a glob of muscle between his lips and sauntered away.

Six.

The word stared up at me. *Six.* The number of months I promised before Nora returned from the Day World, and time was nearly up. I ran the toe of my boot through Baku's note. I didn't need the reminder. Every time I saw Nora with her golden eyes and stained hands, it was glaringly obvious I was on the cusp of losing her.

Once a week I was trapped in a light blue room, suffocating from the scent of eucalyptus-mint. The candle in my therapist's office was supposed to relieve stress, as was the rest of the décor: a brown, buttery leather sofa, ceiling-high windows that let in just the right amount of sunlight, and a barely audible soundtrack of crashing waves to top it all off. None of it negated the fact that I couldn't leave until the minute hand hit twelve.

That was my life now. *Waiting*. Waiting and suffering. I had to run mental rings around everyone in my life, and my body was absolutely finished with the Day World. But just like I was stuck in therapy for an hour, I was stuck in this world for another three weeks.

I glanced at my watch, the silver band stark against the black stain of the Weaver's magic on my skin. *My* magic. Of course, the therapist couldn't see the glove-like markings creeping toward my elbows, the golden veins throbbing beneath, or the gold that swallowed the green in my irises. Not that she would know what to make of it if she could.

Colleen sat in a matching chair, quietly tapping her pen against her knee. "Nora," she said gently. Always gently. Always kind. "You've been coming to see me for a little over five months now, and you've barely said two words."

I slid my sunglasses up my nose, the smallest bit of light too much for my new eyes to handle, and crossed my arms. It wasn't that I didn't want to talk about what happened, but how could I? *Well, you see, Colleen, the Nightmare Lord killed my friends because the Sandman stashed a secret in my dreams. Then I killed him, which means I get to spend the rest of eternity weaving horrible new creatures into existence in his place. Really, it's all Rowan's fault though. She's a nightmare with branch-like wings and a crown of raven beaks that can zap you into oblivion with a single touch. Or, as I like to think of her, she's a double-crossing demon with an army of moaning heathens and an angry, pointy-beaked sidekick, Kail. Anyway, they set me up with this magical knife…* Ugh. It sounded crazy even to me.

So, though I had a lot to say, sweet Colleen with her perfectly curled grey hair and grandma sweaters wouldn't get a single secret from me. This, the coming here, it was for my mother. Because no matter how strained our relationship became, the least I could do was try until the day I returned to the Nightmare Realm.

"This won't work if you aren't willing to talk to me," Colleen said.

I shrugged one shoulder and glanced at my watch again. Five

more minutes.

She sighed and shut her notebook. "Will you at least remove the sunglasses?"

"Why?" I asked, my voice dripping with suspicion. Wearing the glasses got me a few too many strange looks, so I tried not to wear them, but some days I couldn't help it. It just so happened that driving twenty minutes to the therapist's office in the middle of the afternoon exceeded my limits, especially with the pain getting worse each day.

"You've worn them for our last three meetings, and I want to make sure you're all right."

All right. When was the last time I had been all right? Before the Weaver went on a crazed killing spree? Before I met the Sandman? Did a time even exist before him? It felt like another lifetime, like I was another person. I shifted uncomfortably on the couch. I *was* a different person.

"I'm not hiding black eyes or anything, if that's what you're worried about." It certainly felt like I took a couple punches straight to the orbital area though. Actually, that would have been preferable, since that pain would only be temporary.

"I didn't mean to imply that you were." Colleen scooted forward in her chair and leaned toward me, smelling of peppermint. "Have you been crying?"

I laughed, the sound hollow and bitter. I hadn't cried since that day in the hospital.

"Did you fight with your boyfriend?" she further pried.

I took a deep breath and sat up straighter, removing the dark glasses. The sunlight immediately dried my eyes and each blink felt like sandpaper, but I refused to let myself shrink away from the growing discomfort of the Day World. Even the air hurt. It felt too dense against my skin and the universe itself seemed to shove and tug simultaneously in an attempt to be rid of me. My body had grown accustomed to the sharp pain of it all, leaving me with a constant dull ache.

"Ben and I are fine," I assured her.

She set her fingertips on my kneecap, and I fought the urge to slap them away. The pressure felt as if it would crush my leg, though I knew she was barely making contact. "Nora, a lot happened this summer."

"I'm aware." I scratched at the back of my hand, but of course the black stain didn't budge. "I was there."

"I want to help you," she said, almost pleading.

A soft click sounded from the timer on her desk. I forced a smile and settled the glasses back on my face. "Time's up, Colleen. Maybe next week."

"Actually, Nora, I think this will be our last session."

"What?" I froze, halfway off the sofa. "But I—"

"You don't want to be here." She stood and adjusted her cardigan. "I can give your hour to someone who does."

"My mother—"

She raised her hands in surrender. "If you need me to tell her, I will. She can call me tomorrow."

"No, no. Listen, just give me two more appointments, okay? That's it." I held two fingers up. "Two tiny little hours."

"Why two?" she asked with a hint of curiosity.

Because after that I'll be gone. "Let me get through Thanksgiving without letting her down. You can ruin Christmas instead."

"Not coming to therapy isn't going to ruin anything, Nora." Her expression softened. "It's not for everyone, and that's perfectly okay."

Yes, it was okay, but the problem wasn't that therapy wasn't for me. Someone like Colleen would've been a great help if my problem five years ago had truly been my parents' divorce. I stood and slung my bag over my shoulder. "If I promise to talk next Friday, will you let me come back?"

Colleen studied me for a moment, and just when I expected her to say no, she nodded. I let out a breath and grabbed a peppermint candy from the bowl on her desk. Anything to temporarily mask the permanent taste of sulfur that now lived in the back of my throat.

"Thanks. See you then," I called and bolted for the exit.

Outside, the sun was warm, the air cool, and I shivered against the extra jolt of pain the small breeze inflicted. I gave the street a quick visual sweep to ease my paranoia. All day, it felt like someone was watching me, but I was ninety percent convinced the feeling was only caused by my ever-growing magic. Either way, the quiet, residential street seemed safe enough. Nothing rustled in the neighbors' hedges or peeked up from cement storm drains.

Not that I needed to worry when the Dream Lord had my back.

The Sandman leaned against the carved stone railing outside Colleen's home office. My heart attempted to spring from my chest as it did every week, every day, every minute that I saw him. His dark t-shirt pulled against his lean muscles, and the midnight blue and silver flecks tattooed on his arms shone weakly in the sunlight. He turned at the sound of the shutting door, and a smile lit his entire face. My pain faded away, all the tension pouring from my limbs. I took the steps two at a time and flung my arms around his neck. He felt warm and sure against me. The scent of lilacs and something distinctly *him* was intoxicating. I closed my eyes and leaned into his embrace.

"Hi," he said. His breath was warm on my ear.

I smiled into the crook of his neck. "Hi."

"Ready to go?"

"More than ready." I tugged him toward my car, parked on the side of the road, but he didn't budge. "Aren't you coming?"

His violet eyes roamed my face as if he were seeing me for the first time. Or the last. It shook me to the core right there on the sidewalk. A couple walking their dog skirted around us, the woman accidentally nudging me with her shoulder, but I stood firm. I'd learned his expressions quickly over the last few months, but this one was the worst because I still wasn't sure what it meant.

"What's wrong?" I asked in a hoarse whisper. My mind raced over all the problems in the Nightmare Realm he'd brought up recently. We'd agreed on solutions. Did they not work? Was it something new? Something big? It had to be big—the look he gave me almost guaranteed it.

The Sandman's hand came up to cup my face, his thumb skimming my bottom lip. "Maybe we should take the day off from training and do something together."

"Skip training?" I jerked my head back. Sometimes I wondered who pushed harder for training, me or him. He knew the true situation in the Nightmare Realm. Not only *knew*. He saw it while I'd only heard second-hand. New ruler or not, the nightmares would eat me alive over there. Probably literally. "I don't understand," I continued. "Did something happen?"

His eyes flickered with concern, and he pulled me closer, leaning down. Our lips met. The kiss was soft, though anything but careful. It was a kiss of reverence and passion. Sweet. Desperate. I lost myself in the taste of him for the briefest of moments. In the feel of him, of being far away from all life's problems. Right then, it was just me and the Sandman. Like it used to be. But it was a lie—things would never again be like before.

I sighed, easing away so our lips were an inch apart, and tugged at one of his soft brown curls. "You're not telling me something."

"I'm just glad to see you." He nudged my nose with his. "And we've been working so hard."

"Mhm." I didn't believe that for a minute. Our training had turned into make-out sessions more than once, but we'd never skipped one in favor of the other. I really wanted to take him up on it, but time was short, and I wasn't where I needed to be as a fighter yet. "I have to be home for dinner, so we should probably get going."

He winced, and I instantly wished I'd agreed instead. Maybe he really did want to spend time together without all… *this.* I glanced at the black staining my arms, the gold veins throbbing beneath the skin, and heat crept over my face. Deep down, I wanted a day of normalcy too.

But before I could say so, the Sandman walked around my car and opened the door for me.

The hour-long drive out of downtown Cedarbrook was a silent one. The Sandman chewed the inside of his cheek instead of briefing me on the Nightmare Realm, which only made me more curious. I knew whatever was on his mind would come out when he was ready, but that didn't make the wait any easier. Especially when I had a sinking feeling it involved nightmares.

We'd already agreed to let the Dreamers back in despite the risks of me not being there to keep the peace. If it wasn't enough, what else could we do, short of my going back early? Not that three weeks was going to do much good. I scowled out the windshield and cranked the radio to fill the booming silence as we followed the now-familiar roads far away from my mother's network of spies.

Nora skipped therapy today.

Nora jaywalked.

Nora did this. Nora did that.

I tightened my grip on the steering wheel. Leaving my family on a good note was easier said than done, but spending time with the Sandman helped. Going on a *date* with *Ben* gave my mother the impression I was trying to move forward, which cut her constant complaints about not having my GED in half. Sure, I promised I would get it, but only to earn her forgiveness for dropping out of high school. That and the therapy. I had read through a study guide, which apparently didn't count, but I doubted nightmares cared about their Lady's formal education. All they cared about was fear. Theirs. Mine. Dreamers'. Who had the most and who had the least.

I eased the car into the small dirt parking lot near a walking trail and cut the engine. The Sandman stared, unseeing, out the window.

"We can go back," I offered. "Maybe see a movie?"

He pressed his eyes shut and shook his head. "No. You were right. We only have a few more weeks."

"Let's make a deal." I grinned. "If I knock you off your feet first, we leave and do something fun."

Amusement glimmered in his starlit eyes, though not quite as brightly as I'd hoped. "And if I knock you down first?"

I leaned across the car to whisper in his ear. "Winner's choice."

I stole a quick peck on his mouth and darted from the car. The swell of his laughter brushed through my mind but quickly disappeared. Still, that his emotional control slipped even for a second widened my smile. I raced up the trail, jumping over branches, stones, and mud. I didn't have to look to know he was behind me. That's where he stayed until we reached our usual training spot.

At least one good thing came from our training: I could now run and run without getting breathless. I was fast too. Everything else on the other hand… I slowed to a stop in the middle of our clearing. Thick pines circled the oblong patch of overgrown grass, shielding us from the eyes of anyone hiking nearby. Our own little oasis, where I got my butt kicked over and over and over. The Sandman might've taught me how to throw a knife and dodge a punch, but I would never be good enough to beat nightmares like Rowan and Kail if I didn't learn how to use the magic foisted onto me. Magic the Sandman admittedly had no idea how to harness.

"Do you want to warm up first?" the Sandman asked.

It was doubtful any nightmare would give me the chance to stretch, so instead of answering, I bent and swung my leg out to knock the backs of his knees. Despite the lack of warning, he was ready for me and jumped aside. I leapt toward him. He swung out. The moves felt mechanical, rehearsed. Because they were. The same drill on repeat for five months, and I still couldn't figure out how to change it. To be better. To spot an opening and know how to take it in the blink of an eye.

I ducked beneath the Sandman's arm, pivoted, and shoved my palms against his chest. He flew to the ground, his head smacking against the dirt. I blinked down at him in shock. When I suggested knocking him down first, I hadn't believed I would win. I never won. It was an unspoken rule that he never went easy on me, no matter how much it hurt—the nightmares certainly wouldn't. And that was most definitely not him *letting* me get one over on him.

"What's going on with you?" I asked.

He sat up and rubbed the back of his head. "I suppose I'm feeling a little guilty today."

Uh-oh. "Guilty about what?"

The Sandman leaned forward and rested his elbows on his knees. "Baku and I destroyed a nightmare that could've been useful to you."

"So?" *This again?* I wiped the sweat from my forehead. "They aren't exactly in short supply, and I'm sure you had a good reason. I can make more in a few weeks anyway."

"I think—" He winced.

I tensed at the realization of where this was all headed. "If you're going to say a few weeks isn't long enough, the answer is no. We aren't delaying anything."

"It's chaos there, Nora. Anarchy. And Rowan—"

"I don't care," I shouted, then reigned my anger in. "The *only* thing keeping me together right now is that this is almost over. The physical pain, dealing with my family, all of it. I'm tired of standing at the edge of goodbye. The bandage needs to be ripped off so I can learn to be whatever it is I need to be."

He raked a hand through his hair, and a spark of dread flickered inside me. *His* dread. I hated him for it. For letting me know exactly how afraid he was when I was already terrified enough. And I hated that I couldn't hide my feelings. No matter how much I practiced, it was never enough to keep him from knowing everything through our emotional connection as Night World rulers.

"I know," he said quietly. "Don't be angry. I'm just worried about you."

"Then get up and fight me," I growled. Before he had the chance, pain flared in my back, and I let out a soft cry. It felt as if two daggers scraped against my spine. Hateful eyes, hungry and dangerous, tore into me like I was nothing more than fog.

"What is it?" The Sandman was on his feet, his hands on my arms. I couldn't answer. "Nora? What happened?"

"You don't feel it?" I asked, the words barely a breath.

His brow furrowed. "I feel *you*."

"I think someone's watching us."

He removed the pouch of sand from beneath his shirt and turned it upside down while his eyes narrowed, glancing at the edges of the clearing. The sand spread all around us and shot straight out at the trees. A moment later, he let out a breath. "There's nothing here that shouldn't be."

I rolled my shoulders, and the pain lessened. "The stress must be getting to me," I lied. I felt it. Something was out there.

"Hang on a little longer, okay?" He kissed my forehead. "Come on. Let's get out of here."

"But—"

"You won," he said with an encouraging smile.

My phone rang, and I jumped straight into the air. "Sorry. One second." I skipped to my bag, hanging from a low branch, and dug the cell out with shaking hands. *Mom.* My nose wrinkled in disgust. What did she want?

"Hello?" I answered.

"Nora, where are you?" Someone laughed in the background. "Are you on your way home?"

"Not yet." I put my free hand on my hip and stretched my side.

"Well, you need to be."

"Why?"

"I expect you back in half an hour," she said and hung up before I could argue.

I squeezed the phone hard to keep myself from chucking it into the woods. *A half hour.* It was impossible. Now I would have to hear about being late all night. The sinister grin lurking inside me surfaced, a darkness clouding my mind, as it had nearly every day since I woke up in the hospital. Every time my reactions were a little less *Nora* and a little more angry and irrational—a little more… something else. It lured me toward an edge that I wasn't sure was possible to come back from. I pushed back at it, clawing desperately for my normal. It was like standing on ice, hearing it crack, watching the pieces around me splinter, and knowing that one wrong breath was all it would take to plunge me to my death. So I held my breath and waited for the grin to go away, for winter to refreeze the ground beneath my feet. I closed my eyes and searched for bright white snow, but inside my head, it all seemed dark. So, so dark.

The Sandman brushed the hair from the back of my neck and placed a soft kiss on the skin there. "You're okay, Nora."

"Okay?" The word came out strained, and the ice gave out. I shoved the phone back in my purse and wrapped the strap around my hand. "Sure. I'm okay. I only have to learn how to keep myself alive in three weeks when the last five months have proved I'm incapable. It'll be fine. I'll just be the Lady of Nightmares who relies on the Lord of Dreams for the rest of eternity. The nightmares will *love* that."

"I didn't mean—"

"And stop reading my emotions," I snapped.

His jaw muscle twitched. "You know I can't help it."

"Whatever." I stormed back down the path to the parking lot.

"Nora, wait," the Sandman called. "I'm sorry."

I waved a hand through the air without turning around or breaking stride. He was sorry. *Sorry, sorry, sorry.* I'd heard it from him a million times, but it didn't change anything. Just like my being sorry wouldn't turn back time and make me listen to his warning about the balance between our worlds being maintained. I wrenched the car door open and hurled my bag into the passenger seat. *Sorry* was a hollow word, and regrets helped no one. I threw myself behind the wheel, pounded my palms on the steering wheel, and screamed.

The grin darkened, showing its cutting edges.

I jerked back and took a breath. Then another and another until my heart settled in my chest. The cloud lifted but the grin remained, a watermark on my vision, a living scar. It stayed longer and longer these days. My body trembled. *Go away. Please, please, go away.* But it didn't. I jammed the keys into the ignition and peeled out of the small parking lot for home.

Chapter Three

"Nora!" My mother bounced off the couch the moment I stepped through the door. She'd gained weight recently, her cheeks fuller from all the stress-eating, and her hair seemed to be a little greyer every day. "What took you so long? You were supposed to be back a half-hour ago."

I set my purse down on the console table just inside the door and took a deep breath. Be calm, I reminded myself. Be nice. "Ben and I were halfway up a mountain when you called," I said as neutrally as possible.

Her eyes narrowed. "I'm not sure how I feel about you disappearing like that with a boy you won't invite over to meet your family."

"You've met him."

"We say hello to each other when he comes knocking on the door, Nora. I hardly think that counts."

"Colleen thinks it's a good idea," I lied with a shrug.

My mother grunted, clearly unhappy, but unwilling to go against my therapist. "Tell someone next time you decide to go hiking. I want the name of the trail and the time you think you'll be home in case anything happens to you."

Hello to you too, Mother. I chewed the corner of my lip and nodded. I wasn't going to truthfully divulge my entire itinerary, but I wasn't going to argue with her either. "So why did I have to rush home?"

As if on cue, the back-patio door slid open. "You're back!" Katie rushed in from the backyard and maneuvered around the counter. "I thought I heard a car pull up."

My sister's hair was still dyed darker than her natural color, her blond roots barely visible. Instead of the heavy makeup she wore before the Weaver tortured her or the bare face she wore after, her eyes were carefully lined, accented with perfectly blended shadow, and her lips coated in a nude gloss. She looked amazing and so unlike herself that I found myself unable to return her smile.

I cleared my throat. "Yep."

"Took you long enough." She gave me a quick hug that I didn't return. And was that…? *Pot.* She reeked of it. How did our mother not notice? Sure, my sister was hiding it behind a picture-perfect exterior, but I was about to get high just standing next to her. We sat through roughly twenty million *no recreational drug use* speeches, yet this was suddenly fine? But when I didn't mention the Sandman for years, I was still treated like a grenade.

"Come on," Katie said brightly. "I want you to meet someone."

"What are you doing home? Don't you have classes next week?" I asked, holding my breath against the strong odor.

Katie laughed. "Is that the first thing you have to say after not seeing me for three months? A 'Welcome home! I missed you!' would be nice."

"Oh, sister dearest, how I missed you," I said in a flat voice, but her words stung. Was I turning into my mother? *No.* I was turning into an evil overlord. *Some say potato.*

She *tsked* and motioned for me to follow her into the backyard. I hesitated, glancing at my mother for a clue about who was out there, but she was immersed in folding a mound of laundry that had taken over our couch. So, head bent with exhaustion and an utter lack of interest, I joined Katie on the cement patio. She had practically bolted out of Cedarbrook after I was released from the hospital. I could count the number of times she called home on one hand, and now she showed up a week early with someone for us to meet? I watched her carefully. If I didn't know better, I might think she was sleepwalking again instead of being wide awake.

Paul stood in front of the grill with a beer in one hand. He glanced up when he saw me and smiled. I was grateful my mother married him after she divorced my father, if not for how he treated me before, then definitely for how he did after. *The same.*

"I put a burger on for you in case you're hungry."

"Thanks." I folded my arms over my aching stomach. No matter how much I ate, the hunger never left these days. "I am."

"Nora, this is Kellan." Katie clung to a boy with shaggy

brown hair, bloodshot eyes, and a cartoon character on his t-shirt. "Kellan, Nora."

"Hey," he said slowly, dragging out the word. "Nice sunglasses."

My mouth opened, but I wasn't sure what to say so I let the sound of sizzling meat fill the silence. Katie glared at me, imploring me with wide eyes to say something, anything, but I had nothing. A girl can only process so many surprises at once.

Kellan gave a low, uncomfortable chuckle followed by a lopsided grin.

"This is Katie's boyfriend," Paul supplied.

"I thought you were still dating Jen," I blurted.

Katie's eyes shot daggers at me. "She wanted something serious. I wanted… fun. You're only a college freshman once, right?"

Kellan laughed again. Katie and I turned to scowl at him in unison, but he was ignoring us completely in favor of his phone. I gave Katie a withering look and pointed at him. "*That's* what you call fun?"

She grimaced and gripped Kellan's arm. "Let's go set the table."

I gaped openly at them as they walked back to the kitchen. It was like watching a semi barrel down a one-way street at rush hour in the wrong direction, and I couldn't look away. "Did you know she was coming home early?" I asked Paul.

He took a long swig of beer. "Last I heard, she wouldn't be here until next weekend."

"Did I miss the memo that she was bringing someone with her?"

"Nope." He flipped the burgers. "But try to be nice, huh?

Your sister's dealing with things in her own way."

I wasn't sure she was *dealing* with anything. More like avoiding it. With drugs and… Kellan. I glared through the kitchen window where my mother chatted brightly with them and felt myself deflate. That's what she wanted from me—to pretend. To go to therapy, get whatever was troubling me off my chest, and come home with an easy spirit. But I tried doing that for years, and she never talked to me like she was talking to Katie now.

"You can bring Ben over for dinner too, you know." Paul scooped the burgers onto a plate. "We'd like to get to know him."

"Right," I said under my breath. Like I would bring the Sandman here after everything my mother did to make me forget him. Though I supposed if I *had* forgotten him, I wouldn't be in my current predicament. The dark grin prickled inside me. *Yes, you would*, it seemed to say. And it was right. Even if I forgot, I still would've been the Dream Keeper. The Weaver still would've come for me. Still would've taken Katie, killed my boss, my friends, my father—

"Coming, kiddo?" Paul asked, sliding the back door open with his foot. I nodded and followed him into the kitchen, where he leaned over to kiss my mother on top of the head. "Everybody hungry?"

"You know it," Kellan said, followed by another dull laugh.

The table was set with paper plates and cans of soda, a ring of condensation building on the plastic tablecloth around each one. Condiments, potato salad, and corn on the cob waited in the center of the table, while the buns and burger fixings lined the counter. Everyone except me crowded around the steaming meat. My stomach rumbled but I wasn't going to fight my way to the food, brushing against everyone with my aching skin.

"I'm going to wash up first," I said, though I doubted any of them were listening. I removed my sunglasses to avoid my mother's ire. I slipped into the downstairs bathroom and splashed water on my face, careful to avoid the reflection of a girl half-there. A girl that was only half a girl at all, really. I was a creature now—one that only appeared human on the outside. Behind my now-gold eyes laid molten veins and a creeping darkness brimming with untold magic. If a nightmare managed to kill me, would I become human again? Would I regain my green eyes? Or would I rot as I was? Was the original Weaver slowly decomposing? Or was he still sprawled out on the floor of the Keep where I last saw him like some sort of blood-soaked mannequin? I retched into the sink at the thought.

"Are you pregnant?" Katie whispered from the doorway.

"What?" I snagged a washcloth from the towel rack and dried my face. "No. Are *you*?"

"I'm not the one puking."

I snorted. "Right, because that's the only reason someone would be sick."

"Well, when you pair it with your attitude lately and—"

"*My* attitude? What do you know about my attitude? You haven't talked to me since you moved out." I forced my voice to stay low to avoid attracting the others, though I wanted to scream. "I walked through hell to save you but that wasn't enough, was it? No. *You* got to come back from that cave and pretend it never happened. *I* had to go back and make sure the Weaver never bothered us again. Did you ever once think to ask me what I had to do to accomplish that? Do you even care?"

"Shut up," she hissed. "You sound as crazy as Mom thinks you are."

"Maybe I am. But then so are you. You *saw*—"

"I didn't see anything. It was just a dream," she snapped.

"Keep telling yourself that." I tossed the washcloth onto the edge of the sink and moved to push past Katie, but she stepped forward, obstructing my way. "What, Katie?"

"Stop it. You have to move forward. Dwelling on what happened won't change anything. It's all in the past."

"Maybe it's in *your* past." I knew I should stop talking, should lower my voice, but the seal was broken. Each word that escaped was louder than the last. "Denying the truth will change just as much as my dwelling on it. And for the record, there is no moving on for me so why don't you—"

"Nora!" My mother forcefully pushed her way in between us, blocking me inside the bathroom and Katie in the hall. "What's wrong with you, talking to your sister like that?"

"Me?" I laughed bitterly. "What's wrong with *me*? I don't know, Mother. Why don't you drag me to a few more doctors to find out? It worked so well last time."

She gasped, eyes wide. "That's enough."

"No. It was enough when I was twelve." I shoved her arm out of the way and shot a look at my sister. "I thought someone would finally have my back."

"Go to your room." My mother's cheeks were a vibrant shade of red. "Now."

A smirk not my own played on my lips. "Gladly."

I ran to the stairs, but halfway up, Katie called out again, her voice angry yet hesitant. "Nora—"

"You're a coward," I said without turning around.

Kellan's slow laugh echoed in my ears. "Your sister's a savage."

I whirled around mid-step and leaned over the banister looking into the kitchen. "Excuse me?"

Paul's chair scraped the kitchen floor, and he stared at me, confused. "Go cool off."

I bit my tongue and stormed to my room, slamming the door. The string of tiny lights above my bed swayed from the force. I reached above the headboard and ripped them down before falling face first onto the mattress. I hated those lights. Hated them for reminding me every night of the one place I longed for more than any other. For burning my eyes with their taunting glow.

"Sandman." I sobbed angrily into the pillow. "Help me sleep."

But I knew he couldn't hear me. Not since I became the dark to his light.

I let out a long, hard breath and gave myself to the black place that found me every night. It pulled me under just as fast as the Sandman ever had—faster. The grin widened until it felt as if it swallowed me whole, and I opened my eyes to the dark abyss I'd grown accustomed to. At least here my body hurt less for an hour or two, until my mind jerked me awake. I closed my eyes and welcomed the oblivion.

I wasn't sure how long I floated in darkness before light passed in front of my eyelids. The quiet buzz of the emptiness suddenly roared as awareness crept through me, and I cracked my eyes open. Only, I wasn't awake, or, if I was, my body hadn't followed. It felt like waking from anesthesia, but the process halted right before consciousness took hold. This place was nowhere—it was nothing. Nothing except for a white fissure scarring the void. I pressed my eyes shut and opened them again, expecting it to disappear, but the crack didn't move. Nor did it bother my eyes. My body inched forward of its own accord until I stood right in front of it.

A shadow passed on the other side of the uneven opening. My breath hitched, panic bubbling beneath my skin. Maybe it was better to close my eyes and drift away again. But it seemed I was no longer in control of myself. Up close, the fissure was as wide as a window in some places, as narrow as my head in others, which I discovered when I pressed my face into the light. Grey and white layers of stone twisted and turned down a long passageway. The view moved as if I walked the path myself, but my feet were firmly planted. A ragged breath drifted from the scene, followed by a small, pained groan.

"Go," a voice called from behind. I threw a quick glance over my shoulder, but only the nothingness greeted me. "She's coming. We need to *go*."

The familiar voice struck a chord. *Sandman*? What the hell was going on? The scene moved up and down, and I realized I was looking through someone else's eyes. I held my breath, too afraid that if I blinked I would miss something important. This *whole thing* felt important on some instinctual level. My vision tilted and jerked as the person slammed into a wall, then slid down.

A pair of black boots shuffled forward. Knees slammed down on the hard stone. Tattooed arms reached out and shook the person. "Come on." The Sandman tapped the side of my vision and leaned closer. His violet eyes were vivid, the pupils blown wide. Dirt was smeared across his cheeks and chin, and blood trickled from somewhere near his temple. "Stay with me."

"I'm fine." The words sounded anything but fine. They sounded like the man's last. Weak. Broken.

A bloodied arm rose, trembling, to push the Sandman away, and my hands flew to my mouth. Black threads glimmering with gold shone on the man's wrist. *The Weaver.* The Sandman helped him to his feet, then crouched and ran around the next bend. My view clouded, then righted itself, moving in time with the Weaver's unsteady steps.

This was the Weaver's point-of-view. His memory. Was the Weaver so ingrained in the magic that it remembered too? A sour, metallic taste coated my tongue. Knowing some of the things the Weaver had done, I didn't think I could stomach seeing more. And what did it mean? The Sandman said he and the Weaver were friends once, but seeing the look of true fear on his face, the unfiltered terror that the Weaver wouldn't make it… With their combined power, it didn't make sense for them to run from anything.

The fissure snapped shut in my face, and I stumbled back. Icy pinpricks dotted my skin. Everything about this was wrong—the memory, what the memory held. Was it real? A fabrication? I tripped over my own feet, and the world spiraled around me.

Waking was like dropping from the top of a roller coaster, only my cart wasn't connected to the tracks. My heart spasmed. I couldn't breathe. I was weightless, floating, and yet tethered to the instrument of my own death. Then I was suddenly on my bed. Safe. The familiar ache crept back into my bones, and my brain scrambled to reach that semi-peaceful place again. Though after what I saw, I wasn't sure peaceful was the right word. The Sandman and the Weaver were… I scowled. They were what? It all made perfect sense there, but now it seemed out of reach. Like a dream that ceased to exist upon waking. *A dream.* I always remembered mine before. Now, it felt like another person had seen the Weaver's memory. If that's what it was. Maybe I *was* dreaming. I groaned into the pillow.

Just what I needed. More problems and confusion.

My mother's laugh clawed through my door. The soft hum of other voices mingled with it, and I flipped onto my back. Dusk filtered orange light into my room through the open window. Had it been open when I fell asleep? It must have been—I would've woken up if anyone came in. My mother, most likely, had aired the room while I was out, probably as she searched for something incriminating.

I pushed myself up with a grunt. There was no way I was capable of going back downstairs tonight and *not* fighting with Katie. I didn't understand why she was acting like nothing happened. She admitted it was all real in the hospital and even asked a few questions after I woke up. I assumed she hadn't mentioned it again because she was sorting through it, but then she left for college without bringing it up. Even tonight, she more or less admitted she was pretending. Exasperated, I threw myself into my desk chair.

Ungrateful. All of them.

I slid open the top drawer of my desk and dug the tin pencil case out from the clutter at the back. The threads I stole from the Weaver that night in the storage unit thrashed inside, desperately hoping I would release them. How I wished I could. The only thing stopping me was myself, but that was more than enough. However much I longed to absorb their tiny scraps of power, the memory of the threads from the loom clinging violently to my arm was stronger. Sometimes I could still feel where they circled my wrist like a manacle. I pressed the cool metal of the tin against my chest and shut my eyes. *Soon*, I promised. *I'll take you home soon.*

Suddenly, the hair on the back of my neck stood on end.

Something was in the room with me, watching as it had on and off all day. Something familiar and right, but also perverse. *Painful.* My pulse thundered, but I was the Weaver now. Lady of Nightmares. The girl who was supposed to fear nothing. I forced myself to open my eyes, and every last cell in my body froze.

A girl in a threadbare white shift crouched on the desk in front of me. Her knobby knees bent up to her ears, her unusually long shins bare and covered in deep black veins. Chocolate brown eyes stared at me through horizontal pupils. "Hello, Lady." Her voice was a stilted, crackling thing as if she hadn't spoken in years. "Do they want to play?"

Don't be afraid, don't be afraid, don't be afraid. "W-what?" I croaked.

The creature reached out and gently scratched the pencil case with a long, jagged nail. I held my breath, not daring to move. Thick, fanned lashes rose and fell as she blinked. "Wicked, wicked Lady."

Sweat beaded on my forehead, and my knuckles turned white around the tin. What was she doing here? *How* was she here? The nightmares were supposed to be trapped in the Night World. That was the entire reason the Weaver did what he did—to get the secret to releasing his creatures into this world. If they could pop over whenever they wanted, it was all pointless. But it *couldn't* be pointless. People had *died* in the name of his failed mission. There had to be a logical explanation. I sat up straighter and squared my shoulders while my insides screamed to run. "What are you doing here?" I asked in my most authoritative voice. After all, if I couldn't face one of them in my own bedroom, there was no way I could face an entire realm.

She tapped her fingertips absently over her head of wild,

crimped hair. "I'm stuck."

"You're stuck?" I glared at her as the grin inside me turned into a deep frown, setting off tiny explosions of envy and anger. "How so?"

"Came before the walls." She sniffed. "Now I can't get back. So, I'm stuck, you see. Like you, Lady Nightmare. I can show you how to survive here. Would you like that? It's easy. You simply—"

"No," I blurted. "I'm going back, and you should too."

A smirk crept slowly over her face, not reaching her eyes. "Oh yes, Lady. I would like that very much. The last Weaver did not care to help a poor thing like me. Do you know how to take me with you? That's very simple too."

"I—" Heat rose in my cheeks. I didn't even know how to get myself back. "Who are you, exactly?"

"I have many names, Lady." She took a step across the desk, her knee bones shifting at odd angles beneath her skin to accommodate her crouched walk.

Don't back away. Don't give an inch. "Pick one."

The nightmare licked her parched, cracked lips. "Mara."

"It doesn't ring a bell. What are you the nightmare of, exactly?"

"I was never assigned a particular occupation, though I have my preferred methods of entertainment. Did the Weaver force nightmares to be one thing? It wasn't like that before the Night World became separate from the Day World, but, stuck as I am, I know very little about what home is like now."

Something inside me twisted in warning, but I ignored it. She said *before* the worlds were separate, which meant they weren't separate entities at one point. How long ago was that? Long enough that the Sandman didn't think to mention it—not that I should use that to gauge anything. It's not like we had time for intensive history lessons.

"Are there others trapped here?" I asked.

"We are solitary creatures."

I narrowed my eyes. "That's not an answer."

Her facial muscles spasmed, her smile strained. "The Sandman dealt with everyone the Weaver released a few years ago."

"I see." That wasn't an answer either. I stood and placed the pencil case back in the drawer. "I'm not leaving for a few weeks. Come back then."

"Why wait, Lady? You're growing weaker every day, just as I am. Your magic should have been completely absorbed within a week, and yet your arms look as if they've been dipped in paint."

Weaker? But I was training. Preparing. The Sandman wouldn't let me stay if it hurt my chances of protecting myself. The truth of her words hit home, though—I felt it in every ache. But the magic. How would she know the length of time it took to absorb it if the Weaver had always been the Weaver? *Focus, Nora.* I had to get rid of her before my thoughts spiraled.

"I have things to take care of first," I said. "Not that I need to explain myself to you."

Mara hummed. "As you say, Lady Nightmare. But if you want to go back sooner, I can help."

"You should leave." I crossed the room and pulled aside the curtains, then tucked my quaking hands behind me. There was no chance I was leaving her in the Day World to torment anyone. The mere thought of her touching me made me shiver—I could only imagine what she did to mortals. "I'll let you know when it's time to go."

Mara leapt off the desk with surprising dexterity and crept toward me. She barely came up to my waist in her crouched stance. "Call for me, and I'll hear you." She jumped onto the sill and paused, balancing effortlessly. "Don't forget."

Then she shoved herself out the window. I stuck my head out after her, knowing she wouldn't purposely splatter herself on the side lawn but needing to be sure. She landed gracefully beside the fence between my house and Natalie's, then did a frog-like leap into the woods behind the backyard. I stared after her as sweat poured down my neck. The nightmares I'd met in the Nightmare Realm were terrible, but none of them had chilled my blood like Mara. There was something about her—an ancient, foreboding aura.

A light flicked on next door in Natalie's room, and I slammed my window shut with a startled gasp. My back met the wall beside the curtains, and I wished—oh, how I wished—I could disappear into them. My best friend's mother had a new nightly ritual that gutted me. Turn on the light. Sit on Natalie's bed. Smell her pillow. There might have been more after that, but that was as much as I was able to watch. I gripped the fabric of my shirt over my heart and pressed down on the pain. It was my fault Natalie was dead. No matter what anyone told me, I knew it was. I slid down the wall and buried my head in my knees.

All I could do to avenge my friends, I had done.

All I could do to protect the people I was leaving behind, I would do.

Even if that meant taking Mara back with me despite the tiny voice in the back of my head screaming not to.

Sneaking around to see Nora at night was a new experience, one I wasn't exactly fond of. Instead of her simply falling asleep—a perfectly normal human function—and arriving at the beach, I had to turn my gaze inward to her family's cords. Then I had to wait until they glowed brightly enough that there was no fear of anyone waking so I could follow one of them to Nora's house. As if voyeurism wasn't bad enough, creeping into Nora's room made me feel like a criminal.

I stood in the hallway at one a.m. with one hand pressed against Nora's closed door. Her anxiety pulsed through from the other side. I felt it constantly, sometimes mixed with other feelings—anger or fear, mostly, but always with the buzz of nerves. I sucked in a breath. Maybe tonight would help, even if it was only for a little while. Seeing her happy was worth everything. My stomach churned, and I slipped into the dark room, shutting the door with a quiet click.

"Hey." Nora didn't look up, her pencil scratching furiously over paper in the moonlight.

"Hi." Hope fluttered to life. She hadn't picked up her colored pencils since—since *before*. "You're drawing again?"

Her shoulders tensed. "No," she said after a moment.

Disappointment swept the hope away faster than it had come. "Are you busy then?" I asked when she continued to focus on the notebook.

"Not particularly." After a few seconds more, she set the pencil down and splayed her hands on the desk. A list ran the full length of the paper, more than half the notes crossed off. "I'm sorry about the way I treated you earlier. It wasn't right for me to overreact like that."

"You're under a lot of pressure right now," I said, taken slightly aback. She lost her temper more often these days, though not as badly as she had today, and we always pretended it didn't happen. I understood why she would be cranky trapped in the Day World, unable to sleep and in constant pain.

"That's not an excuse." Her shoulders relaxed, and she stood to face me. "It's been a hard day."

I knew. The spikes of hatred I felt earlier told me she'd had another incident with her mother. After the phone call during training, I half expected it, which was why tonight was even more important. I held out a hand with a sheepish smile. "Come with me."

Nora glanced over her shoulder at the window, then back at the paper. A flicker of doubt crossed her face. "Where?"

"It's a surprise," I said playfully. Her gold eyes stared, unblinking, as she chewed her bottom lip. The smile fell from my face. "Nora?"

"Sorry." She let out a quick breath. "I'm trying to figure out what I still need to do before I leave."

My eyes flicked back to the open notebook. Everything was already taken care of—a fake internship with her late father's company in New York, complete with a fake address and a working phone number where her mother could leave messages for us to return later. I estimated it would be at least two months before they suspected anything was amiss. All that was left was to pack a bag to keep up appearances, and even that wasn't completely necessary.

"Can I help?" I asked.

"No." A crease formed between her brows. "Maybe. I'll let you know when I'm done thinking it all through."

I took her hand and laced our fingers together. "Let me give you something in the meantime."

"Oh? The surprise is a present?" She perked up and squeezed my hand. "Tell me it's food, because I could eat a horse right now."

"You'll see," I teased.

She smiled and followed me quietly through the house. The excitement made it hard to move with any real stealth. Nora was going to love it. At least, I hoped so. As we turned toward the kitchen at the bottom of the stairs, something rustled in the living room, and I froze. The blue glow of the TV showed an unfamiliar boy slumped on the couch with Katie's head on his lap, asleep.

Nora bumped into my back, then followed my gaze and

groaned. "Just go," she whispered.

The boy laughed and clawed the air with one hand, mimicking an angry cat. "Careful with that one," the stranger warned benevolently.

I scowled, but Nora nudged me forward. I paused at the back door and pressed the code into the alarm system before swiping an open bag of potato chips from the counter. "I didn't know your sister was home."

"Yeah. You're not the only one with a surprise tonight," she said sarcastically.

I hadn't bothered to check Katie's cord while she was away at college. I doubted she would tell their parents if Nora snuck out, but it was better to play it safe. "Who's with her?"

"Don't ask."

I glanced back at the living room where the guy laughed quietly at something on the screen. Nora was right—I shouldn't ask. Nothing mattered tonight except her. Not the Night World, not magic, not training. Just us.

Nora slipped on a pair of flip-flops left on the patio, and we crossed the backyard to the small shed nestled against a pine tree. I lifted the ladder off the hooks screwed into the siding and propped it against the edge of the roof. "Wait here a minute. Hold these," I added, pressing the chips into her hand.

She wrinkled her nose. "Is this some sort of test?"

"No." Though I could see why she thought that. The last time I dragged her out in the middle of the night was to train after a rather grueling week in the Nightmare Realm. I grazed her cheek with my thumb. "Trust me."

I hurried onto the roof and emptied handfuls of sand onto the shingles, forming it into the perfect nest. A thick, down-filled comforter to lay on with an array of pillows and another heavy blanket, big enough to cover us both. There was only one thing missing, but first... "Close your eyes," I said, peeking down at Nora.

"What?" Her gaze darted to the woods, then back at me. "Why?"

My chest panged. She was still afraid of shadows, and who could blame her? But there was nothing to fear now. Not tonight. "Please?"

She hesitated before complying. I stared at her a moment, taking in each freckle. Warmth radiated through my body, flushing my cheeks. Did anyone in the world love a girl more than I loved her? It didn't seem possible. If someone told me years ago that the Dream Keeper and I would have feelings for each other, I would've laughed at them. She was only meant to serve a purpose, not become the most important thing in my personal life. We became friends one night at a time, despite my attempts to keep distance between us, and then it happened. One night I looked at her, smiling and laughing as she told me about something that happened at school, and new emotions bulldozed me. It took half a second, and I was done for without even knowing I was in danger. But what a wonderful danger to be in.

A warm grin spread across my face as I emptied the rest of the sand onto the blankets. With one upward motion, it soared into the sky and hovered, waiting.

"You can come up now," I called softly.

The ladder creaked almost instantly. It took all my self-control not to rush her, and when her blond hair popped up over the edge, my heart did somersaults. Her lips parted in a wary smile. "What's this?" she asked, patting the blankets.

I held out my hand to help her off the last rung. Once she was on the roof, I lowered myself onto the blankets. She eased down beside me and immediately snuggled into my side. A small groan sounded in my throat before I could stop it. No matter how many times she was close to me, the heat of her skin meeting the heat of mine felt like the first time. It was the most precious feeling in the world to have her pressed into me like I was her anchor. I pulled the top blanket up around us before settling down and loosening a breath. Nora stared at me in the way I always wished she would, but the gold of her eyes was an unwelcome reminder that her feelings might not survive her reign.

When she closed the distance between our lips, I drank her in as if she was the last oasis in the desert. Her hands wound around my neck, and I cupped her face. I kissed her until I was drunk from it. Until everything else fell away, and all I knew was the feel of her. Until the moment a kiss wasn't all I wanted. I pulled back then, because a kiss was all I could allow myself until our relationship stood on undeniably solid ground. If Nora regretted things later, it would crush me a thousand times worse than a thousand kisses ever could.

I pressed my forehead to hers. When my pulse slowed and my breath calmed, I nudged my magic toward the sand hovering overhead and brought my lips to her ear. "Nora?"

"Hmm?" she answered, content.

"I brought you the stars."

She twisted in my arms and gasped. Above us danced a million glimmering stars as bright and brilliant as the ones above the Dream Realm. Hot tears rolled down her cheeks, dripping on my hand where I propped myself up. "Thank you," she breathed.

I kissed her tears away, catching the ones that escaped with my thumbs. Then I kissed her nose, her mouth, her neck, until it felt as if we were glowing just as brightly under our blanket.

"Tell me something," she said when I finally put some space between us again. "Something I don't know yet that isn't about dreams or nightmares or magic."

Those three things took up my entire life. What could I tell her that was new? Not that George Washington dreamed of cheese almost every night or that children used to call to me for more than sleep. They wanted stories and, for a while, I would agree to short ones on the beach, spinning tales before sending them into blissful slumber. Centuries had passed since, but those were other tales of dreams and magic.

"Before you, I never felt real," I admitted reverently. "I was simply a legend. Even when people believed in my existence, that was all people thought of me—that I brought good dreams. They didn't see me as an individual. As a *person*, like you do."

"Of course you're a person," she said defensively. "Different, maybe, but in the ways that count, you're more human than a lot of us are."

Nora's hair slipped between my fingers, smooth as silk, and I lifted another lock. Hopefully she was right. Everything seemed so much heavier than the burdens placed on a mortal. Balancing the Day and Night Worlds wasn't easy to do alone. Nora snuggled into my side, and peace flowed through me. I wasn't alone. Not anymore.

"Stay here with me tonight?" she asked. "Like old times."

I lifted her hand and kissed her knuckles. "I wouldn't leave for anything in the world."

Dawn broke much too soon. I released the magic holding the stars and eased my arm out from beneath Nora's head. "I have to get back." I kissed her, slow and lingering. "And you have to get inside before anyone wakes up."

She stretched out on the blankets with a sleepy grin. "I don't *have* to."

"We have training later," I reminded her, tracing a line down her side. She jerked away, laughing, when I brushed against the ticklish spot above her hip. "I won't be gone long."

She stuck her tongue out at me and sat up. "Thank you. For this."

I kissed her again, cupping her neck, and sighed against her lips. "I miss you."

"I miss you too." She reached up and plucked at one of my curls. "It feels like we haven't talked in a long time."

It was true, but I hated hearing it. Talking was what brought us together. Lately, our conversations centered around rogue nightmares, training, and all the problems in between. I still hadn't told her about the attack on the Dream Realm for fear of overwhelming her. It was over and done with, and soon they would have their Lady to set things right.

"I—I met someone last night," she said quietly.

I reared back as if she had slapped me. There was no way she meant another guy—Nora was a lot of things, but unfaithful wasn't one of them. "Someone?" I asked, my head tilted.

"A nightmare," she clarified.

The blood drained from my face. "That's impossible. I killed everyone the Weaver let out before I bound him."

"She told me that, but I don't think she's technically one of his. She felt… different." She rubbed her forehead as if she had a headache. "She claims to be stuck here because she came before the Day and Night Worlds were separate."

"Before…" My hands shook. "*Mare* was here?"

"She said her name was Mara, but—"

"What did she say to you? Did she do anything? Did she hurt you?" I asked in a rush.

"I'm fine. A little surprised, obviously."

So was I. Mare was banished so long ago that she should've withered away under the stress of the Day World by now. Or, at the very least, been too weak to do any damage. If she tracked Nora down from halfway across the world where the Weaver and I left her, she had to be in minimally decent condition. Unless she had drifted this way without my noticing.

"What did she want?" I asked carefully.

"To go back home." Nora touched my fists thoughtfully. "It'll be okay. We'll take her back with us before she—"

I took Nora's hands, squeezing them hard to make sure she knew I was serious. Enough horrible things had happened because she took my warnings too lightly. "Stay away from her. Promise me."

She frowned. "I don't think we should leave her here. What if she hurts someone? Katie's still here. Paul, my mom—"

"She's been relatively harmless for ages while there's been nothing and no one here to stop her." At least, I thought so. Belief in Mare faded away so long ago that it had to be true. Even her myth wasn't well-known anymore, but I wasn't sure Nora would forgive me for setting Mare loose in the Day World to protect myself. *Ourselves.* The Weaver and I banished her together to protect everything we'd built, though we had no way of knowing the consequences then. Cleaving our worlds in two is what eventually turned us against each other. That set the scales. Light and dark. Dream and nightmare. Good and bad. We each became what we had to become after that.

But at least we existed.

In the Day World, Mare was worn down and nearly powerless, killing Dreamers by sitting on their chest while they slept. She was different in the Night World—a ferocious creature that delighted in tearing things apart with her bare hands and using their bones to pick their flesh from her teeth. People, places. Nightmares. If the Weaver and I hadn't expelled her, there wouldn't be any world at all.

"She's not stuck," I reluctantly told Nora. "The Weaver and I banished her here. If Mare goes back, she'll destroy the Night World, and the Day World will die along with it."

She cringed away from me. "Again with the balance."

"Yes. Always." Fury curled unbidden from my center. "Was becoming the Weaver not proof enough for you?"

"Obviously the balance exists," she snapped back. "But I don't think the consequence of destroying one world will be the destruction of another. The Weaver's death didn't kill you."

"Yes, it did," I shouted. Heat licked up my neck, scalding me with shock. "It *almost* did," I corrected myself, softer. I never wanted her to know what happened to me that day, but maybe it was wrong to keep it a secret. Still, meeting her eyes as I spoke the truth tempered my anger and crushed my soul. "I felt as if I broke into a thousand pieces outside the Weaver's keep that day. I was a single breath away from death. I'm not sure what stopped it, but Nora… We can't take that kind of risk. Mare's not worth it."

"You—" Nora's voice stuck. The color drained from her face until she was as white as snow beneath her freckles. She clutched at her stomach and swayed. "I—" She lunged for the ladder but overshot.

I looped an arm around her waist before she fell from the roof. "I'm sorry."

"For what?" She shook beneath my arm. "What could you possibly be sorry for? I almost *killed* you. And you spent the last five months pretending I didn't."

I winced. "I don't blame you, Nora."

"You *should* blame me." She shoved my arm away and slid down the ladder.

I fought the urge to run after her and tell her that I forgave her, but it wasn't entirely true. She didn't fully trust me—that's what hurt the most. She trusted Rowan and Kail, two strangers, two *nightmares*, more than she trusted me to rebind the Weaver. So, while I understood her actions, the ache they caused still lingered. Hopefully digesting the information would dissuade her from wanting to bring Mare back, not that I would ever allow it.

The Weaver and I had given up too much to get Mare here. Our friendship was destroyed when we bled white and black from grey. *We* were destroyed. And still, it killed me to know that Nora was hurting. I slammed a hand down on the roof, dissolving our nest of blankets. She was the leader of nightmares now, and if she was going to survive, I had to stop coddling her. She needed to understand. But the look of intense pain on her face as I spoke the truth would never fade from my memory.

My lungs struggled to expand, my muscles to move. It was

as if my very existence was weighed down by the growing mound of trouble. First, the Weaver killed Nora's loved ones, then Nora killed him, *then* Rowan took the Keep. Inside, the loom—Nora's source of power—was held hostage. Now Mare. I groaned and gave into the magic, letting it pull me home to the Dream Realm. The quiet serenity of the beach swallowed my thoughts and projected them back tenfold. If I stayed here with my warring feelings of love and hate, anger and understanding, I knew which emotions would win. So, instead of grappling with the desire to make peace with Nora, I forced myself to cross into the Nightmare Realm without looking back.

☾

A narrow path led away from a landscape of open graves, some stacked with rotting corpses, others empty and waiting. I followed where the packed dirt twisted through a crooked cemetery gate with the wails of unseen mourners following at my heel. Before me, tall, skeletal trees lined the walkway as far as the eye could see, reaching into the sky where the tops disappeared in a thin red mist. Red berries lay scattered at their roots. It was silent here. I strained my ears in hopes of hearing a Dreamer in need of saving. Not that I wanted someone to be in danger, but I needed to let off some steam.

"Sandman."

I froze and squinted ahead of me. A figure sat at the very edge of the hazy path. I stepped closer, one hand sliding into my satchel. "Show yourself," I demanded.

"You don't recognize me?" the voice answered, taunting. "I'm wounded."

"You've got to be kidding me." I groaned to myself and took another three steps forward. It wasn't the voice itself that I recognized but the attitude behind it.

Kail perched on a jagged stump, the only tree not identical to the rest. His white pointed mask gleamed in the shadows. An easy smirk played on his lips beneath the curved beak as he picked at his embroidered sleeve, and I closed a fist around my sand. If it wasn't for him, Nora would've gone along with my plan and everything would've gone back to normal. I took a breath, preparing to throw every weapon I could think of at him, but then I paused. This wasn't right. I was looking for a fight, but not this one. At least not until I could get confirmation from my spies if he was still working with Rowan or not. And if he was, I couldn't touch him because Nora needed to avenge herself. I turned and began walking away.

"You'll want to hear what I have to say."

"Doubtful," I said with ire.

"All right, all right. You win. I'll give you a free swing at me first." When I didn't stop walking away, he added, "I know how to help her."

"Help her?" I spun and stormed back down the path before I could stop myself, each step reverberating through my core. "If it wasn't for you and Rowan, Nora wouldn't *need* help." I gripped the collar of his black jacket. "How did you get the knife?"

"I don't know how Rowan got it." He studied his fingernails, seemingly unfazed by my unspoken threats. "But speaking of Rowan—" He brushed my hands away. The tip of his mask skimmed his chest as he smoothed out the wrinkles my clenched fists had left behind. "This used to be her."

I opened my mouth to demand the truth about the blade, but

curiosity won out instead. "What used to be who?"

"Rowan. As in the tree." Kail kicked the jagged stump with the toe of his boot. "The Weaver liked to recycle things on occasion. Seems irrelevant, I know."

"Completely irrelevant," I agreed. "What am I supposed to do with that information?"

Kail shrugged. "Just planting a bug in your ear."

"You said you could help Nora," I snarled. It didn't matter if Rowan started as a tree or a speck of dirt. She was what she was now, and she would pay for what she did. "Why would you want to?"

One blue eye bored into mine while the other flickered through various colors. A small seed of satisfaction grew inside me, knowing that the steady iris was Nora's handiwork.

"When Nora comes back, I think it's only fair she has a fighting chance." Kail shrugged.

"You don't care about her."

"Who said I cared?" Kail laughed. "Maybe I'm just curious what she'll do, given the chance. As an outsider. As a Dreamer."

I swung a fist into his jaw. He stumbled back and looked up at me from behind his mask. "Stay away from her," I warned.

Kail rolled his eyes. "Her magic is too different from yours. You can't help her with this."

"Don't tell me what I can or cannot do. She—"

"But I can," he shouted over me, then stormed away before I could punch him again.

I wanted to run after him and rage. Hit him. Break him. Instead, I shouted wordlessly at the empty space he'd occupied a moment ago, spittle flying. Kail would pay for everything he was part of from the moment Nora fell into the Nightmare

Realm.

Him and Rowan.

I glowered at the jagged stump and imagined it as the woman herself. Imagined white hot flames licking up the sides, crackling the bark. And then they were. My sand fed the conjured blaze, urging it higher and higher, until the exact moment I realized I had lost control of my thoughts. The sand acted on instinct, enacting my will. I pressed the heels of my hands against the throbbing in my temples. *Calm down.* I had to calm down.

After a handful of long, deep breaths, the fire flickered out of existence, and I turned for the Dream World without looking back.

The whirlwind of the mall nearly swept me away. People moved in currents, brushing past me where I stood as if I were a boulder in their river. Some grumbled at me to move, but most moved with silent purpose. My body shook in response to the sensory overload. The people, the lights, the crushing noise. My skin felt raw beneath my layers of clothing. But I was almost done. With this place and this world. If I could just hang on a little longer.

I slid my sunglasses up my nose and clutched the list in my hand. All three presents were checked off. A picture frame for my mother with a family photo inside and an engraved flask for Paul—he would need it after I left. For Katie, I found a pair of black tassel earrings with gold caps. Perhaps gifting my sister a reminder of the Weaver's threads was a bit petty, especially since I braved the same shop where we had watched the cashier stab herself to death to buy them, but she *deserved* petty. She *should* remember, her eyes *should* stay open, so she could look out for herself if she ever needed to.

"Nora?"

My back tightened at the familiar voice. The last time I saw Detective Bell, he was asking my mother for a chance to apologize while I was in the hospital. Her vehement *no* was a relief. I never expected to run into him again, but there he was, cutting through the crowd until he stood in front of me. Instead of his usual shirt and tie, he wore a black hoodie with a jaguar head screen-printed on the front. His silver-framed glasses were missing but had left seemingly permanent divots in the sides of his nose, and his jaw was sprinkled with faint grey stubble.

I forced a small smile and held up my bags. "I'm just on my way out."

"Wait." He cleared his throat. "Please. I only need a minute."

"I'm sort of in a rush so…" I glanced around him to my final stop—a dollar store where I planned on grabbing something colorful to wrap everything in, but the white tissue paper we had at home would serve the same purpose if it meant avoiding the detective. "See you."

He reached out to stop me but dropped his arm at the last moment. "I want to apologize for everything."

"Are you referring to the interrogations, the threats, or just suspecting me in general?" I cringed at my own tone and for opening the door to a conversation by asking the question. I wanted to get away from him, not hear him out. Besides, he wasn't wrong in thinking I was involved. I pressed my arms to my sides and inched further into the flow of the crowd.

"I should never have focused on you," he admitted without hesitation. "You weren't capable of most of those things and obviously had nothing to do with the death you witnessed firsthand, but you were the only link to all the murders. The graphic nature of the crimes affected me more than I'd like to admit. I was exhausted and seeing things by the time everything ended." He paused to draw a long breath.

Exhausted. Seeing things. The internal grin curled in amusement at the words, and I shifted my shopping bags to my other hand. "What kind of things were you seeing?"

"It's not important. I only wanted you to know how sorry I am." He hunched his shoulders, shaking his head as if to clear it, and turned away.

The grin continued to spread, smug. It was almost like the dark part of me recognized something in him. Almost like—*More than one sleepwalker,* the Weaver told me once. It would've been just like him to use the police as another way to pressure me into giving him the dream. It was more than enough that people around me were dying and my sister was missing, but not to him. To the Weaver, it wasn't working. I was still resisting. If life in prison loomed over my head as well… It made sense. Everything the Weaver did made sense.

"Detective Bell?" I called.

He stopped. "I'm not a detective anymore. I resigned."

I scowled, deflating a bit. Another life ruined. "Did anything you imagined actually happen?"

"How did you—" He rubbed a hand over his bald head. "Take care of yourself, Miss Gallagher."

I watched him walk away a different man than I knew over

the summer. Gone was his confidence, his anger, but something else had taken their place. Confusion. Guilt. It wafted off him like bad cologne. *He locked Katie in the storage unit.* The thought came and went so fast it barely had time to register. The residue it left was sticky with truth. He did it.

"Hey," the Sandman whispered.

My heart jumped, one hand flying to my chest, and I spun toward the Sandman while keeping my eyes on Bell. "You scared the crap out of me."

"Sorry." He took my bags and wove his fingers between mine.

I stared at his hand, felt the warmth of him, and fought the urge to rip myself free. To run back home and hide under the covers. How could he dare to touch me after I went behind his back to kill the Weaver? After my brash act nearly killed him? The tell-tale pressure of tears began behind my eyes, and here I thought I had cried them all out in the shower this morning after leaving him on the roof.

His grip tightened as if he sensed my thoughts. "Wasn't that the detective that covered all the murders? He isn't still bothering you, is he?"

I nodded, then realized that only answered one of his questions honestly. With a deep steadying breath, I said, "That's him, but he wasn't bothering me. I think the Weaver used him."

"Used him how?"

"He—" I swallowed hard and looked up into the Sandman's earnest face. He didn't know about the grin I carted around. Mainly because I didn't know how to explain it, but also because I didn't want him to stop looking at me the way he did. There was precisely one person in the entire world—in both worlds—

that put me first in their heart, and I selfishly didn't want that to go away. Each breath became hard won, and the crowd felt as if it was closing in on us. I'd done enough to give him reason to hate me—how much more would it take until he did?

"I can't explain how I know," I said carefully. "But the Weaver made him sleepwalk. He's the one who locked Katie in the storage unit and did who knows what else."

"What do you mean you can't explain it?" the Sandman asked, his voice sounding uncertain.

"It's just something I *know*." I shifted on my feet, desperate for him to drop it and focus on the more pressing revelation: that Bell had been the one to lock Katie up.

"Right." His scowl deepened. "Anyway, we need to talk about something important."

More important than the Weaver using Bell against me? Though I supposed that was a moot point now. "What happened?" I asked warily.

"Come with me."

He pulled me close, tucking me beneath his arm, and we snuck through one of the back exits. Cobwebs filled every corner of the dim hallway, and the beige tiles were stained black from years of wear. Each door had a sign taped haphazardly below a peephole with the name of the store for receiving deliveries. The exits didn't open to any of the customer parking lots, so they were rarely used by anyone other than employees, making them perfect for a private conversation. I leaned against the tiled wall and welcomed the coolness of it seeping through my shirt.

"Okay." I held my breath, knowing this couldn't be good. "Go ahead."

The Sandman ran both hands through his hair and licked his

lips. "Rowan's going to be a bigger problem than we expected."

Anger flared in me, hot enough that the wall would surely have scorch marks afterwards. *Of course she was.* She set me up to kill the Weaver so she could kill me. Then she stole my Keep, loom included, and riled up my nightmares. "What did she do now?" I asked through my teeth.

"The other day when I told you that Baku and I killed a nightmare?" He waited until I nodded to continue. "After, when we went back to the Dream Realm, we found it under attack."

"*What?*"

"Nothing I couldn't handle. A single giant beating at the barrier and some talking mushrooms," he said, hands raised. "I didn't want to say anything until my spies confirmed Rowan sent them, and then today I saw Kail."

"*Kail?*" I screeched.

The Sandman's eyes widened as the sound echoed down the hall, and he shot a look over his shoulder. "He offered his help."

"His help?" I barked a laugh. "He's helped enough, wouldn't you say?"

"Regardless, we can't trust him."

"You think?" I agreed. The grin flickered to life. *Calm down*, I thought to myself. *Don't lose yourself.* The Sandman and I both knew what Kail had done, and neither of us would forget that.

The Sandman paced away from me. "The timing is off. Why would he wait until right before your return?"

"Does it matter? He obviously wants to set me up again."

I rapped my fingers on my thighs in contemplation. Why wasn't Kail in the Keep with Rowan? Did she send him to find the Sandman? They could've had a falling out and delivering me was his way back into her good graces. Or maybe he wanted to be the one to find me first. The one to kill me and take the Weaver's power.

"I think…" The Sandman drew in a deep breath and stared at the exit sign over my head. "I think we should move the date back."

Sweat broke out across my body, and I shoved away from the wall. "I knew this would happen. Are you out of your mind?"

"Not by much," he said in a rush. "An extra week so there's time to find out what their plan is."

"You have eighteen days to figure that out." I scowled, and the grin mirrored the sentiment. Enough was enough. Rowan wasn't going to make claiming my realm easy no matter when I returned. If anything, giving her more time was the worse option. Why let her get any stronger than she already was? We would have the element of surprise if I went back now, but I needed the Sandman to take me. And apparently, he wouldn't. "Is this because you don't want me to go back? You'd rather let Rowan rule in my place?"

He blanched. "Why would I want someone else running the Nightmare Realm? Especially Rowan? As much as I hate admitting it, it's yours. Besides, the nightmares are too unstable to rule each other—they need you."

"*I'm* unstable," I shouted. I doubted I'd be any good at ruling, but anything I did there had to be better than the nothing I was doing here.

"I believe in you, Nora," He said simply.

"Then take me back. Now, not later." I tore off my sunglasses. "Look at me. I don't belong here anymore. Keeping me here is doing more harm than good. If Rowan and Kail are setting a trap for me, we'll deal with it together."

He lifted a hand to my face and ran his thumb over my cheekbone. “Let me get more information before we decide.”

“We decided a long time ago.”

He hesitated before leaning down to kiss me on the corner of my mouth. I wanted not to react, to let him know I couldn’t be sweet-talked into changing my mind, but I leaned into it instead. There was no telling how many more kisses we would have or what would change between us once I got back. I would be busy claiming the Keep and learning how to use the loom in order to cement my authority. And he would be… What would he do? He couldn’t be seen helping or the nightmares would never respect me.

“Give me today to see what I can find, and we’ll talk about it again tonight,” he murmured in my ear.

I turned my head so my lips matched his perfectly and kissed him gently. He could have today to do whatever he wanted, but I wasn’t staying. If Rowan was planning something, it was even more reason to go back and snatch everything away from her. Everything she had given me.

I’d been gone too long already.

Chapter Seven

The glue of the envelope was bitter against my tongue. I pressed the flap down and clicked my pen, doubting myself for the hundredth time. *I won't be home for a while*, I explained in the letter. *I'm safe. Don't look for me.* I would hide it in the bottom of my closet along with their gifts for them to find after they realized the internship was a lie. But what if my mother never found the letter? Or worse, what if she found it before I left? She snooped regularly in both my room and Katie's—mostly mine. It was entirely possible she would happen across it even if I locked it in a box and bricked it up inside a wall. I could only imagine how my last moments here would go then. Still, I had to leave *something* for them.

I tossed the pen down without writing *Mom* across the front and tucked the blank envelope inside a study guide that a certain someone passive-aggressively left on my desk. They wouldn't believe a word of the letter anyway, but what else could I tell them? *Gone to kick a nightmare off my proverbial throne. Back eventually. I hope.* That would be monumentally worse, but Katie would suspect the truth, even if she didn't want to speak it out loud. No one would believe her if she did—a fact I knew all too well.

Coming back to visit after I learned how to Day Walk would be interesting. Who knew how long it would take for me to secure my position? What if they were all dead before I managed it? Being eternal, the only nightmare in a rush was likely Rowan. There were four quarters left on the board and the clock was eternally stalled. I shoved away from the desk, my heart fluttering in my chest. Goodbye was different than *goodbye.*

I lifted my hands and stared at the stained skin. At the gold pulsing beneath. The internal grin cracked its lips, darkness spilling out. It circled my thoughts, twisting them until they almost broke. I strained to hold it back. *I would come home. I would see them again.* I drew a ragged breath.

Then, just as fast as the darkness had spread, a sense of calm washed over me. The Sandman's emotions brushed against mine, and the grin faded. I scrambled to shutter my own feelings. To hide the terrifying thing residing in me from him, but it was pointless. Even if I was an expert at it, the Sandman already felt the desperate fear. That's why he cracked his door open—to offer me the only comfort he could. What would he do if he knew the reason? The truth pressed down on me, begging to come out, but who could I tell if not the Sandman? Definitely not Colleen. I glanced at the wall I shared with my sister and twisted my hands together. It was worth a shot.

I crept from my room and up to her open door. Should I tell her? Katie wanted to forget, but maybe she would stop pretending if we were alone. Five minutes. That's all I needed from her. I leaned against the door frame and watched as she lounged on her bed with one of the random catalogs we got in the mail. She was probably thinking about buying something since more than a few corners were dog-eared, the folds fanning the top of the pages out. My mother always made sure to toss them in the garbage before my sister had a chance to see them, but she'd clearly grown lax while Katie was away at college. I'd never forget the time Katie ordered whoopee cushions in bulk, their purpose still a mystery. Simpler times. Carefree. A pang of longing left me slouching into the wood.

"Where's Kellan?" I asked when she didn't notice me.

Katie jumped, snapping the catalog shut. "Natalie's parents went to California for Thanksgiving, so he offered to walk their dog."

"Dog? When did they get a dog?"

Katie shot me a withering look. "You can talk to them, you know. They miss you."

The blood drained from my face. They had tried more than once to get in touch with me, but I couldn't. Not when I was the reason their daughter was dead. At least Emery's parents gave me a wide berth the few times I had seen them out and about. I was a reminder to them of what they lost, Colleen suggested, but I didn't need a reason. I deserved to be avoided—not hugged like Natalie's mother wanted to do every time she saw me. They should all hate me.

"I thought you said you were done running from your problems," Katie said. "Isn't that what you told me when I was

brushed through the now open window, and I turned to find her perched on the edge of my mattress. Thin lines crinkled around her dark eyes, and she bobbed her head once. "How may I be of service?"

The rational part of my brain screamed at me to send her away. The Sandman had warned me not to interact with her, yet here I was, inviting her into my bedroom. *Don't be stupid.* The thought echoed against my skull, but I was committed. "Do you know the way back?"

She blinked her wide eyes. "If I did, would I be here?"

"Don't play with me. You said you could help." My tone was sharp enough to cut. "Do you know or not?"

"I cannot travel it," she said carefully.

I folded my arms across my chest to cool my temper. "Knowing how and being able to travel it are different things."

"Indeed, indeed." Mara's face twitched. "If you are asking how *you* can get back, I do know a way."

I leaned forward on the balls of my feet. "Tell me."

She grinned. "First, we must come to terms."

"Terms? I already said I would take you back to the Nightmare Realm."

"How do I know you aren't lying?" she asked.

"You don't." *Because I was.* I didn't like leaving Mara in the Day World, but I'd ignored the Sandman's warnings once before. Asking for advice was one thing; bringing her with me was another. "If I have to wait for the Sandman, what do you think your odds will be? He banished you, so something tells me he won't let you just waltz back in."

Mara's thick tongue darted from between her teeth and licked her thin lips. "There's no guarantee he'll ever take you back. He already wants to delay your return by another week."

"He—" I went still while my heart kicked into overdrive. "Have you been *spying* on me?"

"Following. Not spying. How else was I to know when you were ready for me?"

My mouth fell open. *How? Where?* I should've noticed. Should have somehow sensed her lurking. A cold chill prickled my skin. *I had.* That was her I felt watching me the other day during training, and again in my room. There had to be other times, too. What else had she seen? Sweat trickled down my spine. My mind raced over conversations between the Sandman and me. If she knew he warned me about her… No wonder her promise of help was laced with disbelief. Still, there was no guarantee she was near the shed that morning, so I had to play it cool.

"The Sandman will take me back as promised," I said with conviction. "Unless you help me get back sooner."

"*Me?*"

I glared at her. "You what?"

Mara tilted her head. "You said help *me* get back. Not us."

Crap. I schooled my expression into one of indifference. "I'm the best chance you have, and it's now or never. Make a choice."

She was quiet for a moment, her gaze sweeping over my arms. "You might not be strong enough to carry us both back," Mara said at last. "It seems to take a great deal of focus."

The probability was high that she was right. I *was* weak, and, more importantly, my magic was untrained. There was no way to test it here outside of shuttering my emotions, and that continued to be an epic fail. I needed to be in the Nightmare Realm to learn. To test my limits. To reach my full potential. I drew a sharp breath. "Then why are we having this discussion?"

Mara crept along the edge of my room. "You still carry the Sandman's dream which might help… buffer things."

"You know what?" I snapped as my unease grew. "Nevermind. I'll figure it out on my own."

"I'll help, Lady. If you give me your word that I'll go with you."

I had lied to the Weaver, tricked him into leading me to my sister. This would be no different, but if she had heard—if she *did* suspect…The Sandman said she was too weak to do any harm while still in the Day World, but she was strong enough to continue following me undetected. "And if I can't carry you back?"

"Promise to *try*," she seethed.

"I make promises to no one."

Mara's scowl darkened her entire face. The dark veins beneath her skin spread like wildfire, creating a map of twisted lines.

"But," I added, "if you tell me how to get to the Nightmare Realm, and *if* I decide to use that way instead of having the Sandman help me, I will consider it."

"That's not enough."

I nonchalantly shrugged one shoulder. "It has to be."

She hissed. "Let the Dream Lord take you then."

"All right." I waved a hand dismissively. "Leave."

Mara leapt out the window without another word, and I flopped down on the bed, staring at the ceiling. *Double crap*. The Sandman wouldn't leave me here forever, that much I was sure of. He loved me, and it would kill him to watch me completely wither in the Day World. But three weeks was too long to wait.

I closed my eyes and exhaled slowly to calm myself. In and out. Two times. Three. On the fourth inhale, something bore down hard enough to make me wheeze. My eyes flew open to find Mara leering down at me.

"Lady," she said in a grave voice.

Her feet rested on either side of my head as she sat on my chest. I pushed at her knobby knees and attempted to twist my way out from beneath her, but she was like a slab of granite. Hard, heavy, and immovable. She blinked, callous, and a flash of heat raced through me. The taste of sulfur burned up the back of my throat, the grin widening into an angry snarl on my face.

If I couldn't handle one weakened nightmare, the Sandman was right: I wasn't ready to go back. I let instinct focus my energy, let the grin guide it with pinpoint accuracy. Magic built and built, a flooded lake held back by the flimsiest of dams.

Seeming to sense I was about to burst, Mara lifted herself slightly. "Use the threads to take you home. And dare not forget me."

Then she was gone a second time.

I stared at the empty space above me and lifted my head from the pillow. She would not be forgotten; leaving her behind would be a conscious decision. If she thought she could threaten me—*me*—into taking her back, she would learn a hard lesson. One nightmare that thought they were better than their Lady was one nightmare too many, and I already had Rowan. Possibly Kail. There were undoubtedly others too. There was no way I was bringing Mara into the mix.

But she gave me what I needed. The threads I kept locked away were the key all along, and tomorrow I would use them. I would go to the only place I belonged and make my mark on it.

A quietness filled me, my thoughts drifting into silence, save one.

I'm ready.

Chapter Eight

Cool water and mud plastered my pants to my legs. My knees sunk deeper into the riverbed as I wrestled a nightmare covered in a smooth, pod-like shell. It vibrated beneath my bare hands, but I refused to release it. The nightmare's crab legs clawed at the air, the tiny, piercing tips barely missing my forearms. It had followed me since I crossed into the Nightmare Realm—spying, no doubt. Just like I was. If Rowan wanted to know what I was doing, she didn't need to resort to using lesser nightmares as spies. I passed numerous nightmares every time I was here that could easily report back.

If she had to send a nightmare to follow me that meant one of two things: the pod was a decoy meant to distract me from another nightmare tracking my movements, or, more likely,

Rowan wasn't as strong as she wanted us to believe. Either way, it irked me when the thing dove into the water to avoid capture.

I slipped, falling forward, and landed on the shell. It shredded through my vest, but its legs weren't quite sharp enough to go through my tunic and into the flesh underneath. "Enough," I groaned, and I called sand from the satchel at my hip. It spun together in a tight line and dove beneath the nightmare's shell, stealing its mind. A handful of seconds later, the lobster-sized creature stilled. I heaved myself up, tossed it to the shore, and flung mud from my fingertips. It splattered against the nightmare's metallic underbelly, where its legs were now neatly folded.

"Do you speak?" I asked, climbing from the river.

The creature didn't move so I flipped it over with my boot. The shell clicked open into ten even sections, revealing dozens of tiny, open mouths with dull teeth. A bit of black blood dripped from one of them. The lesser nightmares with black blood weren't intelligent; most of them didn't even speak. They simply followed their instincts or direct orders from the Weaver. I winced. *Nora.* They would follow orders from Nora. And, as it appeared, Rowan, because dominance mattered here.

"Let Rowan know Nora is offering a peaceful transition. She can return to leading the Blood Army alongside Kail without retaliation from us," I instructed. A vicious lie, of course. Nora and I both knew she would have to kill Rowan eventually.

The nightmare's legs snapped out, and it scurried over the grassy hill toward the Keep. Something told me I already knew Rowan's answer. Why would she give up such power without a fight after all she'd done to obtain it?

I wasn't sure how Nora would feel about the deal—real or

not—but it was best to delay the fight, especially if she still insisted on coming back sooner than planned. Rowan couldn't be trusted, but if Nora had time to orient herself first… I let out a careful breath and followed the shell's path. It was already out of sight by the time I reached the top of the hill, but I knew the way on my own.

Without my power being pulled in a million directions, it was possible to waltz into the Keep and destroy everything in a single afternoon, but I couldn't simply wipe the Nightmare Realm clean. The balance would be thrown off again, not to mention Rowan would put up a good fight, as would whatever followers she'd gathered.

Besides, I was the Dream Lord. Unfortunately, that meant I couldn't win Nora's power for her. If I tried, if they thought Nora wasn't strong enough to do it on her own, she wouldn't last a day. She would be seen as a puppet—*my* puppet—and no nightmare would allow me to have that kind of power over their Lady. It was bad enough they all knew about our relationship, and worse that there would be creatures coming for her regardless. Nora *was* power, and they would either bow to her or try to seize it as their own.

Anxiety nibbled at my insides, but I pushed it down. There wasn't time to worry, only time to do what had to be done. I crouched in the same patch of cattails Nora and I had hidden in the last time we came to the Keep. Except this time, instead of hiding from me, nightmares covered the entire yard. Large and small, feathered and scaled, hairy and bald. The variety wasn't lacking, but they all had one thing in common: not a single high-minded nightmare graced the lawn. Either Rowan had none willing to stand with her or they found themselves too good to stay outside with the rabble.

The increased number of nightmares wasn't the only change in the last few months. The skeleton of the Weaver's palace—the one destroyed the night I bound him—was no longer in ruins. The stone foundation no longer peeked from the grass, but rose two feet, three in some places, the new stones carefully laid. It followed the same pathways as the old structure, then extended outward on all sides. I scoffed quietly. Rowan wasn't wasting any time.

I quickly and quietly wound my way around the outer wall to get closer to the Keep. It hadn't changed—black marble, veined gold, half-capped with a dome and the other side consisting of open-aired arches. The spy I stole was nowhere in sight, but red mist leaked from the basement windows, which meant Rowan retained at least some of the Blood Army. Probably all of it, as they operated like a hive mind rather than as individuals, but there were too many for them all to fit in the Keep. It begged the question: *Where was the rest of the army?*

A door slammed open, and Rowan appeared on the terrace. Her red dress was a bright wound between two pillars. The black, skeletal wings jutting from her back were hidden in shadow, her skin so pale it nearly glowed. My pulse quickened. There she was. The biggest threat standing in Nora's way stood before me, and I couldn't touch her. It was foolish to even offer a truce, especially without consulting Nora first. Rowan had everything, and my offer gave her nothing. Nora didn't exactly strike fear into anyone yet, nor was she likely to for a while.

A familiar set of clicks rang through the air. My eyes darted across the yard, searching for the spine and bulbous skull that was Despina. The last time I saw her, she was trying her best to defend the Weaver while he worked more threads through his loom. If it weren't for her, maybe things would've ended differently. I could've finished off the other nightmares fast enough to stop Nora from killing the Weaver.

The ivory skull darted down the side of the building, dark hair flowing over her exposed spine. The vertebrae glided back and forth like a snake, and her two-fingered hands guided the way. My hands twitched at my sides, eager to grab sand. *Focus.*

An unseen nightmare chirped behind me, and the cattails rustled as it raced away. I cringed. Despina swiveled toward me, her empty eye sockets locked on their target. There was no hesitation in her approach. She flew toward me as I stood, gathering handfuls of sand. I didn't want to destroy her with more pressing issues at hand, but I would if I had to. My sand circled me, protecting me.

But Despina came to a screeching halt a yard away and tossed the pod-creature at my feet before retreating just as fast. I focused on her until she started back up the wall of the Keep, then turned to the cracked shell at my feet. Carved into the smooth surface was Rowan's answer.

Never.

I kicked the dead nightmare away and glared up at Rowan. She met my eyes from the top of the Keep, the crown of raven's beaks atop her head catching the dull light, and raised her hands as if to say, *Come and get me.* I lifted my chin. If there wouldn't be a peaceful transition, there would be a bloody one. It would just take longer.

I turned on my heel, the sand returning to the satchel, and strode back the way I came. Every nightmare lurking amongst the foundation stared at me. Their gazes followed my face, my hands, my back, but none of them noticed the small line of sand I directed down my leg. They didn't see it glide among the grass and split in three different directions toward their comrades.

One spy for the air: a giant hairy spider with four large, paper-thin wings and legs covered in eyes.

One for the ground: a deer with two heads and the ears of a rabbit.

One for water: a seal without skin.

The sand inched inside each of them, wrapping around their minds like a vice. My magic would kill them eventually, just as it had the others I'd turned over the last few months, but hopefully not before I learned something of importance. I released my grip on the sand so they wouldn't act differently by stilling or focusing too eagerly on me, giving away my secret. Later, when I reclaimed it, everything they knew, I would know too.

But for now, Nora was expecting me.

I only wished I had better news.

Chapter Nine

Nora

Perhaps I should've been a bit more hesitant when I found a new fissure waiting when I fell asleep, but I went straight for the glowing memory. The Weaver's ragged breath filled my ears. Anger painted the hiss of every inhale as he stormed over jagged marble and rock. Black dust coated everything in sight, and fire smoldered beneath pieces of rubble. The Weaver trailed a hand over the walls of his Keep, his arm bare of thread minus a single strand circling his wrist. One last nightmare at his disposal. I squinted, not daring to get any closer to the memory. Dead things littered the yard, many of them half buried and torn apart.

"That bastard," the Weaver shouted. A wave of anguish shuddered through him—through me.

He pounded up the same outer staircase I used the day I

killed him. The image blurred in and out along with his vision, though I wasn't sure why. Was he hurt? He seemed to be moving fine. At the top, he shouldered his way through a door, and the image froze completely. It was like looking at a photograph of the loom, filtered red with rage. The *broken* loom. Treadles were scattered across the floor, the beater snapped in half, the roller missing. There was no reason I should know what those things were called, let alone where they went, but it all felt as obvious as my own name. Was that part of the magic too? Like the memories? Maybe there was more I would simply know once I returned to the Nightmare Realm.

The Weaver fell to his knees at the sight of his loom, and a heart-wrenching cry echoed through the room. His movements were slow, his hands shaking as they collected the treadles. The image quivered with his terror, his hurt. The loom was fixable, but it would take time—time he didn't have. There was a frantic edge to his thoughts, though I did not know what the thoughts were exactly.

I shouldn't know them at all.

The door slammed open behind him. The Weaver spun, clutching the splintered wood to his chest. The Sandman stood in the doorway. His clothes were torn and soggy with blood. Scratches ran along his cheek. My body jolted. I remembered that tear on his chest, the way it seemed to follow the upward curve of the moon tattooed beneath. This was the night we met, only I hadn't seen his face then. I was glad for that now. If it looked anything like it did now with the unspoken threat swirling in his eyes, I would have run in the other direction.

"What have you done?" the Weaver shouted.

The Sandman's gaze flicked down to the loom's broken

pieces, and surprise flashed across his face. "I did not do this," he said carefully.

"Oh?" The Weaver tossed the wood to the floor in a chorus of hollow clanks. "Then who did?"

The Sandman lifted his eyes and looked directly at the Weaver. At me. It felt like I was looking at a stranger. "I swear it, Weaver. This wasn't me."

The Weaver leapt at him, fingers extended toward his throat. There was a quick flick of the Sandman's hand, and something fell from his sleeve. A needle-straight piece of the Weaver's thread, embossed with silver, not gold. Like it was when he used the thread to find Katie. The rest happened in the blink of an eye. The Weaver gripped the Sandman's throat. The Sandman lifted a hand to his chest and shoved the stolen thread into the Nightmare Lord's heart. The Weaver stumbled back with a soft cry.

"I tried talking sense into you." The Sandman winced, his expression clearly pained. "But you wouldn't listen."

The Weaver ripped open his shirt and clawed at a red pinprick on his skin. The picture blurred and cleared and blurred and cleared. His breath was a hoarse wheeze. "What—" He gasped. "What is this?"

There was a short pause before the Sandman answered. "I've bound you to the Nightmare Realm."

"You—you can't do that. Not with so little thread," he said in shocked disbelief.

"I had more," the Sandman replied quietly, sounding almost sorry. "It won't last forever."

"I'll kill you," the Weaver spat. "I'll—"

"Nora." The Sandman's voice drifted in from the dark

nothing outside the glowing memory. It sounded different—the hard edge gone, replaced with the loving concern I was so used to hearing. "Nora, wake up."

I cracked my eyelids open to find his violet pupils inches away and flinched. The way he looked at the Weaver was branded in my mind. Would he look at me like that one day too? They were friends once, after all. I saw them together, as close then as we were now. It was only a matter of time. My stomach churned.

"Let me up." The words came out too high, too panicked.

"Sorry. I didn't mean—" He leaned back, surprised, and ran a finger over my knuckles. They were white where I clenched the sheets. "Are you okay?"

"I was—" I wasn't sure if I should tell him what I saw, but I didn't want to keep anything from him either. *Anything else.* "I think I found some of the Weaver's memories."

He sat down on the edge of the bed. "You said there was nothing there when you slept."

I nodded. "There still is most of the time."

"Most of the time?" A hurt look crossed his face. "How many times have you seen things?"

"Only once before tonight." I rubbed my eyes, pressing a little too hard. "I didn't mention it because I didn't know what to make of it or if I imagined it."

The Sandman tugged at the air near his temple like he used to do with his hood when he felt self-conscious. I didn't have to feel his emotions to understand. That I kept this from him made him miss the security of his hood. He had never known someone like me before, so not only did he lack answers to a lot of my questions, but I held things back from him. Dealt with them on my own. That was new for him—for us. Sometimes I wondered if he doubted my feelings for him too.

"I suppose it's possible," the Sandman started. "Some of his memories could've transferred with the magic, especially since he generated it himself instead of relying on an outward force." He rubbed his thumbs over his navy-blue fingertips, and for the briefest second, I swore it looked like he was jealous. "What did you see?"

"The first time, you helped the Weaver because *she* was coming." I paused to study his face, hoping that rang a bell, but he gave nothing new away. "You said you were friends with the Weaver once."

"A very long time ago," he answered quietly.

"What changed?"

The Sandman shifted uncomfortably. "Things changed for us both after we built the wall to keep Mare out of the Night World. Everything became more black and white." He sighed. "The Weaver became restless, which made him reckless. At the time, I thought he spiraled down his path to darkness rather quickly, but looking back, he was taking steps toward it for a while. It—*we*—"

There it was. A hurt so deep he apparently couldn't finish the sentence, and that's when I knew what I saw was real. The Weaver's magic hadn't conjured up something to make me sympathetic, nor had my own mind put the ideas there. The longing I saw on the Sandman's face today was something that would only exist if the friendship I saw in that first memory was true.

"You never told me the worlds—" Searing pain streaked across my forehead suddenly. I cried out and fell forward into the Sandman. Stars winked behind my eyelids. My head was going to explode. *Oh God.* This was it. The end. "Sandman," I gasped.

His hands were all over me, searching for an explanation. A wound maybe, though he wouldn't find one. This was something else, something dark and biting, and it came from inside.

Then, just as quickly, it was gone, and I took a tentative breath. An echo of it remained, throbbing in my temples, but I could see again. Move again. My stomach settled slowly. Had it been upset? I hadn't noticed.

"It's gone," I whispered.

"What is? What happened?" The Sandman pulled me close, squeezing me as if I would disappear otherwise. "Are you okay?"

"Just a headache." Darkness throbbed in a hollow pocket in my brain. I latched onto the Sandman's arm, forcing him to keep still so I could lean on him a minute more.

"A headache?" he echoed with concern.

"I've been getting them lately, just not this bad." Which was true. Only, I didn't think this was *just* anything. It felt like the Day World's way of saying *get out*, and I had no intention of ignoring its warning. "Did you find what you were looking for in the Nightmare Realm today?"

I felt his muscles twitch. "I created a few spies, and Baku is still trying to get a rough tally of Rowan's followers, but…"

I braced myself and met his gaze. "But what?"

"I offered Rowan a peaceful transition of power."

It felt like he dumped ice water over me. All the pain washed away, only to leave sparks of shock in its wake. Rowan didn't deserve anything less than death for turning me into this—all so she could kill me. I had trusted her, though I knew I shouldn't have, because the nonsense about maintaining a balance had seemed to be exactly that: nonsense. But Rowan knew it was real, and for that she needed her head ripped from her body.

Shh, the darkness cautioned, and I took my first full breath since the Sandman spoke. It was right. The Sandman wanted peace, not war, and I needed him on my side. More than needed. I *wanted* him there the same way I wanted him in my dreams every night, and that counted for more than anything else could.

I took another slow breath to ease the hard edge of anger and asked, "What was her answer?"

He pressed his lips into a straight line and shook his head.

"Of course," I grumbled.

"We have time before you go back. I can draw her out and finish this before then, if it's what you want."

"No." I broke away from him. "The nightmares have to respect me. *Fear* me. If you win this for me, they won't do either, and you know that." He knew it *well* because I shared the same thought months ago only for it to be shot down by his sound logic.

"Nora—"

"This isn't something either of us wanted, but it is what it is. *I'm* what I am." I pushed back at the grin, widening as if it had claim to that sentiment. "How many are going to suffer because of this? How many Dreamers have you saved, and how many more needed to be saved and weren't? I have to take responsibility for what I did to the Weaver, so you can either take me back tomorrow or I'll find my own way."

"We won't know much more than we do now," he argued.

"A lot can happen in twenty-four hours." A lot could happen in twenty-four seconds. A choice. A swing of a blade. A transfer of magic.

"It's too soon," the Sandman said softly.

No. I sighed. *Tomorrow is too late.*

I found myself once again on the eve of betrayal. Only this time, I wasn't uncertain like I had been when we left the Dream Realm for the Weaver's Keep. There was a chance that I wouldn't use the knife then; there was no chance that I wouldn't try to leave now, with or without the Sandman. My chest ached at the thought. How had we managed to get to this place? We were so close for five years. Was five months all it took to change that?

When he stood to leave, I grabbed his arm. My heart pumped, panic racing through me like blood in my veins. I loved him more than anyone or anything, and I was about to risk it all. Again. There was only so much a person could forgive, and I'd already nearly killed him. It wasn't intentional, but if I listened to him, it wouldn't have happened at all. For anyone else, it would've been the final straw. To do this, to go behind his back without ignorance as an excuse—I swallowed hard.

"Don't leave me," I whispered, my voice cracking.

He stared down at me, confused.

Don't abandon me, I wanted to clarify. *Don't hate me.* But I couldn't without giving myself away, so I scooted over and patted the bed instead. He sat without a word and draped an arm over my shoulders. I breathed in his scent. Soaked up his warmth. Reveled in the feel of his skin. "What you did with the stars the other night was amazing. I miss them." I snuggled closer. "I miss you. *Us.*"

His hand tightened on my shoulder. "I'm right here. I'll always be right here."

Not always.

I tilted my head up to kiss the spot beneath his ear. His breath hitched, and I smirked against him. Then I did it again. His fingers drifted from my shoulder up the side of my neck before he lowered his lips to mine. It was a soft reminder that, at least for this moment, he was mine and I was his. Just like we promised. Even if he couldn't forgive me, even if I couldn't forgive *myself*, I knew I would never stop loving him. There was no Nora without the Sandman. I moved closer and leaned in to deepen the kiss. His fingers found the back of my head, weaving into my hair.

I felt each of his movements with every part of me. The sureness in the way he cradled my head, the gentle way he moved against me. The bed shifted, and he knelt in front of me without breaking contact. His free hand dug into my lower back, holding me closer, and in return, I gripped the sides of his vest.

Now, with the Sandman close, the darkness felt far away. It was as if I was *me* again, and I took and took until I wanted more than his kisses. My hands slipped down to his waist. My fingers found the hem of his shirt and slipped beneath it. He shivered as my fingers ran over the sensitive skin just above his pants, and a small moan escaped my throat. I loved that I had this effect on him. My palms flattened against his stomach, and his mouth fell to my cheek, my jaw, my neck. I tilted my head to give him easier access and tugged on his bunched shirt.

The Sandman broke away long enough to let me pull his shirt and vest over his head. The crescent moon tattooed on his chest glowed faintly in the darkness of my room, lifting and falling with each of his rapid breaths. The sight sparked something inside me, and another small groan escaped my lips as he kissed my neck again. His grip tightened on my arms at the sound, almost as if he were forcing himself to keep them in place. But I didn't want him to. I wanted to feel them on me. I needed to—so I wiggled beneath him until I finally managed to remove my shirt too.

The Sandman stared at me, pupils blown wide. "Nora—" I held my breath and waited. Waited for him to tell me again that we should stop. Instead, his eyes trailed down my body before coming back up to my face. I watched as the internal struggle vanished from behind his eyes. "We don't have to do this."

"I want to," I assured him.

His throat bobbed. "Are you sure?"

"I'm more than sure," I whispered and gave the fabric around his hips a little tug, begging him to stop talking and start touching.

Still, he hesitated a moment longer, and then a small trail of sand rose from the pouch around his neck. It floated across the room and disappeared into the crack around the doorknob. There was a faint click of the lock.

I turned back to the Sandman with a playful smile. "Smooth."

"I try." His voice was deeper than I'd ever heard it before.

He kissed me again, slowly. Reverently. My heart hammered in my chest, and my hands shook as I worked the ties at the front of his pants. He lowered himself back over me and nudged my ear with his nose. "I love you."

"I love you too." And I meant it with all that I was.

Chapter Ten

The pen slid smoothly across the envelope. I took my time with each cursive letter, feeling the finality of the words inside. Now that I'd cooled down a bit, I knew I had to leave them something. The explanation of my whereabouts was still vague, but a little more elaborate in that I gave a general idea of where I was going-but-not-really-going. I would scope out New York, live it up a little before the internship started. *Better to ask forgiveness than permission,* I wrote at the end of the letter. So what if it wasn't completely logical to manage such a feat? After not working for months, the money I made from working at Howell's Furniture and Decor wasn't enough to travel for so long in such an expensive place. Most of my savings went into the small arsenal hidden beneath GED books in my bookbag.

I clicked the pen twice and set it carefully on the desk. The letter should probably go to my mother, but I couldn't bring myself to scrawl those three little letters. Instead, Katie's name stared up at me. My sister wouldn't know exactly what happened or where I was, but she *would* know I hadn't hopped the first bus out of town, even if she pretended otherwise.

This was it. I drew a deep breath and placed the envelope at the center of my desk. It was the lone object on the surface, the study guides now in the trash and everything else swept into drawers. If this worked, there would be no going back.

I set my head on the wood and squeezed my eyes shut against the prickle of tears. *Don't cry.* Strength. Fearlessness. Fortitude. *Don't cry.* I couldn't stay. *Do. Not. Cry.* I didn't want to go to that horrible place. *No tears allowed when I can only blame myself.*

My gaze shifted to the bed. The sheets were still rumpled from my time with the Sandman. When he left at dawn, I spent a long time lying there, wrapped up in his scent, before showering. I wondered if the pillow, which still had an indent from his head, would smell like him after so many hours. I bet it would. My heart twisted around itself.

Truly, I was a horrible, selfish person. I knew what being together meant to him. Even though I felt desperate, even though I *wanted* to be with the Sandman—had wanted it for so long—it wasn't right. And the night before I snuck back into the Nightmare Realm? Self-loathing foamed in my throat, threatening to choke me.

I leapt from the chair, fluffed the pillows, and flung the sheets into place so there was no trace of what we did. If only it were that easy to erase my impending betrayal. The grin faded in, spewing its darkness in what felt like impatience. Maybe eagerness. Both.

I felt the same way.

With twitchy movements, I lifted my bookbag from the floor and eased my arms through the straps. Carefully packed inside were a few changes of clothes, necessary toiletries, and a variety of weapons: my Swiss army knife, a Taser, pepper spray, and, most notably, Paul's handgun I pilfered while he was in the bathroom this morning. With luck, I wouldn't have to use any of it, but this was the Nightmare Realm. A place where an unknown percentage of creatures wanted me dead. Who was I kidding? Luck had nothing to do with it.

I removed the pencil box and felt the threads' desperation through the tin. My hands shook as I opened the lid. Gold filament glimmered weakly around the black threads. I stopped breathing as I stared down at the squirming, unborn nightmares. An ache bloomed inside me. Starved. Angry. I picked up one of the threads and closed the pencil box before I could change my mind. A coil of darkness swirled from the grin the moment I shut it back in the drawer, but I held it back. This wasn't something to rush into when I'd never used my magic before. For anything. At all. I gnawed my bottom lip.

With a deep breath, I stared at the thread. My vision blurred, and suddenly I saw—not with my eyes, but some new part of me—exactly what it held. Or, part of the nightmare it would become if given the chance. Off-white skin with pointed thistles along a thick arm, part of a torso, and two nondescript legs. I hadn't exactly been precise when I'd ripped the thread off the Weaver's arm, but it felt like something that could be fixed with a working loom.

"Okay." I held it up in front of me and thought back to the

one time I saw the Weaver turn a strand into a nightmare. He flicked his wrist and it straightened; the Sandman warned him not to create a nightmare in the Dream Realm, and then—then there was that horrifying *thing*, but I didn't want to bring the nightmare to life. I swallowed hard.

"Let it in."

I jumped at the sound of Mara's voice. She crouched in the corner of my room, staring out at me from behind a curtain of coarse hair. "What?" I snapped.

"The Night World. Let it in. The thread is your tether."

Let it in? Wasn't it *already* in? "Have you been spying on me again?"

"You gave me no choice. If I hadn't, you would leave me here." She rocked side-to-side. "Besides, it seemed like you needed further guidance."

"And you think I'll take you now just because you're here?" I clutched the thread to my chest, hiding it from her steady gaze. "I told you I make promises to no one, and you creeping around me twenty-four-seven doesn't exactly make me feel charitable."

"You make promises to the Sandman," she crooned and eyed the bed. "With words and without them."

My face became blistering hot. She was here? She… "You *watched* us?" I shrieked. "What the hell is wrong with you? Are you—"

"Relax, Lady. I didn't stay." Her tongue flicked out in disgust. "I left when he locked the door."

"Oh. My. God." I gaped at her. Enough had happened by that point. "Get out right now."

She parted her hair with her long nails. "There's no need to be embarrassed."

"I'm not embarrassed," I lied. "I'm pissed off."

Mara flicked a look at the fist I still held to my chest. "Are you going to try or not?"

"Not," I growled.

Mara tutted, then vanished.

I slumped in my chair and ran a hand over my face. Did she have to say anything? I could've lived the rest of my hopefully-very-long life without knowing she'd seen us kissing. Shirtless. The memory of what followed sparked through me, and I bit my lip. I was still sore despite how gentle the Sandman had been, but it was a good pain. A reminder of what we shared. It also made the guilt a million times worse. We cemented a bond that was already there, and now—

No.

I couldn't second guess myself. I had to go before the entire Nightmare Realm bowed at Rowan's feet. Before the Day World whittled me down any more than it already had. I swiveled my chair back toward the desk and took a deep breath.

Right. I exhaled slowly. Just let it in…

I willed the dark, muted sense of the Nightmare Realm forward, the grin more than eager to assist, but nothing happened. I huffed and slammed the thread down on top of the envelope. The grin sneered. *Quitter*, it taunted as more wisps caressed its lips. I lifted the thread again.

And stared.

And stared.

I stared at that perfect, watermarked smile. At those curls of black smoke.

The gold filaments on the thread brightened, the impression of the nightmare fading to nothing. The Nightmare Realm rushed toward me in a flurry of chaos. It called to me, a siren song, beckoning me back into its fold. Begging me. I rose from my seat. "Yes," I whispered to its unasked question.

My stomach bottomed out. I careened toward a black shroud, feeling as if I was still and moving all at once. The air burned my eyes, but I kept them wide open out of fear. Fear I would miss something. An obstacle. A danger. The terror of the endless falling sensation gave way to horrified excitement.

Then pain sliced across my shoulders. The pull slowed, held back by something heavy now attached to my back, and I scrambled to lean forward again. The stabbing pain doubled as whatever held me gripped harder. The movement sent my body careening out of control. I flailed, trying desperately to shake it off. My nails scraped against hard, calloused skin, but whatever it was didn't let up. If anything, it held even tighter. A scream burned its way out of my throat.

A thin veil of silver fibers cast a soft glow ahead. I tried to aim for it, but the faster I spun, the harder it became. My stomach clenched, threatening to spew its contents as the spinning continued to intensify. I screamed again, a low, pitiful sound, and black hair whipped into my mouth. I ripped it out and held the coarse locks in my palm. Even with the universe twirling around me, I knew what I was looking at.

Mara.

"No!" I pulled at the shank of hair. Reached back for her head. Tried to bite at her hands. All to no avail. I was too dizzy. Too disoriented. "No!" I cried again. Not Mara. She couldn't be in the Night World. *No, no, no!* She would destroy everything. The Sandman would think—

A silver veil snagged us like a net, stretching around my body like a cocoon. It wrapped tight, cutting off my airway, and stars burst across my eyes. It felt like I was stuck there for ages before it gave way with a loud rip. I gasped for air as the fall suddenly resumed. The spinning, thankfully, did not. But even more concerning was the hard ground rising to meet me at an alarming speed. I twisted myself around in the air to let Mara meet the ground first.

Her body crunched beneath mine, her nails pulling from my shoulders with sickening pops. The world slowed around me. My ears picked up on every little sound my body made, all set to the backdrop of the ringing in my ears. I rolled off Mara, bones grinding, and wheezed. My sneakers scraped against the dirt to find purchase, but it was no use. Jell-O. I was Jell-O.

Mara leapt to her feet and shook her limbs out. "Thank you, Lady," she croaked with a knowing stare.

"Mara," I squeezed out. "Wait."

Instead, she raced away in her loping gait. I shoved myself up to follow, but my knees buckled. My cheek scraped against the rock and dirt, and I groaned. Exhaustion bore down on me with its full weight. I struggled to keep my eyes open, but after five months without any real rest, it was a beast of a thing.

Consciousness hit me like a freight train. I flew up into a sitting position and instantly regretted the movement. My head swam through murky water, my muscles ached. I squinted down at my body, a hiss leaking from between my teeth as my neck throbbed. Everything looked intact, albeit filthy. I wiggled my toes. *All in working order.* It was more than I expected after dropping out of the sky into… My pulse quickened. This was decidedly not the place where I collapsed. When I fell on Mara, it was…I wasn't exactly sure. The whole thing happened so fast—the falling, the landing—but the brown dirt on my clothes proved the overwhelmingly green landscape around me was different.

Green buttons, to be exact. Stacked from largest to smallest to make a forest of pines.

I blinked the last bits of fuzziness from my eyes to find a dozen shapes hidden among them, watching me. I froze and stared back at the woodland nightmares. Rabbits, squirrels, deer, a single raccoon, and tiny birds. Their eyes, made of black buttons, seemed lifeless, but they were undoubtedly alive. Their bodies, made of more stacked buttons of varying colors and shades, clicked gently with every slight movement.

"What the hell is this?" I staggered to my feet.

As I did, the nightmares bowed their heads. The string holding the buttons together peeked through each tiny crack. I gave a quiet, surprised gasp. That was a good sign, but there was no way any of them could have dragged me here, so who did? I reached for the straps of my bookbag to get a weapon, only to find it missing. "No." I spun, searching the carpet of brown and green buttons beneath my feet and slammed my palms over my shoulders as if finding them bare was a mistake.

A rapid burst of pain splintered beneath my hands and sent me reeling back a step. *Mara.* I slid the neck of my shirt over my left shoulder to examine the wounds from her long nails. Black thread dipped in and out of my skin, holding the holes together with a slight pucker. My heart thudded in my chest. Who—

"Lady!" A high, feminine voice cut the air. "You're awake. Splendid."

A female nightmare bustled through the trees. She appeared human in every aspect, though she was clearly modeled after someone's eccentric aunt on an acid trip. Dozens of spools of thread were affixed to her short jacket and strands full of buttons clicked around her neck like pearls. White tights ran down to her floral Mary Janes and her skirt was a rainbow of neon tulle. Her blond hair was divided down the middle in two French braids, and a tiny top hat, no bigger than my thumb, sat cockeyed on her head. She blinked large, owlish eyes and smiled. "Join us, join us!"

"I'm—" I cleared my throat in hopes of sounding more in control. "I'm in a hurry."

"Oh, I'm sure you are," the nightmare said. "You've been asleep so long." She stepped around the button creatures and tucked my arm through hers. "I was just starting a new project, but it can wait. It's not every day the Lady of Nightmares pays a visit."

Project?

She led me through rows of trees into a clearing. Mounds of buttons nearly twice my height were sorted by color on the far side, but it was what sat in the center that stopped me: an elderly woman strapped to the surface of a dinner table by large red ribbons, each bow expertly tied.

"Don't pay her any attention," the nightmare chirped. "The beginning stage is always a bit messy, but she'll be beautiful in no time."

The Dreamer turned her head and large blue buttons stared in our direction, sewed over her eyelids. "Help me, please," she begged, her voice raw.

I wrenched my arm from the nightmare and bit my tongue.

The Weaver wouldn't let this bother him. I needed to win the nightmares to my side, and that wouldn't happen if I outwardly judged and chastised them for doing what they did. I had to be diplomatic. For now. Once I cemented myself as their leader, I could change the rules.

"Who are you?" I asked.

"Oh, goodness. How rude of me." The woman straightened her jacket. "I'm the Doll Maker."

"Ah." I put on the face I wore so often: the calm, unbothered expression my own mother bought for so many years. "Well, don't kill her. We don't need to give the Sandman reason to put the barrier back up."

She bowed slightly. "Of course, Lady, but I would never hurt my dolls."

I watched a bead of blood travel down the old woman's face and held back a cringe. We apparently had very different opinions of what *hurt* meant. My fingers skimmed over the stitches on my shoulder. "Did you do this?"

"Yes, Lady." She tapped her fingers together in front of her and rocked on her heels. "I hope you don't mind. I know you heal quickly, but when I found you, the wounds were bleeding quite badly."

I shook my head. "I appreciate it."

The Doll Maker beamed. "Don't hesitate to come back next time you need stitching. You won't find another nightmare with as light a touch as mine."

Next time. She didn't have to sound so sure about my needing to be mended again. It stood to reason I would, but still, let a girl find her feet before knocking them out from under her.

"How long was I out?" I asked.

"Six hours or so."

Six hours? My family would know I was missing by now. So much for not ruining Thanksgiving. I rubbed at the guilt rolling through my upper abdomen. The Sandman probably knew too. Would he also know about Mara? I had to warn him before Mara hurt anyone else.

"Where's my bag?" I asked.

The Doll Maker flung her hands up and scurried around the table. A moment later, she stood in front of me and gingerly held the black bookbag out as if it were a baby. "I had to remove it to get to your injuries, but it's all there. I didn't even peek."

I nodded slowly as I eased the straps over my shoulders. It hadn't occurred to me that she would steal anything, but now that she brought it up, I would be checking as soon as I got a moment alone. Doing so now would be insulting, and she seemed to like me, which was both lucky and invaluable.

"So." I looked around the button forest. "Which way would the Keep be?"

"Terrible Rowan. Terrible, terrible," the Doll Maker spat. "Taking what's not hers. It would be one thing if the nightmares following her were only doing it because they craved a powerful leader. A majority are, mind you, but there are a few that she's spent decades wooing to her side. Ah—" She cut herself off sheepishly. "Forgive me. That was not your question, Lady. If you head—"

A gloved hand materialized on the Doll Maker's shoulder, followed by a man nearly seven feet tall. I swallowed a scream as he loomed over her with a wide red hat swooping low over his features. People didn't just *appear* like that. But he wasn't a person. He was more dangerous than that, which made staying silent all the harder. When he brought his chin up, a black Venetian mask covered his entire face. Red painted lips swooped up into a cold smirk, and red looping scallops were painted around each eye—or where his eyes should've been if the mask offered holes to see from. The black and red color scheme from his mask continued into the rest of his clothing, from the high, puffed collar to the matte shoes on his feet.

"Halven! My goodness," the Doll Maker chattered. "Two visitors today! Aren't we lucky?" she called to the woman on the table. "Though you did give me a bit of a fright."

Halven gave her a soft squeeze before removing his hand, then stepped toward me. *Don't move* .My legs quaked from the effort to stay still. He extended a hand covered in a black silk glove, and I flinched. He seemed to contemplate the reaction, his head tilted. I could feel him staring, though there was no outward proof of it.

Then Halven bowed deeply.

"Umm…" I glanced between him and the Doll Maker. "Hey."

"Such good timing." The Doll Maker shifted closer to me, almost as if she sensed my discomfort. "There's no one better than Halven to guide you where you're going."

Doubtful. Besides, I was sure his timing was anything but a coincidence. "But he doesn't know where I'm going," I said as neutrally as possible.

"Of course he does." She patted Halven's forearm as if she were a proud mother. "He knows where everyone is, where they've been, and where they're going. Sometimes even before they do, isn't that right?"

Halven, still in his bow, dipped his head lower.

"He can take you right where you're going, my Lady. Don't you doubt that!"

Halven lifted his head, and it felt as if he stitched me to the buttons beneath my feet. "Do you know where I'm going?" I asked, somehow sure he did, though I sure as heck didn't know my destination. Heading straight for Rowan before I got my footing was foolish, and I would need to get in touch with the Sandman before making a move. For his help, and, more importantly, for his forgiveness. If the worst happened, I didn't want to die without apologizing first.

Halven nodded.

"And is it the Keep?" I asked curiously.

He shook his head, and I fidgeted with the straps of my bookbag. "I'll need some things before I face Rowan. Supplies. An army—?" I said carefully, testing their reactions to gauge how bad things really were. I really, *really* didn't want to raise an army. Or lead one. But if Rowan had the Blood Army at her service…

"Army?" The Doll Maker pressed a hand to her chest and glanced quickly over her shoulder toward the woman on the table. She shuffled closer and lowered her voice. "My Lady, you don't need an army to defeat the usurper. All you need is—"

Halven shot up straight and snatched my hand with his. Before the Doll Maker could say another word, we were halfway through the button forest with every step feeling like ten. The darkness inside me reveled in it. Unfortunately, I couldn't share the sentiment.

"Stop," I whispered, trying to shake away the disorientation. When he didn't, I sucked in a breath. "Stop!" The voice was half mine, half something else. A commanding thing. Halven came to an abrupt halt and released me. "I didn't give you permission to touch me."

He bowed low.

"What was she going to tell me?" I snapped. "All I need is what?"

"Your power, my Lady." His voice was deep and forced from behind the mask, as if it took all of him to speak a single word.

I waited for him to continue, but he remained silent. An innocent enough answer, so why rip me out of there? But now wouldn't be the best time to call him on it. We were alone, for one. I took in the desolate landscape. "Where are we?" A fiery geyser blasted up from the ground, and a wave of heat brushed against my face. *Oh, cool.* Death by fire. My favorite. "Nevermind," I muttered.

"I will not betray you," Halven vowed. "Trust me."

"Trust has to be earned."

I had given it too freely before when I took the dagger from Rowan and Kail. I wouldn't make the same mistake twice, but the truth was I didn't have much choice. Not unless I wanted to wander aimlessly and hope the next nightmare I ran across wasn't an enemy. I'd only seen a small amount of my own realm: the cave Katie was tortured in, the Barren, the Blood Tower, and a few other random places on the way to the Keep. Nothing that would offer me shelter.

The straps of my bookbag dug painfully into my shredded shoulders, but I did my best to ignore it in favor of the very real, very big problem in front of me. I stared at the black spaces where Halven's eyes should've been. *Don't do it.* But the grin, half formed and unsure, nudged me forward.

"So earn it," I dared. "And keep your hands to yourself."

Halven gracefully swept an arm out, and I edged past him.

I can do this. I can rule here.

Not that I had much choice.

Chapter Eleven

Snow crunched beneath my boots, my breath clouding in front of my face, but not even the frigid temperature could wipe away my smile. My heart was quieter than it had been in a long time, and my body felt more alive. I could still feel every line Nora traced on my skin. The taste of her lips lingered on mine, along with the memory of her breath on my neck. The shiver that ran over me had nothing to do with the nightmare landscape surrounding me.

Pay attention.

I had a job to do. The three nightmares I took control of on the lawn of the Keep waited at the top of the mountain overlooking the ruined palace. I ignored the booted footprints, large enough for me to lie down in, that lead in the same direction. Either an enormous nightmare lurked nearby, or they were there for the fear factor. That I left no prints of my own did not escape me. It was likely designed to confuse Dreamers when they couldn't retrace their steps, but it benefited me in a way that would've irked the Weaver into altering the entire cliff side.

My smile did waver then. The Weaver was dead, and—Nora's situation aside—I should've been glad of it. Part of me was, but not *every* part. It was strange to know I would never fight him again. There was something like comfort in an enemy one knew and something like grief in the ghost of our friendship. Having both ripped away left me disoriented. Maybe it was a good thing I was too busy to process that aspect; maybe the uncertainty of it would fade away with time.

The two-headed deer trotted toward me, its eyes glazed over with my magic. I laid a palm on its forehead and closed my eyes. My magic skated to the surface just below his fur. An image grew slowly. It warbled and faded, but the message was clear. At least two-thirds of the Blood Army lurked in the swamp near the Keep, biding their time, hidden from view. Their usual near-constant moaning had ceased, likely on Rowan's order. Their black cloaks blended in well with the dark trees. The hiss of the red mist coiling around their ankles could be attributed to the tears of children hitting the scalding swamp water or the cry of the witch dwelling at its center. All-in-all, the swamp was well chosen. I tried not to think about how many of the remaining third were in the basement because even a fraction of the Blood Army was more than enough to pose a threat.

Other images came and went but showed nothing I hadn't already seen with my own eyes. My hand fell to my side, and I willed my magic to fade back into the deer's subconscious. The nightmare's pupils constricted as the creature regained itself, and a moment later it raced back down the mountain with its tail in the air. I had hoped to learn something more. One of Rowan's weaknesses, maybe, or if a more advanced nightmare was helping her. I couldn't take out Rowan, but that didn't mean I couldn't weed out other powerful enemies. Unless the other two spies had anything we could use as a springboard, I didn't see how I could justify bringing Nora back earlier than planned.

There's time, I told myself continuously over the last few months. We would figure it out one step at a time, but now that time was almost up, and we had figured out precisely nothing. The thought of Nora coming here, staying here, ruling here, made my blood run cold.

A quiet buzz of wings zipped down the mountain. The spider's black form cut a line through the stark white horizon. It veered left, then right, as if it were unsure which way to go. *Here,* I called to my magic, but a stone spear whizzed overhead, straight through the spider's wings. The arachnid flipped through the air, legs flailing, and stopped only when its abdomen became impaled on a broken branch. I froze. Between us, the bright white handle of the spear stuck straight into the sky like an icicle. My heart thumped, heavy. A spear that size would need a nightmare even bigger to throw it. The footprints—

The spider's legs quivered and black blood oozed from the base of its missing wings. I scanned the direction the spear sailed from but saw nothing. The obvious thing to do was leave. The spider was dying, and there was no need to pit myself against anything that could help Nora later. But if it learned something, *anything*, it could make the risk worth it. There was a world of possibilities left unaligned. Baku and I hadn't killed so many nightmares saving Dreamers that it would affect—

A cutting gasp of Nora's fear rippled through my veins, yet it was the excitement mixed into that caught me up. It was a dark thrill woven with magic I knew all too well, and it left me with a warm, pooling sense of accomplishment. Nora wouldn't, would she? *Could* she? I rubbed my chest as it grew closer. *No.* Nora had barely mastered basic combat. There was no way she could make it to the Nightmare Realm without help. Then my lungs deflated as every other sensation gave way to blinding terror. I zeroed in on the pain, nearly bright enough to blind me, and reached out desperately for something solid to grab onto. For a cord no longer there. But there were others. I latched onto the closest one and held on to the dull cord as if it were my sole lifeline.

By the time I could see straight again, I stood in Nora's bedroom. I gripped the edge of her dresser, panting, but when I raised my eyes, it wasn't Nora that stood in front of me. Katie faced the desk, and her hand shook as she clutched a piece of paper, her knuckles white. Pieces fell into place. The note. Nora's absence. The emotions.

"No." The word fell from my tongue so quietly I barely heard myself speak, but Katie did. She spun toward me, banging into the desk, and her eyes locked onto me with something between recognition and fear. "Where is she?" I asked from beneath my hood. Katie opened her mouth, either to answer or scream, but nothing came out. I stepped forward and plucked the paper from between her slackened fingers. "She's safe?" I asked, reading over the letter. The page crumpled in my grip. "Taking time to enjoy the city?"

"Why don't *you* tell *me* where she is?" Katie asked in a wavering voice.

The Nightmare Realm. She was in the Nightmare Realm. My body felt numb, my brain scrambling to find answers. How? I glanced at Katie. At least I had an answer for why. Her mother and sister—the only two close blood relatives she had—made her feel like she was out of her mind, and she was starting to believe it.

I flung my hood back and stared Katie right in the eyes. "Are you sure you want to know?"

She slammed one hand over her mouth. "Ben?"

I held the note out for her to take back, waiting for her answer. Katie did everything in her power to pretend nothing happened five months ago, including lying to Nora's face. Why would she want to know now, now that it was too late?

Something hard flickered through her eyes, her expression shuttering. "Or should I call you Sandman?"

"Call me whatever you like," I said, harsher than intended.

When Katie didn't take the note, I set it down on the desk. Dusk had barely settled outside, casting the room in cool light. Already it felt cold and empty, the four walls missing their heart. The sentiment echoed in my chest. Nora asked me to take her back to the Night World, and I failed to give her the answer she wanted last night. So she went anyway. Because she didn't believe in me. I searched out her emotions but found a black wall as hard as granite. I fell onto the edge of her bed. The same bed we… She knew what being together meant to me. I wanted to take things slow and make sure our relationship had a firm foundation so there was no chance for regrets. But still she… Had she planned on leaving with or without me even then? I should've known. The night she found me in the Dream Realm with the knife Rowan gave her, she wanted the same thing from me. It was all to distract me from her lies.

"You won't find her," I said softly to Katie. I covered my face with my hands and fought to breathe. "What have you done, Nora?"

Katie made a disgusted sound in the back of her throat. "It's happening again, isn't it? What did you rope her into this time?"

I pressed the heels of my palms against my eyes. "I can explain."

"No," she said in a low, angry voice. "I don't want to hear your sorry excuses. Get out of my house."

"I—"

The door slammed. When I looked up, I was alone in Nora's room, and my heart tore. *Gone.* Nora was gone. What more could I have done to make her believe in me? When had she stopped? There was a time not so long ago that we were inseparable and had leaned on each other. She told me she trusted me, *loved* me, as I loved her, but she had taken the knife from Rowan. She killed the Weaver, nearly killed me, because she hadn't believed what I said about the balance. And now… She didn't believe me when I told her what she was about to walk into. And yes, part of me selfishly wanted to keep her from the Nightmare Realm to protect her, but I wouldn't have. What I wanted was nothing compared to what she needed. It never was.

And yet—

And yet, I couldn't stop myself from running a hand over the dark wall between me and Nora. "Let me in," I begged softly.

To my surprise, something pulsed in response. A glimmer of silver fractured the stone. My power—the dream Nora carried—

cried out to me, and my chest twisted. *The dream.* Nora got herself back to the Nightmare Realm and, before that, found some of the Weaver's memories. Why hadn't I noticed she was already capable of it? What was to say she couldn't find the dream too?

I followed that small, hopeless piece of magic to the Nightmare Realm and braced myself for the worst.

☾

Though Nora's magic read loud and clear, it seemed no matter which entrance into the Nightmare Realm I used, she seemed just as far away. The center of the realm seemed a logical place for the barrier to spit her out, as that was where the Keep was, but I hoped she was anywhere else. I tried to stuff the hysteria down as the magic lured me into the Doll Maker's domain and focused on Nora. The possibility of Rowan having her—*no.* She couldn't. If Rowan had Nora, she wouldn't waste time killing her.

There.

Just ahead. A massive concentration of Nora's magic. I broke into a run, my boots clattering against a blanket of buttons covering the ground. I wove around trees of the same material, and a smattering of creatures raced further into the forest to distance themselves from me. I slid to a stop at the edge of the clearing, and my chest exploded.

She was there, alive and seemingly safe, flanked by two nightmares. I squinted across a table occupied by a strapped-down elderly Dreamer and past the Doll Maker to the masked nightmare standing beside Nora. One graze of Halven's hand and he could whisk Nora away to anywhere within the Nightmare Realm. Worse, I wouldn't be able to find her, magic or no magic. Not if the nightmare of lost things maintained contact with her. He knew exactly where someone wanted to go and exactly how to take them as far from that place as possible. If he saw me, Nora would be gone in an instant, but I couldn't let her take his offered hand. I held my breath, searching frantically for a solution to get them away from each other, but then Nora spoke.

"I'll need some things before I face Rowan. Supplies. An army—"

An army? My eyes widened. What was she talking about? She didn't need an army. She had *me.* She had someone she could trust.

But she didn't.

After everything, Nora didn't trust me. She couldn't—not if she did this. Ice shrouded my heart as it slipped from its place in my chest and shattered.

"Army?" the Doll Maker exclaimed, then twisted to stare at me across the clearing.

I shifted into the shadows, my mind repeating *Nora doesn't trust me* over and over. My lungs ached, unable to take in air, and I flipped my hood over my head. I leaned into one of the tall button trees. What could I do now? What should I do? I could barge over there and protect her, or I could stand here and do nothing. We were beyond talking now. Nora made it clear she didn't want to listen.

"You can come out, Dream Lord. She's gone," the Doll Maker called in a sour tone after some time. "I haven't hurt her, so I trust you won't hurt me."

I stepped out of my hiding place and forced my shoulders back. Halven was nowhere to be seen, and I nearly crumbled when I saw Nora wasn't either. Had she taken his hand of her own free will? Did he force her to go with him?

"Are you so sure about that?" I asked.

"She's safe with Halven." The Doll Maker plucked a large needle from her hair and circled the table where the old woman thrashed. "Like I was about to tell her, there's no need to build an army. It will only take one person with the right skills to kill the usurper."

I bared my teeth. If it were that easy, I would've brought Nora back a long time ago. "If that's true, if you're so loyal, why don't you kill Rowan yourself?"

The Doll Maker laughed and bent over the Dreamer. "Do I terrify you, Dream Lord? No. I terrify only these precious souls." She ran a hand lovingly over the woman's hair. "Given that, do you think I've survived this long by entwining myself in power struggles?"

"There would be no struggle with Rowan dead."

"Does a snake not still have venom after it's dead? She has those loyal to her." The Doll Maker tied a knot at the end of a string. "Besides, Lady Nightmare has many weaknesses. There will be struggle after struggle until she learns to snuff the rebellion, and when that time comes, Sandman, she will no longer be the girl you knew."

"She will always be Nora," I insisted.

The Doll Maker began stitching the Dreamer's mouth shut, muffling her screams, and my jaw tightened. "Oh, don't look so perturbed. She'll be fine when she wakes up." The Doll Maker rolled her eyes. "And as for the Lady always being Nora, maybe you're right. Or maybe she already isn't. What do I know?"

She *was* Nora. True, she was changing—growing into her new self—but everyone did that over the course of their life. The

Weaver had. I had. Long before the worlds were separate, he wasn't so dark, and I wasn't so light, but we became what we needed to become for things to work. Nora was a new entity though. There were no established rules, no baseline. She could become what she wanted to become, and I wouldn't let her lose herself completely without a fight.

"Where did Halven take her?"

"How should I know?" The Doll Maker tugged thick black thread up in front of her with a small frown. "I'd venture to guess he's going to his twin. They've been more open about their meetings now that Rowan's no longer at the Blood Tower. Don't you fret: Lady Nightmare will be safe for now—unlike the rest of us, now that Mara's back."

The world spiraled out from under me. *No.* Nora wouldn't... I told her who Mare was, *what* she was. She would never... Mare was the worst kind of nightmare. Not even a nightmare, if I was being particular. Mare was something else—an Ancient, like Baku—and they played by no one's rules. That was why the Weaver and I locked them in the Ever Safe not long after we were made. They killed without reason, destroyed things just to feel the despair it caused. And what better place for primal beasts than a world filled with mortals? If Mare had her way, she would take us back to the dark days when danger roamed without borders. Gone were the creatures of legend from the Day World because the Weaver and I took them from it. Lured them into a cage and bolted it shut. Only two ever made it out again. We'd gotten lucky with Baku, who was content as long as his stomach was full. Mare on the other hand would've spent every day of her eternal life trying to break down the doors to the Ever Safe.

Oh, Nora...

I never imagined she would kill the Weaver and destroy the balance, but I hadn't known better then. Now I did. I stared at the place she stood moments ago. There was no catching up to her now that she'd gone with Halven, but even if there was, I didn't have time to follow. With Mare back, I had to reinforce every ward around the Dream Realm. And more. I had to add more. And then—then I would find Nora. Because, if nothing else, I deserved answers.

Chapter Twelve

Nora

Halven's outfit looked more ridiculous the longer I stared at it. His black jacket, piped with red, was covered in an illogical pattern of embossed lines. The collar rose high enough to cover any exposed skin, and the hat shadowed the entirety of his head not hidden behind the mask. From the laces on his boot hung a small key, rusted with age. He oozed a gentlemanly air, while his appearance made him seem more like he belonged in a theatrical group performing satire.

"What are you the nightmare of, exactly?" I asked.

His chest rose with a deep breath, and he forced out an answer. "Being lost."

"What?" My steps slowed. "But the Doll Maker said—and we've been—"

I was duped right off the bat. *Stupid, stupid, stupid.* Even the darkness inside me had hesitated to follow Halven. And the worst part was that this wasn't even the first trick I'd fallen for. Mara fooled me as well, though to my own credit, I never trusted her. And I hadn't purposely brought her back, but she was here nonetheless. Somewhere. Doing who knows what. While I was—*oh, no.* Where was I? I was so busy staring at Halven's ridiculous clothes that I hadn't paid attention to anything else. I whirled around. The button forest was nowhere in sight. Instead, a mountain rose in the distance, pricking at a bad memory, and an orange pond swirled into a whirlpool on our left. How long had we been walking?

Halven patted his chest with a flat hand. "I know where someone is going bec—" His voice cracked. "If not—" He rubbed at his throat through the ruffles. "If I don't know where they *want* to go, I cannot make them lost."

Right. Of course. *Of course.* I was putting my fate in the hands of a nightmare that excelled in getting people lost. Was I too lost for the Sandman to find me? I winced. As if he would even try after what I did. I was on my own now. A weight pressed down on my chest, my heart fluttering, bordering on panic. *Stay calm.* I inhaled slowly and let it out through my mouth. *Calm.* I was the Weaver. This was fine. I would be fine.

Halven motioned me forward with another dramatic sweep of his hand.

Fine, I chanted in my head. I walked alongside him, this time keeping my eyes on my surroundings. Something about them felt familiar, but I hadn't seen this golden prairie before. Small, tan, rodent-like nightmares popped up from the tall grass. They blinked red eyes once, twice, then bobbed their heads in our direction and scurried away, whispering excitedly among themselves.

"Should I be worried about where they're running off to?" I asked.

Halven shook his head.

Still, I watched the grass move as what had to be dozens of them fled from our path. The animals in the button forest had stayed and bowed. Head-bobs could've meant anything. A signal to each other that I was here. That they should rush off and tell Rowan where I was. Or even a signal to Halven that his heinous plan to trap me was ready.

I reached slowly for the small pocket on the side of my bag while keeping one eye on Halven and another on the grass. The zipper made a small sound, and my hand froze. Halven cocked his head toward me and shifted closer. I took a step away from him, my mouth dry. His shoulders rose and fell before he turned to face me fully. He seemed to study me through his mask for a moment, then was behind me in two lightning-fast steps. I leapt away, whirling on him at the sound of my bag's zipper.

Halven held my Swiss Army knife on his palm. "Here," he rasped and held his arm out for me to take it.

I narrowed my eyes at him and carefully plucked the weapon from his hand. So much for keeping my distrust on the down low. "How much farther?"

He held his index finger and thumb a half inch from each other indicating it wouldn't be much longer.

"And where are we going exactly?" I was proud of myself for keeping the fear from my voice, but I doubted it escaped his notice.

"There." He pointed to a tiny black structure past the prairie, an expanse of sand, and a rocky outcrop.

"That looks pretty far to me," I said in a flat voice.

Halven held his hand out for me to take again. "Faster."

"Pass." I gripped the knife harder and let my hands fall to my sides.

He shrugged and led the way out of the dry grass. White sand filled my sneakers as we zig-zagged toward the building. I ignored the grains working their way through my socks to irritate my toes and focused on breathing. The grin inside me, so quiet during the entirety of my journey, now balked. I felt it twisting as if it were my own expression. I touched my mouth with my free hand, but it maintained the neutral mask it was trained to keep. *I am not afraid.* I flicked open the knife just in case.

Halven left more than an arm's length worth of space between us the rest of the trip, coming closer only when the local geography made it necessary. I refused to take his hand again but did allow him to guide me carefully around jagged rocks. The climb was just steep enough to cramp my calves. What I wouldn't give for a bottle of water. Too bad I hadn't packed one. There were probably a lot of things I should've brought that I wouldn't realize until it was too late, but I wasn't up for carting around a fifty-pound bag either.

When Halven paused at the edge of our destination, my body burned with shock. The reality of what stood before me slammed down like a blacksmith's hammer on hot metal, chinking away at my last bit of patience.

Blood flowed between the dark stones of the Blood Tower instead of mortar. The towering double doors and arched windows were all too familiar. My vision blurred, fury gripping me tightly. I snagged the front of Halven's shirt and held my knife to his throat in a movement so smooth even the Sandman would've been impressed. "You lying, traitorous piece of—"

The tower door flew open and banged against the outer wall. Kail braced himself in the doorway, leaning into the stones as if it were the only thing keeping him on his feet. His chest rose and fell quickly beneath the embroidered overlay on his jacket. Behind his white hooked mask, Kail's eye—the one I hadn't stabbed with the corkscrew attachment on my knife—flashed rapidly between colors. I shoved Halven away and pointed the knife at him, my pulse thundering in my ears.

"You," Kail wheezed.

"*You*," I repeated, my words poison. "I'm going to kill you for what you did."

"I didn't do anything." He straightened, completely unfazed, and scanned the landscape behind us. "Did anyone see you? Where's the Sandman?"

"You didn't do anything?" The knife shook in my hand. My skin was hot enough to blister. "You gave me that damn knife and sent me after the Weaver."

He leveled a glare at me. "Problem solved. No? Your family is safe."

I launched myself at him, screaming, and swung at his chest with the knife. His hand circled my wrist and held fast before I could even nick him. "*I hate you.*"

Kail rolled his eyes. "Were you seen, Halven?" he asked again.

Halven made a movement with his hands that seemed to say we were but not to worry.

"Good." Kail glared, not daring to release my arm. "The Sandman sent you? Did he tell you we spoke?"

"Don't worry about the Sandman. Worry about me." I attempted to twist free of his grip, but it was made of iron.

"Yes, yes. You're terrifying." He sighed. "So he didn't tell you I offered to help? Obviously not, I suppose, or you wouldn't look so surprised to see me."

I laughed, the sound bitter. "Just like you wanted to help me last time?"

"I didn't *want* to help you then. Rowan did, and what reason did I have not to go along with it? Other than your failure meaning my impending doom, which was reason enough itself. I'll have you know, my death meant just as much to Rowan as yours did." He eyed the sky. "Let's finish chatting inside."

"Better plan." I finally broke free and strode past him into the tower. A metallic smell swallowed me, and I held my breath against it. "I'll go inside." I whirled around, and Kail nearly bumped into me as I braced myself in the door frame. "And you scurry off to whatever hellhole you crawled out of."

His changing eye slowed. "Are you evicting me?"

"Consider this a hostile takeover." I smiled coldly. "I'm sure Rowan will have a room for you at the Keep. Just make sure you don't get too comfortable, because I'll be taking that too."

"Not without help, you won't," he said matter-of-factly.

I slammed the door in his face and slid a heavy bolt in place with a shaking hand. Tarantulas wallpapered the hallway, and black goop secreted from the floorboards. My stomach rolled. I had locked myself in a torture chamber. *Smart.* It wasn't too late to run out the back door. The grin took on a disgusted edge. *No.* The Weaver did not run. I dug my nails into my palm and strode down the main corridor. I was here. Alone—sort of—and alive, which was an achievement in itself. Now I just had to settle in and make a plan. Easier said than done.

"Face it." I jumped at Kail's voice behind me. He strode down the opposite end of the hallway, hands held out to his sides, smug. "You need me."

"How did you—"

"Did you think I wouldn't know more than one way into my own house?" He *tsk*ed and stalked around me. "Stop worrying, *Lady Nightmare*. If I wanted you dead, you would be."

"Oh geez. What a comfort."

"Let's see it then." He nodded to the bookbag. "What have you brought to exact your revenge?"

My arsenal consisted of the weapons in my bag and the gold in my veins. I couldn't rely on the Sandman to fight this with me, though I was certain he wouldn't fight with Rowan under any circumstance. I puffed my chest out. "The Weaver doesn't need an arsenal."

"*The Weaver* did not. But you—" He gave me a sly grin.

"*I* am the Weaver now. Get used to it."

"No. You are something *else*." He gave a mock bow. "Regardless, I am at your service, and if you'd like to stay alive, I suggest you take me up on the offer. Only a third of the nightmares are in favor of you. The rest are either for Rowan or too stupid to make a conscious decision."

A third? That was less than promising. Hopefully a majority of the others were neutral, though based on the victorious glint in Kail's eyes, I couldn't place stock in it. "And you belong to that last group, I assume," I quipped to cover my uncertainty.

"I am anything but stupid," he said easily.

No, he was not. "So you're for Rowan."

"How many times am I going to have to say it?"

A thousand times wouldn't be enough. Words were nothing more than puffs of air. He could claim loyalty now, but when the wind blew in another direction, his support would go with it. "Oh, Kail," I drawled. "*I* would be the stupid one if I trusted you. You're turning on the woman you spent forever with for one that stabbed you in the eye. What does that say about you?"

He bent to my level and leaned forward until the curve of his beaked mask skimmed my nose, but I refused to yield an inch. "It's *because* you stabbed me that I want to help."

"Okay. You're clearly deranged." I placed my palm against the cool mask and shoved his face away. I raised my knife between us. "I wonder what taking out the other one would get me."

His laugh was short. "I admit to ulterior motives. One being that you fix my eye."

"One," I said pointedly. Another being the chance to stab me in the back. I strode around him and down the hallway, doing my best not to look at the arachnids on the walls. The hair on my arms stood on end at the thought of accidentally brushing against them.

"The Weaver can alter nightmares even after they're born," he called after me.

"So?"

He dashed in front of me and cut off my path. "I'm relying on the human part of you to have a bit of compassion."

The honesty in his eyes shook me. He was a nightmare—the nightmare of the unknown. More importantly, he had tricked me into becoming the Weaver so Rowan could slaughter me. Why would he give me actual answers now? Why be truthful when he clearly had a knack for lying?

“I have compassion for the Dreamers,” I said slowly. “Not for you.”

His eye flashed faster. “Consider it compensation for my assistance then.”

“You’re barking up the wrong tree.” I turned down another hall, searching for another door to lock myself behind. *Aha!* There was one just ahead.

He followed close on my heels. “Where are you going?”

“I’m trying to get away from you,” I hissed.

“Good luck with that.” His arm snapped across a doorway, stopping me again. “Unless you’re able to make me leave?”

I scowled at him, but he didn’t move. Didn’t speak. He just let the question hang there. We both knew the answer was a resounding *no*, and I wasn’t about to give him the satisfaction of hearing it. My fingers flexed, aching to land a punch, but a second before I could swing, he leaned away.

“I didn’t think so.” He straightened his jacket. “Might I offer you Rowan’s old room? We can begin your training tomorrow—the important things the Sandman wasn’t able to teach you. Meaning we start from scratch, really.”

“How about the room I stayed in last time instead?” I asked, ignoring the part about training—not only because he was right that I learned nothing useful, but because there was no way I was going to train with *him* instead. Besides, the idea of sleeping in Rowan’s bed gave me the heebie-jeebies.

“That’s my room,” Kail countered.

I did hit him then: a solid punch to his ribs that produced a satisfying *oof*. He stared at me and, without looking away, kicked his heel against the opposite wall, revealing a hidden room.

Kail said nothing as he stepped away from the entrance.

Inside, soft lights flickered to life, revealing a bed carved into the wide trunk of a low tree. Plush black blankets were piled at the center. Vine-like branches hung from the ceiling with ribbons and small dried flowers dotting the grey-green foliage. It was beautiful and eerie and strangely fitting for Rowan.

"Why don't I just sleep outside?" I asked.

"If you want to, go ahead." He shrugged one shoulder. "The important thing is that *I'm* not out there where something might use me as their midnight snack."

"If that's a possibility, maybe I'll leave the front door open and hope for the best."

He leaned closer and whispered, "What if they find your room first?"

"They wouldn't dare," I said, unsure.

"Wouldn't they? You haven't proven yourself to anyone, and no one fears you nor respects you, though I say we aim for fear in the future." He flicked a piece of hair beside my face. "I hope you're ready to get your hands dirty, *Lady Nightmare*."

"Get out of my tower," I demanded.

"I'll be upstairs in *my* tower if you need anything. You remember the way, don't you?" Kail cracked his knuckles, his face hardening. "Until tomorrow."

"I hate you," I told Kail again.

"So you've said." He sauntered away, tossing a wave over his shoulder.

"Focus," Kail drawled from behind me.

I glared at him over my shoulder and ground my teeth. "I'm so glad you're here to remind me of that every two minutes."

He stood, arms folded, watching me carefully just as he had the last six days, and I instantly regretted ever giving in to *training* with him. To be fair, no one was better than Kail at being annoying. He was my own personal amoeba. For four days he woke me up at regular intervals while my body tried desperately to sleep through whatever adjustments were happening. Then for two days he followed my every zombie-like step while I explored the tower, sometimes never saying anything, sometimes never shutting up. He drained my energy, sending my patience level far into the negatives until I caved.

So there I sat with a pile of the Weaver's thread on the table in front of me. The gold fibers flickered against the black cords as it tried desperately to snake up my arm. My skin ached to let it circle my wrist as it had that day five months ago.

Inside, the grin widened, impossibly cruel, at my denial. The threads were the Weaver's power—my power. I understood that. I *needed* these threads, and they needed me too. But it was exactly because of how much I needed them that I pushed them away. When I ripped them from the Weaver's arm in that storage unit, it took time for him to regain strength. I didn't want the threads to be a crutch for me like they were for him. Darkness poured from the grin, clouding my doubts, pushing me to extend a hand.

"Remember what I said about personal space?" I asked when Kail inched closer.

"I do," he said, unbothered, and his arm brushed against mine.

I gritted my teeth. "What's the point of this anyway? I told you I can see the nightmares inside. Just give me a pair of scissors."

Kail winced. "You can't *cut* them apart. They don't end just like that." He snapped his fingers. "Think of them like holding hands. If you will one of them out, they'll let go."

The image of the disfigured nightmare that brought me to the Night World flashed through my mind, and I wrinkled my nose. "Sure. It's one big pile of comfort and joy."

"It's one big pile of loyalty and respect. Even Rowan wouldn't go hacking her army into pieces," he said with a sharp edge. "Stop whining and try again."

I stared at the threads. At the bits of gold catching the light.

At the rust-colored blood staining nearly half of it. The Weaver's blood, Kail informed me, from the floor of the Keep where he liberated the bundle of thread before Rowan noticed. I glanced down at the gold veins pulsing beneath my stained hands and wondered how true that was. Not that it mattered—the threads were real enough—but I thought all of it hitched a ride when the Sandman took me back to the Dream Realm. It was already established that Kail was a liar, but I couldn't think how else he would have this thread.

"You were the one who said I needed to be feared. Did you think I'd accomplish that by being thoughtful?" I asked.

The beak of his mask skimmed my cheek. "Without those threads, you're nothing."

"I'm the Lady of Nightmares," I ground out. *Like that makes a difference,* my inner voice balked. One day I would be able to utter that title without feeling like I bit into a lemon, but today was not that day.

"A leader without power isn't a leader at all." He set his hands down in the middle of the threads and dragged them across the table to me. I tucked my hands under the table to protect them. "The Weaver understood that, so if you truly want to be the Lady of Nightmares, take them."

I snatched Kail's mask where it touched me and shoved his face hard enough that he stumbled sideways. He studied me from the corners of his eyes with a grim set to his mouth. The air in the room thickened, sparking between us, but I was in charge. If anyone was going to back down, it would be him. And, after what felt like a lifetime, he did.

"You can change it, you know," he said in a careful voice.

"Change what?" I pinned both ends of the threads to the

table with a finger and poked at them with my other hand.

"The mask." When I glanced up at Kail, he tapped the hard, bone-like surface covering his forehead. "You can change it. Remove it even."

"Ah." I rubbed my temples, suddenly tired. "But then where would your mystique go?"

He smirked and resumed his perch behind me. "Try again."

This time it didn't sound like an order. It was more like a friend urging me toward greatness, and I knew that's what these threads were. Greatness. I took a deep breath and closed my eyes. When I reached for the threads again, one end snapped around my finger in a tight coil. "Hold still," I said under my breath. The mass stilled. I cracked my eyes open. *Interesting.* I closed them again and ran a finger down the length of it, pinching where it felt right. A shaggy dog with bulging eyes and steaming drool looked out from the darkness. Its jowls shook in anticipation. Not the most ideal choice for my first nightmare, but I was ready to be finished and that's what I found so—

I focused on his end like Kail told me to. Coaxed it away from the others. Something kicked inside me, the growing darkness throbbing. The grin relaxed, satisfied. I pulled gently at the dog until it frayed, then hesitated. Was this right? Was I hurting it? I scoffed at the concern and resumed the task. *Let it hurt.* But another part of me slapped the thought away, and the thread split, pulling apart fiber by fiber.

I opened one eye at a time to find a six-inch thread between my fingers. The rest of the pile was halfway up my arm, heading straight for the edge of my sleeve. I watched it creep higher with growing fascination. The grin eased forward. Eager. Nervous. Waiting for me to rip it away. The darkness seemed to hold its breath while I decided what to do.

The decision swam slowly from the depths of my thoughts and hovered just out of reach. Suddenly, the darkness wasn't the only one not breathing as I waited for it to take the final step. I held my breath so long my lungs ached. Then, when I exhaled, it was as if I blew the dark cloud away.

Yes. I wanted the threads—and their power—as much as they wanted me.

My body reveled in the sense of completion as the threads fused with the sleeve of my grey t-shirt. The thing I was missing while stuck in the Day World: this was it. One of the things, at least. The power washed over me. Filled me. It radiated with every beat of my heart. I felt larger, bigger than the world. I was Atlas. Nothing could touch me here.

"What is it?" Kail asked, breaking through my euphoria.

"What?" I breathed.

"The nightmare." Kail stared hungrily at the single thread. "What is it? Will it fit in here?"

I held it up and blinked myself fully back to the present. "I think so."

"Good. Then do it."

"Do what?"

"Bring it out." He waved his hands impatiently.

Bring it out. I thought back to the Weaver on the Sandman's beach when he created one of the first nightmares I'd seen. With a flick of his wrist, the thread went straight and stiff. Then there was a burst, followed by the presence of a newly created nightmare. That didn't seem so hard. I wrinkled my nose and flicked. Nothing happened.

"You have to mean it," Kail admonished.

I stared at the thread, at the dog, and flicked it again. It hardened slightly but fell limp. Again and again I tried. Again and again I failed.

"Do what you did last time," Kail suggested, pressing closer until I shot him a death stare. "Just… more."

"Personal. Space." I jabbed a finger into his upper arm. "Do you even know how to do this, or are you guessing?"

"I… don't. But I know what it felt like from the other side."

So they *could* feel it. I twirled the thread between my fingers and looked Kail up and down, marveling at how something so complex could come from something so simple. His mind, his body, his clothing—his abilities, whatever they were, exactly. All of them were once contained in something that wouldn't have been thick enough to sew on a button.

"Enjoying the view?" he purred.

I rolled my eyes. "Don't flatter yourself." He opened his mouth, but I cut him off before he could make a sound. "Are you going to tell me what it felt like or not?"

He was quiet for a long while, staring at the threads on my arm, and just when I thought he wouldn't, he let out a short breath. "Before, it's like—like you exist and don't. It's peaceful, but you desperately want to come out because peace isn't what you were made for. Only you don't know that, so you're trapped in a mild state of constant panic. There are others beside you keeping you from floating away into the nothingness, and you're doing the same for them. Then suddenly there's a pulse of magic and you wake up for the first time. The world becomes so clear. There's this person in front of you—someone you know you want to be closer to—and he's calling you forward so you let go." He cocked his head. "And then you're real."

I rubbed the threads circling my wrist. "They know me then? That I'm the Weaver? Or will I have to assert some sort of dominance the second I give each one life?"

"Anything you make will be loyal to you until you give it a reason not to be." Kail shrugged. "The Weaver gave a lot of us reasons, and most still remained true. It's a sickness, really, but there it is. We don't have time to convince every existing nightmare to believe you're up to par, so if you want to turn the tides—"

An army. Right here on my arm and all I had to do was call it into being. I bit the inside of my cheek and met the fire dancing in Kail's eyes. The grin spread, pleased. I spun back to the table. The thread hung loose between my fingers, taunting me. I pushed my thoughts toward it—*wake up, let go, come this way.* Nothing. So, for the first time, I stared straight at those haunting pearly whites haunting my vision. *A little help?*

The grin brightened as it grew. Coils of darkness spread through me like another set of veins and didn't stop until it felt as if there was nothing left inside me but that sardonic mouth. I winced against it but didn't fight. The Weaver was a being of dark things. If I was going to rule them, create them, I had to let the same darkness in. As long as I kept hold of the key, I could lock it away when I was finished. The thread straightened, and I bolted up in my chair.

Heat zipped from my hand into the thread. It exploded, knocking my chair backward. My head thwacked against the hard floor, and the smell of sulfur nearly choked me as I scrambled to my feet. The table was a pile of splinters, but in front of me was the same brown dog I saw in the thread, only *better.* He was nearly as tall as me with two rows of needle-sharp teeth and silver blades for nails. His green eyes met mine, and he licked the drool from his jowls.

Kail's slow clap filled the room.

"I did it." I laughed. "I did it!"

"Yes." Kail skirted around the room, keeping an eye on the watchful new nightmare. "Though you did say it would fit in here."

"I said I *thought* so." I leaned closer to the nightmare, admiring the hard muscles beneath the fur. With a pack of these, I could do practically anything. "And he does fit. Technically."

Kail leveled me with a hard stare. "He's nearly three times wider than the doorway. How are you going to get him out?"

"You will be loyal to me," I addressed the dog, ignoring Kail's valid point, though the words didn't feel like they were truly mine. "Me and no other." Kail cleared his throat behind me. "And don't eat him—yet," I added.

"Yet?" Kail scoffed. "All I have to do is step into the hallway, and he won't be able to eat me at all."

"If you can make it to the door before he does." I touched the dog's muzzle. Coarse hair followed my hand as if it were a static balloon. "Should we test his speed?"

Kail's eyes widened, not in fear, but with something that almost resembled humor. "Get this giant, frothing thing out of my tower."

"Why?" I asked, enjoying his agitation.

"*Why?* You've got to be—"

The tower walls shook so hard, paintings clattered from their nails. I gasped and gripped the back of the chair for balance. The dog growled, the blades on his feet digging into the area rug, and Kail braced himself in the corner. His warm brown skin paled.

"Was that supposed to happen?" I asked slowly, fearing I already knew the answer.

Kail swore and raced to the window. His knuckles turned white where he gripped the sill. "We're leaving."

I leapt to the second window just as a ball of fire soared toward the tower. I flattened myself against the nearest wall as the impact shook the building again. Black spots danced in my vision. "What the hell is that?" I screeched.

"Not what. *Who*." Kail grabbed my wrist and yanked me into the hallway. "There's no time to explain."

"Wait," I commanded. The giant dog reached a paw out after us, whimpering. "We can't leave him."

"Worry about *us*," Kail shouted over the impact of a third fireball.

My chest twisted. I wasn't sure if it was the human part of me or part of the magic, but I couldn't leave the dog to die. He was a nightmare. He was *my* nightmare. The only thing here I created. Proof that I was capable. A reminder that I was powerful.

"Break the walls down," I ordered him, and his nails ripped through the nearest floorboards in response to my demand. "Escape and find me later."

"In," Kail instructed as he shoved me through another secret door before I could get another word out.

My eyes adjusted quickly to the dark room. Too quickly to be considered normal. Behind us, the inner walls creaked and snapped, while the outer walls continued to shake. Kail kicked aside a woven rug and bent to lift a large trap door. Red and black flecks of dust rained down from the ceiling.

"What are you doing?" I asked.

"Escaping."

He shoved me forward, and I stumbled into the opening, slamming my chin against the edge before falling six feet. The landing sent a bolt of pain up my tailbone. It had to be broken. Could a tailbone break? It was fractured and bruised, at least. My wrists throbbed from catching part of my weight. Kail leapt down beside me, landing perfectly on his feet. A soft thump told me he replaced the trapdoor, though without the rug to hide it, I didn't know why he bothered. I dabbed a finger against my chin and hissed. Blood dripped onto my chest.

"What the hell, Kail?" I cried.

"Would you have jumped if I told you to?" he snapped.

No. Because I would've needed to trust him to jump into a black pit.

"Exactly," he said at my silence and hauled me up by my armpits. "Let's move."

"My bag—"

"It's not worth it."

"I beg to differ," I said, unyielding. My weapons were in there. My clothes. Everything I owned was inside that bag. I jumped, trying to reach the overhead door, but didn't even graze the wood. "I'm not leaving without it."

"The Hours will eat you alive." Kail lifted me up and threw me over his shoulder.

I pounded my fists against his back. "I'd like to see them try."

But he was already racing down a dirt tunnel. Roots reached out for us, and worms snapped tiny mouths when he disturbed their hornet-like nests, but Kail didn't slow. Didn't stop.

"Kail! Put me down."

"Sorry, Lady. You're my only chance at getting fixed." He

swatted the back of my thigh. "Stop squirming before I drop you."

"*Drop me,*" I demanded. Then I fell on my already bruised butt with a groan. *Broken.* Definitely a broken tailbone. "You're such a jerk."

Kail crouched down in front of me. "Keep talking the big talk. See what happens. But Rowan sent the Hours after you, which means she's not planning to wait for you to learn how to walk the walk."

"I'd rather face them than take your advice again." I eased myself to my feet, wincing against the ache in my backside. At least my Swiss Army knife was still in my pocket.

He huffed and stood, looking down at me. "You're a horrible liar."

Dirt rained down on us as another fireball hit the tower, and I wondered how many it would take to bring the whole thing crashing down on our heads. I sobered, anger dissolving under the weight of my survival instincts. "Please tell me there's a way out of here."

"I *did* say we were escaping, didn't I?" Kail held out his hand the same way Halven did, and I narrowed my eyes at the gesture. "Just take it. It's easy to get lost down here, and we have to get to the safe house."

I reluctantly took his hand. "What are the Hours?"

"Twelve nightmares you're nowhere near ready to face," Kail said, stoic.

I swallowed hard and ran beside him, taking turns I didn't see until they were upon us. Not knowing our final destination was anxiety-inducing, but I understood why he wouldn't vocalize it any of the times I asked. Ears were everywhere. I had to wonder if it mattered though, seeing as Rowan had been his partner for so long. Surely she knew the location of Kail's safe house. "Maybe we should go somewhere Rowan doesn't know about so she can't send her minions after us," I suggested.

"Rowan clearly doesn't know or we'd go somewhere else," he replied, guarded.

"Keeping secrets from your bestie?" I asked bitterly. It didn't bode well for me considering I was far from being considered his friend.

Kail's laugh held no humor. "Who do you think I needed safety from, *Lady*?"

Chapter Fourteen

Don't do it. I stalked away from the sand-made sunflower I'd created beneath the brightest star in the Dream Realm. The place Nora and I met every night until we no longer could. *Don't go.*

Nora walked into the Blood Tower of her own free will a week ago. If she wanted to talk, she would've sent a nightmare with a message or let her walls down so I could feel her—her what? Guilt? Remorse? Longing? What did I expect her to feel? I'd done nothing but ask her for more time even though she constantly told me she didn't have more to give. It had to seem like I didn't care, or at the very least, like I didn't take her feelings seriously. And now she no longer trusted me to do what was best. She hadn't even tried to send word that she was okay, though she must've known how worried I would be. That hurt the most—that she would allow me to think the worst.

Well, *almost* the worst.

Everything was upended, my soul ripped apart, but there were bigger things to deal with. If we were to survive long enough to fix this new rift between us, Nora first had to take control of the Nightmare Realm. Then we had to deal with Mara before both the Day and Night Worlds ceased to exist.

I wanted to rage, to break something, to shake some sense into Nora. Instead, I sent a surge of power into the sand, and the perfect likeness of the Weaver swirled together before me. I punched the stupid grin off his face. Then I formed him again. And again and again until I was short of breath and my arm muscles ached.

I ran a hand through my hair, feeling marginally better. *Okay.* Anger later, life-or-death problems now. Both Nora and I had an eternity ahead of us, and I needed to remember that she didn't have the same life experiences I did. She made a choice—a stupid, horrible choice—but it didn't define her. I knew who Nora was, and I would stand beside her so that she would survive, with me or without me.

Stars. I was a lovesick fool. How many betrayals would it take for me to forsake her? The answer was carved in my heart: never. I would never give up loving her. Just as my friendship with the Weaver never stopped haunting me, I would live with this devotion for the rest of my life.

And so I put one foot in front of the other until the sea of glimmering sand disappeared and the muted colors of the Nightmare Realm surrounded me. My chest filled with dread at leaving the beach with Mare loose, but the Dream Realm was as secure as I could make it. It was better protected now than it was when I warded it against the Weaver, and I couldn't stay forever. Ignoring the creatures that scuttled into hiding as I passed, I made straight for the Blood Tower.

Only to find it smoldering.

My heart slammed into my chest hard enough to bruise. *Rowan.* It had to be her. Who else would burn down the tower? *Anyone that wanted to be the next Weaver.* The acrid scent of smoke burned my nostrils as I picked my way through the rubble. Kail wouldn't let anyone else harm Nora. Whatever game he was playing, it had to be for Rowan's benefit. Unless—unless he wanted to rule the Nightmare Realm himself. But he wouldn't need to burn down his own house when he had every opportunity to kill her.

I reached inward, searching for a hint of Nora's magic. Just a scrap. Something to tell me she was safe.

There.

Not in the rubble, but to the far north. I let out a breath, nearly falling to my knees. I had to see her, even if she didn't want to see me. Sand circled my boots, pushing my feet to move faster, faster, faster. The dream Nora held called to my magic, pulling me like a magnet. I wasn't sure how long I had walked before I saw two figures trekking through rows of billowing sheets clipped to clotheslines. I saw only flashes of them between the white linens before they became silhouettes behind it. Red handprints stained some of the fabric, while others were splattered with blood, and the rope they hung from was made of stretched intestines.

I wove my way between the gaps until I found the same row Nora and Kail walked. Seeing her now felt like taking my first breath in a week. I wanted to run to her, to lift her into a tight embrace and tell her how much I loved her in between kisses, but the uncertainty of her reaction shackled my legs. Each of my steps were measured and careful, taking me forward when I suddenly wanted to go in any other direction. I flipped my hood up and swallowed hard.

As I neared, still undetected, I noticed the dirt on her pants and a slight limp, and what was left of my excitement fizzled. Blonde hair clung to her cheeks, bright red from heat and exhaustion, and her shoulders slumped.

Kail slowed when he finally saw me and motioned ahead with one hand. Nora's head snapped up, and her eyes went wide, her body stiff. She said something to Kail, but they were still too far away for me to hear the hushed conversation. They exchanged a few more words while I stood rooted, and then Nora came forward alone.

I waited, not daring to breathe, until she was out of Kail's earshot. She stared up at me, her eyes the brightest gold without any trace of green remaining. There was no apology in her expression, only wary anticipation. "Hi," I forced myself to say.

She blinked a few times and the glow in her eyes faded. She stood with rigid and wiped the sweat from her forehead. A bruise colored her chin. "What are you doing here, Sandman?"

"Did you think I would never come?" My voice scratched its way from deep inside. "That I would find out you left and say *oh well?*"

She blushed, a feat considering how red she was already. "No, but—"

I was vaguely aware of Kail watching us a few sheets away, but with one look from Nora, he trudged further ahead, giving us the illusion of privacy. I stepped closer to Nora anyway. "Why?" I breathed. "I asked you to give me one day. If you insisted on coming after that, I would've brought you here and helped you find safety."

"Would you have?" She winced. "You knew what being in the Day World was doing to me. I told you I couldn't wait anymore."

"You promised me one day, but you barely waited five hours. And we—" I couldn't finish that sentence. Coming back to the Nightmare Realm wasn't the only thing I wanted to wait for, but I stupidly thought that night meant something for both of us. Something good—not the goodbye she intended it as.

"I know." It came out as a reverent whisper. "I'm sorry."

"Why?" I asked again.

"I had to." Her voice was soft but not timid, apologetic but determined.

A lump formed in my throat. "Because you don't trust me anymore."

"No." She gripped my upper arms, meeting my gaze again. "Of course I do. I just needed to take my fate into my own hands instead of waiting around for permission. The Day World was destroying me."

"I only ever wanted you to be safe. This is all so new to you, and you don't understand—"

"I will, Sandman. I'm learning." She lifted her arm to show me the circling threads. "I can see them—the nightmares. When I touch different parts of the thread, I see what each piece will become, and I'm working on bringing them to life. I already did it once. How could I have learned that at home?"

How could she learn that from me? She didn't say it, but she didn't have to. I plucked something white from her hair—a tooth. A human incisor, complete with the root. I flicked it to the side and turned a horrified look to Nora.

"Our escape from the Blood Tower ended in a field of teeth," she explained, shaking her hair out. "I thought I got them all out."

I ran a hand down my face. "You can't trust Kail. Not only has he been with Rowan forever, but there's no incentive for him to turn on her."

"I know I can't trust him." She sighed and pressed the heels of her hands to her eyes. "But this isn't me versus Rowan for him. He admitted he has ulterior motives, but what does that matter? I'm figuring this whole thing out, and soon I won't need him."

"*What does it matter?*" I gripped her face gently with both hands. "Do you really believe that, Nora? Because the last time Kail tried to *help* you get what you wanted, you killed the Weaver. Even if he is telling the truth about helping you take the Nightmare Realm, what then? At what cost?"

She leaned up on her tiptoes and slid my hood off, looking into my eyes, willing me to understand something. Then she kissed me. It lasted only long enough to make me stop talking, but the softness of her broke me. *Please don't let this be the last time.* My heart was hers. My realm was hers. My life. As long as she was okay, I would give any of it freely, but that was dangerous. There were millions of lives unknowingly depending on what we did. Giving the Dream Realm to the darkness would be catastrophic, but that didn't stop my mind from warring between what I *needed* to do versus what I *wanted* to do.

"I need time to figure out who I am," Nora said as gently as she had kissed me.

"You're Nora," I rasped.

"I *was* Nora." She chewed her lip. "Now I'm something more—or less. Maybe I'm someone completely different. That's what I need to figure out, and I can't do that if you're helping me every step of the way."

"You have all the time in the world to figure it out."

"Look at me." She spoke firmly, but her tone remained kind. "*Look at me*. When will I be safe? *When*?"

"After we take care of Rowan and—"

"Stop." She squeezed her eyes shut. "Please, please, stop. I feel this place inside me. I've felt it every moment since I woke up covered in the Weaver's blood, and now that I'm here, it's worse. I need to learn to walk with it, so it doesn't knock me off my feet. But with you, it's like I'm on life support. And Rowan is just one problem. One nightmare. She's who we need to deal with right now, but she's far from the last. I have to embrace the new me in order to be as safe as the Weaver was—if you could ever call him safe. I don't know how much of me will be left." Her eyes fell at the final statement, the words choked.

I reached out to hug her, but Kail's hand landed on my shoulder. "She asked for some time."

In one movement, I flipped him so he landed on his back on the ground. It was more a reflex than anything, but I wasn't sorry it happened. He should've known better than to touch me.

"Unnecessary," he grunted.

"See what happens if you dare lay a hand on Nora," I seethed. He wouldn't have hands left if he tried it again. He wouldn't have *anything* left.

"This is what I mean." Nora touched my arm and sighed

heavily before turning to Kail. "Were you listening?"

"Forgive me, Lady." He stood and brushed himself off with an annoying amount of composure. "The acoustics here don't serve privacy well."

She gave him a pointed look.

"Well, then," he blurted before she could say a word. "Time to be off before we're spotted."

Not yet. It could be days—weeks—before I saw her again. How much time did she want? How much space was too much? But Kail was right. They had to go before the wrong nightmare saw them. It didn't make saying goodbye any easier though. "Nora, I—"

She kissed my cheek, imploring me not to make this harder by allowing her emotions, her aching resolve, to brush through me. "I'll see you soon, okay?"

"Okay," I said reluctantly.

When she left with Kail without so much as a backward glance, she took a piece of me with her. A limb. A lung. A heart. But I would get them back. She just needed time, and I needed to respect that. Nora was the Weaver, and, if she was to survive, she was right. She had to become her new self. That didn't mean I was going to walk away. It only meant I needed to protect her from the sidelines.

Chapter Fifteen

Nora

"Are you listening to me?" Kail asked, clapping his hands in front of my face.

I swatted at him and kept walking. Of course I wasn't listening. He hadn't stopped naming different nightmares and their specialties since we'd walked away from the Sandman over two hours ago. It was like my life had become the worst infomercial ever. *Can't remove the rust from your sink? You need a bunch of extra slimy sucker fish. Starve them of Dreamer blood for a couple days and voila! In a few short minutes, they'll eat your problem away.*

It was an information overload, for one, and I currently didn't care. Also, I *really* needed to stop hearing Kail's voice, so I could replay the entire conversation I had with the Sandman. Every word. The tones. Facial expressions. I wished I removed his hood earlier, but I was too scared to see what was underneath. It would've been better if he looked at me like the traitor I was than the girl I wasn't. Had I made my reasons clear? Maybe I said something wrong. I tried my best, but there was so much left unsaid. He couldn't be expected to forgive me. Not yet. Not ever, maybe.

Kail palmed the top of my head and turned my face toward him. "You're *still* not listening."

"Tell me something I want to hear then," I quipped. Anything—anything *else*—that got my mind off the Sandman and the fracture in my chest.

Kail looked up at the sky and shook his head in disbelief. "How I wish I could kill you without becoming you."

"Yes, well." I shrugged. "Not everyone enjoys self-improvement. You do you."

He glowered at me and spoke in a droning voice. "We're here."

A chain link fence towered over us. On the other side, a long concrete building stretched between two rows of glowing signs. They faced away from the fence, as if intended for someone fleeing whatever dwelled inside, and each was more ominous than the last. My personal favorite was *Danger Lies Beyond*, but I couldn't read them all from this angle. Curling letters decorated the face of the building itself, but I couldn't make those out either.

I laughed. "You're kidding, right?"

"Why would I be kidding?" he asked with a raised brow.

I waved my hands frantically at the yard. "This is *literally* putting a neon sign on your hideout."

"Do any of them mention me? No." Kail pried a piece of

chain link fence away from a post. "In you go."

"No way."

He stared incredulously down at me. "Why not?"

"This is all reverse psychology, right? Don't go out *there* because it's *dangerous*, but what you really have to worry about is what's inside." I crossed my arms, waiting for him to deny it, but he didn't. "What's Plan B?"

Kail rolled his eyes. "It's just a wax museum, *Lady*. Why would I drag you all the way out here if I didn't know we would be safe?"

I grimaced. Why would he? Because he was a cat, and I was a mouse. "Was that supposed to make me change my mind? Because you obviously haven't seen wax figures with their creepy smiles and—"

"Look." He huffed, obviously agitated but trying to control himself. "You can't be afraid of your own nightmares."

"I'm not afraid. I just don't like them," I grumbled, not wanting to admit that he had a point. Besides, my feet were killing me and there was sweat in places I didn't know I could sweat. I grunted and slipped through the hole in the fence.

Kail followed, and the fence clanged perfectly back into place. "Ladies first," he said with sarcastic enthusiasm.

I ground my teeth together and strode past the signs. One was nothing more than a neon red skull, a dozen more were in languages I didn't know, and one was a blank headstone.

"That one adds the Dreamer's name and personal information," Kail whispered conspiratorially when he saw me looking at the carved stone.

Of course it did. I raked a hand over my face and waltzed up to the red door. It opened without a single touch to reveal a grand foyer with black silk wallpaper and a crystal chandelier. A long banquet table sat against the far wall, the entire surface covered with a long, metallic gold tablecloth. A book lay open at its center beside an ink pot and quill. On either side were trays of grapes and cheeses.

"I thought this was a wax museum," I said from the corner of my mouth.

"It is." He stepped across the threshold. "A very *refined* one. Care to sign the guest book?"

I sucked in a breath, ready to explode, while Kail plopped a grape in his mouth before disappearing into a side room. I continued to stand in the doorway. What was I doing? I should've gone with the Sandman. He would never drag me into a place like this. But where else could I go? Not the beach. There was nowhere for the Sandman to take me that guaranteed my wellbeing.

"Keep up," Kail called from the other room.

I scowled. Why did I have to be stuck with *him* though? The moment I stepped fully inside the foyer, the door creaked shut behind me. I stared at the red-painted iron as if it were a living thing. In a way, it was, but… Panic burned its way into my throat. Where was the handle? "Uh, Kail," I shouted. "We can get out of here, right?"

"Worried, Lady?" he asked, leaning out of the other room before vanishing again. "Come on."

I would kill him when this was over. Stab out his other eye and feed it to whatever happened to be nearby. But for now, I followed his voice into a room with several wax figures. No one famous—just a family of four in a seemingly innocent setup: the father in a suit by the fireplace, the mother in a hoop skirt in a chair beside him, and two young girls playing with a puppy on the rug at her feet. I met the mother's glassy stare as I moved toward another door. Her eyes tracked me through the room and her full lips broke into a big smile. Fear drove a spike through my forehead only to meet the dark, steely grin inside and shatter. The grin seemed to recognize the woman. The room. All of it. It softened into something proud and content.

Kail's beak grazed my shoulder, and I nearly fell over. "What part of *keep up* confused you?"

"Something is about to be up," I said in a raised voice. "My foot up your—"

"Now, now. Watch your language around the children." He put a finger to his mouth, shushing me, and winked at the two little girls. The one facing our direction looked up and giggled.

"Holy fudgsicles." I accidentally used the curse my friends and I used around Emery's little brother. *Had* used. When my friends were alive. The memory was sobering. "You're in such a hurry, so move."

"Testy," Kail sang.

In the next room, a cell door stood between us and three wax figures. The inmates wore black and white striped jumpers straight out of the movies. Two of them played cards on a moldy straw mattress and the other clanged his tin cup on the bars. I itched under their gazes and shuffled closer to Kail. The rooms got worse the deeper he led me into the museum. A flailing pig on a hook, a woman crawling from her own grave, and a shipwreck in a sea that swallowed the passengers, even though it appeared as nothing more than a puddle. I shut my eyes against the guillotine setup but still heard the metallic whir of the blade falling toward a man's neck. The thwack of it hitting its mark.

The thump as the head fell into the waiting wicker basket.

When I stepped into the next room and lifted my gaze, I wished I hadn't. A small group of men and women gathered in front of a large, raised platform. The women all wore white caps on their heads, and the men wore top hats. Their clothes were moth-eaten, their skin grimy, but they weren't what stopped me in my tracks. It was a girl no older than me balancing on a stool atop the platform with a noose around her neck.

Kail skipped up the side steps to stand beside her. "Don't just stand there," he said, motioning me forward.

"What are you doing?" I asked, suspicion seeping out.

"This relationship isn't going to go anywhere if you don't learn to trust me a *teensy* bit." He held his fingers up with the slightest space between them.

"I should've gone with the Sandman," I grumbled, regretting my choice yet again, and eased around the wax figures to stand beside him. "For the record, *this* isn't a relationship. It's survival."

Kail gasped dramatically. "Are you breaking up with me?"

I pulled the Swiss Army knife from my pocket and flicked open the corkscrew, twisting it so it caught the harsh lighting.

"No sense of humor, that one," he whispered to the girl on the stool.

"Kail," I warned.

"Excuse me, dear," he said nonchalantly to the girl. Then he kicked the stool out from under her.

"Kail!" I shrieked.

He ignored me in favor of lifting a trap door beneath her swaying feet. I gaped at him. "What?" He flicked a piece of hair from the forehead of his mask. "The longer you stand there, the longer she'll suffer. Once we're gone, the display will reset itself.

So…"

I stared at him, halfway sure he lost whatever sense he had. "What?"

He pointed into the darkness below the platform. "Secret bunker. Geez. Did you land on your head or your butt back at the tower?"

"Is this your thing?" I hissed, ignoring the still swinging wax figure. "Trap doors?"

He glowered. "That's a bit judgmental coming from someone that was *saved* by the fact that I have them."

My blood warmed. *You know what, ya jerk…* I shoved Kail toward the hole the same way he had shoved me into the first one. His knees banged against the edge of the opening, then his beak smacked against the opposite side before he fell in. A soft glow filled the hiding space. I smirked to myself, pleased I was able to catch him off guard. More than pleased. I peered over the edge to find Kail flat on his back and waved at him.

"I'm fine. Thanks for asking," he said, breathless.

I leapt down beside him, not caring that it was nowhere near the graceful landing he managed back at the Blood Tower. The important thing was that *he* was the one on the ground and *I* was the one on my feet. "Keep talking the big talk. See what happens," I repeated the words he'd said to me.

"Touché." He stood slowly and reached up to shut the hatch. "Don't pretend this isn't an ingenious hiding spot." The sound of wood scraping against wood came from above my head, and the creak of the rope ceased. "See?" he added. "Wax Girl is all better."

Pick my battles. Pick. My. Battles.

I turned, taking in the supposed safe house, though it was

more of a safe *box*. A sleeping bag was rolled up in the corner beside a wooden chest, and one of four lanterns was lit with small floating orbs. That was it. Where were the weapons? The food? *Food.* When did I eat last? Not since I arrived in the Nightmare Realm. So why wasn't I hungry? In fact, I felt pleasantly full. But still, what kind of safe house didn't have even basic supplies?

"Kail." I took a breath to center myself. "There's nothing here."

He kicked the trunk with his boot. "What do you call this?"

"That depends on what's inside it."

He lifted the lid to reveal a variety of items. A few coins, a map, and what appeared to be an extra set of the same clothes he was currently wearing, plus a cape. And he made fun of *me* when I wrapped a sheet around myself so the Blood Army wouldn't boil me alive. Not that it would've worked. "Did you raid a five-year-old's toy box?" I asked, my voice high with disbelief. "All you need now is a stuffed parrot and a plastic sword. Where are the weapons? Supplies?"

He huffed. "*We* are your weapons. And what other supplies would I need? Gold in case I need to bribe any nightmares that like to play human, a map of the Nightmare Realm—albeit extremely outdated at this point—and clean clothes."

I lifted the cape with two fingers. "This is a joke, right?" He snatched the fabric from me, and I rolled my eyes, reaching for the map instead. Crudely drawn lines covered the yellowed parchment. "You *did* steal this from a child, didn't you? Is this even accurate? Look at the size of this tree compared to the mountain over here. Is there a giant forest I should know about?"

"Okay, you know what." He snapped the paper from me.

"You can sleep on the floor tonight."

"As opposed to the feather bed?" I asked, crossing my arms. His eyes flared murderously, and I reminded myself that I did, in fact, need to sleep near him. I tugged my t-shirt off, and the threads whipped away from the sleeve in favor of my razorback tank. I wadded the fabric up to use as a pillow. "Forget it. Where's the food?"

"We feed on fear, not food." He snagged the sleeping roll for himself. "Which in turn feeds you. The whole thing where the Sandman banned Dreamers left most of us starved, so you have him to thank if you're feeling a bit peckish."

My stomach growled in protest, as if it missed the food it no longer needed. "You ate a grape when we came in."

"I didn't say we *couldn't* eat. It's instinctual sometimes, especially with the mindless brutes, but there's no reason for me to meal plan for emergencies." He grinned, almost too satisfied with my discomfort. "You'll live."

True enough. If it took me nearly a week to realize I hadn't eaten, there was no point in lugging food across the realm with us. I eased back on the hard cement floor and shoved my shirt beneath my head, too tired to argue with Kail. "See you tomorrow." I said through a yawn.

The last thing that passed through my mind before I fell into a fitful slumber wasn't that he would kill me. He could've done that a hundred times by now. No, the last thought I had was much worse. It was the look of pain on the Sandman's face. A hammer to my chest. I treated him horribly. More than horribly. And, honestly, I wasn't sure there was a way to truly come back from that.

☾

When I saw another fissure waiting for me in my slumber, I hesitated. They had only given me more questions so far, and I didn't have the energy for that tonight. There were enough unanswered things in my life. Why was Kail helping me? How long until this was over? Did Rowan really have no idea where this safe house was? *Real* issues. Not something that I already had a general answer to. The Sandman and the Weaver survived whatever they were running from the first time, and I knew all too well how the Weaver's binding ended.

But, as they say—whoever *they* are—curiosity killed the cat. So I looked anyway.

A woman with long, crimped hair stood with her back to me, surrounded by thick metal bars. The breeze blew a snow-white shift around her body as she hummed.

"A new tune, Mare?" the Weaver asked.

Mare. Wasn't that what the Sandman called Mara? And, true enough, when the woman turned to gaze at the Weaver, it was with the same horizontal pupils as the nightmare in my bedroom. Her knobby knees were visible through the shift, though she stood tall. Nearly eight feet, I would guess, which was extreme compared to the posture I was familiar with.

"Weaver," Mara crooned. "Come again, have you?"

"Tell us how you escaped the Ever Safe," the Weaver demanded.

Mara wrapped her hands around the bars, iron dipped nails clinking against them. "Ask Baku. He followed."

"Baku doesn't speak, and the path is too dark for his dreams to reveal anything useful."

She sneered. "And yet, he is out there while I am in here."

"Because he doesn't want to rip the world out from beneath our feet," the Weaver said with an edge of impatience.

"Weak-minded," she spat.

"Smart," the Weaver corrected.

The breeze around Mara ceased, her clothes and hair utterly still as if she commanded it. Her eyes, on the other hand, were a tempest. "I am caged because I let you cage me." To prove her point, she pried the bars apart and stepped through the opening. "I think, dear one, I will no longer allow it."

The Weaver ran then, screaming for the Sandman, before the memory snapped shut. My sleep was pitch black again, and I let out an aggravated huff. *Every time*. Each memory stopped just before anything important happened. But maybe I'd seen what I had to. Mara as the Sandman knew her.

Mara as Mare.

Chapter Sixteen

"Wakey, wakey," Kail droned.

I rolled over and refused to give him the satisfaction of a groan. It felt as if I aged fifty years the way my joints had stiffened after a night sleeping on the hard floor. "What time is it?" I asked, my words thick with the remnants of sleep.

"Time for task number two," he said.

"What was task number one?" I eased up off the floor, stretching my sore muscles, and yanked the dirty t-shirt back over my head. The glowing orbs still floated around inside their lanterns, and Kail's belongings were gone—probably back in the chest.

"The dog." Kail gripped me by the shoulders and spun me around to face a stained cloth draped over something square.

"*That's* task number two."

I blinked the sleep from my eyes. Where did that come from? It was probably better not to ask or to think about how he got it in here without waking me up. "How long have you been awake?"

"Aren't you going to ask me what's inside?" he asked, sounding far too excited.

"Nope," I quipped, but couldn't stop staring. It was too small to be the loom—not that he could've broken into the Keep and dragged it here—and that was all that mattered right now. Well, that and killing Rowan, which was really the same thing. "We have more important things to deal with." Whatever was underneath the cloth rattled the bars. Hard. I jumped, my back slamming into Kail's chest, and quickly shoved away from him. "Get rid of it."

"You don't even know what it is," he admonished.

"I don't care what it is, Kail. We need to figure out a way to defeat Rowan, not mess around with… *that*."

Kail whipped the sheet off with a dramatic flair to reveal a small cage. Inside, a monkey–or what resembled a monkey—less than a foot tall with dark matted fur bared its tiny fangs. A white moustache curled away from its face like an Emperor tamarin, but in true nightmare fashion, it was deformed. Its arms were short with small hands where elbows should've been, and a bare, rat-like tail twitched behind it. Pointed ears flicked at the edge of a scaled face with black eyes. It had no nose, and its pointed canines hung over its bottom lip.

"Do you know how hard this thing was to catch?" Kail said in a hard voice. "It bit me. Twice. *And* it peed on me."

I smirked at that. "Smart nightmare."

"You're welcome." He crumpled the cloth into a ball and flung it at me.

"What am I supposed to do with it?" I asked, dodging his throw.

"Practice. Obviously."

"Oh, obviously." I rolled my eyes. "Take it outside and let it go."

Kail laughed. "No."

"Yes."

"You seem to have some sort of moral objection to testing on animals, but you need to get over it. We agreed you need to be feared, and that won't happen if you don't want to hurt one of us." He banged on the cage, and the monkey squawked, outraged. "You need to master us before we master you."

He wasn't wrong, but it felt wrong. The monkey hadn't done anything against me, so what good would it do to hurt it? I could be feared and fair at the same time. *No, you can't,* the grin seemed to say with its sarcastic curl. The sentiment filtered through my logic, but I fought against it. I could try.

And fail, the grin implied.

"What exactly do you want me to do?" I asked, weary of my own warring thoughts.

"Change him. You can alter nightmares with almost no effort."

"But…" The monkey's eyes darted between Kail and me, pupils wide. Did it understand what he was saying? I cringed. "It's already alive."

"So?" Kail watched me carefully. "You draw, don't you? Once you finish a picture, is it impossible to tweak anything?"

I narrowed my eyes. "How do you know about that?"

"Rowan," he said dismissively.

For some reason, that made it worse. I ground my teeth together. "How does Rowan know?"

He sighed. "Look, I don't know, okay? Let's not get off topic."

"I don't know how to change nightmares," I admitted. "Besides, it looks fine to me."

He scoffed. "Watch."

Before I could stop him, Kail pressed my hand against his chest. I struggled to escape his grasp, but he cut me a bored, irritated look, and I stilled. Through the fabric of his jacket and the somewhat thicker material of whatever was beneath, I felt it. The thread. It was balled, tightly knotted, and pulsing as if it were a heart. But something about it was off. One end was untucked, dangling, frayed. "What—"

"It's not hard." He shoved my hand away as if the touch had disgusted him and smoothed his clothing. "All you have to do is unknot its thread and coax it into something else."

"I thought the threads were predetermined."

"You're the Weaver. We are whatever you want us to be. A lot about us is decided at the loom, but you can change details. Split us in two even."

"Split you in two? But how? Why?"

"One step at a time, huh?" Kail lifted the cage. "Try it. Turn it blue or give it a mohawk. Something small."

"I'm not touching that thing," I said incredulously.

"Don't be ridiculous."

"You just told me it bites." I scowled, and Kail held the cage closer to my face. He wasn't going to give up, and maybe that's what I needed. To be pushed past my comfort zone. Nothing in this realm was okay with me, but I was here to rule. I had a choice to make: become the Lady of Nightmares or become… dead. I took a deep breath and nodded. "Okay, okay. Just—set it down."

Kail smiled, pleased, and did as I told him.

I knelt and stuck a finger inside the cage. The monkey hissed at me. "Can't we try this with something a little less…?" I motioned to the entire nightmare.

"Where's the challenge in that?" Kail winked, and I almost punched him. He shoved the trap door open. The stool slammed to the floor, and the rope creaked again, the shadow of the girl swaying on the wall outside. "I'm going out for a little bit. Stay in the museum while I'm gone."

My mouth dropped. "You can't leave me here."

"If you want to leave, change it." His expression was more serious than I'd ever seen it. "Learn to control your magic. Until then, you're a liability."

He grabbed the edge of the platform and hauled himself deftly out of our hiding place. "Actually, you know what?" His masked face popped back over the opening. "On second thought, you're right. Maybe this isn't the best nightmare to start on. Hand me the cage."

My heart sang in relief, but somewhere in the back of my mind, a warning bell rang. I pulled the cage protectively toward me. "What's with the sudden change of heart?"

"Just give it to me," he insisted.

I glared at him, but he gave nothing away. No twitch of his lips, no devious gleam in his eyes. His forte, of course, but it was unnerving all the same. The monkey clawed at my fingertips where I held the cage, drawing blood. "Here." I threw the cage up at his face. "Bring something a little less pointy back."

Kail caught the cage and set it next to him. "Actually, that sounds like an awful lot of work." His voice took on a false edge, his eye sparkling for the briefest moment. "On third thought…"

"Kail," I warned slowly. "Whatever you're thinking, don't."

"I'm just giving you a little more incentive."

My eyes widened, my pulse speeding up. "What does that mean?"

He maintained eye contact as he slid the cage to the ledge. And opened it. The monkey fell straight down, landing at my feet with a high-pitched shriek. The door slammed shut overhead.

"Kail, you asshole!" I screamed, dancing away from the nightmare. "Get back here!"

His laugh rumbled overhead, his footsteps receding. The monkey launched itself from wall to ceiling to floor and back up again like a furry bouncy ball. I jumped up to shove open the hatch but couldn't quite reach. Covering my head, I darted over to the chest and kicked it to the center of the room. The monkey whizzed past and grabbed a handful of my hair. It swung around my head, strands wrapping around my mouth. I gave a muffled scream and smacked at the creature until it let go. I leapt onto the chest, heaved the door open, and bolted.

Unfortunately, so did the nightmare.

I shrieked and hurdled off the platform, the mob of wax figures tumbling around me.

There was no telling how long I avoided the ping-ponging nightmare as it followed me from set to set, but the whole debacle ended with us in the foyer, gasping for breath. Bits and pieces of the crystal chandelier were scattered across the floor, and the chandelier itself hung precariously overhead. Each one of the rooms endured different levels of destruction—some more than once after they reset themselves. I was bruised and covered in scrapes from a dozen different props.

And the stupid monkey. It wasn't as funny when it threw waste at me as it was when it peed on Kail. At least it had bad aim, though the mother in front of the fireplace wasn't so lucky. I hadn't gotten close enough to get bitten, but I couldn't complain. Who knew what nasty germs it was carting around? I'd probably end up with some deadly nightmare virus.

"Are you done now?" I rasped and brushed the hair from my sweaty face.

The monkey scowled at me from its place on the overturned banquet table.

"Look, let's just get this over with." I used my softest voice and leaned up onto my knees, but it still stiffened, ready to run. *Not again.* I threw myself forward. It tried to dodge, but its movements were slowed by fatigue, and I caught it by the scruff of its neck. "Just hold still," I urged.

It narrowed its eyes at me and tried to squirm away. After a minute, it sagged, defeated. I hesitated. What should I change? It really did seem fine as it was, but I had to do something. Without a handle on the door, there was no way out unless Kail opened it.

The door.

Kail wanted me to change a nightmare to leave? Fine. I grinned at the monkey. "Want to get out of here?" It perked up, and I set it carefully on the floor. When it didn't try to bolt, I released my hold. "Be good."

I set my palm against the door and closed my eyes, feeling, searching, prodding. The ball of thread writhed at the intrusion, but I held firm. There was no visible end like with Kail's. I didn't know how to pinpoint the door inside the massive knot that made up not only the entire building, but everything inside. I poked at it with my mind, pushed at it, but nothing happened. I clenched my jaw. This was stupid. There was no changing it.

But the grin surfaced, burning bright behind my eyes. One side lifted, smug, and the scent of sulfur hit my nose.

The monkey chirped behind me, and my eyes flew open. Pride swelled at the sight of a round knob in the middle of the door. "I did it," I said breathlessly. "I did it!"

But how? I stared down at my hand in wonder. It just seemed to happen. I didn't really *do* anything. To be honest, it didn't feel like I did anything with the dog either. The grin showed up and ta-da. Maybe that was all it took? To embrace the darkness and let it know what I wanted? That seemed like a slippery slope.

I gripped the warm metal knob and turned it. Gears clicked and whirred inside until the door popped outward. "Out you go," I said to the monkey. It bolted away without another word. I watched it go, scurrying across the lawn, and took a deep, satisfied breath.

Kail appeared, walking between flashing neon signs, slow-clapping, until he stood in front of me. "I was beginning to wonder if you'd ever figure it out or if you were going to chase that thing around all night. Love what you've done with the place, by the way," he added, pointedly looking around me to the knob.

Don't kill him. Don't kill him. "Screw you," I seethed.

He patted my head, and the walls behind me cracked. "Time

to leave."

The foundation shook, and I braced myself in the doorframe. "What's happening?"

"Changing a nightmare isn't exactly a painless process," Kail said, eying the new knob. "It's probably a little pissed."

"What is? The building?"

"Building or not, it's still a nightmare. You had to feel that it was alive while you were messing around in there."

Dust burst from the ceiling, coating me, and I darted outside just as rubble fell into the doorway, sealing the exit.

"So dramatic." Kail straightened his jacket. "Let's go."

"Go where?" I asked, my mouth dry, heart racing. Was that supposed to happen? "Do you have another hidey-hole for us to crawl into?"

"Task number three awaits."

"What?" I shrieked. After hours inside with a deranged nightmare, he wanted me to do something else?

Kail smiled sarcastically and sauntered up to the chain link fence. The realization of what he did settled over me. That bastard set me up! If I got myself out, cool, but if I didn't… How long would he have left me in there? I stomped across the lawn after him.

Do.

Not.

Kill.

Him.

"What's task number three?" I asked skeptically.

"Don't worry. It's nothing you haven't faced before." He pried the fence away from a pole. "After you."

Chapter Seventeen

I stood beside Kail at the edge of a garden full of rotten vegetables, a single step away from cracked, parched ground. My heart fluttered wildly in my chest. At its center stood the rock the firefly had left me at when I first returned to save the Sandman, back before I was the Weaver. Not that he needed it, or that the human-me could've done much. But I remembered all too well what it felt like to be similar to that rock: utterly and completely alone. What it felt like to have my friends and family turn their backs on me. To have the Sandman walk away. Every step I took across the Barren killed me a little more inside.

"You have to face your fear to overcome it," Kail explained when I remained silent and still. He waved his hands in front of us. "Behold! The thing that ensnared you last time."

I didn't want to think about how many things frightened me during my first solo trip to the Nightmare Realm, but this was by far the worst of them. "You're insane if you think I'm going out there," I said, my voice unsteady.

"Your fear is holding you back."

I crossed my arms. "I'm not doing it."

He huffed. "Have I steered you wrong yet?"

"You trapped me in a museum with an angry, poop-flinging mammal," I countered. "That's about as wrong as you can get."

"He flung poop at you?" he asked, too hopeful.

I glared at him. "Be glad he missed."

Kail's laugh was the first genuine one I'd heard. It was warmer than I expected, and even though it was at my expense, I was glad for it. It meant he wasn't cold through-and-through. The relief only lasted until he opened his mouth again.

"Go out there, survive, and meet me back here for a surprise," he said, clapping me roughly on the back.

"Everything you do is a surprise, Kail, and it's never a good one."

"You can't say I don't excel at my job." He watched me playfully. "You'll like this one, I swear."

"Bull."

He held up two fingers and put on a fake smile. "Scout's honor."

"It's three fingers," I said in a flat voice.

He put his ring finger up to join the other two. "Better?"

"I'm not doing it." I turned to walk away, but he was in front of me in the blink of an eye. "I'm *not*—"

He lifted me over his shoulder and stepped into the Barren. The shock of his actions didn't wear off until we were about two feet into the soul-sucking landscape. I shoved away from him and twisted until he finally dropped me on my feet. The effects of the landscape were immediate, sucking away the little joy I had left. The loneliness, the worthlessness… I launched myself at Kail with a roar. Unfortunately, my movements were sluggish here, weighed down by desolation—by my fear of it—and he sidestepped me easily. Soon, I would be a useless heap. Crushed by the solitude of this landscape. Just as I was when Kail and Rowan dragged me out of the Barren so they could use me to kill the Weaver.

"See you on the other side," Kail said with a wave.

Then he turned and walked away. The sight of his retreating back twisted my stomach.

"You can't leave me here!" I screamed, but he had another opinion on that, so I made to follow him. Only, my feet felt frozen to the ground. The hollowness of the Barren inched up my body, and I struggled to shove down the rising panic. Last time I was here, I gave up. If Rowan and Kail hadn't saved me, I would've languished forever. But things were different now. Kail would've preferred me dead last time. *Maybe not so different, then. Could* I die though? The Barren would make for a horrible replacement as Weaver which alone should give him pause.

Ha! Who was I kidding? Kail would let me die without a second thought. He hated me.

No. I shook my head. This wasn't right. Kail was helping me. This place just wanted me to think he wasn't.

Maybe he really *wasn't.* I needed to know what his ulterior motives were. My nails dug into my palms. *Keep it together.* I owned the Barren; the Barren didn't own me. Besides, I was only a few feet into… I spun, searching for something other than the desolate landscape. Nothing. Just the Barren in every direction. Even the mountain I saw the last time was missing. But how? I was barely five steps into this place.

"Kail," I screamed. But he couldn't hear me—or he didn't care. I didn't even know where he was at this point. With a steadying breath, I swallowed my rage. The emptiness surfaced in its place. *Nope.* Anger was better. I let it bubble back to the surface. New plan: Escape. Beat Kail. The grin twitched, amused.

"Okay," I whispered to myself. "I am the Weaver. I am the Lady of Nightmares." I inhaled and exhaled slowly through my mouth. "Got that, Barren? You don't sca—"

A harsh metallic clang sounded right behind me. I spun on my heel, and my heart exploded. Before me stood a woman in a suit of silver armor molded tightly to her body. Intricate chain mail covered both arms, and a heavy leather hood reached up from beneath her collar to hide her hair. The most haunting feature was easily the flat metal mask covering her entire face. Other than the narrow slits that served as eye holes, the only marking was the Roman numeral three stretching from forehead to chin.

I struggled to move my feet, to keep myself from letting the Barren swallow me. *Escape.* I had to run. *Run.*

But before I could act, a fist full of metal plates slammed into my nose. Stars exploded behind my eyelids. Hot blood and tears flowed down my face before I even hit the ground. I gasped for breath only to choke. I forced my eyes open, the lids already swelling, to find the nightmare crouched over me. She reared back for another blow. My mind reeled at the thought of the pain those plates could inflict a second time, and my training took over.

My body moved without having to think. I scrambled back, flipped to my stomach, climbed to my feet, and ran in one seamless move. The Barren made it feel as if I were carrying a small elephant on my back, but I couldn't just lay there, getting pummeled, let alone by a nightmare. A thing I was supposed to control. I scanned the horizon until I found the rock again. The clink of metal told me the nightmare was right on my heels. Then my head snapped back, my feet flying out in front of me, and a scream escaped my throat. The armored nightmare twisted my hair so hard I was sure I would be bald afterward.

She leaned in until the cool metal of her cheek brushed against mine. "You let Mare back in," she whispered in a light voice that somehow also vowed to end me on the spot. Then she slammed me face-first into the dry ground.

The world spun around me. Dizziness erased all coherent thought. There was another blast of pain as my head slammed into the ground again. The grin surfaced, its teeth bared in pure rage, and darkness burst outward, forcing my hands down to splay on the dirt. The knotted thread of the Barren echoed the feeling of despair through my bones.

Sulfur broke through the mind-numbing pain, and my stomach heaved. The pressure on the back of my head disappeared, and the grin gnashed its teeth. *Get up*, it seemed to say. I listened, trusting the darkness, and dragged my feet up from under me. My head swam. My vision was spotty, and my brain tried desperately to shut off, but I had to get to safety. To the Sandman.

No. Not the Sandman. I couldn't run back to his promised safety without at least trying to find it on my own. If it was the Sandman or die, I would turn to him. Otherwise, I needed to turn to myself.

I stumbled to the side and searched for my attacker before she could strike again. Instead, I found a wide circle of saturated dirt. The nightmare was waist deep in the center of it, clawing her way to the edge, but the more she moved, the more it tugged her down. She said something, but I didn't hear the words. Didn't care to hear them, either. All I knew was that, at the edge of the Barren, I could collapse. I left her there with mud inching up her breastplate.

The weight of the landscape rolled off me like rain on a window. I smiled at that. Maybe. My mouth was too numb to be sure. But I did know I conquered this place. At least, in a way. There were worse things out there than being alone. I was alone just now and look at what I accomplished. My magic worked perfectly under duress, though all I wanted was some pain medication, an ice pack, and sleep. Lots of sleep. Unless the magic could do that, I would pat my own back later.

It felt like a lifetime before I stepped back into the spoiled vegetable garden where Kail said he would wait. My eyes were practically swollen shut, and I saw everything through a curtain of eyelashes. There was every chance this wasn't the right place, though the air had the same tang of decay. I fell to my knees, not caring if Kail was nearby, and carefully lowered my aching body into a fetal position. Soggy cabbage was like a pillow beneath my head. *Soft.* I nuzzled into it, letting it cradle me. A quick catnap, then I would find help.

"Nora?" Kail called. It was far off, I thought, but perhaps

not. Reality was fading in and out. Heavy footfalls echoed in my ears. "Nora!"

Kail's hands were on me, lifting me up. I groaned, wanting nothing more than to lie back down.

"What happened?" he barked when I ignored him. If I ignored him. Was he talking a second ago? He gave me a quick shake, and my brain rattled against my skull. "Hey," Kail coaxed again.

Fine. Answer him, *then* nap.

"I—" I coughed blood all over his mask. "Hate you."

"*What happened?*" he asked again, his voice raw.

"I conquered the Barren." I leaned into his grip, letting it hold me up since it was obvious he wasn't going to let me go. Maybe I could sleep like this—

"Nora?" Kail gently tapped my cheek. "Hey, stay awake."

"But I'm tired," I whined.

"You probably have a concussion, among other things. Don't fall asleep."

"I'm the Lady of Nightmares," I said, the words slurred. "Immortal. Strong."

"Yes, yes," he said as if he were talking to a child, and he lifted me into his arms. "Stay with me, Oh Powerful One."

My head nestled perfectly into the crook of his neck. Today he smelled like pumpkin spice, and I wondered, abstractly, if my family had celebrated Thanksgiving without me. "Your surprise better be worth it," I mumbled.

"Stay awake, and I'll tell you all about it."

My eyes slid shut, and I forced them open as much as I could. "Wouldn't that ruin the surprise part?"

"You slipping into a temporary coma would ruin it too." His

hands tightened around me. "I found them. The nightmares that killed your friends."

My breath caught. "What?"

"Rowan promised to take care of the culprits if you killed the Weaver, didn't she?" He sounded defensive. Annoyed. "I figured if she wasn't going to keep her word, it fell to me to get it done."

I shifted in his arms and wheezed. "Why?"

"Think of it as my apology for not stopping Rowan."

Apology. Ha! As if he was capable of such a thing. I couldn't deny the appeal of his gift though. Natalie with her eyes in her hands and Emery with her arms sliced to ribbons. Coils of black swirled through the fog surrounding my mind, clearing it away. My friends would be avenged as brutally as they were killed. Blood would flow, black or red. Mindless or intelligent. Their lives were mine, and I would take them with the entire force of the Nightmare Realm behind me.

This time, when the darkness grinned, I grinned back.

The pounding in my head broke through the blissful silence. My eyes cracked, the lids heavy and swollen, but my vision was no longer obstructed. I sucked in a crackling breath. Everything hurt. Places that I didn't even know existed. But at least I was alive. And awake. I wasn't sure how long I'd been out—just that, at some point on the way here, I gave into exhaustion—wherever *here* was. I was grateful for the cushioned surface beneath me. There were lumps, sure, but it was a thousand times better than the ground.

"Nora?" It was a hesitant whisper, jarring, considering the

source.

I blinked my eyes open and stared up at Kail's masked face as he leaned over me. "Ow," I moaned and batted at the tip of his beak.

He let out a breath that was half-laugh, half-relief. "It took you long enough. I was beginning to think I'd have to kill those nightmares myself."

Ah, yes. The nightmares that killed Natalie and Emery. Everything flooded back to me—the Barren, the armored woman, the magic rushing to save me. "How long have I been asleep?"

"A day and a half." Kail sat on a chair beside the bed and brushed the hair from his forehead. A wet cloth hung off the side of a basin with small bits of green leaves scattered on the tabletop. "How do you feel?"

Better than I should. I eased into a sitting position. "Where are we?"

"Here." Kail held out a wooden cup of water with more tiny leaves floating on top. "This will help with the pain."

I scowled. Rowan had tried to give me something to ease the pain of her touch, and I was glad I refused it. "I'm fine."

He glowered. "Don't be stubborn."

"Why am I always getting head injuries around you anyway?" I snapped.

"Maybe because you pick fights you can't win?" He shoved the cup into my hand and wrapped my fingers around it. "Now drink this. You'll heal quickly thanks to your magic, but this will take the edge off."

"Fine," I said, because I needed relief. Any relief. If Kail wanted to hurt me, he would've done it while I laid there unconscious. "But I need something to write on."

"If I leave, you'll dump it out," he accused.

I downed the entire thing in three gulps. It tasted like grass with a bitter kick, and when it was gone, I threw the cup at him and wiped my mouth on the back of my hand. "Paper. Now."

He batted the cup away before it hit him. It clattered against the concrete. "I doubt there's any here."

I scanned the small, dank room. No, not a room—a cell. Three walls were covered with names and tally marks, the fourth with thick black bars. Thankfully, the door was wide open. "Are we in a prison?" I asked.

"See? Not all my safe houses have trap doors."

I glowered at him.

"I needed somewhere to keep your presents," Kail said with a shrug. "It's as good a place as any."

"I'm sure there are a million other places to lock things up around here." I sighed. It didn't matter—he was right. It was probably one of the better options. "I need something to write on, Kail."

He reached under my pillow, searching.

"What are you—"

"When in Rome." He winked and produced a crude shank. Someone had wrapped half a roll of duct tape around the handle of a warped spoon, filed to a point. "I think there's some free wall space by your head."

I groaned and snatched the sharp object from him. It didn't have to be a fancy image, it just had to get my point across. The more I concentrated on the scraping of metal on concrete, the more my head throbbed, but the shape of the armored woman's face gradually took shape on the wall. Not my best work, but it would do. "What is that?"

Kail stared at it a moment before speaking. "It's Three."

"Three?"

"One of the Hours."

"The Hours? You mean the nightmares that destroyed the Blood Tower?" I asked. Kail nodded, and I swallowed hard, shifting to tuck the shank into my back pocket. "She attacked me in the Barren. Something about my letting Mara back in."

"Ah." Kail stretched his back. "Well, yes. That's bound to be an unpopular move."

"It was an accident. I didn't know she hitched a ride."

"Your intentions won't matter when she decimates the entire realm for the fun of it."

My stomach twisted. The Sandman warned me—unlike with the Weaver, I *had* listened. My mistake was letting Mara think there was a chance. Or maybe it didn't matter either way. She had made up her mind that she was coming, and there had been no changing it. Lying to her had seemed like my only way to return to the Nightmare Realm without the Sandman. I chewed my bottom lip to keep it from quivering. I was such an idiot.

"Don't worry, Lady," Kail said, interrupting my self-pity party. "I'm sure the Sandman will come up with a plan. If he's good at anything, it's that—unless you get in his way yet again." It was a slap in the face yet said without accusation.

"I don't want to rely on the Sandman to fix my mistake," I said quietly and flicked my gaze up to meet his.

His good eye changed slowly, switching between colors almost lazily. "We have to concentrate on Rowan. No one wins when they're fighting a war on two fronts."

"You're right." I slid off the lumpy cot and took a shaky

breath. Moving seemed to push the ache from my muscles, so I bent my joints a few times. "How do I look?"

Kail stood with a smirk. "Two black eyes have never looked so good."

I made a *tsk*ing sound with my tongue. Black eyes were a vast improvement from what I was sure I looked when I stumbled out of the Barren. "Show me these nightmares."

"Now?" His eyes widened.

"Do we have anything better to do?"

"That's a loaded question, Lady. We obviously do," he answered cynically.

I rolled my eyes. "Your ex-girlfriend can wait another day. Let's go."

Kail shrugged and led the way down a hallway full of identical cells, down two flights of stairs, and around a corner. He paused, his hand on a door that said *solitary confinement.* "She's not, you know. For the record."

I bounced on the balls of my feet. The nightmares were close—I knew it. "What?"

His jaw twitched. "Rowan. She's not an ex. Or a girlfriend."

"Oh." That wasn't what I expected. I wondered why he cared what I thought on the matter. I hadn't even meant it when I called her that. "Okay."

"Anyway." He cleared his throat. "I should probably warn you that one of them is pretty strong."

"Don't care," I said and hurried past him into a dimly lit corridor.

Something lunged at the first door on the left, and I peeked curiously through the small window to find a giant wolf-man standing on his haunches. He was covered in coarse, wiry grey hair, his snout pressed in so he looked like a pug with giant fangs. Long pointed claws extended from his hands. He stared out at me, part fear, part hate, part something else.

"He killed Emery?" I asked Kail without looking away from the growling creature.

"I don't know your friends' names," he said with a stiff shrug.

I scowled. It had to be. Something told me this thing wouldn't have bothered asking his victim to hold their own eyes. More likely, he would've eaten them. So. How to make him pay? Werewolves, wolf-men, whatever: they weren't up my alley. All I knew was that they were rumored to change on a full moon, and a person had to shoot them with a silver bullet to kill them. With the nightmare version, all bets were off.

"Does silver affect him?" I asked Kail.

"I wouldn't know."

"You wouldn't know?" I stared at him. "You caught the thing."

"I *lured* it, if you want to get technical. No silver required."

"Worth a shot, then," I mumbled and put my hand on the wall beside the door. The grin rose up, searching for the bundle of thread that was the prison. It came easily without my resistance, and with a quick flick of my magic, molten silver coated every surface in the room. It dripped from the ceiling, flowed down the walls, swirled across the floor. The wolf-man's howl was immediate. His paws sizzled as he jumped from one to the other. The molten liquid ate away at his fur, his skin, his bones. My heart ached at the gruesome sight, but the grin held my resolve firmly between its teeth. He deserved to die for killing Emery. He slammed against the door again, his wild eyes begging me through the small window to make it stop.

"You shouldn't have touched my friend," I said, almost as if my voice weren't my own.

The wolf-man's cries slowly faded as he thrashed, trying desperately not to touch any silver. But there was no escape. I stood there watching, waiting for the moment he drew his last breath.

And I reveled in it.

When his chest finally ceased rising, when he was little more than a skeleton, I turned to Kail and let out a short breath. "Next."

Kail eyed me warily and pointed to the next cell down. "Permission to rescue you if things go bad?"

I snorted. "Sure."

He slid the bolt open and pulled the door outward with a loud screech. Inside the small, musty room, I eyed a figure strapped to a gurney. A straight jacket and brown sack over its head hid its true form.

"What's this?" I asked calmly, stalking around the table. My power crackled in my veins.

"The most beautiful nightmare in the Night World," Kail said in a careful voice. "So beautiful, in fact, that you'll feel unworthy to look upon her and will—"

"Claw your own eyes out. Got it." I swallowed hard at the memory. "How did you catch this one then?"

He looked at me like it was obvious. "Do I strike you as insecure?"

"Far from it." I took a deep breath and steeled myself. "Let's see, then."

Kail stepped up to the gurney and ripped the sack off the

nightmare's head. The room exploded with golden light. It was like staring into the sun, at the purest thing in existence. And when she smiled, I felt no bigger than an ant. A thing to be trampled. Indeed, someone—some*thing*—like me shouldn't look upon her perfection.

"Nora," Kail whispered.

His voice snapped the nightmare's hold on me, and anger blossomed in my chest. *Natalie*. She was pretty and smart. Funny. Loyal. And this… this *thing* made her believe she wasn't. I stared into the nightmare's wide blue eyes and saw no remorse.

"Beautiful." I glanced at Kail over my shoulder with a wicked gleam in my eyes. "We can fix that."

My magic swelled, ready, but killing her that way would be too easy. I took the shank from my back pocket and studied the crude workmanship. *Perfect*. Everything that she was—her golden skin, perfect profile, and glimmering hair—ruined by everything she wasn't. A fitting end.

With the first cut, the nightmare shrieked so hard the gurney shook. It cracked open the box of emotions I'd carried around for months and months. The anger, the hurt, the sorrow, I carved it all into the nightmare's flesh. I took my time doing it. Each new cut flared with golden light that dimmed quickly, leaving behind a blackened wound. I swept my hand over her face, her neck, her collarbones as easily as I would've used a pencil on paper. Her red blood ran thick down the shank. My grip slipped more than once on the taped handle. I felt the blood dripping off my elbows, and I didn't care.

When the nightmare was finally still and the golden glow nonexistent, I dropped the shank to the floor. "I feel better now," I told Kail in a stale voice.

"I'm sure you do," he said in a tone I couldn't quite decipher. "Look at your arms."

I lifted my bloodied hands and sucked in a sharp breath. Beneath the crimson was my own pale skin. No more black. The Weaver's magic was really, truly mine. Fully absorbed. I flexed my fingers. What was I capable of now? A true smile broke across my face.

Kail smiled back, a strangely genuine expression, and pointed down the hallway. "The showers are that way, Lady Nightmare."

For the first time, there was no condescending tone in the title.

Chapter Eighteen

My spies were dying faster than I could make them. An unfortunate side effect of my magic, but at least seeking out new ones kept me from dwelling on Nora. And Mare—I was still having trouble wrapping my head around that problem. The Weaver had experience under his belt when we banished her, but Nora…

I shook my head and focused on the task at hand. Baku crept along the forest ground beside me. The incline to the top of the cliff appeared nearly nonexistent, but it was all an illusion. My thighs started burning halfway to the peak. Now that we were nearly there, I barely noticed it. There wasn't room to worry about personal comfort when we were approaching nightmares as perceptive as the Watchmen. They had one job, one base desire: defend what they were told to defend.

"Remember," I whispered to Baku. "We aren't here to cause a scene. You can't eat these."

Baku's lip curled in annoyance, but his eyes were resigned.

It was smart of Rowan to pull the Watchmen from their assigned landscape to overlook the Keep. The how was the most concerning thing about it though, unless the Weaver had stationed them there before without my noticing or removed their assignment altogether so they could roam where they pleased. My insides twisted at how much I truly neglected the Weaver during his binding. Too little, too late seemed to be my new motto. I needed to rectify that.

As Baku and I crested the top of the hill, solid forms of six giant stone men dotted the far side of the clearing. Some were the color of granite to blend with the rocky outcroppings, others a mixture of browns and greens to blend with the trees. If they shifted so much as a centimeter, their appearance changed to match the backdrop perfectly. The six of them worked as a team so I only needed to secure one to see what all of them saw. The trick was getting close enough. Luckily, their hearing was nowhere near as good as their eyesight.

Baku and I wove between trees, hiding behind thick trunks and boulders until we reached the edge of a wooded shelter. One of the Watchmen turned toward our hiding place in increments—his head, his torso, then his legs. His marble eyes looked out from beneath a sculpted warrior helmet. I cringed. Their hearing wasn't exceptional, but that didn't mean they couldn't hear at all.

I eased a handful of sand from my satchel and dropped it to the ground, directing its path toward the nightmare. It would take twice as much, maybe more, to inhabit something this size, but it could give us valuable information. No, not us. *Me.* It would give *me* information that I would have to get to Nora without her knowing how I came by it. The sand snaked through the sparse tufts of grass and eased into the cracks of rocks, staying as hidden as possible.

The Watchman began to turn back to the cliff but paused. With lightning-fast speed, he slammed the spear in his right hand against the shield in his left. The boom echoed down the hill. Baku bristled, and I pressed myself against the closest tree. One by one, the other five Watchmen twisted toward the forest. Then, in perfect unison, they aimed their spears straight ahead.

"Run," I told Baku.

A spear sliced through the tree right above my head. I ducked and rolled to the side as another soared straight toward my chest. The forest groaned around us as we fled down the mountain. Another spear hit the ground directly in front of me, and I flung myself sideways to avoid running into the swaying stone handle. The fourth ripped through my sleeve before tearing apart a tree to my left. It crashed down, taking me with it, and pinned my leg to the ground. My shin bone shattered under the weight. I swallowed the pained cry that rose in my throat and took a series of shallow breaths.

The Watchmen followed the path of their weapons and reduced the forest to splinters beneath their feet. Each of their steps was worth two dozen of my own. My magic tugged at me, asking to go home, but I couldn't leave Baku. The Watchmen wouldn't kill me; capture me, maybe, and give me to Rowan, but she could never keep me. Baku was another story.

I pried my leg out from beneath the rough bark with a

strained scream. *Run.* I only had to make it out of range of the spears—there would be no prying myself out from one of those. But my leg threatened to crumble beneath me. Baku still hadn't made it far enough to lose them, so I called on the rest of the sand in my satchel. It swept him up and carried him as far as it could before my concentration broke. I nearly vomited as I fell to the ground.

"Over here," I shouted to buy Baku more time.

Using the trees to prop myself up, I hobbled back up the cliff-side. The thunderous footfalls of the Watchmen slowed. I let out a wordless cry to draw their attention, then found it ringing true as I slipped on a mildew-covered rock. Rocks and roots battered my body as gravity pulled me down a slick, muddy trail. When a fallen trunk finally brought me to a halt, I laid there for a long moment, groaning. Bone protruded from my lower leg. I sat up carefully, cringing, and tugged the small bag of emergency sand from beneath my tunic. There was just enough to heal my leg, or at least lessen the pain until I got home.

A twig snapped behind me. Before I could even turn my head, someone latched onto my arm where the spear had ripped the fabric. Red silk flashed in my peripheral vision.

Rowan.

Her name was all I had time to think before the pain of her touch filled me. It cut and burned and suffocated. My magic clawed at the beach in a desperate bid for escape. With a final clear thought, I yanked it back. If I wanted to know what Rowan was doing, where better to be than the Keep? For the Night World, for Nora, the pain would be worth it.

I drew a deep breath and let the agony in.

☾

When my vision cleared again, Rowan had my arms tied around a post at my back. The coarse rope grated against my skin, and the pain of my broken shin lit up my mind like a firecracker. But I stayed still. If I lost consciousness, my magic would drag me back to the beach. Rowan knew that too—it was an open secret in the Nightmare Realm—so she would be careful until she got what she wanted. Whatever that was. Now I simply needed to find something useful to make the upcoming pain worthwhile.

Pieces of straw littered the floor, and I took in the otherwise empty space with growing disappointment. I was going to have to escape from this room and sneak through the tower to learn anything meaningful.

"Hello, Sandman," Rowan said from behind me, her breath hot on my ear. She smelled of licorice and blood. "I know you can hear me. Let's have some fun."

I lifted my head, a gargantuan task, and met her red-flecked eyes as she circled to stand before me. "I think we have different definitions of fun."

"Of course we do." She raised a knife to my chin. "I know what will happen if you pass out, but there are ways around that."

The knife left my chin and nicked my neck. It didn't cut deep enough to hurt, but that wasn't her goal. She plucked the now-broken string holding my bag of sand away from my neck. Her fingers skimmed my skin in the process, sending sparks of pain straight down into my marrow. I ground my teeth to keep quiet, instead directing my anger into my gaze as it followed the pouch. It didn't matter if the sand was in her hands or mine—as long as it was in the same vicinity, I could call on it. But she didn't know that.

"There." Rowan's bright red lips lifted, and she tossed the pouch into the far corner of the room.

Then I saw it.

As Rowan turned to make the throw, everything clicked.

Harsh lines marred the base of her skeletal wings, black and crackled, as if she had been burnt in a fire. I drew in a small breath. Kail had shown me how to defeat her. All this time, the information was right in front of me, but I hadn't given it half a thought because of who it came from. Could he really want Nora to succeed? It was hard to realize everything could end without a single battle.

"Now…" Rowan ripped open the front of my shirt with the knife and cocked her head at the sight of my tattoo. "That's it? The source of your power? I thought it would be… bigger."

My jaw clenched. I had what I came for, so when the edges of my vision began to fade, I let myself succumb.

A quick burning shock lanced my chest before I could fade out. I gasped, the room coming back into sharp focus. Rowan stood in front of me, licking my blood from the tip of the blade. I looked down with sickening dread. She had sliced just above the moon tattooed there. An inch lower and it would've taken months to heal. This would only take two days, maybe three. But I couldn't let her see the relief on my face, so I hung my head as if I were defeated.

"Get comfortable, Sandman," she crooned, content. "We'll be spending a lot of time together."

The distinctive clip of approaching high-heeled shoes filled the stairwell behind Rowan, and she rolled her eyes. "What is it this time?"

A short woman covered in scales practically bounced into the room. Two tiny horns protruded from her green hair, and her dress was made from dripping seaweed. "There's trouble in the courtyard, your queenship," she chirped.

Queenship?

"It can wait," Rowan snapped.

"Unfortunately not," the woman said. "The Devourer has eaten through half your guard already."

Red flared up beneath Rowan's pale skin. "Your *friend* has come to save you?" she hissed, whirling on me.

"He's probably just hungry," I said with as much defiance as I could muster. *Baku, what are you doing?*

"Let's hope your Dream Keeper is a bit more loyal then." She threw the knife to the ground and stormed up the stairs, the scaled woman following close on her heels.

What did that mean? More loyal than who? I strained against the ropes. Whatever Rowan had heard about my tattoo, it didn't need to be intact for the sand to call me home. It only hindered my ability to wield it—a rather large problem at the moment, but it could've been worse. By the time Rowan returned, I would already be cocooned by sand.

Then I would find Nora.

And she would kill Rowan without ever setting eyes on her.

Chapter Nineteen

When Kail returned to the prison mid-afternoon with two horses in tow, I almost locked myself in the nearest cell. They were the same black creatures with clawed feet that carried me from the Barren the first time. Unsurprisingly, he wasn't riding the one that once tried to bite me. My new-found pride wouldn't allow me to be a chicken, so I swung into the saddle made of smooth bone and took the reins. My feet swung at the horse's sides, my legs too short to reach the stirrups attached to the seat by a ball and socket joint. I considered altering it for a second, but the memory of the crumbling museum was too fresh to try.

I glanced back at the brick prison hidden beneath climbing ivy. Concealed among the foliage were faces that screamed obscenities, but beyond that, inside, were the remains of two slain nightmares. Now that the adrenaline had worn off, I wanted to feel guilty.

But I didn't.

I was glad. Satiated.

"Lady?"

"Hm?" I forced myself to turn from the prison and my thoughts. Kail simply motioned me forward. "Bite me, and I'll turn you into dog food," I told the horse before nudging him with my heel. He didn't show the slightest hint of defiance this time, but I kept an eye on the back of his head anyway. From my peripheral vision, I watched Kail. "Where are we going? And don't give me a vague answer."

He smirked as if I stopped him just in time from doing exactly that. "The Blood Tower."

"What?" I asked in disbelief. "You *do* remember it was on fire the last time we were there, right? Is there even a tower left to go to?"

He shrugged. "I wouldn't know, but luckily, Halven and I have you."

"Halven?" I hadn't seen him since he left me with Kail that first day. While I now realized that earned him points in my book, I wouldn't say he *had me*. Nor Kail for that matter. There was still his ulterior motive hanging over our friendship. I cringed at the term. Was Kail my friend? Or a reluctant mentor? "What does he have to do with anything?"

"A lot." Kail hesitated. "He's my brother, you know."

I whipped my head sideways to look at him. His brother? They did have similar traits. The masks, the weirdly elaborate clothes. Halven was much more dramatic in appearance, but Kail made up for it with his sparkling personality. I snorted. "I didn't realize nightmares had siblings. Is it one of those solidarity things between all nightmares or is he your *brother*-brother?"

Kail was silent for a moment, and his hand absently moved to the center of his chest. He seemed to realize it and quickly grabbed the reigns. "He's my brother," he said stiffly.

Oh. That clears things up. I leveled a stare at him. "So you both came from one cord or you were next to each other or—"

"It's not important," he snapped. Then he took a shallow breath and, when he spoke again, sounded much calmer. "I'll teach you that later. First we have to get your loom."

Interesting. I filed his reaction away. "I suppose you know how to weave?" I asked as if he hadn't lost his temper for a hot second.

"No, but you will."

"I hate to break it to you, but I don't even know how to knit a scarf."

Kail sighed. "You didn't know how to bring giant dogs to life or create doorknobs out of nothing before either, but you did it. Listen to the magic, not your doubts."

Was that… I scowled at him. Was he offering moral support? Did we cross into another dimension without my realizing it?

"You'll thank me for everything one day," he said confidently after a moment.

And there he was.

If he was truly loyal—and that was a big if—letting him live would be enough reward.

The threads shifted gently along my arm, and I startled. I had first noticed it during my time in solitary confinement: almost a caress where before they kept a vice-like grip. I couldn't be positive, but it was almost as if they sensed my acceptance. That I now embraced the grin living inside me. That I wanted to be here. To harness their power. They could now relax without fear that I would rip them away as I might have before. No longer were they a parasite. Our relationship was too symbiotic for that. I watched the frayed end thump against the pulse point on my wrist, then suddenly something tickled the skin beneath my sleeve. The threads, now coiled loosely, slithered across my chest and circled my neck. My heart jumped into a frantic rhythm.

"Kail," I called, my voice wavering. Before he could answer, the other end of the thread settled peacefully in the hollow of my throat. When I looked over to him, he smiled wickedly. "What's it doing?"

"It just wanted more room." He eyed the newly visible end as it beat to my pulse like the one on my wrist. "The Weaver used to work them into his clothes to avoid the whole necklace look, but it suits you."

"Was that a compliment?" I joked to hide my unease.

He leveled his gaze at me. "We should use this time for another lesson."

I groaned.

"Pay attention to your surroundings," he continued. "Feel where we are and use it to guide you. The Nightmare Realm is large and has a tendency to confuse even the oldest of nightmares, but the Weaver could navigate it with his eyes closed."

"Does that include you?" I asked, searching my mind for anything that resembled a compass.

He paused. "It never used to, but things change."

"What kind of things?"

"If you're talking, you're not paying attention," he said with a clip to his voice, and he spurred his horse ahead of mine.

The faster I learned, the faster I could be done with his lessons. Then, once I had what was mine, I could see the Sandman again. My chest ached at the thought of him. Days passed since I'd seen him. What was he doing? Was he okay? I hated myself for sending him away, but he didn't want to let me learn. To let me face the dangers. He wanted to fix them for me. That didn't stop me from recalling the way his kisses felt or the way his fingers fit perfectly between mine.

Focus, I reminded myself. There was more than one reason I needed to do this alone. Distraction was one of them. The grin appeared, sarcastic yet ready to help. There was no swirling darkness leaking out this time, but a knowingness filled me. It was almost as if the grin had sprouted limbs as my hands directed the horse to the right.

"This way," I shouted to Kail.

The Blood Tower wasn't nearly as bad as I expected. Fire had scorched the outer walls, but they were still mostly intact, save for the bits of rubble cause by the impact of the fireballs. The front door lay bent on the ground outside, the hinges ripped from the frame. "This was broken from inside," I said, stepping carefully over the dug-up gravel. "Maybe that means the dog escaped."

"Maybe," Kail agreed. But he wasn't looking at the tower. His gaze swept over the area surrounding us, eyes narrow. "Halven should be here by now."

"If he's anything like you, he's probably waiting to make a dramatic entrance." I leaned through the doorway, blinking until my eyes adjusted to the dark interior. The stench of smoke permeated the air, and the walls inside were singed black. Dead tarantulas littered the floor like a carpet. No new ones had sprouted in their place. *Good riddance.*

"We shouldn't stay long," Kail said, suddenly at my side. "I'll do a quick sweep to make sure none of Rowan's minions are inside while you fix it. If Halven hasn't shown up by then, we get what we need and get out of here."

Before I could disagree, he disappeared inside. The spiders crunched under foot, and I placed my hand on the tower to see if I could feel how much damage was done. The blackened stone was still warm. I closed my eyes and searched for the ball of thread. And searched and searched. But it was nowhere to be found.

"All clear," Kail said between quick breaths. I opened my eyes and looked at him with wide eyes. "What?"

"There's no thread," I said softly.

"Look harder." He moved around me and searched the surrounding area for his brother again. "If the thread died, the tower would disappear."

Look harder, I mimicked behind his back, then turned my attention to the tower again. *A little help?* I asked the grin. It surfaced slowly, almost reluctantly. *Lazy*, it seemed to accuse, but I felt it reach into the ruins of the Blood Tower. The withered, throbbing pain echoed through me, and I gasped. The thread *was* there. Huddled. Bound tightly into a tiny ball. I stroked the aching threads soothingly as if it were a wounded bird. The ball shivered and loosened before reaching out to greet me.

The rest happened in a single breath. One inhale that seemed to burn my lungs to ash. The scent of sulfur exploded around me, and I tried to wrench my hand away from the suddenly scalding stone wall. I think a cry escaped from my throat, but it seemed as if I were only a passenger in my own body. Sounds dulled. Vision tunneled. The ground beneath me felt like shifting tiles.

And then it was over.

The stone was cold, the grin gone. I stumbled backward into Kail, tears streaming silently down my face.

"Well done," he said, impressed.

Exhaustion washed over me as I blinked up at the tower. Blood flowed between the stones again with such force that droplets sprayed outward. The old door still sat on the gravel while a large, elaborate black steel door stood in its place. Red metal studs formed a swirling design.

"My Lady," said a painfully hoarse voice.

I turned to find Halven bowing before me. "You're late," I said without an ounce of annoyance. I was too tired for that.

"Forgive me. I underestimated how much slower traveling could be with an army."

"A—what?" I looked between the brothers. "What's he talking about?"

"You told him you needed one," Kail said, irritated. "And Halven lives to serve. Where did you think he was this whole time?"

Scaring Dreamers. Lurking in dark corners. Off doing whatever it was nightmares did in their free time. "Why didn't you tell me?"

"You had to concentrate on your training," Kail said. "An

army is only as strong as its leader."

With a large enough army, I could crush the entire rebellion without using up all my current thread. My chest burst with hope. "Where is it?" I asked Halven.

Halven pointed around the tower where the Blood Army once congregated. I raced forward, all trace of exhaustion gone, and froze at what waited there. Hundreds, maybe thousands, of nightmares sprawled on the ground. They were still alive—their shifting limbs and labored breaths proving that much—but they couldn't crush a soda can, let alone Rowan.

"What happened to them?" I asked, deflated.

"Tired," Halven groaned. "We walked for days."

"They'll be ready to fight on schedule?" Kail asked.

Halven nodded.

"Good." Kail turned on his heel. "Let's go check your clock."

The brothers walked back around the tower together, but I stood there, staring. An army. *My* army. Guilt twisted my stomach. The Sandman said the Weaver relied too much on his nightmares. Look how *that* turned out. And here I was. Doing the same thing. Because, honestly, what had *I* done? Turned a thread into a giant dog? Altered a few buildings? Tortured nightmares? I wanted to be better than the Weaver, but I was following in his footsteps. When I became *this,* I told the Sandman we could create a united Night World, but now… Now I saw the power in what I had. Saw the potential in what I didn't. All these nightmares spread out before me, ready to fight for me, because they believed I would do what was best for them. Or maybe because they were mindlessly loyal. Either way, I understood the Weaver a little more now. His connection to the nightmares warred with his longing for the Sandman's friendship. He told me he wanted things to go back to the way they were before, and so did I. More than anything. The grin surfaced, a contemplative thing. I sucked in a deep breath and hurried after Kail.

"That shouldn't be a problem yet," Kail said, and I followed his voice to the room where he had given me the knife. "Where's Rowan?"

The large hand on the clock moved with a series of soft clicks.

"As expected," he murmured.

"What is?" I asked, and the brothers both startled.

"Rowan's still at the Keep." Kail pointed to a symbol on the clock that looked like an upside-down triangle on a stick.

I stepped closer to the mantel. A dozen gold symbols were emblazoned around the black clock face. "How do you know?" I asked curiously. Surely there was some rhyme or reason to it, but it all seemed like hieroglyphics to me. Were there only twelve nightmares he could find? Who were they?

"Halven asks the clock. Each of the symbols is a location."

I crossed my arms. "Even I know there are more places than that."

"These were the original landscapes. It narrows things down by telling Halven the nearest landscape, then he focuses his energy in that direction to pinpoint the person specifically. It's faster this way."

"You seem to know an awful lot about it," I said carefully.

Kail shrugged.

I squinted at him. "Back to what you were you saying when I walked in. What won't be a problem yet?"

The brothers exchanged a look—or Kail did, at least. Halven turned his masked face in his brother's direction. "Mara's hiding out in a cave at the moment."

"Ah, yes. Her." I chewed on my bottom lip. "Where's the Sandman?"

Halven stiffened.

"What?" I scoffed. "Do only nightmares show up on there?"

"Dreamers, sometimes," Halven rasped.

"I'm sure the Dream Lord is fine," Kail added. "He's giving you the space you asked for."

I winced. He was right, but I wanted to see him. Almost *needed* to.

"Take heart, Lady," Halven said kindly.

I forced a smile, then glared at Kail. "I like your brother so much better than you. Maybe *he* should train me while you manage the rabble outside."

"*Please.*" Kail snorted. "I'm the best nightmare you could get help from."

"I don't know about that." I glanced at Halven. "He talks a lot less than you *and* is nice when he does."

Kail bristled. "Sorry, Lady. You're stuck with me until my eye is fixed."

"Is that all it takes to get rid of you?" I reached toward his face, and he jerked backward.

"How about you practice changing a few moving targets first?" he said, his pupil blown wide. "My eye is a lot more complicated than a doorknob."

"Arrogant bas—"

"Shall we call it a day?" he asked loudly. "I'm exhausted, and you look like you're about to fall over."

Now that the shock of the army's arrival was beginning to fade, the drained feeling crept back in. But I had done it. Fixed the tower. Returned charred remains to their former glory. I smiled to myself, and the grin matched it, equally satisfied. Wanting to be alone, I nudged it.

But it didn't budge.

In fact, it grew.

Panic clawed at my chest. The door I locked the grin behind had disappeared, and the darkness grew heavy in my veins. *We need each other*, it seemed to say with startling clarity. I took a shaky breath. It wasn't wrong.

Besides, we both knew I was only *trying* not to like it.

"What's next?" I asked.

"Now, Lady, we get some rest." Kail flopped down on the couch and put his hands behind his head. "Tomorrow, you take control of your realm."

Chapter Twenty

Hours could have passed. *Days.* It was hard to tell. All I knew was the white-hot pain in my chest. The sand worked fast once it dragged me home, burying me within seconds, but the wound was still there. Skin grew like new over the cut, but beneath, the trapped sand wrestled with interior repairs. Rowan hadn't cut me that deep, but the amount of blood flaking on my skin made it seem otherwise.

I reached up to shake the sand from my hair and winced. How was I going to be of any help like this? I eased back onto the beach and took long, deep breaths. It felt as if a fever was in my bones, making everything ache. But there were other ways to help Nora while I healed. Smaller ways, like getting her a message, would be enough for the moment. She needed to do this alone, after all.

And she had Kail.

Jealousy sparked along my nerve endings, but I shook it away. Nora loved me. This wasn't about us, and Kail was far from being a threat in that respect. Sure, he got to see her every day, all day—a thing I'd never been able to do myself, but one day, maybe I could. I wouldn't lose hope that we would eventually reunite the realms. Forever was a long time.

But what worried me most was why Kail told me how to kill Rowan instead of telling Nora. It seemed like he wanted Rowan dead, so why go through the effort of putting on a show? There must be a reason. Kail never did anything without one—it was just rare that anyone knew what that reason was.

A little longer, and I would get dressed, track Nora down, and tell her everything. This information was too important to trust to a messenger, even one as trustworthy as Baku. And, perhaps, part of it was my desire to see her. Just to make sure she wasn't doing something ridiculously stupid again. I winced at the flash of heat the thought brought along with it and shoved the anger back into its box. Everything in its time.

"Sandman," a voice called down its cord. A voice I knew well enough from five years inside Nora's dreams. "Help me sleep."

I immediately stood on shaky legs and yanked the cord hard, hurtling myself into the Day World with a pained scream in my throat. My legs buckled as the soft blanket of sand became a braided area rug that did little to soften the blow when my knees hit. I fell forward into a puffy bedspread, buried my face into the soft material, and panted for a moment before composing myself enough to stand.

Katie stared slack-jawed at me from the other side of the

bedroom. "It worked," she said in an incredulous voice. "It—it worked."

"Yes." I caught a glimpse of another form under her sheets and stumbled back a step. "Who—"

"Kellan's a sound sleeper," Katie said in a rush. "Plus, he's high as a kite tonight, so if he sees you, don't worry about it."

Don't worry about it. There were an awful lot of things I wasn't supposed to worry about lately, and, in my opinion, they were all very much of concern. Katie rolled her eyes and rushed up to the bed, shaking Kellan violently.

"Don't do th—" I began to protest.

"See? He's out." She let out a disbelieving huff as she turned back to me. "I can't believe it worked."

"It's nice to see you coming around to the truth," I said carefully. The Dream Realm was already pulling at my center. "I'm sort of in the middle of something, so if this is some kind of test—"

"Oh my God. *Oh my God.* Is that blood?"

I stepped around the bed and gripped her upper arms carefully. The strong scent of alcohol permeated from her. "Katie, listen to me." My magic rippled. In another ten seconds, I would be hurtling back to the beach whether I wanted to or not. "We have to finish this conversation somewhere else."

"Wha—"

As quickly as I could, I pinched a bit of sand that was trapped between my shirt and tunic and threw it in her face. The next second, she slammed to the floor. It wasn't my best moment, but it was the only option I had left, because this time, when the beach called me home, there would be no denying it.

If it was any consolation to Nora's sister, my landing back

on the beach wasn't much better. The sand cradled me, softening the blow, but the impact made every warm, throbbing piece of me flash red-hot. My vision was still blanketed in white when a pair of hesitant hands brushed the hair from my face.

"Hey," Katie half-shouted. Or maybe it just felt like she did. "Are you okay?"

"Sorry about your headache," I mumbled.

The hands disappeared. "My what?"

"You'll understand when you wake up." The sand moved to cover me, but now wasn't the best time for another burial. If Katie was going to accept the truth, for Nora's sake, I couldn't risk scaring her off. "Just give me a second."

"Okay," she whispered so softly I barely heard.

I steeled myself by taking deep breaths and focusing on my center. Whatever strength I could pull from the sand within the next few heartbeats, I did, though it wasn't much. My vision cleared, and I forced myself to sit up, but that was all I would be doing. Katie knelt beside me, her face paler than pale as she stared into my pavilion. I knew what she was looking at.

"Nora gave them to me," I said. When she turned back to me with a wild, confused expression, I added, "The drawings."

"This is it, isn't it?" Katie practically flopped backward, propping herself up on her hands. "This is where she came every night. She tried to tell us…"

"Breathe, Katie," I said gently, and she gulped down air. "The place Nora and I met is just under the brightest star, near the water, but yes. This is the Dream Realm. I wouldn't have brought you here if I had another choice."

Her eyes darted back to my chest. "What happened? Is Nora okay?"

"She's fine. I will be too, but you caught me at a bad time."

"Is she here?" Some of her shock gave way to concern. "I know she won't believe it, but our mother is having a horrible time dealing with everything. We all are. So I mean—I thought, if she wasn't with you, you would know where she went."

And there it was. The question I knew was coming. I ran both hands down my face. How was I supposed to tell her what happened? Did Nora even *want* her to know? If she did, she would've found a way to let Katie know, but maybe now… There was no easy path to take.

"She's not here," I said simply.

"Then where is she? I think she wants us to believe she ran off to New York, considering all the work she put into faking an internship, but maybe it was to throw us off." Katie inched closer with each desperate word. "If she's fine, but she's not here, then where is she? *Please.*"

There was no denying how deeply Katie felt Nora's disappearance. It was all over her face, in every syllable of her plea, and she had called me. *Me.* Who she didn't believe existed. And Nora loved her. Nora loved her so deeply that she risked everything to track Katie down in the Nightmare Realm. No matter what happened between them, Nora wouldn't want her sister to be in this much pain. Katie deserved the truth.

I sighed. "Would you like the full version or the quick one?"

"The quick one," she answered immediately.

I nodded. "After we saved you, Nora killed the Weaver, which transferred his magic to her. She rules the Nightmare Realm now."

Katie blanched. "Actually, I think this merits the full version."

It absolutely did. I waved toward the pavilion. "Make yourself at home. This is going to take a while."

☾

Katie was much less patient than Nora had been as I laid everything on the table. The explanation took so many detours that half of it didn't sound logical even to me, but sometime near dawn, I told her of the last time I saw Nora. I left out the part about her haggard appearance.

"So you just let her go off with this other guy? This—this *nightmare*," Katie screeched. "But you *think* he's helping her?"

I swallowed a groan. We'd been over this. "I'm not, nor have I ever been, someone who would force a person to do something." The Weaver, maybe, but that was different. Nora's story wasn't the same as his. "Your sister is smart and capable, Katie. A lot more than anyone likes to give her credit for."

Katie glowered. "She's also ridiculously impulsive. Care to take a stab at where that can get her? Oh, that's right. *Literally* stabbed. By some evil, manipulative tree-woman."

I closed my eyes and willed away the image Katie's words inspired. When it was safe to speak again, I met Katie's gaze and held it. "I promised Nora I would step back so she could figure things out, but don't confuse that with not caring. Every star will fall from the sky before I let anything happen to her. It doesn't matter if the entire Night World collapses. The balance could leave us with nothing but a single stone to stand on and I would step off so that she could survive."

Katie paused to study me. "You really do love her, don't you?"

"She is my soul. Without her, I am nothing."

"Why?" she asked curiously.

I frowned. "Why?"

"Why do you love her?"

Was there supposed to be a *why*? Did love have to make sense? I'd never loved anyone the way I loved Nora. At the time, when my feelings toward her began to grow, I wondered if it was because she was the only person I had significant contact with. It was me, the beach, and a silent Baku without her. It took nearly three months before I accepted that my feelings were real and not because I was lonely. I loved Nora because there was a connection between us that had nothing to do with magic. Her smile lit her eyes, which lit something in me. She had five different laughs, was a talented artist, and had a fortitude that never failed to fill me with pride. Things were easy between us. We were two halves of a single piece, fitting together in each jagged place.

"You're blushing." Katie smirked then, half-glad, half-troubled. "Whatever your reasons, you've got it bad, Sandy. Make sure you don't confuse her right to be an idiot with my right to be alive. I love Nora with my entire heart, but letting her hold the fate of all mankind?"

"She's not holding it alone," I said quietly.

"No." Katie sighed and eased back on the pillows. "I suppose not. But still…"

She wasn't wrong about her sister. My Nora was kind and smart and compassionate, but she was also impatient to a fault. First with killing the Weaver, then returning to the Night World with Mare in tow. If she didn't learn to slow down and think things through, there was no telling what the consequences would be. Suddenly, seeing her again felt increasingly urgent.

"Mind if I stay?" Katie asked. "I'm not ready to wake up and face the real world yet."

I shook my head, though she was no longer looking at me. "Stay as long as you'd like."

"Thanks." And then, after a long pause, "Can I come again? I promise not to get in the way, but it feels like I'm closer to Nora here. Like I'm seeing her in a different way, and I want to understand." She huffed. "I'm probably not making sense."

"You are," I assured her. This was the place where Nora could always be Nora. Even though she wasn't here, it sometimes felt like she *could* be. "Open the drawer on the end there. Take one of the pouches and fill it with sand to use whenever you'd like."

"I'm sorry I called you a freak," she blurted.

My eyes widened, and a laugh burst from my chest. The pain sent me backwards into the sand.

"Sorry about that too," she said nervously.

I smiled and tried not to wheeze too loudly. "I'll live."

"You better." The drawer thumped open then shut again. "Someone needs to look out for my little sister."

I sobered, hoping against hope that both of us were wrong about that. *Please, please let us be wrong.* My exhaustion won then, dragging me into a state of fitful slumber with Nora's name playing on repeat.

Chapter Twenty-One

*N**ora.***

I shifted under the covers.

Nora.

Pulled them up over my head.

Nora.

My eyes flew open. That voice. I recognized it. The Sandman's voice was more familiar to me than my own. I gathered the blankets tighter around me. But how? It felt so very far away now that I was awake, and I couldn't be sure I had really heard it at all. He sounded wrong. Too frantic. Wild. My gut twisted.

"Kail?" I whispered. "Are you out there?"

Silence.

I looked inward to the Sandman, shifting through my own feelings to see if I could catch some glimpse of his. Anything to feel a little less alone. But, unsurprisingly, his walls were barred tight. I lingered anyway. Would he feel me if I reached out? If I knocked on that barrier between us, would he answer after I told him to leave me alone? I shook my head. Of course he would. But doubt still nipped at me as I lifted a finger and tapped three times.

For the briefest of moments, his mental doors cracked, and a burst of pain shot up my leg. I flew out of bed and buckled to the ground with a yelp. "Sandman?" I hobbled around the room, throwing on the first clothes I found. His doors slammed shut again. I beat against them with my mind, begging to be let in, but they didn't budge.

"Kail!" I raced out of Rowan's old room and paused. My thoughts sparked all over the place, making it impossible to focus on my own magic. Desperate, I shouted his name again.

He sauntered down the hall, seemingly out of nowhere, shirtless. His brown skin was covered in a senseless pattern of black lines. "Yes?"

"We have to go." I quickly retrieved my bookbag from inside the door and tossed it over one shoulder. "Now."

Kail squinted at me. "Go where? We don't march until dawn."

"Something's wrong with the Sandman."

"Ah." He scratched the back of his neck. "About that."

Hot fury flooded me. "You knew?"

"There may have been a rumor circulating through the troops last night."

I gripped his beak. The smooth white of his mask darkened

beneath my hand. Cracks spider-webbed up the curve toward his face, the spaces between peeling away like old paint. "What rumor?"

"Nora." His good eye flashed violently. "Stop."

I tightened my grip. "Tell me!"

"He's with Rowan," he said with tangible fear as he gripped my wrist. "Please. I'll explain everything."

"Explain fast," I demanded without relinquishing my hold.

"He was trying to infect the Watchmen." He winced. "Rowan found him and took him to the Keep."

I shoved him into the wall. Half his beak crumbled, leaving a burnt, jagged crater in place of its curve. I wiped the residue on my jeans and adjusted my bag over both shoulders. "Get whatever you need," I instructed. "We're going." He remained against the wall and dragged air in through his mouth. I raised my brows. "*Now.*"

"He let himself be caught," Kail said in a tone I'd never heard him use before. Defeated. Like he knew this was a battle he would never win. "He could've let the sand call him home at any time, but he didn't. For whatever reason, he wanted to be there."

"Were part of my instructions unclear?" I raised my hand to grip his beak again.

"Fine," he snapped before striding back the way he came. "Give me two minutes."

The threads pulsed against my arm and neck. *Soon*, I promised them. They could come out and do their job soon. All of them. If Rowan thought I would let her take the Sandman, she was mistaken. She had my Keep. My loom. But she would never have my heart. I proved that much when I took the knife from her. When I plunged it into the Weaver's chest to protect everyone—the Sandman included. I was wrong then, but I wouldn't be wrong now. The Nightmare Realm was mine and she was done pretending otherwise.

"This is a horrible idea," Kail muttered as he brushed by me on his way to the staircase.

I stormed after him. "Did you really think I'd leave him there?"

"I *think* the Sandman is perfectly capable of taking care of himself, just as he's done since the dawn of time. Rowan is a fool to think she's caught him." He shouldered out the front door. "But what I think obviously doesn't matter, does it? I'm just a stupid nightmare. What would I possibly know about anything? Especially compared to the newest member of our world."

"Watch yourself," I warned in a voice not quite my own.

"He *wants* to be there," Kail said again, insistent.

I scoffed. "Why would he? He's not a masochist, and he certainly wouldn't want to become bait to lure me in."

"And here I thought you knew him better than anyone," Kail snapped.

"I do."

"No." Kail kept walking, his shoulders stiff, in what I assumed was the direction of the Keep. "You know a different Sandman than the rest of us. He's always been *good*, as subjective as that is, but when he's around you, he's almost human. When he's alone, he blazes a path of destruction through this place."

"What's that supposed to mean?"

"It means, the last time you were in the Blood Tower, he didn't just look for you. He murdered every nightmare he came across." His expression turned stony. "Didn't know that, did you?"

I wasn't going to dignify that with an answer. Wasn't going to feed into Kail's agenda. The last time I was in the Blood Tower, I would've rejoiced to hear he killed them. The only thing that had changed since then was me.

"Really, *Lady*," Kail continued. "Aren't you even a little concerned that the Sandman was traipsing around your realm, messing with your nightmares?"

"They weren't *my* nightmares then."

He leaned a bit closer. "They're yours now."

I opened my mouth to reply, but nothing came out. Nothing could when Kail made such a valid point. I hadn't known the Sandman was a killer then, but that didn't matter. It was in the past. Maybe they attacked him first. There were a lot of things only the Sandman could clarify. And I would let him. One day, when this was all over. What *was* important was that he wasn't killing any of the nightmares now. Infecting them—taking their minds—was another matter. Until he proved otherwise, I trusted the Sandman in my realm. With my life.

"Well, as you've so keenly shown that you're able to exert your will," he said sarcastically, motioning to his mask, "why don't you bid the entire army to follow us? Might as well get everything over with at once, right? Priorities and all."

I shoved past him, my shoulder knocking his arm. "Stop talking before I burn off the rest of your face."

"At least try to remember what those threads are for. They're all you have until you learn how to weave, and Halven did a lot of work to make sure you kept them." He caught up to me and grabbed my arm. "Actually, you know what? If I'm going to march you toward Rowan—who, might I add, probably wants to kill me *slightly* more than you at this point—I want my eye fixed first."

"You were going to lead me to her in a few hours anyway." I ripped myself free of him and skirted around a puddle surrounded by a ring of three-eyed frogs. A hundred more puddles dotted the next quarter-mile, filling my head with croaks from their inhabitants. "What's the difference?"

Kail leapt over a pile of what looked like beige bird eggs covered in jelly. "Look around you. Where's the army? Where's Halven?"

I rolled my eyes. "He's *your* brother. Where did you see him last?"

"Asleep!" he shouted. "Because it's the middle of the night!"

"It's technically always night here, Kail," I quipped, weary. It was the darkest part of it, but I wouldn't concede the point.

He let out a frustrated groan. "Please, just think about this."

"Hm." I held a finger up to the edge of my mouth. "Okay, thought about it. Not leaving the Sandman to be tortured by your maniacal friend."

"So torture is only okay if you're the one doing it?" He waved to his face. "Look at me."

I refused. If I did, I might waver. Or, more likely, I would slam my fist straight into the gaping hole, snapping the entire beak clean off. "You're the one that said I needed to be feared. Besides, you can still see out of your eye, can't you?"

His jaw twitched. "It's. My. Eye."

I glared at him, unamused. "And your mask is your mask. You'll live."

"I regret every minute of helping you," he snarled.

I stiffened at that. If Kail wasn't helping me, he would likely be helping Rowan instead. He never struck me as the type to sit on the sidelines to wait and see what happened. Then again, he was the embodiment of the unknown. There was so much I didn't know about him. So much I didn't understand. And chances were, I never would. Especially since, after this was all over, I was booting him back to the Blood Tower where he wouldn't be able to harass me anymore. That day was still too far in the future to plan, so for right now, as much as I loathed it, I needed him.

"Fine. Your eye or your mask? I'll try to fix one now and the other after we get back from the Keep."

"If you die in there, Rowan won't fix either one," he said, eyes glittering with rage. "You may not know this, but I'm rather vain."

I rolled my eyes. "Shocking development, but let's be real. If I fix both now, what incentive would you have to not turn on me?"

"Would you like a list?" He held up a finger. "Let's start with *Rowan wants to kill me*. I chose a side—*your* side. There's no going back for me now."

"Pick one," I said, cutting off his tirade.

He exhaled slowly and spoke through his teeth. "The mask."

I swiveled to face him and set my palm over his charred beak. The grin twitched lazily, lending me its power, and the curve rose up beneath my hand until his mask was as good as new.

"There. Happy? Now let's go."

Chapter Twenty-Two

When Nora tapped against my mind, phantom pain answered. I scrambled to regain consciousness and shove it down before it was too late, but I wasn't quick enough. By the time I pulled myself together to send her another message—that I was fine—her mind was whirling too fast to listen. It was a massive tornado of worry and anger, crushing any calm thought I sent at it, which only left me with one option. I had to find Nora before she did something stupid, like tackling Rowan head on. I climbed from beneath the sand to find Katie gone and eased the strap of my satchel over my head. I winced as the new skin over my cut stretched from the movement. It felt as if there were shards of glass inside my chest, but I could function well enough for this.

Baku lounged near the water's edge, and relief washed over me. He climbed to his feet as I neared. "You made it," I said. He shot me a look as though the mere thought that he wouldn't was offensive. I chuckled. "It's good to see you."

He nodded once and eyed my ripped shirt. I should've taken a minute to change so Nora would believe that nothing was wrong. *Too late now.* It was everything I could do to keep moving forward; there was no way I was going to backtrack.

I cleared my throat. "Any idea where she is?"

Baku trudged by my side into the Nightmare Realm, skirting around the place burned by the acid rain. He cast a glance in my direction that let me know his exact thought: *idiot.*

"You didn't have to come," I said playfully to lighten the mood.

He exhaled in what I interpreted as a sarcastic laugh.

"We won't be long." I hoped. Her magic registered within this side of the realm, which was a small miracle, but it was moving in the direction of the Keep, which was decidedly not. "I need to talk to her for a second. That's all."

The only thing that might keep me true to my word was that I needed the sand for another day. After that, I would be able to resume normal activity. The pain might linger for a few days, but it was of no true consequence. In that much time, Nora would've already destroyed Rowan's tree and taken the realm. By the time we had to join forces against Mare, I would be as good as new.

On and on we walked, following the trail left by Nora's magic. Baku leaned into me at one point to offer his support, but I could walk on my own. By the time the Keep was in view, I was beginning to regret not taking him up on the offer. The Watchmen looked down at us accusingly. Was there no other path she could've chosen? Their stone eyes bored into me, angry at having missed their mark and annoyed at not being able to leave their post to finish the job.

Baku snorted. I followed his gaze to find Nora near the base of the cliff with Kail behind her. My heart leapt, my legs pumping before I even realized I was running or that Baku had taken off in the opposite direction.

"Nora," I called.

She stopped mid-step and stumbled forward, while Kail simply turned to face me.

"Finally," Kail called back. "I was beginning to think we'd actually have to go in there to save you."

"In where?" I stepped up beside Nora. She still hadn't faced me, her eyes fixed on the ground, but just being next to her made it easier to breathe. With her blond hair flowing loosely over her shoulders and the pink knit sweater she wore, it almost seemed as if she didn't belong here. *Almost.* Because the threads circling her neck told the truth. "Are you okay?"

There was a pregnant pause.

"Define 'okay'," Kail drawled. "Does walking away from your army to launch a suicide—sorry, *rescue*—mission, count as okay?"

"Can you give us a second?" I asked Kail, and he backed away. Indeed, wishes *were* sometimes only wishes. Of course Nora would mount a foolish attempt to save me. I knew she would the moment she felt my pain. "Nora, look at me."

"No," she said, determined.

I placed a hand gently on her shoulder, and she shivered beneath the touch. "Why not?"

She was silent for a heartbeat. "Because, Sandman. I'm

supposed to be figuring myself out and claiming the realm, but do you know what I'm doing instead?" Her voice grew tighter, more irritated, by the second. "Instead of marching my army to the Keep this morning as planned, I rushed here to save you. But Kail was right: you obviously let yourself be caught, or you wouldn't be in front of me. So now, I'm having trouble deciding if I'm angrier at you for going with her or myself for not believing it."

She was going to make her final stand today? Without sending word to me first? It was one thing if she didn't want my help, another to take on her enemy without giving me a heads up. A *goodbye* in case things went poorly. If she failed, if I hadn't had another moment with her—how was I supposed to live with myself? Did she understand my feelings for her? Truly and completely? Even now that things were different? Did I understand hers? We deserved a five-minute conversation before she marched off to her potential death.

"Were you going to tell me?" I breathed. "So I could see you again before—"

She spun around, and I drew in a sharp breath. Faint reddish-purple bruises fanned out beneath her gold eyes. "So you could tell me not to attack? So you could blame Kail for something out of his control?" She held her hands up. "Or how about so you could see that my hands are back to normal? Care to ask how I accomplished *that* one?"

"Nora, I—"

"I'll tell you." Tears rimmed her eyes, but I wasn't sure if they were caused by sorrow or rage. "The secret to absorbing the Weaver's power was torture. I carved up the nightmares that killed my friends, and I didn't even think twice about it."

"Nor—"

"And that's not all I've done. Kail's mask? I burnt half of it to ash with my bare hands because he tried to talk some sense into me, and I only put it back together because I needed his help. Not because I regretted it."

I wrapped my arms around her and held tight. If she wouldn't let me talk, this was the next best thing. Despite the terrible things she just told me, I loved her. No matter what she did or would do, she was the brightest star in my sky. "Shh," I said quietly. "None of that matters. You're doing what you need to. It will calm down one day, and you'll be able to control your actions." *Urges*, the Weaver had always called them. After banishing Mare, after drawing a clear line between Day and Night, his mind became a more volatile place, just as mine became less so. If the Weaver could control himself, if he could learn to be more pragmatic with his violence, Nora could too.

"Of course it matters." Her hands gripped my shirt, and she buried her face in my chest.

I winced against the pain but held tight. "Not to me. When I said always, I meant it."

"I'm sorry," she said quietly. "I—I can't be—"

Kail cleared his throat.

I glared at him over Nora's head. "There's a reason I came," I said into her ear. "I realized something important."

She stared up at me, gold eyes gleaming, and continued to hold me close. "What?"

"Kail showed me a tree that he said used to be Rowan." I toyed absently with the ends of Nora's hair, wrapping them around my fingers, though all I wanted to do was kiss her. "When I was with her in the Keep, I noticed her wings were burned."

"So?"

"So, I set the stump on fire that day. It burnt out within seconds, but it was long enough to do some damage. I think if you destroy the nightmare she *was*, it will kill them both," I explained.

She glanced at Kail, who had crept closer. "You knew about this?"

He sighed loudly. "Obviously."

"Then what was all *this* about?" she shouted, pushing away from me to advance on him.

"Training," Kail ticked off a finger. "Gaining loyalty."

She slammed her palms against his shoulders, and he stumbled back. "I could've trained in the Keep."

"Which is why I told *him*, thinking he would understand. But when he didn't, I took it as a sign. You've got an army now, and, when you take the Keep back, it will be with a show of force. No one will doubt you then."

"An army *Halven* built," she argued.

"Nora," I said gently, scanning the area in case the Watchmen alerted anyone. The trees remained still. "He's not wrong about the show of force, and it's my fault for not realizing what would happen if—"

"Stop. I don't want to play the blame game right now," she said. My chest crackled, the sound like plastic crumpling, and Nora glanced at the torn fabric of my shirt. "What was that?"

"Nothing important." I rubbed the skin just below the tattoo where it wasn't sore. The movement shifted the ever-moving magic beneath, and there was a small pop. "I have to get back to the beach, but there's one more thing I wanted to tell you."

Her eyes widened with worry. "Tell me what happened."

I shook my head. "Your sister called to me tonight."

"Katie?" She jerked back in surprise. "Why?"

"She was looking for you." It was all I felt right saying, especially now. Her mother was a sore subject, and she didn't need to be distracted if she was about to take down Rowan. "I told her everything. She took it well, considering."

Nora chewed her bottom lip, looking askance. "Thanks. I'll… I mean, can you make sure she doesn't come here? Use your sand on her until this is all over?"

So she doesn't become a weapon to use against me again, is what Nora didn't say, but she didn't have to. "Of course," I promised. "She already has some."

"Okay, thank you." Nora closed her eyes and took a deep, centering breath. "I'll check in with you soon. After I take care of a few things," she said, glancing at the Keep in the distance. It was smart not to say her plan out loud with so many ears nearby—it was enough of a risk that I had.

"Stay safe."

She nodded and turned to Kail. "We're going back to the tower to have a little chat."

I took her wrist before I could stop myself. Nora looked over her shoulder at me, and her expression softened. "I love you," I said, wistfully.

She turned, stretched up on her toes, and kissed me. "Wait for me?" she breathed against my lips but didn't stay for my answer.

Letting her walk away was like watching the sun go down for the final time. When she was out of sight, Baku nudged my leg with a tusk. "I'm okay," I said, my voice hoarse. But I wasn't.

Chapter Twenty-Three

Nora

Maybe I deserved this pain. This exhaustion.

The hurt was no less than what I put my family through. Katie had called out to the Sandman, for crying out loud. How desperate was she? There had to be something I could do to ease their fears. I couldn't go back, and Katie couldn't come here. The last thing I needed was something snatching her up again or her seeing me like this.

And then there was Kail's betrayal.

I definitely, absolutely deserved that, but I didn't expect to feel so stung by it. Kail was good at what he did. At making me believe he was on my side even though I knew he was up to no good. It was hard to tell which bothered me more—that he lied or that I bought it.

"Are you going to ignore me the *entire* walk back to the Blood Tower?" Kail asked in the cool voice he used the first time I met him.

"Ideally."

"You're not going to snap my mask off or stab my other eye?"

"Don't tempt me," I warned.

"You're angry with me," he said, suddenly chipper. "I'm willing to let bygones be bygones if you think hurting me again will help you get over it."

I stared at him harder. Was he serious? Was this another ploy to win me over to his side so he could use me like a puppet? Or was that honestly what he expected of me? Was it what Rowan had done? I balled my hands into fists. "I won't apologize for what happened earlier, if that's what you're fishing for."

He snorted. "I don't expect you to. That's the ruthlessness that will save you."

"Then what?" I whirled on him, arms raised to my sides. "What do you want me to get over, Kail? That we've been running all over the Nightmare Realm like fugitives for weeks now, *hiding*, when this all could've ended the moment I got here? That you lied and lied and lied? Every day, you spun your web around me, but do you know the worst part? I was starting to believe you were on my side."

"We weren't simply hiding, and you know that," he said quietly.

"Oh, right. I was *training*. Learning how to use my magic so I could claim my realm when *I should already have it*." I stepped closer and poked his chest. "You were going to let me risk my life—all those nightmares' lives—for what?"

He hesitated. "The show of strength would've earned you the surviving dissenters' loyalty."

"What makes you think I'd allow survivors?" I ground my teeth together until they ached. "How about some straight answers?"

The corner of his lip twitched. "When have I ever given you a straight answer?"

"Exactly my point." I ran a hand down my face, forcing myself to calm down. Kail filled in the blanks when it suited him and talked in circles when it didn't. It was time that changed. "You're going to tell me the truth. Now."

He lowered his chin, cocking his head to the side. "About?"

"Why did you show the Sandman the way to defeat Rowan? Why didn't you take me right to the tree?"

"I wanted you to trust me first," he said warily.

"Trust you?" I burst out laughing. I couldn't help it. "You wanted to earn my trust by lying to me?"

He bristled. "I *did* help Rowan last time you were here. Would you have believed me if I took you there right away? The Sandman didn't even bother to think on what I said until now. Besides, Halven and I wouldn't have let Rowan kill you."

The laugh died in my throat. "There's nothing you could ever do that would make me trust you."

Except he had made me trust him already. Barely. Day after day, he worked a little magic on me. Not real magic like mine, but his own twisted charm. Each new thing he taught me was another fold of a paper airplane. But now I tossed that plane into the wind and watched as it dove nose-first into the ground.

"Then it really shouldn't bother you that I omitted things," he said with a stiff shrug.

"What's your motive?" I demanded. "You said you had one."

He thought for a moment—really thought. "I think I'd rather wait and tell you when you're in a better mood."

Then he turned on his heel and strode away. I gaped at his back for a long moment before my mouth caught up to my brain. "Hey, you don't get to walk away from me," I shouted, storming after him. "You were the one who started this whole conversation. I was perfectly fine with the silence, but *no*. You just *had* to pick at it, didn't you? Well, now it's time to fess up before I decide to throw you to Rowan as a parting gift."

When he didn't turn around, I snagged his elbow and attempted to pull him to a stop. "Keep walking," he said in a deathly low voice and easily extracted himself from my grip.

Oh, no. He wasn't going to feign danger to avoid the truth. "After you answer my question."

"Remember how Three attacked you in the Barren, and I didn't ask questions?"

"What about it?" My fingers unconsciously went to my healed nose.

"You did kill her, right?" His eyes slid to mine, one flickering too quickly. "That's how you got away?"

"Not exactly," I said slowly as my nerves began to tingle. "Why?"

"Don't look back but—"

I threw a glance over my shoulder.

"Or ignore me. What else is new?" Kail droned.

"I don't see anything," I whispered.

He sighed. "Three of the Hours are following us, so the sooner we get back to the Blood Tower and the army, the better."

"What do they think killing me will accomplish?" I hissed. "It's not going to make Mara disappear."

He *tsk*ed. "Mara? What does she have to do with this? The Hours are working with Rowan."

"No," I said slowly. "If they were working with Rowan, Three wouldn't have tried to kill me. She would've taken me back to the Keep for Rowan to do it. She was mad that I brought Mara back."

Kail's body grew more rigid, and he eased sideways to stand closer to me. His eyes were the only part of him moving as he scanned the riverbed on our left all the way to the landscape of dense yellow fog on our far right. "That makes sense," he said finally. "Unfortunately, that means we can't reason with them. First you killed their creator, then you sent an Ancient back to destroy their world, which in turn will destroy *all* the worlds. They're probably seeking vengeance."

"I didn't *send* her back," I shot back defensively.

"There you go again." Kail slid an arm around my shoulders to encourage me to walk faster. "Splitting hairs."

I fought the urge to turn around and search for the Hours. My heart slammed into my chest with enough force I swore it would break through bone. Rowan wanted me dead. Twelve nightmarish knight-like people were hunting me. I couldn't push the Sandman further away if I tried. My family thought I ran away, and the only person standing in my corner was someone I could no longer believe in.

Someone I never should've believed in to begin with.

"This is your fault. I could be in the Day World living my real life right now," I told him.

"You wound me with your accusations," he said sarcastically.

"I clearly let you know my feelings on the matter before Rowan sent you off with Elkmar. Don't blame me for your choices."

Elkmar. The shadowy nightmare with ribbed horns and webbed hands that was meant to deliver me to the Weaver after Rowan gave me the knife. He still filled me with unease. The clicking of his voice, the way he stayed so close no matter how I changed my gait… A shiver ran over me. Where was he these days? "Why would you go along with it if you—"

"Really? *Now* is the best time for this conversation?"

I attempted to step out from beneath his arm, but his fingers dug into my shoulder. "You can talk and walk at the same time."

He grunted in frustration. "We all have our weaknesses, okay? Just… leave it alone. Please."

I opened my mouth to let him know just how much I *wasn't* going to let it go—but had he just said *please*? An arrow whizzed by my head. I tucked my face into Kail's side with a small shriek.

"Be fearless," he said into my hair. "Duck."

"Wha—"

Kail slammed us both to the ground as a hail of arrows soared through the sky, landing around us in a perfect circle.

"Run!" I ordered, climbing to my hands and knees.

"No." He pressed me harder into the ground so I couldn't move. "If the Hours wanted you dead, you would be. Six doesn't miss."

"Or they want to make me die a slow and painful death." My voice rose so high it cracked.

"We don't care about the method," said a deep male voice. "Only the outcome."

Kail's arm shifted, allowing me to scramble to my feet. Three stood before me, her arms folded tight across her chest. Beside her was a second woman in similar armor, a long black braid trailing over her shoulder, the Roman numeral six on her mask. She nocked another arrow but kept it pointed at the ground. The third nightmare, the one that had spoken, wore a black fur cloak around his shoulders that nearly hid all the shining metal beneath. An X was carved over his face mask.

"Hello, Ten," Kail said, dusting himself off.

Ten didn't acknowledge the greeting, his eyes remaining on me. Though I couldn't see them, I felt them, like nettles. It was ages before the burning ceased, and Ten spoke. "Three has something she would like to say." When the woman beside him didn't speak, he gripped her arm and pulled her forward a step. "We discussed this as a group," he whispered to her.

"I'm sorry for trying to kill you," she said as unapologetically as possible. Ten cleared his throat, and she added, "Lady."

My eyes widened in surprise. She was seriously apologizing? Because someone made her? Like a scolded child reluctant to admit to poor behavior? I glanced at Kail who looked equally perplexed. "Um." I elbowed Kail hard in the ribs.

"Ow! What was that for?" he mumbled.

"Say something," I hissed from the corner of my mouth.

He opened and shut his mouth a few times. "Like what?"

"I don't know. Think of someth—"

"Lady," Ten interrupted. "The Hours have decided to honor you as the rightful ruler of the Nightmare Realm as long as you have a plan to deal with Mare. If you don't, we will remove you."

I blinked in surprise and eyed Six's bow. The grin sneered. *How dare they?* They were giving me an ultimatum? As if it were up to them. The only one here that should be making decisions was me, and right now I had half a mind to turn them into a living Dali painting. You're welcome, Dreamers. Hope you enjoy your melting clock-people. I filled my lungs until they were near bursting and opened my mouth wordlessly.

"And," the Hour continued, "as a show of good faith, you'll heal Four."

Oh, good. *More* demands. "If I don't?"

"She's a little busy at the moment," Kail interjected. He flashed a quick look in my direction as if begging me not to freak out.

"This can't wait. Neither can Mare," Six said in a light, airy voice. "You need to kill her now before she regains too much strength."

I huffed. "Yeah, well, like Kail said, I'm busy."

"If Four dies, you die," Three spit.

Kail leaned into my side. "Healing the Hour might be faster than arguing about it."

"What happened?" I asked reluctantly.

"Mare attacked him. We've brought him with us, there." Ten pointed behind them.

While I couldn't see anything in the direction he indicated, I did notice the blood coating his metal gauntlet. Not just a few drops either. My shoulder ached at the phantom memory of Mara's claws, but I had worn no armor. Assuming Four dressed like the other Hours, he was covered in it, so how was he that bloody? It might be worth healing him simply to see what Mara was capable of against a real opponent. Again, I wished the Weaver's memory of Mara lasted a bit longer.

"I'll look at him," I agreed.

Kail gave no outward sign that he approved or otherwise, which was both helpful and stressful. I didn't want him second-guessing me in front of the Hours, but a bit of validation would've gone a long way. It would have to be enough that he stayed beside me when the Hours lead me toward their injured comrade.

Nestled beside the river, directly beside a chain that disappeared below the water's surface, Mara's victim laid lifeless. Blood seeped into the short, bleached grass at the water's edge, then into the stream itself. Small parasitic worms coasted on the surface, soaking up the murky red liquid.

It took me a long moment before I allowed my gaze to seek out Four's wounds. The silver breastplate was dented an inch deep, and chunks of his arm were missing, along with the protective chainmail. Claw marks on his neck left him nearly decapitated. Both legs were turned at unnatural angles, and there wasn't much of his body *not* covered in crimson. I hardly believed he wasn't dead already.

"Not the safest place to leave him," I commented. "Who knows what lives at the other end of these chains, and with all that blood? It's like you were asking for trouble."

"Clearly, we were in the right," Three said defensively. "Now heal him."

Was she giving me orders again? Where did she get off? I—

Kail touched my elbow. "All or nothing, Lady."

Kill all of them or none of them. One was more satisfying, the other more expedient, and I wasn't exactly out on a leisure stroll. There were other things to do, so I crouched at Four's side. With a sigh, I placed a hand on his chest, wincing against the feel of his blood beneath my palm. The thread squirmed weakly, though still very determined to survive. The grin helped—urged my power into the thread, pumping it full of strength.

Just before the final pieces were tucked neatly back into the knotted ball, I broke contact. The dent remained in Four's breastplate, though less pronounced, the scratches on his neck still red and angry, and his arms were now covered in scabs. Four moaned weakly.

"Good as new," I lied.

"Finish it," Three commanded.

I stood, feeling even smaller than I was in Three's shadow. "He'll live. Now, if you'll excuse us."

Six's bow flew out in front of me before I could make it more than two steps. "If Mare can do that to one of us, imagine what else she's capable of."

A chill ran up my spine. "I'll deal with Mara. As soon as I finish my other business."

"You have an army now," Three snapped. "Let them take Rowan out while you deal with the real threat."

I barked a laugh, which was probably not the wisest idea, and Kail glared at me. "I'm going to kill Rowan with my own two hands, thank you. Who do you think you are? You can't tell me how to rule."

"Lady or not, you're no nightmare," Three snarled, lunging at me.

Ten yanked her back by the collar before I could react and dragged her away. "We will have words with her again, Lady," Six promised. "But be warned. Next time we see you, you will need to have a plan ready, or we will appoint a ruler who does."

"Your friends are leaving." I motioned behind her where Ten and Three continued to move away, practically dragging Four between them. "Might want to go with them."

Six made a small sound of annoyance in the back of her throat, though I wasn't sure who it was directed at, and hurried after the others.

"See?" I hissed the moment they were out of earshot. "This has nothing to do with Rowan and everything to do with that evil hag."

Kail cuffed the back of my head. "Do you have any idea what they're going to do now?"

"Talk to Three again, obviously." I rubbed the back of my head and started walking toward the Tower. "I bought myself some time to come up with a plan, at any rate."

"Right. Time. From the Hours," he said in a dull voice. "And when that time runs out, they'll expect you to take down an ancient being. If you don't? *Poof*, you're dead."

I stepped over the chain, and at the other end, a large metal cage broke the surface of the water. Small ripples, like those made from a light spring rain, danced around it. The grin widened as something inside gurgled.

I grimaced, ignoring the tormented sound. "Mara was always going to have to die, but like you said, one thing at a time."

"And you choose now to start listening to me? Mara will kill you before you can even raise a sword."

"What did you want me to tell them, Kail? That I was busy? Because that was *so* helpful," I snapped.

"This is serious." His eyes narrowed to slits. "You do know what's in the Ever Safe, don't you? And what will happen if you don't take care of Mara?"

"I don't even know what the Ever Safe *is*," I admitted. My head throbbed. Rowan, Mara, Hours, the liar next to me. There was only so much more doom and gloom a girl could take. "But go ahead. We have a long way to go so you might as well enlighten me."

He let out a small huff. "Story time really isn't my thing."

"*Make* it your thing."

He waved his hands out in front of him, and his voice took on a monotone edge. "A long, long time ago, before the world as you knew it—"

I silenced him with a look. "Cliff notes version."

"Boring," he said with a dramatic sigh. "Basically, this place used to be full of what we call the Ancients. Blah, blah, blah, the Weaver and Sandman came into existence when your world needed to balance things out, or some such nonsense. That whole bit's kind of iffy for me. Anyway, things went down. They locked the Ancients in the Ever Safe where they've been dormant ever since."

Seemed like a non-issue then. "What does that have to do with Mara?"

"She escaped. Clearly." He made eye contact with me and held it. "Everything you've been hearing about her destroying our worlds? It's because she wants to open the safe and let her friends out to play."

My stomach dropped. I assumed she wanted to come back because the Day World sucked so much for us, but if Kail was right… My mouth ran dry. *Screwed.* I was so screwed. "Can she do that?"

"If she didn't know how, would the night lords have messed with the balance to exile her?" Kail's gaze dulled, his thoughts taking him far away.

"Perfect," I mumbled around a lump in my throat. "Just perfect."

Since I was going to die—either by Rowan before I found her stump or by Mara after—I needed to do a better job of saying goodbye. My family needed closure. There was only one way to do that given my current situation, so it would have to do. I poked at the grin in hopes that it would have a better idea, but it snapped its lips shut.

Fine. That settled that then. Option number two it was.

Afterward, I would make things right with the Sandman. Who knew—he could already have a plan. Maybe it was time I tried to remember the girl who thought we could unite the realms. The grin thinned, but it didn't have to like everything I did.

☾

When Kail and I finally dragged ourselves back inside the Blood Tower, my feet felt raw. Almost as raw as my nerves. But nothing else attacked us along the way. A few mindless nightmares stopped to watch us with something like reverence, and a tall flower with a face waved her leaves in greeting. The only thing keeping me from falling asleep right there on the hallway floor was the fact that tonight could be my last chance. I paused beside Halven, where he waited just inside the door, and waited for Kail to shuffle to the staircase.

"We leave at dawn," I announced to both brothers. Then I whispered so only Halven would hear, "Meet me outside in two hours."

Chapter Twenty-Four

Katie flopped down on the edge of the pavilion with a plastic bag. "Good evening, Mr. Sandman," she said in a poorly-executed English accent.

"Hello again." I didn't bother climbing out from my half-buried state. It felt too good with the sand covering my bare torso to get up before it was necessary.

"I come bearing gifts." Katie dug into the plastic bag and produced a spiral notebook. "My mother was tearing Nora's room apart earlier, so I liberated this."

Her notebook. "How did you know where to find it?" I asked carefully.

Katie pointed to the drawings on the wall. "No one gets that good without practice, so I may have done a little digging of my own. Don't tell Nora though."

"Your secret is safe with me." I eyed the notebook hungrily. Nora hadn't let me go through her drawings in a long time, and it would be a lie to say I wasn't curious. I knew I shouldn't look, that it was private, but the temptation was palpable. "Why did you bring it here?"

"Are you kidding me?" She reached back in the bag and pulled out a large box of colored pencils, setting both items on the pillow beside her leg, before stuffing the empty bag into the pocket of her plaid pajama pants. "My room isn't safe from expert snooping, and I clearly can't go back to college in the middle of this crisis. If my mother saw this, she would absolutely lose it. It was either try bringing the pictures here—victory!—or use them to start a bonfire."

I nodded, glad she opted for the first choice. "I'm sorry. About your mother." I looked away then, toward the stars. "If it wasn't for me, she and Nora would've been closer, and you wouldn't have to deal with her invading your space so often."

Katie snorted. "Maybe. Or maybe she's always been like this."

"You don't have to say that to spare my feelings. I know what I've done," I said quietly.

Her laugh filled the beach. "Please. Like I care about that. You've definitely screwed a lot of stuff up, but credit needs to go where credit is due. My mother's issues are her own. Plentiful as they are."

"Okay," I said, strangely amused. "Then, in your opinion, what do I need to apologize to you for? You deserve that much from me."

Silence fell as Katie picked at her bottom lip, her gaze

faraway. "Nothing," she said after an eternity. "If I had believed Nora, she wouldn't have hidden so much, and if I knew, then maybe I would've had a pouch of sand to keep me from the Weaver when I needed it."

I sat up then, sand cascading down my chest. She couldn't find me completely blameless. If the situation were boiled down to bare facts, I stole her sister away. She had the dream because of me, the Weaver went after her to get it, and now—

"So *that's* the tattoo, huh?" Katie said with a playful smirk. "I'm dying to know why Nora saw you shirtless way back then."

"Back *when*?" I asked and hurried into the pavilion for a shirt. The black fabric clung to my body, putting just enough pressure over my breastbone to make it uncomfortable.

"The day we saw you at the mall, Nora said you had tattoos." Katie wagged her eyebrows. "Interesting development."

"She was talking about the ones on my arms," I clarified. "Not my chest."

Katie burrowed into the pillows. "Sure. Whatever you say."

I leaned my back against the wall, legs crossed. "What about Kellan?" I asked, feeling slightly defensive.

"He's gone. I broke up with him." Her words were unbothered and lacked emotion. "Jen came home for Thanksgiving and wanted to meet up, so… you know." She waved a hand through the air. When I stayed silent, she added, "We talked. I begged forgiveness and plead with her for another shot."

"I knew what you meant." Because I felt like doing the same thing with Nora—but at the same time, it was her that needed to apologize. She asked me to wait, so I would. I would wait forever, but there were still conversations that needed to be had.

"I hope you two work it out. Nora told me you guys were great together."

"So." Katie forced a cough, her voice rising, and motioned to the notebook. "Have you looked at them before?"

I stared hungrily at the cover and shook my head. "She didn't talk about drawing much. I had to ask for the ones on my wall."

"Maybe you should." She gave me a pitying look before snuggling deeper into the pillows and closing her eyes.

Katie was giving me privacy to take her advice, but I wasn't entirely sure I should. These were Nora's. If she wanted me to see her drawings, she would've shared them herself. Then again, she wouldn't have left the notebook behind if she didn't want anyone to eventually find it. Nora admitted more than once that her mother went through her belongings and would again after she was gone. Maybe she wanted her mother to see what was inside.

Against my better judgment, I slid the glossy black book into my lap and cracked it open. The first page was a spectacular rendering of the beach. So was the second, as well as the third. Pages and pages of a starlit sky, then one of Katie with her pink hair, followed by a portrait of Natalie, then Emery. Me with my hood up and another with my hood down. And finally, drawn with a regular pencil, so light that the page almost looked blank, was a knowing grin. Who would it have been if she finished?

I went to shut the book when Katie quietly said, "There's one more."

I jumped at the sound of her voice breaking my reverie and carefully turned the page, the crisp crinkle of it loud in the silence. My heart dropped. I wished I hadn't seen this until I was alone. Maybe not at all. Mostly, I wished Katie hadn't seen it. My finger traced the pencil marks in the corner. It was another one of me, this time with my head on Nora's pillow as I slept. She captured every shimmering mark on my bare arms and followed the path across my collarbones, where the tattoos disappeared beneath the sheet. It wasn't hard to figure out when she'd drawn this. I had only been shirtless in her bed once. Heat flooded my face, and the ache in my chest had nothing to do with my healing body. With shaking fingers, I closed the notebook and placed it back on the pillows.

"I'm never going to see my sister again, am I?" Katie looked up at the sky, the bright stars reflected in her watery eyes, and her chin trembled.

"You will," I promised. "Someday, when she's ready."

The silence that followed was a heavy, painful thing, but something about it felt easier with Katie there. A shared sadness stretched between us. I hadn't realized how much I needed another soul to share the burden, if only for a few minutes.

"You two look comfortable," drawled a familiar voice. "Moving on so soon, Sandman?"

I flew to my feet and faced Kail. "How did you get in here?"

"Like Mara's the only one who knows how to hitch a ride?" He flicked a piece of hair from his forehead. "Baku's back."

There were only a dozen things wrong with what he just said. "Where is he?"

"He'll be along when he wakes up," he said casually, eyeing Katie with interest.

My jaw hung open, speechless.

Kail huffed. "Oh, don't give me that look. He wanted to eat me; it was purely self-defense."

I scanned behind him for Nora, but she was nowhere in

sight. "What are you doing here, Kail?"

"I'll give you two guesses." He looked around me to Katie. "Should we talk in front of the human?"

"Is it about Nora?" Katie eased to her feet and took in Kail from head to toe. A worried gleam shone in her eyes as if she thought he would snatch her away at any moment. It wasn't impossible.

"Ah." Understanding lit Kail's face. "You must be the famous sister. Is she around?"

"Is who around?" I asked.

"Nora, obviously. Who do you think?" he snapped, suddenly impatient.

My pulse roared, my magic grating against my insides. *Stay calm. Think. Process.* "What do you mean, 'Is she around'? She's supposed to be with *you*."

He made a low, thoughtful noise in his throat. "Well, this is less than ideal."

"Nora's supposed to be with him?" Katie asked. "*This* is the guy?"

"She could do worse," Kail quipped. "A clown, perhaps."

The blood drained from Katie's face at the mention of clowns. If Katie was afraid of them before the Weaver trapped her inside a cave with one, she had to be absolutely terrified of them now.

"Enough," I demanded. Kail pulled a piece of yellowed paper from inside his jacket and held it out. I accepted it only to find Nora's handwriting filled the center: *I'll be back soon. Wait here.* "What does that mean?"

Kail scowled at me. "I'm pretty sure it means she'll be back soon and for me to wait there."

"Give me that." Katie ripped the letter from my hand. She scanned the words a dozen times, as if something new would appear before clutching it to her chest. "Where did she go?"

"Well, I rather thought she'd be here," Kail said cynically.

My insides flipped. "You're telling me you don't have any idea where Nora is?"

"I'd ask Halven to find her, but he seems to be aiding and abetting her little jaunt."

"Let me get this straight." I sucked in air, trying desperately to keep myself from murdering Kail on the spot. No burst of emotions broke through Nora's walls signaling she was in trouble, so that had to count for something. "Nora took off with your brother? And you have no clue where?"

"As I said, I *had* an idea." He motioned around us at the never-ending sand. "It didn't pan out."

"You were supposed to be taking care of her," I shouted. White-hot rage blasted through my head. I trusted Kail against my better judgment because Nora seemed to, but he couldn't even keep track of her, let alone stop her from storming the Keep when she thought I was held captive. For someone as old as he was, he was completely incompetent. He had *one job*—keep Nora safe.

"Don't try to pin this all on me," Kail shouted back. "If you hadn't dragged my name into this earlier—"

"Don't you dare," I said through my teeth. "She had a right to know about the tree. You might be okay with lying to her, but I'm not."

"Oh, *that's* rich." Kail laughed, stepping close enough that we nearly touched. "You lied to her for years."

A knife to the gut. "And look how things turned out."

"Wow. You two are being ridiculous." Katie stepped between us and held her hands out to keep us apart. "I don't give a rat's behind whose fault it is, but one of you better come up with a way to find her, *pronto*."

I inhaled, and a shudder ran through my body. *Don't kill him.* Nora needed him. *Him. Not me.* The thought barreled through me like a freight train, but now wasn't the time. "Katie's right," I admitted reluctantly.

"She's definitely with Halven," Kail said slowly. Then, to Katie, he added, "Before you get your panties in a twist, he's trustworthy."

"Oh, I highly doubt that," Katie scoffed.

"What about the army?" I asked.

Kail's lips parted in disbelief. "If the army was missing too, would I have assumed she snuck away to visit her lover?"

"You two are talking like Nora's your prisoner," Katie sharply interjected.

"Of course she isn't," I said, her outburst stealing my anger. "But she's still learning to use her power."

"And you remember our realm, don't you Bubble Gum Princess?" Kail smirked. "Nice dye job, by the way."

Katie blanched. "You seriously trust this guy with my sister's life?"

"Don't worry. If I was going to hurt her, I would've done it a long time ago. She's rather infuriating, though I'm sure you know that." Kail smiled, then paled. "Oh, look. Someone's awake."

Baku stormed toward the three of us, swaying slightly on his feet. A cloud of glimmering sand followed him down the nearest dune.

"That's my cue to leave. I'll wait at the Blood Tower in case she comes back," Kail called as he raced in the opposite direction.

For a moment, I entertained the thought of keeping him locked inside the barrier. Let him sweat a bit. But now wasn't the time to be petty. I sighed and, with a quick flick of my wrist, opened the barrier into the Nightmare Realm just long enough for him to escape. Baku chuffed at my side, his brindle fur sparkling with sand.

"Sorry, but you'll have to wait a little longer to eat that one." I looked Baku over. "Are you okay?"

He nodded once and eyed Katie.

"Katie, this is Baku. Baku, meet Nora's sister."

"My head's about to explode," Katie said in a strained voice, and she wobbled where she stood.

"You should probably sit down." I took her elbow and eased her down onto the pillows. "I need to talk to him for a minute."

Katie wordlessly tucked her head between her knees.

I knelt beside Baku, my chest aching worse than before, and lifted a handful of sand. Tapping into his dreams, I let the grains fall from between my fingers, and what took shape chilled me to the core. The Blood Army marched behind Rowan, her face a thing of fury. Then, from behind the red mist, another large group of nightmares broke away, veering right while Rowan kept left.

"She knows," I breathed. "About the tree. She knows we know." I stared at the dream, hoping for a clue about where the second group was headed. "Where did they go?"

Baku shifted his feet nervously and gave a small shrug.

My stomach twisted. One battalion to protect the stump,

another to hunt Nora down. That's what made sense. I would've done the same thing in Rowan's position. "We have to find Nora. *Now.*" And warn Kail. If he was going back to the Blood Tower alone, he might run into them before he got there.

"Katie." I put my hands on her shoulders. "Stay here as long as you want—Baku will stay with you. When you're ready to leave, all you have to do is wake up."

She looked up at me with wide eyes. "Tell me she's going to be okay."

"It's Nora." I did my best to smile reassuringly, but my entire being screamed in terror. "She'll always be okay."

Katie glanced over at Nora's drawings again and winced. "You better hurry."

Chapter Twenty-Five

Nora

Halven stopped at the edge of a black and white floor caked with dried muck. With no walls around the tiled area, a breeze sent dry leaves rustling across the surface. I gagged at the pungent scent of rotting meat that it brought along with it and swatted at the swarm of tiny flies that greeted us. Couldn't Detective Bell have been afraid of kittens or something? A rhythmic thwacking drew my attention to the table in the center of the floor. A squat, wrinkled nightmare with green skin and no nose stood on a tall stool. His long, pointed ears shook with each thud of his meat cleaver. Blood splattered around him as he hacked at what looked like ribs. Entrails, piles of skin, and fur covered nearly every inch of the table, and unidentifiable liquid dripped from the edges.

"That's disgusting," I said from behind my hand.

Halven shrugged and pointed to the far end of the table. I squinted, and a human figure took shape near the table leg. A large man with dark skin was gagged and bound to the blood-slick wood.

"Detective Bell." I let out a relieved breath. "Thanks, Halven."

"I'm at your service, Lady," he rasped.

The Weaver had used Detective Bell against me before, so I didn't see a reason not to use him for a bit of good now. He said he was sorry, and I believed he meant it. Maybe he felt guilty enough that I shouldn't feel bad for hijacking his body. Either way, this was my only feasible option. I needed Bell in particular. My parents knew him, trusted him, and I doubted they were aware that he was no longer a detective. In fact, I was banking on it.

Darkness swelled in my chest. It was probably dangerous to try this without any of Kail's instructions, but the grin hadn't let me down yet. I had to trust my power. Trust myself. Besides, Kail's *instructions* were basically to toss a problem at me and wait to see if I sank or swam.

"Lady?" Halven asked, concerned.

I brought my head up, shoulders squared. "Wait here. We'll go back to the Blood Tower when I'm finished."

I called upon every ounce of confidence I had and strode out to the table. *Please don't be one of Rowan's.* But Halven was with me. I trusted him at least this much.

The nightmare looked up from his work to reveal pupil-less white eyes covered in pulsating blue veins. "Lady Nightmare," he said in a high, shocked voice. "I didn't do it!"

"Do what?" I asked suspiciously.

"Anything." He blinked rapidly. "I swear it."

Halven stepped up behind me, and I let out a breath. "Watch him," I told Halven in a low voice, then nodded at Bell. "I need to borrow your Dreamer."

"But I'm hungry," the nightmare whined like a small child.

"I'll give him back when I'm finished. It won't take long."

"Yes, Lady." He pouted. "Thank you, Lady."

I knelt in front of Bell and picked at the knotted rope around his wrists. He shrieked and thrashed at the touch. "Enough," I shouted. "Relax. It's Nora."

"Nora?" His pupils blew wide as he focused on my face. "Run! Run before he catches you."

My hands stilled, the knot still intact, and I sat back on my haunches. There wasn't time to chase Bell all over the Nightmare Realm. This would have to happen here. With a deep breath—one I instantly regretted making this close to the spoiled meat—I reached inward toward the grin. It was waiting for me, lips curled in contemplation, and a wisp of black guided my hand until my pointer finger pressed against Bell's forehead. His mind exploded through me. Every fear, every want, all spread out before me like a buffet on Halloween. Only, instead of chocolate severed fingers and ghost-shaped Peeps, they were the real thing. I gasped at the shock of it all, but the darkness urged me onward. Deeper and deeper. Until I came to a small orb of glowing light.

Take it, the grin seemed to say.

I wrapped my fingers around the gentle warmth, and the ground fell out from beneath me. My body felt as if it was expanding. Changing. Rational thought came and went. Up and down. Side-to-side. Dizziness dug its claws in deep. Then it stopped in an instant, a head-on collision at eighty miles an hour.

My neck whipped back. My ears rang so loudly I felt it echoing in my skull. I sat up gingerly and massaged my head. Only it wasn't *my* head. Not unless someone had shaved it in the last sixty seconds, and if that was the case, there were going to be *big* problems.

But it only took a moment to understand I wasn't in the Nightmare Realm. Instead, I was in a room lit only by a small television atop a dresser. A striped comforter covered the lower half of my body. No, not mine. Bell's. I did it. I was in. I flexed his hands, testing out the motions, and the mattress shifted beside me.

"What's wrong, baby?" A dark-skinned woman, her hair covered with a colorful scarf, leaned up on one elbow, frantically blinking the sleep away.

"Nothing," Bell—I—said. The darkness guided me from beneath the covers. Coaxing—but not forcing—his actions so they seemed natural. "Just a bad dream."

"I told you not to watch that movie before bed," she half-mumbled, rolling back onto her side.

I padded across the room and grabbed a pair of pants from the back of a chair. I stood back and let the grin do the work as it led him through the steps of making himself presentable.

"What are you doing?" the woman asked.

"I'm going to take a drive," I said, Bell's voice robotic. "Clear my head."

The woman didn't say anything else after that, and within five minutes, I was driving to my house in a silver sedan.

I stole glances in the rearview mirror every so often. His facial expression remained blank the entire trip, and the grin kept trying to poke at his thoughts. *No.* I snapped the unspoken order at it. This already felt uncomfortable—I didn't need to know Bell's deepest, darkest secrets. I wondered if he was aware of what I was doing or if it felt like a dream. Maybe neither. Maybe he would have flashes of this later and wonder, like he seemed to with what happened before.

I parked his car in my driveway, walked to my door, and knocked. Panic burst in my chest, and I scrambled to back away. To exit Bell's head. Suddenly, I didn't want to do this. To see them. But the grin held tight as Paul answered the door. His mouth parted, and he stared for what seemed like an eternity before slipping outside. "Detective." He closed the door with a soft thud. "Tell me you're not here for the reason I think you are."

"What reason would that be?" I pressed. The darkness seemed to shush me.

Paul paled. "A homicide detective shows up in the middle of the night while my daughter is missing—"

"No, no," I said. "Nora's fine."

Paul blew out a breath. "Come in. My wife will want to talk to you."

Ha! My mother had threatened him with a lawyer the last time he had me at the station. But the grin ignored me, and I followed Paul into the living room. Everything was in perfect order which somehow made seeing my house again worse. My favorite blanket was folded over the back of the couch and the dancing stuffed turkey remained at the center of the coffee table even though it was well into December now. The automatic air freshener periodically spritzed a pumpkin spice scent into the air. Usually by now, the tree would be up in the corner and our stockings would be tacked up above the television. Seeing the house Thanksgiving-ready, like it was when I left, was a gut-punch.

"Val?" Paul paused at the top of the stairs. "Can you come down here a minute?" I heard my mother mumble a reply, then Paul turned back to me. "Would you like a cup of coffee?"

I shook my head just as my mother appeared at the top of the stairs in holey sweats and a stained sweater. Her hair was matted with grease, and I swore it had thinned since I left. Her dead gaze found mine, and she started down the staircase like a zombie. The closer she got, the more the shock wore off, and I realized that she was wearing *my* sweater. One I wore to bed a lot during the winter, printed with the words 'I don't do mornings'. Except when I left, it was in much better shape. Had she been living in it? I sneered at the thought. Clutched in her hand was a small stuffed bear my dad gave me when I was little that I hadn't seen in years. If only she had held me as close.

"You remember Detective Bell, don't you?" Paul said gently.

"Hello," I said. "I have some good news and some bad news, if you'd like to come sit down."

"Good news?" My mother perked up and rushed into the living room. "You found Nora?"

I nodded. "She called the precinct from a restricted number when she found out you reported her missing. She's safe in Nevada with a friend."

"A friend? What friend?" She twisted to look at Paul with wild eyes. "She doesn't know anyone in Nevada."

"Is it her boyfriend, Ben?" Paul asked. "Have you found him yet?"

Ah, crap. I hadn't thought about the fact that the Sandman wouldn't be Day Walking anymore. Of course they would think he was either with me or guilty of something. Probably the latter, in my mother's case, since she liked to believe the worst of everyone. "They're together," the grin made me say.

"She wouldn't do this to me," my mom insisted, nearing hysterics. "There's no reason for them to run off together. We never stopped them from being together. Why would she—"

"Mom." Katie rushed down the stairs, glaring at Bell as if she knew, or at least suspected, it wasn't really him. "It's true. Nora called me too."

Paul shifted to address Katie. "She called you? When?"

"Tonight. I was going to tell you." The lies rolled easily off Katie's tongue. "She wanted you to know that she loves you and she's sorry."

My mother leapt to her feet and began pacing. "Send someone to bring her back. She's a minor."

"I'm afraid it's not as simple as that," I said.

"Maybe we should go to Nevada and talk to her face-to-face," Paul suggested.

"You're right." My mother squeezed the tiny bear so hard I expected its head to pop off. "I'll pack right now. We'll catch the next flight out and talk some sense into her."

"Mom," Katie implored. "We can't just show up and hope we stumble into her. She wouldn't tell me where she was staying, let alone what city she's in. It's a big state."

"Your sister lied about an internship and then took off in the middle of the night with her boyfriend. I'm going to track her down and drag her back by her ears if it's the last thing I do," my mother insisted and headed for the stairs. "I don't care if I have to comb every square inch of Nevada to do it."

"Katie's right, Val," Paul said. "Please think about this. We should go, but only once we have a plan in place." Paul followed her up the stairs, his voice fading away.

Katie stepped closer to me and narrowed her eyes. "Nora didn't call, did she?"

"Of course she did," the grin insisted, though I didn't know why it bothered.

"Liar." Katie waved a hand through the air to cut off any forthcoming denial. "I don't know what's going on here, but I do know where she is. If you talk to her again, tell her that Rowan knows, and she's marching."

My breath caught. *How?* How did Rowan know? How far was she from the Keep? I pressed forward to beg for details, but the darkness was faster. "Who is Rowan?"

"I hope Nora gets there first," Katie said with a knowing scowl.

The grin flew into action, sending Bell's body racing back to his car. The tires squealed as I sped away from my house. I took corners so fast the vehicle nearly tipped, and at the first red light, I slammed the car into park. The darkness pulled back, and I struggled to hold on. I couldn't leave him in his car in the middle of the street—a million things could happen after I let go. But the grin bared its teeth, insistent.

In the next moment, I was back in the Nightmare Realm beside an unconscious Bell. I sucked in a breath, my heart pounding a mile a minute. There was no time—he was on his own now. I stood and wheeled on Halven. "We have to hurry."

"Goodbye, Lady." The green creature resumed his chopping, but I blocked it out.

Rowan knows. There was only one thing Katie could've meant.

"She knows we're going for the tree." I looked at up at

Halven and knew that behind his mask, his face reflected my own fear. "We have to get there first."

"Kail—"

Kail. He could handle himself, but I needed that army. Just in case. I held my hand out. "It's too far to walk. Do the thing you did to me at the Doll Maker's."

Halven didn't hesitate as he clasped my hand and sped us back to the Blood Tower.

Chapter Twenty-Six

The Blood Army's moans filled the courtyard of the tower and carried into the neighboring tundra where Halven and I stopped. Rocks rolled away from the sound, bumping into each other, into us, with tiny, surprised *oofs*. Small pixie-like nightmares dressed in furs fled from patches of dried grass, filling the air like a swarm of dragonflies, tiny sacks in their arms. Halven and I stood there in mutual terror.

"This isn't right," I breathed. It didn't make sense. Why would Rowan be *here*? If she thought I was heading for her tree, what purpose would she have coming to the Blood Tower? "Where is the army? Why aren't they doing something?"

Halven shook his head.

"'No' what?" I whisper-yelled.

He pointed to the top of the tower where a plume of red mist billowed upward. "You don't have one anymore," he croaked.

"No. No, no, no. They can't *all* be dead." There were so many—and the Blood Army was the main force I expected to face. My army should've been prepared to fight them. My mouth ran dry, and I stepped forward. Halven put his arm out to stop me. "We have to do *something*," I insisted.

But what could we do? My army was dead. And Kail—no. There was no way he was dead too. The army may not have been ready, but he always was. He was the king of hidey-holes and escape routes. A virtual Houdini. The Blood Tower probably had more hidden passages than Paris had Catacomb tunnels.

A scream rose above the low moaning, and the familiarity of it cut me in two. *Oh. Oh, no.* Kail was alive… but he hadn't escaped. After the quaking pain of his cry, I wasn't sure if I should be glad he was still breathing.

Halven was the one to step forward this time, but I dug my fingers into his forearm. "I know another way inside." His chest rose and fell with heavy, labored breaths, but that was the only part of him to move. "Come on, before it's too late."

That got his attention, and he locked my hand in a death grip. "Where?" The question was harsher than usual.

"There's a hidden door beneath all those teeth on the—"

We were running then, faster than ever before. The wind stung my eyes, and each inhale felt like I was suffocating, but the discomfort was nothing compared to the gut-wrenching fear. It was like thinking the Sandman was dead all over again. Like turning on that lamp in Emery's living room and knowing what I would find when I looked up. I shouldn't care if Kail lived or died. What I *should* be doing was racing to the trees while I knew Rowan was occupied. But maybe she wasn't. Maybe someone else led the Blood Army here. I shook my head. It didn't matter who was hurting Kail—it only mattered that I stop them.

A blanket of teeth crunched beneath our feet. If one didn't look too closely, they could be mistaken for pebbles ranging from the whitest of whites to yellow to black. "The door is—"

I took a shuddering breath and tried to regulate my breathing. To calm down. Focus. It was buried somewhere near the center, but I hadn't been paying much attention when Kail and I escaped the fiery attack. Halven and I didn't have time to dig through this entire place, so I jabbed at the grin. It popped open with impatience. I let go completely, and the darkness urged me forward. "Here," I shouted, and fell to my knees a few paces away.

Halven joined me, and we scooped handfuls of teeth out of the way. Some of them still had bloody roots attached, others slimy with what I assumed was saliva. The small piece of rope finally appeared. Halven wrenched the hatch upward and a shower of teeth flew into the air. More funneled into the dark opening with a chorus of tiny pings. I jumped inside, teeth pelting my head, catching in my hair, with Halven right behind me.

The door slammed shut, casting us in darkness, but my feet moved as confidently as if the tunnel was brightly lit. The walls stretched out in front of me as solid shadows, and Halven's outline was perfectly clear against the grey haze. Another scream echoed somewhere overhead. I shivered, my fury needing an outlet, and ran.

"I can't reach," I huffed when we reached the overhead

door.

Halven reached up and paused to let out a long, shaky breath. Then he eased the trap door open a crack. After what felt like an eternity of him looking into the room above, he lifted it open the rest of the way and climbed out. A moment later, he reached down for my hand, swinging me up with graceful ease. I shook teeth from my hair. Focus. I had to focus. There was no telling how many things were lurking inside the tower right now.

A loud thud bounced down the hallway. "Where is she?" Rowan shrieked.

Her voice slithered over me, blinding me with rage, and I barreled from the room. I didn't think. Didn't pause for a moment. The blackest part of me ruled my movements, and I let it take me straight to Rowan's old room. What I found inside had my own lips mimicking the grin's internal sneer. Rowan's burnt wings blocked the doorway, but between the charred branches, I saw Kail, bloodied and broken on the floor.

"Just kill me," he wheezed, blood gushing from his mouth.

"You'd like that, wouldn't you?" Rowan growled.

She bent and grabbed Kail's chin. Her touch ripped a cry from his throat and brought every scream I'd ever heard crashing through me. Starting with Katie's. Ending with my own. No more—there would be no more screaming because of me.

"I'm right here," I said in a deadly voice.

Rowan whipped around, her red-flecked eyes wide. "Dream Keeper. I was looking for you," she said confidently.

"Oh." I released a mirthless laugh. "I think you mean *Lady Nightmare*, though I'm not sure how you could make that mistake. This is your fault, after all."

Her expression tightened. "You left the Nightmare Realm

before I could congratulate you."

"*Kill* me. I left before you could kill me. We're past pretending otherwise."

My gaze slid to Kail, his head hanging in defeat, and anger roared in my ears. *End her now*, the grin demanded. Energy crackled over my skin, and I lunged. Mindless. Unseeing. My body was a wild, reckless blur of magic. I was in the backseat, watching myself move with an ease that couldn't be taught. My shoulder slammed into Rowan's chest, and she tumbled backward into the giant bed.

But instead of yielding, she gave me a predatory smile. "The Weaver's magic has done wonders for you." *Imagine what it could do for me*. She didn't say it, but the thought hung in the air between us.

Until I smashed through it, fists flying.

They each met her face with a sickening crunch, and the sureness faded from her eyes. My next blow met her palm. Her fingers dug into the back of my hand, and the blazing pain had me crawling back into the driver's seat. A scream built rapidly in my chest, and it wouldn't be long before it escaped. Whatever force oversaw my body slammed down on the gas pedal. My body moved without my mind, twisting and turning in ways neither the Sandman nor Kail had ever trained me. I tried to stop it. To move another way. *Any* way that would show I still had control.

But nothing worked.

Rowan was off me. My hands were around her throat, and the pain registered behind a brick wall. She slammed me into one of the Keep's walls. Her wings rose higher. Shifted. The tips pointed at me. And then Rowan screeched.

With her grip loosened, I scrambled away, gasping for air, and my limbs slowly returned to me. *What was that?* My heart became heavier with each beat. Kail stood in the center of the room with half of Rowan's right wing in his hands, and Halven slipped in front of his brother in a protective stance. My mind scrambled to find a solution, but my thoughts were twisted with the agony of Rowan's touch. I was just now able to feel the terror at having my body stolen away.

Rowan shot to her feet. I punched her again. She sailed sideways, her head cracking against the wall, and slumped to the floor, knocked out.

"Tie her up somewhere before she regains consciousness," I croaked to Halven. He was covered from head to toe, making him the only one of us who could safely touch her. I needed a minute to still my shaking body and relearn how to move properly. "Then find me something to kill her with."

Halven nodded and swept across the room, where he gripped Rowan by the crown of raven beaks adhered to the top of her head, dragging her from the room. Her intact wing snagged on the door frame. With one swift kick from Halven, the offending piece of burnt branch crumbled into ash, and the two of them disappeared down the hall. And, just like that, I was alone with Kail. Without a single idea of what to say or how to act.

"You're picking up on the whole grand entrance thing," Kail said after a long, heavy moment. "I had ideas on how to teach you that particular skill, but I suppose this will have to do."

I cut him a sharp look. "You're welcome."

"For?" he asked in a pained voice.

"Saving your life."

He laughed and slid down the wall to sit beside me. *When had I sat down?* "I'm pretty sure *I* saved *your* life," he said lightly.

"What?" I blurted, and he tossed the broken branch at our feet. "That doesn't count. Halven and I didn't have to sneak in here, you know. We could've let Rowan kill you and gone for the stump instead."

"*You* didn't have to save me, true." He sighed and dabbed carefully at his bruising jaw.

I opened my mouth to say I should've let him die but swallowed the words. Kail's cheek was already swelling, and there was a huge dent in the mask above his right temple. Each shallow breath ended with a crackle. Bones in one of his hands jutted out at unnatural angles, and scratches marked the side of his neck—yet still he hadn't told Rowan where I was. My note hadn't been very specific, of course, but he could've told her that I would be back. To hide and ambush me when I walked through the door. There had to be a million ways to double-cross me just waiting inside his head.

I cleared my throat and shifted to kneel in front of him. "This doesn't change anything," I said carefully. "If you told me about the tree sooner, none of this would've happened."

He gave me a sad smile. "I didn't protect you to change anything."

"Then why? You could've easily played your cards to save yourself."

"I told you." He coughed and clutched at his ribs. "I have my reasons."

I rolled my eyes. "When I got here, you said these ulterior motives of yours depended on my humanity, which I assume means you'll want a favor one day. You might as well fess up while I'm feeling generous."

He closed his eyes and licked the corner of his cracked lip. "Perceptive."

When he didn't elaborate, I bit down on my tongue. *Later.* When Rowan wasn't tied up in the other room—when she was dead. "I need gloves. And a turtleneck, maybe. Does your brother have spare masks lying around?"

Kail cracked his eyes open, unamused. "Do you have spare faces lying around?"

I opened my mouth, only to shut it again. *Touché.* "Are you going to help me kill her or not? I need to be able to touch her without worrying about her shredding my insides again."

"I'm afraid I'll have to sit this one out." He winced. "But you're welcome to raid my closet for gloves. Or, you know, take the easy route and use the gun in your bag."

"You went through my stuff?" I shouted. Lies. Snooping. More lies. It shouldn't surprise me, but he'd made such a big deal out of my trusting him. And he'd actually succeeded to a degree. I stared at him as his muscles twitched beneath his skin, and my anger left in a whoosh. He bore the pain well—well enough that I knew it wasn't his first rodeo. After decades—maybe longer—at Rowan's side, how could it be? He deserved to watch her die. I licked my lips. If I could heal Four, I could heal him too. I pressed my hand against his chest before I could change my mind.

Kail jerked. "What are you doing?"

"Shut up," I snapped, then called on the grin.

It unfurled, and the magic flowed from my fingertips, finding Kail's knotted thread without a drop of effort. The thread throbbed against the magic, and the grin did the work, as always.

It tucked gold fibers back in place, smoothed down snagged bits, and molded it all back into a neat ball. Except for the frayed end—that still dangled helplessly. I nudged the magic at it, but Kail pushed my hand away.

"Not that," he said hoarsely.

I looked him in the eyes and startled. His blue eye flashed colors in unison with the other. "Your eye is better," I whispered.

"About time," he muttered, though he couldn't seem to help the boyish glint that surfaced in his irises. He stood. "Come on, Lady."

He was halfway through the door before I climbed to my feet. "Kail?"

"What?" he asked without turning around.

"You said I could've left you here to die…" I chewed my bottom lip for a moment. It wasn't what he said, but how he said it. "Why couldn't Halven have done the same?"

"Ah." He cracked his knuckles. "Careful, Lady. You might stumble upon all my secrets."

"Something tells me *you* don't even know them all," I joked.

"You might be right," he said with a laugh as he stepped into the hallway. "Let's go. You've got a murder to commit."

Murder. The word twisted my gut. I knew it was what I was going to do—what I had already done. On top of torture. But it didn't feel right to be so numb to it. I winced. Now was not a good time to regain my conscience. Rowan had to be dealt with while I had the chance, so I stood tall and followed Kail.

Outside, the Blood Army's moaning took on a deeper note, and I glanced out the nearest window. Each robed figure drifted toward the same point, circling their unseen prey. *No.* Deal with Rowan first, the Blood Army second. Whatever nightmare they were attacking was—

"Sandman?" His name left my tongue before I could stop it.

Kail leaned back on his heel to follow my gaze. "Ah. Don't worry. He can handle himself."

"Don't worry?" It felt as if I were the one out there, surrounded by the enemy. "He can't possibly take that many on by himself."

Kail snorted. "Looks like he's doing fine to me."

A silver tornado made of sand blew a path through the onslaught. Still, my heart raced. I remembered exactly how that mist felt. The Sandman needed help. The grin puckered in obvious denial at the idea of assistance.

"I may have told him you were missing," Kail admitted, nonplussed.

"I wasn't missing." I sucked in a breath. "Wait—you what? How? When?"

He shrugged. "I got your note and assumed you'd be there."

I gripped the windowsill. "So you what? Went to drag me back?"

"Oh, I don't think the Sandman would've let me drag you anywhere. You, on the other hand…" He winked and pressed a stone in the wall to open a hidden door.

"Not another step," Rowan ordered from inside.

I froze, a million curses on my tongue. Halven's back was pressed against Rowan's front, a long, jagged piece of her broken wing pressed against his throat. Before I could move, before I could speak, Kail let out a low wail at the sight of his brother in danger. "Don't," he pleaded. The word was brittle and desperate, and it nearly ruined me hearing it from him.

"I could do it," Rowan said. "Take you both out, then the

girl. But the Sandman is another story."

"Rowan." Kail sounded small. Lost. "Please."

"Send the Dream Keeper in, and I'll let him go."

Kail shook with fear, or maybe anger, but he didn't move. I shoved him aside. Despite the ruffles around Halven's neck, Rowan's weapon placement was perfect.

"Let him go," I demanded.

Rowan dug the tip in a little deeper, but Halven didn't move a muscle. "You're not in any place to be making demands."

"Nora," Kail begged. "Let her go."

"*What?*" I spun on him. "Are you kidding me? This is the moment we've been training for."

He shook his head. "Let her walk out of here. Promise the Sandman won't touch her on the way out, and maybe she'll let us all live to fight another day."

"I'd much rather see you all dead," Rowan snapped.

All of us.

Kail and Halven wouldn't matter much to the Dream Lord fighting an army singlehandedly, but I would. And no matter what he believed about the balance, the Sandman would never let anyone get away with killing me.

"You could kill us all," I agreed slowly. "But then you would die too. What you didn't see inside the Keep the day I killed the Weaver was that I died too." Not true, of course, though it felt like I had. The words flowed so easily, it didn't feel like a lie. "The magic killed me and then brought me back as this. So I suppose the question you need to ask yourself is whether or not you would have time to be reborn before the Sandman finds you."

She hesitated. The grin inside me gnashed against my self-constraint. *End her, end her, end her*, it chanted. Let Halven die. Let anyone die, as long as she did too. Now. While she was in the Blood Tower. Trapped. Alone. Vulnerable.

"You'll never survive this realm," Rowan spat, holding Halven against her chest. They moved toward us in unison without her hand leaving the weapon. "Every day you breathe is another day borrowed."

I shrugged, feigning confidence. "Take it up with my bank."

"Move," she insisted. "I'll release him when I'm outside."

Don't you dare, the grin warned me, but the desperate look on Kail's face as he obeyed was enough for me. This wasn't letting Rowan escape—this was saving Kail's brother. This was earning the loyalty he had given me. *No*. More than that. This was a way to keep my humanity in a place built for the inhumane.

We followed Rowan all the way to the front door as she used Halven as a human shield. "I know you think you've figured out how to win," she said, slipping the door open with her heel. "But you'll never succeed."

"We'll see," I vowed.

Rowan shoved Halven toward us a split second before the door slammed between us. I bolted around the brothers and threw it open again, but she was already halfway across the tundra, surrounded by what was left of the Blood Army. The ones the Sandman managed to kill lay scattered around the tower, their bodies slowly evaporating into red mist. There was no getting past it—we were trapped until the bodies finished decomposing unless we wanted to be boiled alive.

"Rowan," I screamed so loud my throat burned.

Mistake, the grin chastised. *Big, big mistake.*

It wasn't wrong.

Chapter Twenty-Seven

Nora

The steady thud of a meat cleaver greeted me, followed immediately by the stench of what could only be a dozen corpses. They were skinned and chopped into large sections, rotting away on a tall table. I held my breath as I approached a small green nightmare standing on a stool beside the table. "Where is she?" I demanded, the sense of déjà vu not lost on me.

The creature didn't bother to look up from his work. "Who, Dream Lord?"

"You know who."

"She left." He paused to slide a pile of rancid meat across the table and resumed chopping. "Needed to borrow my Dreamer, then took off in a bit of a hurry."

"Your Dreamer?" I asked, confused. The nightmare nodded to the other end of the table, and I picked my way closer, avoiding the thick liquid dripping to the floor. My eyes widened. "Detective Bell?" The Dreamer muttered incoherently as his eyes darted around behind his lids.

"She broke him," the nightmare complained. "He's not scared anymore, but he won't wake up either."

I pressed my fingers against his throat to find a pulse. It was barely there, unsteady and fading. "What happened?"

"Don't ask me." He waved his knife at Bell and kept talking. "The Lady took him sleepwalking and stayed in his head the whole time. Fried his brain, I suppose, but he'll still make for some tasty meat. Chop him up and—"

I tuned the nightmare out and stared at Bell. Sleepwalking was foreign to me. The *how* of it. The Weaver never stayed. He went in, did whatever brainwashing he had to do, and got out. Anything could've happened inside Bell's head while Nora was in there. "I'm sorry," I whispered. Hopefully, he would wake up with no lasting effects. I reached for my satchel. After everything he'd been through, starting with the Weaver's first murder, he deserved the peace of the Dream Realm.

Blood bubbled from Bell's mouth. His head fell back, and his eyes rolled so far back all I could see were their whites.

"No fair," the nightmare cried.

I gripped my sand, but in the next moment, Bell vanished. "*No!*"

"She didn't say she was going to kill him," the nightmare whined to itself.

I leveled a stare at the creature, my heart thumping wildly. "Which way did Nora go?"

"Not sure. Halven took her," he said, pouting.

I reached out with my magic until I found Nora's. That way. *The Blood Tower.* She was on her way back to the very place Rowan would expect to find her. A low, frustrated scream lodged in my throat. Until this was over, Nora had to stop taking off without thinking, and we needed to know where she was. All of us—me, Kail, Baku, Halven. As unlikely as it was, we were working together toward the same goal of putting Nora in her rightful place. While I understood her desire to figure herself out, she needed to believe in us. Not even I was delusional enough to think I didn't need help from time to time. I didn't *like* needing someone like Kail to watch Nora's back, but what I liked made no difference.

With a shallow breath, I forced myself to stand and move in the direction of Nora's power. I ran a hand through my hair, holding it off my forehead. My jaw ached as I clenched it shut. I was angry with Nora, but I should be even angrier. It wasn't possible though. She was in a bad place right now and doing what she thought was best, even if she was actually selecting the worst option. I kept telling myself during my entire journey through the Nightmare Realm.

When I reached the Blood Tower, I froze, my heart dropping. Whatever I expected to see at the Blood Tower, it wasn't this. Rowan was supposed to be marching the Blood Army to defend her tree stump. That's what made sense. The second set of nightmares should've come here, not Rowan herself. Nora could already be halfway across the Nightmare Realm for all Rowan knew. So why?

But Nora wasn't halfway anywhere—she was inside. Her anger raked along my mental wall like thorns. Fighting the entire

Blood Army wasn't at the top of my to-do list, but there was no getting around them. I stayed away from Nora all this time and still it came down to this. There would be ways to fix her image later if she survived. I steeled myself for what had to be done, and *only* what had to be done. If I held back now, Rowan might not realize I'd regained my strength until it was too late. She had already underestimated me once when she took me to the Keep.

The weary, heartsick boy in me had no place here so I looked across the tundra through the eyes of the Lord of Dreams. I registered everything with lightning precision. Tower entrances, Blood Army weaknesses, numbers, the density of the red mist. Alone it meant nothing. Together, it gave me an exact plan of attack. I took my gloves from my belt and shoved my hands inside to protect my skin.

"Forgive me, Nora," I said without an ounce of apology and snapped my hood up.

As I ran toward the tower, I felt nothing. Not the anger and vengeance I felt when I scoured the Nightmare Realm for Nora the first time. Not worry for her wellbeing because she already had help—and her own strength. I didn't even feel the burn of the army's mist where it snuck into the crevices of my clothing. I felt nothing except perhaps resignation. This wasn't Nora and me anymore. This was Dream and Nightmare. Day and Night. And it was my duty to protect all of it.

The Blood Army drifted toward me as a unit, circling me. I poured half of my satchel to the ground by my feet and waited. Waited for them to come closer. To press together into a tighter pack. Then I swept my arm out. A tornado ripped through their ranks, snuffing them out. The other robed figures wailed and pressed forward to fill in the gaps.

"I don't have time for this," I mumbled and lifted my hand again.

Only, my arm froze midair. Rowan's red silk gown caught my eye from the doorway. She hugged Halven to her chest, a jagged stick in her hand. I noticed right away a large portion of her wings were missing. The Army swiveled away from me, moving toward her instead. I regained myself and threw my hand out to make another twister. More figures fell, but not enough. The door slammed shut. Rowan was alone. And running. The Blood Army circled her, their mist seeming to propel her faster and faster. I took two steps when Nora's voice cut through me.

Her scream was for Rowan, but it obliterated my sense of nothingness. It felt as if my heart started beating anew, and my stomach dropped. *I'm in trouble.* How could I be what the universe needed if, even in these circumstances, Nora filled my every breath? Unfortunately, there was no cure for love. Not that I would take it if there were.

"Sandman," Nora called, waving me forward.

I jerked, and the first true blast of pain went straight through me. Red mist rose through the entire courtyard, higher and higher, as the bodies evaporated. I rushed from the carnage and over the threshold before any of the blistering cloud could make it inside. The door barely shut behind me before Nora's arms wrapped around my middle.

"Hi," she breathed.

"Hi." I melted into her, my anxiety falling away. "Are you okay?"

"Fine." She stepped back and cleared her throat. "We're all fine."

"What are you doing here?" Kail's two flashing eyes scanned

me critically.

I pushed my hood off and glared at him. When had she fixed him? Last I knew, she was fuming over his earlier omission and refusing to make his requested repairs. "Finding Nora," I said simply.

"You were supposed to check between here and the trees," he said grumpily.

"Obviously she wasn't there," I snapped.

"Enough. Let's all take a minute. Or five," Nora said. She eyed the red mist pressing against the windowpane. "We're clearly not going anywhere right now."

"The tunnel—" Kail started.

"Five minutes," she barked. "Then we'll meet in the room with the clock to make a plan."

I watched her walk away, shoulders squared, and instantly knew how she was going to spend that time. It made sense that she would want to hide her weakness from Kail and Halven, but was I included now? Would she still allow me to see her vulnerability? I wasn't brave enough to find out. But, in those minutes, Nora was going to crumble under pressure only to pull herself together, stronger than before.

"She's stalling," Kail said with a sigh.

Halven shook his head. "Our lady is right. Without a plan, we're going into a fight blinded by hatred."

"We need options." I massaged my temples. "You have five minutes to fill me in about this tunnel."

Kail studied me for a long moment, then led the way into the tower.

Chapter Twenty-Eight

We were not trapped in this forsaken tower of death. I refused to allow it. But no matter what part of the Blood Tower I touched, it was the only knot I could feel. Nothing beyond the walls, nothing within them. Some part of me knew it wouldn't be possible to change anything without touching it, but I couldn't help trying. The grin turned smug, and I punched the nearest surface, which happened to be a decorative metal sculpture that spiraled up from the floor. My knuckles throbbed, the skin peeling away, and the grin seemed to chuckle.

"Fine," I whispered at it. "Do you have a solution?"

Silence.

Of course.

Because the grin wasn't an actual, physical thing—it was just part of the magic. It didn't have a mind of its own even if it felt like it sometimes. *Okay.* Think. Rowan came here believing she had the upper hand. I was sure she didn't expect things to go as they did, so what would her backup plan be? Retreat to the tree? Plan another ambush?

"Hey." Kail poked the back of my head. "When you say five minutes, do you usually mean twenty?"

I whipped around. "Oh, I'm sorry. Did you have somewhere else to be?"

"It would be good to know for future reference," he said.

"Bold of you to assume we'll have a future." What did I know about any of this? I was a seventeen-year-old high school drop out from the Day World. My biggest problems should be picking out the perfect prom dress, studying for the SAT, and applying to colleges I didn't want to attend, but no. Instead, I had to become an expert at strategy so I could plot the death of my mortal enemy. I shouldn't even *have* a mortal enemy.

Kail rolled his eyes. "Everyone's waiting to hash out our next move."

There was no more stalling. No more hiding. I stared down the grin, letting my resentment harden my nerves, and joined the others. Halven stood in front of his clock and the Sandman sat on one end of the sofa, pinching the bridge of his nose. He smiled when I walked through the door, and I couldn't help but return it. *God.* He was the most beautiful man in existence. It was all I could do not to bury myself in him right there in front of the brothers.

"It takes about six hours for the bodies to disappear and the mist to dissipate," Kail said. "Are you sure you don't want to take the tunnel?"

"Can Halven whisk us all across the Nightmare Realm at once?" I asked. Halven shook his head without looking away from the symbols.

"It would take longer to go through the tunnel and backtrack in the direction of the trees than it would to wait," the Sandman said, his tone dry. He had probably told them the same thing a dozen times while they waited for me.

"It would take the same amount of time," Kail corrected.

Anger flared inside me, and I said, "In that case, there's really no benefit to leaving just now."

"Let's not get sidetracked," the Sandman said and placed his hands on his knees. "It doesn't matter how we get there—it matters what we do after."

I took a seat beside him, careful to avoid physical contact. We needed to focus on the plan, and if I touched him, I would give into the urge to fold myself into him. To soak up the warmth, the love, of him instead of feeling like a rock plunked into dark, icy water.

"We should all lay our cards on the table first," I said. "There seems to be a lot of things the four of us are sharing with one or two others instead of with the group." Not that we were really a group—more like pairs. Me and the Sandman, Kail and Halven, me and Kail. But we hadn't been a cohesive gathering until now. "I'll start," I added when they were silent. I turned to the Sandman. "Those bruises you saw? I was attacked by one of the Hours, who are also responsible for burning down the tower."

"The Hours?" The Sandman sat up straight. "Rowan has the Hours behind her?"

Kail snorted. "That would make our lives too easy."

"They're upset about Mara," I said, cutting a look at Kail.

"Some more than others," Kail added. "Three wants her dead. Six and Ten want a plan to take care of the problem, or they'll kill her. The others could be anywhere in between."

"If they kill you, they'll be the new Weaver," the Sandman stated.

"Not sure they thought the process through," I admitted. "Anyway. Your turn."

The Sandman cocked his head and locked eyes with me. "I don't have any secrets. You know I've been making spies and that I let Rowan capture me. There's nothing else to tell."

My first instinct was to scream *liar*, but while the Sandman hid things sometimes, he didn't lie. Especially not to my face. My heart throbbed painfully with guilt for even thinking it. "Okay." I looked to Kail. "Go ahead. And remember we only have six hours."

He crossed his arms and leaned against the wall beside his brother. "Sure. Believe everyone but me."

Yup. I shrugged. "I'll always believe the Sandman, and I haven't asked Halven yet."

"Kail and I will tell you the same thing," Halven supplied in his usual raspy voice. "Forgive me, but it's easier for him to explain."

"Not yet," Kail hissed.

Halven looked away from the clock for the first time. "Then when?" he asked his brother.

"No," I interrupted with finality. "Now is perfect."

Kail shook his head. "You won't agree yet. We still have to prove ourselves."

"Put us back together," Halven blurted so quickly it sounded as if his throat were made of gravel. He coughed and rubbed at his breastbone. "Please, Lady. It hurts to be apart."

Pieces clicked together. The frayed end of Kail's thread, the cryptic answers when it came to Halven. They weren't brothers. They were the same nightmare cut in two. Kail's ulterior motive was to be whole again. Even the grin's lips parted in surprise. I sucked in a breath at the agonized look on Kail's face and Halven's rigid stance. The Weaver wouldn't put them back together because he didn't care how they felt about being apart. That's why he needed my humanity. My heart cracked a little for them both.

"That's why Halven couldn't leave you to die?" I asked in a low voice. "Because if you die, he dies?"

Kail clenched his jaw and nodded once. "Pain aside, I don't particularly like having my biggest weakness wandering the Nightmare Realm alone."

"It's safer to wander than to work with Rowan," Halven said softly.

"I didn't have a choice," Kail snapped, his face instantly red. The break in his voice nearly did me in as he said, "Go ahead, Lady. Get it over with. Tell us you won't help so we can let go of the hope."

The backs of my eyes prickled with tears. *That* was what he wanted. Why he was helping me. I wasn't sure why I felt it so deeply, but it was a weight lifted to know his reasons weren't underhanded. "Of course I will." My voice wavered, and I felt my face flush.

They said nothing, but Kail's eyes fixed on the floor. Had they really thought I wouldn't do it? After all they'd done for me? But an image of Kail's crumbled beak flashed before me, and my ears rang with the fight we had when I found out he knew how to kill Rowan. Why *wouldn't* he expect me to refuse? He betrayed me with the knife many months ago, and he probably only knew the unforgiving nature of the Weaver and Rowan. He was right to want to build loyalty and trust first.

"After," Kail finally said. "When you've got your loom back and have practiced on something else first. It's a lot harder to put things back together than it is to rip them apart."

"Okay," I agreed.

The Sandman reached over and took my hand, squeezing gently. His expression said everything he couldn't say in front of the others, and my heart swelled. *I love you, I love you, I love you.* But also, a painful twist deep beneath that. *You don't deserve him*, it said. And it was right. So, so right. I squeezed his hand back anyway.

"So, where's Rowan?" I asked Halven.

"The trees," he said, pointing. "The Blood Army too."

The Sandman tensed. "I saw what Baku saw—there should be more than the Blood Army with her."

"A few." Halven confirmed.

"Does it say where they went?" The Sandman's violet, starlit eyes scanned the clock almost frantically.

Halven rubbed at his throat. "Who, specifically?"

A crease formed between the Sandman's brows. What had he seen exactly? Another army? "Where's Baku?" I asked, trying not to think about it. One disaster at a time. "Is he going to help?"

"He does what he wants when he wants," the Sandman said in a distant voice.

"Oh, he'll come," Kail said with certainty. "At the end. To eat the corpses."

"We leave when the mist lifts," Halven rasped, steering the

conversation back on track. The four of us exchanged looks and nodded in agreement.

"And when we get there?" I asked.

"We fight," Kail said as if it were obvious.

"This is my first real battle," I said. "I'm going to want to fight with something a little more concrete."

"Trust yourself," the Sandman whispered. "Use what you've learned. Rowan may have nightmares on her side, but they aren't there. Even if they are, they'll switch sides if you give them reason to. Make a show of force."

"And the second you get the chance—" Kail dragged a finger across his throat. "It doesn't matter if it's Rowan or the tree, as long as you take one of them out."

Take one of them out. Right. That was the plan, and yet the action itself always seemed so far away. So *doable*, yet so unreachable. Standing at the starting gate turned out to be a whole other beast. Suddenly, I wasn't sure this was a race I could win. I was *not* ready for this. Not even a little bit. I was nothing more than a puppy who just learned to eat solid food stepping into a fighting pit with the top dog—but what other choice did I have? It didn't matter if I was ready; this was happening, and I was going to win.

I took a fortifying breath. "What about you guys?"

"We'll watch your back." Kail glanced at the clock. "Don't worry. I know all Rowan's tricks. You just worry about killing her and leave the rest to us."

Even now that I had all this magic, her touch was too much. Telling me not to worry was about as helpful as telling water not to be wet. The Sandman ran his thumb over my scraped knuckles, and I jumped.

"Sorry," he whispered. "I didn't mean to hurt you."

"You didn't. I just realized something." I smiled and turned to Kail. "Rowan's clothes?"

"What about them?" he asked, curious.

"Show me where they are."

He shrugged and pushed off the wall.

I moved to follow him into the hall when the Sandman grabbed for my hand again, stopping me in my tracks. "Can I see you later? Alone?"

"Please," I answered, my heart fluttering at the thought, and I gave him a quick kiss.

Maybe we really could win this. Together. All of us.

Chapter Twenty-Nine

This was the first time since I told Nora that I loved her that I was *this* nervous to see her. All our time apart washed away the moment she returned my smile in the sitting room, and holding her hand felt like it did the first time, sparks and all. I had to believe things wouldn't go badly when we left to face Rowan, but if they did—if they did, I wanted her to know how I still felt. I leaned my head on the doorframe of Nora's room and watched her chew her bottom lip as she stared at the clothing scattered over the floor. When she didn't notice me after thirty seconds, I tapped my knuckles on the wood.

Nora jumped at the sound, then smiled as her gaze fell on me. "Hi."

"Hi." I motioned to the heap of fabric. "Need help?"

Nora snorted and pointed to a pile of red silk in the corner. "Raiding Rowan's closet was a flop. All she had were three identical red gowns. I'm trying to decide what will offer the most coverage so she can't touch me, but I guess it doesn't matter what I wear. Nothing here would cover my neck."

"Layers," I suggested.

Nora plucked up a camisole, a t-shirt, and a purple sweater and tossed them onto the bed. "I should've packed some of my scarves," she lamented.

I stepped into the room, closing the door behind me, and took my gloves from my belt. "Here." They were too big for her, but it was better than nothing.

"I can't take those." She climbed to her feet. "You'll need them if you fight the Blood Army."

"You need them more than I do." I took her hand and set them in her palm, holding tight. "How are you?"

"I'm o—"

I silenced her by tracing a line across her forehead. "I mean in here."

Nora's breath caught. "It's like there's another person in there with me sometimes," she admitted with a grimace. "But it's getting better. I just need to get through this, you know?"

"I know." I pulled her against me, and she nuzzled into my chest. "We will."

We clung to each other for what felt like an eternity, silently soaking each other in. It was almost like before. *Almost.* A hint of sulfur clung to the air about her, where before she smelled like autumn giving way to winter—a fresh, crisp scent that was distinctly Nora. It was still there, under everything. All of her was. The Weaver's magic hadn't destroyed her completely, which meant there was hope. Maybe it wouldn't—maybe she really could be both. Her reaction to Kail's secret, that she didn't hesitate to grant their request, proved it.

"Are you sure I should go?" I asked.

She held me a bit tighter. "I'm sure."

"You've come so far without me…"

"I've learned a lot being here." She set her chin on my chest and looked up at me with as much longing in her expression as I felt. "But my head feels messy, so I'm going to listen to something else instead."

"Kail?" I joked.

"Ha-ha." She tapped her fingers over my chest. "My heart."

My own heart swelled painfully. I tried not to think about all the hurt she caused me. This could be our last time together for a while, and I wanted to enjoy it. There was plenty of time for anger later, because Nora would survive this battle if I had to kill Rowan myself—but I wouldn't dredge it all up now. She had to focus on what came next.

"Sandman," she whispered. "Where did you go?"

"What?"

"Just now. You looked like you were a million miles away."

I shook my head.

"We used to talk about everything," she said wistfully. "Now look at us."

"Now isn't the time," I said.

"Now is the only time. If I don't make it back tomorrow, I'll die with a lot of things left unsaid, and I don't want that." It wasn't said with fear, but resolve.

"You're not going to die, Nora," I promised.

"You don't know that." She stepped back suddenly and

covered her face. When her hands dropped, her gold eyes shimmered with tears. "I've done so many horrible things to you, Sandman. Why are you still here?"

I clutched the fabric over my heart. Another blow, though I knew she didn't mean it to be. My love for her was strong enough that I wouldn't walk away instead of trying to work things out. "I promised you that I would be yours no matter what, and I meant it."

"I don't—" She growled wordlessly. "I don't want you to be here because of some promise you made before I lied to you." I stepped forward, but she stepped back, keeping the same amount of distance between us. It sparked a match inside me. "Am I angry? Yes," I said, the words bitter. "But we can talk through it after you've taken your realm. I'm not here because of some sense of obligation. The promise will always be true, no matter how many lies you tell, because I've lied too. For five years, I kept secrets that would eventually destroy your life. *More* than your life. Because of me, there are a lot of devastated people in the Day World right now, and while I can't be sorry for saving the rest of the world, I *am* sorry for the cost. I understand lying when you feel it's the only option for the greater good. You did what you thought you had to do, and I don't blame you for it. I only wish you had *talked* to me instead. That, after everything, you trusted me." My voice cracked. "Have I not always done what you wanted? I admit I was being selfish about you coming back here because I didn't want to lose you, but if you insisted… You had to know I would've brought you here, Nora."

"I'm sorry," she said. Her voice warbled, and she pinched her lips together to stop them from quivering.

"It's not over, you know," I said with an edge. "Learning

who you are. You've barely scratched the surface, so when this is done, I'll give you the space you need."

Tears flooded down her cheeks. "Without you, I'm this other thing, but I don't want to be. I want to keep being Nora."

"You are." And she was. I wanted to believe she would stay that way forever, but some part of me knew she would eventually adapt to her surroundings. Maybe not to the extent the Weaver had, but enough. Besides, she was young. It was natural she would grow and change.

She shook her head and fell to her knees. "I'm sorry. This wasn't supposed to be about me. When you asked to see me, I wanted to apologize about everything, but especially—" She paused and wiped her face off. "Especially that last night in the Day World."

"You needed to distract me," I said and swallowed a lump in my throat.

"No." She winced. "No, that wasn't why. You said you were selfish for keeping me in the Day World because you didn't want to lose me. I didn't want to lose you either. And, before you say it, I know logically that I wouldn't have, but I stopped thinking logically a long time ago. I knew what it meant to you, but I didn't let it stop me. So just hate me, okay? I need you to hate me."

My heart broke for us both. Its contents were a swirling mass of anger and sorrow and regret. Everyone had their breaking point, and, while this would be it for some, I wasn't close to mine. Not when I understood first-hand how hard learning to be a new version of yourself was. Before the Weaver and I banished Mare, altering the Night World and ourselves, I was less kind. Just as the Weaver wasn't always wholly malicious.

Hot tears stung my check, and I joined Nora on the clothes-covered floor. "I love you." When she opened her mouth to issue a rebuttal, I stopped her with a kiss. "I love you, Nora. Always."

Her hands trembled as she cupped my face. "I'm sorry," she whispered softly.

"Shh," I said against her mouth and kissed her again. "We've forgiven each other. Whatever comes next, we'll figure it out."

Nora kissed me then, her lips scalding. It was a desperate thing seeking comfort. I matched it and poured every second of longing into her. Her touch erased everything, leaving nothing but us. This time, it was me who tugged off my shirt. Me who guided hers over her head. The black threads winding over her skin drew my attention, and she paused.

"I can't take them off," she said, drawing away.

My eyes met hers, and I pressed her hand against my exposed tattoo. "I can't take mine off either."

Her breath caught, a small smile appearing across her lips, and she climbed onto my lap. Our kisses softened and slowed, grew explorative. Until we couldn't take it anymore.

"Are you sure you want to do this again?" Nora asked.

My body shook in anticipation. "Absolutely sure. Are you?"

"Oh, I'm sure," she said with a hint of laughter.

And that was all either of us needed to hear.

That night, on the cusp of a new future, we brought the Dream and Nightmare Realms together. Only time would tell if we could keep it that way.

Chapter Thirty

Blue and white crystal pillars stabbed the sky in all directions. The columns stretched for miles, forming a dense maze of tunnels and holes for us to climb through. After an hour, I was covered in sweat and more than ready to level the entire landscape, but that would ruin the whole sneak-until-we-can't-sneak-anymore plan. And, on the other side of this ridiculous obstacle course, we would rendezvous—Kail's word, not mine—with the Sandman after he replenished his sand supply.

I leapt at the side of an extra wide piece of fallen crystal, searching and failing to find something to grab onto. Halven made climbing over it look so easy. Of course, Halven was practically a giant compared to me. But then, most people were.

Suddenly, Kail grabbed my ankle. I squeaked and kicked out.

"Kail!" I hissed. But he just grabbed my other leg and slid me up the side of the chipped pillar.

"Sorry," he said, sounding anything but. I straddled the crystal and glared down at him. "What? Would you rather keep practicing for your breakout roll as a rabbit?" He gripped my thigh, just above my knee, and pretended to yank me back down.

"No," I said quickly, squeezing my legs to stay put.

Kail chuckled and hauled himself up beside me with an embarrassing amount of grace. "A little trust, Lady."

"There *is* no trusting you," I mumbled. I was beginning to sound like a broken record.

He gave me a withering look. "I thought we were past all that."

I wanted to be, but there was no reason he would stay loyal after he got what he wanted. True trust didn't come with an expiration date. "You scratch my back, I scratch yours. Don't read too much into it."

"I won't kill you," he insisted, suddenly serious.

"Do you say that to all the girls?" I batted my eyelashes at him sarcastically. "Rowan trusted you enough to show her weakness, and look where that got her."

"For what it's worth, she didn't trust me either," he said, aloof. "Listen, I don't like being vulnerable. Halven and I waltzing around separately puts us both at risk."

It did. And it gave me something to hold over them. Halven was much better company. I could keep him at my side and use Kail to do my dirty work. It would serve Kail right for deceiving me for so long. I wrinkled my nose, annoyed with myself for even thinking it. "Who isn't trusting who now? I said I would put you back together."

The muscles in his jaw twitched. "All I'm saying is, if you do this for us, we will always be grateful enough not to stab you in the back."

"The Weaver was stabbed in the front," I deadpanned.

Kail rolled his eyes. "And make myself the most wanted man in the Night World? Pass. If the Sandman didn't kill me, everyone else would try. At least take comfort in my instinct for self-preservation."

Now *that* I could trust.

He slid down the other side of the pillar, landing neatly on his feet. I followed suit, though much less smoothly, and we walked the rest of the way in a strangely comfortable silence. My ears picked up on every little sound, just as Halven's and Kail's seemed to, but the three of us were together. For now. Maybe I should give them long-term benefit of the doubt. Or maybe that was what they wanted. Once they were put back together, who would they be? Kail or Halven? Neither? Which personality would stay, and which would go?

"Hey," the Sandman whispered, suddenly at my side.

My heart jumped, and I reached out for him. He took my hand. "Baku can't find any trace of Rowan's second group of nightmares, but the Blood Army is waiting on the other side of this landscape."

The tell-tale sign of red mist reflected through the crystal, distorted. We had to be close. "How did they know we were coming this way?" My voice shook. If the Blood Army was waiting for us, there was no getting out of this end of the landscape unseen, and it would be all too easy to send nightmares after us from behind. We would be fish in a barrel.

"We need to distract them," Halven said. "I'll go."

"Like hell you will," Kail shot. "We are not dying today."

"Someone needs to."

"No, they don't," the Sandman said. "They're not overly intelligent, right?"

Kail shook his head. "They follow orders. Nothing more."

The Sandman dipped his hand into his satchel and tossed sand straight up into the air. As it fell, the particles swirled into a shape. *My* shape. It wasn't a completely believable clone—the image was slightly grainy and partially transparent—but it was definitely me, down to every last freckle.

"Good enough for them?" the Sandman asked.

Kail nodded, impressed. "Should be."

Tiny wrinkles formed around the Sandman's eyes as he concentrated on the figure. She—it—disappeared to the left, and the Sandman motioned for us to follow him in the opposite direction. A few more hurdles, and the end of the crystal obstacle course peeked through the openings. Mist licked at the very edges, but there was only silence, which set me on edge worse than if the robed figures of the Blood Army had moaned. We approached slowly, all of us wary. My heart beat wildly in contrast, and I barely drew breath for fear something would hear. The Sandman looked down at me with a small smile. *It'll be okay*, his smile said. *You can do this*. I hoped he was right.

Suddenly, the Blood Army wailed violently.

My head swam. *They saw us*. This was it. We wouldn't even make it to Rowan. I closed my eyes and waited for the blistering pain.

"Nora," the Sandman whispered. "It's working."

My eyes snapped open to find the Blood Army drifting away from us. The mist receded, leaving a straight line of sight to a row of trees. Only, they weren't really trees at all. Dozens of stumps of various heights lined a dirt path, and the tall, scraggly trees lay to the side like a hundred corpses. "It's supposed to look like that, right?" I asked with rising dread.

They didn't have to answer. The Sandman and Kail both wore matching looks of shock while Halven shook his head in disbelief.

"We'll buy you time," the Sandman said. "As much as we can."

I swallowed hard. "But—"

He kissed me, quick and passionate. "Go, before they realize they're chasing the wrong Nora."

The grin rose to the challenge, forcing my feet to move. I didn't want to go. Didn't want to fight. To fail. Forget looking like a strong, powerful leader. I needed help. What were they thinking, sending me after Rowan on my own? The darkness in me didn't care how afraid I was, and it kept me on a direct path all the way to the edge of the tree trunks.

A loud growl echoed from the other end of the path. I stumbled on a pile of crushed red berries, but the grin widened. It only took a moment to know why. A dog—the first nightmare I created—leapt off one of the tall crystal pillars and raced after the Blood Army. I didn't know how he found me. Didn't care. Relief that he made it out of the tower swept over me, only to vanish the moment I heard a familiar voice.

"I was beginning to think my informant was wrong," Rowan crowed.

My brain fired a million thoughts all at once, but I understood zero of them. *Hot.* It was so hot here. The ground dropped out from under me, but the darkness broke the fall.

Black talons dug into my muscles, fused with my bones. The grin twitched eagerly as my hand reached unconsciously for a thread.

A flick of the wrist.

A puff of sulfur.

Beside me stood a creature nearly as tall as I was. Its elongated body was made of layers of thick, overlapping triangular plates the color of new copper. Its nose came to a sharp point, capped in tiny burrs. I didn't have to say a word for it to identify the enemy. Red berries popped under its hooved feet as it barreled toward Rowan.

The darkness didn't bother watching what happened next. Instead, it slammed my hands against the nearest trunk, and the grin pursed in concentration. The knotted thread that emerged was bigger than the one in the museum, bigger than the one in the Blood Tower. It shifted around itself like a ball of snakes, feeding the entire tree-lined path. How was I ever going to find the right piece in time? I would need to destroy the entire landscape.

The nightmare that went after Rowan let out a death squeal that rang in my ears and flamed my anger. I almost didn't look, but I had to. Rowan's jagged, broken wings bent over her shoulders, spearing the nightmare through the eyes. *More time.* The need for it pounded through me almost as fast as my pulse.

Two more threads exploded before I realized I pulled them from my arm. An orange dragon the size of my palm zipped overhead. The other—a purple alien-like creature with oozing pustules and wheels for feet—cackled. It was hard throwing them at Rowan when I knew their inevitable fate. Harder still not to lunge in and take care of her myself. Sadly, the Weaver's powers didn't grant me the same ability the Sandman's did. The nightmares *were* my power, my strength, and they were doing their job. I had to do mine.

I pressed my palms against the nearest stump again, feeling desperately for a frayed end. A weakened middle. Anything that would tell me where to press. How to destroy it. An orange blur thwacked the side of my face. I gasped as the small dragon flopped over, dead, at my feet.

"You're just like your predecessor," Rowan called, sounding almost bored. "But what you've failed to realize is that I'm the Weaver's strongest creation. I couldn't kill him, but there are no nightmares that can kill me."

More time, more time, more time. I pressed my palm harder against the rough bark. *Where are you?*

Rowan's wings flared behind her. The black blood of her victims oozed down the jutting branches and dripped onto the red silk of her dress. She eyed the thread on my arm with hungry eyes. "Give me the threads, Dream Keeper. You never wanted them anyway."

As if the threads were what mattered. Without the magic in my veins, in my head, my body, the threads might as well be given to the Doll Maker to sew on buttons. "I'm not a Dream Keeper anymore," I said with all the bravado I could muster. "I'm the Lady of Nightmares, and you will stand down."

Her laugh was genuine and harsh. "So much confidence." She stalked toward me. "Though I suppose it's hard not to feel like you've won when your lapdogs are circling."

Lapdogs. The darkness sent out a silent thrum that left me feeling as if I were in the passenger seat again. "It's only fair we do this one-on-one," I forced myself to say. "No armies. No tricks. Just you and me."

The grin snarled at me, the threads convulsing against my skin. *Relax*, I snapped at it.

"Come on," I goaded, abandoning my search for the frayed thread. "Let's get this over with."

Rowan plowed into me before I saw her move and knocked me off my feet. My back hit the ground, the air whooshing from my lungs, as she reached for my exposed throat.

Immediately, I wrapped one of my legs around hers and flipped us so I was on top of her. And that was the last thing I remembered. The Sandman's training, everything I'd learned since, all of it swirled in technicolor as the darkness regained control. I blinked rapidly, trying to get my eyes to focus, but it was as if I was looking through a frosted window. Things faded. Blurred. I floated away to that place where I'd been every night after I'd fallen asleep in the Day World.

The next moment, everything was crystal clear. I was on my back, and the large dog I created was dragging Rowan down the path by her broken wing like she was nothing more than a stick to play fetch with. I staggered to my feet at the same moment Rowan grabbed one of the dog's back legs. His howl of pain would forever scar my mind. I screamed my rage and leaned forward to tackle her. That was as far as I got before the grin peeled upward, and the blackness shoved me down to my knees. Things swirled again. Nothingness. Everything. Hypersensitivity followed by numbness.

The grin grew and grew, and my face bunched against it. The dog continued howling as he dragged Rowan to me. Mentally, I beat against the spreading grin, tears welling in desperation, but it ignored me completely. With one hand still pressed against the ground, pinning the frayed thread down, my other palm slammed against Rowan's chest. My vision blurred, allowing only snapshots to register. Rowan's panic-filled gaze. The frayed thread pounding violently at both ends. Creaking wood. Screams—so many screams. My throat burned as if I was the one crying out, but my teeth were bared in agonized concentration.

The world washed over me like a tidal wave. The sharp ache of the alteration. The shredding pain of Rowan's touch on the exposed skin right above the Sandman's glove. Flashes of gold as the thread knitted back together. Each reattached fiber sent jolts of electricity through every cell of my body. The darkness swept over me again, numbing me to the pain.

And then something cold and wet brushed against my cheek.

My eyes flew open with a startled gasp only to find the massive dog nudging me with his nose. *No*. Rowan hadn't won, or I wouldn't be here. But where was she? I flew off the ground and spun around. My heart stopped. Instead of a field of broken trunks, there was a path neatly lined with bare trees. A fresh layer of red berries coated the ground. More noticeable was the tree now towering over me. Branches were missing and broken, its trunk covered with charred bark.

"Oh," was all I could say. Hundreds of ravens croaked in response, their wings beating like drums overhead.

Rowan. The tree. Rowan *was* the tree. I wanted her dead, but this—this was almost better. In death, she could become a martyr. In life, she could become a warning. But to be so peacefully rejoined with her former self seemed almost like a reward. I scanned the other trees—all of them connected—and knelt in the center of the path.

There was no crippling pain this time, no black moment. It

was as easy as adding the doorknob to the museum door or turning a cell into liquid silver. The grin looked greedily on as the darkness helped me ease pieces of their thread away and mold it into something different. They were slight changes, all carefully calculated. A sense of hearing for Rowan, a voice for the others, causing just enough pain for them each to cry out in a chorus of different pitches. Paired with the rhythm of raven wings, even I was delightfully horrified.

"Let this be a warning to anyone who thinks they can do better than Rowan," I said to the dog. He hunched on the dirt, licking his leg. "Thank you," I softly told him.

He let out a small whine and glared at Rowan's trunk. Eyes narrowed, he stood and lifted his leg.

I gaped, the shock quickly fading, and I laughed. A real laugh. It was a weightless thing, a helium balloon pulling me up, up, up. Every moment leading to this had sucked something away from me. Stolen seconds, minutes, hours of my life exchanged for fear and doubt. But now—now I was buoyed by relief. It was over.

It's never over, the grin jeered.

But it was. *This* was. That deserved a moment of quiet victory.

Chapter Thirty-One

Nora was halfway to the broken tree line when Halven slammed face-first into the ground beside me.

Sand burst from my satchel in a protective bubble as I looked around wildly for the cause. Kail lurched toward his brother. I ground my teeth and sent sand out in all directions, searching. It found our enemy in record time—an invisible humanoid nightmare. The fine coating of sand revealed his form, a masculine body with hammers instead of hands. The sand wrapped around him like a second skin. "Duck!" I shouted.

Kail crouched just as one of the hammers swung at the back of his head. I squeezed my fists, and the sand squeezed too. The nightmare buckled under the pressure. He lay on the ground as stiff as a board. With another wave of sand scouring the area, I straddled the nightmare and slammed my knees into his upper arms.

"Kill it," Kail urged. He carefully flipped Halven over, examining him for wounds. "What are you waiting for?"

"Answers." My sand returned empty-handed, and I met Kail's angry stare. "Rowan knows too much about our movements, and I want to know how."

Kail flicked a look over my shoulder. "Not the best time for an inquisition."

I followed his gaze to find the Blood Army backtracking. They funneled straight for the fallen trees, and a curse flew off my tongue. "Watch this thing," I snapped.

"Where are you going?" he asked, laying Halven's head carefully on the ground.

"Watching Nora's back like you promised we would."

I lifted myself off the nightmare with a building sense of purpose and drew in a breath, letting it out slowly. With it, my qualms faded. I became the Lord of Dreams—a powerful being responsible for defending both worlds. For protecting them. Such was my penance for what the Weaver and I did when we banished Mare long ago, but this was about so much more. This was about Nora.

I stepped out from the shelter of crystal pillars, and the Blood Army paused. *Decisions*, I thought. Me or Nora. But orders were orders. Half of the robed figures shifted toward me, while the rest continued along their original path. It didn't matter—they would all be dead in a moment. Sand poured from my satchel to circle my hands. A silver glowing orb of pure dream magic hardened around both my hands, and sparks of navy blue popped with anticipation. I drew myself up and shot into the center of the red mist. The other sand I carried flew out in an attempt at snuffing the painful cloud, but there was too much of it.

That didn't matter either.

My lips curled in vengeful triumph, and I crossed my wrists in front of my chest. When I threw them back down to my sides, silver and blue light exploded through the Blood Army. I winced against the brightness as their moaning died off. My chest panged with the sudden explosion of power. I rubbed at my tattoo, reveling in the fact that I wasn't depleted like I would've been months ago. When the white light finally faded, I stared down at the entire Blood Army. Dead. A quick snap of my fingers and the last bit of sand I had domed the bodies, trapping their mist.

"That would've been helpful back at the tower," Kail screamed from the other side of the pillars.

I cast a wistful glance at the tree line before rejoining Kail and our prisoner. Nora was okay. If not, I would feel her die. And then I would beg Kail to kill me too, because Kail as the new Sandman was better than living with such a destructive loss. *She's fine.*

"I'm serious," Kail said the moment I was beside him again. "We waited hours to leave when you could've done *that.*"

"We needed time to make a plan," I said. *I needed time to mend things with Nora.* A selfish thing, I knew, but a few hours wouldn't have made a difference. "Besides, I wasn't supposed to be helping, remember? Nora made that quite clear."

Kail huffed. "What do you call leveling the entire Blood Army?"

I cut him a hard look and knelt beside the still-glimmering

nightmare.

"Whatever," Kail mumbled.

Halven chuckled, and I jerked at the sound. "You're awake." He held his arms up as if to say *obviously*. I shook my head to clear the ringing in my ears. "Has he said anything?"

"We were waiting for you," Kail said, shrugging. "You're the one with questions."

I rolled my shoulders. Of course Kail would still be difficult. "Who told Rowan where we were?" I asked with an exasperated sigh.

Silence.

"Do either of you have a preferred method of torture?" I asked Kail and Halven.

"Break a finger?" Kail suggested, half-hearted. "Rip out a toenail, maybe?"

I stretched my fingers in an attempt to control myself. It was no wonder Nora broke his mask—too long around him and I would probably break his *neck*. "Are you going to help with this?"

Kail crossed his arms. "Why do you assume I enjoy torturing things?"

"I *assume* you want to know who Rowan has spying on you," I snapped.

Kail opened his mouth to reply when the nightmare whispered, "Mara. It was Mara."

"Wow," Kail scoffed. "Just threatening bodily harm got him to spill his guts."

"Hush," Halven said, leaning forward.

"How did Mare know?" I asked.

Silence. Then: "I don't know."

That was his answer for every following question I asked.

Where was Mare? He didn't know. Was Rowan alone in the trees? He didn't know. I pushed away from him with a strangled scream. There had to be more. Why would he know Mare told Rowan our location and not know anything else? I ran my hands through my hair and looked out at the tree line. The now *unbroken* tree line. I froze.

"Interesting," Kail contemplated. That wasn't the word I would have chosen. "Maybe she put them back up to find the one remaining stump."

A large, shaggy nightmare broke through the trees. I searched for Nora's feelings but only got a quick flash of exhaustion. The dog-like creature ambled away in the opposite direction, but nothing else moved. "I'm going down there," I said, the not knowing finally breaking me.

"Don't." Kail stepped up beside me. "Nora made him."

Nora made that thing? I shook the thought away. She was learning her magic, which included making nightmares. Kail nudged me with his elbow and motioned a few yards down, where another figure walked straight for us. I recognized that purple sweater. My heart ricocheted in my chest. There was no holding me back this time. I ran toward Nora as fast as my legs could carry me. The closer I got, the louder a hundred different screams became—unlike those of the Blood Army, but no less fearsome. I scanned the area behind her, waiting for something else to emerge from the trees. Nothing came.

Nora stopped where she was and waited for me. A tired smile tugged at the corners of her mouth. Her arms circled me when I reached her, holding tight. "It's done," she breathed.

"Yes." I ran a hand over the back of her head, toying with the ends of her hair. "What's that noise?"

"The trees."

"The trees?" I asked.

"I changed them." She sighed and eased out of my embrace. "This is the Nightmare Realm, and there's only one way to survive."

"One way?"

Something hardened in her eyes. "Rule by fear."

Concern flickered through me at the ease in which she said it. A bit tired sounding, yes, but the words flowed from her mouth as if they meant nothing. "It was Mare," I said, changing the subject.

She winced. "Mara? What was her?"

"She told Rowan where we would be."

"But how did she know?" Nora said loudly, eyes wide. "How do *you* know?"

I motioned behind us. "We caught an assassin."

"Did he say anything else?" she asked, quickly regaining her calm demeanor.

"Unfortunately not."

Nora hung her head and placed the top of it against my chest. "I suppose that means there's no time to catch our breaths, huh? What are we going to do about Mara?"

"We?" I asked.

She squirmed uncomfortably. "You worked together with the Weaver to stop her the first time, didn't you?"

Yes. And that was the thing that finally destroyed our relationship. "We did. I like hearing you call us 'us' though."

"We can do this, can't we?" She squeezed my hand. "Bring the realms together. Or, as together as they used to be."

"We can do anything." I took her cheeks in my hands and

lifted her head so I could see her face. "Including breathe, Nora. We can't run after Mare without thinking things through." She wasn't a nightmare—she was an Ancient. An Ancient that knew how to escape the Ever Safe where the rest of the old beings slumbered.

"Tell me what to do, and I'll do it," she whispered.

I was quiet for a moment as different scenarios played through my mind. We needed to know where Mare was and what she was after. If we could take her to the Day World again, she would be trapped. The alterations the Weaver and I did were still there—still strong. If Nora didn't have the dream in her, Mare wouldn't have made it back the first time.

"Give me the dream," I said haltingly.

"What?" she asked, confused.

"It's the reason Mare could come back with you. Both Nightmare and Dream magic together—"

"Yes," she said quickly. Understanding smoothed her features. "Take it."

I pressed the pads of my middle fingers against her temples, my palms shielding her eyes, and felt a pang of regret. This dream was what brought us together and eventually was what tore Nora apart. I was sorry I ever asked her to hold it—but at the same time, if I hadn't, we never would've fallen in love. No matter what Nora became, I trusted her with this information. It hadn't occurred to me to take the dream before, because—even if Nora could access it—she would never let the nightmares into the Day World. Not with her family there. This wasn't about trust, though. I closed my eyes and called my magic home.

It raced frantically to meet my call, and when I opened my eyes, a flickering orb floated in the air between us. I hurried to cup it in my hands without looking down at the sand-made images swirling inside. Without another Dreamer, it would be reabsorbed into me. But a Dreamer with a true heart and a true mind could fuel the magic themselves.

"I won't spy or step foot in your realm, so you can build a name for yourself, but give me use of Halven," I said quickly.

"Halven?" she blurted. "I promised I would put him and Kail back together, and I just proved I could do that."

I took a long breath. "No one knows that but the four of us. Everyone will think Halven is off doing what Halven does while Kail stays to help you. I need eyes here if I'm going to figure out what Mare is doing and how to stop her."

"Use Baku," she said defensively.

"Baku doesn't speak," I explained. "And everyone knows we have a relationship."

She chewed her bottom lip. "Fine. But only until you know what's going on."

"Of course." I kissed the top of her head. "Kail and Halven are where you left them."

Nora's gaze snapped up. "Aren't you coming?"

"No." I held the orb closer. "I have to do something with this."

She eyed the glowing sphere hidden in my hands and nodded. "But I'll see you soon?"

"Soon," I said, though I wasn't sure how long things would take. I smiled anyway. "You can do this, Lady Nightmare. Go on. They're waiting."

Nora toyed with the threads near her wrist until the worried gleam faded from her eyes. Her shoulders slowly squared. "I can do this," she repeated softly to herself and walked away from me.

I didn't watch her long. She was safe, she was strong, and she had allies.

Instead, I let the beach pull me home, my magic already skimming over the cords in search of one in particular. One that Nora would never dream of hurting, in case dealing with Mare affected Nora the same way it had the Weaver.

"What is *that*?" Katie cried, shocked.

I spun to face her, surprised by her presence enough to forget my search for her cord. "Katie. I was just coming to see you." This felt wrong. A betrayal, almost, but I also knew it was the best option for both worlds, so I held her gaze. "I have something important to ask you."

Chapter Thirty-Two

The walk to the Keep was fueled by adrenaline. Excitement. Anticipation. After I met back up with Kail and Halven, after they killed the assassin, everything became a blur. My eyes focused on what was in front of me—a clear pathway to the Keep. Nightmares bowed when I passed, Kail close at my heels. *Word spreads fast*, I thought but didn't look away from my destination despite the urge to take in each of their faces. The Lady of Nightmares would rule by fear, and no one feared a thing they knew. I watched Kail from my peripheral vision and understood him a bit better. We were all more than the face we presented to the world. I was Nora to my family. To the Sandman. Maybe to Kail and Halven. To everyone else, I would be something untouchable.

"Welcome home," Kail said with a small smile.

Another step up an incline, and I saw it. The Keep. Half walls rose throughout the entire lawn where before there was nothing. No, not nothing. The Sandman said the Keep was much bigger before his battle with the Weaver. I studied the lines that formed room after room and smiled. An imposing palace for an imposing position.

"Have them continue rebuilding," I told Kail. "I want it completed within the month."

Kail's eyes widened. "You could finish it yourself in a fraction of the time."

I could, yes. If I wanted a palace made of spies. The walls here could be like those of the Blood Tower—alive with nightmares—but I didn't want to be watched. First my mother, then the Sandman in my dreams, and here, it was Kail. Defensive measures would be taken to protect myself, but the walls themselves would be painstakingly built using whatever materials my nightmares could find. I wove my way through the construction. It seemed like a waste of resources with Mara still out there somewhere, but I would rule this place and these creatures in my own way. And I would do it without a permanent audience.

"Have them continue," I repeated and paused at the door to the Keep. The darkness grinned wide along with me. "Stay here."

"Lady." Kail bowed and took two steps back.

Inside, the stillness of the Keep washed over me, and I took my first easy breath. *Mine.* Finally. Lights flickered to life as I shut the door, revealing four other doorways and a set of spiraling stone stairs that wrapped around the entire interior. I stared at the hatch above, knowing exactly what was there, but before I ascended them, I peeked into each annexed room. The closest had a bed covered with a soft, gold-spun blanket, a chest similar to the one Kail had in the museum, and a bookshelf full of trinkets. The next room was arranged as some sort of a macabre living room—the moving heads of nightmares mounted to the walls would be the first thing to go—and the third housed only stairs leading to the basement.

The final room was instantly my favorite. A large oak table ran the length of each wall with floor-to-ceiling cabinets on either side of the doorframe. Papers covered nearly every inch of the table, and worn bits of charcoal crunched beneath my feet. The walls played host to hundreds of charcoal sketches of nightmares. Their eyes seemed to follow my every step, though I knew it was only an illusion. I plucked the nearest drawing off the wall, and a sense of peace settled over me. The Weaver's technique was good—more than good. Every imagined light reflected off a sketched bubble with a tiny person trapped inside. While I wasn't sure if the inhabitant was part of the nightmare or a rendering of what the bubble would do to Dreamers, I felt every ounce of the Weaver's creativity. It shook hands with the artist in me, eager to pick up a pencil. A brush. Anything that would get the sudden rush of creative thoughts onto paper. I smiled, biting my bottom lip.

There was work to do.

Nightmares to weave.

Mara to hunt.

Mara to kill.

These drawings would help until she was taken care of. The Weaver spent eons at this, so they were undoubtedly valuable outlines. Perfect for learning the loom. I set the bubble drawing on the table and slipped from the room, reluctant to go. But there was something else I had to see. Touch. Feel.

The hatch to the domed upper level creaked open. I slipped inside and tried not to remember the feeling of the knife as it slid into the Weaver's chest. The lingering scent of sulfur helped clear my head, but the rust-colored stain coating the floor like paint nearly sent me spiraling. *Blood.* This was the place where the old Nora died and I was born.

The loom creaked, seemingly aching for my touch just as much as I ached to touch it. The threads vibrated against my skin when at last I reached out and made contact with the machine. *More*, they seemed to say.

"Yes. So many more," I whispered, though I wasn't sure what they wanted more of. More of me? More nightmares? It didn't matter—I would give them both. I would give them everything.

The bench was still knocked over from where the Weaver once stood to face me, so I picked it up and sat behind the loom. A flash of power stole my breath as I ran my hands along the aged wood. It felt better than anything I'd done with my magic so far. Like I was finally alive again after months on my deathbed. A sigh rattled my body with a breath that wasn't mine, ripping the ecstasy away. I felt it with every drop of blood in my veins. Freezing. Burning. Tearing through me.

Then a voice slowly emerged inside me, gentle, playful even, but carrying a thunderstorm on its back. I recognized it at once.

"Lady, Lady, quite contrary," it crooned, "how does your darkness grow? With bloody claws and snapping jaws and pretty nightmares all in a row."

My blood drained to my feet in one painful whoosh, and I gripped the loom so I wouldn't fall from the stool. The darkness thrummed. Swelled. Invaded and conquered every bit of my body. It couldn't be…

"Weaver?" I croaked.

"Hello, Keeper," the grin replied.

NIGHT WARDEN

Chapter One

R*ule by fear.*

Nightmares respected a ruthless, vicious, unforgiving leader, and it was easy enough to wear those traits as armor. Too easy perhaps. No one knew my decisions were made by asking myself: *what would the Weaver do?* Nor did they know I got the answer right from the horse's mouth.

Rule by fear, I told myself again.

If the nightmares didn't fear me, they were going to make certain I feared *them*. Whatever initial notion I had of making the Nightmare Realm a better place was now a distant memory. Maybe one worth revisiting down the road, one small change at a time, but first I had to bring each and every living thing to heel.

"Nora," Kail said from the corner of his mouth. He stood on my right, arms crossed, gaze ever vigilant. "Sometime today?"

I took a deep breath from where I stood atop the half-completed palace roof. The building was supposed to be finished within a month, not a month and three days. There had to be repercussions. Already, the last two days were more productive thanks to my new form of motivation. It didn't bother me, what I was doing, but it bothered me that it *didn't*. Killing should never be effortless.

"The palace still isn't finished. You know what that means," I called to the nightmares below in my most authoritative voice. It was stern and unyielding, making me feel every bit the villain.

The nightmares building the palace filled the lawn, stretching out in every direction. They were big brutes, mainly. Trolls who doubled as security, a couple giants with ladders grown into their lumpy, jaundiced skin, and a pack of garden gnomes that worked as well and as hard as any colony of ants. Wyverns were outfitted with ropes to carry materials back and forth from wherever they were mined, the digging done by lanky, alien-esc creatures with extendable arms that ended in curved paddles. A smattering of nondescript nightmares helped in whatever way they could, but mostly they just got in the way.

Yesterday, it was one of those that suffered the consequences.

A medium-sized nightmare with black fur, run through with pink scars, hunched and crooked, murdered with a single bullet from my stepfather's liberated gun. The day before it was a gnome in a red hat, and a giant the morning before that. The choices weren't intentional. I simply held the firearm up and sighted the first forehead that came into view. My aim was far from perfect, but the bullets never missed. Not when I wove them on the Weaver's loom to be sure of it.

I didn't bother explaining what would happen next. They knew. All of them knew. I lifted my arm, aimed at the first thing I saw and squeezed the trigger. A troll flew backward from the impact, blood spraying his neighbors. No one moved. Their eyes were trained on me, sharp as daggers.

"Tomorrow, it will be two of you," I promised before I passed the gun to Kail and turned from the crowd.

"Two, huh?" he asked. I leapt through a hole in the roof and into an empty room with him close on my heels. "At this rate, you won't have anyone left to finish the palace."

I leveled a stare at him. His eyes flickered almost lazily, color after color, as he looked at me from beneath his lashes. The white curved beak of his half mask brushed his chest. A sarcastic smile lifted my lips. "Then I'll make more."

That's my girl, the Weaver cooed inside my head.

I blanched at the sound. It was a near constant thing that sponged away my patience and my sanity. Talking, warning, tormenting. Sometimes I woke to him chanting eerie rhymes, old songs twisted and darkened. Other times, it was flashes of emotion that cut through me like a sword, though I didn't think those were intentional. My days were full of commentary. *Criticism.* Praise. Praise that I considered criticism. Having my life narrated by the man who ruined it was a special kind of hell.

"Feeling alright, Lady?" Kail asked. His words dripped with something like concern, something like accusation.

I waved a hand at the construction overhead, focusing my anger on that—*that* I could change. "I will be when there isn't a giant hole over my head big enough for anything or anyone to creep through."

"Yes." Kail pursed his lips and turned his gaze upward. "It's certainly a security risk."

I said nothing. It was easier that way. All the things I couldn't say, the things I wasn't ready to tell, would feel smaller as soon as I reached the art room. With a pencil in my hand and a blank page before me, things felt right again. Normal. A lie, but one I clung to. Because eventually I would have to tell Kail about the voice in my head. The Sandman too—the Sandman *first*. But not yet. Not until he came with news of Mara. I would let myself pretend there was a possibility of getting rid of the Weaver until the very moment one of them told me otherwise.

"Would you like to go out today?" Kail asked. "Explore? Create? Maim? Anything, really, that doesn't involve you holed up in the Keep again."

All excellent ideas. If only leaving didn't make the Weaver more active. "My strength is my thread." The existing coil of black thread, flecked with gold, tightened affectionately around my arm. "If we're going to take down Mara, I'll need as much of it as I can get."

Kail sighed, defeated, and held out Paul's gun. "Where do you want this thing?"

I looked down at the Day World weapon and something inside me wriggled uncomfortably. If the threads were my strength, I should be showing them off. Embracing the power of the Nightmare Realm instead of leaning on what I knew from my old life. "I don't need it anymore," I said carefully. It was time I killed more creatively.

Kail's eyes flicked faster in response.

Rule by fear.

I *was* fear. A Lady made from it as much as controlled by it.

My heart thudded heavily. I hadn't realized before now that acting as the cruel, unmerciful lady would slowly stain my heart. It would burn the edges black, leaving the smallest sliver of red beating at its center. There, Nora lived. *There*, I cared. I loved. In that tiny pocket, I felt pain and regret and even the occasional joy. Mostly, I feared. Feared that one day, I would feel nothing at all.

You will always feel, the Weaver said in a smug voice. *One day, you will feel as I have felt. Then you will understand me as I now understand you.*

New terror seized me. Maybe he was right, and one day I would wake up very much the monster he was, because when I killed those nightmares outside, I felt nothing. No regret, no shame. No *anything*. How long until I was like him? *Truly* like him—the Nightmare Lord that killed my friends and family. *No.* I would never allow myself to be that savage. I was the Lady of Nightmares, but I was also human.

Humanity in an inhumane world, the Weaver mused. *I tried that as well.*

Not hard enough, I thought back, my teeth bared.

Kail waved a hand in front of my face. He tilted his head and eyed me suspiciously. "Is there a problem?"

"No." I jumped away from him, walking quickly into the nearest room. "You're dismissed."

I slammed the door shut in his face and slumped against the heavy wood. Wyverns soared over the open courtyard on the way to pick up their first load of the day. The Keep stood before me, surrounded by a wide circle of grass. I had planted tall, neon-colored flowers around its base to brighten the courtyard, but the fact that they shot poison darts didn't hurt either. If anyone other than Kail and Halven made it into my private sanctuary, it would be the last thing they did.

Rule by fear, I promised myself again and again. Fear would keep my body alive. The rest I needed to protect another way. Bottle it up and keep it safe.

You're wrong, the Weaver said wistfully.

"Shut up," I snarled.

I tried, he said simply. *For him, I did.*

"I will dig you out of there with my bare hands," I threatened. Empty words, we both knew, because I wasn't even able to block him out.

My hands twitched, eager for the relief drawing would bring. I closed my eyes for a moment to center myself. Everything would be fine. Soon, the Sandman would come back, and we would make everything right again. I nodded to myself, and with a deep breath, strode straight for the Keep.

Everything would be fine.

It would.

It won't.

Deep down, I knew my last thought was the most probable.

One month later

Time was strange.

A second could feel like a lifetime.

A lifetime could feel like a second.

The quiet made it feel as if everything was peaceful and calm in the Dream Realm when that was the furthest thing from the truth. My magic vibrated mercilessly beneath the domed barrier that kept the nightmares out. I felt it in my bones. My breastbone hummed constantly beneath the tattoo of a crescent moon. The navy blue and silver flecks rising from its center flowed down my arms. They had multiplied, become denser, and moved along my skin with an almost frantic edge. It made me want to scream to break the tense silence, but I didn't. Instead, I shoved down the anxiety prowling inside me like a caged beast, so I could channel it later.

Mare had been quiet too. *Too quiet.*

For nearly two weeks now.

That was also a deception. She had spent the majority of the last two months waging mental warfare against both Nora and myself. Her last act toward me was to create a straw man full of nightmare rats, which she then left at the edge of my realm on fire. Mare was fast and deadly, but she was never *quiet.* This long break was simply meant to heighten the anticipation while she schemed. I hated that it was working.

Fingers snapped next to my ear. "Earth to Sandy."

I blinked at the sudden noise and found Katie standing beside me. How long had I stood there, staring blankly ahead? "Sorry." I cleared my throat. "I was…"

"Pining for Nora again?" Katie rolled her eyes. "It's obvious. Really, you have bigger problems, don't you think?"

No.

Yes.

True to my word, I hadn't stepped foot in the Nightmare Realm since Nora defeated Rowan. It was for the best. In a short amount of time, Nora rebuilt the palace entirely, created loyal nightmares of her own, and convinced enough of the others not to cross her. From what I gathered, she was finally able to sleep with both eyes shut.

Halven, being a nightmare of few words, never offered any details when he came to deliver news. In return, I didn't ask how Nora managed to accomplish so much, so fast. I wanted her to tell me herself when we saw each other again. *Soon,* I prayed to the stars. This distance made me feel like a stranger to her despite logic telling me that was absurd.

"No," I finally said to Katie. I hadn't been thinking of her sister *right* then. "I was wondering if the proverbial dam was about to burst."

Katie snorted and plopped down on the edge of my pavilion like she owned the place. "Pretty sure it's been leaking for a while now. At least, it has if your mysterious informant is telling the truth. Rumbling landscapes. Hundreds of nightmares disappearing from the grid. Sounds like time's wearing thin."

I said nothing. Until Halven found Mare, there was nothing to be done. She was an Ancient and there was no rushing into this if we wanted to win. Mare had it all—strength, speed, intelligence. We needed to catch her off guard before she found a way to open the Ever Safe, which was easier said than done, or it wouldn't only be Mare that wanted to crush us. There were fourteen other Ancients, most of them larger, stronger, and undoubtedly more pissed off after so long in captivity. I ran my hands through my hair and blew out a slow breath.

"Bring up the map again." Katie flicked her hand at the sand and leaned back on her elbows, only to fly up with a shriek.

Baku lifted his head from beneath the mound of pillows, blinking sleepy eyes, and I laughed.

"Oh, yeah," Katie snapped. Baku glared at Nora's sister and used his elephant trunk to pull the pillows close again. "*So* funny."

"Didn't you tell me you were getting used to this place?" I asked, trying not to smile too wide.

"This place. Not..." She pointed to the yawning chimera. "Is he *always* here?"

More often than not these days…

"Nora never got used to him either," I said wistfully. She hadn't gotten the chance, but I was sure they would've gotten along. Before she became the Lady of Nightmares and the ruler of Baku's food supply.

"Cool, cool," Katie said. Queen of sarcasm, as always. "So, the map."

I sighed and lifted my hands, palms up. Sand rose, a million glittering flecks forming an incomplete map of the Nightmare Realm. Every landscape I knew of was represented. The rest were filled in piece by piece when Halven checked in. The outer lines were jagged and uneven. The Dream Realm was at one end, bordered on all sides by nightmares.

"Fewer areas are glowing," Katie contemplated.

I nodded. The places we'd ruled out as Mare's hiding place were faded while the places she might be gave off a faint blue glow. Unfortunately, the closer to the Ever Safe the map went, the more options were left open. The Weaver wouldn't have hidden the key to the safe that close, but—not for the first time—I wished he was here to ask *where*. I clasped my hands together behind my back to keep from fidgeting. Knowing the key's location would put my mind at ease, because if Mare didn't know where the key was, that meant she was going to have to break in. When she broke out all those years ago, Baku following, we sealed that exit with magic and buried it under an icy landscape.

"Halven stopped by while you were awake and cleared an entire sector," I explained before Katie accused me of zoning out again.

"The palace looks safe."

"Yes," I agreed carefully. The building at the center of the Nightmare Realm was surrounded by devoted landscapes, and routinely patrolled by equally loyal nightmares.

"I want to see my sister," Katie said abruptly. She met my gaze, her brown eyes hard and unrelenting. "Take me there."

I barely suppressed a groan. "We've been over this."

"I don't care what awful things I see," she insisted, "and I certainly don't care if Nora *wants* me there. I'm her sister. You don't abandon family."

"I…" I promised Nora. Not only that I would keep Katie away but that I wouldn't go into the Nightmare Realm until we found Mare. We went through enough, Nora and I, and we needed to heal. Not make the wounds deeper. "Please don't ask me to break promises to your sister."

She folded her arms. "Fine. Keep your promises, but I'm *going* to see her."

"Stars." I rubbed a hand over my face. "You're as stubborn as she is."

"You mean, she's as stubborn as I am," Katie said with a satisfied smirk. "I'm older."

Baku groaned from within the pavilion, echoing my own sentiment. Katie had grown on me the last two months, more than I thought she would, but my penchant for humor was drained dry. First Nora inherited the Weaver's power when she killed him, then she snuck back into the Nightmare Realm behind my back. Those two betrayals were enough to dim even the loudest laughter, but it didn't end there. Rowan was taken care of—reunited with her stump amid a now-wailing path of trees—but Mare was very much *not.* The Hours weren't going to wait forever before making good on their threat to dethrone

Nora if Mare wasn't dealt with. They probably weren't alone in that mindset either. I turned my attention back to the map.

"Sandman," said a low, rasping voice.

Katie bolted behind me, and I sighed. "Hello, Halven. I thought we agreed you wouldn't come if a certain person was visiting."

"I have important news." He tilted his head, moonlight sneaking beneath his wide hat. The bright red lips painted on his mask were curled in a permanently cold smirk and a red scalloped design circled where the mask's eyeholes should've been. "Hello," he added to Katie as if it would erase any sense of threat from him.

She poked my back with her finger. "Well?"

"Halven is fine," I told her, growing wearier by the second. When had I slept last?

"That has to be the creepiest mask I've ever seen in my life. Can he even see?" she asked as if he weren't standing right in front of her.

Before I could remind her not to offend our ally, Halven spoke, his words forced as always. "I see many things. As for the mask, I believe that was the intent."

"Five stars to the Weaver," she stuttered.

"What's the news?" I asked before the conversation could sink any lower.

Halven was suddenly at the far edge of the map near the Ever Safe, pointing at a landscape full of metal globes. I tapped it with a finger, and it dimmed.

"No." Halven's excitement rippled around him. "She's there."

Baku immediately leapt from the pavilion. He barely spared Halven a glance after his first few visits. I supposed it was because Baku knew that, if the worlds ended, so would he, and that was slightly more important than a full belly. "Stay away from it," I said calmly. "We can't tip Mare off that we know where she is."

"Now what happens? What do we do?" Katie asked, chewing nervously on her thumbnail.

"*We* don't do anything." I took her by the arms and looked her in the eye. "Stay put."

"I—"

"Katherine Gallagher, I swear on my power that if you try to follow us…"

"Fine." She wrenched herself from my grip and threw herself onto the vacant pile of pillows. "I wouldn't want to be a liability or anything. I *am* a weak, pitiful mortal after all."

I raised a brow at Halven in a way that let him know that I knew she was a handful. Apparently, all of the Gallagher women were. I made for the barrier between realms, grabbing my full satchel of sand on the way and throwing its strap across my chest. "Don't walk with me," I said to Halven. "It's too soon to blow your cover."

Halven was already headed toward a different landscape, my magic allowing him—and only him—to pass through.

The soft clack of moving loom pieces filled the air. I closed my eyes where I sat beneath the domed half of the Keep and let the sound fill my head too. Magic in. Thread out. Mindlessness was key. The wooden pieces were smooth beneath my hands as I worked. The machine moved flawlessly, drawing from the darkness inside me to create a pile of newly woven nightmares that coiled at my feet. The images I drew a few days ago floated through my mind. A brood of headless chickens gave way to an angry old woman in a cardigan with a forked tongue and then a winged man brandishing an ax.

Magic in.

Thread out.

Magic i—

Are you going to do this little chant every *time you weave? I must tell you, it's extremely irritating,* the Weaver drawled.

I blanched, my hands jerking away from the loom. Two months with a sarcastic, murderous, psychopath in my head and—

I resent that last bit.

"Shut up!" I screamed so loud it echoed off the ceiling.

"I didn't say anything," Kail called back.

My eyes flew open, but there was no sign of my somewhat reluctant right-hand. I scanned the room, knowing he was nearby. Not because I'd heard him—because he was never far. Ever. Which was as infuriating as it was a comfort. Movement caught my eye across the room. Kail's black boots dangled through the hatch that led to the open half of the Keep's roof, and the bottom of his black trench coat hung to one side of his thighs.

"What are you doing up there?" I asked.

He was quiet for a moment. "Enjoying the corpse-free view."

"Go enjoy it somewhere else," I grumbled. Hundreds of human-like nightmares impaled on stakes greeted me from atop the hill yesterday morning, their silhouettes lining the horizon like macabre scarecrows. Mara's choice of creature wasn't lost on me—it was a personal threat. The bodies had barely been gone twenty-four hours now. Not long enough for jokes.

"It's almost as if you don't enjoy my company, Lady Nightmare." He casually propped one foot up on the opposite edge of the hatch. "Though I know that's a lie."

I slipped from the stool as quietly as I could and tip-toed up to the grey light filtering in. With quick movements, I grabbed his still-dangling foot and yanked. Kail tumbled through the opening in a flurry of flapping fabric and curse words.

He landed flat on his back, his embroidered coat pooled out beneath him, and he stared up at me with his ever-changing irises—blue, red, black, yellow, green, and every color in between. A dimple formed on one side of his warm brown cheeks. "I'm beginning to think this is a form of foreplay for you."

"You wish," I snapped. I was still happily in love with the Sandman. Whom I hadn't seen since the day I took the Nightmare Realm. I ached for him every minute, and I had to remind myself that we had, quite literally, forever. In the meantime, it was important to firmly establish my rule over the nightmares. Then, when the Sandman did come with news of Mara, I had news of my own to share. I had to tell him that the Weaver was alive and well inside my head. I cringed at the thought of that conversation.

"You don't have to try quite so hard." Kail's fingers grazed my ankle, and I kicked him in the ribs. "I was kidding," he wheezed. "Totally kidding."

You have so much pent-up anger, the Weaver said with an undercurrent of amusement. *He could relieve some of it.*

"I swear to God if you don't stop—"

"Okay, okay." Kail eyed me curiously and sat up. "I was just trying to lighten the mood."

I spun back to the loom, to my work, so he wouldn't see the pink in my cheeks and think it was caused by his *joke*. Losing my temper and speaking out loud to the Weaver was becoming too common. Exhaustion settled into my bones. How long had I worked? An hour? A day? *Two?* The loom had a way of stealing time from me.

Kail stood and dusted his jacket off. "Lady," he said softly when he was finished. "Please rest."

"Since when is the word '*please*' part of your vocabulary?" I blew out a harsh breath. "Anyway, you know I can't."

"You've been weaving for a very long time." He stepped up to my side and eyed the giant pile of new thread coiled on the floor.

"Mara…" I explained, my voice hollow.

"Where will you put it all?"

I touched my arm where thread already covered so much space that my skin was barely visible. "It's not for wearing."

"You can't keep creating nightmares this fast." His tone was so unlike him. Gentle. Sensible. "There's a balance—"

"*There's a balance,*" I mocked. "I hate to break it to you, but I'm an Aquarius, not a Libra."

"You know I don't understand these references," he said, folding his arms.

"The zodiac sign with a woman holding scales. *Balance.* Nevermind." I waved my hand through the air, brushing the conversation away, and filed the idea away for possible nightmares. The zodiac signs would be interesting to work with. A man-eating crab, a fire-breathing bull. The twins could be interesting to work with…

"Nora." Kail took my chin between his index finger and thumb and lifted my face. When I met his gaze, he lifted a brow. "Do you hear yourself? Not only are you speaking nonsense, but you're extremely distracted."

I swatted his hand away. I thought I was doing a decent job of hiding those facts, but apparently not. "So?"

"You've been off since you defeated Rowan, and it's getting worse."

I approached the pile of thread, giving up on the idea of losing myself in more work, and lifted the weighty material in my arms. With a quick thrum of magic, the part nearest the loom eased away, leaving the rest attached to the loom to finish later. I cradled the humming unborn nightmares as if they were a swaddled newborn baby. "I'm fine, Kail." I strode around him to the spiral staircase leading down to the main floor of the Keep.

Are you? the Weaver teased.

"You are most decidedly *not* fine." Kail stormed after me. "I can't help you if you won't talk to me."

"We don't talk. We bicker." I reached the bottom of the stairs and bumped a door open with my hip. Inside, all the Weaver's charcoal drawings were gone, used up as I learned the loom. Most of his expertly-done sketches existed out there in the Nightmare Realm as physical manifestations, but a few of the more impressive ones I hung onto. It was my own drawings that covered the walls and tables now. Our styles were different—my lines cleaner—but no matter how many new creations I produced and hung, the voice in my head wouldn't allow me to appreciate my art. The process, yes, but the Weaver was a perfectionist. The moment I thought a design was finished, he ripped apart its flaws.

"Nora," Kail practically begged.

I opened the nearest cabinet and carefully set the new thread in beside the last pile I wove. "Leave me alone."

If only I could, the Weaver said wistfully at the same time Kail said, "Just tell me what's wrong and I'll—"

"Get out!" I screamed at the former. Kail paled, and my anger drained, leaving me even more tired than before. "Seriously, I'm fine," I said in a much calmer voice. "Okay?"

His eyes narrowed suspiciously.

"You're right. I should get some rest," I added to appease him. The last thing I needed was him catching on that I wasn't alone in my own head before I could talk to the Sandman about it. Kail was too shrewd—which was helpful when it was directed at the nightmares that came to beg favors, but generally speaking, his mouth was too big and his words too loose. "I'll be better after I sleep."

He stood stiff as a statue when I eased past him and fled from the tower. Outside, the muted sky illuminated my new palace. It was worth waiting an extra ten days for the nightmares to finish. Unless you asked one of the nightmares I killed, though that was worth it too. It struck fear into the masses. Maybe I would get a sign: *No assassination attempts in nineteen days.*

I stood in the circular courtyard, the Keep surrounded by palace walls on all sides. Kail was the only one I allowed into the courtyard or the Keep, and that was mostly due to necessity. Emergencies I needed to be aware of while weaving, rooms swept out. Kail had become quite handy with a broom.

I thought you were going to sleep, the Weaver taunted.

"What do you care?" I growled under my breath and shoved through the door into a vacant room. Most of the rooms were empty since I had nothing to fill them with. I rarely spent time outside of the Keep or my bedroom, so it didn't bother me apart from the annoying echo it created.

I wove through the maze-like corridors of gleaming black stone lit with torches bolted to the walls. No part of the new structure was made from nightmares—I wouldn't risk them spying on me—so I had to get creative with functionality. To keep the palace lit, I created a small, easy-access landscape of cacti that belched flames from purple flowers. It was a rather pretty sight if you ignored the sounds and smells. Luckily the fire itself was odorless.

"Lady Nightmare."

I winced at the voice—child-like, yet prim and proper at the same time. The owner, one of the Weaver's remaining designs, bustled toward me. She was swathed in layers of light pink fabric stained red with blood. The garment hid her figure completely, wrapping her from neck to floor, and her face mirrored the features of whoever looked at her. An extremely unsettling feeling that left me unable to look higher than her waist. Unfortunately, the nightmares didn't always come with names, so I called her Bloody Mary. Not that anyone here appreciated my humor.

"Who let you in here?" I snapped.

"Your guards thought I was the lesser of two evils," she said, bowing low.

My eye twitched as I caught a glimpse of her blonde hair, the same color as mine. "Meaning what?"

Nothing good, the Weaver commented, and I ground my teeth.

"The Hours are requesting an audience," Bloody Mary informed me.

A spark of fear ignited in my chest. The last time I saw them, they threatened my life if I didn't take care of Mara. Threatened me with a hail of arrows. But they weren't pushing their way inside, though I knew they were capable of it if they wanted to badly enough. Where was Kail? We needed to double—no, triple—security.

Your arm is about to break beneath the weight of all those threads, and you're worried? the Weaver scoffed.

"Of course I am." I stretched my right arm out until my elbow popped. The long thread was heavier than I expected it would be when I put it on.

Bloody Mary shifted. "You are what, Lady Nightmare?"

The Hours should be afraid of you, not the other way around.

Easy for him to say. If the twelve of them thought they could do better, they'd kill me and take over as the new Weaver.

False. I put myself here on purpose.

"What?" I shrieked. The shock of his statement made the room blur around me. That couldn't be true.

"Lady?" Bloody Mary asked, her curious tone fading to concern.

"Get out!" I shouted at her, then spun on my heel, heart hammering.

Two months. The Weaver made his grand appearance two months ago and *now* he'd dropped another bomb. Assuming it wasn't a lie. The Sandman would know. I winced. *No.* He clearly thought it was an automatic transfer of magic because he said to kill the Weaver was to become the Weaver. No one had ever killed a Lord of the Night World before. No one would know what really happened—no one except the Weaver. *Oh, God.* He did this to me on purpose.

It was less doing this to you, *and more doing it* for me.

Six of one, half a dozen of the other. Either way, the Weaver chose to invade my body, and the room tilted. It would've been nice to know so I could've passed the information along to the nightmares that wanted to butcher me.

Then how would we know who the enemies were?

"Call me crazy, but I'd rather not find out by them shoving a blade in my gut."

That only happened once.

Once was enough. It took two days for my stomach to stop hurting even though it only took a handful of hours to heal the wound. That was the last time I saw a nightmare without a thorough body search, and even then, they didn't need a weapon. They *were* weapons. I put a hand on the wall to stay myself.

"Anything else you feel like sharing?" I asked, feeling breathless.

Not at the moment, no.

That didn't mean *no*. My vision blurred again, a combination of pure exhaustion and, quite possibly, shock. I had to lay down—to think, process. I hurried blindly through empty hallways until I reached my private chambers. A soft gold rug took up the center of the room—a gift from the Doll Maker as was my entire wardrobe minus the few items I had originally brought with me—and a soft mattress piled high with pillows filled a canopied frame. The only other piece of furniture in the windowless room was a giant wardrobe Kail found…somewhere.

Are we really going to rest? the Weaver asked, contradicting himself. *With so much to do.*

I slammed my door. "Stop saying *we*! I'm *me* and you're a *soul-sucking parasite.*"

It wouldn't kill you to say thank you.

"Thank you?" I pried off my boots, my socks sticking inside, and stumbled across the room. "There's nothing to thank you for."

No? The grin glimmered faintly. *If I hadn't fused my essence with the magic before it was too late, your Sandman would be dead, and both our worlds would be imploding.*

My mind exploded with events of my reign, starting with the moment I woke up in the Doll Maker's forest. I stared down at my hands. It still wasn't clear how much of what I'd done was me and how much was the Weaver. Though, either way, I'd brought this situation on myself. But now…*now* it was the Weaver's choice. Sure, I had killed him, but it was to save the Day World. He did this to me to save himself.

Actually, I saved two worlds *with my actions,* the Weaver said. *I only hid because I was letting you gain confidence without me.*

"What do I have to be confident in? That you'll keep me alive until you find a better host?" I said through my teeth. "You destroyed my entire life."

It's called supply and demand, but, trust me, Keeper, being in your head isn't fun for me either. Oh, woe-is-me, it's been so long since I stared into the Sandman's eyes. And, gasp, what does my family think about me being gone all this time? I trust Kail. I don't trust Kail. I hate being the Lady of Nightmares. I love being the Lady of Nightmares. I—

"Yes, yes," I hissed. "You're privy to my every thought. I get it. Your eternal commentary is equally thrilling."

He let out a low, disgusted sound. *Go meet the Hours.*

"They can wait." I peeled back the covers of my bed and climbed under them fully clothed. It didn't take long for sleep to find me. It swept me under like a riptide, and I tossed and turned against the echoing screams of the Weaver trying to get me to remain conscious. My body won in the end, and all resistance faded.

Wake up, Keeper. Wake up, wake up, wake—

A hand slammed over my mouth, another gripping my thread covered arm. My eyes flew open to find two silver masks staring down at me with the Roman numerals for one and two embossed from forehead to chin. My body grew hot with fear.

I hate to say I told you so, the Weaver said with resignation. *But I told you so.*

I tried to scream, but One's metal gauntlet bit into my lips, muffling any sound. My fingers dug uselessly into the chain mail around her wrist. Two's bare hand gripped my throat and, with expertly placed fingers, ushered me into oblivion.

Chapter Four

Any time now.

The Weaver's words cut through my unconscious state, and a small groan built in the back of my throat. I scrambled to piece my current surroundings together and find my footing, but I couldn't because I wasn't in control of my body. The Weaver was driving, and he wouldn't so much as let me open my eyes.

Don't, the Weaver warned. *They don't need to know you're awake yet.*

Awake. Was I awake? It felt as if I were just dragged over a bed of nails by…whoever *they* were. This had to be a bad dream, but I didn't dream anymore. Working constantly for days on end must've stressed me out so much I was hallucinating as I slept.

A few seconds of pressure to your jugular doesn't wipe your memory. Snap out of it, Keeper.

Jugular. Right. The Hours. New Hours—One and Two—had burst into my bedroom and attacked me. All fogginess fled, leaving me acutely aware of my precarious state. Judging by the hard surface beneath me, I was no longer in my bed which meant they kidnapped me. *Bastards.* Mara or no Mara, this was unacceptable.

Bingo.

I swallowed a retort to the Weaver and listened hard to see if I could determine whether I was alone.

You know you don't have to say it for me to hear it, he purred.

Can you truly feel a death threat if I don't scream it at you? I thought back.

Oh, indeed. It's delicious either way. He released the vice grip on my bodily functions. *Stay still and don't open your eyes yet.*

I huffed. A mistake.

"I see you're coming around," someone said a few feet to my left.

That was the end of my ruse. I steeled myself and sat up. My muscles cried at the movement, but I didn't allow myself to voice any complaints. *Power. Authority. Be the Weaver.*

Before me, Six perched on a chair in an otherwise empty room made of dulled brass. Her elbows rested on her knees as she leaned forward, spinning an arrow between her fingers. Her dark braid hung nearly to her lap, and I could see a blurry reflection of myself in the flat, shiny metal mask covering her face. The last time we met, when Kail and I were on our way back to the Blood Tower, she shot a ring of arrows around us.

Then she and two other Hours forced me to heal their comrade after a run-in with Mara.

"You," I growled.

"I had nothing to do with this," she said casually. "Those who brought you here are with the Chime now."

"The Chime?"

Six leaned back in the chair and crossed her arms. "Thirteen."

Before you say that everyone told you there were twelve Hours, Thirteen isn't an Hour, the Weaver supplied. *The Chime has final say over the clock. Now try to stop making yourself look incompetent. You need to gain the upper hand and let them know just how unacceptable this is.*

If you're not going to work some of your mojo, stop talking, I thought back, then to Six, "what am I doing here?"

"Mara is still a problem," she said simply. "I'm sure you haven't forgotten."

Mara was more of a problem than even *she* knew. Entire landscapes were razed to the ground, nightmares slaughtered, all by the Ancient's hand. The problem was that she waited until just before she moved on to disturb anything, so it was difficult to track her. She left me presents, too. Unnecessary reminders that she was out there. The impaled corpses that greeted me when I left the palace were only the latest in a string of gifts.

Considering that the Sandman and I hadn't made a single move in two months, the Hours probably thought we weren't going to hold up our end of the bargain. I was willing to bet they thought I was stupid enough to brush it off in favor of my other mounting responsibilities, but I had to be smart about it and trust the Sandman's judgment.

I lifted my hands to brush the hair from my face and found them bound, wrapped from the wrist all the way to the tips of my fingers with smooth rope. "What the—"

Six cocked her head. "We couldn't let you create anything new inside the clock."

Things kept getting better and better. Without the ability to create nightmares or use the existing ones around me, all I had were my own innate skills. Which were basically nonexistent even though I was getting better thanks to my continued training with Kail. *Kail.* Had he noticed I was gone yet? It was only a matter of time, but even he wouldn't think to look for me here.

"Kail will find me," I said in a rush of faked confidence.

Shut up.

Finally, some sound advice.

"He could call upon his brother to find you, but Halven can only find *where* someone is. Not when."

I couldn't see her face behind her mask—if there was a face there at all—but still, I felt the smug smile. *Shut up, shut up, shut up*, the Weaver urged.

"Make me," I growled under my breath.

"What?" Six asked, confused.

Again, I can hear you without speaking.

I thought the loudest shriek I could and leveled my gaze at Six. Two months of killing nightmares without mercy gave me a decent chunk of respect. Or fear. But if anyone found out the Hours kidnapped me, *poof.* All of it a waste. Not only did I need to escape, but I had to do it quietly and without any additional notice. Then punish an entire group of powerful nightmares because nothing ever stayed a secret here.

"Do you think I need Kail or Halven to rescue me?" I asked Six.

You're backtracking. Why would you say Kail would find you if you didn't need him to? If you're going to play tough, at least do it right.

Ignore him. I had to ignore him.

Six laughed. "If you could escape alone, you wouldn't be sitting here right now."

She has a point. All talk, no action.

For someone that depended on my life to keep himself alive, the Weaver was awfully quick to side with the enemy.

I *am your enemy*, he snarled.

All talk, no action, I said, throwing his own words back at him. The Weaver was absolutely my enemy, but until we figured out how to get him out of me, we were forced to accept a truce. Or, at least, to press pause on killing each other.

I cleared my throat and raised my chin. "Take me to the Chime so we can get this taken care of."

"You don't get *taken* to the Chime. The Chime summons you."

It was my turn to laugh. "I'm the Lady of Nightmares. No one *summons* me." I stood, poking at the internal grin that was the Weaver. His sigh breathed through me as he let the darkness swirl violently. A decent trick we came up with to our mutual benefit. The air darkened around me, pulling in energy from surrounding nightmares, feeding me like a banquet for one. The magic took from Six until she visibly struggled to stay upright. I shoved at the grin until the Weaver reluctantly cut off the surge of power.

"The Chime," I demanded. *"Now."*

Six straightened, her shoulders stiff. She said nothing as she stood with a chorus of clinking chainmail and spun a cogwheel set in the wall, hidden behind her chair. That wheel set off another, then two more, then four. A panel of wall slid away to reveal the inner workings with each new piece that turned until the entire wall spun. A weight dropped from the middle of the ceiling and dangled there, waiting. With a terrible grinding sound, a slab shifted overhead, and with another few grinding clicks, stairs popped from the far wall.

"We have to go up," Six said when I didn't move.

I took a deep breath and tread carefully into the brighter chamber above. The walls glowed faintly, illuminating more moving pieces. The floor was a blanket of nuts and bolts, and the pieces pressed into my bare feet. A window served as the roof with an inverted Roman numeral six painted black across the surface. I stepped around the shadow it cast and followed the curve of the room. *The clock face.* I knew it without the Weaver's input. Six said Halven wouldn't know *when* I was...did that mean I time traveled to six o'clock? What time was it really? There was no sign of the clock hands.

No one can time travel, the Weaver said rather blandly. *She was messing with you. Honestly, you make it too easy.*

"After you," Six said, and spun another cog.

I held my breath and waited for the next opening to appear. It took longer this time. More sliding pieces. More clacking mechanics. When the door finally slid up, my heart rammed into my chest. The other eleven hours stood around the perimeter of the circular room. On the floor, black lines marked white marble, forming the blank face of a clock. But it was what was in the middle that drew my attention.

Standing at the center of the clock face was a man swathed in layers of glimmering bronze material. His robe flowed around him like water. A heavy matching chain ran down from the ceiling, attaching itself to the nightmare's back. True to his name, each slight movement sent a musical tinkling through the chamber.

When the door clanged to a stop over my head, every eye found me, and I struggled to keep my composure. "What's wrong?" My voice miraculously sounded commanding and sure. "Not expecting me just yet?"

"Six," one of the Hours snapped. I refused to look away from the Chime to see which one spoke.

The Weaver lashed out unbidden, sucking away what little energy Six had left. She fell to the floor just inside the room, unconscious. "You." I held my bound arms out to the nearest Hour, guided partially by the true Nightmare Lord, and glared at the knife on Seven's hip. "Free my hands."

When he hesitated, I poked at the darkness again, letting it dim the bright room. Slowly, Seven pulled the knife free and carefully sliced through my bindings without harming my threat. I rubbed my wrists, glancing at each Hour in turn, before meeting the Chime's gaze.

Say nothing, the Weaver said quietly as if he were talking to a spooked animal. *Just turn and walk out.*

Ha! Like that was happening. Not only because I wanted revenge first. They didn't go through all of this to let me waltz out the door.

You showed your strength, Keeper. Leave now before they see a weakness. "Lady Nightmare—" the Chime began.

"First, I was brutally attacked by Three in the Barren, then threatened by her again along with two others. Now, you've stolen me from my bed." It flowed off my tongue so fast, I couldn't have stopped it if I wanted to.

"Lady—"

My eyebrows rose, and I glared pointedly at the glimmering figure. "Be glad I gave you so many chances. Others weren't so lucky." I backed out of the room, setting off a flurry of motion from the Hours. "This better work," I mumbled both to myself and the Weaver.

The Weaver didn't bother to hide his disdain as I pressed my hand against the same cog wheel Six used to open the chamber, but he lent me his power anyway. I didn't always need his help—I was learning to harness it on my own—but right now, speed was a major factor, especially since the Hours were already lunging after me. With a lightning-fast bolt of energy, the door slammed down between us. Bodies rammed into the other side, armor clattered against armor. Another brush of power melted the moving pieces, effectively sealing them inside. At least from this entrance.

There, I thought at the Weaver, and practically felt his eyes roll.

You could've maimed them a smidge.

You literally told me to get out of there two seconds ago.

The Weaver settled, his magic relaxing, and said nothing because he knew that would get under my skin the most. His back-and-forth instructions were one thing, but his indifference when I called him on it set my nerves on edge.

A shadow passed over the floor, drawing my attention to the glass ceiling just in time to see a figure vanish. That was quick.

Another exit had to lead directly to the exterior of the clock face for the Hours to be there already.

That wasn't an Hour.

My stomach twisted with unease. "Great. Let's get out of here before—"

A loud crash reverberated through the tower. I covered my head, biting back a scream, but when nothing fell down around me, I dared to look up. Cracks webbed across the ceiling, stemming from the room I just sealed.

"Please tell me that's one of their buddies," I said softly.

Shouts rose up on the other side of the door.

Doesn't sound like it, the Weaver said. *You'll want to take a right up ahead.*

I took one step and paused. My fingers twitched at my sides. The Hours threatened me, beat me, and broke into my palace to kidnap me. They were probably planning to kill me like they said they would—I still had no plan to deal with Mara, after all.

And yet…

Leave them.

I should. It would be the smart thing to do. Leave and let something else kill the Hours for me. They had a fighting chance. Thirteen against one, a home turf advantage, undoubtedly more exits if they wanted to run.

Don't get soft now, Keeper.

Don't get soft? I winced. Did he think I had hardened *that* much? So soon after picking up the mantle of Lady Nightmare?

Not completely, the Weaver said. *Or you wouldn't hesitate to leave them to their fate.*

That was true. He certainly wouldn't have cared—not unless it served a purpose for him. But I didn't want to be like the

Weaver. Whatever scraps of humanity I had left needed to be guarded, so I put my hand back on the wall and reopened the door.

Inside, chaos reigned.

Hours ran and leapt, swung weapons and fired arrows, all with carefully executed precision. The Chime shouted orders and dodged projectiles. But only one thing sent my pulse roaring.

Mara.

She stood taller than I remembered, her legs at ninety-degree angles instead of bent up to her ears. A hump bubbled between her shoulder blades, but it didn't slow her movements as she sliced at the Hours. Her nails—once jagged—now shone like blades on the tips of each finger.

"Summon the Hands!" the Chime shouted above the melee.

One of the Hours jumped over the Chime's head and scurried up the chain to the ceiling. She ripped open an overhead chamber and two black blobs fell to the floor with a splat.

If you're just going to stand here, it's better to leave, the Weaver commented.

I jolted at his words. Right. *Do something.*

This was your idea.

My nostrils flared. I pulled a thread from my wrist at the same time a loud gong blasted everyone in the room backward. We froze in the air, moving ever-so slightly, as two enormous figures rose from the black blobs. They took the shape of humans dunked in tar with unnaturally long limbs and featureless faces. With lightning-fast movements, they each grabbed onto the Chime's throat with one hand and opposing walls with the other.

Another gong sounded, low and impossibly drawn out. I was still flying back, almost as if frozen in time, but Mara wasn't. She fought her way forward with seemingly forced steps and dug her nails into the nearest Hour: Four—the same one I healed near the river two months ago.

You might want to snap out of it if you want to save them.

Why the hell would they slow down time and put themselves at risk? *You do the snapping,* I told the Weaver. *I'll do the stopping.*

I'd rather do it all, he said casually.

The next moment, my body wasn't my own—it was the Weaver's. He pushed against the invisible force holding us in place so hard that I swore my bones would break. I cried out, but he was the only one to hear my internal scream.

The Weaver used the thread I pulled to create a molted grey scorpion with two tails, both tipped with three stingers. On the inside of its claws were hundreds of smaller ones pinching at the air. It took off straight for Mara.

The black figures—the Hands—began moving in unison, spinning the clock face, and the Hours shimmered in and out. It only lasted a handful of seconds before they flashed out of the room altogether.

Are you serious? I screeched inside my head.

The Weaver smirked using my mouth. *I told you that we should've left them.*

Mara stumbled forward with Four gone and spun to face the scorpion. Her thick tongue darted out with a low *tsk*. She launched herself forward without missing another beat and spun through the air like a torpedo.

One moment, the scorpion stood there.

The next, it split down the middle and black blood splashed all around us.

"We meet again, Lady," Mara crooned. She stood in the middle of the carnage, covered in nearly as much black as the two figures that fell from the ceiling. It trailed down her face and mixed with chunks of scorpion flesh that clung to her skin. "You look well."

Do something, do something, do something, I chanted at the Weaver.

Before he could, Mara scuttled across the floor, hunched as she was in the Day World, and sliced the backs of my ankles. Stars burst before my eyes and the Weaver's control slipped in and out.

Don't you dare give my body back now, I warned.

The Weaver's grip tightened, but Mara was already sitting on my back, her breath hot on my ear. "I'd love to see what you look like on the inside." Her fingernail cut a line down my cheek and hot blood raced toward my chin. "Such a pretty color. Sadly, I haven't decided if you'll be useful to me yet. Until then, I must leave you alive."

The Weaver rolled us, and Mara leapt off, fleeing through the hole she made in the ceiling. *Your body has more limits than mine,* he thought bitterly. *The least you could do is not let pain get in the way.*

Excuse me? How was I supposed to react when my tendons were severed?

You're not supposed to react at all. Then the Weaver receded, leaving me to figure out how to move on my own.

Don't react at all? As if that were possible.

Chimes tinkled softly, drawing my attention back to the center of the room. The black figures were blobs again, and they inched up the Chime's chains to the hatch they fell from.

"As you see," the Chime said in a stern voice. "Mara needs to be eliminated."

I glowered at him and sat up the best I could. Blood pooled around my feet—mine and the scorpion's. "You fared well enough," I accused.

"She wasn't controlled by the slowing of time," he said as if that should've meant something.

It means she isn't affected by us. Why do you think it took both the Sandman and me to get rid of her the first time?

If this was some sort of set up to show me how dangerous Mara was, I was seriously going to lose it. It felt like too much of a coincidence to be anything else, but seeing Mara again blew on the fire raging inside me. "I'll deal with Mara," I warned him. "Just stay out of my way." *We should leave before the Hours return.*

Finally, a suggestion I couldn't argue with. The problem was actually moving. I bit my lip and snagged someone's bow from the floor. Slowly and with blinding pain, I used it to pull myself onto my feet. The wall was the only thing keeping me up, the bow the only thing helping me shuffle back into the corridor. How the hell was I supposed to walk like this?

Turn right, the Weaver instructed. Heat burst through my legs, almost too hot for comfort, but it stole away the pain. *Don't say I never helped you out.*

I look a tentative step and nearly fell flat on my face. The pain was dulled, but tendons were rather important if one expected to use their limbs. Thankfully they would heal thanks to my Nightmare magic. I leaned on the bow again and shuffled from the room the best I could.

After a few more guided turns, I found myself outside a giant grandfather clock. And I wasn't alone.

"Lady Nightmare," Halven said, bowing.

I gasped for breath, sweat dripping down my face. The sight of him with his ridiculously frivolous outfit and cruel mask brought tears to my eyes. Never had I been so glad to see a nightmare in all my life. "What are you doing here?" I asked, allowing every ounce of relief to leak into the question.

"You called to me," he said in his rough voice.

"I did?" I asked, mostly to myself.

You're welcome.

"Of course," I snapped back. "I thought you said I didn't need them."

No. I said you shouldn't let the Hours know *you needed help.*

"You're hurt?" Halven asked, his head cocked.

"I'll live." I turned my gaze up to the face of the massive clock, half expecting to see figures through the broken glass racing after me. Hobbling as I was, I couldn't chance that happening, so I touched the outer wall. Heat flowed between my palm and the bronze panel as I fixed the damage Mara caused. Then I sealed every door that led outside.

"Let's get back to the palace before your brother ends up with an ulcer." I took a step toward Halven and tumbled to the ground. "Actually, we're making a stop somewhere else first. I'm going to need a little help though."

Halven lifted me from the ground without another word and began walking without my having to tell him the destination. A perk of having the nightmare of lost things come to your aide. "Thanks," I breathed.

It wasn't just his help I was grateful for. Around Halven, I didn't have to worry about judgment if I showed everything wasn't okay. He gave me a small squeeze as if to say *you're welcome,* and I rested my head on his shoulder. Weakness didn't feel so wrong around the right people.

Chapter Five

Nora

The pain in my ankles faded to a sharp prickle by the time Halven carried me into the Doll Maker's clearing. Forest animals made of buttons trekked behind us with curious gazes. Soft clicks surrounded us as they moved among the trees while the carpet of green buttons crunched beneath Halven's feet. I liked to imagine the button trees smelled like pine, but they honestly smelled like nothing at all.

"Put me down," I told Halven. It was bad enough I was going to ask the Doll Maker for stitches again—I could at least look as if I got there on my own two feet.

Halven immediately set me on my feet but stood close, arm at the ready in case I needed it. I wasn't entirely sure I wouldn't. Dropping that bow awhile back wasn't my best move.

"Lady Nightmare!" The Doll Maker rounded one of her gigantic mounds of color-coded buttons in the clearing. A tiny top hat sat crooked on her head and a basket hung off one arm. Around her neck clicked a necklace of more buttons, and her skirt was the brightest tulle, making her look like an eccentric middle-aged woman. "Do you need another garment?"

I shook my head and fought off a wave of nausea the action sent through me. Suddenly, sitting down seemed more than ideal. "You told me to come back next time I needed to be stitched up."

"Oh." She dropped her basket with wide eyes. Ribbons and buttons spilled across the ground. "Of course, of course. Come to the table."

The table where she tied Dreamers down to sew buttons over their eyes, adorn them with frills, and paint their skin as if they were her personal toys. *Great.* Beggars couldn't be choosers, and the surface was blissfully empty tonight. All traces of blood were scrubbed away, though the red ribbons she used to hold down the Dreamers' limbs dangled like entrails.

Ugh. I've spent way too much time in the Nightmare Realm.

The Weaver chuckled, but otherwise remained silent. A shock, honestly. I was showing multiple weaknesses to the Doll Maker when Halven could've simply whisked me back to the palace and let the cuts heal naturally over the next day or two. It was my residual human side that wanted medical attention because my nightmare side certainly didn't *need* it. Sure, it helped, but it wasn't necessary. I'd given up so much of my former life though that I felt no regret.

"What are we patching today?" The Doll Maker patted the tabletop.

I sighed and allowed Halven to hold my elbow while I stumbled up to the table. Once there, I brushed him off and hoisted myself onto the cool surface. "My ankles."

"Rather important, those are." The Doll Maker rummaged through her braided hair until she found a needle. "Nothing will topple a Dreamer faster than putting them in shoes that their ankles can't support. The older they are, the lower the heel has to be. More than once I've had them just *pop* right out of place and no one wants a broken doll. They're never the same if you try to fix them either. Limping around and such."

"I'm sure you do your best," I said without conviction.

"Always, my lady. Now, let's see." She bent over, threading the needle without looking, and let out a low whistle. "The tendons are nearly cut through. What happened?"

I peered at Halven where he stood a foot away and wondered if I should tell the Doll Maker the truth. It wouldn't do any good for the nightmares to know I couldn't handle Mara, but the Hours would escape eventually. Plus, with all the trouble the Ancient stirred up, it was no secret she was on the loose. Still…

"I'd rather not talk about it," I hedged. "Can you fix it?"

The Doll Maker smiled brightly. "I can fix anything, though, if you don't mind me saying, you shouldn't be walking on it."

"It would take months to heal in the Day World if I were still human, so I think I can handle a day or two off," I reassured her.

Can we though? the Weaver asked.

Of course we couldn't. *What else do you want me to say?*

He grunted. *Let her sew you up if it settles your mind. I'll work on internal repairs so we can put this whole ordeal behind us.*

You could've been doing that since I walked out of the clock tower, I thought harshly. It was as if he enjoyed withholding help just to torture me.

One must get their thrills where they can. Be happy I assisted with the pain.

I sucked in a breath, but the Doll Maker's needle pierced my skin, erasing the scathing reply from my mind. It was strange how I could force myself to walk around like this, albeit with the Weaver's help, but the Doll Maker's stitches sent my head spinning. I laid back on the table and bit my lip.

"I hear Mara decorated your hill a few days ago," the Doll Maker said conversationally. "Though, clearly she stole the idea from one of the Weaver's landscapes. Ivan the Impactor? No, that doesn't sound right."

"Vlad the Impaler?" *Original,* I tacked on in my head for the Weaver's benefit.

The classics never go out of style, Keeper.

"That's it!"

The Doll Maker chattered happily as she worked. Something about one of her dolls escaping and ending up on one of Vlad's pikes decades ago. It was such a waste of her hard work, blah, blah, blah. I focused on her cheerful voice to take the edge off the pain, but the words blurred together. At least, until she brought Mara up again.

"What?" I bolted up onto my elbows.

"Stay still, Lady."

"Repeat what you just said."

"Mara." The Doll Maker brought the needle up with a gentle tug. "She collapsed a nearby landscape. From what I hear, she burrowed into the ground without realizing a system of caves was beneath."

Or she did *know.* My skin prickled with goosebumps. It would really help if someone remembered the exact location of the Ever Safe door or the key to open it, but no. The Weaver made it disappear, even from himself. Apparently, that was a Night Lord trait, but unlike the Sandman, there was no Dream Keeper to retrieve the information from.

Halven did what he does best, he said, sounding slightly offended. *The less I knew about its location, the better.*

"The whole thing crumbled into itself, killing everyone down there. I don't know who or where it was, mind you, as I only heard second hand. A real shame though."

"Yes. A shame," I agreed and looked to Halven. Did he know about this? He was spying for the Sandman, but that didn't make him any less a nightmare. I needed to be kept in the loop.

Wait. Halven hid the key?

The Weaver didn't bother to reply with words—he didn't need to. I felt his withering glare as clearly as I felt each stitch slide through my skin. Of course Halven hid it. Who else?

The sharp snap of metal scissors signaled the end of the Doll Maker's work. "Good as new."

"I appreciate it."

The Doll Maker waved off the words. "I'm working on something new for you. I'll send it to the palace when I've finished."

"I have enough clothes," I promised her.

"That isn't possible. Besides, your pants aren't any good like this. Look at the holes!"

A small smile spread on my lips. There was no arguing with her. "Thank you."

"Off you go now." She tucked the still-bloody needle back into her braid and wiped her hands on her skirt.

I held a hand out to Halven again, but instead of taking it, he wordlessly lifted me in his arms. *Right.* I wasn't supposed to walk on my own yet.

I only need a little while to make the tendons functional, the Weaver said. *Not that it won't still hurt.*

"Such a good boy," the Doll Maker said with a pat to Halven's arm.

He bobbed his head to the Doll Maker and carried me back to the palace. Part of me wanted him to slow down so I could avoid Kail's hissy fit a little longer, but I wanted to be back in my own space more. Mostly, I wanted to sleep. For a very, very long time.

Chapter Six

Nora's new palace was impressive. Her security, on the other hand, was not. Sentries lined the walls and manned the entrances, but there were no built-in defenses that I could detect. I strode straight for the front door where a rather gruesome nightmare sat on a bench, one hand hovering over my satchel. A multitude of nightmare eyes burned through the layers of my clothes, and I swept my gaze from one end of the wall to the other. No one moved to stop me which made the hair on my arms stand on end. Nora couldn't think this was enough, and if she did, Kail should've known otherwise.

I stopped in front of the nightmare just outside the main entrance. Pink, blood-stained fabric swallowed her shapeless body. When I looked up from the clothing, I startled. My face stared back at me, curly ash brown hair, violet eyes…it was like staring in a mirror, except where I knew my jaw hung open, the nightmare smiled coyly.

"Where is the Lady of Nightmares?" I asked.

The nightmare scrambled to her feet, stumbling on the hem of her outfit to give a minute bow. "Dream Lord."

I glared expectantly. "Well?"

"Kail said to wait," she fumbled. "That I had to wait."

"Sandman." Kail burst through the massive doors and glanced at the waiting nightmare. "What are you doing here?"

"Waiting," she said again.

He shook his head, eyes rolling. "There's no time today. Leave."

"But you said—"

"I said your problems could wait, not that you should." Kail grabbed her by the upper arms and shoved her unceremoniously away from the building before dragging me inside. The slam of the door echoed through the empty entryway. With a quick look down the hallway, Kail looked me straight in the eyes, his irises flashing wildly. "Nora's gone."

"Gone." I tested the word. "As in out taking a stroll?"

"Damned if I know." Kail stormed down the hallway with sure, angry steps. "She said she was going to sleep, but her room is empty. As well as the Keep and the interior courtyard."

I rubbed my forehead. Everyone had to be somewhere. Gone didn't mean *gone*, especially when Nora was Lady of this realm. She knew better than to disappear without telling someone when things hadn't fully settled yet. The way Kail acted, I knew this wasn't commonplace. "Where would she go?"

"There's a movie she's been wanting to see at the theater. Oh, and Suzie from down the street has become her new bestie. Maybe they're painting each other's nails and talking about boys." His sarcastic tirade ended with him sucking in a deep breath and holding it while his fingers curled in and out of fists at his side.

I waited two beats for him to gain some semblance of sobriety before remembering who I was dealing with. "Don't test me, Kail."

He paced the patchwork of shadows in the windowless hall, dim torches burning every few feet. "She spends most of her time in the Keep. Occasionally meets with nightmares when they show up if she's feeling restless. That doesn't happen much," he added, then paused. "The meetings usually end with her killing one of the nightmares."

"The Keep…" I started, ignoring the last part. How bad had Nora gotten since we parted? It took the Weaver a few years after banishing Mara to enjoy killing, but Kail hadn't said Nora *liked* it. Just that she did it. I took a moment to center my thoughts in an attempt to ward off an avalanche of fear.

"The Keep!" he shouted in mock surprise. "Why didn't I think to look there? Thank goodness you showed up when you did."

"Kail," I warned in a low voice.

"What are you doing here?" Kail whirled on me as if he were angry at himself for not asking before. "Maybe I should be asking *you* where she is?"

"What?" A flash of anger cracked the word.

"You show up here the same day Nora disappears." He looked me up and down. "That's what I like to call suspicious."

What did he think I'd done? Whisked her away to the Dream Realm where she would taint my sand? Forced her back to the Day World where she would wither? More importantly, *why* would I? I inhaled slowly, forcing myself to calm down. "Halven found Mare. I came so Nora and I could take care of her before she disappears again." A thought hit me like a lightning bolt, and my body went cold. "Mare…you don't think she—"

"No. Mara wouldn't bother to take her anywhere. If she did get in here, Nora would already be dead." The certainty in Kail's voice was enough to make me believe it. He picked at his bottom lip and fidgeted nervously. "Something's wrong with her."

"Everything is wrong with her. Which is why we need to send her back to the Day World where she isn't a threat."

"Not Mara," he said so softly that I barely heard. The front door slammed open before I could ask for clarification and Halven swept in. Kail brushed past me to greet him.

Halven reached out to take Kail's hand. "Sorry we're late," he croaked.

"*Please*." Nora's voice barreled through the entrance like a battering ram. "Your Lady is always on time."

Kail practically shoved his brother out of the way to reveal Nora in the doorway. His shoulders visibly relaxed, but his sarcasm hid any hint of relief. "Nice of you to join the party."

Nora snorted. "Yeah. This place is a real rager."

Her eyes landed on me, and she froze, her lips parting. I didn't dare move though my heart was beating so fast I was sure she could see it pounding against my chest. Her hair framed her face, her freckles stark against already pale skin, made only paler by her black sweater and dark pants. A line of dried blood marked her cheek, though the wound had already healed. The gold of her eyes burned bright, but beneath them, a familiar haunted expression lurked.

"…you been?" Kail's voice drifted to my ears, interrupting my thoughts.

"Visiting the Hours," Nora said off-handedly.

Silence.

Nora kicked the front door shut. "Don't give me that look, Kail. It wasn't *my* idea."

Kail whirled on Halven.

"It wasn't his either." Nora tucked a piece of hair behind her ear and let out a slow breath. "I'm not really in the mood to explain, but they won't be giving us any more trouble." She wrinkled her nose in the way I loved best. "I think. Not for a while anyway."

I stepped forward and Kail tossed an arm out to bar my way. "Not in the mood? I just spent half the day—"

"I'm fine." She stared at him hard, then turned on her heel. There was a slight limp in her steps and, at the back of her ankles, torn, bloody fabric that said otherwise.

"Where are you going?" he asked frantically.

"To bed." She flicked a quick look at me and bobbed her head as if telling me to follow.

I did, of course, as quickly as my feet would carry me. When I got to Nora's side, she took my hand. Her fingers were freezing, trembling, but they sent jolts of fire straight to my core. Kail called after us, but we didn't stop until we were in another set of rooms deep inside the palace. Thick black curtains hung around a massive wooden bed frame. The four posts were sculpted with care, each long swirl brushed lightly with gold, and a rich, brocade fabric covered the mattress. A large matching wardrobe and plush golden carpet were the only other items of note in the otherwise nondescript chamber. Nora's bedroom, I guessed, noticing the bookbag thrown haphazardly in the corner. A far cry from her old room with its sheer curtains, white mini lights, and pastel color palette.

I turned to ask if she wanted me to bring her anything from home, but before I could get the question out, her lips were on mine. They were warm and pliant, almost reverent. My fingers tangled in her hair, and I pulled her close, hands against her lower back. I breathed her in, and a low noise caught in my throat. That sound was a key twisting open a lock.

Our kisses became more frantic, more eager to make up for lost time. I shuffled back, pulling her along with me, but misjudged the bed's location. Her lips quirked into a smile without leaving mine as my back hit the wall. We kissed until I was drunk on the taste, and my hands burned with the desire to touch every inch of her.

Just when I thought I would combust, her lips trailed along my jaw and down my neck. My grip on her hips tightened. "I missed you," she breathed against my skin.

"I see that," I teased, and she nipped at my ear. "I missed you too."

"Let's never stay away from each other this long again?" she asked lightly, though I could tell she meant it.

If only we could promise that. "Mare—"

"Can wait until tomorrow," she interjected. "I've been awake for days, more or less, and there's something more important to talk about."

The lingering heat from our kiss cooled. *Days?* Even I got regular rest to keep my mind clear and decisions judicious. "No,"

I said, though I was dying to ask what happened to her ankles. "Now, you sleep. We can talk when you wake up."

She glanced longingly at her bed and shuddered. "You need to know."

"All I need to know—" I gave her another quick kiss, "is that you're okay."

I guided Nora to the bed, and she eased down onto the rumpled blankets. When she looked up at me, every ounce of exhaustion showed on her face. There was a sadness there, too. *Something is wrong with her.* I shook Kail's words away. Of course there was something wrong. A strong, dark power surged through her, twisting her into something she was never meant to be, and she was dealing with it the best she could. Nora was good at that, at adjusting, but she was also good at hiding things. It was one thing for her to let me see her struggle because she'd always allowed me in, but for Kail to notice…

"Close your eyes," I said softly and bent to remove her pants. There was nothing worse than prying fabric away from a wound after blood cemented them together.

"I thought you wanted me to sleep," she said with a tiny smirk.

I smiled back and kissed her bare stomach just above the ties on her pants. "You are going to sleep, but not in bloody clothes."

She made a soft sound of consent.

"What happened?" I asked when the fabric peeled free. There were black stitches over jagged, semi-healed cuts. I ran my thumb over the skin near it, careful not to touch too close.

"Mara needs a manicure."

My eyes shot up to Nora's. Halven found Mare, and it wasn't anywhere near the clock tower. "Excuse me?"

"I suppose there are two things I need to tell you." Her eyelids shut. She took a deep breath, then shimmied under the covers. "Tomorrow?"

The exhaustion and stress hardening her features injected me with a dull ache. "Tomorrow," I reluctantly agreed.

Nora relaxed slightly and held open the blankets. "Will you stay with me?"

She didn't have to ask. I would've sat outside her door just to listen to her breathe, outside the palace even, just to be in the same realm, anything to be allowed near her again. But, as I crawled into the bed beside her and she snuggled against my side, I was glad she had invited me to stay. I took my first easy breath in two months and ran my fingers through her hair until she finally fell into a deep slumber.

Fire danced. It swayed and spread, crackled and popped. An entire town became an instrument, the screams of its residents an orchestra. Smoke billowed into the sky and blotted out the sunrise. Perhaps the orange glow coming from behind was another fire. Another town.

The image moved, my view through another's eyes: through the Weaver's. This was another memory, a fissure in the dark of sleep. I usually had to approach the glowing fissures to see inside—or ignore them, if it suited me, but this time it sucked me in without warning. If I had seen it from a distance, I would've ignored it this once instead of approaching to peek inside, but as it was, I was too weary to fight my way out. Even my strange, false sense of a body ached at the thought of forcing my mind away.

The Weaver coughed as he walked straight into the burning streets, boots sloshing in the mud. Judging by the curved roofs, he appeared to be somewhere in the far east. A man with a long braid of hair stumbled away from the inferno, his arm around a woman. Their white silk clothing was stained black with soot.

The Weaver passed by them without hesitation, and they didn't appear to see him at all. He moved with purpose. Steps steady. Focus locked. It took a moment before I realized what exactly he was staring at.

A dark figure stood atop a building. Despite the smoke swirling, I knew it was Mara. Her posture was the same as it was in the clock tower—partially hunched—but when she leapt from her perch in front of the Weaver, it was with a pained expression.

Mara stood slowly, wincing, limbs bending at crooked angles, but her head…that was held high. She hissed like an animal at the Weaver, then bound around him to slit the couple's throats. They fell right there in the muck without knowing they were in danger.

"Come to take me home, Lord?" Mara taunted.

"Stop this," he replied, arms held out to imply the destruction.

She feigned surprise with a hand going to her chest. "Lord, you've given me a new home. I only seek to change it to my liking."

The Weaver looked down at the threads on his arm but made no move to touch them. They were useless to him in the Day World. "The worlds have already changed, Mare."

"Because *you* changed them," she spat.

"No." He stepped toward her carefully. "Men did. They chased the magic from this world, but they've breathed their own sort into it. You and I are the ones out of place here. You can't make this place something it isn't."

"This is a means to an end." She leaned over the corpses, jabbed her finger in the man's open throat, then sucked the blood off like it was brownie batter. "If I have to destroy this world first, so be it, but I will live again in chaos. Darkness is my home, Nightmare Lord. Ashes and dust and bone. My brethren and I will have it as such again."

"Then who will be left for you to kill?" the Weaver tried to reason.

Mara smiled, her teeth tinged red. "That's the point—to be rid of the vermin."

Kindly step away from my memory. The Weaver's thought broke through the scene and everything froze.

If you don't want me to see something, don't show it to me.

He huffed. *No one can have control of their thoughts a hundred percent of the time.*

I've seen this much. Might as well let me see how it ends.

It ends with my burying her a thousand feet in the ground, he said simply. *I had to stop her from destroying the Day World—my nightmares need Dreamers to survive.*

I would've loved to see that. Served her right. Too bad she didn't stay buried. Though, it was probably less about his nightmares and more about him not wanting to die along with everything else.

How exactly did you manage that feat by yourself?

Do you underestimate me, Keeper? the Weaver asked, feigning offense. *Mara was wreaking havoc in your world for a long time by then. She was weaker than she was when the Sandman and I banished her.*

Still, to dig so far down, get Mara inside the hole, and fill the dirt back in over her? Not to mention that he had no nightmares to help—threads yes, but not actual nightmares. The next thought I sent his way was less of a thought and more of a wordless annoyance.

You should've seen what she did before that, he said, indignant. *Moving entire landmasses, hurling fiery comets—*

Okay, okay. Evil. Got it. Not in the mood for a complete recap. I was exhausted. Was one night too much to ask for? One night free of being reminded of my mistake in accidentally letting Mara back in? Just one night?

The paused memory vanished, and I loosened a breath. Distantly, I heard the steady *thump thump thump* of a heartbeat and felt the Sandman's warmth against me. I held onto that instead of the gnawing fear and let my mind rest.

My fingers danced over the gleaming crescent moon on the Sandman's chest while he slept beside me. I had no idea when he removed his shirt, but his skin was hot beneath my touch. Almost too hot, just like mine, which I suspected was the reason I couldn't fall back asleep. Still, I didn't have the heart to get up yet. I would have to crawl over him to leave the bed and I hated to wake him. The Sandman looked peaceful, so at ease. I missed the days when sleep brought me the same sensation. I tried—I really had—but even when the Weaver was quiet, his magic buzzed in my head like a swarm of bees.

There were also the memories to deal with—but last night was different. Silly me for thinking nightmares were impossible for me to have anymore. The Weaver in my head was like having a night terror every moment of my life, asleep or otherwise.

Pity party for one.

I will kill you one day, I vowed to the Weaver, counting it a miracle I managed not to say the threat out loud.

You promise that a lot, Keeper, but what will happen to you if I'm dead?

I didn't want to know. Only part of me cared at this point. Maybe I would go back to being human, or maybe I would die along with him, but a literal eternity with the Weaver lodged in my brain was nothing short of torture. I had to do *something* because there was no living like this forever.

Tell him about me, the Weaver suggested. *See what happens. See how he looks at you once he knows.*

I bit my bottom lip. My killing the Weaver was enough of a disappointment to both of us, but this…this was another ball game. The Sandman had to know—I would've told him last night if I weren't so exhausted. When he woke up, I'd try harder.

If you wanted, this could be a symbiotic relationship. I'll keep you strong.

I am *strong*, I shot back. And I was. The Weaver lent me his strength when I needed it, but it was me who built this new life. The palace. Me that spread new fear through the Nightmare Realm. Besides, however the Weaver expected to benefit in return was sure to be too steep a price.

"Morning," the Sandman said in a husky, sleep-filled voice.

I jerked my hand away from his tattoo and looked up to find his violet eyes cracked open. "Morning," I replied, almost shy.

"What's wrong?" he asked and skimmed my cheekbone with his thumb.

"Nothing." I shook my head. No—he wouldn't believe that. "Mara," I amended. "Facing her yesterday was a wakeup call. She's been taunting me for weeks but seeing her was different."

A flash of fear crossed his face, disappearing as fast as it came, replaced by a playful smirk. "You know, there's a way to make you less afraid for a little while."

"How?"

He was on top of me so fast that I'd barely realized he'd moved. Then his grin widened, and he buried his face in my neck, tickling me with play bites. I squealed with laughter and shoved him away. "You don't play fair."

"Not always," he admitted.

Staring at his bright, smiling face, my gut twisted. No more lies. No more stalling. But the Weaver's ever-so-sure warning that the Sandman would look at me differently sent a wave of prickling shame down my back. It didn't matter—the truth had to come out before he learned it another way. "There's still something else I need to tell you."

A hard knock shook the door. "Are we going to deal with Mara or not?" Kail droned from the other side.

"Go away," I called.

"No rest for the wicked," he replied.

I rolled onto my back and stared at the bunched fabric hanging above the bed. Wasn't he *just* telling me that I needed to rest? A throbbing ache began in my jaw, and I forced myself to unclench it. "That explains why you're constantly around like a tiny, yappy dog."

The sound of the Sandman's quiet laugh warmed me from the inside out and chased away my irritation. A small smirk lifted my lips.

"Woof," Kail deadpanned.

Fine. There was no ignoring Kail. I'd tried. Almost every day. He only became more and more annoying, as if that were possible. I climbed reluctantly from bed and hurried into a clean pair of soft black pants, a green shirt of the same mystery material, and a long black jacket with a stiff winged collar of gold, all gifts from the Doll Maker.

With a resigned huff, I yanked the door open to face Kail. "What?"

He mimicked knocking again before raising a quizzical brow. "I already said what I wanted."

"We're coming," the Sandman told him, then, to me, "we need a place to practice."

"Practice what?" Kail asked before I could.

The Sandman met my eyes. "Day Walking."

The basement of the Keep provided both the privacy we wanted and the caution we needed. I'd only been down here a few times, once to check it out, a handful more to scream where no one could hear. It was spacious, nearly four times bigger than the Keep above, with massive support beams running down the center. The floor was made of large stones, artfully placed in a jagged circle, while the walls were the same black and gold marble as above. Pieces of straw littered the floor, though I wasn't sure why, and any nightmares the Weaver or Rowan kept here were long gone.

The Sandman stood at the bottom of the stairs, whispering to Halven. Halven nodded once, then caught me watching. "Lady," he said with a bob of his head.

"Ready?" the Sandman asked, walking to my side.

Halven strode back up the stairs, leaving us alone with Kail who stood, brooding, in the corner.

I waved a hand toward the empty staircase. "What was the about?"

"I asked him to make sure Mare didn't move again after yesterday's attack."

That made sense. I stared at where Halven just was, unsure what answer I wanted him to return with. If she was still there, we could make our move. If she wasn't, well… It bought a little more time for my ankles to stop feeling weak.

"Nora? Are you ready?" the Sandman asked again.

"I don't want to do this," I whispered, my voice cracking. Day Walking was at the bottom of my to-do list, right under being boiled in hot oil. The pain of the Day World was still fresh—both the physical and mental. It ached down to my very bones, the air grating my skin, but my family…they were there. Thinking I ran away with *Ben*. Except Katie, anyway, because it took her until I was gone to realize I'd always spoken the truth about the Sandman. What if I suddenly popped up in my living room? I wasn't ready to deal with that particular confrontation.

"We won't go to your house," the Sandman promised with a smile that let me know he understood my worries without voicing them.

Perceptive, isn't he? the Weaver pondered.

The Sandman brushed a kiss over my knuckles. "Mare can't cross into the Day World without our combined power to carry her, and now that you don't have the dream …"

I nodded. Mara could only hitch a ride back to the Night World with me because I had carried a small sliver of the Sandman's power. Now that the dream was gone, the barrier wouldn't let the Ancient back through unless we worked together. Putting her back in the Day World wasn't my first choice though. I wanted her dead and buried, but clearly that was more difficult than it sounded. So the Day World it was. Sure, it would keep Mara from opening the Ever Safe and destroying everything and everyone, but there would still be a cost. The people who had no idea of the danger of this world would be the ones paying it.

I knew that should bother me. It didn't.

Much.

But I *wanted* it to which had to count for something.

"I follow Dreamers' cords to get to the Day World," the Sandman continued. He looked between Kail and me and shifted uncomfortably.

"I don't have that ability." My voice was hard-edged with frustration.

"Is there a place inside you that feels like it would help?" he asked, eager.

If he only knew, the Weaver taunted.

"Not really." Kail's presence burned at my back. No way was I spilling the beans about the Weaver in front of him, so I shut my eyes instead. "I'll try."

Okay. What's the secret to this whole Day Walking business? I demanded from the Weaver.

Why don't I do it for you?

My stomach twisted at the thought of him taking control of my body like he had when I found Rowan and when I woke up in the clock tower. The helplessness, the fear. *No—*

"Nora!" The Sandman's voice cut through the silent conversation, and my eyes flew open. A crease formed between his brows. "We have to go together."

"Right. Sorry." Had I almost gone somewhere? I flicked my gaze over to Kail. He eyed me suspiciously, and I squeezed the Sandman's hand. The Weaver's near-giddy laugh lingered in the back of my head, his claws sunk in deep. It was a miracle I was able to speak at all. To hold onto the Sandman. It was almost a certainty that I wouldn't be able to move without setting off something terrible. A domino effect, starting with the Weaver's talons slicing through my brain and ending with me dangling off a cliff somewhere in the Day World. *He needs me alive*, I reminded myself. "On the count of three?"

The Sandman nodded and began the count. Time seemed to slow, his words blurring, and my body felt fuzzy. Weightless. I focused on the Sandman's eyes and let them ground me as the Weaver's manic energy fizzled through my veins.

"That wasn't so bad, was it?" the Sandman asked.

I blinked and the hair on my arms rose. Not because I was unnerved—I was—but because it was freezing. Wind whipped around us, pelting us with hard bits of snow. It blew in sheets that seemed to erase the world beyond. I winced and huddled closer to the Sandman.

"Snow isn't supposed to hurt," I cried as it stung my face.

Snow was supposed to be fluffy. Pretty. It wasn't supposed to attack you. It was everywhere, as far as the eye could see, endless blankets of white. "What is this place?"

"You've never seen snow, so I thought I'd show you." He cringed when a particularly large piece landed in his left eye. "Sleet is admittedly less exciting."

"I think I've seen enough," I said, unamused. "Can we go back, or do we have to do something first?"

He scanned the area through slitted eyes. "This will be a good place to bring Mare, don't you think?"

I tensed at the reminder. But yes, this was a good place. Frigid, which would hopefully take a toll on her, and not a building in sight. Not that we could see far in this weather. Maybe by the time she found anyone, she would be too weak to do much damage.

Don't lie to yourself.

I pursed my lips. The Weaver was right—it was a lie. Mara survived centuries—

More than centuries, the Weaver corrected.

—without losing her touch. Why would a little cold weather change that?

"We can't bring her here." I met his eyes. Curse my stupid desire to be empathetic. "She'll eventually find a way to kill people."

The truth of it flickered across his face. "Losing some lives is better than losing them all, which is what will happen if Mare opens the Ever Safe."

"I don't accept that." I stepped away from him, shaking my head against the buzz of power. I *couldn't* accept that. My family was here, my friends' families. I owed it to Natalie and Emery to protect their kin. Even if their loved ones weren't a factor, even if this was happening a hundred years from now when everyone I knew was dead, I couldn't willingly allow people to be killed. Everyone was important to someone, even if they didn't know it. Like I hadn't known how important I was to my mother. It was still hard to reconcile that fact with the way she treated me.

The darkness in me pulsed. It wrapped itself around the thoughts of loved ones and grief and squeezed. And squeezed. And squeezed some more. *Stop it,* I hissed mentally.

I'm not doing that, the Weaver said, his voice honest, intrigued.

Panic boiled, but as each bubble popped, it left behind resignation. Tranquility. A void. Maybe the Sandman was right. Mara could kill a handful of people to keep the rest of our worlds alive. Thousands, even, which was more likely. But what did I care? I wouldn't die.

That last thought tore through the suffocating darkness. "I'm going back," I managed to say in a crackling voice.

And I did.

I sacrificed the thread nearest my wrist and used it to go home the same way I had used the one in my pencil box, not trusting the Weaver to help. Not trusting the power to not grow into something worse.

"You're missing something," Kail said carefully when I reappeared in the basement alone.

I took deep breaths to situate myself and flung the melting sleet from my hands. It hit the ground with a splat. "Don't start."

"You didn't toss the Sandman into some deep, dark abyss or anything, did you?"

More snow and ice melted from my hair, running down my face, and I glared at him. "Shut. Up. Kail."

He pushed away from the wall and straightened. "You aren't denying it."

My patience plunged into the negatives, and I snapped. I lunged at him, knocking him back into the wall. My fists balled into the front of his jacket. "I said, *shut up*."

With one slow, confident swipe of his arm, Kail knocked my hands away. "Thou doth protest too much. Did it cross your mind, then?"

"Can you tell what's crossing my mind right now?"

Kail's eyes flashed in beats—three quick changes, a slower one, and then back to their usual steady pace. He gripped my chin between his thumb and forefinger, then blocked the slap I brought up to remove his hand. "You may think I'm a fool, Nora, but I'm nothing if not observant."

Oh, I knew he was no fool.

"I'll find out what's going on with you," he vowed.

The Sandman stepped up to us. "What's going on?"

I jerked away from Kail with my heart in my throat. Why did he insist on silently popping up out of nowhere all the time?

"Someone needs to get you a bell," Kail said.

A wonderful idea for Christmas. "He thought I tried to hurt you."

The Sandman glared at each of us in turn with no expression to give away his thoughts. That in itself told me he was utterly confused. "Right," he said carefully after a long, strained silence. "Can you do that again? At a moment's notice?"

I opened my mouth to say no, but the Weaver gripped my head and nodded for me. *We have to take care of Mara, dear Keeper. Deal with your personal demons later.*

You *are my personal demon,* I shot back.

Maybe the Weaver was right. Maybe it was something else, something *me*. The darkness left a stain, because now very little felt truly heinous. It felt almost justified that the Day World should make a few sacrifices of its own. Just like killing all those nightmares had, but people weren't nightmares. I scowled. That should matter. Why didn't it matter?

"Halven's waiting outside," Kail said with measured words. "Are we doing this?"

I sighed, resigned. "Yes."

We walked single file out of the Keep's basement and back into the palace. Melted snow and ice dripped around my shoulders from where it had crusted my hair. I gathered the ends and squeezed the excess water out.

"Lady Nightmare?" I winced at the sound of Bloody Mary's voice. The slap of her footsteps filled the hallway as she rushed toward us. "I've been waiting so long to speak with you."

"Not now," Kail told her impatiently.

"It will only take one moment." The nightmare turned to me and clasped her hands in front of her chest. "Please, Lady?"

I ran a hand down my face, careful not to look at hers. Seeing my features on her was unnerving, and she'd been lurking for days. If hearing her out got rid of her, then by all means. "Fine. What?"

"Can I have the meat?" she squeaked, as if she suddenly lost her nerve. "It's old now and you haven't touched it."

I shot Kail a questioning look, only to find his brows lowered in equal confusion. The Sandman tensed beside me. "What meat?" I asked, half-certain I didn't want the answer.

"I…I wasn't snooping around," Blood Mary assured me quickly. "I came to ask you to fix the damage to my territory and smelled it."

"What meat?" I repeated, with growing irritation. We had things to do, an Ancient to see.

Blood Mary pointed to a set of double doors. They led to a room with a long dining room table—no chairs, because no one actually ate there—that spanned the length of the room and ended with an identical set of doors. The other set opened almost directly across from the main palace entrance. Had one of the nightmares come in to ask a favor and died inside, waiting? I hadn't been slacking *that* badly, had I?

"Sure." I spoke slowly, regretting the words as they left my mouth. "Take it and leave."

"Thank you, Lady!" Blood Mary wasted no time tugging on the doorknob.

The heavy wood barely budged, but it didn't seem to faze her. She simply kept pulling, making progress one centimeter at a time. If she knew there was meat inside, she had managed to open them before. How long had it taken then and why hadn't we noticed?

I looked to Kail again and bobbed my head, signaling him to follow her.

"I'd really rather not," he glowered.

"If there's something dead in there, I want to know what it is," I said from the corner of my mouth. Bloody Mary didn't need to know it worried me, and Kail was better than me at hiding emotions.

"Well, then. By all means, after you, Lady." He held an arm out to usher me forward.

The Sandman exhaled heavily and eased between us to follow the nightmare. Bloody Mary looked up at him and cringed away. "Shortcut out of here," he said as an excuse to help, and pulled the doors open with one yank.

The smell was immediate, overwhelming, and utterly fatal. Fatal for me. Not for whatever creature was decaying in my would-be dining room. They had already perished—clearly—though if they hadn't, this odor would've surely done them in. There was no possible way these doors could trap every trace of this catastrophe.

Quality craftsmanship, the Weaver said with a touch of admiration.

What? Oh, dear lord. I was going to throw up everything I'd eaten in the last eighteen years.

It's air tight, he mused.

Not now, Weaver.

"Do you want the note?" Bloody Mary asked before entering the room.

"Note?" I wheezed, and stifled a gag as best I could, bile burning my throat. The Sandman stepped away from the doors, his face white, a hand clamped over his nose and mouth. I desperately wanted to follow him away from the source. We were going to have to burn the palace down and start over if I was ever going to be rid of this stench.

"What does it say?" Kail asked calmly. As if we hadn't entered the devil's lower intestine.

"I didn't read it. Only saw there was one," Bloody Mary replied.

Ah, hell. The sooner I went in there, the faster it would be over. "Yes, I want it."

With watery eyes and a hand firmly clasped over my nose, I followed Bloody Mary inside. A mound of carefully cut meat was stacked at the center of the table in a semicircle. Each piece resembled a pork chop, except the two center pieces that looked more like a roast. It was as if they were waiting to be packaged and sold at the grocery store, minus the huge rotten black spots.

"It's there," Bloody Mary practically sang as she pulled the front of her dress out to create a pouch.

I struggled not to inhale and approached the table. A butcher knife stuck out of the wood at an angle, pinning a piece of parchment down. My pulse beat erratically. Every piece of me screamed not to look at the words scrawled across the page. In rusty colored ink.

Blood, the Weaver interjected.

My stomach roiled. *Yes, I got that.*

Read it, he urged.

"I can still have it?" Blood Mary asked, eying me with one hand hovering above the top cuts. "The meat?"

I scowled at her, disgusted. "Why do you want this?"

"It's a delicacy, even if it's spoiled." She slopped the round pieces of meat into the pouch she made from her dress. "Dreamer meat is nearly impossible to come by."

My body jerked to attention. Dreamer meat? She couldn't mean…

The note, the Weaver reminded me. *Read the note.*

I stumbled up to the table, doing my best not to vomit all over it as Bloody Mary hummed happily beside me, and snatched the paper up. It slid free of the knife with a soft rip. Blocky letters stared up at me.

Humans say not to play with their food. If they only knew how much fun it could be…don't you agree?

I crumpled the message in both hands. *Mara.* She didn't sign it, but she didn't have to. No one else would be brazen enough to cut up a Dreamer and leave them here. In my palace. With a note that taunted my human side.

"Get it out of here," I said breathlessly to Bloody Mary. "All of it. Now."

In that moment, it didn't matter that it was a Dreamer. A person. Chopped up. I needed it out of my sight and out of my palace, along with anything that could link me to it. If nightmares thought I forbid them from killing Dreamers while I feasted on them, there would be trouble. And I had enough of that already.

Get Kail, the Weaver ordered.

As if on cue, he waltzed into the room with a large wooden crate. "Here," he said to Bloody Mary. "Hurry up." His eyes fell to the meat on the table and, for the first time, he paled. His throat bobbed with a hard swallow.

"It's a Dreamer," I supplied.

He looked at me from the corners of his eyes. "You don't say."

"It's very recognizable," Bloody Mary commented as if it backed him up. She then dumped the pile of meat from her dress into the crate with a *squick.*

The sound sent me reeling, and I chucked the balled-up note at Kail's feet. "Another gift from Mara."

"Someone really needs to redefine the word *gift* to her. Get her to send a nice fruit basket, perhaps."

"How did she get in here?"

She got in, the Weaver said matter-of-factly, *because you built yourself a house of stone instead of a palace of nightmares.*

My stomach dropped. He was right—this wasn't an impenetrable sanctuary. The Hours waltzed in and kidnapped me, so why had I expected Mara not to get in? I stormed from the room without letting Kail answer.

"Let's go kill her," I called when he didn't follow me out.

Kail moved then, barking orders at not only Bloody Mary, but every nightmare within hearing distance. Inspect every inch of the palace. Destroy anyone unauthorized. Clean the dining room until they could see their reflections in every surface.

I joined the Sandman and Halven just outside the main doors while Kail set everyone into motion, my jaw clenched. When we returned, if there was a single cell from an unwanted nightmare within a five-mile radius, it would die a slow, painful death.

"Lady?" Halven croaked.

"Not now." Not until we were far away, and the scent of rancid Dreamer meat was gone from my nostrils. Not until I knew exactly what features I would add to the palace walls for security purposes. "Where's Mara?"

"Halven just confirmed her current hiding place." The Sandman opened his mouth to say something else, but Kail bustled up to the group, out of breath, and his focus shifted. "What happened in there?"

"What happened?" Kail scoffed, glancing quickly at me, then followed Bloody Mary with his gaze as she dragged a full crate of meat out the front doors. "Ask me again when I feel less like saying *I told you so.*"

Chapter Eight

Nora

I knew I wasn't the only one thinking it was too easy to toss Mara back into the Day World, but they acted like it was as simple as dragging the garbage out to the side of the road. Our *trash* had no intention of going anywhere though. We had to get close, had to touch her. A chill crawled up my spine at the thought of grabbing her dry skin, of her coarse hair and sharp nails. She would undoubtedly use her teeth too, if it came to that, and her knees were big enough to act as sledgehammers.

But here I was, making my way through the Nightmare Realm with the Sandman, Halven, and Kail. The Sandman assured me Day Walking would be as effortless as when we practiced. The hard work was done already. He and the Weaver erected the barrier between worlds, and it had proven effective at keeping her out. But what they considered effortless, I considered dangerous. The dark coil that tarnished my conscience earlier sat poised to strike again. Was that the price I had to pay for the Weaver's power? Was it becoming more like him and less like me?

I feel the same as always, the Weaver chimed in.

My eyes twitched with the effort not to respond. If the magic was turning me into something else, why had it waited the better part of a year? Maybe the Day World kept it at bay. If I had come back sooner, maybe this would've happened a long time ago. And speaking of coming back, how did the Sandman Day Walk alone if the barrier needed both Dream and Nightmare magic? The Weaver had to have the same ability too.

Before I was bound, the Weaver added, grumpy.

I sighed. *Are you ever going to let that go?*

Unlikely.

If that wasn't the truth, I didn't know what was.

We can pass through the barrier to Day Walk because we're made of pure magic. There was a way around it for my nightmares before the Sandman stole the information and hid it in your head, but the Ancients are made of something else.

Super.

For the record… The Weaver hesitated. *No one here thinks this will be easy, but it has to be done either way. Why splash around in a puddle of fear and doubt when it solves nothing? A brave face can go a long way, and you of all people should know that.*

I made a low, contemplative sound, and Kail whipped around to stare at me. The Sandman and Halven were too deep in a hushed conversation about our destination to notice—

something about a map and symbols and the clock in the Blood Tower.

"What?" I snapped.

"Nothing," he replied, every syllable full of sarcasm.

I bristled. The least he could do was voice his thoughts if he insisted on being so obvious, and not the same *what's wrong* spiel. "Liar."

A blur of black and orange zipped past me, and I jumped, my heart in my throat. When the creature skidded to a halt at the Sandman's side, my pulse only beat faster. Baku, your friendly neighborhood nightmare eater and all-around sketchy chimera. I tried to convince myself the increasingly bad vibe I got from him was because he looked at me like a juicy burger fresh off the grill. With his elephant trunk and tusks large enough to skewer me, tiger paws to shred me, and the same watchful eyes as a rhinoceros, I would be a fool not to be wary, but it was something else. The watchfulness was tinged with a sense of anger. Of resentment.

"Hello," the Sandman greeted cheerfully. "Where did you run off to yesterday?"

Baku gave no reply, of course, as he couldn't speak. It was just as well because I doubted I could stomach hearing about his hunts.

Kail gripped my wrist and slowly tried to pry my clenched hand from his forearm. When had I grabbed him? "Sorry," I whispered and relinquished my death grip.

"Relax. He won't eat you in front of us," he said, impassive.

"I wouldn't be so sure." What could they do to stop him? If a few nightmares were all it took to bring Baku down, he wouldn't currently be a thorn in the side of my realm, but I kept my mouth shut for the Sandman's sake. He was alone in the Dream Realm with the chimera as his only steady companion now that I couldn't visit the beach.

Kail let out a small breath. "I'm sure of nothing."

"Except maybe yourself." I shot him a knowing smile, but his eyes were glued ahead on Baku.

"True. But him… even I can't figure him out."

The statement was lacking, as if a whole story needed to follow. And I would hear it, just not with Baku three feet away. My guess was the chimera's presence put Kail on edge too because he wasn't one to hold his tongue. And with the Sandman's proximity, we couldn't exactly speak freely about his friend without putting him on the defense. Plus, we were on the way to fry a bigger fish. A whale, really.

"You won't need Halven to spy after today." Kail's voice wavered. "Mara will be gone."

My guard melted away, replaced by the familiar tang of guilt. I was almost relieved that I could still feel that way, but it was hard to be glad when it hurt so much. Not as painful as Kail and Halven must have felt being torn in two…

"I'm sorry it's taking so long to make good on my promise," I told him sincerely. I hadn't wanted to wait at all, but we needed them apart to keep up our ruse.

He shrugged, glib. "What's an extra two months when I'm withering away on the inside?"

I held back a wince. They were apart for a long while now, and the side-effect was constant pain. Though they both hid it extremely well, I knew first-hand how exhausting it was. Day after day. Week after week. For them, decade after decade. Maybe even longer as I actually had no idea how old they were or when the split happened. I hated delaying their reunion, but it wouldn't matter if they were in one body or two if Mara opened the Ever Safe.

"You're easily the most irritating thing in my life but—"

"The *most* irritating? I can think of a dozen other problems that should come before me. The Doll Maker's constant gifting of ridiculous clothes—" He ticked off a finger, staring pointedly at my collar. "That bloody creature hanging around the palace—really, I don't know why you didn't kill her." He ticked off another finger. "The Hours."

"Some of those clothes are cool," I shot back. The jacket I had on made me feel like I belonged in an action movie, kicking butts and taking names, which I happened to be doing. Well, the butt kicking anyway. I didn't care about their names. "Bloody Mary probably won't come back for a while now that she took off with the Dreamer..." I couldn't bring myself to say *meat* out loud. "And the Hours are locked up at the moment, so, you win."

"Those are all temporary fixes. Mine would be permanent."

"If you had let me finish." I purposely cleared my throat. "You're the most annoying thing in my life, but you deserve this. Tonight, after Mara is gone, I'll put you and your brother back together."

"Tonight?" he asked skeptically. "You won't be too tired?"

I lifted a brow. "Do you want to wait until tomorrow?"

"I'm just saying, the Sandman stayed over last night and—"

"Kail." I elbowed him hard in the ribs. "Quit while you're ahead."

"Right." He stood a little straighter and sniffed. "Tonight is fine, I suppose."

"That's what I thought."

He rewarded me with an extremely rare true smile, then quickly tried to hide it. Maybe he would be freer with his feelings once he was back with Halven. His brother was kind and empathetic, so with any luck, some of it would rub off on him, if only to give me a break from his constant attitude. It would be nice to have someone I could hold an actual conversation with.

In front of us, Halven and the Sandman slowed. "This is the place?" the Sandman asked him.

Halven nodded.

Braided metal, knotted and tarnished, stretched high above our heads. Hundreds of spires, maybe more, in groups of four and five, held up globes. Some of the spires were misshapen, others tilted, the shine gone, and each sporting holes rimmed with crumbling rust, while the spheres ranged from colossal to minuscule and everywhere between. A decaying city in the sky. Occasional sprinkles of dust fell like autumn leaves. Metal creaked around us, sounding as if the slightest breeze would knock everything over, and a chill ran over my skin.

"You're sure about this?" I felt less brave than ever as we hid behind half of a rusted globe that had fallen to the ground. "Because it *sounds* easy and all, but I've seen how agile she is now."

The Sandman tucked a piece of errant hair behind my ear. "It's not easy to kill an Ancient. This is the fastest and most effective way to stop Mare. We can monitor her in the Day World and, if she's out of control, we can kill her there, where she's weaker."

If. The Weaver laughed. *Might as well stay when you get to the other side and finish the job.*

You're awfully sure we'll get her there without her ripping us to shreds.

Oh, she most certainly will. Especially with you *in charge of* us.

"Stop." It was almost as if I could feel the smoke from his memory snuffing the air from my lungs. Those people... She killed them without reason. What would she do now that she had a personal vendetta and my home address? At the first whisper of the Weaver's breath, I rushed to stop him from telling me *exactly* what Mara would do. "Just stop!"

The Sandman cocked his head. "Stop what?"

"Not you." I squeezed my eyes shut. Right. *That* conversation still had to happen, but not right before we faced the big bad. I flicked a hand casually through the air. "Myself. Doubts or whatever. Mara knows what we'll try to do, and she'll never let us get to her at the same time."

Kail glowered around the Sandman at me, the suspicious look returning. "On what planet did you expect her to *let* you?"

"It's okay, Nora," the Sandman said calmly. Though it was obvious he wasn't convinced . "You know the plan. We both need to have a good grip on her, then Day Walk. The second we're there, we let go and come back."

He forgot to add 'and hope she lets go too'. Remember how well she latched onto your back? It's not often a lord—sorry, lady*—requires stitches. Twice now. Not that I'm keeping count, but I'd really love to stop wasting energy fixing you for stupid mistakes.*

"That's not much of a plan," I said softly. There were too many holes. Too many things that could go wrong.

"Try, try again," Kail said in a flat voice. "And again, and again, and—"

"You're not helping," I hissed.

Fallen crumbs of rust *crunched* behind us, and I whirled to see Baku trotting straight into the landscape. He wove expertly

broken record player used to make. I waited to see if it would happen again. If it were simply a wrong note or a broken piece of the landscape. Echoes came instead, one right after the other. *Footsteps.*

My mouth ran dry. "Do you hear that?"

Another scratch like the first.

The Sandman and I stopped in our tracks. My hand went for the thread around my arm while his dove deep into his satchel of sand. Whatever it was, it was close, but it wasn't necessarily Mara. Other nightmares had to live here—the globes were too perfect a habitat to pass up. My heart hammered, the sound filling my ears. I flexed my fingers. Maybe I should alter the landscape. Make it silent just until this was over so we could hear where—

A figure launched itself from the globe in front of us. A flurry of white fabric and wild brown hair. *Mara.* She landed on her feet, crouched and ready to pounce. Her long shins stretched up to knobby knees that bent near her head. Deep black veins covered her pale skin. She smiled viciously.

No words were exchanged. No quips or threats. They weren't necessary when Mara's next attack said everything. She lunged at me faster than a whip. Her nails were longer now, sharper than they were in the clock tower, her teeth filed to points. Spittle sprayed from her mouth on a hiss.

I froze.

Move! the Weaver screeched.

A net made of glimmering sand shot in from the side. Mara leapt over it and gouged my arm on her way past me. Her nails dug in hard as she swung herself around my torso and landed a few yards away. The pain jarred something in me. Darkness swirled rapidly. Its energy rose up around me, and my vision tunneled to the hideous ancient creature. It was as if someone flipped a switch inside me. Nora off, Lady Nightmare on. Any sense of self evaporated, and I plucked a thread from my wrist. Gave it life. Heard its first vicious roar. A great beast with a head of horns and sparse red feathers decorating its thick hide leaned back on its haunches in front of me.

Mara made the most inhuman of sounds and skittered backwards. A hail of dream-made weapons flew through the air—knives and grenades and throwing stars. My nightmare chose that moment to charge, and my chest tightened.

"No!" But my cry was too late. The nightmare took nearly every one of the weapons meant for Mara.

You have more, the Weaver reminded me.

Yes. I had more nightmares woven than I could count, but it wasn't about the nightmare. It was about all those lost chances for a weapon to strike Mara. To slow her down. But it was done, so I loosened threads from my wrist, one after another. A floating saber-tooth shark and monsters made of muck. Human-like fodder beside things that would never pass as such. Thorns and teeth. Archers and mountain men with picks.

"Nora." The Sandman stopped me from pulling another thread. "It's too many. She'll run, and we'll never catch her."

"They'll slow her down," I disagreed. Mara would cut every nightmare down—I knew that—but they weren't meant to do my job. They were meant to make my job easier.

He winced and pointed the long spear in his hand at the worn pillar holding the sphere above our heads. "Look."

Mara scrambled up the knotted metal as easily as a monkey climbed a tree, and my nightmares attempted to follow. Tried and failed. The corroded, weakened post disintegrated beneath their weight and the whole construction groaned against the pressure. Rust rained down around us, and I shielded my eyes. Panic flashed through me, hot and tingling.

"Enough," I screamed at them. They would bring the entire thing down and the close, confined quarters of the sphere would make it easier to get our hands on Mara. "Stop!"

The nightmares eased away reluctantly. Mara was a bone to chew, and I had taken it away from a pack of loyal dogs. They surrounded the base, immobile yet waiting. Waiting for Mara to fall. Waiting for me to let them attack again. They wanted an order from their lady, but my brain scrambled to think of a purpose for them on the ground. The archers could still shoot, and if any of them had aerial abilities—

Screw the nightmares right now, the Weaver practically roared in my head.

The Sandman pulled me to him with an arm around my waist and shot a grappling hook straight at the top of the globe. "Hang on."

Handy, that sand of his… I was beginning to see why the Weaver was jealous.

I'm not jealous.

The next moment, my feet were off the ground. The Sandman and I hurtled toward the globe at an alarming speed, and my stomach churned. How did you stop these things? Mara squeezed up through a small hole at the base of the globe. *Perfect.* Now, if we could only get—

The Sandman let go of the hook.

I would've screamed if I remembered how. Or if I was able to breathe. Or do anything except cling to the Sandman for dear life. Which was exactly was I did. Why would he let go? He just told me to hang on. My hands balled into the fabric of his shirt, and I fought the urge to close my eyes as we free-fell straight down.

The sphere was getting closer and closer, and a scream stuck in my throat. A moment later, we hit a large rusted area near the top. The Sandman twisted so his back broke through the metal instead of mine, and the thin material crumbled like dust. We continued to fall. And fall. And fall. Shards of muted light pierced the interior of the globe. The entire thing was hollow save for the pillar that went from the north pole to the south pole.

Mara scurried around the center post, eyes fixed on us. She wouldn't have to wait long at the speed we were going.

Oh, this was going to hurt…

The Sandman produced a short scythe and drove it into the pole. It sliced through the metal with a loud screech, tearing a jagged line behind us. "Hang on," he said again in my ear.

Not a problem. My eyes tracked Mara's every movement until she disappeared into our blind spot. *Nightmares.* I needed to make more in here. Two or three… They could pin her down and we could—

Something hard slammed into me from behind, causing the Sandman to lose his grip on the scythe handle. We broke apart and we careened the rest of the way down. His sand shot out to catch me, but while he loved me, his magic didn't. I fell straight through the sand and hit the bottom of the sphere with a resounding *thwak.* It echoed through the metal interior and through my ears. My head. My bones. Did I still have bones that weren't broken?

Shake it off.

The sound of fighting filled the globe. Mara screeching. The Sandman calling my name. Metal striking metal. A loud thud.

Help him! The Weaver's shout bounced through me alongside the pain.

He was right. I had to get up. Help. Move. Make a nightmare. Something. Anything. But my body refused to listen to commands.

Worthless, the Weaver snarled.

Darkness swooped in. My vision faded, returning only in brief flashes. The ceiling. Mara sitting on the Sandman's chest, digging her nails into his face. A wall of sand rising.

My shoulder exploded into fiery agony. Mara was beneath me, said shoulder rammed into her ridiculously hard sternum.

"Quickly," I said to the Sandman. Only it wasn't *me.*

I scrambled to regain control of myself, but everything spun violently. Turned black and suffocating.

The next instant, Mara's face lit up with a victorious smile.

Metal creaked.

Metal crumbled.

Metal gave way.

The Weaver clenched my jaw. *We'll be fine, Keeper. The Sandman is safe.*

But all I knew was the ground outside quickly rising to greet us. The déjà vu didn't escape me in that very brief moment. I fell into this life with Mara clinging to me, and now I was falling out of it with a single difference. She wasn't going to break my fall—I was going to break hers. And, likely, my neck.

A fissure glowed bright in the darkness. I stared at it for a long time, struggling to connect the dots. The only time I saw these was when I was asleep, but we were just fighting Mara…

Look, Keeper, the Weaver's voice urged quietly.

At what? I asked, the thought feeling far away.

He didn't answer, but there was a deep knowing inside me. At the memory. He wanted me to see this one. I crept closer, steeling myself against the unknown. The other memories I had seen of him and the Sandman weren't exactly informative. Insightful, maybe, but not in a way that helped me rule. *Here goes nothing…* I swallowed hard and peeked inside.

A knife sat in the Weaver's palm. His threads throbbed weakly over the pulse point in his wrist. There weren't many left—a single long strand that housed maybe a dozen nightmares. He turned the blade over carefully, and I jerked forward. It was *the* knife. The one I used to kill him. Only the handle wasn't glowing with magic.

"This will likely have dire effects," the Sandman warned.

The image shifted up as the Weaver looked at him. He was covered in filth, his violet eyes dull. "What choice do we have?"

"It's not too late. We could still find a way to put Mare back into the Ever Safe."

The Weaver shook his head. "Baku can't remember how she lured him out, and there's no time left. If we don't stop her now, she'll let more Ancients out. We both know there are worse things still locked up."

"The balance…"

"Will compensate," the Weaver said. "We've been over this. It's decided."

His gaze went back to the knife, and I felt his sigh as if it were my own. The thread slithered away from his wrist and toward the heel of his hand where it reached up to circle the handle. A piece of it separated and wrapped itself around the hollow hilt in the same pattern it had when I held it.

"Your turn," he said.

The Sandman held out his hand, sand cupped at its center, and the Weaver set the handle down on top of it. A slight sizzling filled the air as the sand coated the spaces between the thread. The two lords looked at each other and a sense of foreboding swelled within me—within the Weaver. The same feeling was written all over the Sandman's face.

Without looking away, the Sandman sliced his forearm with the tip of the blade. His blood ran down the center chamber of the gleaming metal, and the Weaver held his own arm out. "Be quick about it," he said.

A moment after the Weaver's blood mixed with the Sandman's and reached the interior of the hilt, the knife glowed brightly. The space around them rippled with magic so strong that the hair on my neck stood straight up. The Sandman handed the knife back to the Weaver and pulled out a handful of sand.

"We'll be fine, right?" he asked.

The Weaver tightened his grip on the knife. "Hurry before Mara finds a door back to the Night World."

The Sandman pursed his lips and tossed the sand into the air above them. It clung to an invisible sheet riddled with holes. *The fabric between worlds.* The Weaver stepped up to it. With a single swipe of his arm, he sliced it open. The tear released hurricane level winds, ripping a line down its entire length. The Weaver stumbled back. He shouted to the Sandman, but it was impossible to hear him. Dark hair whipped across his face, obstructing his vision. The rest of the scene became an erratic flash of images as strands were blown from his eyes and back again.

The Sandman hurried in front of him, struggling to control his sand. There were barrels worth of it in the air. It spun and spun, half of it blowing away. The Sandman's arms were raised, his head angled against the wind, knees bent in a struggle to stay on his feet.

After what felt like an eternity, some of the sand reached the cut, flashing bright blue on contact. The rest of the Weaver's final thread flew off his arm. Together, their combined magic stitched the fabric between the worlds back together. The ground grumbled, tilted, groaned—

The fissure slammed shut.

Wait! I called.

You've seen what you needed to see, the Weaver said. *A knife powerful enough to split worlds will surely be powerful enough to kill Mara.*

We couldn't even touch *her at the same time,* I cried. If we couldn't manage to grab two random body parts, how did he expect us to be precise enough to deliver a fatal blow?

The Sandman's plan failed. Now it's your turn.

My turn. The words sunk in. As the Lady of Nightmares, it was only natural that I should get equal say.

Don't forget, Keeper, we need to take a little side trip. Send the Sandman and Halven out to find Mara again, but bring Kail along with us. He might prove useful.

Care to expand on that?

He paused before answering. *Not yet, but it needs to be done whether or not you comply.*

Anger rose hot as his words reminded me of my last few conscious moments before he took control again to attack Mara. *He* was the reason the plan failed. The Sandman had direct contact—all I had to do was lay a hand on Mara and it would've been over.

I saved him, the Weaver said, *and you know it's true.*

It wasn't true. Yes, I was having trouble moving, but he didn't have to tackle Mara off the Sandman. All he had to do was touch her, then we could've warped to the Day World and ended this. We had her. *We had her.*

If the Sandman was hurt further, he would've gone back to the Dream Realm, leaving you all alone.

"I hate you," I screamed, and the action yanked me fully back into consciousness.

Three familiar faces greeted me along with the smell of burning pine. I sat up with a start. The sudden movement set my head spinning, and I groaned, digging the heels of my hands into my forehead. *Deep breaths.* There would be no sorting things out until I calmed down. Until I shifted through all the new information. Even if the Sandman was too hurt to continue with the original plan, which I immensely doubted, there was time. A split second more and—

"Take it easy," the Sandman said softly. His hand landed, feather-light, on my back.

I nodded stiffly and cracked my eyes open. We were surrounded by a forest of black and white. Greying leaves coated the ground, each balanced upright on their narrow tips, and white flames licked a pile of black sticks inside a freshly dug pit. "Where are we?"

"Did you expect us to carry you all the way back to the Keep?" Kail poked at the fire with a long stick. "You're not as light as you look."

I dabbed at the lingering ache at the back of my head. A knot rose beneath my hair, but not so big that one would think I fell dozens of feet to the ground. Hooray for magic healing. I was lucky my neck wasn't broken. At least, not any more. Who knew what state I was in when they had dragged me here? Judging by how dark the muted sky was, I had been out nearly all day.

"It wouldn't be a good idea to let the nightmares see you weak," the Sandman explained. "They shouldn't see you as something they can defeat."

"Mara isn't exactly the same caliber as nightmares." Not to mention that we were surrounded by nightmares at that very moment, even if it seemed like an empty forest. Other things surely lurked nearby, and Rowan proved that even trees weren't to be trusted. I stretched my back and groaned. "Besides, Halven could've whisked me back to the Keep unseen."

"Forgive me, Lady," Halven said in his usual raspy voice. "That would be difficult."

I opened my mouth to ask why when I saw the answer. Blood flowed freely from his arm and bones jabbed through his skin in two places. "What happened?" I demanded.

"*That* happened," Kail growled, pointing a finger into the wooded area behind me.

I twisted around to see Baku prowling among the trees. "Baku did that?" I asked with raised brows and leveled a look at the Sandman. "Why didn't you stop him?"

"Don't look at me," he said, staring into the flames. "He's his own creature."

"Perhaps he misread my intentions," Halven suggested painfully.

Kail and I snorted in disbelief at the same time. "He tried to attack me before," I said. "He'd eat me if he could."

"Hunger?" Halven proposed.

"Hunger," Kail echoed. "After he gorges himself almost nightly? Is that why he bit *you*?"

"Wait. Let's focus." I scowled at the shadow moving around us in giant, predatory circles. "Give me your arm."

Halven held out the mangled limb, and I took his hand. Closing my eyes, I quickly found his knot of thread and stitched the injured part together. When it was finished seconds later, I let go, and Halven flexed his arm. "Thank you, Lady."

"Sorry I couldn't do more." I looked between him and Kail. They should've been back together by now, like I promised Kail this morning. Bitterness coated my tongue.

"So," I began carefully. "What's next?"

"I was thinking about our next move." The Sandman paused and stared into the flames for a long stretch of time.

"Oh? It seems as if this new plan upsets you. I like it already. Tell us. What offends your morals so?" Kail leaned back on his elbows, smug.

The Sandman's jaw twitched. "We should gather forces and lay a trap. Mare was able to run off because there was no second line."

"That sounds like it would take too long," I said.

"You have enough thread to pack the Nightmare Realm full of nightmares," Kail reminded me.

"Fine." I had to pick my battles. The truth was, I wasn't worried about making the necessary nightmares. I was worried that it was going to take time to find Mara again and sneak this second line into position without her realizing it. There was almost no chance she wouldn't see us coming if we traveled with an entourage. "I'll make whatever you think we need, but this time, we're doing it my way."

Kail looked me over. "We're to pace back and forth through the Keep and avoid the problem?"

"No. We're getting the knife I used on the Weaver." I met the Sandman's eyes and held his troubled gaze. He knew where I was going with this without my voicing it, but the others didn't. "We're putting it in Mara's heart."

That's not quite what I had in mind, but it'll do.

What else could you possibly have meant? I snapped. *You literally said the knife could kill her.*

"Why not all of the above?" Kail offered. "Trap her in the Day World. Stab her with the knife. Deposit her somewhere far from civilization. If she's not completely dead, she'll still be weak. And not to mention, *gone.*"

It felt like overkill, but with Mara, was *anything* overkill? The Sandman and I held each other's stare for an entire minute. He knew he was fighting a losing battle—I could see it in his expression—but I could also see his hesitation. That knife was responsible for changing so many things. Now it was time for it to do some good.

"We have a plan then," I said finally.

"Right." The Sandman gnawed on the inside of his cheek. "I'll travel back to the Keep with you, then get the knife by myself."

By himself. The Weaver sounded as bitter as a grapefruit. *Always doing things alone. Always thinking he knows better than everyone else. Watch out, Keeper. You might be next.*

"I won't," I hissed.

The Sandman's eyes narrowed. "Won't what?"

Kail flew up straight, staring at me as if the Sandman sharing his suspicions somehow validated everything. "Yes, Lady," he added in a cynical voice. "Won't what?"

"Let you go alone," I said quickly, panicking. "Halven will find Mara's location while the rest of us retrieve the knife."

"It won't take three of us to—"

Kail cleared his throat, and the Sandman cocked his head. A curious look passed over his face as he looked at me. He might as well have been Medusa the way I froze under the scrutiny. If the two of them were going to team up on me, I was in trouble.

"If you insist," he finally said.

I stood and wiped my hands on my pants. "You have no idea where the knife is or what you'll have to do to get it, so yes. I do insist."

Chapter Ten

Kail was right. Something was wrong with Nora.

She came up with an alternative plan to deal with Mare rather quickly. A very *specific* alternative including the knife. There were the strange things Nora said, the comments that had nothing to do with the conversation. Something was off, but I couldn't place my finger on the cause. So, if Nora wanted to come with me to get the knife, fine. Hopefully it would give me a chance to ask her for the truth.

"Yo," Katie called. She floated in the water at the edge of the beach, letting the luminescent waves push and pull her gently. Her arms were flung out wide as if she were in her own private swimming pool, complete with bathing suit and foam noodle. My nostrils flared in annoyance, though I knew it was uncalled for. We were out there risking everything while she was taking a dip, but what was Katie supposed to do? We had banned her from entering the Nightmare Realm.

"Enjoying yourself?" I asked neutrally.

The knife. I had to find the location of the knife. Too much was going on right after Nora became the Weaver to give it much thought so I hid the blade as well as I could on short notice.

First stop, the second Dream Keeper. Katie could only hold one dream, so I had to use another. The problem was that I didn't bother keeping an eye on whoever it was. Nora, Kail, and Halven were the only ones who knew I took the knife, and none of them would go looking. *Yet.* Not when we had to get rid of Mare, and the brothers still needed Nora. It was safe for the moment, but the plan was to move it somewhere more secure as soon as I had the chance.

"I am, in fact," Katie answered, gliding her arms through the water.

"You do know there are sharks in there, right?"

Katie bolted upright and swam frantically toward shore. When she hit sand again, huffing and puffing, I couldn't help but laugh.

"I was kidding."

She glared up at me. "I liked you for a hot second there."

I crouched in the sand and shoveled some into my satchel. "Do you want me to whip up an inflatable chair before I go?"

"You just got here." There was a slight whine in her voice, but she hid it well as she shook glowing water from her hair.

"Yes, well…" I rubbed the back of my neck and stood. "Things with Mare didn't exactly go according to plan so we're busy putting together a new one."

Katie's eyes widened. "That was today? What happened? Where's Nora?"

"She's okay." There was no reason to mention the ten-story fall, Nora's temporarily broken back, or the way her skull had cracked open like an egg. The magic healed her, aided by the fear siphoned off from nearby nightmares, but I wasn't ready to relive it. I probably never would be. There's something about seeing the brain matter of the person you love…I shivered. "She's at her palace now."

Katie pursed her lips like she did whenever I said a word like *palace*, *Lady*, or *ruler*. "No one got hurt?"

"Nothing we won't recover from," I hedged.

She crossed her arms. "Your face is literally covered in blood."

I scrubbed at my cheek with the back of my hand. "Just some scratches, but as you see, no lasting damage."

"You strike such confidence in a gal."

"Don't take this the wrong way, but I'm in a hurry." Retrieving the weapon required at least two steps—finding the Dream Keeper and fetching the knife—but it was possible I threw in a couple side tasks to get to the final hiding place. We had to be ready to go as soon as Halven found Mare's new hideout.

I strode back toward the barrier, and Katie followed at my heels. "What are you going to do that you didn't do last time?"

"Bring a weapon."

"That sounds suspiciously like you didn't bring one this time." She hurried in front of me and walked backward. "But that would've been dumb, so I know that's not the case."

"We did." Nora and I were technically weapons, if used as such.

Katie made a low disbelieving sound and tied her hair back with a band from her wrist.

"Alright, well, you have fun." I slipped the satchel across my chest.

"Wait!" She grabbed my wrist before I could I turn away. "How was she?"

Somehow, it was an entirely different question than when she asked where Nora was and what happened. It was also a loaded inquiry that I had no idea how to answer so I didn't, which was undoubtedly worse.

"Did she…" Katie winced. "Did she ask about me? Or Mom? Paul, even?"

I shook my head slowly. "We didn't have much time to talk."

She quickly shuttered the splash of hurt on her face. "So, where are we going?"

"*I'm* going to get a knife. You're staying here."

"Like hell!"

I pinched the bridge of my nose. "I can't take you into another person's dream."

"Nice try. You were heading toward the Nightmare Realm."

Touché. My impatience to be near Nora again got the better of me. "I can do it from anywhere."

"Safely?" She quirked an eyebrow and paused for my answer. I stayed silent. "I didn't think so. You never know what's waiting in the shadows, eh?"

"Katie, listen. Please," I begged. "I really can't take you into someone else's dreams. *Can't,* not won't."

"Fine." She plopped down on the beach. "You go do whatever you've got to do inside someone's head, and I'll sit right here until you get back. Then we'll go back to Nora together."

I lifted my satchel off and dropped it to the ground. There wasn't time to argue but…our first attempt to get rid of Mare failed. Worst case scenario, if I took Katie with me, she would get a chance to say goodbye before Mare wrestled the knife from us and destroyed both worlds. Best case, Katie would see Nora and give some insight into what was wrong. I always thought I was the closest person to Nora—I *was* at one point. Now…was anyone? Not even Kail knew, and he was beside her nearly every second of every day.

"Wait here." I gave in. How could I not? There was no way I'd let anything hurt Katie, and it would put her at ease to see her sister alive. Nora though, that was another story.

She stretched her arms over her head. "As I said."

I bit my tongue and shut my eyes. The cords stretched out before me, a tapestry of glowing strings mingled among duller counterparts. I mentally ran a hand over them, sending out a spark of power and waiting for the dream to answer in kind. Like with Nora, it would be an ache, almost a cry, begging to come home. All I had to do was let it. The trick was getting the Dreamer to relinquish the information, and for that, I needed to spin a dream that would make them happy enough—*distracted* enough—to say yes.

There.

A wobble down a dull cord. Of course the Dreamer would be awake right now. I gripped the connection anyway and followed it to a quiet cobblestone street, letting sand cloak my presence. The scent of freshly baked bread filled the air, and a middle-aged woman hummed while watering a potted shrub beside a sign reading *kleintierpraxis*. The sun wasn't completely over the terracotta roofs, yet which meant this early bird would be up for quite a while. I groaned impatiently as I hovered beside the woman.

The veterinarian took her time—another two minutes admiring the flowers followed by ten minutes plucking dead leaves from a range of potted shrubs—before heading inside. I followed on her heels, waiting until I could safely put her to sleep. A dog barked from somewhere in the back of the house-turned-animal clinic. She cooed reassuringly that their mama would be there to pick them up that afternoon and slid behind her desk, humming again.

I took the smallest pinch of sand from the pouch around my neck. She had to be awake for her job, after all, and it would only take a moment to get what I needed. The vet opened an appointment book and skimmed a finger down the page. *Now or never.* I tossed it in her eyes and whispered, "sleep."

A second later, her head flew toward the desk. I flung my palm out, catching her forehead before it slammed into the wood, and brought her arm up to cradle her cheek.

I pulled on the magic inside her, and it dragged me inside the vet's dream. We sat at a fire at the foot of snowcapped mountains with three other people. Stars hung in the sky as the group laughed and passed a flask to each other. I eased onto the log beside the vet.

"May I please have the dream back?" I whispered in German. The woman jerked out of the scenario to stare at me with wide, frightened eyes. I exhaled quickly and dumped more sand into my palm. It swirled into an elderly man that immediately drew her attention.

"Klara?" he asked in an awed voice.

She stood with tears in her eyes. "Papa?"

"The dream?" I prodded. "Will you give it to me?"

"Papa?" she asked again.

I let the image of her father fall back into its original form. "He will come back, but first, the dream. Please allow me to take it," I urged in a gentle voice. It was an awful thing to do, using her dead father to blackmail her into cooperation, but time was short. I would make it up to her when I could, just like I had with the children I'd stolen dreams from. A years' worth of dreams with her entire family, dead and alive.

"*Ja*." She blinked at the sand scattered at her feet and repeated her consent. Three times. Four.

I willed the sand into her father again just as the dream flew from nowhere and slammed into my chest. The location of the knife flooded through me along with images following my steps as I hid it. I was a little disappointed in myself for the lack of tasks required to get to it. I knew it was a possibility, but still…two stops and a weapon capable of killing Nora could've ended up in enemy hands. Though the final resting place made it fairly improbable…I shook my head. Next time I hid it, after Mare was dead, there would be more time to think it through.

When I returned, Katie was dressed in jeans and a faded yellow t-shirt with a setting sun printed across the chest. "We good to go?" she asked without preamble.

"Not yet." I stared at the sea. Somewhere out there was the only token capable of calling to The Spectral, which we could use to sail to the knife. There were two options—swimming down to the bottom of the very deep water or letting my sand do the work—and I wasn't in the mood for a dip. With a flick of my wrist, a thin veil of sand shot across the water like a pool cover, and I sat down beside Katie to wait. "Did you wake up to change?" I asked to fill the silence.

"The power of the dream is mine." A proud smile stretched her lips, and her t-shirt darkened to orange.

"Nora never figured that out." I chuckled, but reality wiped away the sliver of amusement. Nora asked me to keep her sister out of the Nightmare Realm, yet here I was, preparing to do the exact opposite. "I should probably fill you in on a few things while we wait."

Katie raised her brows. "I'm all ears."

Chapter Eleven

Nora

My hand flew furiously over the paper, creating a rough human figure. Anything to distract myself while we waited for the Sandman to come back. Anything to stay busy.

You know what would keep you busy? the Weaver asked, though it wasn't really a question.

"We are not going to the Blood Tower," I retorted.

I need to see if I'm right about something.

"We have more important things to do."

It could be related.

I stood, flinging a stack of half-completed sketches at the wall of my studio. They fluttered to the ground when what I needed them to do was slam into the marble. Shatter. Crack. Break. Then I could pretend it was the Weaver I was hurting.

Anxiety swelled, reaching peak levels, and I knew that, given another chance—if the Weaver stood in front of me now—I would kill him all over again.

My breath came too fast, my heart like a hummingbird. My stomach rose up, up, up amid remembered flashes of falling from the globe. The Weaver practically threw me out of that sphere to save the Sandman. In his warped little mind, he did it to save me from fighting Mara on my own. If it were true, I should've felt grateful, but I didn't. The Weaver didn't try another option first. The resulting wounds would've been worth it if we had completed our goal.

You like the kill plan better, he said matter-of-factly.

"Yes, I like it better!" I screamed. "Only a fool would want—" The rest of the sentence stuck in my throat as I turned to find Kail leaning against the door frame. How long had he been standing there? "Kail," I breathed, ignoring the growing tightness in my chest. "What do you want?"

"That's hardly relevant at the moment." He stared at me as if he knew. As if I had just confirmed something. The slow, thoughtful shift in his eye color held me frozen as he stalked toward me. "Hello, Weaver."

A nervous laugh bubbled from me. "What are you talking about?"

"It took me a long time to put the pieces together." Kail tilted his head. "You used your power expertly at times, but two minutes later struggled with the easiest problems. You've been distracted, troubled, and talking to yourself. I don't claim to know your every side, Nora, but it wasn't hard to pick up on the fact that something wasn't right."

"It's been a learning curve. How would you know what's *easy* for me to do? You don't have this magic inside you," I snapped. There was no way he could come up with the truth on his own. *No way.* "In case you haven't noticed, I'm stressed."

He made a low sound of assent and stared into my eyes. "I'm sure you are. Being held hostage is no walk in the park. I would know."

"I'm—"

"Tell me." Kail leaned in until his mask skimmed my nose. "Are you working yourself so hard because *he's* making you or because *you* want to?"

"I don't do anything I don't want to." I lifted my chin, my hands balled into fists. "I'm the Lady of Nightmares."

Kail jumped up to sit on the long table, his knees bumping into my hip. Paper, pencils, and charcoal scattered. He stared at his lap, and his long beak skimmed his chest. "Don't lie. You're not good at it."

"I'm not—"

You're a terrible *liar,* the Weaver agreed. *The Sandman only believes your untruths because he loves you and* wants *to believe you're speaking honestly.*

Shut up, Weaver.

This is getting ridiculous, the Weaver said, impatient and cutting. *Why deny it? Kail knows.*

I haven't told the Sandman yet.

"You're talking to him now, aren't you?" Kail smirked knowingly and watched me from beneath his lashes. "You can admit it any time now. Just say the words, *Kail, your observant ways paid off once again.*"

The world shifted, pushing me down, burying me. Flashes of color broke through the darkness as it grew. My knuckles throbbed. The Weaver's low growl filled my head, and my muscles strained to hold him back. To stay *me.*

Did you not train with the Sandman to build your strength? he quipped. He knew very well I had. Apparently, he was there the entire time. *A lot…of good…it did,* hė strained.

Weight bore down on my chest. I struggled to breathe as memories of Mara sitting on me in my bedroom intensified the pressure. Mental warfare on top of physical assault. The Weaver's specialty. Then my vision cleared in an instant, though the weight remained, and I found myself held against the floor. My arms were pinned behind me, fists digging into my lower back, with Kail's thighs firmly securing my own to the ground. This close, I could almost taste the pinch of fear mixed with the light scent of cinnamon that he'd smelled like for nearly two days now. The beak of his mask pressed roughly into my cheek.

"Kail," I managed to squeak. "I can't breathe."

He shifted his weight slightly, lifting his head to meet my gaze, but kept me trapped. "Explain."

"You first," I wheezed.

His eyes narrowed. "Lady or no lady, I'm not going to let you attack me without cause."

"There's always cause with you."

"You're in no position for jokes." A small flicker of enjoyment crossed his face.

I wriggled beneath him. "As much as you love knocking me down a peg or two, would you mind?"

"That depends. Would you mind terribly *not* lunging at me like a maniac?"

"Get up. I'm not going to do anything." *Probably* not going to do anything. If my hands ever regained feeling, I might use one to punch him for this.

"Are sure about that?" His voice rose an octave at the end.

"It was him," I admitted. "The Weaver. Are you happy now? Let me up, and I'll explain."

Kail lifted himself slowly, one limb at a time. As if he didn't quite believe me. If I were being honest, I wouldn't have either if our roles were reversed. I would probably chain him to a chair and make him talk to me from behind a concrete wall. But Kail was too curious a creature not to get all the juicy details of my possession.

I'm not a demon, the Weaver said. *But if you want to see a real possession, I can tell you which landscape to visit.*

I ignored him as best I could. Kail crouched in front of me, his expression blank. Waiting. This could be my practice run for telling the Sandman. Get an outsider's opinion. Test out reactions. I sighed and pulled my hair back into a ponytail. "Ever since I killed the Weaver, a grin has haunted me. Only that grin turned out to be your friendly neighborhood serial killer." Then I launched into the shortest version of events possible, starting with the day I beat Rowan.

When I finished, the exposed bottom half of Kail's face was drained of color. The hollows of his cheeks seemed to deepen as his flashing irises studied my face. "He's really in there?"

"I thought you figured that out on your own?" I accused.

"I'm usually only ever ninety percent sure about my theories."

My eyes widened. "Considering the risks you have me take, those are terrible odds."

Kail shrugged, unbothered, and continued to stare. It was more of a curious study than a judgment, but still I fidgeted under the scrutiny.

"Trust me," I grumbled after a long minute. "It's worse for me than it is for you."

"There are…options…" He grimaced. "I'm sure there are."

The only way to get me out of your head is if you're dead, the Weaver said to me. *Though, seeing as their whole theory is wrong about what would happen next, it would only create bigger problems for everyone.*

"Oddly enough, I like living," I said to them both.

Kail offered a lopsided grin that didn't reach the rest of his face and eased back until he sat against one of the cupboards. "You should've told me," he said. "If he can take over like that, it was a dangerous truth to keep to yourself."

"He's only done it a couple times." More than a couple, but not more times than I could count on my fingers. It felt almost shameful. A stupid sentiment, but one I couldn't shake.

Kail glared at me like that wasn't an excuse. Because it wasn't. "Has he said anything about what you promised me?" he asked. "He won't try to stop it, will he?"

I have bigger problems than you and Halven, he said dismissively.

"No," I said. "Even if he did have a problem with it, I'll keep my word."

Kail stared at my forehead with a crease in his brow.

"You can't see him," I said, my voice flat.

His eyes darted away. "Thank goodness for small miracles."

Tell him that I want to go to the Blood Tower.

Why?

I practically felt his eyes roll. *Just do it.*

Fine, I'll play along. If out of my own growing curiosity than anything else. The Weaver was this insistent about very few things. I think he enjoyed watching me fail too much. "He wants us to go to the Blood Tower."

Kail licked his lips. "Why?"

I don't know yet.

"You don't know?" I half-shouted.

Trust me.

Never going to happen. He killed my boss, slaughtered a girl with a glitter pen, tortured my friends to death, and gave my father a heart attack. Not to mention kidnapping my sister and making Detective Bell turn his sole focus on me because apparently there wasn't enough pressure already without adding possible murder charges to the mix.

There was never enough to actually charge you, the Weaver said in his defense.

"This is creepy," Kail said, watching me through narrowed eyes. "And, coming from me, that says a lot."

"You have no idea."

The Blood Tower was exactly how we left it. Blood flowed in place of mortar and the new front doors stood intimidatingly tall. Unlike before, it was somewhat comforting to see the stone tower before me. It felt almost like a childhood home. In a way, I supposed, it was. I became the Lady of Nightmares within these walls alongside what some might consider a new family. One corner of my mouth twitched into a smile, and I stole a quick peek at Kail. I thought of him as a brother of sorts, so yes. A weird, dysfunctional, messed up family.

Not such a different family then, the Weaver said, not unkindly.

I snorted. My family was messed up—there was no denying it—but I couldn't help wondering if I would feel this calm walking up to my mother's house. Odd that Kail's domain would be the one I felt most connected to when it was where Rowan instigated my demise. I told Kail the tower was his to do with as he pleased, though I wasn't sure what his plans were. Or if he even wanted it. There was an unspoken rule that I did not ask specifics about his time with Rowan, but it was obviously unpleasant for him. Just because I liked the tower didn't mean he did. To my knowledge, he hadn't come back since before we dealt with Rowan, but I hoped, for selfish reasons, he had set something up to keep scavengers out.

You actually have to go inside, the Weaver said when I simply stared at the exterior.

"We came this far." I looked to Kail, completely aware of how awkward this was. The two of us...doing something because the Weaver wanted. When he was supposed to be dead by my hand. Because of something Kail helped orchestrate, willingly or not. I grimaced. "Might as well do this."

He pushed the door open with his shoulder, eying me. "If only we knew what *this* was."

Rowan was very detail-oriented. She liked lists. I think it had something to do with the tree line being so perfectly spaced and orderly. Even the berries—

I don't care, I hissed. Rowan was back as her perfectly-spaced self, suffering eternally. Exactly where she belonged.

You'll care if she kept notes from her spies.

My brows lifted. "Rowan had spies?"

"Of course," Kail answered. I startled at the realization that I had spoken out loud. "Many."

"You didn't think that might be important information to share?"

"I thought it was obvious," he said with an edge. "Did you think she had some sort of all-seeing eye? Really, Lady. Where's your head?"

I chewed on the idea as we entered the tower. It *was* obvious—as obvious as the tarantulas on the wallpaper. Medallions, at first sight. Furry, eight-legged horrors, at the second. Rowan knew a lot. Too much. I thought she was following me that day she and Kail found me in the Barren, but maybe not. She also knew which people the Weaver personally killed, and which murders he delegated to other nightmares. *Why* he delegated to other nightmares. *He was busy with the Sandman at the time*, Rowan told me. How was it that she knew what the Weaver was doing at the exact time my friends died? Unless someone told her…

Yes, yes. Spies, the Weaver said, impatient. *Now that you're caught up, pay attention.*

Oh, I was going to pay attention, alright. To who these spies were, where I could find them, and how best to kill them. "Kail." I paused when I noticed he was no longer beside me, but halfway down the hall. I raced after him. "These spies—"

"Don't know." He didn't slow or stop.

"I didn't—"

"You were going to ask me who they are. Why would Rowan tell me her secrets when she could use them against me instead?" He shot me a sarcastic smile over his shoulder and paused at the bottom of the stairs. "I don't know who spied for her because they probably spied on me too."

My mouth opened, but no words came out. I knew Kail didn't want to follow Rowan, knew they didn't exactly see eye-to-eye, but if she didn't trust him, why keep him around? She had the Blood Army and a single brush of her skin was enough to bring down an elephant while Kail was just good at…being Kail. He was smart, sure, but so was Rowan.

Nightmares have the same emotions as humans, the Weaver said. *The intelligent ones anyway. Just because something delights in the dark doesn't mean they're incapable of love.*

Love? I thought a bit too loudly.

Perhaps not your version of it, he conceded.

I would say not, though Rowan did seem to love herself. Did she have feelings for Kail too? The idea of that gave me a squicky feeling.

No. Rowan loved power. Kail did too, though not quite as much. She kept him because he was able to convince *other nightmares to see things her way, and he stayed because she had leverage.*

Leverage?

"You're talking to him again," Kail stated with a flicker of hatred. "About me?"

I wanted to deny it but couldn't. Instead, I would ask Kail the questions I wanted answers to. It was the fair thing to do, and I would accept if he chose to keep something to himself. The Weaver had no right telling personal secrets.

"Why did you stay when Rowan was so awful to you?" It felt much *too* personal the second the words left my mouth, so I quickly added, "You don't need to tell me if you don't want to."

"Better the enemy you know than the enemy you don't." His voice was dreary, his irises yellow for nearly fifteen seconds—the longest I'd ever seen them stay one color—before he spoke again. "I'm going to get a few things while we're here. I'll find you when I'm finished."

He climbed the staircase with stiff shoulders, and a part of me—a part that felt far away and almost wrong now—wanted to comfort him. Even if that feeling wasn't faint, buried deep inside, I would never have followed. Not when I knew Kail wouldn't want me to. I could only imagine his reaction if I tried to hug him.

Halven.

"What?" I turned away from the stairs.

The leverage. It was Halven.

"What happened to paying attention?" I asked, steering the conversation away from things I had no right knowing. "We're here for the notes, not a history lesson."

He's a little like you, you know. Halven may not be his brother in the literal sense, but they care for each other the same way you care for Katie.

"Focus," I insisted. "We're short on time. What am I looking for?"

The Weaver was silent for so long I thought he wasn't going to answer. *Her room. Go there.* I tensed at the command. *Just do it, Keeper, before I make this easier on all of us and take over.*

I shivered. He was in my head; he knew how much I loathed him controlling my every move. It made it even easier to hate him when he used my emotions against me. "You should really learn to keep your mouth shut."

Oh, I deserve an award for that after five months.

I groaned and reluctantly turned toward Rowan's room, the hidden door familiar to me after my temporary stay. Inside, the bed was nestled in the trunk of a thick tree that grew from the ground, twisting upward until it hit the ceiling where vine-like branches hung down. Red ribbons were knotted on the thinner areas, intermingled with small dried flowers.

"You know I already tore this place apart," I reminded him.

The obvious places, yes. Be more inventive this time.

"I hope you didn't bring me here on some stupid whim," I warned.

None of my whims are stupid.

I begged to differ, but that was a fight he'd never concede. So, I opened Rowan's closet and kicked aside the pile of her clothes where I had left them crumpled on the floor. With a long exhale, I ran my fingers along the wall, looking for the smallest inconsistency.

"There's nothing here." I flopped onto Rowan's bed nearly an hour later. Kail shuffled around the room, having joined me almost fifteen minutes ago. Why it took him forty-five minutes to *get a few things* was beyond me, especially since he returned empty handed. If I didn't know any better, I would've said it was a ploy to keep from helping me with this wild goose chase. "Maybe she hid them somewhere else." *If the notes existed at all.*

"No. She would've kept them here." Kail picked at the bark of the tree, listless, and completely unhelpful.

"Why?" I asked. "This place has more unused space than the palace."

"That's hardly true. And where would *you* keep top secret records?" He looked me over as if entertaining the idea that I might, in fact, have a cache of files squirreled away somewhere.

"I wouldn't."

"If you did. And if I were living with you," he pried. "Would you keep them anywhere except close?"

I rolled onto my back. "First off, you do live with me. Second, I wouldn't keep evidence around for anyone to find."

Kail made a loud beeping sound. "Wrong answer."

I wasn't sure why I bothered to question him—Kail knew Rowan. Her habits. Her daily routine. Plus, he never gave me real answers. The whole search seemed like a waste of time, which was what got under my skin. That, and allowing the Weaver to talk me into something, even if it was something as stupid as hunting down—

There.

I flinched at the Weaver's sudden exclamation after a long stretch of blissful silence. *What?*

There. The ribbons.

I zeroed in on the red knotted strips of satin. Some were brighter than others, a handful fraying, as if they were a collection Rowan gathered over time. I flew up from the bed and jumped, snagging the nearest vine. It strained as I held it down low enough to pick at the knot.

"What are you doing now?"

"They've been in front of us the whole time," I breathed.

The first ribbon fell away. My hands shook as I straightened the length of cloth to reveal a message written in fading black ink: Kail seen in the spaceship. Elkmar.

"Spaceship?" I held the note out to Kail, my pulse thumping. Seeing Elkmar's name sent a shiver down my spine, almost as if the shadowy nightmare were standing right behind me. Watching. Waiting. Standing too close on legs that bent backward with his ribbed horns and webbed feet. I rolled my shoulders against the sensation, knowing it was just my imagination. My magic would tell me if it were true.

Kail pulled the ribbon slowly from my fingers and scanned it. "One of my first safe houses." His gaze traveled to the hundreds of ribbons overhead. "Compromised, obviously, hence the others."

"So Elkmar was her spy?" It made sense. Rowan trusted him to deliver me to the Weaver, but she also didn't tell him that I wasn't meant to make it there. Did that mean Elkmar was loyal to the Weaver or to Rowan? Was he under the impression Rowan was working as the Weaver's hand?

You give him too much credit, Keeper. Elkmar simply likes to shadow things, and she gave him cause.

I jumped for another ribbon at the same time Kail snapped a vine clean off. Note after note. Secret after secret. There were names written that I didn't recognize, ones the Weaver assured me were no longer a problem, but there was one that appeared over and over that left me speechless.

Baku.

Each new note naming him as spy crushed me a little more. My soul floundered, a predator dragging it down into a murky grave. The Sandman…this was going to destroy him. They were friends. *How could he…?* I tore down each and every ribbon with shaking hands.

"He's been spying on the Sandman this whole time?" The words were hard to say. Harder to believe. How did he even communicate with Rowan?

"And you," Kail added.

Things made sense now. So many things. "We have to tell the Sandman."

Do we?

"Are you kidding me?" I said in a single breath. Kail watched me carefully as if I were a grenade ready to blow. "The Weaver doesn't think we should tell him," I clarified.

"Maybe we shouldn't," he agreed reluctantly.

My jaw dropped. "Okay. Both of you have clearly lost your minds."

"Better the enemy you know," Kail echoed his words from earlier.

I flung the latest unfurled note to the ground and whirled on him. "Rowan's gone. This isn't the same thing."

Meaning Baku is still hanging around because he found someone else to spy for.

"We *are* telling him. That's final." I met Kail's stare and held it. There was already enough the Sandman didn't know. When he found out about the Weaver, it would be a hard blow, but knowing I kept it to myself would be worse. I wouldn't repeat the mistake. "What we do after, we decide together. All of us."

Kail ran a tongue over his front teeth. "Can we hold hands and skip merrily into this fantasyland you've imagined?"

"What?"

"Nothing." He bowed with a flourish, making it perfectly clear he didn't mean the action. "You're the Lady."

"Damn right I am." I kicked at the pile of red ribbons. "Now find something to carry those back home in."

Chapter Twelve

Nora's palace stretched out before us with its harsh, intimidating lines and numerous watchful nightmares. I tried to see it through Katie's eyes, as something new and frightening, instead of the simple building it was. For her, this wasn't reality like it was for Nora. It certainly wasn't something Nora wanted her to see. I winced at the imagined potential tirade I would receive the second I crossed the threshold with Katie in tow.

"I can't believe I let you talk me into this." I snapped my hood up, hiding. "Your sister is going to kill me."

"I'll take the blame," Katie said, unconcerned, as her gaze traveled from one end of the palace to the other. "It's not like I gave you much choice anyway."

"You gave me *no* choice," I clarified.

She smacked my upper arm lightly with the back of her hand. "Then you have nothing to worry about."

Katie took off down the narrow path worn through the grass like the surrounding area wasn't crawling with nightmares. Two mangled trolls with crooked swords stood on either side of the path, and a woman with four eyes and skin a rainbow of color splotches trailed our movements from behind the easel she held. The massive dog I saw that day at the Rowan trees lounged against the outer wall. Yet, Katie's expression remained a blank slate the entire way up to the massive main doors. I almost had to wonder if she saw them at all. They were rather hard to miss, especially when the trolls grunted with each exhale and the artist reeked of paint and turpentine.

The dog lifted his head, ears perked, as Katie flew by him and flung open the doors. "Nora!"

A stunned Kail leapt back, arms flying out to catch the heavy wood before it smashed him in the face. "The hell…?" His eyes flicked over Katie's shoulder to me. "She's some sort of sand illusion, right? Or did the door actually hit me and I'm hallucinating Nora's sister? Because we can fix brain damage."

"She's real," Halven whispered from further inside.

Kail's irises flashed faster, his hands sliding higher up the door to bar the entrance. "Oh, no. No, no. You can't be here."

Katie's laugh was sharp. "Try and stop me, Tweety."

His brow lowered in obvious confusion, and I stepped forward to diffuse the situation. "It's fine," I assured him.

"That's rather hard to believe," he shot as Katie shoved her way past him. "Nora is going skin you alive."

Kail wasn't wrong, but here we were. There was no changing my mind now.

"There's an emergency back in the Day World?" Kail asked hopefully.

"No." I sighed.

A muscle jumped in his jaw. "Halven, don't let her find Nora. And keep her quiet." To his credit, Halven hesitated before obeying Kail's orders. Katie deserved at least that much fear with her stubborn temper. "In case you've forgotten, we *do* have an emergency here," Kail said under his breath the moment we were alone.

"I'm well aware of the threat Mare—"

"Not Mara, you idiot," he hissed. "Nora. I *told you* something was wrong with her."

My brows lowered. "She was fine when I left a few hours ago."

"Was she?" He dragged out the words.

It wasn't really a question. We both knew she was keeping something from us, but objectively speaking, Nora was okay. She was alive, and the Nightmare Realm accepted her. She would never be safe just as the Weaver never truly was, but there was a solution to every problem. Katie was hopefully the key to figuring out what was bothering her.

"Sandman!" Nora's voice bounced down the bare hallways. It was still echoing down the far end of the palace when she flew into view. Rage colored her pale cheeks red. "What were you thinking?"

Katie ran at her heels. "I was coming whether he brought me or not."

"Did you tell her to say that?" Nora asked.

The accusation grated. "Did I tell her to use the same reasoning you used to sneak back here? No. She just happens to be as stubborn as you are."

"Don't turn this around on me." Nora narrowed her eyes. "I specifically asked you *not* to let Katie come. What if something took her? There are still nightmares that want me dead. The Hours won't stay locked up forever, and Mara's running around."

"Mara is in the ice caves," Halven said calmly.

Nora shot him an angry glare before turning her fury back to me. "Now is not the time for a family reunion."

"You're just embarrassed," Katie snapped. "You don't want me to see you like this. Like one of *them*."

She spat the last word. I couldn't blame her—the Weaver had strapped her down inside a cave with an enormous serpent and a crazed clown as her babysitters—but I knew the hatred stung Nora. I felt the hurt as if it were my own. But Nora knew how her sister would react, which was another reason she asked me to keep Katie away. Seeing it in action only intensified my regret at bringing the two of them together.

"I'm not one of them," Nora snarled.

"Your eyes are glowing, Nora, and look at your arm. Look at this *place*." Katie flung her arms out toward the walls. "You left home for this? Mom has been inconsolable."

Nora balled her hands. "Detective Bell gave her my alibi."

"That you ran away with Ben?" She laughed bitterly. "Why would that make her feel better? You could be living in a cardboard box for all she knows."

"She never liked me anyway!" Nora shouted. A vein throbbed in her temple. "She should be happy I'm gone. No more *'crazy Nora'* to worry about."

Katie's face turned a deep shade of magenta. "You know that isn't true."

"Isn't it?"

"Alright," I said calmly. "Let's take a breath. Katie hasn't seen you in months and wanted to make sure you were okay before we went after Mare again."

"Why? To say goodbye?" Nora gave me a scathing look. "I don't intend on dying, Sandman."

"No one ever *intends* to die," Katie said in a hard voice.

Nora's laugh was hollow and unamused. "You want to make sure I'm okay? Well, I'm not, but I won't die. Ever."

"You can't know that," I said gently. "The Weaver never expected to die either." Our magic kept us alive, kept him alive, until it killed him.

She scoffed. "The Weaver isn't going to die a second time."

One Weaver wasn't more powerful than the last. In fact, I would say Nora was much weaker. That didn't mean she wouldn't grow to be as strong as her predecessor, but she was still learning. It wasn't possible to gain the kind of experience she needed to be considered his equal in so little time. She had the same amount of magic, yes, but the ability to wield it? The knowledge of when to go all out and when to hold back? She needed longer to master those skills.

"Your magic won't protect you from the knife if Mare gets hold of it," I said.

"That's not what she means." Kail's demeanor shifted, half fearful, half reverent. "*The Weaver* won't die again."

The Weaver, yes—Nora. But that didn't seem to be what he was hinting at. I scowled. "I don't understand."

Katie gripped Nora's arms and regained her sister's attention. "You're not indestructible."

Nora shot daggers at Kail as she replied to her sister, "I'm as close to it as someone can be."

Katie took a steadying breath. "Come home. This Mara chick can't get you there, right?"

Nora brushed her sister's hands off, her expression tight. "I *am* home, and if we don't stop Mara, you won't have a home to go back to."

"Then come see Mom first," Katie begged.

Kail groaned. "There isn't time for this. Really, Sandman? This is what you brought her here for? Now? It couldn't have waited a few more nights?"

"It should've waited until I was ready to go to her," Nora said to the empty space between us. "We all know this place isn't safe for Dreamers."

A sense of foreboding hung in the hallway. Words not yet spoken seemed to drip from the ceiling like heavy condensation. In a moment, I knew Nora would open her mouth to say something—perhaps *the* something—and I also knew I no longer wanted to know. Needed to, maybe, but wanted to? No.

"The Weaver didn't die," she said.

I couldn't tell if she whispered it or not over the roaring in my ears. "I saw his body."

"That doesn't mean he died."

I held my hands out at my sides. "That's exactly what seeing a body means."

"He attached himself to the magic that day in the Keep," Nora explained. "His body is dead, but he's inside my head. Talking. Constantly, constantly talking." She winced. "It's getting harder to know where he starts and I end. Or if there are ends at all anymore."

Breathing became impossible. My hands tingled. The Weaver was inside her head, filling her mind with his poison this whole time? "Since the day in the Keep?" I forced out. "That was almost ten months ago."

Nora blanched, and her eyes shifted almost unwillingly to Kail. "I didn't know," she said after a long moment. "That he was there. I didn't know. Not until the night we defeated Rowan, but I've only seen you once since then. I was going to tell you."

"When?" I demanded.

Nora gripped the sides of her head, her features twisting. "Knock it off," she said through clenched teeth.

"Nora?" Katie touched her shoulder. "Are you okay? What's going on?" Silence. Nora drew in a deep breath and clenched her jaw, lips tightly pursed, as if holding back a scream. "I don't understand what's going on. Do something!" Katie yelled at me.

Nora straightened before I could move. Her head tilted, chin up, shoulders square, and the look she leveled at me wasn't Nora at all. The world slowed. Nora—the Weaver—drew every drop of oxygen from the palace. To see him so boldly looking out from the face of the woman I loved was a new sort of torment.

Kail swore under his breath and slipped behind me. "As entertaining as this has been, may I suggest immobilizing her now?"

"Don't even try it," Katie warned.

The person before me ignored them both, eyes only for me. "Always taking things so personally, old friend."

It was Nora's voice, but it wasn't Nora speaking. An icy death crept up my spine.

"You." Kail hurried toward Katie when no one else spoke. "It would be a good time to wake up."

"Fat chance."

Kail took another step toward her, and Nora grabbed his arm. "Touch my sister, and you can forget about our deal."

"You can't leverage that," he breathed.

Her gold eyes shifted to his. "You can forget about it because you will be dead."

"Get out," I boomed, my voice hoarse. Katie wasn't the Weaver's sister and for him to call her that was a slap in Nora's face. If it had been up to him, Katie would be long dead by now. "Get out of her right now."

Nora winced and stumbled back. "Bastard," she said between heavy breaths.

"What the ever-loving hell was *that*?" Katie's demand was a boulder crashing into an otherwise silent ravine.

Nora launched into a detailed timeline of the last two months. Every fragment of information swirled through me like a storm. *The Weaver wasn't dead.* A bigger part of me than I wanted to admit rejoiced. I wanted only to hate him, to condemn him and find a way to kill him all over again for violating Nora, but I couldn't.

"I tried to tell you the night you came," Nora insisted.

She had, and I made her rest. She tried again the next morning too. That didn't stop the betrayal from fraying the edges of my heart. She could've sent word with Halven—he stopped here as well as the beach—or sent another messenger. Something. *Anything.*

And worse, Kail knew. The nightmare no one should ever trust.

"There's more," she whispered.

"More?" Katie raked her fingers down her cheeks. "What else could there possibly be?"

Halven stepped forward and held out a fist. I stood frozen, staring at the gloved hand. More. There was more. I wasn't sure I could handle it.

"Take it," Halven said in a sympathetic voice.

I held my palm out. A moment later, it was full of red ribbons. "What's this?" I forced myself to ask. None of them answered me. Nora's cheeks flushed, and she kept her eyes on her boots. Even Kail avoided my gaze.

"For crying out loud," Katie huffed. She took a ribbon from me and turned it over. "The Sandman has a Dream Keeper. Baku." Katie frowned. "What does that mean? Baku's a Dream Keeper too?"

"He was spying on you for Rowan," Nora said softly.

I balled the ribbons in my fist. "That's not possible."

"It makes sense." She winced, hesitating. "Rowan knew a lot about me."

"That doesn't mean anything," I said harshly. Baku was my friend long before Nora was born. We were alone in our solitude, bonded by it. The trusted chimera would never turn on me. "What does *he* say about it? That Baku was his spy too?"

Nora looked as if I slapped her but shook her head. "The Weaver didn't know until today."

"I don't believe it." Was it hot in here? Why was it so hot? I tugged at the neck of my shirt. "It's another lie, isn't it?"

Nora flinched. "I didn't lie to you."

"You didn't tell me something as important as the Weaver being alive." It was a near shout edged with panic. Sand inched slowly, cautiously, from my satchel, circling my hand. It sensed my anger and hurt and was ready to strike in my defense. "You know what? Nevermind. I can't talk about this right now. We need to go see the Wish Granter and get the knife so we can put Mare down."

"Sandman." Nora's voice was low as she reached for my arm.

I spun away from her and stalked back past the dog. The artist. The trolls. It was almost a half night's walk to get where we were going. Maybe by then I would be pulled together enough to hold a conversation. *Maybe.*

The Green Sea smelled of decaying fish, making me loathe to touch it, but we would need the token to get back from the island, so I couldn't toss it in. I took the gold medallion from inside my vest and ignored the curious stares at my back. I hadn't looked at Nora since we left, though I desperately wanted to. We had to talk. Really talk. I shook my head before thoughts of Nora could cloud it. The chipped token was heavy in my palm.

First, the knife.

With a sigh, I curled my fingers around the token and dunked my fist into the water. The reaction was immediate. Water hissed and rippled as a sail rose from the sea. Barnacles grew along the mast of a great, rotting ship, and Katie gasped at the skeleton crew leering down from the deck. I opted to avoid looking at them.

It only took a few moments for The Spectral to bob on top of the water. I stood, flashing the token that made me their commander, and one of the crew members tossed a rope ladder over the railing. The end dangled into the festering water a few yards from shore. No matter. I spared a pinch of sand to form a dock and strode straight for the waiting vessel.

Chapter Thirteen

Every curse word in the English language filled my head. *Repeatedly*. Katie was here in the Nightmare Realm. She was watching me like I had horns and a forked tail. The exact place, the exact look, the exact everything I wanted to avoid. Well, perhaps not the *exact* place. A rickety pirate ship run by a literal skeleton crew never came up in my imagined scenarios.

The first mate hovered nearby, pieces of sinew hanging from his exposed jaw, staring at me with his one good eye. *Good* being objective; the other dangled from its socket, covered with bot flies. It took everything in me to suppress the memory of Natalie with both of her eyes clawed out. The way the blood coated her cheeks. The two black, haunting pits in her beautiful face. I pushed away the image of her dull, lifeless eyes sitting in her hands, not because I didn't want to feel sorrow, but because I was terrified of *not* feeling it.

Your friend died well, the Weaver supplied.

Bile rose. "I hope, whoever this Wish Granter is, she grinds you to dust."

Your threats are so… He made a sharp, disgusted sound. *The Wish Granter isn't a miracle worker. Even* if *she didn't twist wishes around, she can't do anything about us.*

"We'll see about that," I mumbled.

You'll see your secret outed to the entire realm. I wonder what the nightmares will do if they know I'm in here…

"I know what *I* would do."

"Okay." Katie's voice was short and sharp. "You've been talking to yourself for the last half hour."

I gave her a withering look. "Talking to myself would be the preferred alternative, don't you think?"

"There's a lot I'm thinking." My sister pushed away from the mildew-coated railing and pointed at the first mate. "First, that *that thing* is a complete creeper."

"He's..." *Star struck made* it seem like I was full of myself, but it was the Lady they were awed to see. Whether it was the rarity of me leaving home or that I was *made* was anyone's guess. "He's fascinated. It happens sometimes."

"Privacy. It's a thing." She rushed at him, waving her arms wildly.

It reminded me of the day at the mall when she threatened the boys sitting next to us in the food court. They wanted to ask about my boss' death, but after she snapped at them, they bolted out of there, much like the nightmarish first mate did now. My lips tugged up into a smile. It fell the moment my sister turned her wild stare back on me. There was a reason I didn't want her in the Nightmare Realm—a reason other than her safety. I needed to let go of my life in the Day World, of the person I was then, in order to be the person I had to be now. Not forever, I hoped, but long enough to grow here. To let old anger fade away.

"I've got the basics of your situation," Katie started in a voice full of forced calm. "But it's the newest twist I'm struggling with."

"It's only new to everyone else," I said, shrugging.

"So, he's really in there?" She circled the air around my head with a finger.

"Lucky me, I know." I stared at the endless water. Emerald green waves lapped against the hull, appearing quiet and calm, but it was a lie. I felt the anticipation inside me. The waiting. When one of the cackling grey seagulls from above swooped down, red eyes trained on something beneath the surface, a large, frothy hand snapped it out of the air. It was gone so fast it didn't know what hit it. Not that I personally had anything to fear, but not all of us on board had that luxury.

"Nora Jane Gallagher."

I cringed and peeked over at my sister again. A mistake. Sorrow scarred her face. Anger, too. Frustration. "What?" I demanded.

Katie launched herself at me, wrapping me in a tight hug. I stood stiff, but not for long. Slowly, her hug thawed something inside me, and my arms lifted, returning it. "I hate you so much," she sniffled into my hair.

My heart panged. "I know."

"Why didn't you tell me what was going on?"

And that was the end of that. I pulled away. "Katie." I swallowed the bitter laugh but failed to do the same with the razor-sharp disbelief. "I tried to talk to you about it, and you denied anything happened. Repeatedly."

She opened her mouth and snapped it shut again. What could she say? There wasn't a time after my sister left for college that she didn't vehemently insist there was no truth to the Sandman or any of the things she'd seen.

"You destroyed so much when you left," Katie said, brittle.

"I'm sure I did." *My fault.* Everything was, even if it wasn't. "My choices were to lie and leave or tell the truth and leave. Either way, I couldn't stay and lying was obviously the better option. What do you think Mom would've done with the truth?"

"She wouldn't have believed you," Katie admitted.

"Oh, she would have. She would've believed I was ready for an institution."

"Nora…"

"Did you come all the way here to drag me through a guilt-trip?" She could've saved herself the trouble. I already felt guilty…when I managed to feel at all.

They didn't deserve you, the Weaver chimed in.

"I came to make sure you were okay," she said.

Laughable. We all knew I wasn't, and yet, I was. The old Nora was in trouble, but the me now? I chewed my bottom lip. "I'm sure the Sandman kept you updated."

"Seeing is believing." She plucked at the threads near my wrist, and they squirmed away from her touch.

My cheeks warmed, and I tucked my arms behind my back. "I need to check in with Kail."

I spun on my heel, leaving Katie alone at the bow of the ship, before I wasted another minute dwelling on the past. We had to focus on the now. Except my *now* stood like a statue at the bottom of the stairs leading to a raised tier at the center of the ship. The Sandman's violet eyes followed me across the deck, and I forced myself not to meet them. As hard as that was. If I was going to get to Kail, I had to go right past him. However poorly Katie looked at me, I was convinced his gaze would be worse. I lied, then lied again, and now it looked as if I was doing it a third time. I'd learned my lesson though. I had only needed more time. An opportunity to talk uninterrupted…

"Nora?" the Sandman whispered as I passed.

I ignored him.

Until he grabbed my wrist. "We need to talk about this."

"We don't need to do anything." I tried to pull away, but his grip tightened. It felt as if he held my heart instead of my wrist, squeezing, squeezing, squeezing. "I know, okay?" I admitted softly. "We do, I know, but not now."

"*Right now*," he insisted.

I wanted to use his own training against him, to lay him out flat right there on the slimy, mildew coated wood, but that would create a scene. And if he turned the tables on me, I would look weak in front of all these nightmares, which I couldn't afford. "You want to talk now? Okay. Let's start with how you lead my sister straight to the heart of the Nightmare Realm after you *promised* to keep her away."

"I'm sorry," he said through his teeth. "But she was going to come with or without me. It seemed safer for it to be *with*."

Ah, there it was. The first barb. Yes, it was better to come to the Nightmare Realm with him. For Katie, at least. But was it better for me? Did I not have enough to make up for here without having to make amends to my family at the same time? "Have we learned *nothing*?" I asked in a low voice. "You let me make my own choices, humored me, and look at us now."

His eyes narrowed. "I didn't *let* you do anything, Nora. You're your own person, and I never tried to control you."

"Didn't you, though?" I regretted the words instantly because they weren't true. He urged me one way or another, but he never forced me to take the advice.

"No!" His shout boomed across the ship. I'd never heard that tone from him before, and it held me in place like cement. When he spoke again, the anger was a quiet undertone as he spoke low enough for only me to hear. "We are in this place because of your repeated deceptions."

I opened my mouth, unsure what was going to come out, but he continued without giving me a chance to speak.

"*You* trusted Rowan and Kail. *You* killed the Weaver. *You* snuck into the Nightmare Realm like some sort of outlaw and brought back the only being who knows how to open the Ever Safe. And now? *Now?* You kept the Weaver a secret from everyone who helped you. It's been *two months.* What do you expect from us? From me? Do you expect me to continue forgiving you? You asked if we learned nothing, and the answer is no. *I* learned something though. Ironically, it was the Weaver who taught me to know when enough was enough."

My mouth ran dry. Was he going to bind me too? I wouldn't hurt the Day World. Heck, we were on our way to *save* it. Not that I wanted to go back, but the idea of being chained anywhere rubbed me the wrong way. "What's that supposed to mean?"

"It means, when this is done." He swallowed hard, his throat bobbing. "When Mare is dealt with and the Weaver is…contained elsewhere, I will go back to the Dream Realm and let you self-destruct in whatever world you choose. But, should you decide to stay in the Night World, it will not be the Dream Realm that you call home." He flicked a grim look behind me and let go of my wrist. "We're here."

The crew moved hastily about the ship as a tall structure appeared through the thickening fog, but I didn't care. Not when I finally *felt* something. Really and truly felt it. The pain nearly brought me straight to my knees. *No.* I *had* learned something. A lot of things. But right now, I needed to lean on one of my old truths—pretending to be fine. After Katie was home safe and sound, after we had the knife, I would talk to the Sandman. Would better explain. Make him understand. This couldn't be it between us. We'd come so far together.

Trust lost is the hardest to regain, the Weaver said sympathetically.

"You would know," I seethed.

Unlike the Weaver, I wasn't a homicidal maniac. Plus, I had a literal eternity. The Sandman couldn't stay angry at me *forever*, could he?

"Are you coming, Lady?" Kail called from across the deck.

I rubbed my aching chest, my heart breaking beneath the surface, and urged my heart to be patient, to keep hope alive. Then I raised my chin, threw back my shoulders, and strode across the ship like I owned it.

Chapter Fourteen

Nora

A gargantuan hedge maze towered over us. The dark, muted green shrubbery was both perfectly trimmed and a hot mess. It was as if a landscaper purposely missed an overgrown patch every few feet, the long finger-like vines swaying in an eerie dance. Somewhere inside the tangle of foliage, wind howled. I glanced back at the pirate ship, but the only part visible through the fog was the crow's nest as it sailed away from the island.

Perfect. We're stuck here.

The Sandman can call it back, the Weaver reminded me. Not that it helped ease my fears. *Besides, you're right where you want to be, aren't you?*

I rolled my eyes. *Yes. I* want *to go into a maze full of who knows what and—*

You're in the best company for it, he said with nonchalance. *Between Halven and myself, you have a map to the center.*

Halven turned his head slowly in what I could only assume was an examination of the outer wall through his eye-less mask. He knew how to get around, to read the clock in the Blood Tower, to pin-point exact locations, but we were technically *at* our destination. Could he see how to get from here to the center? Was the center even where we needed to go?

Relax, Keeper. I'll share a secret with you: all roads lead to the Wish Granter. It's just a matter of how long it takes.

I scowled.

What good is it if the Dreamer never reaches the nightmare? Residual fear is a nice appetizer, but who wants a veggie platter when you could have a nice juicy steak?

Vegetarians, I said, my voice flat. His laugh seemed genuinely amused.

"Hey," Kail said, loudly, in my ear. "Are you going to throw your two cents into this conversation or not?"

Conversation? Were they talking? My face warmed, my ears buzzing. "What was the question?"

"Halven can only see a direct line to the center so we have to find our way through the maze. Are we splitting up?" he asked like he was speaking to a child.

"What?" My eyes popped. "No way. Are you nuts?"

"We would cover more ground," he argued.

I looked at the Sandman, and my heart seized painfully. The muscle in his jaw jumped. "No," I said. "It doesn't matter which way we go. We'll get there without getting permanently lost."

Kail shot Halven an exasperated look. "It would be *faster*—"

"How do you know?" Katie asked me. "That we won't get lost, I mean."

I sighed and trudged toward the entrance without looking back, "because we're steak."

Their confusion and reluctance pulsed against my back, but it didn't stop them from following. Kail was close on my heels, Halven close on his, while the Sandman and Katie kept their distance. The quiet hush of their conversation filled me with emotions I couldn't decipher. Jealousy, perhaps, that my sister spent the last two months at the beach when I couldn't. That *they* could be close. It was stupid, and I had no right to feel that way, but when had that ever stopped someone? Emotions had no master. The only thing a person could control was their outward reactions.

"Listen, about being steak…" Kail eased up beside me and held his hands up questioningly.

"No one's going to eat you," I said, knowing where his train of thought was headed. "Unless you don't shut up."

The moment we were all inside the maze, the walls surrounding us rustled. Branches shook, starting at the far end and racing closer. All the stray pieces sticking out disappeared into the center of the greenery, only to shoot out across the entrance. They tangled together, pulling and twisting, until there was no opening at all. Only perfectly manicured hedges.

"Yeah, okay," Katie said, her voice wavering. "I'm out."

"I don't blame you," I said, part of me wishing I had the same option. Besides, saying *I told you so* wouldn't help anyone and antagonizing her would probably make her tough it out.

"This isn't over," she promised. "I'm coming back."

Before I could tell her not to, that things would only get worse before they got better, my sister woke up, vanishing from the maze. "Anyone else want to chicken out?" I looked at each of them.

"Seems a little late for that," Kail said with a raised brow.

We all knew it wasn't. I could force the maze to open if I needed to, but whatever fed his courage was fine by me. If Kail needed to convince himself this was mandatory in order to keep going, then that's what it was. I cracked my knuckles and focused on the landscape instead.

The maze was silent again now that we were locked in, and I led the way down the straight passageway. It didn't appear to turn anywhere. The longer we walked, the more I began to wonder if this was a maze at all. It felt like we'd walked miles and miles in a straight line. There were no off-shoots, no other ways to turn.

Sure there are, the Weaver interrupted. *It's an illusion. Look for the darker green patches.*

I ran my hand down the thread on my arm, taking comfort in its presence. *Right. Okay. Nice of you to mention that before.* I squinted at the walls, seeing no difference. *Darker green patches, darker green patch*...my gaze swept over the other side of the passage, and I noticed a single protruding leaf. The wall sucked it back in like it knew I noticed the mistake. I stopped and walked up to the spot, licking my lips. It was slightly darker, but not much. I would never have noticed if it weren't for the leaf. *Are you sure about this?* I asked the Weaver. Walking straight into a wall would be completely embarrassing.

Try it, he drawled.

I scowled at the wall, debating whether I should trust him on this one or not. He wouldn't let me get hurt because he needed me, but there was nothing stopping him from torturing me mentally. In fact, I was pretty sure that was his favorite pastime. The ground boomed once beneath our feet. The sharp penetrating sound rung through the air as if someone were using it as a snare drum.

"What possessed you to leave the knife with the Wish Granter?" Kail chided the Sandman.

"She's stationary," he answered, sounding unsure of himself. "I don't remember doing it, but the Dream Keeper…"

He trailed off at the title. *My* title. Before…

"That seems like a rather weak reason," Kail went on. "What if someone wished for it?"

"Why would anyone wish for it?" His frustration cut the air. "They would have to know she had it first."

"Or," Kail dragged the word out, "they could wish for something to kill one of the Night World rulers and ta-da! Knife on a platter."

The Sandman didn't have time to defend himself further because something small and white zipped across the opening. It was too fast to make out a shape, but it left a trail of smoke in its wake. I stumbled backwards into Halven's chest. "You guys saw that, right?"

"Saw what?" Kail asked.

Another one like the first darted by, scampering up the hedge wall. "That."

A flurry of angry chirps traveled from inside the hidden passage. That was our only warning before a scurry of white squirrels launched themselves at us. Streaks of smoke trailed behind them. They pelted into us before we could duck, their little nails and teeth digging in. I gripped the one on my shoulder and screamed as its abdomen scorched my hand. It fell to the ground, lowered itself into a crouch, and chattered loudly. Its body was solid white, its tail formed solely from the smoke drifting off its back. Beady black eyes swirled. My hand throbbed while another squirrel gnawed its way down my back.

"They're made of dry ice," the Sandman said in a rush, plucking the creature from my back. "Don't touch them with your bare hands."

I kicked at the squirrel still snarling in front of me without making contact. It took off, hopping into the hedges, and I shook out my hand. "This is stupid. I'll just change the maze to open a direct path."

Bad plan.

I clenched my fists. *Great plan.*

There are more nightmares separate from the maze living here. Disrupt their home, and you'll be attacked again.

We'll be attacked again anyway. Being the Lady of Nightmares only offered so much protection. Nightmares had to recognize me first, and that took the mindless ones longer to do sometimes.

"What are you waiting for?" Kail asked.

Freaking Weaver. It would be stupid not to listen to him and invite more trouble than necessary. "We're going—"

Halven shoved me straight through the camouflaged opening, and I tumbled head first into the hedge on the other side. Tiny barbs scratched at my face and hands. I hissed at the burning pain.

"What was that for?" I shouted, extracting myself from the shrubbery. But when I turned around, I was alone.

The opening was gone, replaced with a solid hedge wall, spliced through with giant iron spikes. Blades of grass floated, settling on the ground where I stood a moment before. If Halven hadn't pushed me, I would've been crushed. Or impaled. A shiver ran up my back.

"Sandman?" I called. "Kail?"

There was no reply. I eased open my connection to the Sandman and felt his confused terror pulse through me as if it were my own. Maybe some of it was. But he was alive which was enough for now. I stuck my hands carefully between the spikes and felt around the shrub for any way to get it to open again. Leaves wrapped around my hand, grinding bone against bone. I ripped myself free and stared at the wall.

"Screw it." I pushed up my sleeves and reached out to touch the maze, to find its knotted thread. To tear down its walls.

Don't do it, the Weaver warned again. *They know where you're going, and therefore where to find you.*

"I can't do this alone." I pressed my hand to the ground and searched for what I needed.

You aren't alone, Keeper, but even if you were, you'd manage.

Thread. Thread, thread, thread. Where was it?

Keeper, if you don't trust me, at least trust yourself.

I froze. My nerves calmed, settling into place. Didn't I promise myself to do just that when the Weaver was tormenting me from his own body? Hadn't I been trying to prove myself capable since then? I lifted my hand from the grass and stood.

"Fine."

Good. Then turn left.

"We just came from that way."

Did we?

We definitely had. The entrance to the maze was in that direction, but I went left anyway, making sure the threads on my arm were visible in case anything else wanted to try its luck.

You're turning out to be quite the GPS system, I told him.

He ignored the comment in favor of another order. *Chop, chop. This isn't a leisurely stroll.*

I rolled my eyes. "Stick to directions before I change my mind."

☾

It only took a few uninterrupted turns before a gentle humming filled the air, the sound as soft as a mother's lullaby. I blinked, instantly charmed, which was always dangerous in the Nightmare Realm. "Is that something good or something I'll need to fight?" I asked in an airy voice.

You don't need to fight anything, the Weaver answered.

"You…" I blinked again as my thoughts turned fuzzy. "You didn't say it was good."

It's the Wish Granter, he said, sounding slightly mystified himself.

"Good," I breathed. Surely, she was *not* good if the Weaver refused to answer the question, but I needed to see her regardless. "That's good."

Very good indeed because my feet were already carrying me toward the warmth and comfort the song promised. My mind conjured up an image of a beautiful woman, curvy and tall, with a welcoming smile. In my mind, she sat in rocking chair with a warm mug of chocolate. She held it out to me, her lap an open invitation, and a bedtime story waited on her lips.

Wrong, the Weaver promised.

It felt right. I wanted it to be right.

I rounded the curve to find a red glow waiting where the path widened into the heart of the maze. The color faded as I approached the source. When I finally stepped into the very center of the maze, I found out how right he was. There was no woman. No human-like nightmare at all.

Instead, a heart twice my height greeted me. Veins clung to the ground like roots and blood sprayed in a fine mist from the artery. The organ contracted, revealing bluish shapes nestled within. Was that…a *squelch*?

"Some warning would've been nice," I told the Weaver as I clutched my churning stomach.

The mist ceased, leaving no trace on the ground or surrounding hedges. For one awful moment, nothing happened. The following second, my definition of *awful* changed drastically. Veins plucked themselves off the grass with sickening pops, and without their support, the heart fell to its side with a wet splat. The organ twitched violently. Flickers of blue and red emanated from its center, and a tiny trickle of white pus dribbled from the artery. The humming resumed, mixed with the mere whisper of a voice. "Lady Nightmare. Why have you come?"

I swallowed bile. It *talked.* Did it have to talk? "I need something from you."

"Do you?" It sounded intrigued. "What can I possibly give you that you could not take?" I opened my mouth to answer. "Hush now. Show me your wish or I cannot grant it."

"Err..." I patted my jacket, hoping I still had my mini sketchbook in one of the pockets. "It's a—"

No, Keeper. Show *her.*

"I didn't know I needed a photo of the thing," I snapped.

"Come now," the Wish Granter beckoned. The veins crept across the grass toward me. "It will only take a moment."

I stared at the heart, willing myself to step back, but I needed the knife if we were going to stop Mara. "Am I...I mean, I can draw it for you? I don't seem to have any paper, but I could..."

The humming hitched into what I assumed was a laugh before falling back into its previous rhythm. In the next second, the veins snapped forward. Sucker-like appendages latched onto my skin, my clothes no barrier to them, and dragged me forward. My own heart pounded frantically in response, and I pulled in air to scream. The Weaver pushed out against it, silencing me.

Now, now, he cooed. *Save the dramatics.*

Before I could even consider shoving him back into submission, the veins hoisted me, head-first, into the oozing artery.

Chapter Fifteen

Halven rammed into Nora, sending her sailing straight through a hidden opening in the maze, just as the hedge snapped shut. Iron spikes skewered the foliage, and I dove sideways. Metal sliced through my calf. My jaw slammed into the ground, making my head ring. The spikes impaled the opposite side of the passageway with a heavy thud.

I rolled over, the large cut on my leg burning, to find two dozen projectiles spanning the space separating me from Kail. He stared, wide-eyed, at the metal, and seemed to be holding his breath whereas mine was too fast. His eyes stilled halfway between red and green.

"Kail?" I asked when he remained motionless. "Are you hurt?"

He snapped out of his stupor at the sound of my voice and moved lightning fast, leaping between spikes. "Halven!"

Halven was on his stomach right next to the hedge, a spike protruding from the back of his shirt near his side. "I'm fine," he rasped and slid himself free. "It's only a scratch."

Kail spun his brother around, frantically checking for wounds, but I simply stared at the newly formed wall. Nora was on the other side of it…had the spikes attacked there as well? I couldn't feel her emotions—I hadn't for a long while now. My heart flew into a crazed rhythm.

"Nora?" It was a croak. I sucked in a breath and rushed to the hedge, digging at the leaves. "Nora! Nora, can you hear me? Are you okay?"

Halven gripped my arm and hauled me away. *"Run."*

I ripped free of him. There was no way I was going to leave Nora. She would heal from any wound, but that didn't mean she wasn't hurt. She could be injured and bleeding or trapped against the opposite hedge. *Impaled.* Something even worse could've happened on her side…

Kail leapt feet-first between the last two spikes. "Nora's more capable than we are," he said in a rush. "We have to move."

And then I saw why. Halfway down the passage, a zombie-like man stood, watching us. His head was bent at an unnatural angle, his eyes blank. Soiled clothes hung from his emaciated body like a sack. A half-groan, half-laugh echoed around me, but more worrisome was the approaching multitude of voices.

I reached for my sand, but Kail grabbed my wrist. "Save it for when we really need it."

"I'd say we need it," I hissed.

"You Lords and your magic." Kail narrowed his eyes. "There's nothing wrong with running away."

"Nora is—"

"We have a long way to the center of the maze. Don't make me abandon you here," he pressed.

The center of the maze? No. We weren't going anywhere except to find Nora. I scooped a handful of sand from my bag and prepared to throw up a barrier between the three of us and the nightmares when the sky turned yellow. Hail fell—small pellets of molten lava. It singed my hair, burned my face, melted holes in my clothes. Kail cursed loudly at my back. I threw the barrier up overhead instead, but the sheet of pellets shifted to fall at a severe angle. The relentless hail flew around my protection at the same time the zombie moved closer. Behind him, dozens just like him emerged.

"Okay. Run," I agreed. If I ran out of sand and was hurt too badly, my magic would pull me to the beach, and there wasn't time for me to travel back here.

Kail and Halven wasted no time, and neither did I. The lava pellets turned their fury toward the easier, unprotected targets, and the howling cries of the zombie-like nightmares were all that chased after us. Kail trailed a hand along the hedge as we ran. The moment his hand passed an empty space, we veered into it. A claw-foot bathtub greeted us in a small alcove. Bubbles foamed high, a few floating ethereally into the air, and rose petals were sprinkled over the grass.

"A dead-end," Kail groaned, running his hands over the walls.

Halven peered into the bubbles with a cocked head. One of the bubbles floated right up to his face and popped, releasing a high, taunting laugh. The faucet turned on by itself with a low creak, topping off the tub and releasing a strong floral scent. Halven leaned even closer, then jerked back as another bubble popped against the brim of his hat. This time the laugh was nothing short of demonic.

"Do you think it's a fear of bubbles, bathing, or outdoor nudity?" Kail asked.

"Does it matter?" I snapped. "Get away from it before something drags you into the water." I flexed my hands. *Nora, Nora, Nora.* Where was she now? Looking for us? Fighting off other creatures? "We have to find her."

"Something here..." Halven struggled to say. "It stirs a memory."

"This isn't the time," I said, too harshly.

"Nora will be fine." Kail didn't tear his curious gaze away from his brother. "You really should step away from that."

Halven did as he was told and rubbed at his throat. "I've smelled this before."

"Forget about the bathtub," I shouted. "Nora—"

Kail blew out a frustrated breath. "She has the literal creator of this maze inside her head, so if you can just focus on *us* getting to the Wish Granter, that would be great."

It was a truth I didn't want to acknowledge and didn't know how to process. The pain, the anger, of it was too fresh. My trust was broken, my heart too. Unfortunately, love wasn't so easy to shatter. I meant what I said to her on the ship—every word of it—but now...now I would take it all back to see her in one piece.

Would the Weaver help her make it to the center of the maze or would he sabotage our plans? Did he want Mare dead? It was more likely he was playing us—playing *me*. We both agreed to create the knife to get rid of Mare, but he took the consequences harder than I had.

Deep down I knew, even if he was reliving any past pain, the Weaver wasn't suicidal. That had to count for something.

Kail hoisted his brother up from a crouched position by the tub. "Put the petals down. What are you doing?"

I shook my head. "Let's move."

I threw my back up against the wall, gasping for breath. My satchel was half empty now after saving us from a variety of nightmares. Hair that sprung out of the hedges and attempted to strangle us, disembodied feet that tried to stomp us into the ground, flesh-eating snails. The complicated scientific equations floating around our heads now were more annoying than dangerous, but my patience had long reached its limit.

"Haven't you done this before?" Kail wheezed. "When you hid the knife?"

I swatted at the numbers and letters drifting around my head. "I wasn't attacked then, obviously."

"Why wouldn't—*oh…*"

"Oh?" I repeated.

Kail waved a hand through the air. "Things were chaotic then."

"Yes." I leveled a hard stare. "Which made things *more* violent."

He gave me a withering look. "Rowan wasted no time snapping up the reins. Everyone was too busy either tormenting each other or hiding before her spies could...*recruit* them. They're not going to give up their hiding place to fight a losing battle with you. Rowan needed you to bring Nora back so there were orders not to touch you."

"You're saying I played into Rowan's hands?"

"No," he said, his tone clipped. "Are you always this tiring, Dream Lord? Though, since you brought it up, if you *had* played into Rowan's hands and brought Nora back, we wouldn't have to deal with Mara. Maybe we've been blaming the wrong person this whole time."

I bristled, torn between anger and guilt, but there wasn't time to settle on which. A quick buzzing sounded within the hedge at my back. I eased away from it and turned slowly. "Did you hear that?"

Silver-winged insects burst from the foliage in a swarm large enough to circle all three of us. They bit and stung and bit and stung. "Enough," I shouted. Sand burst from my satchel and turned each bug to ash. "This is ridiculous."

Halven brushed grey powder from the ruffles of his collar. "We're here." Kail and I exchanged a confused look. "Nearly."

"How nearly?" Kail asked.

Halven pointed to a corner of the millionth dead-end we found. "Nearly," he repeated.

Finally, with a direction to aim for, I used my sand to blow a hole in the hedge. The leaves squealed as the exposed brambles burned. "After you," I told the brothers.

Chapter Sixteen

There was nothing.

No light.

No weight.

No air, though my body didn't seem to miss it.

Panic lurked deep inside, but the humming filled me like air filled a tire. Slow, heavy pressure that churned my insides. I wasn't sure I existed anymore. Everything was too peaceful; too calm. Even the Weaver was utterly silent—not the slightest hint of a grin to be seen.

"What is your wish, Lady Nightmare?" the Wish Granter asked, her voice slightly garbled. I tried to open my mouth to reply, but the cocoon constricted around me. "Shhh. I must look for myself."

That was the last moment of comfort I felt before the warmth of the heart squeezed me to the point of breaking. Bones snapped and cracked. A scream built in my throat, but then I was suddenly in a familiar living room. *My* living room. All traces of pain vanished, and I gasped with relief. The scent of cookies overwhelmed me in the best way, sweet and a little spicy, like gingerbread. I breathed in the sweet air, let it settle in the cracks of my old memories, and turned to see the house I left months ago.

It looked like someone bought out the entire holiday decoration aisle. Garland with red berries circled the banister, fake poinsettia flowers were pinned to the curtains, and the TV stand was covered with sparkly white fabric. Little snowmen figurines sat on every flat surface of the room. A nativity set took up most of the space on the coffee table and Santa throw pillows lined the couch. My jaw dropped. Never in the history of Gallagher family Christmases had my mother gone this overboard with decorating.

"Nora," my mother called. "It's time to lick the spoon!"

I followed her voice to the kitchen and blanched when I found her in a coordinating Christmas apron and Santa hat. "Mom…?"

"Hurry, silly," she said warmly. "Your father will be home soon with the tree."

The walls around me constricted again, dragging me from the home—the mother—I never had. All of it was gone in the blink of an eye, replaced by the Keep. The exterior door leading to the loom swung open and an unseen force pushed me inside before slamming it shut again. The Weaver's gold eyes flared at the sight of me as they had when I met him there that fateful day.

Only, when he stood, knocking the bench over, the door flew open again. The Sandman raced in, throwing handfuls of glimmering sand into the air. Hands were on me. Kail's.

"Give me the knife," he pleaded. "Don't listen to Rowan."

My heart slammed into my breastbone. "Take it," I said in a rush and reached for the knife hidden beneath my vest. Only it wasn't there.

The scene paused, the entire room completely still. "What's this?" the Wish Granter asked. I opened my mouth to ask her the exact same thing when she spoke again. "Hello, Lord. I did not expect to find you here."

"No one does," the Weaver answered, only this time, his voice wasn't in my head. It was the real thing standing in front of me. He swatted the sand, frozen in time, away from his path and came to stand in front of me. Dark hair was swept back into a low bun at the back of his neck, highlighting high cheekbones and a strong jaw. "Do they, Keeper?"

"What a predicament," the warm voice said thoughtfully. "Only one body is allowed in at a time, as you know, Lord. As you also know, I can only grant the body one wish."

"Quite the predicament, indeed." His lips curled up in a familiar grin, and my knees shook. "Which of us shall it be, Keeper? You or me?"

"Weaver," I addressed him carefully. He couldn't steal my wish, could he? What would he ask for? Would he wish to have never died? If he wished for that, I wouldn't have become the ruler of the Nightmare Realm. I wouldn't have brought Mara back. The Sandman and I would find our way back to *us*, but…but if I hadn't killed the Weaver, something worse might have happened. Like him torturing the dream out of me and unleashing his nightmares into the Day World. That was a huge *if* that I couldn't risk. "We need the knife."

"You could be you again." He cocked his head, looking at me like it was the first time. Assessing. Quizzical. "I could be me."

I licked my lips. "What's done is done."

"It can be undone." His gaze softened slightly. "I could wish that you never met the Sandman. That way, you'd never have the chance to kill me and your boss, your friends…your dad, they would be alive. You could have a normal life. A mother like you saw a moment ago."

Never meet the Sandman? My blood drained to my feet at the thought. "My mother was *never* like that," I said around my parched tongue. Our problems aside, she wasn't the type to put in more effort than necessary. Especially when it came to her kids. "The Sandman was all I had growing up."

"That's not true. You had your sister."

I choked on a humorless laugh. "Sisters *hate* each other growing up as much as they love each other."

"Is that your wish then?" the Wish Granter asked.

"I wish for the knife," I shouted before the Weaver could say otherwise. "The knife the Sandman gave you. I wish for it."

The Weaver's grin widened, revealing perfectly straight teeth. "She will only grant that which is most wanted."

"You are Lord and Lady, I will not twist the wish as I usually do. I'll give you exactly what you ask for in respect of your titles," she assured me.

"That's what I want the most," I insisted. "To get the knife so I can right my wrong."

"Ah," the Wish Granter said thoughtfully. "Now *that* is the right kind of wish, but, Lord, if I may…knowing you are here, if I must choose sides…"

The Weaver waved a lazy hand. "Your loyalty is appreciated."

No. *No, no, no,* this couldn't be happening. It was *my* body she swallowed up which meant it should be *my* wish she granted. "Please." My voice cracked. "Please, don't. This is all messed up—so, so messed up—but I accept it. I…" I wanted this place—to rule here. I didn't understand that until this very moment, didn't want to accept it, but I was doing something here. Something worthwhile and good. In a strange way, I *belonged.* Even if my old feelings were fading, and I was becoming less. I was also becoming more.

The Weaver closed the space between us so that we breathed the same air. Tears burned at the backs of my eyes, but I refused to back down. I *needed* the knife, and we weren't leaving without it. He lifted his hand, empty of thread, and ran one finger down the side of my face before cupping my cheek. My eyes widened at the gentle touch. This was the Weaver. *Gentle* wasn't part of his vocabulary.

"Keeper," he whispered. A spiteful, predatory sound, as if he were thinking seriously about snapping my neck.

"Tell her you want the knife," I growled.

A brow quirked and his chuckle brushed over my lips, his grin never wavering. "Are we going to play nice with each other?"

"I already told you that we will *never* be friends." I tucked my hands behind my back to keep from punching him. One didn't befriend a murderer, especially when his victims were close friends and family, but I couldn't afford to piss him off at the moment.

The Weaver held my gaze, and my breath caught at what stared out from the depths of his golden eyes. It wasn't a monster. It was a little something like what I saw in the mirror. Different, but the same. Hurt. Regret. Desperation. *Want.* His felt crueler, hardened by countless years. Still, in that lingering moment, I felt a connection to him, a deep understanding. I hated it…but I also didn't.

His eyes fell to my lips, the grin fading. Before I could process what that meant, he was kissing me. His lips were warm and soft, the pressure full of pliant desperation. I forgot how to move, the appalling act stealing my ability to function, but it only lasted for a brief moment before I tore myself away. I wanted to scream at him—*how dare he!* My lips burned with the acrid memory, and I was sure it would take years to scrub away.

"What was that?" I demanded. "You can't just go around kissing people when you *know* they loathe you."

His grin returned, but his eyes remained glossy. Wistful, almost. "Relax. The Sandman seems to like doing that very much, so I wanted to see what the big deal was. Alas, I still don't understand the appeal."

My mouth gaped open and shut. He couldn't be serious. *Rat bastard.*

"You'll forgive me," he said, unworried.

I most certainly would *not.* My cheeks blazed with fury. Who did he think he was? Maybe I *should* let him wish himself back into his body, if only so I could kill him all over again. Stab him a few times instead of the once.

"I wish for the knife the Sandman gave you," the Weaver said in the quietest of voices.

My heart skipped a beat. "You... *what?*"

"Looks like we'll be stuck with each other for a while longer." He tried to grin wider before giving up and it dropped off his face completely. "Maybe now you'll reconsider my offer of friendship."

"Fat chance," I said, but the Weaver's body crumpled to the floor before I finished speaking. His blood seeped around him as it had when I drove the knife into his heart. The frozen image of the Sandman and Kail vanished, and a hard weight dug into the base of my spine. I moved languidly, twisting my arm around to grip what I knew would be cold metal.

The moment my fingers wrapped around the handle of the knife, the entire setting dropped away. The *nothing* was back, only the humming was alarmingly absent, and this time I desperately needed air. Panic overflowed my nervous system. I twisted and turned in an attempt to free myself, only to find I didn't need freeing because grass tickled my skin. When I opened my eyes, I saw the muted blue sky of the Nightmare Realm above me. The giant heart was back in place, the veins holding it in an upright position as a light spray of blood fanned out from the top of the aorta. I scrambled to my feet and clutched the knife—*the knife*—to my chest. "Weaver?" I whispered.

Still here.

I closed my eyes, hating the words I was about to say. Especially after the stunt he pulled. "Thanks. For this."

He was silent for a moment. *You're welcome, Nora.*

I jerked at the sound of his voice forming my name for the first time.

"There!" Kail shouted.

Three sets of feet pounded the ground behind me. I turned slowly to face them, and it took everything I had not to run to the Sandman. It was a jackhammer to my insides knowing I couldn't. At least, not until we figured things out. What he said on the ship…a shallow, pained breath left my lungs.

The Sandman stood beside Kail and Halven, all three of them looking like they braved a war single-handedly. They stared at the knife with matching looks of surprise. A sudden wave of exhaustion hit me, a weariness not of my body but my heart. A fierce battle I didn't know I was fighting, finally won. Or maybe lost.

But over.

I shuffled toward the single path out of the maze's center on wobbly legs. On my way by, I shoved the knife against Kail's blood-soaked chest. The hedges whipped back, creating a clear path to the foggy shore of the Green Sea. I heard the others behind me: slow, hesitant. I was too tired to see if they were actually following or if the maze was working to swallow them back up.

Chapter Seventeen

The ship ride and following trek to Nora's palace was deathly quiet. Tension did the speaking for everyone. Nora's headspace was clear to read—angry, exhausted, and determined. I didn't know what her determination was focused on—Mare or something that happened inside the Wish Granter—but it was impossible to ask after our fight. I didn't know how to fix things, especially when I was still so angry, but the way I felt when the hedge separated us told me we had to speak again. Only, not today.

I held my hand out to Kail. "Knife."

Kail, for once, did as he was asked without commentary. He simply extracted the blade from inside his coat and handed it over. I turned the knife over in my hand, feeling its power throb almost painfully up my arm, before tucking it away in my satchel. It was time to go back to the Dream Realm to replenish my sand supply, but my feet refused to move.

Nora drew in a steady breath. "Sandman…"

"Don't." My voice was firm, the crack barely held beneath the surface, and I couldn't bring myself to look at her. There was little worse than being at war with yourself. "Not right now."

Luckily, she had enough mercy for me not to push it, though the air still thickened further.

"We'll meet again in a few hours then," Kail said, uneasy. "Get this done."

I nodded once, my head heavy, my heart heavier, but this time my limbs obeyed. They carried me away from Nora. I was halfway to the cattails near the palace when I spun on my heel and walked part of the way back. "You're okay?" I asked, my gaze steadily directed at Nora's boots. "You weren't injured?"

There was a heavy pause before Nora answered, "No. I'm fine."

"Good." I cleared my throat and, this time when I walked away, I didn't look back.

☾

Halven waited at the barrier to the Dream Realm. His back was to me, his hands folded carefully behind his back. "You wasted no time." My steps slowed. "What are you doing here?"

Halven's hat tilted as he looked up. "We must speak."

"We could've spoken on the ship ride back." I walked past him and onto a sea of glimmering sand. "Did something else happen since I left?"

He followed me inside. "No."

His voice gave nothing away, and there was no telling what his expression was behind the mask. I removed the knife from my empty satchel as I bent to refill it. "What is it?"

Halven fiddled with the voluminous fabric around his neck, saying nothing.

Though he was a man of few words, his words carried weight which meant his silence did too. "Did you think I would run off with the knife?" My eyes narrowed with realization. "They sent you to make sure I came back?"

"You are paranoid." Halven angled his head toward me and pounded on his chest as if he could break up whatever held his voice hostage. "I understand why."

I shifted uncomfortably, turning my attention to the sand beneath my hands. Paranoid wasn't the right word. My trust was broken, along with a certain vital organ, but that accusation was unfounded. Nora distrusted me—she proved that again and again—but thinking I would run off without killing Mare first was too much. I shouldn't have voiced otherwise.

"I came beca—" Halven's swallow was audible. "Becau—" He paused, his agitation radiating around him. "Roses."

My satchel full, I removed my stained shirt while the sand scrubbed the dried blood from my skin. "Roses?"

"The Weaver gave me a key." His words were quickly becoming more and more hoarse.

My eyes snapped up. The key to the Ever Safe was lost, likely destroyed by now, since it was created shortly after the first humans. Even nightmares crumbled with age without proper care. The pavilion now standing in the Dream Realm was the fifth or sixth version. There was no way a metal key almost as old as I was survived the elements this long. "A key to what?"

Halven shook his head. "Never said."

I raised my brows. "I'm not sure I'm following."

He drew a long breath as if readying himself for the pain of speaking. "He told me to lose it so—" A cough wracked his body, and he bent to hold his knees until it passed. When he had, he managed to squeeze out, "I am lost."

"You're lost," I repeated, almost a question. The meaning of his words struck ten seconds later. *He was lost.* "You have it. The key he gave you—you kept it because if it was with you, it wouldn't be found."

Halven nodded.

"Is it..." I pressed my eyes shut. Maybe it was better if I didn't know what the key opened—better if *he* didn't know. If it was for the Ever Safe that meant Mare's prize was within reach this entire time.

Halven touched my arm tentatively. When I opened my eyes, he kicked out a leg and pointed to his boot.

A thousand lifetimes passed since I last saw the key to the Ever Safe, yet I recognized it immediately. The metal was worn, eroding away slowly, though it had clearly been cared for enough to survive this long. "You should have destroyed that," I said, breathless.

"That is different than lost."

Weaver. If I could strangle him for this, I would. I flopped down on the sand and hung my head between my knees. A tired, humorless laugh flowed out of me and I was powerless to stop it.

So many beings would've killed for that key.

Halven wore it like a trinket.

A moment later, he sat beside me, silently waiting for my hysteria to pass. Having a nightmare sit beside me, tainting the sand around him, in a show of support only made it worse. I flopped back and threw an arm over my eyes. The laughter instantly gave way to tears. I let them come, let my sleeve soak up each drop without leaving a trace for Halven to see.

"Sandman?" he asked when my silence stretched on.

"Just go," I pleaded. I needed a few minutes to myself. "Don't tell anyone else about the key until I return to the Keep."

I felt him shift, felt the sand crumble as he stood, but he hadn't made it a single step before a distant boom sounded. It was far enough away that it sounded like nothing more than lumber dropped onto the back a truck, and, based on the way it echoed, it was indeed a long distance off. Nightmares occasionally acted up; loud sounds weren't uncommon and occasional lights flared on the horizon.

However, this didn't feel like something that innocent.

"Should I investigate?" Halven rasped.

I took a moment to gather myself and tuck away my emotions. "No. We should get back to Nora."

Baku burst through the barrier, heading straight for us, and I held up a hand to silence Halven. If Nora was right and Baku was Rowan's spy, it was best not to say anything important in front of him. Why take an unnecessary risk? Rowan might be gone, but my trust was shaken. If he sided with Rowan, what was to say he hadn't sided with someone else since then? Baku pranced closer to me, his eyes shifting side-to-side.

"Baku." I managed to keep the suspicion from my voice. Acting differently could tip him off, but what I would've said under normal circumstances failed me. Would I ask about the sound or have him look into it while I went back to the palace? Whatever it was, I had to say something. "Do you know where that noise came from?"

Halven listened to Baku's silence for a moment, then pointed to our right. "That way."

Baku nudged me with his tusk and pointed his trunk in the opposite direction. His hearing was impeccable, but Halven had his way of *knowing* where nightmares were.

"I thought the same as Halven." I squinted into the distance. Unease settled deeper into my soul. Perhaps it would be best to test Baku's loyalty and settle things once and for all. "We'll check that way, and if there's nothing there, we can double back."

Baku's lips curled up. "We can't both be right," I reasoned. "Halven is going that way anyway." I pointed in the direction Baku gave. "He'll look around while we go this way."

I stared at where Halven's eyes should've been, willing myself to catch some sort of clue to his thoughts, but he simply nodded in agreement.

Baku chuffed, and I barely stopped from wincing.

The sound echoed and *could* have come from either direction, but something felt off. "Did you see anything strange on your way here?" I asked him.

Baku shook his head.

"I can read your dreams," I offered, reaching for my sand. He turned and sauntered back toward the barrier. I stared at Halven, willing him to understand that I didn't like this. Not one bit. "Let them know I'll be there soon."

Halven pressed a hand to his chest and bobbed his head. I watched him leave, aching with uncertainty. Nora. Baku. Even

Halven who told me about the key instead of Nora… When would enough be enough?

Baku pounded his tiger paws into the sand, the small thuds drawing my attention. "Coming."

☾

There was no way to know where I needed to go. Landscapes stretched on and on, none appearing to have been disturbed, and it wasn't like sound left a trail. Instead, I turned each way Baku tried to stop me from going. If I veered north, he would urge me east. If I went east, he wanted to go west. Each time I ignored his suggestions, he grew more anxious. His ears twitched, his lips quivering.

"What's gotten into you?" I asked.

Baku unhinged his jaw, stretched it from side to side, and shut it again.

I inhaled and moved into a new landscape. The ground was covered in grey pits with raised ridges of purple and orange, like coral. It crunched slightly beneath my boots but held its shape. The air smelled of salt. A low growl came from Baku, and I scanned the area for any approaching nightmares. There were none that I could see, though I was sure they were around. For the first time, I wondered if it wasn't me Baku was warning, but them.

"Maybe I'm wrong," I said with faked sincerity. "There's no harm looking here first."

Baku's nails raked across the surface, creating a crackling sound as bits of coral broke away. Then he ran, nothing more than a blur of black and orange fur. I stood immobile for two seconds. They felt like twenty because, though Baku couldn't speak, I could sense his annoyance. I didn't know if he expected me to follow him or stay my path. Was he running toward his spy-master, to warn them I was close, or away from them in hopes of keeping me from the truth?

I sent sand after Baku. A bug formed, no larger than a flea, and attached itself to the ridge of his ear. Through it, I saw what he saw. I didn't dare give it my full attention, but I got flashes each time I blinked. The further Baku went, the faster my heart sped. *Ice caves.* He was headed straight for them. The coral ground gradually gave way to snow, a dusting at first, then inches, then feet. Baku moved so quickly he didn't sink into the soft powder. So quickly, in fact, that he was just outside the caves in a matter of minutes.

He wasn't alone.

The second half of the army was there—the one I saw in Baku's dream the day we confronted Rowan. We never found where they went, but Halven had scoured most of the Nightmare Realm and a group this size was hard to hide...we assumed it disbanded without Rowan there to give orders.

We were wrong.

Very wrong.

Chapter Eighteen

"Ding dong," Kail said, breezing into my art studio.

I didn't bother to look up from my latest drawing. It wasn't clear yet what the finished design would be, but the head was triangular, and tentacles filled half the page. So far, it was strangely elegant.

"No one's home."

"We're supposed to be getting ready to go slash up an Ancient, and you're doodling?"

His beak skimmed my shoulder, and I brought my elbow back into his stomach. "I'm *designing*, and it helps me relax."

Relax and take my mind off things. A lot of things. The Sandman, mainly, but also what happened inside the Wish Granter. I couldn't erase the taste of the Weaver's lips from my own. Bitter. Metallic. Wholly awful. If cutting them from my face would erase what happened, I'd do it.

Come now, the Weaver said. *It wasn't so bad.*

It was worse, I snapped. If *he* was my last kiss, I would invent a way to physically torture him if it took a hundred years. It wasn't like I would move on from the Sandman. Even if I wanted to, my choices as Lady Nightmare were zero, so if he never forgave me…

"Plus," I added with a pointed stare, "as you know, I need to stop things like you from barging into places they shouldn't."

Kail ignored my comment and lifted a paper. He studied the sketch of the new front doors I installed earlier. The once-wooden doors were now strong metal, ten inches thick. There was only one door now instead of two, and the frame was shaped like an old-fashioned keyhole. It wasn't the most aesthetically pleasing with oddly shaped patches bolted together every which way, interior rods exposed in places as if the metal had melted around them. No part of it matched the rest of the palace—it would really only look right in a scrap yard—but if anyone tried breaking in, they wouldn't escape.

Behind each of those different patches was something murderous. A family of sprites was in charge of the inner workings, their home a series of connecting tunnels inside the door. Their skin was soft as velvet but potent pollen fell from them like dandruff, causing anaphylaxis. There were other deadly things waiting too; In case of emergency, the sprites would open the appropriate piece, unleashing anything from poisonous gas to a swarm of hornets that wouldn't stop stinging until their victim was dead. It wasn't my most creative work, but time was short.

"There seems to be a tiny problem," Kail said when it was obvious I wasn't going to ask what he wanted.

I sketched in rough edges of webbed hands. "There are never *tiny* problems here."

"Ah, but there are." He walked the length of the room and tapped the edge of the table with his fingertips. "The east side of the castle is overrun with hedgehogs."

A laugh burst from my mouth. "Nice try. Go away, I'm busy."

"I'm completely serious," he said, horrified. "They're all different colors and smell like dirty feet. Also, they keep *hissing* at me."

"Animal instinct is so spot on, don't you think?" Part of me wanted to race to the far side of the palace and squeal over how cute they were. I'd always wanted a hedgehog, but my mother was worried they would give me salmonella. Dad let us have a dog, but when he left, we weren't even allowed to keep a goldfish. I sighed. The nightmare version of hedgehogs wouldn't be anything like the ones in the Day World anyway. Seeing them harass Kail would be worth the walk though.

Kail's taps became more insistent. "This amuses you?"

"Oh, you have no idea how much." I smiled wide. "How did they get in?"

"I'm assuming they waddled."

The frustration in his voice only brightened my smile, and I set my pencil down to look at him. "Are you really bothering me with this? Get them out of there. Or don't. I don't use that side of the palace."

He scowled. "Because you gave it to *me*."

My amusement bloomed. "Merry Christmas, Kail. You're now a proud pet parent."

"Get rid of them," he said, teeth bared.

"*You* get rid of them."

"Nora—" He paused and took a deep breath, gathering himself. "They shoot their quills. It's very unpleasant."

"That's just a myth." Returning to my drawing, I added long, narrow eyes to the design. Next, I had to decide whether to give it a nose or gills.

"Is it?" He pulled the neck of his shirt down to expose countless little red welts. "Not only that, but they're coated in some sort of…agitator…because, why not?"

I sniffed the air. "Do you smell that?"

"What? Nora. Focus. Hedgehogs—"

"Fear." I abandoned my sketch and stepped up to Kail to inhale the air around him. It was entirely possible I was enjoying this too much. "Ah, yes. Definitely fear."

He leapt away. "I'm not afraid of them. I just want them *gone*."

It's true. He's not afraid of them, the Weaver chimed in like a co-conspirator. *He's afraid of things touching him while he sleeps.*

I shuffled the information around in my head. Had I ever seen him sleep? All those nights he spent training me away from the Blood Tower, I was always the first to pass out. The last to wake. His bedroom in the tower had no door to keep things out—was that something Rowan did on purpose? He had kept to a different cell the night we spent in the prison too. Maybe it was some sort of strange paranoia about his own specialty. He was the unknown to Dreamers, so maybe he hated other nightmares sneaking up on him.

Where do you come up with your theories? He was asleep when I broke him in two, the Weaver explained. *It's that simple.*

It felt as if he splashed cold water against my insides. Any nugget of playfulness—of wanting to use the information against Kail—vanished in an instant. "Come on, ya big baby."

☾

Laughter poured from me, an endless well, until I sat on the ground struggling to breathe. When Kail said the east side of the palace was *overrun*, I thought it was an exaggeration. It was more of an understatement, if anything.

"I'm *so* glad you think this is funny," Kail growled.

"I'm sorry," I lied between breaths. "It's just—"

"If you tell me how cute they are one more time, I swear I'll open that door and throw you inside."

"All right, all right." I dabbed the tears from my eyes and stood up. The closed door to Kail's personal quarters was riddled with quills. A few were there before I came, most after I waltzed in like it was no big deal. A point to me for avoiding them. "We need something to use as a shield."

"What? No. Use your Weaver mojo to make them impale each other. Problem solved."

I raised my upper lip in disgust. They were too cute for that. Too cute to be nightmares. The brief look I got when I opened the door revealed a blanket of rainbow hedgehogs covering nearly every surface. Reds and oranges, blues and purples, yellows and greens. I doubted there were two of the exact same shade. They were smaller than the ones people owned as pets. Smaller nearly always meant cuter. They had beady black eyes that shimmered as if they were about to cry and adorably twitchy noses. But those flying quills were definitely an issue.

"I highly doubt you're interested in the cleanup that would leave," I told him.

Kail folded his arms across his chest. "Fine. You like them so much, turn them into stuffed animals and keep them on your bed."

"Alterations hurt, remember? We'll usher them out the same way they got in."

"We don't know *how* they got in." He tilted his head to stare at me as if I had checked out of the conversation. "Besides, that's hardly important."

"If things are slipping inside my safe space, it's extremely important. Now, shield," I repeated. Granted, these were less an issue than the Hours or Mara, but the obvious entrances were covered now. If there was something we missed, I'd have to add it to my growing list of structural changes. When Kail didn't move, I flicked my hands at him. "Unless you want to volunteer yourself for the job?"

You don't need a shield, the Weaver said. *Just tell them to cease.*

I grinned as Kail disappeared around the corner, grumbling under his breath. *I know,* I told him. *But it's more fun this way.*

Poor Kail.

Poor Kail, my rear-end. He locked me in a museum with a very angry monkey.

The Weaver chuckled. *I thought that was rather genius. A test within a test.*

You would.

Kail returned, dragging a piece of driftwood down the hall with one hand, the bottom scraping against the stone floor. It wasn't wide enough to protect one of my arms, let alone my entire body. "Here." He held it out between us. "This should work."

I took it, pretending to examine its worth. I found small notches and areas that appeared to be purposely scraped down. "Where did you find this?"

"We all have our secrets, Lady. Especially me."

"That's exactly what worries me." I dropped the wood to the ground. It hit with a hollow clunk. "Stand over there."

"What happened to needing a shield?" he asked, wary, but moved away from the door where the hedgehogs' projectiles wouldn't reach.

I plucked a quill from the door and flicked it at him. "Stand over there and *shush*," I clarified.

With a deep breath, I reached for the knob. A surge of darkness flowed through my veins. *All taken care of*, the Weaver said, smug. *All you have to do now is shoo them away.*

I didn't ask for your help. I ground my teeth together to keep from speaking out loud. Kail knowing the Weaver talked to me didn't mean it wasn't awkward if I talked back in front of him.

Do friends need to ask? It seemed like a genuine question.

"*You* need to," I snarled. We weren't friends. Our interests might align for the moment, but they wouldn't always. If there wasn't a life-or-death situation, I expected him to stay seated. Even then, if I was about to die, a heads up would be nice. Especially since his idea of *help* included tossing me out of a rusted-out globe.

I wasn't helping you. I was helping the Sandman.

With a quiet *tsk*, I eased open the door to the east side of the castle, half expecting the Weaver to have played a practical joke on me. But, when no quills came flying, I loosened a breath and stepped inside. The hedgehogs sounded almost human when a wave of v*ooshlada*—their way of saying *our lady*—swept through the room and echoed through the hallways.

"You can't be in here. Go out the same way you came in," I ordered.

It took a moment for any of them to move, but slowly they crept away. More hedgehogs filed into the hall from open rooms. Everything about their departure was neat and orderly, the way highway traffic could be if people weren't jerks about merging. I almost hated to see them go, if only for the fact that they bothered Kail. As their numbers thinned, I was happy to see they left…presents behind that were as colorful as they were.

"Are they gone?" Kail called.

"Almost." I picked my way carefully through the excrement. "Come on. We need to follow them."

"I'll do it," he said quickly, popping up beside me. "You can go back to your drawings."

My brows rose at the eagerness in his voice and inched further up my forehead when I saw the edge of panic in his eyes. "What's with the sudden change of attitude?"

"What?" He forced a laugh. "I can manage following them out and overseeing the hole patched up. You were only needed to make them stand down."

"Uh huh," I said slowly. There was no way I was walking away now. Kail should've known that much after all our time together. Curiosity was one of my worst vices.

"It's fine, really," he insisted when I didn't turn away.

"It is," I agreed. It was fine for me to investigate my own palace's weak spots.

I eased inside after the last of the hedgehogs and froze. Rocks, once cemented into place with whatever material the nightmares used, were scattered on the ground. Dust and tiny chunks of stone coated the floor. But it wasn't those things that had my heart racing. It was the hammer and chisel leaning in the corner, and the way the broken stone around the hole pressed slightly outward. As if someone were breaking *out*, not in.

"Nora, I can explain," Kail said quickly. "It's not what you think."

"Not what I think?" I repeated in a whisper. "What is it you think I'm thinking exactly?" Even I wasn't sure.

Kail took wide steps to the side. "That I was letting nightmares in to harm you."

I jerked at the accusation. While I didn't know what to think, it wasn't that. Maybe it needed to be—he had turned on Rowan, and even helped train me to kill her. He still needed me though. He needed me to put him and Halven back together, and to kill Mara. After both those things were accomplished, maybe I would doubt him, but not until then.

"I don't think that," I promised, "but start explaining before I do."

Kail rushed to the hole, jacket flowing, and began stuffing rocks back into the wall. "It's just…you know…"

When he didn't elaborate I said, "no, I don't know."

"Me and all my *hidey holes*," he supplied flippantly, though the carelessness didn't ring true.

That's what I called his escape route out of the Blood Tower. His secret passage to run away from Rowan. My shoulders fell at what that implied. As much as I wasn't completely sure of Kail, I *wanted* to be. And I wanted him to be sure of me too. Sure that

I wouldn't blackmail him or hold him here against his will. If Kail didn't trust me, how could I expect any of the others to?

There you were, worried your emotions were fading.

Shut up, Weaver. Not that he was wrong, but he wasn't entirely right either. Apparently, I had only lost my ability to feel guilty about slaughtering things.

For what it's worth, I never stopped caring about personal relationships either, he supplied.

I wasn't sure if that made things better or worse.

"Kail, if you ever want to leave, you're welcome to use the front door," I said in a strained voice.

He nodded.

"You don't have to keep helping me if you don't want to." *That* hurt to say. Because I needed him. Very much. Especially if the Sandman was serious about what he said on the ship. "I appreciate your help—Halven's too—but if you really don't want to be here, you can go. I'll still make good on my promise."

"I know you will," he said quietly, still sifting through rocks to puzzle the wall back together.

I chewed on my bottom lip. "Then what's with all this?"

Without turning around to look at me, he shrugged. "Old habits are hard to break, I suppose, but I'll fix it." His voice was thin and nervous. I hated it, and not in the same way I hated his sarcasm and occasional underhanded tricks.

"Good," I said, whether he meant mending the wall or fixing whatever made him feel as if a secret door was necessary. "We wouldn't want any raccoons to catch wind of today's adventure and pay a visit."

"We can't have that." He lifted another stone and froze. "Nora?" he asked, his voice hard and steady.

His abrupt change in tone raised the hair on my arms. "What?"

There was a long, heavy pause. "Remind me what your sister looks like."

"Katie?" I blinked in surprise. "You know what she looks like; she was just here a day ago."

"Humor me."

"A few inches taller than me, dark hair—" I sucked in a breath, my head cocked. If he didn't care what Katie looked like yesterday, he shouldn't care what she looked like today. Unless…I tried to see past him, outside, but his shoulders were too wide. "What's with the sudden interest?"

"Because I'm pretty sure that's her."

My heart bottomed out. I was across the room in three steps, shoving him away from the hole. Across the lawn, Katie trudged between two nightmares—one a centaur with incredibly long antlers and the other a large blob of clear gel. Bits and pieces of nightmares floated inside its formless torso as if it hadn't finished digesting its last meal. Katie's hands were bound in front of her, a dirty cloth shoved in her mouth, and yet, the closer they got, the more defiance shone on my sister's face.

"This has to be a joke," I half-yelled.

Kail leaned down beside me to peek outside. "It looks rather serious to me."

I growled wordlessly. Of course it was serious—my sister was taken hostage by nightmares. *Again.* The very thing I wanted to avoid. I kicked the rocks loose from the wall, squeezed outside, and bolted straight for them.

"What's this?" I called in my best Lady Nightmare voice.

The blob waited until I was close enough to speak normally. "We wanted her, but she claimed to be under your protection."

My nostrils flared. "Did she?"

"Along with other things," the centaur added.

Katie reached her bound hands up and yanked out the gag, flexing her jaw from side to side. "Are we done with this whole charade yet?"

The centaur stomped an overgrown hoof. "No one said you could speak!"

I held up a hand. "Thank you for bringing her to me. I'll take it from here."

I grabbed Katie's upper arm and led her toward the front of the palace. *Under my protection.* Of course she would come up with something like that. Something that would ultimately hurt my reputation. Protecting Dreamers was the Sandman's signature move.

"What are you doing here?" I hissed the second we were out of earshot.

"I told you this wasn't over," she said calmly. "I came back for the full Nora-version-of-events and promise to listen judgment free."

Like that was possible, but once my sister set her mind to something, that was it. "You're an idiot," I said and hauled her inside.

☾

Apparently, it *was* possible for Katie to listen without implying I was off my rocker. Or that I was selfish. Or stupid for trusting people I shouldn't, not trusting people I should, and keeping the

Weaver's presence a secret. She didn't say much at all, really. A welcomed surprise.

"Side note," my sister said after a long period of contemplative silence. We were sprawled out together on my bed, staring at the ceiling, our legs tangled together. "I'm seeing your old psychologist now."

"Colleen?"

"Yup. She's really helping me. I can't tell her what's actually going on, of course, but she's ace at picking up on things anyway."

"That's great, Katie," I said, and I meant it. Colleen was sweet. It was me that had been the problem during our sessions, but if she helped Katie despite a laundry list of un-truths, I was glad. "You should try the Italian restaurant down the street from the office. Their bread is to die for."

"Noted."

She picked nervously at a hangnail, and I scrambled to find a topic to break the tension. It was information overload, I knew, but she couldn't keep coming to the Nightmare Realm. Now that she knew about my new reality, she needed to stay away. Let me come to her. Assuming all the nightmares would listen to her claims of protection was foolish when many of them were nothing but horrendous looking wild animals.

But, for now, I wanted to take advantage of this chance to enjoy a few minutes together. And if it stoked the flames of my fading self, all the better.

"Do you know what I miss? Hot apple pie, cheesy lasagna, *chocolate*..." I sighed wistfully.

She turned her head to look at me, thoughts churning behind her eyes. "Come home, and I'll personally make all of that for you."

"Okay, when I said I missed those things, I meant the *good* kind—"

Katie pinched my arm and laughed for the first time. "My cooking has improved."

"Improving charred food isn't difficult. It just means you learned to set the timer on the stove. *Oww*," I cried as she pinched me again.

"Jen is teaching me," she said, her cheeks pink.

"Jen?" Last I knew, they broke up because Jen wanted something more serious and Katie was seeing that guy… Kevin? Keenan? "Spill," I demanded.

She did. The edge in her voice smoothed as she talked about her ex-girlfriend, or her *ex*-ex girlfriend. I wasn't going to interrupt to ask when her words and body language told me all I needed to know—that they were still crazy about each other. She avoided talking about Mom and Paul while I avoided talking about the Sandman. There was no need to rub salt in old wounds when we were finally having a conversation that didn't leave us at each other's throats. We talked instead about TV shows I missed and new movies that came out. Internet memes. The possibility of Katie dying her hair again—blue this time, or maybe purple.

The conversation went on and on until my cheeks hurt from smiling and my eyelids grew heavy.

Chapter Nineteen

Nora

The bed shifted, rolling me off my side and onto my back. I groaned into the pillow. How long was I out? Two minutes? Three? Not long enough, whatever it was.

"What, Kail?" I grumbled.

"It's me."

I flew up in a tangle of sheets. The Sandman sat on the edge of the mattress, elbows resting on his knees, and my heart flip-flopped. Was he here to talk? Forgive me? Hear me out, at least? A hundred unvoiced thoughts rushed to my tongue, all of them fighting for a chance to go first. Excuses, excuses, and more excuses. They all seemed equally wanting, but I had to say something. Anything.

"Hi," I breathed. Not helpful, but a better greeting than *I swear I was going to tell you everything.*

"You might be right." He stared at the floor, soft brown curls floating around his forehead, and I fought not to reach out to touch them. "About Baku, I mean."

Baku? He came here to talk to me about that good for nothing nightmare eater? That's why the Sandman was in my bedroom: to tell me that I was right about his *"friend"* being a spy.

"I might be right…" I repeated, my shoulders slumped.

"Most likely right," he amended.

I pursed my lips. I already knew I was right. It was completely obvious Baku was working against us; Rowan wasn't going to forge her own notes, and it connected a lot of dots. How she knew exactly what to say to manipulate me into killing the Weaver, and how Kail knew I liked to draw when I had never mentioned it.

But…Baku wasn't my friend. He was the Sandman's. This visit wasn't because he forgave me; it was because he needed me. We were each other's safe space. He needed comfort now, and, outside of this moment, it didn't mean anything would change. Not yet anyway.

I exhaled quietly and slid up further in the bed, rubbing my arms though I wasn't cold. "I'm sorry, Sandman," I said, genuinely disappointed on his behalf. "I know you two were close."

He let out a dry laugh. "Well, I suppose I shouldn't be surprised. It was always friends by default for us, right? We were all the other had."

That was how he described Baku to me at first. Enemy of his enemy. His associate. That didn't make the betrayal any less painful, I imagined. "It doesn't matter how you became friends," I whispered.

"Only that it was a lie." His voice was low, broken. "Like so many things are."

I flinched. "Sandman—"

"It doesn't matter." He stood quickly and brushed his palms off on his thighs. The spell was broken. An icy wall slammed down on his desperate grief almost immediately. "Rowan's second army still exists, and Baku knew all this time."

I untangled myself from the covers and slid from the bed. If Baku knew and didn't tell us, that meant he was on their side. The question was, who controlled the army? I thought Kail and I had weeded out the rebels capable of starting an uprising, but we must have missed someone. We couldn't fight Mara *and* someone else with an army at the same time. "What should we do?"

"Take care of Mare." The Sandman kept his gaze anywhere but on me. "Once the immediate danger is gone, you can deal with your nightmares, and I can deal with Baku. If it's true he's betraying us, that is."

If it's true, the Weaver scoffed.

I zeroed in on another part of his words, my insides twisting. This was it then. He wanted to kill Mara and go our separate ways, but he hadn't heard me out yet. He *had* to hear me out first…right?

This is hardly the time to worry about your love life, the Weaver reasoned.

"Have you heard anything from Halven about a key?" he asked suddenly.

"A key? To what?" I spoke quietly, not trusting my voice.

"Nevermind. We'll leave in a few hours for the ice caves," he said, then left without a backward glance.

We aren't waiting until Mara is dead to deal with the army? the Weaver asked.

"There isn't time to deal with it." I stared at the door, hoping the Sandman would come back in, knowing he wouldn't.

You're forgetting the first law of ruling this realm.

I sighed and headed for my wardrobe. "And what would that be?"

The grin lifted. *Delegate.*

This isn't the best of ideas, the Weaver told me for the fifth time. *When I said delegate, I meant…really anything other than this.*

"The Hours are motivated."

Motivated to kill you, perhaps.

I chewed my lip, regretting that I told Kail to hang back, and stared up at the clock tower. They would break out eventually. Releasing them meant they would have less reason to be angry, and it would give them a purpose. At least, I hoped.

"I'll have to kill them first, but something tells me they want Mara dead more than me. Besides, the Sandman and I have a solid plan which is what they wanted." Of course, I wasn't about to divulge what the plan was. Betrayal was nearly impossible to see coming, and I already didn't trust the Hours.

The Weaver scoffed. *There are twelve of them, not including the Chime and the Hands. They can handle killing two things at once.*

"You've been in my head too long." I rubbed my sweaty palms together. "The Weaver I know wouldn't worry about some measly *nightmares*. Especially since the Sandman is back at full power. The only thing holding him back is the whole balance thing. And morals."

Don't those hold you back too?

Did they? I supposed so, though I assumed it was my humanity that kept me in check. My morals were greying, but the balance was important. I believed in it enough to follow in the Sandman's footsteps when it came to not blowing up my every problem. Not that I didn't *want* to…

"I should go in there now."

Is there a game plan?

Right. Game plan. "Walk in, walk out?"

Guns-a-blazin' then? Shall we let some darkness out?

It wasn't a horrible idea, actually. The Hours knew I was powerful enough to trap them, but there was no harm in flaunting it. It worked well enough the first time.

Wonderful, the Weaver said buoyantly.

The darkness swirled faster and faster. Leaking out. Snaking around me like a cloak. I forced myself to ignore the tendrils in my peripheral vision and focus on the clock. Everything appeared frozen, the same time as when I left. Maybe that meant they were all dead, and this was a waste of time.

Don't get your hopes up.

Whatever. I dragged my feet up to the sealed door. "Here goes nothing."

The Weaver was silent.

"You could offer a little encouragement, you know."

Why bother? Every time I try, you get angry.

"Jerk." I clenched my jaw and laid a hand on the door. "Open sesame."

I felt the Weaver's eye roll, but he worked his magic much faster than I could have. The door made a small hiss and fell inward. *The fastest route then?* he asked. *Assuming I'll be your tour guide yet again.*

"Can it, Weaver." I stepped into the dark interior of the clock. It smelled of dust, metal, and oil. The only splash of color came from the many golden cogwheels. I hadn't noticed the beauty of it before. The intricately designed gears were interspersed with black, creating wonderfully elaborate patterns on the walls, but not a single one moved. The stillness sent a chill up my spine. "Fine. Yes. Directions."

I wanted to close my eyes and let the Weaver do the walking, but unfortunately my eyes were his. So I endured his carefree instructions. *Turn left. Go straight. Pull this lever.* It was like he didn't even have to try. Maybe he didn't, but how he kept so many landscapes straight was beyond me.

There, he said. *The door to the Chime.*

I paused, my hand on the lever that would open it. The Hours had to know I was inside, but they were nowhere to be seen. Their strange absence could've meant a lot of things, but my money was on an ambush. What better way to hurt me than to wait until I was in the very center of their lair to attack as a unit. My free hand drifted to the threads around my arm.

I would wait to attack. You do want their help, after all.

Sure, I snapped back. *Wait until it's too late for backup. Great plan.*

You die, I die, he cautioned. *Trust me.*

Trust him. *Ha!* I trusted his self-preservation, but what was to say he wouldn't simply transfer himself into the next person? He didn't need me specifically—he only needed a body.

It wasn't easy putting myself here. There's no guarantee it would work a second time, so just go in there.

No wonder he'd stuck around when there were stronger creatures to body snatch. Something mindless, even, where he wouldn't need to share headspace.

Nora, he said in exasperation.

Fine, fine. I pulled the lever. Because I was an idiot. And because the Weaver loved the Sandman in his own way. He wouldn't hurt him by hurting me. *Probably* wouldn't. There was always the chance it was like when Katie and I were growing up. *We* could hurt each other, but no one else was allowed.

As the door lifted, a clatter of metal on metal filled the chamber, and I braced myself for whatever came next: arrows, fists, swords. Something was bound to come flying out. The movement intensified, and shadows filled the gap between the floor and the half-lifted door.

"Don't," someone demanded, and everything fell silent.

This is a good sign, right? I asked.

I hope so.

The door came to a stop with a resounding thud. The Hours stood around the room, their hatred thick and cloying. Their hands held weapons—bows, swords, whips, shining metal objects I didn't know the names of. I held my breath and counted all twelve of them which meant I only had to worry about protecting my front.

The Chime shifted at the center, chains clanking. "Lady Nightmare."

The darkness around me flared. *Play it cool,* I reminded myself. I was in charge. I was in power. Throwing my shoulders back, I strode into the room with a hammering heart. "I'm surprised to find you here," I said as calmly as possible. "No luck breaking out or did you decide to be good nightmares for a change?"

"Lady," the Chime said again, his voice strained. His face was more angelic than I remembered. Or maybe it was a matter of not bothering to notice the first time when I had been under duress. There was a faint bronze shimmer to his skin that matched his clothing, and small bells pierced his ears, six on each side. "We—"

"Save it." I gave an exaggerated sigh. "I have a job for you."

The Chime stared. After a long moment, he took hold of his chain. "I cannot leave the clock."

"They can." I gestured at the Hours. They hadn't moved a muscle since I stepped into the room. "And they will."

"We will never take orders from a Dreamer," Three shouted.

"Won't you?" I quirked an eyebrow and, with a smooth slip of a finger, extracted a thread.

Interesting choice, the Weaver mused.

I flicked the thread, and he pushed magic into it. One second, Three was openly defying me from the center of the clock face. The next, when the puff of sulfuric smoke dissipated, she screamed from inside an iron maiden. Her mask shone behind the rectangular opening, her fingers slipping up to the hole. The inner spikes wouldn't emerge unless she tried to escape, which I anticipated happening any moment now.

"Anyone else?" I asked.

They all stared at Three in awed silence. One by one, their masked faces drifted to the other iron maidens now positioned menacingly at their backs. The contraptions were open, ready to snap them up. Two and Seven shifted. I was sure they would seal their own fate by running, but an agonized cry wiped that notion away. Three's armor crunched, giving beneath the sharp spikes. Her scream faded to a whimper, then the only sound was her rasping breaths.

"What would you have the Hours do?" the Chime asked slowly.

"Rowan sent part of her army to a snowy landscape near some ice caves." I rolled my shoulders and tried to downplay the significance. "I don't know which one exactly. You will find them, and you will kill them all without making a scene."

Eleven cleared his throat. "What of Mara?"

I smirked, annoyed. Questioning my orders, questioning my plans…all of that was over. "Take care of it today. I want them gone before I get there."

Walk out, the Weaver said.

I spun on my heel. My orders were given. There was no other reason to stay. No reason except that they hadn't agreed and leaving without any reassurance made me jittery. What if they decided not to obey? What if they decided to follow me from the clock and exact revenge away from the threat of the iron maidens?

"What of Three?" one of them called. "Release her."

A dreadful laugh came from deep inside me. I spared a single, fleeting look over my shoulder and said, "No."

I flipped the lever on my way out, and the door slammed shut behind me. *Any chance this solves my problems with them?*

They've seen enough of your power, the Weaver said thoughtfully. *But unless you kill Mara, I don't imagine it's enough. Honestly, you should probably kill them too.*

I snorted. *There's still time for that.*

Nora? The Weaver's tone changed. Hardened. *They're at the ice caves.*

That's what the Sandman said.

Find him. Now.

Baku lurked at the edge of the Dream Realm, tail swishing in aggravation. My eyes narrowed as I tracked his movements. The chimera had no idea that I knew he was a spy. If he did, I wouldn't be able to feed him false information, but pretending was difficult when we had worked together for so long. *If* we had ever truly worked together at all. Were we ever true friends? Maybe Baku only came to see me because someone sent him.

"Hungry?" I called from where I stood beneath the brightest star. *Our* spot—Nora's and mine. Apparently, I enjoyed reminiscing about people that wanted to rip me down to nothing. There were so many lies, so much deceit, that it would surprise me more now if someone told the truth. Myself included since I was currently beginning to weave my own web of untruths. "If you want to go hunting, I'll come along. I promised I would meet Nora shortly anyway."

Baku slowed then nodded, and I followed him through the barrier into the Nightmare Realm.

I couldn't come right out and accuse him of treachery. In truth, Baku was always a spy. He passed important information to me for centuries, but was it always complete? There were times he cut off the dreams I read before I was finished, and others when he refused to let me read his dreams at all. I never thought much of it then because everyone deserved their privacy, but now?

Outside the Dream Realm, Baku went straight for Rowan's second army. I wanted to believe it didn't mean he was controlling them himself. Without being able to speak, he couldn't give orders, but that only proved he was indeed working for someone else.

"Have you seen any sign of Mara?" I asked, careful to keep my tone light.

He gave a small shake of his head.

My fingers twitched nervously against my legs. "Halven mentioned seeing her in the west near the vampire farm. Maybe you could take a look later."

He waved his trunk noncommittally.

"I'm sorry I keep asking you for help. This isn't your fight, but there *has to* be some sign of her," I ventured. How far would I have pressed him before? "Maybe if I read your dreams, I can pick up on something you missed. A clue or a—"

Baku pounced away, lips curling up in disgust, when he eyed me sticking a hand into my satchel.

"Are you mad at me?" I closed my fist gently around the sand in case I needed to use it for self-defense. Against Baku. A thing I never expected to worry about. "If I've done something to upset you, it wasn't intentional."

We stared at one another other, letting the silence speak for us both. Then he took off at lightning speed. His course altered slightly to the right, away from the army, and straight for the ice caves. It was possible that was a coincidence, but not likely. My doubts vanished in a cloud of smoke. Baku was working against me, Nora, and both worlds. There was only danger in denying the truth.

Chapter Twenty-One

Nora

Kail droned on and on about issues that needed my attention when we returned from killing Mara. I only half-listened from almost the moment he opened his mouth. Minor squabbles from miscreants were the absolute least of my problems. Had the Weaver bothered with this nonsense? I doubted it. He probably ate popcorn while he watched them tear each other apart. Got a problem? Don't worry—the Weaver will let you settle it gladiator style. It wasn't a bad idea, really.

Hmm? the Weaver asked as if thinking his name summoned him from whatever dark pit he hid away in. *I stopped listening a long time ago.*

Ditto. I sighed.

He made a noise like clucking his tongue. *I've been thinking.*

I told you twenty times, I'm not going out to find the Sandman. He'll be here soon, and you can tell him whatever revelation you had then. Unless you want to fill me in? Honestly, it was ridiculous that he wouldn't tell me what relevance the ice caves had until everyone was together.

I've been thinking about something else, he clarified.

Oh? I nodded to Kail, so it looked like I was listening. *That's never good.*

Ha. Ha. How easily you forgot the mention of a key.

I didn't forget. It just didn't seem important enough to worry about, considering. "Okay," I agreed without knowing what Kail suggested.

I want to try something.

Absolute pass.

Hear me out, the Weaver urged. *You've seen my memories before, but what if we found one together?*

That was unexpected and rather unnecessary when he could just tell me whatever he wanted me to know. "Got it," I told Kail absently and rapped my fingers on the table. *What's your angle?*

The Weaver grunted, annoyed. *Must I have one? Honestly, Keeper—*

What happened to Nora?

Nora, he clipped. *I'm not sure what the memory is, but I'm more than happy to watch it myself.*

You have to watch your own memories?

I do now, he grumbled. *This arrangement isn't exactly all sunshine and rainbows for me either.*

"Are we almost done?" I asked Kail.

Kail leveled a hard look at me. "All we're doing is waiting for the Sandman, so we might as well sort this out now."

"Why? You want our ducks in a row in case someone kills me?" I joked, but I knew why he was doing this now. He wanted a plan for later because it made him feel as if there would *be* a later.

The muscle in his jaw twitched. "I didn't say that."

Are you joining me or not?

Fine. I leaned back in my seat and motioned for Kail to continue. *Multitasking for the win.*

Lovely.

Darkness clouded my vision almost instantly. I blinked to be sure my eyes weren't closed, though I wasn't sure which was more terrifying—the Weaver controlling my eyelids or being temporarily blinded. Glowing fissures whizzed by. The Weaver hummed a monotone song that was like a hammer to my head. I rubbed my temples against the growing pain.

This is weird, I thought at him.

Ah. A fissure eased to a stop in front of us. *Here we are. After you…*

Kail's voice felt far away, his help even further. Would he notice if this was the Weaver's way of trapping me in the passenger seat? If not, the Sandman would, and he'd be along any time now. I needed to get this over with before Kail noticed my mind was somewhere else completely and freaked out. *Here goes nothing.* I shoved my head into the fissure as I had the other times a memory appeared and waited.

A landscape spread around me with tunnel-like cobwebs spiraling straight up toward the sky. Rose petals shot out of the tops. They were red at first but quickly blackened before hitting the ground where they disintegrated. Footprints marked the flat, ash-covered ground as if it were snow. One set. The Weaver looked around slowly, and cleared his throat.

"Lord," rasped a familiar voice.

"Halven." The Weaver spun around, and the masked nightmare bowed low. "It took you long enough."

Halven straightened. "Forgive me."

The Weaver stepped closer and spoke in a low whisper. "I need you to do something."

"Anything, Lord."

The Weaver held out a fist, and Halven brought his palm up to meet it. "This needs to be permanently lost."

Kail slammed his palms down on the table in front of me, and the fissure snapped shut. His masked face hovered in front of me, eyes flashing violently through colors. "Did you hear what I just said?"

"No." My voice felt lost somewhere between here and there. What did the Weaver give Halven? Why did he want us both to watch the exchange? "Are we done?" I asked again.

"*Are we done?*" His ever-changing eyes narrowed. "Do you have no opinion on the matter? You have an opinion on *everything*."

I shrugged and shoved myself out of the chair. "Do what you think is best."

Kail lifted his hands to my face and slapped my cheeks between them. "I don't think you want me to do that."

I leaned away from his palms and rolled my eyes. "Fine. Do whatever you think I would tell you to do."

The key, the Weaver blurted.

Let the key go.

Halven had it. The key to the Ever Safe. We have to make sure it's secure.

Every muscle within my body tensed. To give the key to a nightmare, especially one with a brother at Rowan's mercy, was the stupidest way to dispose of something so important to the safety of both worlds.

Halven had it? I sucked in a breath, willing the frustration to stay within a manageable parameter. For half a second, I succeeded. Then I was on my feet. "That's the key you gave him? Seriously?"

Kail startled. "I didn't—"

"Not you," I snarled. "You gave Halven the key to the Ever Safe, and you didn't think that was something I should know?" I snapped at the Weaver.

Obviously, I thought you should know.

"He's been the front man in the search for Mara for months. What if she caught him and tortured the location out of him?" I shrieked, then whipped around to face Kail. "And you. Did you know? Wait—" I held up my hands. "Don't answer that. Where is the key now?"

Kail straightened. "I wish I did know. It would make this entire…*conversation*…a lot more interesting."

Halven never knew what it was. It was of little importance to him—just another job I asked of him in a long line of tasks.

I struggled for breath. Struggled to see straight. To not punch something. Halven was out there looking for Mara all this time with the key *on him*. Alone. And there I was, feeling like the only one who made mistakes. Because mistakes were for rookies.

Breathe, the Weaver reminded me.

I exhaled through my mouth. In through my nose. "Why am I just hearing about this?"

Kail shifted nervously. "Halven wouldn't tell Mara anything." *Ah…*

"*Ah?* So you did know about this?" I ground out. Kail started to reply, but I closed my fingers together, mimicking a shut mouth. "Not. You."

It's possible that I forgot giving it to him, hence the memory, but I've seen it recently…

Kail paused, obviously hesitant to continue. *Tied on Halven's boot.*

"You forgot." That was completely insane. No way could not one, but *two* people, forget where the key to the Ever Safe was. "What's wrong with you people? You act like it's a bike lock we're dealing with here and not the damn apocalypse."

Do you think after millennia, you'll remember everything that happened this year?

"It's kind of hard to forget!" I screamed. My entire life changed this year. The Sandman turned out to be real, I lost friends and family to horrific murders, I killed the Weaver, became the Weaver, abandoned my family, gained a realm…gained darkness and a parasite. A certain…*fondness* for it all and a spark of hatred for myself. No, I wouldn't forget this year. This was the year Nora died and was reborn.

You would be surprised.

"Okay. Okay." I paced the room, fingers digging into my scalp, while Kail looked on, intrigued. "So, he has the key." A nervous laugh burst from my chest. "We need to get it from him and destroy it."

What a novel idea, the Weaver said in a flat voice.

"It's indestructible," Kail whispered. "If it wasn't, they wouldn't have bothered giving it to Halven. The lords would've blown it up themselves."

Of course it was. I covered my face and screamed, attempting to give my frustration an outlet. "Fine. Great. Then what? We hide it somewhere? That worked so well with the knife you and Rowan gave me."

This time there's no Baku to spy and retrieve the key.

"I have an idea." Kail smiled a plastic smile, and I knew his suggestion was going to be the icing on my cake. "We can give it to your sister."

Forget frosting—that was some baking show level fancy fondant.

I whirled on him. "Want to run that by me again?"

Mara was in the Day World when I gave it to Halven…it makes sense since she can't get back there.

"You *would* be on his side," I retorted.

Kail pursed his lips. "Calm down before the vein in your forehead ruptures."

"Don't tell me to calm down!" My throat burned with the words. I bent over, gripping my sides, and dragged in air like it was in short supply. Right, rational. I had to be rational. I closed my eyes and counted to ten. "I want Mara dead, I want *him* out of my head, and I want things to just be *normal* again. Every time I think things can't possibly get worse, they do."

The Sandman will forgive you, the Weaver said with surety.

"Shut up, shut up, *shut up!*" I covered my ears, hunching over. This had nothing to do with the Sandman.

After a long minute, Kail's hand settled on my shoulder. I stiffened but allowed it to stay. "The key will be safe in the Day

World. Mara won't be able to get it, and there aren't any nightmares left on that side."

My hands dropped, and I met his gaze. "First, are you sure there's no one left over there? Because I'm not. Maybe everyone *forgot* about some random evil they tossed over the fence into the neighbor's yard. Second, stop bringing my sister into this mess."

"She doesn't seem like the type that's going to let us keep her out of it," he said.

God, I hated him for being right. "Screw you, Kail."

He rolled his neck with a humorless laugh. "My whole life is one big *screw you*. We're giving it to your sister. End of story."

Chapter Twenty-Two

Seeing Nora made my chest ache only slightly more than not seeing her, and slightly less than knowing Baku was a spy for both Rowan and Mare. I couldn't look at her yet, but I felt her. It was as if the entire room was hyper-sensitive to her presence. The air shifted with her every movement, and the silence waited with bated breath for the sound of her voice. I stood near the door to the empty chamber while Nora paced along the far wall about ten feet away. Halven and Kail stood between us, anxiety rippling off them both. I wanted it to be due to the situation, but I knew better. The tension between Nora and me was nearly unbearable.

"So," Kail ventured. "Is there a purpose to this get-together or are we going to stand around all day?"

Nora's lips moved as if she were talking, but no sound left her. At least not until she bent over, hands digging into her abdomen, and dragged in a shallow breath. "The ice caves." She stood upright again, eyes squeezed shut. "The Weaver said that the Ever Safe is beneath the ice caves."

No one moved. No one breathed.

"No. It was in a jungle." I could still remember how rudimentary it was—one of the Weaver's first full landscapes. He created it just to help lure the Ancients in, either out of curiosity or anger at the *blight* we left in their charred world. There were dense trees, sweeping vines, and the violent screams of cicadas, but not much else.

"Apparently, he thought it would be better after Mara broke out to change things," Nora said, her face ghostly white. "Throw her off the scent."

Kail fell against the wall with a bitter laugh, and Halven reached out to steady him. He swatted his brother's hand away. "Welcome to the end of days."

No one replied. What could any of us say? If the Weaver really had altered the jungle into ice caves—and there was no reason for him to lie about it—then Mare already found what she was looking for. If we didn't get there before she found a way into the Ever Safe, everything we did was for nothing.

"And *you*—" Kail seethed to Halven. "You have the key?"

Halven nodded and bent to untie it from his boot. "I didn't know."

Kail snatched it from his brother's hand. "I'll deal with *this* the way it should've been dealt with before."

I stepped forward, heart thumping wildly at the sight of Kail with the key. "Give it to me."

"What do you think I'm going to do, Sandman? Hand it over to the enemy?" He glowered. "After all I've done to keep us alive?"

"I don't trust anyone," I stated. "Especially not you."

Kail opened his mouth to argue, but Nora grabbed his fist where the key was tucked. "Let me have it," she whispered. "You need to give it to someone who can make your plan happen."

"Fine." Kail barred his teeth and relinquished the key to her.

Nora tucked it away in her pocket. "I'm giving it to Katie."

She *wanted* to involve Katie? I couldn't deny it was a good idea, but hadn't she wanted her sister away from all this?

"What about Mara?" Kail asked.

A plan formed in my head, buried beneath the emotional heaviness that lurked there. "Baku won't let us near the ice caves if he thinks we know Mare's there." He was trying to keep us away regardless, and I didn't want to bait him into an outright attack. "I'll leave a false trail for him to follow."

"Wise," Kail agreed, nodding. "I don't want to be eaten."

Nora groaned. "Kail, be constructive or be quiet."

"You want constructive? Is no one going to talk about what happens to the rest of us if the two of you fail?"

"We know what will happen," Nora muttered.

Halven cleared his throat and spoke in a low voice. "If the Ever Safe is opened, nightmares will perish first."

He wasn't incorrect, but it didn't matter who died first. If the safe opened, nightmares died, the realm crumbled, taking the Dream Realm with it, and finally, the Day World. Without night, there could be no day. Without darkness, no light. Each piece of our worlds was a support beam—lose one, and they all fell.

There wasn't an alternative sequence of events, unless…I sucked in a shallow breath. Unless there was a contingency plan.

Would it be worth it? If Nora and I couldn't keep the safe closed, would anyone else be able to shut it? After all it took from the Weaver and me the first time…I looked at the threads around Nora's arm as the pieces of my plan coalesced. It was worth a try.

"Give them an army," I said, hardly believing my own suggestion.

Nora took half a step toward me. "Give *who* an army?"

"Them." I motioned to Kail and Halven. "Give them a chance to go down fighting in case we fail."

Halven stiffened while Kail didn't move a muscle. It was a risk, I knew. Giving nightmares an army that they could march against Nora later, against me, was asking for trouble, but it could also get us *out* of trouble. If either of them wanted Nora dead, they had enough opportunity already. Besides, they both seemed to care about Nora, in their own way.

"That's absolutely the *worst* advice I've ever heard," Nora said. "Kail had the Blood Army and look what he did with it."

Kail whirled on her and, suddenly, our tension wasn't the only source of discomfort in the room. "*Rowan* had an army. Not me."

I stared at her chin, not daring to look higher. It seemed like she wouldn't say anything for the longest time, but then she nodded. "Right. You're right." Her fingers drifted to the thread at her wrist. "I'll do it if you promise to get us out of the ice caves should we need assistance."

"Of course," Halven agreed quickly.

If we were stuck in the ice caves, it would be because things went poorly, but if it made her feel better…I only hoped I wasn't setting us up for bigger problems in the future—should we *have* a future. "It's settled then," I said quietly.

Nora sighed. "As long as the Hours are doing what I told them to, Mara's force shouldn't be a problem."

"Sure," Kail said nervously. "As long as they are…"

Nora pulled her hair back and twisted it into a severe bun. "They will, or I'll do a lot worse than locking them in a clock."

A chill ran through me at the easily tossed out implication. I didn't doubt she meant it. How much of that was the Weaver's doing? She had to rule the nightmares with an iron fist, but not around us. Not around *me*.

"There are giant trees full of nests that overlook the ice caves. Meet me there as soon as you can," I said, looking to Nora's boots.

☾

When I got back, I found Baku curled up like a cat just outside of the waters' reach. His elephant ears were relaxed against his body and his trunk was snugly tucked between his tiger paws. *Even traitors needed sleep.*

I paused a few feet away and stared. It would be easy enough to end him now if Nora were with me. The knife suddenly weighed a million pounds. Even if it worked without nightmare magic, I couldn't do it. Baku wasn't who I thought he was, but that didn't erase all those years together. He was the only thing that had kept me from crushing loneliness. I wasn't sure I could ever kill him, but if I did, it wouldn't be like this. He would see it coming, and he would understand why.

Now however, it was time for my performance.

"Baku," I called, forcing my voice to sound strained.

The chimera rolled from his side, ears perked, and sand fell from one side of his face. His innocent, dazed expression was a blow.

"Halven thinks Mare moved again." I bent to my knees to refill my satchel. No matter how much I tried, I couldn't remember if he was around when I learned about the ice caves. "He saw her near the ant hill, but soon lost sight of her. She must be hiding inside the colony."

It made sense to hide there. Giant ants could be troublesome, but there were endless places to hide within their tunnels. Baku launched to his feet, uncertainty flashing in his eyes. *Ah, yes.* The first phase of betrayal. Only, it had to be Mare's loyalty he was contemplating. Wheels visibly turned in his head, and it wasn't hard for me to guess his thoughts. Why would she move without telling him? Did something happen in the caves?

"We have a plan," I admitted. The key to a successful lie was keeping to the truth as much as possible. "Nora's making an army to search the tunnels for Mare, and I'll meet her at the palace. Can you stake out the hill? If she leaves, we need to know which direction she goes."

Baku shook the sand from his brindle coat and studied me as if deciding what to do.

I stood, the satchel bursting with sand at my hip, and injected near-panic into my voice. "Please, Baku. I promised to meet Nora, but there's only one way out of that ant hill. We can't lose our best chance."

He nodded slowly but didn't move until I did. I felt his sharp gaze at my back as I raced in the direction of Nora's palace. I caught glimpses of him as he followed me part of the way, running parallel to my path when he should have veered right a long time ago.

As I neared the outskirts of a landscape that bordered the palace, Baku finally turned away. Using as little sand as I could, I used the same technique that lured the Blood Army away from the Rowan trees. *Just in case.* A replica of myself continued forward, carrying the name of Baku's spymaster, while I slunk away in the opposite direction. I held my breath, waiting to hear the sound of Baku's footfalls behind me, but after none came, I bolted.

Chapter Twenty-Three

Thread flowed through my fingers so fast, it burned. Treadles clacked against one another. My breath was shallow. Baku was working with Mara. *Mara.* Each time the thought passed through my mind, it was like a fresh slice of a knife. It made sense, I supposed, seeing as both he and Mara were *other* in a world of dreams and nightmares, but it didn't excuse him. Weaseling his way into the Sandman's affections only to turn around and use that closeness, that trust, to spy…

You're taking this rather personally.

"It *is* personal." I jerked the loom too hard, fraying the thread. "If you betray the Sandman, you betray me."

You betrayed him.

I winced. It was true twice over, but it hadn't been intentional. Or maybe it was intentional, but I never set out with that goal. It just…*happened.* I felt cornered. I shoved away from the loom. "No one asked you, Weaver."

"These private conversations with your predecessor make me extremely uncomfortable," Kail said.

"No one asked you either," I shot at him where he stood against the wall.

He rolled his eyes. "I don't know why you're so surprised about Baku. Keep your enemy close and whatnot."

"What does that say about you?"

Kail simply smirked.

Should we not be asking Baku's motives?

My breath stuck for a moment. It felt different now that the Sandman acknowledged it as the truth. I couldn't pretend it might all be in my head, or that I was making something out of nothing. "His motives are that he's a heathen nightmare, obviously," I said in a huff. "Evil and calculating and eager to mess with everyone."

You make it sound like those are bad things.

"You…" Before I could take the bait, a thought hit me—*really* hit me—and I spun to look at Kail. "Baku isn't a nightmare."

Kail scoffed. "You think the Weaver would create something that ate the rest of us?"

I stared at him, my face stoic. "Yes."

You wound me, Keeper.

"The Weaver wasn't always…" Kail pinched his lips tight together in a grimace. "Nevermind. He doesn't need me inflating his ego."

"Definitely not," I agreed.

"You know how you feel about your nightmares," he continued. "Would you create something like Baku?"

He knew I wouldn't. "He's an Ancient too? That would explain why he's working with Mara." There was another creature like him now, so he wasn't alone, and if he helped Mara open the Ever Safe, he never would be again.

"Figuring that out just now, eh? Anyway, I think you can stop now." Kail waved a hand at the loom. "You'll never be able to create this many nightmares without passing out, and the Sandman said to meet him in a few hours. It's been at least seven."

I stared at the pile of threads heaped in front of me. The newest additions to my growing army. Undoubtedly loyal and ready to go in case Kail needed them to pull our sorry butts out of whatever predicament we found ourselves in. Ice caves didn't exactly scream prime fighting conditions when Mara could corner us as easily as we could corner her.

When the Sandman suggested letting Kail have command over a nightmare army, I thought I entered the twilight zone. I mean, it was *Kail*, for one, and a huge risk regardless. If Kail was waiting for the perfect moment to strike, this would be it. He'd have the manpower and, after fighting with Mara, weakened prey. With enough power, he could try forcing me to reunite him with Halven even though I promised…*keep your enemies close.* Baku had played his cards well enough to fool everyone, and Kail was undoubtedly more conniving.

Did I have enough nightmares? Yes; but I had to delay the inevitable somehow.

“Right.” I slipped from the bench and gathered the threads in my arms.

It was time. We needed to meet the Sandman west of the Ever Safe doors, far from where our enemy made camp. While the Hours kept them distracted, we would sneak into the caves. Before that, I had to deliver the key to the Dream Realm.

“Chin up, Lady. You’ll stop her,” Kail said with certainty.

That was probably the best motivational speech I was going to get, but I appreciated him trying. I hugged the unborn nightmares to my chest. “Guess we should get this show on the road.”

Kail nodded solemnly and took the pile of thread from my arms.

“Chivalry isn’t dead after all,” I said with a forced smile. There were so many nightmares to make, so many pieces of myself—of the Weaver—to give away. But this was a long-term plan. A failsafe for the realm and, in turn, both worlds.

A long-term plan with short-term deadlines, the Weaver commented.

That’s why I have you, I quipped. He didn’t get to second guess the plan in the final hour when he hadn’t bothered to come up with an alternative before now, and he could’ve. I was positive he had more devious plots left in him than cheetahs had spots.

I followed Kail down the Keep’s outer staircase and through the courtyard surrounding the Keep. My bottom lip was raw from where I anxiously gnawed on it, but I couldn’t stop as I exited the palace. The sound of the pixies sliding bolts into place reverberated in my ears. It wasn’t exactly *home,* but it was the closest thing I had.

Which is why we must defend it.

I blew out a breath. *Stop being so…*

Contrary? the Weaver offered. *It's called being realistic. Very few things are ever all or nothing.*

"Lady." Halven stepped up from behind me and inclined his head.

I quickly patted the secret pocket sewn inside my shirt to feel the press of the key. It was like carrying air, an impossibility if one didn't consider magic, but the shape of it still dug into my skin beneath my new clothes.

Each layer of fabric the Doll Maker used for my battle outfit was as thin as paper. The darkest of blues pressed against my skin with the lightest blue—nearly white—over all eight varying shades. Despite the whimsical feel, the cut was fiercer than I was. Jagged, rough lines, raw edges, and decorative, studded gold buttons. The left sleeve wrapped around my arm like a bandage, the fabric darkening back to the deepest shade at my wrist, while my right arm was bare, save for my threads. The ends of them thrummed against my pulse points on my wrist and at the soft hollow of my neck where they laid like a choker. It paired perfectly with shimmering black pants made of thick, flexible fabric. I had returned these clothes back when they were first sent, or I thought I had before Kail produced them this morning. *They should fit you now,* he had told me as he sauntered away.

They always *fit.* But that wasn't what Kail meant.

I drew from his confidence in me, and it brushed up against the budding kernel of my own. *Okay, Nora. You're doing okay.* The Sandman and I were going to do this. We were going to kill Mara.

You two are quite the dynamic duo. Maybe now that you're both on the same page, you won't screw this up.

Seriously?

His sigh breezed through me. *I'm tired, Keeper.*

Yeah, but that's the gloomiest encouragement I've ever heard. Do you even want me to succeed?

Take it or leave it, he said, grumpier than I'd ever heard him. For that reason alone, I would take it.

Someone had already moved the other threads from my art room—most likely Halven given they were separated into neat piles. I scooped up the end of one, letting the rest trail on the ground. This was too many…*what was I thinking?* Though some were future landscapes which needed to be stored for later use…

Kail shifted in front of me and caught my gaze. In his, I saw conflict. Each flickering color said something different. Sorrow, worry, eagerness, determination, affection. I looked away before any of it could rock my decisions. Kail needed to think I would make it back for me to believe it, as ridiculous as that felt. Apparently, I still had more work to do on trusting myself.

"You might want to move," I told him, and he stepped back to stand beside Halven.

I coaxed the first nightmare free and snapped the thread. An iron rhinoceros emerged, held together with shifting panels, her nostrils steaming. The scent of burning wool filled the courtyard as another nightmare followed. And another and another. The sky darkened with sulfuric smoke, and my muscles begged for a break.

Nora, came the Weaver's voice. Gentle. Wary. *Let me finish for you.*

"No way." I wasn't going to give him permission to wear my body like a costume.

I don't need your permission, he hedged.

"Don't even think about it."

I can only help so much this way.

It will have to be enough, I snapped.

Then I waited.

Waited for the swooping sensation of him ignoring my wishes. The fading. The loss of control. I made as many nightmares as I could in those few precious moments, but when nothing happened—when nothing even *tried* to happen—my arms dropped heavily to my sides.

What? he asked, unamused. *Did you* want *me to force my way to the surface? I daresay that it isn't fun for either of us.*

For either of us? It sucked for me, but it seemed like he enjoyed it enough. Especially when he was firmly in control.

It's rather like forcing myself into a latex suit two sizes too small, but let's stay on task, yes? Do you want me to do it or not?

I looked out at the array of newly created nightmares—the birds of prey, the hobgoblins, the possessed farm equipment, and things with no known names—then down to the remaining piles of thread. The Sandman expected us soon, and there was still my side quest with the key to take care of.

"Fine," I said reluctantly. "Do it."

There was an immediate pull at my center. Brisk and painful.

Are you sure?

"I said so, didn't *I*?"

Then relax. When I didn't, the Weaver added a withering, *Please.*

I took a deep breath and let it out through my mouth. Kail and Halven were moving about the crowd, organizing the new nightmares into formation. Would they notice if the Weaver tried anything sketchy? He already attacked Kail once…

A moment later, my concerns didn't matter. The Weaver was pushing too hard for me to concentrate on *what ifs,* so I exhaled again, letting it knock down my defenses. The Weaver slithered by them and right up to the surface with a slimy feeling that made me shudder. He didn't bother to comment on my repulsion, nor did he try to sabotage anything. No, the Weaver simply took up where I left off, and I watched my body move in response to his commands.

Magic bubbled. Fizzled. Stretched. I felt myself drifting further back the longer he worked. As he strained. We were nearly finished with the usable threads, but what strength would we have left over? The Sandman said we were of equal strength, but it depended on where we allocated our power. I was giving mine to the nightmares—they would fight for me while I regained the depleted magic—but *I* needed to fight Mara. Not them.

Weaver, I called weakly. *We have enough.* My thoughts slammed into something solid, and I spun around with a gasp. A clear box brimming with black swirling tendrils burned through the darkness. *What is this?*

"That, Nora dear, is why I continued to call you *Keeper* after the dream was gone."

It shook me to hear him speak with my voice. *What?* I assumed he called me Keeper out of habit, or maybe because I 'kept' him. *Explain.*

"I couldn't let you play with *all* our magic before you learned to control yourself."

My lips parted, and I pressed up against the box. *So much.* There was so much. What I used all this time was a mere raindrop in a thunderstorm. If I had access to this much power, we could've stopped Mara the first time. The Sandman had an equal amount? He was holding back way more than I had ever imagined, all in the name of maintaining balance.

"The power you used in the globe is not the same power that's in there," he said with a sense of glee.

Then he let go. The sudden, unexpected control of my body hit like a tidal wave, and I fell to my knees into the grass. "Jerk," I croaked.

"Nora!" Kail flew to my side and skidded across the lawn to grip my shoulders. "What happened?"

Give yourself a few moments. You won't feel tired for long.

"Nothing," I breathed. Then, to the Weaver, *you're not getting out of an explanation.*

"But—"

"No *buts*." I forced myself to my feet. "Get Halven over here."

He hesitated. "Right. You have to take the key to the—"

"No." Taking the key to Katie wasn't all I had to do before I left. I fought back a smirk. "I'm going to give you what you asked for."

His chest expanded with a deep, silent breath. "Now?"

"Well, I am walking off to potential doom and all that, but if you'd rather wait—"

"Halven!" he screamed.

I laughed a real, true laugh. There was enough magic left inside me, box or no box, to make good on my promise. Kail deserved it. As did Halven. Sure, I wasn't exactly happy about the army thing, but they'd already done plenty for me.

Halven appeared next to me. "Lady?"

"You still want to be put back together, right?" I placed my hand on his shoulder. "This might be our last shot."

Halven stiffened beneath my touch. "No, Lady."

"No?" My brows shot up. "But I thought…"

"It won't be our last chance."

Kail shoved between us. "What are you talking about, brother?"

"I meant to be reassuring," Halven clarified.

"Yes, yes," Kail gripped his brother's hand and tugged him closer. "All is fine and dandy. Let's do this."

Eager, aren't they, the Weaver thought.

Why wouldn't they be? They were kept apart and in pain for years. "It…might hurt," I said because I had no idea if the process would be painless. It had hurt them coming apart, and I *hoped* it hurt Rowan when I put her back into her tree.

"It's worth it," Kail insisted

I reached out to them with closed eyes. Their knots, different yet the same, throbbed inside their chests. Unlike with Rowan, I saw everything perfectly. The frayed edges, hanging limp and grey, and the spark that traveled through each one until those decaying ends flared to life. The threads reached for each other. Tugged and stretched along the bridge I created until, with one final, blinding flash of gold, there was only one knot.

I stepped back, my body aching as if I had a fever deep in my bones and cracked my eyes open. One pair of boots stood before me. Matte black. *It worked.* I beamed. *It worked!* My eyes were fixed on those boots so unlike Kail's worn pair or Halven's ridiculous, court jester style shoes. What were they…or was he…now?

My eyes trailed up fitted black pants, the flare of Kail's trench coat missing. Bare hands, the same warm brown tone I was used to, tugged the bottom of a red shirt up. Crimson lines snaked over his skin in the same irregular pattern that decorated Halven's coat, the same pattern that seemed to scar Kail's abdomen before. The astonished laugh was half Kail, half Halven's rasp. No longer a strained sound, but rougher, more masculine.

Finally, I gathered the courage to look at his face. The long beak was no more. The mask now hugged his nose with a gentle curve . Instead of white, the half mask was decorated with the same black and red design from Halven's Venetian mask. Only it wasn't black and red for long. The red quickly morphed to purple, then blue, yellow, green, while his eyes were two orbs absent of any color but black. On his head, sat a large black hat. The brim was smaller than Halven's, less ostentatious, but more mysterious.

I didn't know how to react or what to think. Maybe it was because I had gotten used to them, but he was a hundred times more intimidating like this…more…*nightmarish.* Until he smiled. It was a beautiful thing full of Halven's kindness and Kail's swagger. "Hello," I said, matching his smile. "And you are?"

"Kail," he said quickly. "We were always Kail."

I folded my arms and pretended to study him. "I suppose this body will do."

Kail held his arms out as if to ask '*what's wrong with it?*' "It's my natural form."

"Yes," I agreed. "It's yours. Unless you betray me."

"Lady—"

I held up a hand. "I'll trust the Halven part of you not to use *an army* against me."

"Only to save you," he promised with more sincerity than I expected.

"Good." I patted him on the shoulder and turned on my heel. "Then you know what to do."

When I was almost out of earshot, Kail whispered. "Good luck, Nora."

☾

"Please be here," I whispered at the edge of the Sandman's domed barrier. If Katie wasn't asleep, we would need a lightning-fast backup plan because the Sandman was too occupied to Day Walk and find her. I hesitated outside of the barrier. The magic emanated from it, tingling against my skin in warning. The Weaver wasn't meant to be in the Dream Realm, but how I longed for it. The stars, the sand, the luminescent water. Memories that made up so much of the last five years, but I wanted the beach to be here tomorrow so today, I had to do my job.

My hand slipped past the glowing barrier, the magic zap-zap-zapping like tiny electrical currents. I jumped the rest of the way through and was instantly surrounded by the familiar scent of lilac and fresh air. It was almost cloying, but I still gulped it down. The scent was game boards drawn in the sand and fantastical tales of legends, known and unknown. Math homework gone unfinished when the Sandman said he had no idea what x equaled and *why were there letters in math anyway*? A thousand dancing, swirling, twisting dreams given life. Seeing the

Sandman's face for the first time. Leaving this place for the last time. All of that and more.

My gaze automatically drifted up to the sky to find the brightest star. It pulled me forward as if my feet weren't my own. Slowly, slowly, I inched across the beach from the far side until the water became visible. It was every bit as majestic as I remembered, but my focus unexpectedly zeroed in on something else. A tall, sand-made sunflower stood in our spot, staring up at the sky, petals gleaming, and my heart shattered right there on the beach.

"Hey, Nora," Katie said from behind me. "What are you doing here? I thought you couldn't come because you messed up the beach or whatever?"

I jumped and spun around, hand over my racing heart. "How long has that been here?"

"What? The flower? As long as I've been coming. Why?"

"No reason." *Every reason.* It was still there which meant either the Sandman still cared about me or he hadn't bothered to get rid of it yet. A pit formed in my stomach. "You're right. I shouldn't be here, so I'll get right to it. I need you to take something back to the Day World to keep safe."

"What is it this time?" she asked, curious.

I opened my mouth to tell her about the key, but the words stuck as I contemplated her question. "What do you mean *this time*?"

"First the dream, now this. I'm not a safety deposit box."

My world spun. *She couldn't mean…* "*You're* the new Dream Keeper?" I blurted.

Her hands rose between us in surrender. "Calm down there, killer. Didn't the Sandman tell you?"

"Does it *sound* like he told me?" I asked with dismay. "He's supposed to be *protecting* you. He promised to keep you out of all of this."

"Right." Katie rolled her eyes. "I'm pretty sure the one he's protecting is you. The rest of the world comes second."

That was a lie—the balance came first—but he had promised me. *He promised.* Katie wasn't supposed to get involved in any Night World business. Instead, the Sandman walked her right to my door and had the audacity to get upset with me for holding back information? At least I tried to tell him about the Weaver.

You're about to involve your sister with the key, the Weaver chimed in.

That's different, I shot back. *I didn't put anything in her head. All she has to do is stick the key in a drawer or melt it down.*

"Everything okay?" Katie touched my arm. "You look a little pale."

"I'm peachy," I answered through my teeth. I dug the key from my pocket and held it out to her. "Take this key back with you and hide it somewhere. Anywhere."

She plucked it from my outstretched hand and turned it over. "What's it for?"

"I'm going to err on the side of caution and say *don't ask, don't tell.* Just keep it on your side of the barrier."

"But—"

"Please," I begged.

Katie drew in a slow breath, closed her fingers around the key, and lunged at me. I didn't have time to move before her arms wrapped around me in a tight hug. "I love you."

"I love you too." I gingerly returned the hug. Katie was a lot of things, but most importantly, she was my sister. "I'm really sorry about all of this."

She squeezed a little harder. "I know you are."

"I can't come home again," I said carefully. "Ever."

Katie swallowed hard. "Lucky for me, I know where you live so you'll never get rid of me."

Except one day, Katie would grow old and die. Decades from now, hopefully, but what was that to someone like me? We would have to make every day count. And if I didn't make it back from killing Mara, she had to stay away. From here *and* the Nightmare Realm, for as long as they stood.

"Don't just waltz into the Nightmare Realm, okay? I never want you to get hurt because of me again." The sand shifted beneath my boots, disintegrating from the prolonged contact. "I have to go, but I'll see you soon."

Katie pulled away and held up the key. "I'll take care of this."

"Thank you."

I gave my sister a small smile and spared another glimpse at the sunflower before leaving them both behind.

Chapter Twenty-Four

The Hours were methodical. I watched them work from the giant eagle's nest on the other side of the ice caves, pleased they were taking their assignment seriously. A death cry carried across the landscapes followed by a shifting of the army. They moved in a confused, frantic fashion, rallying around the death, or so it appeared from this distance. The Hours kept the panic at a slow burn—a benefit of the nightmares' mindless nature—so I doubted Mare knew anything was wrong yet.

I expected Nora to be here by now, but I was confident she would come. Soon, I hoped, before the Ancient grew suspicious. Or Baku. Kail's army would stay far enough away that I wouldn't be able to see it, even from this height. Instead, I kept my eyes peeled for a single figure. Nora would be coming from the direction where cut logs gave way into towering trees.

One of the green and black speckled eggs in the nest rolled up against my leg. I shoved it away and moved a few of the loose sticks to form a barrier between the two unhatched nightmares. I doubted they were ever meant to hatch, but still, the way the other eagles watched me from their own nearby nests let me know they wouldn't hesitate to protect them. The only thing likely holding them back was the fact that I vaporized the owner of this one.

A shadow wove between neatly stacked, chopped logs below. I leaned over the edge of the nest and squinted. My heart ricocheted against my chest. *Nora.* She shone as bright as the sun, as dark as pitch, and my anger burned away like a flame to paper. The Lady of Nightmares never seemed so fitting a title as it did in this moment.

Nora was an enigma—a being made of Day and Night, of light and dark, and she glowed with them both. She moved languidly, unafraid of any nightmares lurking nearby, and it finally hit me. *Rule by fear,* Kail taught her.

And she did.

She could walk as fearlessly as she did. At the palace, hearing her threaten the Hours worried me, but now I understood. She had indeed become a lady with kindness in her heart and steel in her soul. I had to make things right with her before we took on Mare.

I slid down the tree, guided by sand. Nora must've seen me because when I landed on the pine-covered ground, she was waiting. "Any trouble?" I asked at the sight of her pinched expression.

She shrugged silently and refused to look at me. Was it because I hadn't looked at her in the palace? My brows lowered. No, she wasn't that petty—but there was something bothering her. Judging by the severe clenching of her jaw, it was anger fueling whatever this was.

"Nora?" I asked. "What happened? Did Kail—"

She huffed. "Kail? What would Kail do?"

"Well…" Confusion settled in. "You gave him an army, right?"

"It was your idea," she snapped, stepping closer. Her gold eyes blazed when she finally looked up. "But, no. Kail hasn't done anything. You on the other hand…"

I sucked in a breath. "Me?"

"I asked you to leave Katie *out of this world*." She jabbed a finger into my chest. "And you made her the new *Dream Keeper*?"

Oh. That. Given everything else that happened, I'd almost forgotten Nora didn't know. "Nora, I—"

"You had the audacity to get mad at me, to walk away from *us*, because I didn't have a chance to tell you about the Weaver—even though I tried to tell you and I would have—when you did this? To my *sister*? You broke your promise to keep her safe twice, but somehow *I'm* the bad guy?" Scarlet colored her cheeks, tears brimmed at her eyes, and she took a ragged breath. "I've done a lot of things I shouldn't have, and you always forgave me. I would've forgiven you too."

"Would have?" I asked desperately.

"It doesn't matter." Her shoulders jerked in a shrug. "When we're done here, you can leave me to my own destruction."

Suddenly, I was two inches tall. I was in shock on the ship, allowing my emotions to rule me, when I said those things. They were words of anger, nothing more, and I had every right to be mad. It would've taken me time to process Nora's revelation, well-deserved time, but I loved her more than I loved anything.

"You're right," I croaked. "We kept things from each other, both of us."

Nora's lip quivered. "She's my *sister*."

"I know." Before I had time to worry that she would push me away, I crushed her to my chest. "I'm sorry, Nora. She was the safest choice, but I'll move it to someone else. I swear I will."

"Forget it. This isn't the time," she mumbled into my shirt. "Let's call a truce until Mara is dead."

She was right. This was absolutely the worst time, but it could be our last if anything went wrong. I lifted her chin and wiped escaped tears off each cheek. "Can I kiss you?"

Nora leaned up on her toes and pressed her lips to mine. It said all the things we didn't have time to say, most importantly that we were sorry and still loved each other. The kiss didn't last long—*couldn't* last long—but it was enough to put me at ease. Nora set her forehead on my chest with a relieved sigh before stepping back.

"Ready?" she asked.

I took the knife from my belt and turned it over in my hand, feeling its capacity for destruction. It scared me. The last time I used it, worlds were cleaved in two. "As I'll ever be," I admitted.

Gusts of frigid air cut through my clothes. It swirled out of the round opening to the ice caves, whistling in a way that seemed to speak. *Come inside*, it beckoned. *Bask in my splendor.*

It was beautiful in a way that only made it more dangerous. The grotesque nightmares held no surprise when they released their fearsome attacks, but the pretty ones? The landscapes, the creatures, that calmed Dreamers before snapping them up with hidden horrors…those were the ones to look out for because you never knew what to expect.

Nora inched closer until our arms brushed. I ran a finger along her jaw, memorizing her profile. "We can do this," I whispered.

She nodded, but her focus remained on the dark opening. Up close, the ice was a brilliant aquamarine with ripples just beneath the surface. It was as smooth as glass up close and, from a distance, as reflective as a mirror. Deep inside the opening, the ice appeared to glow from within, but from where we stood, it was cloaked in shadow. I took the first step, knowing it was that or stand at the opening all day, but I didn't mind. Let me be the one to step into a trap.

When nothing jumped out at us or scurried off to spread the news of our arrival, it only felt more wrong. We crept further and further toward the glowing interior, our steps nearly silent on the icy ground. I scanned the ceiling to be sure nothing hung over our heads, and that the dips and curves of the tunnel were clear of danger—at least, any visible danger. Beside me, Nora took in our surroundings as if in slow motion, her luminous eyes absorbing the entirety of the cave mouth. I was too afraid to speak and have my words travel to Mare's ears, so when her eyes finally landed on me, I offered a reassuring smile. She returned it and silently pointed forward.

On and on we went, slowly choosing which branches to take. Right, right, left, right, straight…on and on the system went with nothing noticeably amiss. The glow of the caves stayed in front of and behind us, trapping us in a bubble of semi-darkness. Another left. Straight again. It was quickly becoming clear this was going to take too long, and we needed to reassess. I slowed to a stop and ran a hand down my face.

Unfortunately, Nora must not have noticed because she slammed into my back a moment later. Her loud gasp filled the tunnel as her feet flew out from under her. She landed on the slippery ice and slid a few feet away. The soft *thump* of the impact echoed around us. And echoed and echoed. I winced, not daring to move, and waited. Nora stared at me, wide-eyed, not breathing.

Seconds ticked by, minutes perhaps, but nothing happened. Nora eased to her feet and mouthed *sorry*. I wasn't convinced we were in the clear yet and gave her a terse smile. Something had heard that, without doubt. Nora took small steps back to my side and rubbed at what had to be sore palms from trying to catch her fall.

She wasn't the only thing to move. Within the glossy surface of the walls, at the edge of the lit area, there was a flutter of white fabric. I sucked in a breath, pulse racing, just as Mare materialized behind Nora.

"There you are, darlings."

Chapter Twenty-Five

My entire body quivered at the sound of Mara's voice. She sounded stronger with the way her voice bounced off the walls. When I spun around, my chest heaved at the sight of her. Her hair was matted and the shift she wore a tattered mess, but everything else about her seemed fiercer than when I last saw her. The bones of her legs were visible still, but now muscle surrounded them, her face was now full, and eyes no longer sunken. *How?* It wasn't that long ago I saw her in the clock tower.

The Ever Safe, the Weaver said cautiously. *She must be feeding off its energy somehow.*

My eyes widened. *Can she do that?*

"When you began picking off the nightmares outside, I knew it would only be a matter of time before you came yourselves."

Mara trailed her sharp nails along the ice, leaving white trails across the glossy surface. "We can do this a number of ways. You could give me the key—"

The Sandman let out a harsh growl. "You're *not* opening the gates."

"Or I can kill you and take it," she finished.

"Yeah, okay," I said before either of them could squeeze in another word. "We aren't doing the whole threatening conversation bit. You're not going to give up, we're not going to give up, so let's just get this over with."

Mara snarled wordlessly. "Eager to die, Lady? I can get back in without the key. It's just more difficult."

"The key is in the only place you'll never get it, so all this—" I motioned between us, ignoring the second half of her proclamation, "is pointless."

"I was wrong. You aren't useful to me," she roared, launching herself at us before she finished speaking.

Her blows were fueled by rage, but they were no less precise. It was only thanks to the Sandman's quick reflexes that we both managed to avoid her nails swiping toward our faces. He blasted her back with a sand-made bowling ball to the chest and unsheathed the knife.

The power slammed into me like a wrecking ball, and I stumbled back into the wall. A giant fish stared out of the ice beside my head with red eyes and rows upon rows of needle-like teeth. A small scream fell from my lips before I realized it was frozen solid. Mara's hiss drew my attention away.

Sand circled the Ancient. Stabbing, cutting, gripping, but Mara continued to lash out. The Sandman slashed with the knife, but never quickly enough. He needed help. If I could immobilize her, this would be over in seconds.

Delegate! the Weaver screamed as I flew forward. *Delegate!*

I drew a thread from my wrist and created a large Venus fly trap. Its roots scrambled to find a patch of dirt to dig into, and it flexed a giant blue and green mouth. A lock of Mara's hair must've touched one of the hair triggers when she leapt away from the sand, and the trap slammed shut on her shoulder, the rest of her body dangling between its blades.

Stupid plant, the Weaver grumbled.

Mara shrieked, and the Sandman drove the knife toward her chest. I held my breath and braced for the impact. But the flytrap instinctively flung its head upward and attempted to suck Mara in further. The knife hit empty air.

Terrible choice.

"If you have a better plan, be my guest," I fumed.

Mara's hand emerged from one side of the leathery plant, clear liquid dripping to the floor. The nightmare opened its mouth, dropping its prey, and flailed until it lay still on the ground. The Sandman spun, trying to take out our enemy before she regained her footing. I took a single step with a new thread ready between my fingers.

Don't you dare go over there with him swinging that knife around, the Weaver said in a hard voice.

He was right. The Sandman was acting like a man possessed. His movements were panic-driven and messy, while Mara's were made of pure determination. If I got in the way, or if Mara threw me in his path, I was a goner. We needed to use the knife together, so I wasn't doing much good over here by myself.

I tossed a nightmare out as a distraction. A ten-foot yeti covered in white fur hunched over to keep his head from scraping against the ceiling. Thick spittle rained down on both Mara and the Sandman, and there was a split second of terror when I wasn't sure who the yeti would attack—the Sandman or Mara. If the Sandman was too badly injured, he would disappear to his realm, leaving me here alone. A huge *hell no.*

I had to do my part. I placed my palms on the wall and tracked the knot belonging to the ice caves. My breath was ragged, my palms sweating. I had to be exact. And Mara had to stop moving. *Oh God, oh God.* I was going to miss. I was going to—

There, the Weaver barked. *Hurry.*

I plucked at the piece of thread he indicated without a second thought and launched myself at the frozen wall now blocking the middle of the tunnel. Inside, Mara was frozen mid-attack. Nails out. Teeth bared. Behind her, the yeti pounded against the thick ice with little effect.

"Nice move," the Sandman wheezed. He stretched his back, fists pressing into his lower vertebrae. "Ready?"

Did he even have to ask? "Ready."

He held the knife with his left hand and wrapped my right around his. Quickly, he placed the knife just above Mara's heart, then positioned his other palm at the end of the knife. "I'll use sand to push it through the ice," he informed me. Sand swirled around his hand a moment later, glowing blue. He brought it away, readying to slam the blade straight though to its target when something body slammed the yeti into the wall. Blood streaked across the clear surface as he slid to the ground, lifeless.

The Sandman's hand hovered, and my heart nearly gave out. "Do it," I urged.

His hand moved in what felt like slow motion. Closer. Closer. The tip dug into the ice. One more second and—

The ice exploded.

Baku's tusks tore through the wall, sending us both flying back amid hunks of ice. The knife clattered out of the Sandman's hand. It slid down the tunnel along with us. Baku dug his claws deep into the ice floor and snarled. I knew he was strong—no one would fear him if he wasn't and the Weaver would've ended him a long time ago.

Fifty-fifty shot back then, he glowered. *But now? End him.*

I wasn't sure if *could* kill him. He had burst through a three-foot-thick wall of ice like it was a banner at the start of a football game. Mara now stood behind him, shaking clumps of ice from her hair.

"Sandman?" I breathed.

He stared at Baku as if he'd never truly seen him before. I supposed he hadn't. "Baku, what are you doing?" It wasn't a question, but a plea. "If she lets the Ancients out, they'll destroy everything."

Baku's lips curled in disgust.

"That's the point," Mara stated with an air of superiority. "To end the worlds and get back to *my* version. When things were dark and violent, and everyone *liked* it that way. When *we* were the only living things to walk a dead, scorched earth."

Worse than the nightmares who needed fear to survive, worse than the Weaver who killed with warped purpose, the Ancients wanted to destroy for the fun of it. Something told me it wouldn't be a quick, painless death for anyone.

Least of all us, the Weaver chimed in.

The last thing on my mind was *us.* It was Katie. It was my mom and Paul. Kail. The people depending on us, even though not all of them knew it. I scrambled to my feet and scurried for the knife. Without it, this was over. All of it.

"No!" the Sandman cried.

His yell echoed off the smooth walls, echoed down to my bones, but I didn't dare look back. Instead, I dove for the knife, hard pebbles of ice digging into my stomach and chest, and my fingers closed around the handle a second before Mara's foot came down. I ground my teeth against the pain of what was surely five broken knuckles.

With my free hand, I pulled a thread from my wrist, quick as lightning, and flicked it without bringing the nightmare out. Then I drove the needle-sharp thread into the top of her foot. It went straight through, protruding from her calloused sole, and into my hand trapped underneath. I swallowed a cry when she shrieked and lost her balance on the ice, toppling over, taking the thread with her.

The Sandman dragged me to my feet. Blood flowed into one of his eyes from a gash in his forehead.

"Baku?" I asked.

"Gone."

I wasn't sure if he meant gone as in *gone* or gone as in dead, but I had little time to dwell on it. The Sandman held a hand out and sand shot from his satchel. With a snap of his fingers, the sand circled Mara and turned to thick, white glue. She clawed at it, unable to tear it apart. Unable to escape. I fought the urge to cry. It would be done. *Done.*

The Sandman covered my broken hand with his and together, we slammed the knife straight into Mara's chest. She gasped, eyes bulging. Blood bubbled from between her lips, and she writhed against the hilt of the knife. We withdrew the blade. The Sandman slid it back into its sheath, and I fell to me knees to watch her die.

The sand fell away from Mara's body, leaving her sprawled and bleeding on the ice. Each breath was tattered and wet. Her eyes…they were as bright as ever. Not dull. Not near death. I shifted back to my feet and leaned toward the Sandman.

"We should stab her again," I suggested.

A few times, perhaps, the Weaver added.

"Fools." The blood garbled Mara's voice. "I was made from the world, and it will take the world to end me."

No. No, no, no. This wasn't right. This was supposed to *work*.

"Quickly," the Sandman said, grabbing Mara's wrist. "We'll take her to the Day World while she's weak. She won't be able to heal there."

Yes. It was better than nothing. I lunged at the idea, at Mara—but my hand met ice. The Sandman fell forward at the sudden disappearance of Mara's body. Her laugh echoed behind us, chilling me more than the ice caves ever could.

"Hurry!" I shouted. Mara was wounded—she had to be easier to catch while weakened. "We can still—"

The tunnel collapsed with a mighty roar right over the yeti's corpse. The ice fell in sheets. Jagged shards splintered up from the ground and icicles dangled precariously overhead.

Like hell, I growled to myself. Mara wasn't going to trap us in here and run off. I placed my uninjured hand on the nearest wall and snatched the knotted thread. All it would take was the squeeze of my fist and the entire landscape would die.

I wouldn't.

Why not? I snapped back.

It's ice, Nora. When it dies, it will either, A: melt. There's miles of it, so getting washed away is actually counterproductive. Or, B: it will collapse on your pretty little head.

"Crap," I groaned.

The Sandman held the knife out in front of him as if he'd never seen it before.

I stormed back to where the red-eyed fish stared out at us and placed my palm over the thin veneer of ice that separated us. It was a quick fix, turning its body temperature up until the ice melted around it. It twitched inside its own personal bubble of water. "Follow Mara," I told it, then turned back to the Sandman. "Please tell me we have another backup plan."

His violet eyes churned as he looked helplessly at me. "I do."

Chapter Twenty-Six

The Sandman's voice went through me like an electric shock. I knew…I *knew* whatever he said next wouldn't be good. "Nevermind," I said and held up my hands to silence him. "I'll come up with something. Just give me a minute."

"Nora." This time his voice didn't tremble. "It's not enough. Us—you and me—we aren't enough like this."

We had to be enough. If we weren't, who was? There was a way to stop Mara—there was always a way. No problem was unsolvable. "We'll make it work," I said, pacing. "We'll…find where she snuck out of the Ever Safe, shove her back inside, and seal it off."

"It's already sealed," the Sandman said quietly. "Why do you think she hasn't used it again?"

Okay. I scowled and twisted my hands together. "Then we'll chop her up and put the pieces in different corners of the Night World."

The Sandman eased up to my side and placed one hand over my swollen knuckles. "The Weaver and I were never fully good or bad, dream or nightmare, before we banished Mare. We weren't balanced by one another, but together we had equal parts of both realms. He and I…we needed each other. Cleaving our worlds in two took something from us that we shouldn't have gambled with."

"Right, right. The balance righted itself," I said quickly, the words all blending together. This wasn't the time for a history lesson. So what if they used to be sixty-forty good and evil or whatever; I'd come to learn it was all relative. Good people did bad things all the time. Both worlds had their monsters. "You were right. We should try to get her back to the Day World. It's worth a try, though my vote is still for dismemberment."

"Nora."

"Of course, if we go with your plan, we'd probably have to stay for a while to make sure she wasn't a threat. She does look stronger now," I mused. "We'll need to get the key back from Katie."

My muscles shivered, the thought of extended Day Walking enough to send me running for the hills. We wouldn't have to stay as long this time though, and we could always take shifts. A few days here, a few days there. It wouldn't be like before—it couldn't. And when Mara was weak enough, we could leave her to rot.

"*Nora.*"

I froze at the Sandman's harsh tone. *Definitely, definitely wasn't going to like this.*

He gently lifted my chin, forcing me to look at him, and I instantly wished with everything inside me that I hadn't. A full year hadn't passed since I saw his face for the first time. This was an expression I'd yet to encounter. One I never wanted to again. There were elements I recognized—determination, resignation, adoration. Sorrow, even. What it lacked, I realized with a bolt of terror, was hope.

Oh no. The Weaver's words breezed through me, echoing my own thoughts.

"What?" I squeaked.

"I love you," he said, truth dripping from every syllable.

He did, yes, but that wasn't what he was saying. Not really. I backed out of his grip. "*What?*" I repeated.

"Nora, listen to me." He spoke slowly and moved even slower, his palms cupping my face. The knife was still in his right hand and now pressed gently against my cheek. "Mare said *world.* The *world* created her."

Whatever that meant.

It means, the Weaver paused, seemingly at a loss for words. *He better not be taking this where I think he is…*

"Okay." I struggled to inhale. "I'm not following."

"The world," he said again, his gaze piercing me.

I placed my hands over his. "Sandman, you're scaring me."

"You're going to be fine. Everyone's going to be fine," he said, broken. His eyes glazed over with a thin layer of unshed tears, and suddenly, I was broken too.

"Explain before I completely lose it," I begged.

The world, the Weaver supplied, *created the Ancients. They were made from the violence of the world coming together, whereas the Sandman and I were made from magic afterwards.*

"Spell it out for me!" I shouted to them.

The Sandman flinched. "If we can restore balance in the Night World, it should balance *both* worlds."

A single, completely balanced being could destroy her, the Weaver agreed bitterly.

"How *exactly* does that happen?" I asked warily.

"The Weaver's magic taints my beach, and my magic inside a nightmare will kill it. Can something like that truly work together?" His throat bobbed as he swallowed hard. "It's not cohesive enough."

My body went cold. If our magic couldn't work together, taking her to the Day World was our only option. Why did it feel like that wasn't his pending suggestion? "And?" I urged. "Do you want to use the knife to rip open the barrier between Day and Night again? Is it even possible?"

"If it were, that information died along with the Dream Keeper I used to hold it." The Sandman's hands fell from my face, and he pulled the knife from its sheath, the blade still coated black with Mara's blood. "You killed the Weaver with this."

Don't you dare say another word! the Weaver raged.

"Stop," I said, breathless, the Weaver's panic sparking my own.

"You have his power in you," he said, ignoring me.

"I have *him* in me," I corrected. "And that's only because he put himself there. It's not an automatic transfer."

He ran a hand through his hair. "If you had both dark and light powers—"

"No," I said before he could finish. "Did you hear me? That's not how it works."

"I could put myself there too," he insisted.

I leapt away from him and the knife. If my pulse was any faster, my heart would explode. Everything around me faded, my focus sharpening on the man before me. "I'm not killing you. Are you crazy?"

He took a step toward me and I took another back. "I wouldn't be dead," he said patiently.

I had *major* opinions on that, but it didn't matter because I wasn't going to do it. Even if it worked, even if the Sandman claimed another pocket inside my head and we successfully killed Mara, there was absolutely no chance I would be able to drive a knife into his chest. Stabbing the Weaver had been traumatic enough. If I killed the person I loved most, what did that make me?

"I don't need a third voice in my head—especially when you two would be fighting with each other twenty-four-seven. Besides, what's to say the magic would combine inside me? Maybe they would eat at the other until all three of us were dead. *Really* dead."

"They wouldn't." The Sandman held up the knife. Black and gold, blue and silver. A patchwork of both magics, held together with the blood of two Night Lords. "It worked before."

"Yes. *Before you changed things.*" I took a deep breath to keep myself from falling apart. Even if there was a guarantee that killing him wouldn't change things again, make them worse, it wasn't an option. "It's not going to happen, Sandman."

He darted forward and crushed me to him before I could flee. "You had me long before any of this happened, and you'll have me long after it ends."

"Not if you're dead, I won't." My throat constricted, my words coming out choked.

"If the worlds end, it won't matter. We'll be gone. All of us. Me, you, Kail. Katie…" He pulled away and his star-flecked eyes bored into me. "Do it, Nora. I've lived a long time, and I've made an eternity's worth of mistakes. Let me fix them. Later we can work on getting the Weaver and me into separate bodies."

Tears burned the backs of my eyes. "You're clearly having a moment—"

"We'll put him in a hamster or something, of course," he said, the joke not quite reaching its mark.

A hamster? the Weaver growled. *Do not do this, Nora. There's a strong chance all of us will die.*

He didn't need to convince me. Not even a little. "I love you. That's why I'm saying no. We'll find another way."

The Sandman backed out of our embrace, taking my hands, and wrapped them around the knife's handle. The Weaver exploded into a wordless shriek that mirrored my own feelings. Just touching the knife made my entire body go numb. I tried to yank myself from his grip, but he was stronger. It felt as if my brain was about to short circuit. My back hit the side of an icy tunnel, and I felt the frigid temperature with every molecule.

"Stop," I begged.

Gently, the Sandman aimed the tip of the knife between his ribs, resting it against the skin underneath. "Here."

"No!" I flexed my fingers to drop the knife, but he squeezed harder.

"It's okay," he promised.

Enough, the Weaver roared and, in the blink of an eye, rammed himself forward, taking control of my body.

The Sandman's eyes widened. Warm liquid flowed over my hand, and I screamed. Only the sound didn't come out because the Weaver held fast.

"Forgive me, old friend," he rasped in that voice that was only partially mine. "This wasn't your wrong to set right."

There was a groan then. From me. *Me.*

The world spun ever-so-slowly. As I fell to my knees, I noticed the distinct lack of a weapon protruding from the Sandman's chest. Because it was in mine.

Hold onto the darkness, Nora, the Weaver instructed. *Hold it tight.*

"What?" I breathed to the Weaver and slumped to the side.

The Sandman caught me. His lips were moving. His beautiful lips. I lifted my hand to touch them—or at least, I tried. Darkness stole them away. It stole everything. My vision. Sound. Feeling. It didn't even hurt, being stabbed in the heart.

Chapter Twenty-Seven

Keeper, called a familiar voice. *Nora.*

The blackest black surrounded me, but I knew I wasn't alone. A golden orb emerged out of nowhere, surrounded by a mass of dark spirals. The faint glow shone through strands of swirling darkness and peeked out from tiny holes. I drifted toward it as it called my name again. The swirls reached toward me. Beckoned. I stretched out a hand. The threads on my arm slid down, the ends fraying out as if eager.

Hold tight, the voice said again. How many times had it repeated those words now? A thousand? How long had I been like…this? Here? Where was I?

The spirals brushed over my fingertips, and I gasped. Pure, unfiltered power burst through my body. The spirals pulled me in. Cradled me until I was cocooned in their golden light. I gripped the coils as hard as I could.

Now, listen.

Listen? I was listening. Hanging onto every word. Grasping onto them for life itself.

"Nora!" cried another voice. It was the sound of breaking. Of a window shattering. A million little pieces of pebbled glass cascading over cement. But it was also the sound of warmth, of dreams and promises. Memories. Reality filtered in. The knife…it was imbedded in my chest. A dull, throbbing pain pounded around it. Faintly. So faintly. Fading, fading, fading.

Do not let go, the Weaver urged.

You killed me. It wasn't an accusation, merely a statement. I didn't have it in me to feel angry or betrayed. *You saved him.*

I saved us all, the Weaver said, terse. *Unless you let go.*

A part of me, distant and tired, wanted to loosen my grip. To let go and drift away. *Why save everyone? What do you get out of it?*

I get to live, he stated as if it were obvious. *It was your hand that held the knife. Where could my power escape to if we're in a closed loop? I can't let you die because I can't get out of your body. So, if you don't listen to me, if you don't hang on, you die. I die. He dies.*

If I killed myself, there would be no more Weaver. Without the Weaver, there would be no more balance. He acted out of self-preservation, but that wasn't the only reason. I felt him in this space, whatever it was. Where I would've expected him to feel like a bed of nails, the Weaver's essence wrapped around me like a warm blanket. A bit of a coarse blanket, perhaps, and made of the itchiest wool, but if I was going to die, I would take it over the alternative.

The balance always rights itself, the Weaver said, slightly smug. *Follow the Sandman's voice. Wake us up and let's find out what our new existence looks like.*

New existence. Did I want to see what that looked like? Changing the first time was brutal enough. What if it was worse this time? What if I lost more of myself until nothing was left? The numbness couldn't extend much more if I wanted to keep my humanity, but perhaps living without it was better than not living at all. I stared into the swirling darkness. I had to make a choice: live as the Weaver or die as Nora.

But…maybe I wouldn't have to choose. A new existence had potential.

"Nora, please," the Sandman called.

The sound was far away. Reaching it felt impossible, but I had to try. I forced myself to move, pushing my way through time and space, dragging the bundle of light behind me like a ball and chain.

"Not again," he whispered repeatedly. "Open your eyes, Nora."

Regret filled me. I stabbed the Weaver, and now the Weaver had stabbed me in return. Both times, the Sandman was there, thinking me either dead or dying. I was glad I didn't experience this part the first time. It had been like a dreamless sleep then—one moment I was awake, the next I was waking.

Now it was more like clawing my way out of a coffin buried six-feet underground. Freedom was there above me, and I scratched my way toward it with lungs ready to burst.

Hold tight, the Weaver reminded me when my grip loosened.

So I did. I held so tight that it hurt.

Blue caves glistened overhead. I gasped for breath and rolled onto my hands and knees. Ice bit into my palms as I coughed and coughed, drawing ragged breaths between each painful heave.

Relax, the Weaver droned. *We're alive. Try to remember that requires breathing.*

Hot tears flowed down my cheeks. They dripped to the ground and melted small divots into the ice. My fingers curled over the smooth ground. Without warning, blood spurted from my mouth, over and over until I thought I would die all over again, the coughing picking up it where it had left off. The Sandman rubbed my back in slow circles until it slowed to a stop. I focused on his touch. Let it pull me back.

I wiped my mouth on the back of my hand and fought the urge to collapse. "I'm okay," I lied. My chest felt exactly like one would expect after being stabbed. "Help me sit?"

The Sandman eased me back off my shaky arms to sit against the tunnel wall. Tear tracks stained his face, and his shoulders were slumped. In pain, in relief. "Why did you do that?" he croaked.

"It wasn't me. It was—" I gasped. Threads of gold broke through his violet irises, weaving neatly between the silver specks, and bled into the whites of his eyes. Or, what used to be the whites, but were now black as pitch.

"Nora?"

I flew to my feet, woozy and nauseous, and patted at my chest. The hole remained in my shirt, but the knife itself was gone, as was the pain…and the wound. "Where is it? The knife, where is it?"

I pulled the magic out to save us. It's gone.

"We need it," I rasped. "To kill Mara, we need it."

The Sandman gave me a gentle *shh* and ran his fingers through my hair. "It didn't kill her, remember? It won't help us."

My mind was blank except for pain and shock. Mostly shock. Without the knife, without us being a single, completely balanced being, what were we supposed to do?

"What do I look like?" the Sandman asked quietly.

"Like... you?"

He shook his head and inched closer to me, inches from my face. "What do I look like? Your eyes. They're gold from corner to corner, except for the very center. It's dark blue with..." His lips parted with an awed gasp. "With silver flecks."

We are remade, the Weaver said in wonder.

I met his gaze, a smile creeping over my face. *It worked.* "Yours too. Are different, I mean."

The Sandman crushed me in his arms. "I love you. I love you, I love you, I love you," he repeated in a single breath.

"I'm sorry," I said, returning the embrace with every ounce of strength I had left. "The Weaver—"

"I know." He tightened his grip and placed a kiss on my shoulder. "I'm going to kill him a thousand times for this."

Tell him I said good luck.

I'm not telling him that, I replied.

His breathing was uneven against my neck. "I will never forget what he did."

Tough crowd, the Weaver said with a sigh. *At least ask him which part.*

"He wants to know which part," I relayed.

The Sandman pulled back and cracked a smile—a thing I hadn't seen in what felt like forever. "Weaver," he paused as if unsure he could speak to me to reach him. "I'm not sure if I'll be able to forgive all that you've done. You've acted rashly and put people in danger for as long as I can remember, but…it's always gone as you planned."

Except that once, he grumbled.

"What you did was reckless," the Sandman continued. Then he stopped, though I could tell there was more he wanted to say by the way he paused.

You're welcome.

"We're alive," I said slowly.

"We're new," he corrected. "And old."

I shrugged one shoulder. "New or old, we're *both* alive."

"Yes." The Sandman rubbed his chin thoughtfully. "His heinous plan worked."

He'll be grateful one day when he recovers from seeing you dead. Again.

Not sure he'll ever get over that, I said tersely. If our roles were reversed, I never would.

"Do you feel it?" he asked, almost reverently. "My power alongside yours?"

I tilted my head and looked inward. There was the darkness I became so accustomed to, but above it, propped up like a new bud on a dying stem, was a cloud of silver. "I feel it," I said quietly. "It's small, but I feel it."

You are aware Mara's likely banging away at the safe by now, yes?

"Crap." I leapt to my feet. "Mara."

The Sandman stood, his movements achingly slow. He probably *did* ache—the stabbing wound wasn't my only source of pain. The Dream magic inside me was heavy, as I'm sure the Nightmare magic was to him. He flexed his hands carefully as if testing their new strength, or, perhaps, fearing the sand wouldn't respond to him anymore. I waited silently next to him as the worry drained ever-so-slowly from his expression. Then with a flick of his wrist, the blocked passage shattered outward. "After you."

I looked down the icy tunnel and shivered, though not from the cold. Mara was so close, and there wasn't time to waste exploring empty passages. I placed a hand on the wall and felt for the fish's thread. "That way," I said, pointing to the tunnel that tilted down at the fork in front of us.

☾

We followed the fish down, up, and down again until we were only a few steps away. It swam in a horseshoe around the opening to another tunnel. Mara had to be down there, if not because of the fish leading us this way, then because of the repetitive thuds coming from inside. I shooed the fish away, so it wouldn't inadvertently rat us out. It took off like a rocket, the water pocket refreezing.

"What do you think she's doing in there?" I whispered.

The Sandman tapped the flat side of an exposed sand-made blade against his palm. "I don't know."

"You're going to cut yourself," I said, placing a hand on his forearm to still his nervous movements.

"If it doesn't work this time…" He winced.

"Don't make me be the optimistic one."

There wasn't anything else we could do except try. Most of me still belonged to the Nightmare Realm which made me feel less balanced instead of more, but maybe Mara needed that chaos to kill her. Not two halves of a whole, but jagged pieces to a puzzle.

I really didn't want to have magic twist me up and spit me out a third time, so if this didn't work, it was the Day World or bust. Taking the Sandman's hand, I led the way without another word. If he came out with another doubtful sentence, I'd probably crumble anyway.

We followed the tunnel where it veered off, filled with skeletal remains. A mammoth's skull took up the entire space and more, the ice partially swallowing the bone. The tusks were twice as long as the Sandman was tall, two jutting up into the ceiling and another two down into the ground. There were three sets of eye sockets on each side—the largest near the top, another slightly smaller toward the front, and an even smaller one in between. Behind the skull, the ribcage acted as support for the tunnel.

The Sandman slipped through a gap between the top and bottom jaw, and I eased through behind him. A large blue scorpion shifted near the top of the skull, tail clicking. I glared at it, daring it to make a move, and tugged the Sandman away. We proceeded slowly beneath the spinal cord. We came to the end of the ribcage to find a long tail with a spiked harness for drilling tunnels, perhaps, or battle, chained to the tip.

On it was Baku.

He lifted his lips in a silent growl and slunk down from his perch with more grace than I would have thought possible. The chimera lowered into a crawl-like stance, prowling toward us. *Crap.* I glanced at the Sandman. Baku dead would be fine with me, but it was still his call. His face gave nothing away other than the pain of seeing his friend prepared to attack.

"He's going to give us away," I whispered.

"I know."

I clenched my jaw. "Do something."

"I can't..." he admitted reluctantly.

But I could. I was so close to the wall that all I had to do was tilt my hand to make contact. It was harder finding the cave's thread with only the tip of my pinky finger, but not impossible. I didn't dare move more than that and risk Baku noticing. My hands trembled as the nightmare eater got closer and closer. If I had another few seconds, I could easily—

Excuse me, the Weaver said, slipping forward and waiting. I wrinkled my nose and let him do the work. It was over in a second. The ice beneath Baku melted, the water sucking him under, the ice immediately reforming around him. I stared in horror at the frozen form a few feet away. Looking at the Sandman was too hard.

"Come on," I whispered.

We didn't have far to go because Mara stood in the shadows, watching. Something long and curved spun in her hands. At her back a hole was gouged into the ice. I didn't know what she hoped to accomplish by unearthing the doors when she had no key, but it didn't make a difference.

She ran at us, her scream vibrating against my eardrums. A glint of metal was the only warning of her weapon swiping out. It sliced just above my kneecap, and I fell with a strangled scream of my own. The Sandman wasted no time hurling sand-made weapons at her. He parried her thrusts with a pipe and used it to knock her feet out from under her. She leapt up with ease. I stopped watching then and scanned our surroundings.

Think, Nora, think, I told myself. We had to get the advantage, even if it was only for a moment. The Sandman slammed back into one of the skeleton's ribs with a resounding crack, and an idea formed.

Do it. Do something, the Weaver urged.

I took a thread from my wrist and produced a four-foot, 3D diamond puzzle made of the same stone. It held its shape until I climbed to my feet and hobbled two steps, then it collapsed into a heap that no Dreamer would ever be able to piece back together.

That's what you chose? the Weaver yelled. *Why not the heavy-weight boxer or the—*

"Shut up," I growled and picked up one of the L-shaped pieces.

Mara swooped in front of me, and I swung at her head. The puzzle piece connected, snapping her neck sideways. The Sandman followed as she slid down the tunnel toward the spiked ball. I took the moment to hook the puzzle piece around one of the exposed ribs and pulled. I could sense the bone giving—getting ready to snap, but it just needed a little more strength. Swallowing a scream, I lifted my injured leg up, leveraged my foot on the icy wall, and shoved my whole body back. The bone splintered. Sweat beaded on my forehead as I readjusted myself and did it again.

This time the bone snapped in two, splinters flying. I landed hard and stopped sliding backward when my head cracked against the opposite wall. There was no time to clear the ringing from my ears. I grasped another thread. This time a large, ivory-toned creature with four arms covered in suction cups emerged, somewhere between a starfish and an octopus. It barreled into the fight, knocking the Sandman back. He landed in front of me, a deep cut from ear to collar bone bleeding freely.

"We have to get her on the bone," I urged and climbed to my feet. "She won't be able to get free without ripping herself apart."

The new nightmare fell backward with Mara wrapped against its chest. The suction cups pulsed, and dark veins popped up along its rubbery arms. The Sandman cursed and lifted his knife.

"Wait!" I cried.

But it was too late. He swung down at the same time Mara flipped the nightmare over, shielding herself from the blade. The nightmare shuddered and, one-by-one, the suction cups turned black and still. I grunted wordlessly. My plan was *going to work*. The Sandman leapt onto the nightmare's back, pressing them both into the ice. Mara wriggled and squirmed, nearly toppling him.

"Screw this." I grabbed a long piece of the diamond puzzle from the floor. The sharp edge ripped open my palm, but I barely felt the sting. There was only the briefest of moments where I paused to consider my plan. Too brief for the Weaver to tell me not to do it. For *me* to talk myself out of it. I drove the puzzle piece through the Sandman's shoulder, bones grinding against gemstone. It slid effortlessly into the boneless nightmare beneath, and then into Mara like a pick into stone. It wasn't clear who screamed first. Me or one of them.

"I'm so sorry." I took the knife from the floor where the Sandman had dropped it before it turned into a pile of sand. "So, so, so sorry."

Hurry, the Weaver urged. *It won't hold her for long.*

The pile of impaled bodies was already shifting as Mara scrambled to escape. My heart was a hummingbird ready to flit away, taking me with it. My entire body shook as I ignored the Sandman's face, pinched in pain, and the nightmare's ever-blackening form. My body flowed through the motions as if it were nothing but a dream. A bad, *bad* dream.

The knife slammed into the side of Mara's head with a dull, wet *thunk*.

I froze, hand still wrapped around the handle, waiting. *Waiting*. Waiting.

For her to move.

For her to speak.

For something, anything to happen.

It felt like days but couldn't have been more than twenty seconds.

The Sandman lifted himself up, tearing the diamond shard the rest of the way through his body. He grunted and clutched at the wound. Blood flowed down onto the decaying nightmare. I fixated on that. On his hand, slick with thick red blood. It leaked between his fingers. Ran down his forearm to his elbow.

"I'm sorry," I croaked, the words not even close to enough.

"Don't be sorry," he rasped. "I'll heal."

I nodded. *Right.* Heal. He would heal. But he was still in a lot of pain. It was a miracle he wasn't swept back to the beach, but nothing vital was hit. He could still fight if he absolutely needed to.

How about a little less gloom and doom, and a little more 'yay, mission accomplished'?

"Is it?" I asked aloud.

"Is what?" The Sandman rolled the nightmare off Mara's body with his good arm. "Nora?"

"Is it mission accomplished?" I blinked a dozen times until my vision cleared. "She's dead, right?"

He offered me a smile, as pained as it was. "Yes. She's dead."

She didn't look dead. Not like other things looked dead, and I would know. Mara looked more like a photograph—a moment frozen in time. Her palms still pressed to the ground and one leg bent upward, foot planted as if she were about to shove herself up and make a run for it. If it weren't for the knife still sticking out of her skull…

"You're sure?" I squeaked.

How much more dead do you want her to be? the Weaver asked, annoyed. *You used the blood of two lords. It's the closest you'll get to how the world used to be.*

The Sandman ran a hand from my cheek down to my shoulder, and gave it a reassuring squeeze. "I promise."

I let out a breath and leaned back onto my heels. My leg screamed all over again with the motion, and I hissed. "I'm fine," I said when I saw the Sandman open his mouth to ask. The blood of two lords. I wiped the sticky blood from the backs of my hands onto my pants. Was that what did it? Our blood? Mine on the knife, his on the diamond shard? Did it matter? It took less than a heartbeat to answer my own question. *No.* It didn't. "What should we do with the body?" I asked.

"I don't think it matters." The Sandman ripped the blade from Mara's head, globs of brain matter showering the area, and slipped the filthy knife back into its sheath. I cringed. Did he have to keep it?

"I don't feel comfortable leaving it here." I studied the chiseled part of the ice cave and did a quick patch job. Whatever Mara was after was going to stay hidden.

"We could burn it."

I nodded. "But not in here."

The Sandman rolled Mara onto her side. "We could…" He paused, blushing.

"What?" I pried open my hand to assess the cut and nearly blacked out when the cold air hit the wound. It was deep enough to see bone.

"Nevermind," he faltered. "It's a bad idea."

Oh? the Weaver said curiously.

I clenched my fist shut again—it felt marginally better that way—and pressed it against my chest. "What's a bad idea?"

"I…" He took a deep breath, unable to meet my eyes. "I don't want to leave him like that."

"Wh—" *Oh,* was right. I looked toward the chimera frozen a few yards away. "Baku."

"It's a bad idea," he said again.

It was. It was a horrible idea. He was a spy. An enemy. Still, he had been a friend once which deserved some level of respect. Just as the Sandman didn't punish the Weaver more harshly than he could have, he couldn't punish Baku to an eternity in frozen terror. I understood. I didn't agree, but I understood.

"Okay." The word was sour. "I'll let him out, but he has to stay caged."

Not here, the Weaver added. *If you're going to be stupid about this, at least make sure he's far away from this place.*

I couldn't argue with that. With my jaw clenched so hard my teeth ached, I found the thread yet again and cut the ice around the chimera, leaving him completely frozen, but easily transportable with the right equipment.

"Consider it my *sorry for stabbing you* gift," I said with a half-smile. "I'll go get Kail to help with the heavy lifting."

"I've got him," the Sandman said quietly.

I gave a terse laugh and stood. "And miss out on the chance for Kail to do more work? I would never."

"Thank you," he said so quietly I barely heard.

He didn't have to thank me. It wasn't any less than he would do for me. I kissed him on top of the head, sparing a long moment to breathe him in. The lilac scent I knew so well blended with the harsh, cold scent of ice and the metallic tang of blood, but underneath was something else. Something new, something old. Something…*us.* I kissed his hair again. "Wait here," I said softly, and left.

When I finally limped my way to where Kail waited with the nightmare army, it was everything I could do not to collapse. He would've caught me, I was sure, as long as I waited until he was close enough to manage it. That wasn't the problem. The problem was my image. I still really, *really* didn't want another revolt on my hands.

Smart, the Weaver said.

Please stop talking, I snapped, too exhausted to deal with him. Or anyone, really.

"Nora!" Kail shoved his way out of the formation and gripped my arms painfully tight. "Are you okay? What happened? Where's the Sandman? Is Mara—"

"Dead." I patted his chest with the edge of my fist. *We did it,* I wanted to shout. Now that I was out of the caves, the gravity of that sunk in, but as much as I'd come to love Kail, I wanted to celebrate with the Sandman first. "Send three of the strongest nightmares in. There are a couple of…things to carry out, and then I need you to help the Sandman with something. I sort of stabbed him so…"

Kail's eyes blew wide. "Repeat that."

"I stabbed him." I scanned the nightmares and leaned closer to whisper in his ear. "Before you go, bring me the Hours."

He pulled away and tilted his head. "Why?"

They were traitors. Though they obeyed me this once, it didn't mean they always would. I was finished looking over my shoulder. There was one chance for loyalty, and they blew it before I even sat at the loom.

Yes. I would avoid a revolt.

Today.

Tomorrow.

Always.

The Hours would be my latest example.

"*Why?*" I met his gaze. "I'm not as forgiving as the Dream Lord."

Understanding filled Kail's expression and he bowed, the gesture his brother's influence. "Of course, Lady."

Long, tattered ribbons in all shades of yellow and blue hung from overhead coils. Some brushed against the dirt while others floated obnoxiously in my face. I wasn't sure what fear the landscape was supposed to instill in Dreamers, but it was far from the ice caves and I was tired down to my very core. Dragging a frozen solid Baku across the Nightmare Realm—assisted by the new Kail or not—wasn't easy when my shoulder still oozed blood. A few inches over and the shard would've hit my heart, sending me straight back to the beach.

"This works for now," I said and leaned against one of the coil supports.

Kail lifted the rope of a sand-made sled and bent over, gasping. "He's heavier than he looks."

"It's his diet," I said with a small smile.

Kail glared at me, his new appearance jarring. It was the eyes—black orbs didn't exactly inspire confidence in someone's benevolence. I wish Nora had waited until after we took care of Mare to put him back together with Halven so she wouldn't be completely alone right now. I sighed. It didn't matter. She sent Kail with me specifically, claiming she had something to take care of. I'd ask what later.

"Nora should've stabbed you a couple more times when she had the chance," Kail griped.

I pinched my lips. *She should've stabbed me* first. But then I would be gone, and Nora would be what? Playing host to two warring Night Lords? The Weaver made the right decision, even if it was irresponsible. I'd make him pay for it one day, regardless. When he was out of Nora's head and locked away somewhere. When we no longer had to worry about fighting for our survival. But that was the distant future. There were too many uncertainties, mainly what would happen to Nora without the Weaver, but one day…

One day, we *would* have to fight to survive again. The threat could come from nowhere or it could bloom closer to home, but it would come. Eventually. By then, Nora would undoubtedly be able to fight without help. She'd come so far in such a short amount of time that I could only imagine the powerhouse she would be in a few hundred years.

"You should probably kill him," Kail said, interrupting my musing, and motioned to Baku.

"Probably," I agreed. Unlike with the Weaver, I would reinforce his binding and often, but his prison wasn't what worried me. There was no caging an idea. Baku's ideas, his desire to help Mare open the Ever Safe, were a danger to everyone. I studied my former companion through the thick layer of ice. "He betrayed me."

"Everyone seems to betray the ones they love at some point," Kail said sincerely.

"Yes." I winced. "We didn't all try to release ancient monsters and destroy the world though."

Kail shrugged.

"What about you?" I asked quietly. "Who have you betrayed?"

"Me?" He laughed mirthlessly. "I think the question should be who *haven't* I betrayed. A nightmare of the unknown wouldn't live up to his name otherwise."

I narrowed my eyes at his admission. "Then how many have you loved?"

The amusement drained from Kail's face, and he fiddled with a worn yellow ribbon. "Ah, you have me there, Dream Lord. I've never betrayed a loved one."

"Right, because you've never loved anyone but yourself." It sounded cruel, perhaps, but Kail had always been nothing if not self-centered.

"That's not true. Or…" One side of his mouth quirked into a rueful grin. "I guess it is seeing as Halven was my other half."

I rolled my eyes and backtracked the way we came. My shoulder itched where it slowly mended and screamed where it hadn't yet started. A day or two from now, when it was nothing but a pink mark, I was going to think more on the fact that Nora ran me through without a second thought. It was smart—unexpected from Mare's point-of-view—but…she didn't even flinch until after the job was done.

"I know what you're thinking," Kail called, running after me. "That I can't love."

"Am I so transparent?" I asked.

Outside the ribbons, I turned to Baku and began the painstaking process of creating a prison large enough, *strong* enough, to hold him. It would have to allow other nightmares to wander in; I couldn't starve him. Though I knew nothing I did would make him forget he was locked up, I hoped there was something salvageable between us. At the very least, maybe we would stop hating each other one day.

"I can, you know," Kail continued as I worked.

I lifted a brow at him. Was he still fixated on this? This was what I got for trying to confide in a nightmare. "You're taking this rather seriously when I only asked for personal reasons."

He groaned and folded his arms across his chest. "This is harder than I thought it would be. Halven was the one that knew how to talk to people while I was the one left with the ability to be articulate. He learned, sort of, but…I guess I'm out of practice."

"Kail." I paused with a handful of sand resting in my hand and shifted uncomfortably. "This new attitude of yours is putting me on edge. Say what you want to say so I can focus on my work."

His cheeks flushed. "I won't betray Nora. That's where you were going with your questions, right?"

"No." I dragged out the syllable. It was entirely about my situation with Baku. "I'm not worried about that because if you do, I'll personally hunt you down, and you know that."

Kail gave me a half-hearted salute.

I shook my head and put the finishing touches on Baku's cell. The walls glowed a faint blue with flecks of gold where the light hit. I liberally threw another layer of magic at it to be safe, then turned to Kail. "You probably don't want to be here for the next part."

He wasted no time leaving me there alone. Maybe it was the awkwardness that sent him sprinting toward the palace, or that he was as worried about Nora's solo plan as I was. It wasn't that she was incapable—she had proved otherwise over and over—but her choices weren't always the wisest. Killing the Weaver, taking Mare's advice on traveling back to the Night World…the consequences should've deterred her from future rash decisions, but with the Weaver in her head doing things like making Nora stab herself in the heart…I pressed my eyes shut and shook the thought from my mind. It was over and done, but Baku wasn't.

As I added the final layer of sand to the underground slab, I allowed myself a final moment to rein in my emotions. Then it was time. I dumped the remaining sand from my satchel and ushered it through. It coated Baku's body, eroding the ice from head to toe. It took longer than I anticipated, and I refused to look as he made a variety of grunts and groans. Being half frozen had to be uncomfortable, but it would pass. Unlike the pain in my chest. Baku might as well have run me through like Nora had, one tusk at a time.

I waited patiently when it was over for Baku to stop throwing himself against the walls. He dug pits in the soft dirt and climbed the coils to scratch at the ceiling until he swayed with exhaustion. Finally, when he fell to the ground with a sorrowful huff, I approached and removed the pouch from around my neck to read his dreams. I had to know why he did it. The sand fell from between my fingers and spun into an empty plateau, then, when the sand was almost gone, it twisted up in the center. A tiny Baku sat at the center. Alone.

"You were lonely," I said in a hoarse whisper. "Did you want to open the door because you wanted to see others like you?"

Baku flopped his ears over his face.

"I'm sorry I never realized how you felt," I choked. *I'm sorry that I wasn't enough of a friend for you.* We were never really friends like the Weaver and I once were. Baku and I spent time together because we were both completely alone, and while that turned into something like affection, it wasn't what either of us needed.

When Nora started coming to the beach, I should've put two and two together. She was more like me than Baku was and with every passing night, we grew closer. I asked Baku not to come to the beach when she was expected without considering his feelings. He thought I traded him in for a different type of friendship, and I supposed I had. If I included him from the beginning, maybe we wouldn't be in our current situation. Or, maybe, it still wouldn't have filled his void.

"I'm sorry," I said again, a mere whisper.

I walked away. One heavy, heartbreaking step at a time.

Chapter Twenty-Nine

Three months later

The Hours' masks were stark against the black marble of the Keep. Kail leaned over the edge of the roof, holding the final one—number six—in place. The masks circled the open half of the building starting with one, ending with twelve, staring out in almost every direction, yet visible no matter where one looked.

"A little to the left," I yelled from my place in the courtyard. He slid the numbered mask over an inch. "There. That's perfect."

His string of curses blurred together as he struggled to attach one of the heavy-duty command strips Katie brought from the

Day World. She loved the idea of hanging the masks as a warning, though I couldn't say the same for anyone else.

"Make sure the hook is straight," I shouted.

"So you've told me," he called back. "At least a hundred times."

I chuckled. He was a different nightmare lately. More helpful, less snarky. *More* meaning he asked fewer questions when I told him to do something like hang the Hours' masks. *Less* meaning I got a sincere *good morning* out of him now before he switched off the polite, Halven-side of his personality.

You would be bored if he were polite, the Weaver said.

It was true enough. It was one of the only things that still felt normal. The Dream magic left me feeling diluted, weaker, and there was a constant vibrating itch that seemed to travel through my bones. But that same sense of dilution made me stronger in another way. The blackness swirling inside my head was more of a dark grey now. My thoughts were clearer, though still void of guilt over killing random nightmares.

The Hours deserved what they got, just like the nightmares that killed my friends. Mara most of all. If the nightmares that killed Natalie and Emery deserved the horrible deaths I gave them, what did that mean the Weaver deserved? He was the one that had given the orders. I didn't regret killing those creatures, nor would I regret torturing the Weaver should we ever discover a way to extract him.

I closed my eyes and counted to ten. Calm…I had to be calm. If things became too much, if I let the anger overwhelm me, that little box of power the Weaver stashed away threatened to crack open.

I deserve a lot of things, the Weaver breezed. *But until you figure things out, we've decided to play nice, remember?*

I remembered. The decisions at uncomfortably, but he was right. We were forced to deal with each other for now, and that could be as hard or as easy as we wanted to make it. So, despite the fact that he murdered me, we would be…on friendly terms.

I didn't do anything to you that you didn't do to me.

Yes, yes, I snapped. *Truce.*

"What's going on here?" the Sandman asked as he stepped up behind me.

A smile cracked my face, and I leaned back against him. "A little redecorating. I didn't hear you come in."

"I know." He snaked his arms around me in a hug. "Are you ready to go?"

Just like that, my smile fell. Was I ready? Would I ever be? I left home months ago and used Detective Bell to spin the lie about Nevada. My mother and Paul probably hated me now, but I promised I would visit today. Katie stood beside me in this place—she would stand by me there too.

Suddenly, I regretted not seeing my sister since giving her the key to the Ever Safe. The Sandman kept her in the loop, passed messages between us, and delivered gifts, but I'd been so busy culling nightmares that there wasn't time. So, when the invitation came for today, I felt obligated to accept.

"Fine." I let out a harsh breath. "Let's get this over with."

"Good luck," Kail called from the top of Keep. He stood, straightening his clothes, the final mask in place. "You'll need it."

"That one's crooked," I shouted and took the Sandman's hand. "Fix it."

"What? Which one?" he cried in outrage.

I suppressed my giggle just long enough to dart out of the courtyard. "None of them," I whispered conspiratorially. The Sandman's answering laugh warmed me. "Are you sure you want to come?"

"Of course," he said, giving my hand a squeeze. "I'll wait at the end of the street like we discussed in case you need me."

☾

I knocked. On my own door. *No.* It *wasn't* my door anymore. Discomfort twisted my insides. What was I supposed to say? How was I supposed to act? I wasn't the Nora they knew anymore—if you could say they ever truly knew me at all. I was a killer, a ruler, a creator. I was fearsome.

Say the opposite of what you want to say, the Weaver suggested.

"I'm not taking advice from you today," I said under my breath.

The door swung open, and for a moment, my mother stared at me like a deer caught in oncoming headlights. Did Katie not tell them I was coming? Oh, I was going to strangle her the next time she fell asleep. The joke was on her. I'd bring clowns. Lots and lots of clowns.

Right now however, one of us had to do something. Speak. Move. *Breathe.*

"Hi, Mom," I blurted, surprising myself.

She flung herself at me, crushing me in a hug. Tears splashed my neck a moment before her sob broke. I froze and stared over her shoulder at Katie, unsure what to do next. My sister stood in the middle of the living room with a smug grin. *Hug her*, she urged, mimicking the act with both arms.

That's the logical response, the Weaver added.

How would you know? Have you ever hugged anyone?

Ouch, he droned. *No need to be spiteful.*

I'll give you spiteful, you s—

"I missed you so much," my mother cried. "Oh, my baby girl."

My arms raised slowly as if they were no longer part of my body. I didn't know what to do. To think or say. Nothing would be enough to make up for the hurt I caused.

"Mom," Katie said, stepping up and resting one hand on her shoulder. "Let her inside."

"Right." My mother sniffled and pulled back. "Right, of course."

There wasn't any hesitation from my mother after that. She led me into the house without breaking physical contact. Her nails dug into my arm so I hard I thought she would draw blood, but I said nothing. The thud of the door behind us felt like the closing of a tomb.

If you can survive the Nightmare Realm, you can survive a single afternoon here, the Weaver said.

Like he would know. This *was* a nightmare. Mine. I had to look my family in the face and take responsibility for a lot that wasn't true. All while they pretended the things that *were* my reality didn't exist. Not that I was still bitter or anything…

You're the absolute worst at pep talks, Weaver. Seriously. Shut up.

First you want them, now you don't. Make up your mind.

Paul came in from the backyard and nearly dropped the plate of ribs in his hands. "Nora." He quickly slid the food onto the counter and rushed around the counter to hug me. It was less invasive, more welcoming, than the one my mom greeted me with. "It's so good to see you. When did you get here?"

"Right now," I said, numb.

"I made your favorites for dinner." He motioned to the table. "I hope you're hungry."

I nodded, though I wasn't. Not even a little. The nightmares kept me well satisfied.

My mother pulled out a chair and patted the seat. "Come sit next to me. I want to hear all about Nevada." She moved with a frantic energy, touching everything, turning plates just so, adjusting silverware.

"You didn't have to do all this," I said, taking in the extensive spread. "I…I can't stay long."

My mother's eyes widened. "You just got here."

I'm fairly certain you're going to regret coming at all, the Weaver whispered.

I already do, I thought back at him. But, at the same time, it was good being here. I hated to admit that even if it was only to myself. I didn't *want* to think of this place as a comfort zone. It was too…I suppressed a cringe. Too soft. Smelling the familiar smells, *feeling* the memories. Not all of them were good, but all of them were like the sun on a winter day. If I took any of this place back with me, it would get me killed.

"Where are you staying? You could stay here." My mom hesitated before she continued. "Ben, too, if he's with you."

"Mom," Katie warned. "You promised not to grill her."

"I'm not. I was only asking a question," she insisted.

I eased up to the table and into the chair. "I can't stay long," I said again.

"Why?" my mom asked. "Why did you leave?"

Ah, here we go.

"Mom," Katie said at the same time Paul said, "Val."

Her eyes bored into me. "I want to understand. Were you in trouble? Do you need help?"

I looked at Katie, begging her to step in. She took the hint without missing a beat. "You're going to scare her off," she warned. "Let's have a nice dinner, okay?"

Cancel the clowns, the Weaver said, enjoying himself far too much.

"Yes," Paul agreed. "We all have a lot to say, I'm sure, but we should go into this slowly and enjoy what time we have together."

"But—" My mother sucked in a breath and sat beside me. "Okay. Okay."

And just like that, she was piling my plate with ribs, corn on the cob, and macaroni salad, none of which were my favorites. But today they were. For them.

Three hours later, after a forced second helping because I *looked too thin*, and a giant slice of belated birthday cake, I said goodbye. For the tenth time.

"I really have to go," I repeated. "I'll be back, okay? I promise."

"What's your number, at least?" My mother grabbed a pad of paper and searched frantically for a pen. "At least give us that. Or your address."

"I have her number," Katie said quickly and gave me a subtle wink as if to say *I've got you.*

I like her, the Weaver said. *She's got a flare for extensive planning. Would you like to bet that she has a second phone stashed somewhere so she can message them under your name?*

I studied my older sister. My brave sister. My too-stubborn-for-her-own-good sister. And I smiled. *Sorry, I don't take bets I know I'll lose.*

Hugs followed. More hugs. So many hugs. I took a deep breath and endured it because it was the least I could do. Then I left. They watched—I knew they did. Their gazes clung to me like leeches. I shoved my hands into the pocket of my hooded sweater as I stepped onto the sidewalk and breathed in air heavy with the promise of rain. My steps were brisk, nearly a run.

He'll be there, the Weaver promised.

It wasn't a question of whether the Sandman was waiting or not. He promised he would, so he would, but that didn't mean my heart didn't flutter in anticipation of seeing him. Or that my skin didn't tingle in want of his touch. After all that had happened, he was still my addiction. The thing that kept my world spinning.

Hate to interrupt the internal love fest but would now be a good time to ask for a favor? the Weaver asked slowly.

"For you? Every time is a bad time for that," I said under my breath.

He paused. *Permission is overrated. I'd like for you to hold off on getting me out of here.*

I barked out a laugh. "Are you serious? Not a chance."

What if I'm quiet...er? Quieter.

As if that were possible. It still amazed me he was silent for a solid five months. "Why would you *possibly* want that?"

Because.

He fell silent when the Sandman came into view, and a sense of yearning filled the silence. Mine. And his. *Ah,* I thought bitterly. *You want to use me to get in his good graces before he has a chance to knock you into the next millennium.*

No. The Weaver huffed. *Fine, yes, but that's not the only reason. If I'm not...you know,* you... *Then I'm nothing to him.*

My heart skipped a beat as I flung my arms around the Sandman. This was where I belonged. With him. Things were better between us lately—the events in the ice cave seemed to have reset more than our magic. We hadn't talked about our fights, but somehow, we didn't need to.

"Hey." His smile was brighter than any star in the sky. "How was it?"

I winced. "Ugh."

"That good, huh?" he asked with a small laugh.

"Even better." I pressed my cheek against his chest, reveling in the steady *thump, thump, thump* of his heartbeat.

Then, to the Weaver, *You're wrong. You're not nothing to him.* He was a thorn in both our sides. A weed to rip out by its roots. The Weaver was our enemy, but it was never that cut and dry. History was fixed. The future was not. Ahead was a road shrouded in dense fog, and the only way we would know what it hid, was to travel through it.

I was not forgiving—I couldn't afford to be—but the Sandman was. All it took was one person to believe in you for change to happen.

"Let's go home," I breathed into the Sandman's chest.

Let's go home.

Chapter Thirty

Home.

The beach stretched out around us, and Nora didn't relinquish her hold on me as we snuggled into the pillows covering the pavilion.

Yes, we were home. *Our* home, now that Nora's magic didn't taint the beach. No nightmares, no fear, no death…those stayed in the Nightmare Realm where they belonged.

Not everything changed. We had, but the realms were largely the same. The Weaver and I cleaved the world apart—Nora and I put it back together. Not completely, but it was a start. I could feel the scratch of the Weaver's magic inside me now. It was a manageable enough sensation that I hoped to get used to it.

"I've been thinking." Nora propped her chin on my chest, and a small smile played on her lips. The stars reflected in her eyes, on her face, and in my heart. "Specifically, about you not having a name…"

"Oh?" I chuckled at the reminder of her past suggestions. "This should be good."

She *tsked* playfully, her nose wrinkling. "I've actually come up with a good one this time. Or, at least, I hope it is."

"I'm intrigued."

She pulled back slightly and toyed with the ties on my vest. "Do you remember how I was really into astronomy?"

I remembered her crying the night she threw her books away, but that wasn't a memory worth having. "I do, yes."

"For the record, there are *a lot* of stupid star names, so my options were limited." Her cheeks burned bright red. "There are two stars nicknamed *'the twins'* so I thought with the balance and everything that it sort of fit, but now that I'm saying it, it sounds dumb."

"It doesn't," I assured her. "Go on."

"Obviously I'm not going to suggest calling you Pollux." She gave a nervous laugh and lightly drummed her fingers against my abdomen. "Castor is weird too, but—and be honest if you hate it—what about Cas?"

"Cas," I repeated, testing the name. It felt strangely…good. I wasn't sure I needed a name, and I wouldn't want anyone but Nora using it, but I liked the idea. The thought of having a role outside of the Lord of Dreams as Nora's equal, not only in magic, but in life. My chest swelled with pride, with love and adoration. "I love it," I whispered and leaned in to kiss her. "I love *you*."

"I love you too," she vowed and leaned up on the pile of pillows until we were nose-to-nose. Every trace of her uncertainty melted away beneath my lips. The kiss was slow and tender, a promise of forever.

I hadn't dared hope for a future like this for us—one where we were together and safe. We had become the guardians of two worlds, rulers of one, as Lord and Lady of Night. There was a lot we needed to figure out, but one thing was always certain: I loved Nora more than anyone could love another living thing.

She and I were twin fires burning bright and eternal. I would fill her darkest moments with hope, and I knew without question, she would fill mine. Because, after all, for every light there was a shadow, for every dream, a nightmare.

Acknowledgements

Now's the part where I say thank you and pray I don't forget anyone!

First, my editor, Kate—you're an absolute gift from the editing gods!

My endlessly supportive critique partners: Lauren, Kalyn, Loretta, and Candace.

As always, my Saltmates!

Lindsay & Judy.

Priscilla, Katie, Elle, Melissa, Stacy.

And, of course, all the thanks to my family! My husband, my boys, Nonny, Kathy, Mom, Dad, Heather, and my Georgia family.

Thank you, thank you, thank you!

Also by Amber R. Duell

Young Adult

When Stars Are Bright

New Adult

The Prince's Wing
Fragile Chaos

Sins of Blood Trilogy:
Sins of Blood and Wrath
Sins of Blood and Malice
Sins of Blood and Ruin

Faeries of Oz series (co-written with Candace Robinson):
Lion (ebook prequel short story)
Tin
Crow
Ozma
Tik-Tok

Vampires in Wonderland (co-written with Candace Robinson):
Rav (ebook prequel short story)
Maddie
Chess
Knave

Once Upon a Wicked Villain (co-written with Candace Robinson):
Spindle of Sin
Tower of Shadows

www.ingramcontent.com/pod-product-compliance
Lightning Source LLC
Chambersburg PA
CBHW020344310726
48979CB00015B/2503/J

* 9 7 8 1 9 6 0 9 4 9 5 7 8 *